Phineas Finn

Anthony Trollope

Copyright © 2017 Okitoks Press

ISBN: 1548822914

ISBN-13: 978-1548822910

Table of Contents

CHAPTER I

Phineas Finn Proposes to Stand for Loughshane

Dr. Finn, of Killaloe, in county Clare, was as well known in those parts,—the confines, that is, of the counties Clare, Limerick, Tipperary, and Galway,—as was the bishop himself who lived in the same town, and was as much respected. Many said that the doctor was the richer man of the two, and the practice of his profession was extended over almost as wide a district. Indeed the bishop whom he was privileged to attend, although a Roman Catholic, always spoke of their dioceses being conterminate. It will therefore be understood that Dr. Finn,—Malachi Finn was his full name,—had obtained a wide reputation as a country practitioner in the west of Ireland. And he was a man sufficiently well to do, though that boast made by his friends, that he was as warm a man as the bishop, had but little truth to support it. Bishops in Ireland, if they live at home, even in these days, are very warm men; and Dr. Finn had not a penny in the world for which he had not worked hard. He had, moreover, a costly family, five daughters and one son, and, at the time of which we are speaking, no provision in the way of marriage or profession had been made for any of them. Of the one son, Phineas, the hero of the following pages, the mother and five sisters were very proud. The doctor was accustomed to say that his goose was as good as any other man's goose, as far as he could see as yet; but that he should like some very strong evidence before he allowed himself to express an opinion that the young bird partook, in any degree, of the qualities of a swan. From which it may be gathered that Dr. Finn was a man of common-sense.

Phineas had come to be a swan in the estimation of his mother and sisters by reason of certain early successes at college. His father, whose religion was not of that bitter kind in which we in England are apt to suppose that all the Irish Roman Catholics indulge, had sent his son to Trinity; and there were some in the neighbourhood of Killaloe,—patients, probably, of Dr. Duggin, of Castle Connell, a learned physician who had spent a fruitless life in endeavouring to make head against Dr. Finn,—who declared that old Finn would not be sorry if his son were to turn Protestant and go in for a fellowship. Mrs. Finn was a Protestant, and the five Miss Finns were Protestants, and the doctor himself was very much given to dining out among his Protestant friends on a Friday. Our Phineas, however, did not turn Protestant up in Dublin, whatever his father's secret wishes on that subject may have been. He did join a debating society, to success in which his religion was no bar; and he there achieved a sort of distinction which was both easy and pleasant, and which, making its way down to Killaloe, assisted in engendering those ideas as to swanhood of which maternal and sisterly minds are so sweetly susceptible. "I know half a dozen old windbags at the present moment," said the doctor, "who were great fellows at debating clubs when they were boys." "Phineas is not a boy any longer," said Mrs. Finn. "And windbags don't get college scholarships," said Matilda Finn, the second daughter. "But papa always snubs Phinny," said Barbara, the youngest. "I'll snub you, if you don't take care," said the doctor, taking Barbara tenderly by the ear;—for his youngest daughter was the doctor's pet.

The doctor certainly did not snub his son, for he allowed him to go over to London when he was twenty-two years of age, in order that he might read with an English barrister. It was the doctor's wish that his son might be called to the Irish Bar, and the young man's desire that he might go to the English Bar. The doctor so far gave way, under the influence of Phineas himself, and of all the young women of the family, as to pay the usual fee to a very competent and learned gentleman in the Middle Temple, and to allow his son one hundred and fifty pounds per annum for three years. Dr. Finn, however, was still firm in his intention that his son should settle in Dublin, and take the Munster Circuit,—believing that Phineas might come to want home influences and home connections, in spite of the swanhood which was attributed to him.

Phineas sat his terms for three years, and was duly called to the Bar; but no evidence came home as to the acquirement of any considerable amount of law lore, or even as to much law study, on the part of the young aspirant. The learned pundit at whose feet he had been sitting was not especially loud in praise of his pupil's industry, though he did say a pleasant word or two as to his pupil's intelligence. Phineas himself did not boast much of his own hard work when at home during the long vacation. No rumours of expected successes,—of expected professional successes,—reached the ears of any of the Finn family at Killaloe. But, nevertheless, there came tidings which maintained those high ideas in the maternal bosom of which mention has been made, and which were of sufficient strength to induce the doctor, in opposition to his own judgment, to consent to the continued residence of his son in London. Phineas belonged to an excellent club,—the Reform Club,—and went into very good society. He was hand in glove with the Hon. Laurence Fitzgibbon, the youngest son of Lord Claddagh. He was intimate with Barrington Erle, who had been private secretary,—one of the private secretaries,—to the great Whig Prime Minister who was lately in but was now out. He had dined three or four times with that great Whig nobleman, the Earl of Brentford. And he had been assured that if he stuck to the English Bar he would certainly do well. Though he might fail to succeed in court or in chambers, he would doubtless have given to him some one of those numerous appointments for which none but clever young barristers are supposed to be fitting candidates. The old doctor yielded for another year, although at the end of the second year he was called upon to pay a sum of three hundred pounds, which was then due by Phineas to creditors in London. When the doctor's male friends in and about Killaloe heard that he had done so, they said that he was doting. Not one of the Miss Finns was as yet married; and, after all that had been said about the doctor's wealth, it was supposed that there would not be above five hundred pounds a year among them all, were he to give up his profession. But the doctor, when he paid that three hundred pounds for his son, buckled to his work again, though he had for twelve months talked of giving up the midwifery. He buckled to again, to the great disgust of Dr. Duggin, who at this time said very ill-natured things about young Phineas.

At the end of the three years Phineas was called to the Bar, and immediately received a letter from his father asking minutely as to his professional intentions. His father recommended him to settle in Dublin, and promised the one hundred and fifty pounds for three more years, on condition that this advice was followed. He did not absolutely say that the allowance would be stopped if the advice were not followed, but that was plainly to be implied. That letter came at the moment of a dissolution of Parliament. Lord de Terrier, the Conservative Prime Minister, who had now been in office for the almost unprecedentedly long period of fifteen months, had found that he could not face continued majorities against him in the House of Commons, and had dissolved the House. Rumour declared that he would have much preferred to resign, and betake himself once again to the easy glories of opposition; but his party had naturally been obdurate with him, and he had resolved to appeal to the country. When Phineas received his father's letter, it had just been suggested to him at the Reform Club that he should stand for the Irish borough of Loughshane.

This proposition had taken Phineas Finn so much by surprise that when first made to him by Barrington Erle it took his breath away. What! he stand for Parliament, twenty-four years old, with no vestige of property belonging to him, without a penny in his purse, as completely dependent on his father as he was when he first went to school at eleven years of age! And for Loughshane, a little borough in the county Galway, for which a brother of that fine old Irish peer, the Earl of Tulla, had been sitting for the last twenty years,—a fine, high-minded representative of the thorough-going Orange Protestant feeling of Ireland! And the Earl of Tulla, to whom almost all Loughshane belonged,—or at any rate the land about Loughshane,—was one of his father's staunchest friends! Loughshane is in county Galway, but the Earl of Tulla usually lived at his seat in county Clare, not more than ten miles from Killaloe, and always confided his gouty feet, and the weak nerves of the old countess, and the stomachs of all his domestics, to the care of Dr. Finn. How was it possible that Phineas should stand for Loughshane? From whence was the money to come for such a contest? It was a beautiful dream, a grand idea, lifting Phineas almost off the earth by its glory. When the proposition was first made to him in the smoking-room at the Reform Club by his friend Erle, he was aware that he blushed like a girl, and that he was unable at the moment to express himself plainly,—so great was his astonishment and so great his gratification. But before ten minutes had passed by, while Barrington Erle was still sitting over his shoulder on the club sofa, and before the blushes had altogether vanished, he had seen the improbability of the scheme, and had explained to his friend that the thing could not be done. But to his increased astonishment, his friend made nothing of the difficulties. Loughshane, according to Barrington Erle, was so small a place, that the expense would be very little. There were altogether no more than 307 registered electors. The inhabitants were so far removed from the world, and were so ignorant of the world's good things, that they knew nothing about bribery. The Hon. George Morris, who had sat for the last twenty years, was very unpopular. He had not been near the borough since the last election, he had hardly done more than show himself in Parliament, and had neither given a shilling in the town nor got a place under Government for a single son of Loughshane. "And he has quarrelled with his brother," said Barrington Erle. "The devil he has!" said Phineas. "I thought they always swore by each other." "It's at each other they swear now," said Barrington; "George has asked the Earl for more money, and the Earl has cut up rusty." Then the negotiator went on to explain that the expenses of the election would be defrayed out of a certain fund collected for such purposes, that Loughshane had been chosen as a cheap place, and that Phineas Finn had been chosen as a safe and promising young man. As for qualification, if any question were raised, that should be made all right. An Irish candidate was wanted, and a Roman Catholic. So much the Loughshaners would require on their own account when instigated to dismiss from their service that thorough-going Protestant, the Hon. George Morris. Then "the party,"—by which Barrington Erle probably meant the great man in whose service he himself had become a politician,—required that the candidate should be a safe man, one who would support "the party,"—not a cantankerous, red-hot semi-Fenian, running about to meetings at the Rotunda, and such-like, with views of his own about tenant-right and the Irish Church. "But I have views of my own," said Phineas, blushing again. "Of course you have, my dear boy," said Barrington, clapping him on the back. "I shouldn't come to you unless you had views. But your views and ours are the same, and you're just the lad for Galway. You mightn't have such an opening again in your life, and of course you'll stand for Loughshane." Then the conversation was over, the private secretary went away to arrange some other little matter of the kind, and Phineas Finn was left alone to consider the proposition that had been made to him.

To become a member of the British Parliament! In all those hot contests at the two debating clubs to which he had belonged, this had been the ambition which had moved him. For, after all, to what purpose of their own had those empty debates ever tended? He and three or four others who had called themselves Liberals had been pitted against four or five who had called themselves Conservatives, and night after night they had discussed some ponderous subject without any idea that one would ever persuade another, or that their talking would ever conduce to any action or to any result. But each of these combatants had felt,—without daring to announce a hope on the subject among themselves,—that the present arena was only a trial-ground for some possible greater amphitheatre, for some future debating club in which debates would lead to action, and in which eloquence would have power, even though persuasion might be out of the question.

Phineas certainly had never dared to speak, even to himself, of such a hope. The labours of the Bar had to be encountered before the dawn of such a hope could come to him. And he had gradually learned to feel that his prospects at the Bar were not as yet very promising. As regarded professional work he had been idle, and how then could he have a hope?

And now this thing, which he regarded as being of all things in the world the most honourable, had come to him all at once, and was possibly within his reach! If he could believe Barrington Erle, he had only to lift up his hand, and he might be in Parliament within two months. And who was to be believed on such a subject if not Barrington Erle? This was Erle's special business, and such a man would not have come to him on such a subject had he not been in earnest, and had he not himself believed in success. There was an opening ready, an opening to this great glory,—if only it might be possible for him to fill it!

What would his father say? His father would of course oppose the plan. And if he opposed his father, his father would of course stop his income. And such an income as it was! Could it be that a man should sit in Parliament and live upon a hundred and fifty pounds a year? Since that payment of his debts he had become again embarrassed,—to a slight amount. He owed a tailor a trifle, and a bootmaker a trifle,—and something to the man who sold gloves and shirts; and yet he had done his best to keep out of debt with more than Irish pertinacity, living very closely, breakfasting upon tea and a roll, and dining frequently for a shilling at a luncheon-house up a court near Lincoln's Inn. Where should he dine if the Loughshaners elected him to Parliament? And then he painted to himself a not untrue picture of the probable miseries of a man who begins life too high up on the ladder,—who succeeds in mounting before he has learned how to hold on when he is aloft. For our Phineas Finn was a young man not without sense,—not entirely a windbag. If he did this thing the probability was that he might become utterly a castaway, and go entirely to the dogs before he was thirty. He had heard of penniless men who had got into Parliament, and to whom had come such a fate. He was able to name to himself a man or two whose barks, carrying more sail than they could bear, had gone to pieces among early breakers in this way. But then, would it not be better to go to pieces early than never to carry any sail at all? And there was, at any rate, the chance of success. He was already a barrister, and there were so many things open to a barrister with a seat in Parliament! And as he knew of men who had been utterly ruined by such early mounting, so also did he know of others whose fortunes had been made by happy audacity when they were young. He almost thought that he could die happy if he had once taken his seat in Parliament,—if he had received one letter with those grand initials written after his name on the address. Young men in battle are called upon to lead forlorn hopes. Three fall, perhaps, to one who gets through; but the one who gets through will have the Victoria Cross to carry for the rest of his life. This was his forlorn hope; and as he had been invited to undertake the work, he would not turn from the danger. On the following morning he again saw Barrington Erle by appointment, and then wrote the following letter to his father:—

Reform Club, Feb., 186—.

My dear Father,

I am afraid that the purport of this letter will startle you, but I hope that when you have finished it you will think that I am right in my decision as to what I am going to do. You are no doubt aware that the dissolution of Parliament will take place at once, and that we shall be in all the turmoil of a general election by the middle of March. I have been invited to stand for Loughshane, and have consented. The proposition has been made to me by my friend Barrington Erle, Mr. Mildmay's private secretary, and has been made on behalf of the Political Committee of the Reform Club. I need hardly say that I should not have thought of such a thing with a less thorough promise of support than this gives me, nor should I think of it now had I not been assured that none of the expense of the election would fall upon me. Of course I could not have asked you to pay for it.

But to such a proposition, so made, I have felt that it would be cowardly to give a refusal. I cannot but regard such a selection as a great honour. I own that I am fond of politics, and have taken great delight in their study—("Stupid young fool!" his father said to himself as he read this)—and it has been my dream for years past to have a seat in Parliament at some future time. ("Dream! yes; I wonder whether he has ever dreamed what he is to live upon.") The chance has now come to me much earlier than I have looked for it, but I do not think that it should on that account be thrown away. Looking to my profession, I find that many things are open to a barrister with a seat in Parliament, and that the House need not interfere much with a man's practice. ("Not if he has got to the top of his tree," said the doctor.)

My chief doubt arose from the fact of your old friendship with Lord Tulla, whose brother has filled the seat for I don't know how many years. But it seems that George Morris must go; or, at least, that he must be opposed by a Liberal candidate. If I do not stand, some one else will, and I should think that Lord Tulla will be too much of a man to make any personal quarrel on such a subject. If he is to lose the borough, why should not I have it as well as another?

I can fancy, my dear father, all that you will say as to my imprudence, and I quite confess that I have not a word to answer. I have told myself more than once, since last night, that I shall probably ruin myself. ("I wonder whether he has ever told himself that he will probably ruin me also," said the doctor.) But I am prepared to ruin myself in such a cause. I have no one dependent on me; and, as long as I do nothing to disgrace my name, I may dispose of myself as I please. If you decide on stopping my allowance, I shall have no feeling of anger against you. ("How very considerate!" said the doctor.) And in that case I shall endeavour to support myself by my pen. I have already done a little for the magazines.

Give my best love to my mother and sisters. If you will receive me during the time of the election, I shall see them soon. Perhaps it will be best for me to say that I have positively decided on making the attempt; that is to say, if the Club Committee is as good as its promise. I have weighed the matter all round, and I regard the prize as being so great, that I am prepared to run any risk to obtain it. Indeed, to me, with my views about politics, the running of such a risk is no more than a duty. I cannot keep my hand from the work now that the work has come in the way of my hand. I shall be most anxious to get a line from you in answer to this.

Your most affectionate son,

Phineas Finn.

I question whether Dr. Finn, when he read this letter, did not feel more of pride than of anger,—whether he was not rather gratified than displeased, in spite of all that his common-sense told him on the subject. His wife and daughters, when they heard the news, were clearly on the side of the young man. Mrs. Finn immediately expressed an opinion that Parliament would be the making of her son, and that everybody would be sure to employ so distinguished a barrister. The girls declared that Phineas ought, at any rate, to have his chance, and almost asserted that it would be brutal in their father to stand in their brother's way. It was in vain that the doctor tried to explain that going into Parliament could not help a young barrister, whatever it might do for one thoroughly established in his profession; that Phineas, if successful at Loughshane, would at once abandon all idea of earning any income,—that the proposition, coming from so poor a man, was a monstrosity,—that such an opposition to the Morris family, coming from a son of his, would be gross ingratitude to Lord Tulla. Mrs. Finn and the girls talked him down, and the doctor himself was almost carried away by something like vanity in regard to his son's future position.

Nevertheless he wrote a letter strongly advising Phineas to abandon the project. But he himself was aware that the letter which he wrote was not one from which any success could be expected. He advised his son, but did not command him. He made no threats as to stopping his income. He did not tell Phineas, in so many words, that he was proposing to make an ass of himself. He argued very prudently against the plan, and Phineas, when he received his father's letter, of course felt that it was tantamount to a paternal permission to proceed with the matter. On the next day he got a letter from his mother full of affection, full of pride,—not exactly telling him to stand for Loughshane by all means, for Mrs. Finn was not the woman to run openly counter to her husband in any advice given by her to their son,—but giving him every encouragement which motherly affection and motherly pride could bestow. "Of course you will come to us," she said, "if you do make up your mind to be member for Loughshane. We shall all of us be so delighted to have you!" Phineas, who had fallen into a sea of doubt after writing to his father, and who had demanded a week from Barrington Erle to consider the matter, was elated to positive certainty by the joint effect of the two letters from home. He understood it all. His mother and sisters were altogether in favour of his audacity, and even his father was not disposed to quarrel with him on the subject.

"I shall take you at your word," he said to Barrington Erle at the club that evening.

"What word?" said Erle, who had too many irons in the fire to be thinking always of Loughshane and Phineas Finn,—or who at any rate did not choose to let his anxiety on the subject be seen.

"About Loughshane."

"All right, old fellow; we shall be sure to carry you through. The Irish writs will be out on the third of March, and the sooner you're there the better."

CHAPTER II
Phineas Finn is Elected for Loughshane

One great difficulty about the borough vanished in a very wonderful way at the first touch. Dr. Finn, who was a man stout at heart, and by no means afraid of his great friends, drove himself over to Castlemorris to tell his news to the Earl, as soon as he got a second letter from his son declaring his intention of proceeding with the business, let the results be what they might. Lord Tulla was a passionate old man, and the doctor expected that there would be a quarrel;—but he was prepared to face that. He was under no special debt of gratitude to the lord, having given as much as he had taken in the long intercourse which had existed between them;—and he agreed with his son in thinking that if there was to be a Liberal candidate at Loughshane, no consideration of old pill-boxes and gallipots should deter his son Phineas from standing. Other considerations might very probably deter him, but not that. The Earl probably would be of a different opinion, and the doctor felt it to be incumbent on him to break the news to Lord Tulla.

"The devil he is!" said the Earl, when the doctor had told his story. "Then I'll tell you what, Finn, I'll support him."

"You support him, Lord Tulla!"

"Yes;—why shouldn't I support him? I suppose it's not so bad with me in the country that my support will rob him of his chance! I'll tell you one thing for certain, I won't support George Morris."

"But, my lord—"

"Well; go on."

"I've never taken much part in politics myself, as you know; but my boy Phineas is on the other side."

"I don't care a —— for sides. What has my party done for me? Look at my cousin, Dick Morris. There's not a clergyman in Ireland stauncher to them than he has been, and now they've given the deanery of Kilfenora to a man that never had a father, though I condescended to ask for it for my cousin. Let them wait till I ask for anything again." Dr. Finn, who knew all about Dick Morris's debts, and who had heard of his modes of preaching, was not surprised at the decision of the Conservative bestower of Irish Church patronage; but on this subject he said nothing. "And as for George," continued the Earl, "I will never lift my hand again for him. His standing for Loughshane would be quite out of the question. My own tenants wouldn't vote for him if I were to ask them myself. Peter Blake"—Mr. Peter Blake was the lord's agent—"told me only a week ago that it would be useless. The whole thing is gone, and for my part I wish they'd disenfranchise the borough. I wish they'd disenfranchise the whole country, and send us a military governor. What's the use of such members as we send? There isn't one gentleman among ten of them. Your son is welcome for me. What support I can give him he shall have, but it isn't much. I suppose he had better come and see me."

The doctor promised that his son should ride over to Castlemorris, and then took his leave,—not specially flattered, as he felt that were his son to be returned, the Earl would not regard him as the one gentleman among ten whom the county might send to leaven the remainder of its members,—but aware that the greatest impediment in his son's way was already removed. He certainly had not gone to Castlemorris with any idea of canvassing for his son, and yet he had canvassed for him most satisfactorily. When he got home he did not know how to speak of the matter otherwise than triumphantly to his wife and daughters. Though he desired to curse, his mouth would speak blessings. Before that evening was over the prospects of Phineas at Loughshane were spoken of with open enthusiasm before the doctor, and by the next day's post a letter was written to him by Matilda, informing him that the Earl was prepared to receive him with open arms. "Papa has been over there and managed it all," said Matilda.

"I'm told George Morris isn't going to stand," said Barrington Erle to Phineas the night before his departure.

"His brother won't support him. His brother means to support me," said Phineas.

"That can hardly be so."

"But I tell you it is. My father has known the Earl these twenty years, and has managed it."

"I say, Finn, you're not going to play us a trick, are you?" said Mr. Erle, with something like dismay in his voice.

"What sort of trick?"

"You're not coming out on the other side?"

"Not if I know it," said Phineas, proudly. "Let me assure you I wouldn't change my views in politics either for you or for the Earl, though each of you carried seats in your breeches pockets. If I go into Parliament, I shall go there as a sound Liberal,—not to support a party, but to do the best I can for the country. I tell you so, and I shall tell the Earl the same."

Barrington Erle turned away in disgust. Such language was to him simply disgusting. It fell upon his ears as false maudlin sentiment falls on the ears of the ordinary honest man of the world. Barrington Erle was a man ordinarily honest. He would not have been untrue to his mother's brother, William Mildmay, the great Whig Minister of the day, for any earthly consideration. He was ready to work with wages or without wages. He was really zealous in the cause, not asking very much for himself. He had some undefined belief that it was much better for the country that Mr. Mildmay should be in power than that Lord de Terrier should be there. He was convinced that Liberal politics were good for Englishmen, and that Liberal politics and the Mildmay party were one and the same thing. It would be unfair to Barrington Erle to deny to him some praise for patriotism. But he hated the very name of independence in Parliament, and when he was told of any man, that that man intended to look to measures and not to men, he regarded that man as being both unstable as water and dishonest as the wind. No good could possibly come from such a one, and much evil might and probably would come. Such a politician was a Greek to Barrington Erle, from whose hands he feared to accept even the gift of a vote. Parliamentary hermits were distasteful to him, and dwellers in political caves were regarded by him with aversion as being either knavish or impractical. With a good Conservative opponent he could shake hands almost as readily as with a good Whig ally; but the man who was neither flesh nor fowl was odious to him. According to his theory of parliamentary government, the House of Commons should be divided by a marked line, and every member should be required to stand on one side of it or on the other. "If not with me, at any rate be against me," he would have said to every representative of the people in the name of the great leader whom he followed. He thought that debates were good, because of the people outside,—because they served to create that public opinion which was hereafter to be used in creating some future House of Commons; but he did not think it possible that any vote should be given on a great question, either this way or that, as the result of a debate; and he was certainly assured in his own opinion that any such changing of votes would be dangerous, revolutionary, and almost unparliamentary. A member's vote,—except on some small crotchety open question thrown out for the amusement of crotchety members,—was due to the leader of that member's party. Such was Mr. Erle's idea of the English system of Parliament, and, lending semi-official assistance as he did frequently to the introduction of candidates into the House, he was naturally anxious that his candidates should be candidates after his own heart. When, therefore, Phineas Finn talked of measures and not men, Barrington Erle turned away in open disgust. But he remembered the youth and extreme rawness of the lad, and he remembered also the careers of other men.

Barrington Erle was forty, and experience had taught him something. After a few seconds, he brought himself to think mildly of the young man's vanity,—as of the vanity of a plunging colt who resents the liberty even of a touch. "By the end of the first session the thong will be cracked over his head, as he patiently assists in pulling the coach up hill, without producing from him even a flick of his tail," said Barrington Erle to an old parliamentary friend.

"If he were to come out after all on the wrong side," said the parliamentary friend.

Erle admitted that such a trick as that would be unpleasant, but he thought that old Lord Tulla was hardly equal to so clever a stratagem.

Phineas went to Ireland, and walked over the course at Loughshane. He called upon Lord Tulla, and heard that venerable nobleman talk a great deal of nonsense. To tell the truth of Phineas, I must confess that he wished to talk the nonsense himself; but the Earl would not hear him, and put him down very quickly. "We won't discuss politics, if you please, Mr. Finn; because, as I have already said, I am throwing aside all political considerations." Phineas, therefore, was not allowed to express his views on the government of the country in the Earl's sitting-room at Castlemorris. There was, however, a good time coming; and so, for the present, he allowed the Earl to ramble on about the sins of his brother George, and the want of all proper pedigree on the part of the new Dean of Kilfenora. The conference ended with an assurance on the part of Lord Tulla that if the Loughshaners chose to elect Mr. Phineas Finn he would not be in the least offended. The electors did elect Mr. Phineas Finn,—perhaps for the reason given by one of the Dublin Conservative papers, which declared that it was all the fault of the Carlton Club in not sending a proper candidate. There was a great deal said about the matter, both in London and Dublin, and the blame was supposed to fall on the joint shoulders of George Morris and his elder brother. In the meantime, our hero, Phineas Finn, had been duly elected member of Parliament for the borough of Loughshane.

The Finn family could not restrain their triumphings at Killaloe, and I do not know that it would have been natural had they done so. A gosling from such a flock does become something of a real swan by getting into Parliament. The doctor had his misgivings,—had great misgivings, fearful forebodings; but there was the young man elected, and he could not help it. He could not refuse his right hand to his son or withdraw his paternal assistance because that son had been specially honoured among the young men of his country. So he pulled out of his hoard what sufficed to pay off outstanding debts,—they were not heavy,—and undertook to allow Phineas two hundred and fifty pounds a year as long as the session should last.

There was a widow lady living at Killaloe who was named Mrs. Flood Jones, and she had a daughter. She had a son also, born to inherit the property of the late Floscabel Flood Jones of Floodborough, as soon as that property should have disembarrassed itself; but with him, now serving with his regiment in India, we shall have no concern. Mrs. Flood Jones was living modestly at Killaloe on her widow's jointure,—Floodborough having, to tell the truth, pretty nearly fallen into absolute ruin,—and with her one daughter, Mary. Now on the evening before the return of Phineas Finn, Esq., M.P., to London, Mrs. and Miss Flood Jones drank tea at the doctor's house.

"It won't make a bit of change in him," Barbara Finn said to her friend Mary, up in some bedroom privacy before the tea-drinking ceremonies had altogether commenced.

"Oh, it must," said Mary.

"I tell you it won't, my dear; he is so good and so true."

"I know he is good, Barbara; and as for truth, there is no question about it, because he has never said a word to me that he might not say to any girl."

"That's nonsense, Mary."

"He never has, then, as sure as the blessed Virgin watches over us;—only you don't believe she does."

"Never mind about the Virgin now, Mary."

"But he never has. Your brother is nothing to me, Barbara."

"Then I hope he will be before the evening is over. He was walking with you all yesterday and the day before."

"Why shouldn't he,—and we that have known each other all our lives? But, Barbara, pray, pray never say a word of this to any one!"

"Is it I? Wouldn't I cut out my tongue first?"

"I don't know why I let you talk to me in this way. There has never been anything between me and Phineas,—your brother I mean."

"I know whom you mean very well."

"And I feel quite sure that there never will be. Why should there? He'll go out among great people and be a great man; and I've already found out that there's a certain Lady Laura Standish whom he admires very much."

"Lady Laura Fiddlestick!"

"A man in Parliament, you know, may look up to anybody," said Miss Mary Flood Jones.

"I want Phin to look up to you, my dear."

"That wouldn't be looking up. Placed as he is now, that would be looking down; and he is so proud that he'll never do that. But come down, dear, else they'll wonder where we are."

Mary Flood Jones was a little girl about twenty years of age, with the softest hair in the world, of a colour varying between brown and auburn,—for sometimes you would swear it was the one and sometimes the other; and she was as pretty as ever she could be. She was one of those girls, so common in Ireland, whom men, with tastes that way given, feel inclined to take up and devour on the spur of the moment; and when she liked her lion, she had a look about her which seemed to ask to be devoured. There are girls so cold-looking,—pretty girls, too, ladylike, discreet, and armed with all accomplishments,—whom to attack seems to require the same sort of courage, and the same sort of preparation, as a journey in quest of the north-west passage. One thinks of a pedestal near the Athenaeum as the most appropriate and most honourable reward of such courage. But, again, there are other girls to abstain from attacking whom is, to a man of any warmth of temperament, quite impossible. They are like water when one is athirst, like plovers' eggs in March, like cigars when one is out in the autumn. No one ever dreams of denying himself when such temptation comes in the way. It often happens, however, that in spite of appearances, the water will not come from the well, nor the egg from its shell, nor will the cigar allow itself to be lit. A girl of such appearance, so charming, was Mary Flood Jones of Killaloe, and our hero Phineas was not allowed to thirst in vain for a drop from the cool spring.

When the girls went down into the drawing-room Mary was careful to go to a part of the room quite remote from Phineas, so as to seat herself between Mrs. Finn and Dr. Finn's young partner, Mr. Elias Bodkin, from Ballinasloe. But Mrs. Finn and the Miss Finns and all Killaloe knew that Mary had no love for Mr. Bodkin, and when Mr. Bodkin handed her the hot cake she hardly so much as smiled at him. But in two minutes Phineas was behind her chair, and then she smiled; and in five minutes more she had got herself so twisted round that she was sitting in a corner with Phineas and his sister Barbara; and in two more minutes Barbara had returned to Mr. Elias Bodkin, so that Phineas and Mary were uninterrupted. They manage these things very quickly and very cleverly in Killaloe.

"I shall be off to-morrow morning by the early train," said Phineas.

"So soon;—and when will you have to begin,—in Parliament, I mean?"

"I shall have to take my seat on Friday. I'm going back just in time."

"But when shall we hear of your saying something?"

"Never, probably. Not one in ten who go into Parliament ever do say anything."

"But you will; won't you? I hope you will. I do so hope you will distinguish yourself;—because of your sister, and for the sake of the town, you know."

"And is that all, Mary?"

"Isn't that enough?"

"You don't care a bit about myself, then?"

"You know that I do. Haven't we been friends ever since we were children? Of course it will be a great pride to me that a person whom I have known so intimately should come to be talked about as a great man."

"I shall never be talked about as a great man."

"You're a great man to me already, being in Parliament. Only think;—I never saw a member of Parliament in my life before."

"You've seen the bishop scores of times."

"Is he in Parliament? Ah, but not like you. He couldn't come to be a Cabinet Minister, and one never reads anything about him in the newspapers. I shall expect to see your name, very often, and I shall always look for it. 'Mr. Phineas Finn paired off with Mr. Mildmay.' What is the meaning of pairing off?"

"I'll explain it all to you when I come back, after learning my lesson."

"Mind you do come back. But I don't suppose you ever will. You will be going somewhere to see Lady Laura Standish when you are not wanted in Parliament."

"Lady Laura Standish!"

"And why shouldn't you? Of course, with your prospects, you should go as much as possible among people of that sort. Is Lady Laura very pretty?"

"She's about six feet high."

"Nonsense. I don't believe that."

"She would look as though she were, standing by you."

"Because I am so insignificant and small."

"Because your figure is perfect, and because she is straggling. She is as unlike you as possible in everything. She has thick lumpy red hair, while yours is all silk and softness. She has large hands and feet, and—"

"Why, Phineas, you are making her out to be an ogress, and yet I know that you admire her."

"So I do, because she possesses such an appearance of power. And after all, in spite of the lumpy hair, and in spite of large hands and straggling figure, she is handsome. One can't tell what it is. One can see that she is quite contented with herself, and intends to make others contented with her. And so she does."

"I see you are in love with her, Phineas."

"No; not in love,—not with her at least. Of all men in the world, I suppose that I am the last that has a right to be in love. I daresay I shall marry some day."

"I'm sure I hope you will."

"But not till I'm forty or perhaps fifty years old. If I was not fool enough to have what men call a high ambition I might venture to be in love now."

"I'm sure I'm very glad that you've got a high ambition. It is what every man ought to have; and I've no doubt that we shall hear of your marriage soon,—very soon. And then,—if she can help you in your ambition, we—shall—all—be so—glad."

Phineas did not say a word further then. Perhaps some commotion among the party broke up the little private conversation in the corner. And he was not alone with Mary again till there came a moment for him to put her cloak over her shoulders in the back parlour, while Mrs.

Flood Jones was finishing some important narrative to his mother. It was Barbara, I think, who stood in some doorway, and prevented people from passing, and so gave him the opportunity which he abused.

"Mary," said he, taking her in his arms, without a single word of love-making beyond what the reader has heard,—"one kiss before we part."

"No, Phineas, no!" But the kiss had been taken and given before she had even answered him. "Oh, Phineas, you shouldn't!"

"I should. Why shouldn't I? And, Mary, I will have one morsel of your hair."

"You shall not; indeed you shall not!" But the scissors were at hand, and the ringlet was cut and in his pocket before she was ready with her resistance. There was nothing further;—not a word more, and Mary went away with her veil down, under her mother's wing, weeping sweet silent tears which no one saw.

"You do love her; don't you, Phineas?" asked Barbara.

"Bother! Do you go to bed, and don't trouble yourself about such trifles. But mind you're up, old girl, to see me off in the morning."

Everybody was up to see him off in the morning, to give him coffee and good advice, and kisses, and to throw all manner of old shoes after him as he started on his great expedition to Parliament. His father gave him an extra twenty-pound note, and begged him for God's sake to be careful about his money. His mother told him always to have an orange in his pocket when he intended to speak longer than usual. And Barbara in a last whisper begged him never to forget dear Mary Flood Jones.

CHAPTER III
Phineas Finn Takes His Seat

Phineas had many serious, almost solemn thoughts on his journey towards London. I am sorry I must assure my female readers that very few of them had reference to Mary Flood Jones. He had, however, very carefully packed up the tress, and could bring that out for proper acts of erotic worship at seasons in which his mind might be less engaged with affairs of state than it was at present. Would he make a failure of this great matter which he had taken in hand? He could not but tell himself that the chances were twenty to one against him. Now that he looked nearer at it all, the difficulties loomed larger than ever, and the rewards seemed to be less, more difficult of approach, and more evanescent. How many members were there who could never get a hearing! How many who only spoke to fail! How many, who spoke well, who could speak to no effect as far as their own worldly prospects were concerned! He had already known many members of Parliament to whom no outward respect or sign of honour was ever given by any one; and it seemed to him, as he thought over it, that Irish members of Parliament were generally treated with more indifference than any others. There were O'B—— and O'C—— and O'D——, for whom no one cared a straw, who could hardly get men to dine with them at the club, and yet they were genuine members of Parliament. Why should he ever be better than O'B——, or O'C——, or O'D——? And in what way should he begin to be better? He had an idea of the fashion after which it would be his duty to strive that he might excel those gentlemen. He did not give any of them credit for much earnestness in their country's behalf, and he was minded to be very earnest. He would go to his work honestly and conscientiously, determined to do his duty as best he might, let the results to himself be what they would. This was a noble resolution, and might have been pleasant to him,—had he not remembered that smile of derision which had come over his friend Erle's face when he declared his intention of doing his duty to his country as a Liberal, and not of supporting a party. O'B—— and O'C—— and O'D—— were keen enough to support their party, only they were sometimes a little astray at knowing which was their party for the nonce. He knew that Erle and such men would despise him if he did not fall into the regular groove,—and if the Barrington Erles despised him, what would then be left for him?

His moody thoughts were somewhat dissipated when he found one Laurence Fitzgibbon,—the Honourable Laurence Fitzgibbon,—a special friend of his own, and a very clever fellow, on board the boat as it steamed out of Kingston harbour. Laurence Fitzgibbon had also just been over about his election, and had been returned as a matter of course for his father's county. Laurence Fitzgibbon had sat in the House for the last fifteen years, and was yet well-nigh as young a man as any in it. And he was a man altogether different from the O'B——s, O'C——s, and O'D——s. Laurence Fitzgibbon could always get the ear of the House if he chose to speak, and his friends declared that he might have been high up in office long since if he would have taken the trouble to work. He was a welcome guest at the houses of the very best people, and was a friend of whom any one might be proud. It had for two years been a feather in the cap of Phineas that he knew Laurence Fitzgibbon. And yet people said that Laurence Fitzgibbon had nothing of his own, and men wondered how he lived. He was the youngest son of Lord Claddagh, an Irish peer with a large family, who could do nothing for Laurence, his favourite child, beyond finding him a seat in Parliament.

"Well, Finn, my boy," said Laurence, shaking hands with the young member on board the steamer, "so you've made it all right at Loughshane." Then Phineas was beginning to tell all the story, the wonderful story, of George Morris and the Earl of Tulla,—how the men of Loughshane had elected him without opposition; how he had been supported by Conservatives as well as Liberals;—how unanimous Loughshane had been in electing him, Phineas Finn, as its representative. But Mr. Fitzgibbon seemed to care very little about all this, and went so far as to declare that those things were accidents which fell out sometimes one way and sometimes another, and were altogether independent of any merit or demerit on the part of the candidate himself. And it was marvellous and almost painful to Phineas that his friend Fitzgibbon should accept the fact of his membership with so little of congratulation,—with absolutely no blowing of trumpets whatever. Had he been elected a member of the municipal corporation of Loughshane, instead of its representative in the British Parliament, Laurence Fitzgibbon could not have made less fuss about it. Phineas was disappointed, but he took the cue from his friend too quickly to show his disappointment. And when, half an hour after their meeting, Fitzgibbon had to be reminded that his companion was not in the House during the last session, Phineas was able to make the remark as though he thought as little about the House as did the old-accustomed member himself.

"As far as I can see as yet," said Fitzgibbon, "we are sure to have seventeen."

"Seventeen?" said Phineas, not quite understanding the meaning of the number quoted.

"A majority of seventeen. There are four Irish counties and three Scotch which haven't returned as yet; but we know pretty well what they'll do. There's a doubt about Tipperary, of course, but whichever gets in of the seven who are standing, it will be a vote on our side. Now the Government can't live against that. The uphill strain is too much for them."

"According to my idea, nothing can justify them in trying to live against a majority."

"That's gammon. When the thing is so equal, anything is fair. But you see they don't like it. Of course there are some among them as hungry as we are; and Dubby would give his toes and fingers to remain in." Dubby was the ordinary name by which, among friends and foes, Mr. Daubeny was known: Mr. Daubeny, who at that time was the leader of the Conservative party in the House of Commons. "But most of them," continued Mr. Fitzgibbon, "prefer the other game, and if you don't care about money, upon my word it's the pleasanter game of the two."

"But the country gets nothing done by a Tory Government."

"As to that, it's six of one and half a dozen of the other. I never knew a government yet that wanted to do anything. Give a government a real strong majority, as the Tories used to have half a century since, and as a matter of course it will do nothing. Why should it? Doing things, as you call it, is only bidding for power,—for patronage and pay."

"And is the country to have no service done?"

"The country gets quite as much service as it pays for,—and perhaps a little more. The clerks in the offices work for the country. And the Ministers work too, if they've got anything to manage. There is plenty of work done;—but of work in Parliament, the less the better, according to my ideas. It's very little that ever is done, and that little is generally too much."

"But the people—"

"Come down and have a glass of brandy-and-water, and leave the people alone for the present. The people can take care of themselves a great deal better than we can take care of them." Mr. Fitzgibbon's doctrine as to the commonwealth was very different from that of Barrington Erle, and was still less to the taste of the new member. Barrington Erle considered that his leader, Mr. Mildmay, should be intrusted to make all necessary changes in the laws, and that an obedient House of Commons should implicitly obey that leader in authorising all changes proposed by him;—but according to Barrington Erle, such changes should be numerous and of great importance, and would, if duly passed into law at his lord's behest, gradually produce such a Whig Utopia in England as has never yet been seen on the face of the earth. Now, according to Mr. Fitzgibbon, the present Utopia would be good enough,—if only he himself might be once more put into possession of a certain semi-political place about the Court, from which he had heretofore drawn £1,000 per annum, without any work, much to his comfort. He made no secret of his ambition, and was chagrined simply at the prospect of having to return to his electors before he could enjoy those good things which he expected to receive from the undoubted majority of seventeen, which had been, or would be, achieved.

"I hate all change as a rule," said Fitzgibbon; "but, upon my word, we ought to alter that. When a fellow has got a crumb of comfort, after waiting for it years and years, and perhaps spending thousands in elections, he has to go back and try his hand again at the last moment, merely in obedience to some antiquated prejudice. Look at poor Jack Bond,—the best friend I ever had in the world. He was wrecked upon that rock for ever. He spent every shilling he had in contesting Romford three times running,—and three times running he got in. Then they made him Vice-Comptroller of the Granaries, and I'm shot if he didn't get spilt at Romford on standing for his re-election!"

"And what became of him?"

"God knows. I think I heard that he married an old woman and settled down somewhere. I know he never came up again. Now, I call that a confounded shame. I suppose I'm safe down in Mayo, but there's no knowing what may happen in these days."

As they parted at Euston Square, Phineas asked his friend some little nervous question as to the best mode of making a first entrance into the House. Would Laurence Fitzgibbon see him through the difficulties of the oath-taking? But Laurence Fitzgibbon made very little of the difficulty. "Oh;—you just come down, and there'll be a rush of fellows, and you'll know everybody. You'll have to hang about for an hour or so, and then you'll get pushed through. There isn't time for much ceremony after a general election."

Phineas reached London early in the morning, and went home to bed for an hour or so. The House was to meet on that very day, and he intended to begin his parliamentary duties at once if he should find it possible to get some one to accompany him; He felt that he should lack courage to go down to Westminster Hall alone, and explain to the policeman and door-keepers that he was the man who had just been elected member for Loughshane. So about noon he went into the Reform Club, and there he found a great crowd of men, among whom there was a plentiful sprinkling of members. Erle saw him in a moment, and came to him with congratulations.

"So you're all right, Finn," said he.

"Yes; I'm all right,—I didn't have much doubt about it when I went over."

"I never heard of a fellow with such a run of luck," said Erle. "It's just one of those flukes that occur once in a dozen elections. Any one on earth might have got in without spending a shilling."

Phineas didn't at all like this. "I don't think any one could have got in," said he, "without knowing Lord Tulla."

"Lord Tulla was nowhere, my dear boy, and could have nothing to say to it. But never mind that. You meet me in the lobby at two. There'll be a lot of us there, and we'll go in together. Have you seen Fitzgibbon?" Then Barrington Erle went off to other business, and Finn was congratulated by other men. But it seemed to him that the congratulations of his friends were not hearty. He spoke to some men, of whom he thought that he knew they would have given their eyes to be in Parliament;—and yet they spoke of his success as being a very ordinary thing. "Well, my boy, I hope you like it," said one middle-aged gentleman whom he had known ever since he came up to London. "The difference is between working for nothing and working for money. You'll have to work for nothing now."

"That's about it, I suppose," said Phineas.

"They say the House is a comfortable club," said the middle-aged friend, "but I confess that I shouldn't like being rung away from my dinner myself."

At two punctually Phineas was in the lobby at Westminster, and then he found himself taken into the House with a crowd of other men. The old and young, and they who were neither old nor young, were mingled together, and there seemed to be very little respect of persons. On three or four occasions there was some cheering when a popular man or a great leader came in; but the work of the day left but little clear impression on the mind of the young member. He was confused, half elated, half disappointed, and had not his wits about him. He found himself constantly regretting that he was there; and as constantly telling himself that he, hardly yet twenty-five, without a shilling of his own, had achieved an entrance into that assembly which by the consent of all men is the greatest in the world, and which many of the rich magnates of the country had in vain spent heaps of treasure in their endeavours to open to their own footsteps. He tried hard to realise what he had gained, but the dust and the noise and the crowds and the want of something august to the eye were almost too strong for him. He managed, however, to take the oath early among those who took it, and heard the Queen's speech read and the Address moved and seconded. He was seated very uncomfortably, high up on a back seat, between two men whom he did not know; and he found the speeches to be very long. He had been in the habit of seeing such speeches reported in about a column, and he thought that these speeches must take at least four columns each. He sat out the debate on the Address till the House was adjourned, and then he went away to dine at his club. He did go into the dining-room of the House, but there was a crowd there, and he found himself alone,—and to tell the truth, he was afraid to order his dinner.

The nearest approach to a triumph which he had in London came to him from the glory which his election reflected upon his landlady. She was a kindly good motherly soul, whose husband was a journeyman law-stationer, and who kept a very decent house in Great Marlborough Street. Here Phineas had lodged since he had been in London, and was a great favourite. "God bless my soul, Mr. Phineas," said she, "only think of your being a member of Parliament!"

"Yes, I'm a member of Parliament, Mrs. Bunce."

"And you'll go on with the rooms the same as ever? Well, I never thought to have a member of Parliament in 'em."

Mrs. Bunce really had realised the magnitude of the step which her lodger had taken, and Phineas was grateful to her.

CHAPTER IV
Lady Laura Standish

Phineas, in describing Lady Laura Standish to Mary Flood Jones at Killaloe, had not painted her in very glowing colours. Nevertheless he admired Lady Laura very much, and she was worthy of admiration. It was probably the greatest pride of our hero's life that Lady Laura Standish was his friend, and that she had instigated him to undertake the risk of parliamentary life. Lady Laura was intimate also with Barrington Erle, who was, in some distant degree, her cousin; and Phineas was not without a suspicion that his selection for Loughshane, from out of all the young liberal candidates, may have been in some degree owing to Lady Laura's influence with Barrington Erle. He was not unwilling that it should be so; for though, as he had repeatedly told himself, he was by no means in love with Lady Laura,—who was, as he imagined, somewhat older than himself,—nevertheless, he would feel gratified at accepting anything from her hands, and he felt a keen desire for some increase to those ties of friendship which bound them together. No;—he was not in love with Lady Laura Standish. He had not the remotest idea of asking her to be his wife. So he told himself, both before he went over for his election, and after his return. When he had found himself in a corner with poor little Mary Flood Jones, he had kissed her as a matter of course; but he did not think that he could, in any circumstances, be tempted to kiss Lady Laura. He supposed that he was in love with his darling little Mary,—after a fashion. Of course, it could never come to anything, because of the circumstances of his life, which were so imperious to him. He was not in love with Lady Laura, and yet he hoped that his intimacy with her might come to much. He had more than once asked himself how he would feel when somebody else came to be really in love with Lady Laura,—for she was by no means a woman to lack lovers,—when some one else should be in love with her, and be received by her as a lover; but this question he had never been able to answer. There were many questions about himself which he usually answered by telling himself that it was his fate to walk over volcanoes. "Of course, I shall be blown into atoms some fine day," he would say; "but after all, that is better than being slowly boiled down into pulp."

The House had met on a Friday, again on the Saturday morning, and the debate on the Address had been adjourned till the Monday. On the Sunday, Phineas determined that he would see Lady Laura. She professed to be always at home on Sunday, and from three to four in the afternoon her drawing-room would probably be half full of people. There would, at any rate, be comers and goers, who would prevent anything like real conversation between himself and her. But for a few minutes before that he might probably find her alone, and he was most anxious to see whether her reception of him, as a member of Parliament, would be in any degree warmer than that of his other friends. Hitherto he had found no such warmth since he came to London, excepting that which had glowed in the bosom of Mrs. Bunce.

Lady Laura Standish was the daughter of the Earl of Brentford, and was the only remaining lady of the Earl's family. The Countess had been long dead; and Lady Emily, the younger daughter, who had been the great beauty of her day, was now the wife of a Russian nobleman whom she had persisted in preferring to any of her English suitors, and lived at St. Petersburg. There was an aunt, old Lady Laura, who came up to town about the middle of May; but she was always in the country except for some six weeks in the season. There was a certain Lord Chiltern, the Earl's son and heir, who did indeed live at the family town house in Portman Square; but Lord Chiltern was a man of whom Lady Laura's set did not often speak, and Phineas, frequently as he had been at the house, had never seen Lord Chiltern there. He was a young nobleman of whom various accounts were given by various people; but I fear that the account most readily accepted in London attributed to him a great intimacy with the affairs at Newmarket, and a partiality for convivial pleasures. Respecting Lord Chiltern Phineas had never as yet exchanged a word with Lady Laura. With her father he was acquainted, as he had dined perhaps half a dozen times at the house. The point in Lord Brentford's character which had more than any other struck our hero, was the unlimited confidence which he seemed to place in his daughter. Lady Laura seemed to have perfect power of doing what she pleased. She was much more mistress of herself than if she had been the wife instead of the daughter of the Earl of Brentford,—and she seemed to be quite as much mistress of the house.

Phineas had declared at Killaloe that Lady Laura was six feet high, that she had red hair, that her figure was straggling, and that her hands and feet were large. She was in fact about five feet seven in height, and she carried her height well. There was something of nobility in her gait, and she seemed thus to be taller than her inches. Her hair was in truth red,—of a deep thorough redness. Her brother's hair was the same; and so had been that of her father, before it had become sandy with age. Her sister's had been of a soft auburn hue, and hers had been said to be the prettiest head of hair in Europe at the time of her marriage. But in these days we have got to like red hair, and Lady Laura's was not supposed to stand in the way of her being considered a beauty. Her face was very fair, though it lacked that softness which we all love in women. Her eyes, which were large and bright, and very clear, never seemed to quail, never rose and sunk or showed themselves to be afraid of their own power. Indeed, Lady Laura Standish had nothing of fear about her. Her nose was perfectly cut, but was rather large, having the slightest possible tendency to be aquiline. Her mouth also was large, but was full of expression, and her teeth were perfect. Her complexion was very bright, but in spite of its brightness she never blushed. The shades of her complexion were set and steady. Those who knew her said that her heart was so fully under command that nothing could stir her blood to any sudden motion. As to that accusation of straggling which had been made against her, it had sprung from ill-natured observation of her modes of sitting. She never straggled when she stood or walked; but she would lean forward when sitting, as a man does, and would use her arms in talking, and would put her hand over her face, and pass her fingers through her hair,—after the fashion of men rather than of women;—and she seemed to despise that soft quiescence of her sex in which are generally found so many charms. Her hands and feet were large,—as was her whole frame. Such was Lady Laura Standish; and Phineas Finn had been untrue to himself and to his own appreciation of the lady when he had described her in disparaging terms to Mary Flood Jones. But, though he had spoken of Lady Laura in disparaging terms, he had so spoken of her as to make Miss Flood Jones quite understand that he thought a great deal about Lady Laura.

And now, early on the Sunday, he made his way to Portman Square in order that he might learn whether there might be any sympathy for him there. Hitherto he had found none. Everything had been terribly dry and hard, and he had gathered as yet none of the fruit which he had expected that his good fortune would bear for him. It is true that he had not as yet gone among any friends, except those of his club, and men who were in the House along with him;—and at the club it might be that there were some who envied him his good fortune, and others who thought nothing of it because it had been theirs for years. Now he would try a friend who, he hoped, could sympathise; and therefore he called in Portman Square at about half-past two on the Sunday morning. Yes,—Lady Laura was in the drawing-room. The hall-porter admitted as much, but evidently seemed to think that he had been disturbed from his dinner before his time. Phineas did not care a straw for the hall-porter. If Lady Laura were not kind to him, he would never trouble that hall-porter again. He was especially sore at this moment because a valued friend, the barrister with whom he had been reading for the last three years, had spent the best part of an hour that Sunday morning in proving to him that he had as good as ruined himself. "When I first heard it, of course I thought you had inherited a fortune," said Mr. Low. "I have inherited nothing," Phineas replied;—"not a penny; and I never shall." Then Mr. Low had opened his eyes very wide, and shaken his head very sadly, and had whistled.

"I am so glad you have come, Mr. Finn," said Lady Laura, meeting Phineas half-way across the large room.

"Thanks," said he, as he took her hand.

"I thought that perhaps you would manage to see me before any one else was here."

"Well;—to tell the truth, I have wished it; though I can hardly tell why."

"I can tell you why, Mr. Finn. But never mind;—come and sit down. I am so very glad that you have been successful;—so very glad. You know I told you that I should never think much of you if you did not at least try it."

"And therefore I did try."

"And have succeeded. Faint heart, you know, never did any good. I think it is a man's duty to make his way into the House;—that is, if he ever means to be anybody. Of course it is not every man who can get there by the time that he is five-and-twenty."

"Every friend that I have in the world says that I have ruined myself."

"No;—I don't say so," said Lady Laura.

"And you are worth all the others put together. It is such a comfort to have some one to say a cheery word to one."

"You shall hear nothing but cheery words here. Papa shall say cheery words to you that shall be better than mine, because they shall be weighted with the wisdom of age. I have heard him say twenty times that the earlier a man goes into the House the better. There is much to learn."

"But your father was thinking of men of fortune."

"Not at all;—of younger brothers, and barristers, and of men who have their way to make, as you have. Let me see,—can you dine here on Wednesday? There will be no party, of course, but papa will want to shake hands with you; and you legislators of the Lower House are more easily reached on Wednesdays than on any other day."

"I shall be delighted," said Phineas, feeling, however, that he did not expect much sympathy from Lord Brentford.

"Mr. Kennedy dines here;—you know Mr. Kennedy, of Loughlinter; and we will ask your friend Mr. Fitzgibbon. There will be nobody else. As for catching Barrington Erle, that is out of the question at such a time as this."

"But going back to my being ruined—" said Phineas, after a pause.

"Don't think of anything so disagreeable."

"You must not suppose that I am afraid of it. I was going to say that there are worse things than ruin,—or, at any rate, than the chance of ruin. Supposing that I have to emigrate and skin sheep, what does it matter? I myself, being unencumbered, have myself as my own property to do what I like with. With Nelson it was Westminster Abbey or a peerage. With me it is parliamentary success or sheep-skinning."

"There shall be no sheep-skinning, Mr. Finn. I will guarantee you."

"Then I shall be safe."

At that moment the door of the room was opened, and a man entered with quick steps, came a few yards in, and then retreated, slamming the door after him. He was a man with thick short red hair, and an abundance of very red beard. And his face was red,—and, as it seemed to Phineas, his very eyes. There was something in the countenance of the man which struck him almost with dread,—something approaching to ferocity.

There was a pause a moment after the door was closed, and then Lady Laura spoke. "It was my brother Chiltern. I do not think that you have ever met him."

CHAPTER V

14

That terrible apparition of the red Lord Chiltern had disturbed Phineas in the moment of his happiness as he sat listening to the kind flatteries of Lady Laura; and though Lord Chiltern had vanished as quickly as he had appeared, there had come no return of his joy. Lady Laura had said some word about her brother, and Phineas had replied that he had never chanced to see Lord Chiltern. Then there had been an awkward silence, and almost immediately other persons had come in. After greeting one or two old acquaintances, among whom an elder sister of Laurence Fitzgibbon was one, he took his leave and escaped out into the square. "Miss Fitzgibbon is going to dine with us on Wednesday," said Lady Laura. "She says she won't answer for her brother, but she will bring him if she can."

"And you're a member of Parliament now too, they tell me," said Miss Fitzgibbon, holding up her hands. "I think everybody will be in Parliament before long. I wish I knew some man who wasn't, that I might think of changing my condition."

But Phineas cared very little what Miss Fitzgibbon said to him. Everybody knew Aspasia Fitzgibbon, and all who knew her were accustomed to put up with the violence of her jokes and the bitterness of her remarks. She was an old maid, over forty, very plain, who, having reconciled herself to the fact that she was an old maid, chose to take advantage of such poor privileges as the position gave her. Within the last few years a considerable fortune had fallen into her hands, some twenty-five thousand pounds, which had come to her unexpectedly,—a wonderful windfall. And now she was the only one of her family who had money at command. She lived in a small house by herself, in one of the smallest streets of May Fair, and walked about sturdily by herself, and spoke her mind about everything. She was greatly devoted to her brother Laurence,—so devoted that there was nothing she would not do for him, short of lending him money.

But Phineas when he found himself out in the square thought nothing of Aspasia Fitzgibbon. He had gone to Lady Laura Standish for sympathy, and she had given it to him in full measure. She understood him and his aspirations if no one else did so on the face of the earth. She rejoiced in his triumph, and was not too hard to tell him that she looked forward to his success. And in what delightful language she had done so! "Faint heart never won fair lady." It was thus, or almost thus, that she had encouraged him. He knew well that she had in truth meant nothing more than her words had seemed to signify. He did not for a moment attribute to her aught else. But might not he get another lesson from them? He had often told himself that he was not in love with Laura Standish;—but why should he not how tell himself that he was in love with her? Of course there would be difficulty. But was it not the business of his life to overcome difficulties? Had he not already overcome one difficulty almost as great; and why should he be afraid of this other? Faint heart never won fair lady! And this fair lady,—for at this moment he was ready to swear that she was very fair,—was already half won. She could not have taken him by the hand so warmly, and looked into his face so keenly, had she not felt for him something stronger than common friendship.

He had turned down Baker Street from the square, and was now walking towards the Regent's Park. He would go and see the beasts in the Zoological Gardens, and make up his mind as to his future mode of life in that delightful Sunday solitude. There was very much as to which it was necessary that he should make up his mind. If he resolved that he would ask Lady Laura Standish to be his wife, when should he ask her, and in what manner might he propose to her that they should live? It would hardly suit him to postpone his courtship indefinitely, knowing, as he did know, that he would be one among many suitors. He could not expect her to wait for him if he did not declare himself. And yet he could hardly ask her to come and share with him the allowance made to him by his father! Whether she had much fortune of her own, or little, or none at all, he did not in the least know. He did know that the Earl had been distressed by his son's extravagance, and that there had been some money difficulties arising from this source.

But his great desire would be to support his own wife by his own labour. At present he was hardly in a fair way to do that, unless he could get paid for his parliamentary work. Those fortunate gentlemen who form "The Government" are so paid. Yes;—there was the Treasury Bench open to him, and he must resolve that he would seat himself there. He would make Lady Laura understand this, and then he would ask his question. It was true that at present his political opponents had possession of the Treasury Bench;—but all governments are mortal, and Conservative governments in this country are especially prone to die. It was true that he could not hold even a Treasury lordship with a poor thousand a year for his salary without having to face the electors of Loughshane again before he entered upon the enjoyment of his place;— but if he could only do something to give a grace to his name, to show that he was a rising man, the electors of Loughshane, who had once been so easy with him, would surely not be cruel to him when he showed himself a second time among them. Lord Tulla was his friend, and he had those points of law in his favour which possession bestows. And then he remembered that Lady Laura was related to almost everybody who was anybody among the high Whigs. She was, he knew, second cousin to Mr. Mildmay, who for years had been the leader of the Whigs, and was third cousin to Barrington Erle. The late President of the Council, the Duke of St. Bungay, and Lord Brentford had married sisters, and the St. Bungay people, and the Mildmay people, and the Brentford people had all some sort of connection with the Palliser people, of whom the heir and coming chief, Plantagenet Palliser, would certainly be Chancellor of the Exchequer in the next Government. Simply as an introduction into official life nothing could be more conducive to chances of success than a matrimonial alliance with Lady Laura. Not that he would have thought of such a thing on that account! No;—he thought of it because he loved her; honestly because he loved her. He swore to that half a dozen times, for his own satisfaction. But, loving her as he did, and resolving that in spite of all difficulties she should become his wife, there could be no reason why he should not,—on her account as well as on his own,—take advantage of any circumstances that there might be in his favour.

As he wandered among the unsavoury beasts, elbowed on every side by the Sunday visitors to the garden, he made up his mind that he would first let Lady Laura understand what were his intentions with regard to his future career, and then he would ask her to join her lot to his. At every turn the chances would of course be very much against him;—ten to one against him, perhaps, on every point; but it was his lot in life to have to face such odds. Twelve months since it had been much more than ten to one against his getting into Parliament; and yet he was there. He expected to be blown into fragments,—to sheep-skinning in Australia, or packing preserved meats on the plains of Paraguay; but when the blowing into atoms should come, he was resolved that courage to bear the ruin should not be wanting. Then he quoted a line or two of a Latin poet, and felt himself to be comfortable.

"So, here you are again, Mr. Finn," said a voice in his ear.

"Yes, Miss Fitzgibbon; here I am again."

"I fancied you members of Parliament had something else to do besides looking at wild beasts. I thought you always spent Sunday in arranging how you might most effectually badger each other on Monday."

"We got through all that early this morning, Miss Fitzgibbon, while you were saying your prayers."

"Here is Mr. Kennedy too;—you know him I daresay. He also is a member; but then he can afford to be idle." But it so happened that Phineas did not know Mr. Kennedy, and consequently there was some slight form of introduction.

"I believe I am to meet you at dinner on Wednesday,"—said Phineas,—"at Lord Brentford's."

"And me too," said Miss Fitzgibbon.

"Which will be the greatest possible addition to our pleasure," said Phineas.

Mr. Kennedy, who seemed to be afflicted with some difficulty in speaking, and whose bow to our hero had hardly done more than produce the slightest possible motion to the top of his hat, hereupon muttered something which was taken to mean an assent to the proposition as to Wednesday's dinner. Then he stood perfectly still, with his two hands fixed on the top of his umbrella, and gazed at the great monkeys' cage. But it was clear that he was not looking at any special monkey, for his eyes never wandered.

"Did you ever see such a contrast in your life?" said Miss Fitzgibbon to Phineas,—hardly in a whisper.

"Between what?" said Phineas.

"Between Mr. Kennedy and a monkey. The monkey has so much to say for himself, and is so delightfully wicked! I don't suppose that Mr. Kennedy ever did anything wrong in his life."

Mr. Kennedy was a man who had very little temptation to do anything wrong. He was possessed of over a million and a half of money, which he was mistaken enough to suppose he had made himself; whereas it may be doubted whether he had ever earned a penny. His father and his uncle had created a business in Glasgow, and that business now belonged to him. But his father and his uncle, who had toiled through their long lives, had left behind them servants who understood the work, and the business now went on prospering almost by its own momentum. The Mr. Kennedy of the present day, the sole owner of the business, though he did occasionally go to Glasgow, certainly did nothing towards maintaining it. He had a magnificent place in Perthshire, called Loughlinter, and he sat for a Scotch group of boroughs, and he had a house in London, and a stud of horses in Leicestershire, which he rarely visited, and was unmarried. He never spoke much to any one, although he was constantly in society. He rarely did anything, although he had the means of doing everything. He had very seldom been on his legs in the House of Commons, though he had sat there for ten years. He was seen about everywhere, sometimes with one acquaintance and sometimes with another;—but it may be doubted whether he had any friend. It may be doubted whether he had ever talked enough to any man to make that man his friend. Laurence Fitzgibbon tried him for one season, and after a month or two asked for a loan of a few hundred pounds. "I never lend money to any one under any circumstances," said Mr. Kennedy, and it was the longest speech which had ever fallen from his mouth in the hearing of Laurence Fitzgibbon. But though he would not lend money, he gave a great deal,—and he would give it for almost every object. "Mr. Robert Kennedy, M.P., Loughlinter, £105," appeared on almost every charitable list that was advertised. No one ever spoke to him as to this expenditure, nor did he ever speak to any one. Circulars came to him and the cheques were returned. The duty was a very easy one to him, and he performed it willingly. Had any amount of inquiry been necessary, it is possible that the labour would have been too much for him. Such was Mr. Robert Kennedy, as to whom Phineas had heard that he had during the last winter entertained Lord Brentford and Lady Laura, with very many other people of note, at his place in Perthshire.

"I very much prefer the monkey," said Phineas to Miss Fitzgibbon.

"I thought you would," said she. "Like to like, you know. You have both of you the same aptitude for climbing. But the monkeys never fall, they tell me."

Phineas, knowing that he could gain nothing by sparring with Miss Fitzgibbon, raised his hat and took his leave. Going out of a narrow gate he found himself again brought into contact with Mr. Kennedy. "What a crowd there is here," he said, finding himself bound to say something. Mr. Kennedy, who was behind him, answered him not a word. Then Phineas made up his mind that Mr. Kennedy was insolent with the insolence of riches, and that he would hate Mr. Kennedy.

He was engaged to dine on this Sunday with Mr. Low, the barrister, with whom he had been reading for the last three years. Mr. Low had taken a strong liking to Phineas, as had also Mrs. Low, and the tutor had more than once told his pupil that success in his profession was certainly open to him if he would only stick to his work. Mr. Low was himself an ambitious man, looking forward to entering Parliament at some future time, when the exigencies of his life of labour might enable him to do so; but he was prudent, given to close calculation, and resolved to make the ground sure beneath his feet in every step that he took forward. When he first heard that Finn intended to stand for Loughshane he was stricken with dismay, and strongly dissuaded him. "The electors may probably reject him. That's his only chance now," Mr. Low had said to his wife, when he found that Phineas was, as he thought, foolhardy. But the electors of Loughshane had not rejected Mr. Low's pupil, and Mr. Low was now called upon to advise what Phineas should do in his present circumstances. There is nothing to prevent the work of a Chancery barrister being done by a member of Parliament. Indeed, the most successful barristers are members of Parliament. But Phineas Finn was beginning at the wrong end, and Mr. Low knew that no good would come of it.

"Only think of your being in Parliament, Mr. Finn," said Mrs. Low.

"It is wonderful, isn't it?" said Phineas.

"It took us so much by surprise!" said Mrs. Low. "As a rule one never hears of a barrister going into Parliament till after he's forty."

"And I'm only twenty-five. I do feel that I've disgraced myself. I do, indeed, Mrs. Low."

"No;—you've not disgraced yourself, Mr. Finn. The only question is, whether it's prudent. I hope it will all turn out for the best, most heartily." Mrs. Low was a very matter-of-fact lady, four or five years older than her husband, who had had a little money of her own, and was possessed of every virtue under the sun. Nevertheless she did not quite like the idea of her husband's pupil having got into Parliament. If her husband and Phineas Finn were dining anywhere together, Phineas, who had come to them quite a boy, would walk out of the room before her husband. This could hardly be right! Nevertheless she helped Phineas to the nicest bit of fish she could find, and had he been ill, would have nursed him with the greatest care.

After dinner, when Mrs. Low had gone up-stairs, there came the great discussion between the tutor and the pupil, for the sake of which this little dinner had been given. When Phineas had last been with Mr. Low,—on the occasion of his showing himself at his tutor's chambers after his return from Ireland,—he had not made up his mind so thoroughly on certain points as he had done since he had seen Lady Laura. The discussion could hardly be of any avail now,—but it could not be avoided.

"Well, Phineas, and what do you mean to do?" said Mr. Low. Everybody who knew our hero, or nearly everybody, called him by his Christian name. There are men who seem to be so treated by general consent in all societies. Even Mrs. Low, who was very prosaic, and unlikely to be familiar in her mode of address, had fallen into the way of doing it before the election. But she had dropped it, when the Phineas whom she used to know became a member of Parliament.

"That's the question;—isn't it?" said Phineas.

"Of course you'll stick to your work?"

"What;—to the Bar?"

"Yes;—to the Bar."

"I am not thinking of giving it up permanently."

"Giving it up," said Mr. Low, raising his hands in surprise. "If you give it up, how do you intend to live? Men are not paid for being members of Parliament."

"Not exactly. But, as I said before, I am not thinking of giving it up,—permanently."

"You mustn't give it up at all,—not for a day; that is, if you ever mean to do any good."

"There I think that perhaps you may be wrong, Low!"

"How can I be wrong? Did a period of idleness ever help a man in any profession? And is it not acknowledged by all who know anything about it, that continuous labour is more necessary in our profession than in any other?"

"I do not mean to be idle."

"What is it you do mean, Phineas?"

"Why simply this. Here I am in Parliament. We must take that as a fact."

"I don't doubt the fact."

"And if it be a misfortune, we must make the best of it. Even you wouldn't advise me to apply for the Chiltern Hundreds at once."

"I would;—to-morrow. My dear fellow, though I do not like to give you pain, if you come to me I can only tell you what I think. My advice to you is to give it up to-morrow. Men would laugh at you for a few weeks, but that is better than being ruined for life."

"I can't do that," said Phineas, sadly.

"Very well;—then let us go on," said Mr. Low. "If you won't give up your seat, the next best thing will be to take care that it shall interfere as little as possible with your work. I suppose you must sit upon some Committees."

"My idea is this,—that I will give up one year to learning the practices of the House."

"And do nothing?"

"Nothing but that. Why, the thing is a study in itself. As for learning it in a year, that is out of the question. But I am convinced that if a man intends to be a useful member of Parliament, he should make a study of it."

"And how do you mean to live in the meantime?" Mr. Low, who was an energetic man, had assumed almost an angry tone of voice. Phineas for awhile sat silent;—not that he felt himself to be without words for a reply, but that he was thinking in what fewest words he might best convey his ideas. "You have a very modest allowance from your father, on which you have never been able to keep yourself free from debt," continued Mr. Low.

"He has increased it."

"And will it satisfy you to live here, in what will turn out to be parliamentary club idleness, on the savings of his industrious life? I think you will find yourself unhappy if you do that. Phineas, my dear fellow, as far as I have as yet been able to see the world, men don't begin either very good or very bad. They have generally good aspirations with infirm purposes;—or, as we may say, strong bodies with weak legs to carry them. Then, because their legs are weak, they drift into idleness and ruin. During all this drifting they are wretched, and when they have thoroughly drifted they are still wretched. The agony of their old disappointment still clings to them. In nine cases out of ten it is some one small unfortunate event that puts a man astray at first. He sees some woman and loses himself with her;—or he is taken to a racecourse and unluckily wins money;—or some devil in the shape of a friend lures him to tobacco and brandy. Your temptation has come in the shape of this accursed seat in Parliament." Mr. Low had never said a soft word in his life to any woman but the wife of his bosom, had never seen a racehorse, always confined himself to two glasses of port after dinner, and looked upon smoking as the darkest of all the vices.

"You have made up your mind, then, that I mean to be idle?"

"I have made up my mind that your time will be wholly unprofitable,—if you do as you say you intend to do."

"But you do not know my plan;—just listen to me." Then Mr. Low did listen, and Phineas explained his plan,—saying, of course, nothing of his love for Lady Laura, but giving Mr. Low to understand that he intended to assist in turning out the existing Government and to mount up to some seat,—a humble seat at first,—on the Treasury bench, by the help of his exalted friends and by the use of his own gifts of eloquence. Mr. Low heard him without a word. "Of course," said Phineas, "after the first year my time will not be fully employed, unless I succeed. And if I fail totally,—for, of course, I may fail altogether—"

"It is possible," said Mr. Low.

"If you are resolved to turn yourself against me, I must not say another word," said Phineas, with anger.

"Turn myself against you! I would turn myself any way so that I might save you from the sort of life which you are preparing for yourself. I see nothing in it that can satisfy any manly heart. Even if you are successful, what are you to become? You will be the creature of some minister, not his colleague. You are to make your way up the ladder by pretending to agree whenever agreement is demanded from you, and by voting whether you agree or do not. And what is to be your reward? Some few precarious hundreds a year, lasting just so long as a party may remain in power and you can retain a seat in Parliament! It is at the best slavery and degradation,—even if you are lucky enough to achieve the slavery."

"You yourself hope to go into Parliament and join a ministry some day," said Phineas.

Mr. Low was not quick to answer, but he did answer at last. "That is true, though I have never told you so. Indeed, it is hardly true to say that I hope it. I have my dreams, and sometimes dare to tell myself that they may possibly become waking facts. But if ever I sit on a Treasury bench I shall sit there by special invitation, having been summoned to take a high place because of my professional success. It is but a dream after all, and I would not have you repeat what I have said to any one. I had no intention to talk about myself."

"I am sure that you will succeed," said Phineas.

"Yes;—I shall succeed. I am succeeding. I live upon what I earn, like a gentleman, and can already afford to be indifferent to work that I dislike. After all, the other part of it,—that of which I dream,—is but an unnecessary adjunct; the gilding on the gingerbread. I am inclined to think that the cake is more wholesome without it."

Phineas did not go up-stairs into Mrs. Low's drawing-room on that evening, nor did he stay very late with Mr. Low. He had heard enough of counsel to make him very unhappy,—to shake from him much of the audacity which he had acquired for himself during his morning's walk,—and to make him almost doubt whether, after all, the Chiltern Hundreds would not be for him the safest escape from his difficulties. But in that case he must never venture to see Lady Laura Standish again.

CHAPTER VI
Lord Brentford's Dinner

No;—in such case as that,—should he resolve upon taking the advice of his old friend Mr. Low, Phineas Finn must make up his mind never to see Lady Laura Standish again! And he was in love with Lady Laura Standish;—and, for aught he knew, Lady Laura Standish might be in love with him. As he walked home from Mr. Low's house in Bedford Square, he was by no means a triumphant man. There had been much more said between him and Mr. Low than could be laid before the reader in the last chapter. Mr. Low had urged him again and again, and had prevailed so far that Phineas, before he left the house, had promised to consider that suicidal expedient of the Chiltern Hundreds. What a by-word he would become if he were to give up Parliament, having sat there for about a week! But such immediate giving up was one of the necessities of Mr. Low's programme. According to Mr. Low's teaching, a single year passed amidst the miasma of the House of Commons would be altogether fatal to any chance of professional success. And Mr. Low had at any rate succeeded in making Phineas believe that he was right in this lesson. There was his profession, as to which Mr. Low assured him that success was within his reach; and there was Parliament on the other side, as to which he knew that the chances were all against him, in spite of his advantage of a seat. That he could not combine the two, beginning with Parliament, he did believe. Which should it be? That was the question which he tried to decide as he walked home from Bedford Square to Great Marlborough Street. He could not answer the question satisfactorily, and went to bed an unhappy man.

He must at any rate go to Lord Brentford's dinner on Wednesday, and, to enable him to join in the conversation there, must attend the debates on Monday and Tuesday. The reader may perhaps be best made to understand how terrible was our hero's state of doubt by being told that for awhile he thought of absenting himself from these debates, as being likely to weaken his purpose of withdrawing altogether from the House. It is not very often that so strong a fury rages between party and party at the commencement of the session that a division is taken upon the Address. It is customary for the leader of the opposition on such occasions to express his opinion in the most courteous language, that his right honourable friend, sitting opposite to him on the Treasury bench, has been, is, and will be wrong in everything that he thinks, says, or does in public life; but that, as anything like factious opposition is never adopted on that side of the House, the Address to the Queen, in answer to that most fatuous speech which has been put into her Majesty's gracious mouth, shall be allowed to pass unquestioned. Then the leader of the House thanks his adversary for his consideration, explains to all men how happy the country ought to be that the Government has not fallen into the disgracefully incapable hands of his right honourable friend opposite; and after that the Address is carried amidst universal serenity. But such was not the order of the day on the present occasion. Mr. Mildmay, the veteran leader of the liberal side of the House, had moved an amendment to the Address, and had urged upon the House, in very strong language, the expediency of showing, at the very commencement of the session, that the country had returned to Parliament a strong majority determined not to put up with Conservative inactivity. "I conceive it to be my duty," Mr. Mildmay had said, "at once to assume that the country is unwilling that the right honourable gentlemen opposite should keep their seats on the bench upon which they sit, and in the performance of that duty I am called upon to divide the House upon the Address to her Majesty." And if Mr. Mildmay used strong language, the reader may be sure that Mr. Mildmay's followers used language much stronger. And Mr. Daubeny, who was the present leader of the House, and representative there of the Ministry,—Lord de Terrier, the Premier, sitting in the House of Lords,—was not the man to allow these amenities to pass by without adequate replies. He and his friends were very strong in sarcasm, if they failed in argument, and lacked nothing for words, though it might perhaps be proved that they were short in numbers. It was considered that the speech in which Mr. Daubeny reviewed the long political life of Mr. Mildmay, and showed that Mr. Mildmay had been at one time a bugbear, and then a nightmare, and latterly simply a fungus, was one of the severest attacks, if not the most severe, that had been heard in that House since the Reform Bill. Mr. Mildmay, the while, was sitting with his hat low down over his eyes, and many men said that he did not like it. But this speech was not made till after that dinner at Lord Brentford's, of which a short account must be given.

Had it not been for the overwhelming interest of the doings in Parliament at the commencement of the session, Phineas might have perhaps abstained from attending, in spite of the charm of novelty. For, in truth, Mr. Low's words had moved him much. But if it was to be his fate to be a member of Parliament only for ten days, surely it would be well that he should take advantage of the time to hear such a debate as this. It would be a thing to talk of to his children in twenty years' time, or to his grandchildren in fifty;—and it would be essentially necessary that he should be able to talk of it to Lady Laura Standish. He did, therefore, sit in the House till one on the Monday night, and till two on the Tuesday night, and heard the debate adjourned till the Thursday. On the Thursday Mr. Daubeny was to make his great speech, and then the division would come.

When Phineas entered Lady Laura's drawing-room on the Wednesday before dinner, he found the other guests all assembled. Why men should have been earlier in keeping their dinner engagements on that day than on any other he did not understand; but it was the fact, probably, that the great anxiety of the time made those who were at all concerned in the matter very keen to hear and to be heard. During these days everybody was in a hurry,—everybody was eager; and there was a common feeling that not a minute was to be lost. There were three ladies in the room,—Lady Laura, Miss Fitzgibbon, and Mrs. Bonteen. The latter was the wife of a gentleman who had been a junior Lord of the Admiralty in the late Government, and who lived in the expectation of filling, perhaps, some higher office in the Government which, as he hoped, was soon to be called into existence. There were five gentlemen besides Phineas Finn himself,—Mr. Bonteen, Mr. Kennedy, Mr. Fitzgibbon, Barrington Erle, who had been caught in spite of all that Lady Laura had said as to the difficulty of such an operation, and Lord Brentford. Phineas was quick to observe that every male guest was in Parliament, and to tell himself that he would not have been there unless he also had had a seat.

"We are all here now," said the Earl, ringing the bell.

"I hope I've not kept you waiting," said Phineas.

"Not at all," said Lady Laura. "I do not know why we are in such a hurry. And how many do you say it will be, Mr. Finn?"

"Seventeen, I suppose," said Phineas.

"More likely twenty-two," said Mr. Bonteen. "There is Colcleugh so ill they can't possibly bring him up, and young Rochester is at Vienna, and Gunning is sulking about something, and Moody has lost his eldest son. By George! they pressed him to come up, although Frank Moody won't be buried till Friday."

"I don't believe it," said Lord Brentford.

"You ask some of the Carlton fellows, and they'll own it."

"If I'd lost every relation I had in the world," said Fitzgibbon, "I'd vote on such a question as this. Staying away won't bring poor Frank Moody back to life."

"But there's a decency in these matters, is there not, Mr. Fitzgibbon?" said Lady Laura.

"I thought they had thrown all that kind of thing overboard long ago," said Miss Fitzgibbon. "It would be better that they should have no veil, than squabble about the thickness of it."

Then dinner was announced. The Earl walked off with Miss Fitzgibbon, Barrington Erle took Mrs. Bonteen, and Mr. Fitzgibbon took Lady Laura.

"I'll bet four pounds to two it's over nineteen," said Mr. Bonteen, as he passed through the drawing-room door. The remark seemed to have been addressed to Mr. Kennedy, and Phineas therefore made no reply.

"I daresay it will," said Kennedy, "but I never bet."

"But you vote—sometimes, I hope," said Bonteen.

"Sometimes," said Mr. Kennedy.

"I think he is the most odious man that ever I set my eyes on," said Phineas to himself as he followed Mr. Kennedy into the dining-room. He had observed that Mr. Kennedy had been standing very near to Lady Laura in the drawing-room, and that Lady Laura had said a few words to him. He was more determined than ever that he would hate Mr. Kennedy, and would probably have been moody and unhappy throughout the whole dinner had not Lady Laura called him to a chair at her left hand. It was very generous of her; and the more so, as Mr. Kennedy had, in a half-hesitating manner, prepared to seat himself in that very place. As it was, Phineas and Mr. Kennedy were neighbours, but Phineas had the place of honour.

"I suppose you will not speak during the debate?" said Lady Laura.

"Who? I? Certainly not. In the first place, I could not get a hearing, and, in the next place, I should not think of commencing on such an occasion. I do not know that I shall ever speak at all."

"Indeed you will. You are just the sort of man who will succeed with the House. What I doubt is, whether you will do as well in office."

"I wish I might have the chance."

"Of course you can have the chance if you try for it. Beginning so early, and being on the right side,—and, if you will allow me to say so, among the right set,—there can be no doubt that you may take office if you will. But I am not sure that you will be tractable. You cannot begin, you know, by being Prime Minister."

"I have seen enough to realise that already," said Phineas.

"If you will only keep that little fact steadily before your eyes, there is nothing you may not reach in official life. But Pitt was Prime Minister at four-and-twenty, and that precedent has ruined half our young politicians."

"It has not affected me, Lady Laura."

"As far as I can see, there is no great difficulty in government. A man must learn to have words at command when he is on his legs in the House of Commons, in the same way as he would if he were talking to his own servants. He must keep his temper; and he must be very patient. As far as I have seen Cabinet Ministers, they are not more clever than other people."

"I think there are generally one or two men of ability in the Cabinet."

"Yes, of fair ability. Mr. Mildmay is a good specimen. There is not, and never was, anything brilliant in him. He is not eloquent, nor, as far as I am aware, did he ever create anything. But he has always been a steady, honest, persevering man, and circumstances have made politics come easy to him."

"Think of the momentous questions which he has been called upon to decide," said Phineas.

"Every question so handled by him has been decided rightly according to his own party, and wrongly according to the party opposite. A political leader is so sure of support and so sure of attack, that it is hardly necessary for him to be even anxious to be right. For the country's sake, he should have officials under him who know the routine of business."

"You think very badly then of politics as a profession."

"No; I think of them very highly. It must be better to deal with the repeal of laws than the defending of criminals. But all this is papa's wisdom, not mine. Papa has never been in the Cabinet yet, and therefore of course he is a little caustic."

"I think he was quite right," said Barrington Erle stoutly. He spoke so stoutly that everybody at the table listened to him.

"I don't exactly see the necessity for such internecine war just at present," said Lord Brentford.

"I must say I do," said the other. "Lord de Terrier took office knowing that he was in a minority. We had a fair majority of nearly thirty when he came in."

"Then how very soft you must have been to go out," said Miss Fitzgibbon.

"Not in the least soft," continued Barrington Erle. "We could not command our men, and were bound to go out. For aught we knew, some score of them might have chosen to support Lord de Terrier, and then we should have owned ourselves beaten for the time."

"You were beaten,—hollow," said Miss Fitzgibbon.

"Then why did Lord de Terrier dissolve?"

"A Prime Minister is quite right to dissolve in such a position," said Lord Brentford. "He must do so for the Queen's sake. It is his only chance."

"Just so. It is, as you say, his only chance, and it is his right. His very possession of power will give him near a score of votes, and if he thinks that he has a chance, let him try it. We maintain that he had no chance, and that he must have known that he had none;—that if he could not get on with the late House, he certainly could not get on with a new House. We let him have his own way as far as we could in February. We had failed last summer, and if he could get along he was welcome. But he could not get along."

"I must say I think he was right to dissolve," said Lady Laura.

"And we are right to force the consequences upon him as quickly as we can. He practically lost nine seats by his dissolution. Look at Loughshane."

"Yes; look at Loughshane," said Miss Fitzgibbon. "The country at any rate has gained something there."

"It's an ill wind that blows nobody any good, Mr. Finn," said the Earl.

"What on earth is to become of poor George?" said Mr. Fitzgibbon. "I wonder whether any one knows where he is. George wasn't a bad sort of fellow."

"Roby used to think that he was a very bad fellow," said Mr. Bonteen. "Roby used to swear that it was hopeless trying to catch him." It may be as well to explain that Mr. Roby was a Conservative gentleman of great fame who had for years acted as Whip under Mr. Daubeny, and who now filled the high office of Patronage Secretary to the Treasury. "I believe in my heart," continued Mr. Bonteen, "that Roby is rejoiced that poor George Morris should be out in the cold."

"If seats were halveable, he should share mine, for the sake of auld lang syne," said Laurence Fitzgibbon.

"But not to-morrow night," said Barrington Erle; "the division to-morrow will be a thing not to be joked with. Upon my word I think they're right about old Moody. All private considerations should give way. And as for Gunning, I'd have him up or I'd know the reason why."

"And shall we have no defaulters, Barrington?" asked Lady Laura.

"I'm not going to boast, but I don't know of one for whom we need blush. Sir Everard Powell is so bad with gout that he can't even bear any one to look at him, but Ratler says that he'll bring him up." Mr. Ratler was in those days the Whip on the liberal side of the House.

"Unfortunate wretch!" said Miss Fitzgibbon.

"The worst of it is that he screams in his paroxysms," said Mr. Bonteen.

"And you mean to say that you'll take him into the lobby," said Lady Laura.

"Undoubtedly," said Barrington Erle. "Why not? He has no business with a seat if he can't vote. But Sir Everard is a good man, and he'll be there if laudanum and bath-chair make it possible."

The same kind of conversation went on during the whole of dinner, and became, if anything, more animated when the three ladies had left the room. Mr. Kennedy made but one remark, and then he observed that as far as he could see a majority of nineteen would be as serviceable as a majority of twenty. This he said in a very mild voice, and in a tone that was intended to be expressive of doubt; but in spite of his humility Barrington Erle flew at him almost savagely,—as though a liberal member of the House of Commons was disgraced by so mean a spirit; and Phineas found himself despising the man for his want of zeal.

"If we are to beat them, let us beat them well," said Phineas.

"Let there be no doubt about it," said Barrington Erle.

"I should like to see every man with a seat polled," said Bonteen.

"Poor Sir Everard!" said Lord Brentford. "It will kill him, no doubt, but I suppose the seat is safe."

"Oh, yes; Llanwrwsth is quite safe," said Barrington, in his eagerness omitting to catch Lord Brentford's grim joke.

Phineas went up into the drawing-room for a few minutes after dinner, and was eagerly desirous of saying a few more words,—he knew not what words,—to Lady Laura. Mr. Kennedy and Mr. Bonteen had left the dining-room first, and Phineas again found Mr. Kennedy standing close to Lady Laura's shoulder. Could it be possible that there was anything in it? Mr. Kennedy was an unmarried man, with an immense fortune, a magnificent place, a seat in Parliament, and was not perhaps above forty years of age. There could be no reason why he should not ask Lady Laura to be his wife,—except, indeed, that he did not seem to have sufficient words at command to ask anybody for anything. But could it be that such a woman as Lady Laura could accept such a man as Mr. Kennedy because of his wealth, and because of his fine place,—a man who had not a word to throw to a dog, who did not seem to be possessed of an idea, who hardly looked like a gentleman;—so Phineas told himself. But in truth Mr. Kennedy, though he was a plain, unattractive man, with nothing in his personal appearance to call for remark, was not unlike a gentleman in his usual demeanour. Phineas himself, it may be here said, was six feet high, and very handsome, with bright blue eyes, and brown wavy hair, and light silken beard. Mrs. Low had told her husband more than once that he was much too handsome to do any good. Mr. Low, however, had replied that young Finn had never shown himself to be conscious of his own personal advantages. "He'll learn it soon enough," said Mrs. Low. "Some woman will tell him, and then he'll be spoilt." I do not think that Phineas depended much as yet on his own good looks, but he felt that Mr. Kennedy ought to be despised by such a one as Lady Laura Standish, because his looks were not good. And she must despise him! It could not be that a woman so full of life should be willing to put up with a man who absolutely seemed to have no life within him. And yet why was he there, and why was he allowed to hang about just over her shoulders? Phineas Finn began to feel himself to be an injured man.

But Lady Laura had the power of dispelling instantly this sense of injury. She had done it effectually in the dining-room by calling him to the seat by her side, to the express exclusion of the millionaire, and she did it again now by walking away from Mr. Kennedy to the spot on which Phineas had placed himself somewhat sulkily.

"Of course you'll be at the club on Friday morning after the division," she said.

"No doubt."

"When you leave it, come and tell me what are your impressions, and what you think of Mr. Daubeny's speech. There'll be nothing done in the House before four, and you'll be able to run up to me."

"Certainly I will."

"I have asked Mr. Kennedy to come, and Mr. Fitzgibbon. I am so anxious about it, that I want to hear what different people say. You know, perhaps, that papa is to be in the Cabinet if there's a change."

"Is he indeed?"

"Oh yes;—and you'll come up?"

"Of course I will. Do you expect to hear much of an opinion from Mr. Kennedy?"

"Yes, I do. You don't quite know Mr. Kennedy yet. And you must remember that he will say more to me than he will to you. He's not quick, you know, as you are, and he has no enthusiasm on any subject;—but he has opinions, and sound opinions too." Phineas felt that Lady Laura was in a slight degree scolding him for the disrespectful manner in which he had spoken of Mr. Kennedy; and he felt also that he had committed himself,—that he had shown himself to be sore, and that she had seen and understood his soreness.

"The truth is I do not know him," said he, trying to correct his blunder.

"No;—not as yet. But I hope that you may some day, as he is one of those men who are both useful and estimable."

"I do not know that I can use him," said Phineas; "but if you wish it, I will endeavour to esteem him."

"I wish you to do both;—but that will all come in due time. I think it probable that in the early autumn there will be a great gathering of the real Whig Liberals at Loughlinter;—of those, I mean, who have their heart in it, and are at the same time gentlemen. If it is so, I should be sorry that you should not be there. You need not mention it, but Mr. Kennedy has just said a word about it to papa, and a word from him always means so much! Well;—good-night; and mind you come up on Friday. You are going to the club, now, of course. I envy you men your clubs more than I do the House;—though I feel that a woman's life is only half a life, as she cannot have a seat in Parliament."

Then Phineas went away, and walked down to Pall Mall with Laurence Fitzgibbon. He would have preferred to take his walk alone, but he could not get rid of his affectionate countryman. He wanted to think over what had taken place during the evening; and, indeed, he did so in spite of his friend's conversation. Lady Laura, when she first saw him after his return to London, had told him how anxious her father was to congratulate him on his seat, but the Earl had not spoken a word to him on the subject. The Earl had been courteous, as hosts customarily are, but had been in no way specially kind to him. And then Mr. Kennedy! As to going to Loughlinter, he would not do such a thing,—not though the success of the liberal party were to depend on it. He declared to himself that there were some things which a man could not do. But although he was not altogether satisfied with what had occurred in Portman Square, he felt as he walked down arm-in-arm with Fitzgibbon that Mr. Low and Mr. Low's counsels must be scattered to the winds. He had thrown the die in consenting to stand for Loughshane, and must stand the hazard of the cast.

"Bedad, Phin, my boy, I don't think you're listening to me at all," said Laurence Fitzgibbon.

"I'm listening to every word you say," said Phineas.

"And if I have to go down to the ould country again this session, you'll go with me?"

"If I can I will."

"That's my boy! And it's I that hope you'll have the chance. What's the good of turning these fellows out if one isn't to get something for one's trouble?"

CHAPTER VII
Mr. and Mrs. Bunce

It was three o'clock on the Thursday night before Mr. Daubeny's speech was finished. I do not think that there was any truth in the allegation made at the time, that he continued on his legs an hour longer than the necessities of his speech required, in order that five or six very ancient Whigs might be wearied out and shrink to their beds. Let a Whig have been ever so ancient and ever so weary, he would not have been allowed to depart from Westminster Hall that night. Sir Everard Powell was there in his bath-chair at twelve, with a doctor on one side of him and a friend on the other, in some purlieu of the House, and did his duty like a fine old Briton as he was. That speech of Mr. Daubeny's will never be forgotten by any one who heard it. Its studied bitterness had perhaps never been equalled, and yet not a word was uttered for the saying of which he could be accused of going beyond the limits of parliamentary antagonism. It is true that personalities could not have been closer, that accusations of political dishonesty and of almost worse than political cowardice and falsehood could not have been clearer, that no words in the language could have attributed meaner motives or more unscrupulous conduct. But, nevertheless, Mr. Daubeny in all that he said was parliamentary, and showed himself to be a gladiator thoroughly well trained for the arena in which he had descended to the combat. His arrows were poisoned, and his lance was barbed, and his shot was heated red,—because such things are allowed. He did not poison his enemies' wells or use Greek fire, because those things are not allowed. He knew exactly the rules of the combat. Mr. Mildmay sat and heard him without once raising his hat from his brow, or speaking a word to his neighbour. Men on both sides of the House said that Mr. Mildmay suffered terribly; but as Mr. Mildmay uttered no word of complaint to any one, and was quite ready to take Mr. Daubeny by the hand the next time they met in company, I do not know that any one was able to form a true idea of Mr. Mildmay's feelings. Mr. Mildmay was an impassive man who rarely spoke of his own feelings, and no doubt sat with his hat low down over his eyes in order that no man might judge of them on that occasion by the impression on his features. "If he could have left off half an hour earlier it would have been perfect as an attack," said Barrington Erle in criticising Mr. Daubeny's speech, "but he allowed himself to sink into comparative weakness, and the glory of it was over before the end."—Then came the division. The Liberals had 333 votes to 314 for the Conservatives, and therefore counted a majority of 19. It was said that so large a number of members had never before voted at any division.

"I own I'm disappointed," said Barrington Erle to Mr. Ratler.

"I thought there would be twenty," said Mr. Ratler. "I never went beyond that. I knew they would have old Moody up, but I thought Gunning would have been too hard for them."

"They say they've promised them both peerages."

"Yes;—if they remain in. But they know they're going out."

"They must go, with such a majority against them," said Barrington Erle.

"Of course they must," said Mr. Ratler. "Lord de Terrier wants nothing better, but it is rather hard upon poor Daubeny. I never saw such an unfortunate old Tantalus."

"He gets a good drop of real water now and again, and I don't pity him in the least. He's clever of course, and has made his own way, but I've always a feeling that he has no business where he is. I suppose we shall know all about it at Brooks's by one o'clock to-morrow."

Phineas, though it had been past five before he went to bed,—for there had been much triumphant talking to be done among liberal members after the division,—was up at his breakfast at Mrs. Bunce's lodgings by nine. There was a matter which he was called upon to settle immediately in which Mrs. Bunce herself was much interested, and respecting which he had promised to give an answer on this very morning. A set of very dingy chambers up two pairs of stairs at No. 9, Old Square, Lincoln's Inn, to which Mr. Low had recommended him to transfer himself and all his belongings, were waiting his occupation, should he resolve upon occupying them. If he intended to commence operations as a barrister, it would be necessary that he should have chambers and a clerk; and before he had left Mr. Low's house on Sunday evening he had almost given that gentleman authority to secure for him these rooms at No. 9. "Whether you remain in Parliament or no, you must make a beginning," Mr. Low had said; "and how are you even to pretend to begin if you don't have chambers?" Mr. Low hoped that he might be able to wean Phineas away from his Parliament bauble;—that he might induce the young barrister to give up his madness, if not this session or the next, at any rate before a third year had commenced. Mr. Low was a persistent man, liking very much when he did like, and loving very strongly when he did love. He would have many a tug for Phineas Finn before he would allow that false Westminster Satan to carry off the prey as altogether his own. If he could only get Phineas into the dingy chambers he might do much!

But Phineas had now become so imbued with the atmosphere of politics, had been so breathed upon by Lady Laura and Barrington Erle, that he could no longer endure the thought of any other life than that of a life spent among the lobbies. A desire to help to beat the Conservatives had fastened on his very soul, and almost made Mr. Low odious in his eyes. He was afraid of Mr. Low, and for the nonce would not go to him any more;—but he must see the porter at Lincoln's Inn, he must write a line to Mr. Low, and he must tell Mrs. Bunce that for the present he would still keep on her rooms. His letter to Mr. Low was as follows:—

Great Marlborough Street, May, 186—.

My dear Low,

I have made up my mind against taking the chambers, and am now off to the Inn to say that I shall not want them. Of course, I know what you will think of me, and it is very grievous to me to have to bear the hard judgment of a man whose opinion I value so highly; but, in the teeth of your terribly strong arguments, I think that there is something to be said on my side of the question. This seat in Parliament has come in my way by chance, and I think it would be pusillanimous in me to reject it, feeling, as I do, that a seat in Parliament confers very great honour. I am, too, very fond of politics, and regard legislation as the finest profession going. Had I any one dependent on me, I probably might not be justified in following the bent of my inclination. But I am all alone in the world, and therefore have a right to make the attempt. If, after a trial of one or two sessions, I should fail in that which I am attempting, it will not even then be too late to go back to the better way. I can assure you that at any rate it is not my intention to be idle.

I know very well how you will fret and fume over what I say, and how utterly I shall fail in bringing you round to my way of thinking; but as I must write to tell you of my decision, I cannot refrain from defending myself to the best of my ability.

Yours always faithfully,

Phineas Finn.

Mr. Low received this letter at his chambers, and when he had read it, he simply pressed his lips closely together, placed the sheet of paper back in its envelope, and put it into a drawer at his left hand. Having done this, he went on with what work he had before him, as though his friend's decision were a matter of no consequence to him. As far as he was concerned the thing was done, and there should be an end of it. So he told himself; but nevertheless his mind was full of it all day; and, though he wrote not a word of answer to Phineas, he made a reply within his own mind to every one of the arguments used in the letter. "Great honour! How can there be honour in what comes, as he says, by chance? He hasn't sense enough to understand that the honour comes from the mode of winning it, and from the mode of wearing it; and that the very fact of his being member for Loughshane at this instant simply proves that Loughshane should have had no privilege to return a member! No one dependent on him! Are not his father and his mother and his sisters dependent on him as long as he must eat their bread till he can earn bread of his own? He will never earn bread of his own. He will always be eating bread that others have earned." In this way, before the day was over, Mr. Low became very angry, and swore to himself that he would have nothing more to say to Phineas Finn. But yet he found himself creating plans for encountering and conquering the parliamentary fiend who was at present so cruelly potent with his pupil. It was not till the third evening that he told his wife that Finn had made up his mind not to take chambers. "Then I would have nothing more to say to him," said Mrs. Low, savagely. "For the present I can have nothing more to say to him." "But neither now nor ever," said Mrs. Low, with great emphasis; "he has been false to you." "No," said Mr. Low, who was a man thoroughly and thoughtfully just at all points; "he has not been false to me. He has always meant what he has said, when he was saying it. But he is weak and blind, and flies like a moth to the candle; one pities the poor moth, and would save him a stump of his wing if it be possible."

Phineas, when he had written his letter to Mr. Low, started off for Lincoln's Inn, making his way through the well-known dreary streets of Soho, and through St. Giles's, to Long Acre. He knew every corner well, for he had walked the same road almost daily for the last three years. He had conceived a liking for the route, which he might easily have changed without much addition to the distance, by passing through Oxford Street and Holborn; but there was an air of business on which he prided himself in going by the most direct passage, and he declared to himself very often that things dreary and dingy to the eye might be good in themselves. Lincoln's Inn itself is dingy, and the Law Courts therein are perhaps the meanest in which Equity ever disclosed herself. Mr. Low's three rooms in the Old Square, each of them brown with the binding of law books and with the dust collected on law papers, and with furniture that had been brown always, and had become browner with years, were perhaps as unattractive to the eye of a young pupil as any rooms which were ever entered. And the study of the Chancery law itself is not an alluring pursuit till the mind has come to have some insight into the beauty of its ultimate object. Phineas, during his three years' course of reasoning on these things, had taught himself to believe that things ugly on the outside might be very beautiful within; and had therefore come to prefer crossing Poland Street and Soho Square, and so continuing his travels by the Seven Dials and Long Acre. His morning walk was of a piece with his morning studies, and he took pleasure in the gloom of both. But now the taste of his palate had been already changed by the glare of the lamps in and about palatial Westminster, and he found that St. Giles's was disagreeable. The ways about Pall Mall and across the Park to Parliament Street, or to the Treasury, were much pleasanter, and the new offices in Downing Street, already half built, absorbed all that interest which he had hitherto been able to take in the suggested but uncommenced erection of new Law Courts in the neighbourhood of Lincoln's Inn. As he made his way to the porter's lodge under the great gateway of Lincoln's Inn, he told himself that he was glad that he had escaped, at any rate for a while, from a life so dull and dreary. If he could only sit in chambers at the Treasury instead of chambers in that old court, how much pleasanter it would be! After all, as regarded that question of income, it might well be that the Treasury chambers should be the more remunerative, and the more quickly remunerative, of the two. And, as he thought, Lady Laura might be compatible with the Treasury chambers and Parliament, but could not possibly be made compatible with Old Square, Lincoln's Inn.

But nevertheless there came upon him a feeling of sorrow when the old man at the lodge seemed to be rather glad than otherwise that he did not want the chambers. "Then Mr. Green can have them," said the porter; "that'll be good news for Mr. Green. I don't know what the gen'lemen 'll do for chambers if things goes on as they're going." Mr. Green was welcome to the chambers as far as Phineas was concerned; but Phineas felt nevertheless a certain amount of regret that he should have been compelled to abandon a thing which was regarded both by the porter and by Mr. Green as being so desirable. He had however written his letter to Mr. Low, and made his promise to Barrington Erle, and was bound to Lady Laura Standish; and he walked out through the old gateway into Chancery Lane, resolving that he would not even visit Lincoln's Inn again for a year. There were certain books,—law books,—which he would read at such intervals of leisure as politics might give him; but within the precincts of the Inns of Court he would not again put his foot for twelve months, let learned pundits of the law,— such for instance as Mr. and Mrs. Low,—say what they might.

He had told Mrs. Bunce, before he left his home after breakfast, that he should for the present remain under her roof. She had been much gratified, not simply because lodgings in Great Marlborough Street are less readily let than chambers in Lincoln's Inn, but also because it was a great honour to her to have a member of Parliament in her house. Members of Parliament are not so common about Oxford Street as they are in the neighbourhood of Pall Mall and St. James's Square. But Mr. Bunce, when he came home to his dinner, did not join as heartily as he should have done in his wife's rejoicing. Mr. Bunce was in the employment of certain copying law-stationers in Carey Street, and had a strong belief in the law as a profession;—but he had none whatever in the House of Commons. "And he's given up going into chambers?" said Mr. Bunce to his wife.

"Given it up altogether for the present," said Mrs. Bunce.

"And he don't mean to have no clerk?" said Mr. Bunce.

"Not unless it is for his Parliament work."

"There ain't no clerks wanted for that, and what's worse, there ain't no fees to pay 'em. I'll tell you what it is, Jane;—if you don't look sharp there won't be nothing to pay you before long."

"And he in Parliament, Jacob!"

"There ain't no salary for being in Parliament. There are scores of them Parliament gents ain't got so much as'll pay their dinners for 'em. And then if anybody does trust 'em, there's no getting at 'em to make 'em pay as there is at other folk."

"I don't know that our Mr. Phineas will ever be like that, Jacob."

"That's gammon, Jane. That's the way as women gets themselves took in always. Our Mr. Phineas! Why should our Mr. Phineas be better than anybody else?"

"He's always acted handsome, Jacob."

"There was one time he could not pay his lodgings for wellnigh nine months, till his governor come down with the money. I don't know whether that was handsome. It knocked me about terrible, I know."

"He always meant honest, Jacob."

"I don't know that I care much for a man's meaning when he runs short of money. How is he going to see his way, with his seat in Parliament, and this giving up of his profession? He owes us near a quarter now."

"He paid me two months this morning, Jacob; so he don't owe a farthing."

"Very well;—so much the better for us. I shall just have a few words with Mr. Low, and see what he says to it. For myself I don't think half so much of Parliament folk as some do. They're for promising everything before they's elected; but not one in twenty of 'em is as good as his word when he gets there."

Mr. Bunce was a copying journeyman, who spent ten hours a day in Carey Street with a pen between his fingers; and after that he would often spend two or three hours of the night with a pen between his fingers in Marlborough Street. He was a thoroughly hard-working man, doing pretty well in the world, for he had a good house over his head, and always could find raiment and bread for his wife and eight children; but, nevertheless, he was an unhappy man because he suffered from political grievances, or, I should more correctly say, that his grievances were semi-political and semi-social. He had no vote, not being himself the tenant of the house in Great Marlborough Street. The tenant was a tailor who occupied the shop, whereas Bunce occupied the whole of the remainder of the premises. He was a lodger, and lodgers were not as yet trusted with the franchise. And he had ideas, which he himself admitted to be very raw, as to the injustice of the manner in which he was paid for his work. So much a folio, without reference to the way in which his work was done, without regard to the success of his work, with no questions asked of himself, was, as he thought, no proper way of remunerating a man for his labours. He had long since joined a Trade Union, and for two years past had paid a subscription of a shilling a week towards its funds. He longed to be doing some battle against his superiors, and to be putting himself in opposition to his employers;—not that he objected personally to Messrs. Foolscap, Margin, and Vellum, who always made much of him as a useful man;—but because some such antagonism would be manly, and the fighting of some battle would be the right thing to do. "If Labour don't mean to go to the wall himself," Bunce would say to his wife, "Labour must look alive, and put somebody else there."

Mrs. Bunce was a comfortable motherly woman, who loved her husband but hated politics. As he had an aversion to his superiors in the world because they were superiors, so had she a liking for them for the same reason. She despised people poorer than herself, and thought it a fair subject for boasting that her children always had meat for dinner. If it was ever so small a morsel, she took care that they had it, in order that the boast might be maintained. The world had once or twice been almost too much for her,—when, for instance, her husband had been ill; and again, to tell the truth, for the last three months of that long period in which Phineas had omitted to pay his bills; but she had kept a fine brave heart during those troubles, and could honestly swear that the children always had a bit of meat, though she herself had been occasionally without it for days together. At such times she would be more than ordinarily meek to Mr. Margin, and especially courteous to the old lady who lodged in her first-floor drawing-room,—for Phineas lived up two pairs of stairs,—and she would excuse such servility by declaring that there was no knowing how soon she might want assistance. But her husband, in such emergencies, would become furious and quarrelsome, and would declare that Labour was going to the wall, and that something very strong must be done at once. That shilling which Bunce paid weekly to the Union she regarded as being absolutely thrown away,—as much so as though he cast it weekly into the Thames. And she had told him so, over and over again, making heart-piercing allusions to the eight children and to the bit of meat. He would always endeavour to explain to her that there was no other way under the sun for keeping Labour from being sent to the wall;—but he would do so hopelessly and altogether ineffectually, and she had come to regard him as a lunatic to the extent of that one weekly shilling.

She had a woman's instinctive partiality for comeliness in a man, and was very fond of Phineas Finn because he was handsome. And now she was very proud of him because he was a member of Parliament. She had heard,—from her husband, who had told her the fact with much disgust,—that the sons of Dukes and Earls go into Parliament, and she liked to think that the fine young man to whom she talked more or less every day should sit with the sons of Dukes and Earls. When Phineas had really brought distress upon her by owing her some thirty or forty pounds, she could never bring herself to be angry with him,—because he was handsome and because he dined out with Lords. And she had triumphed greatly over her husband, who had desired to be severe upon his aristocratic debtor, when the money had all been paid in a lump.

"I don't know that he's any great catch," Bunce had said, when the prospect of their lodger's departure had been debated between them.

"Jacob," said his wife, "I don't think you feel it when you've got people respectable about you."

"The only respectable man I know," said Jacob, "is the man as earns his bread; and Mr. Finn, as I take it, is a long way from that yet."

Phineas returned to his lodgings before he went down to his club, and again told Mrs. Bunce that he had altogether made up his mind about the chambers. "If you'll keep me I shall stay here for the first session I daresay."

"Of course we shall be only too proud, Mr. Finn; and though it mayn't perhaps be quite the place for a member of Parliament—"

"But I think it is quite the place."

"It's very good of you to say so, Mr. Finn, and we'll do our very best to make you comfortable. Respectable we are, I may say; and though Bunce is a bit rough sometimes—"

"Never to me, Mrs. Bunce."

"But he is rough,—and silly, too, with his radical nonsense, paying a shilling a week to a nasty Union just for nothing. Still he means well, and there ain't a man who works harder for his wife and children;—that I will say of him. And if he do talk politics—"

"But I like a man to talk politics, Mrs. Bunce."

"For a gentleman in Parliament of course it's proper; but I never could see what good it could do to a law-stationer; and when he talks of Labour going to the wall, I always ask him whether he didn't get his wages regular last Saturday. But, Lord love you, Mr. Finn, when a man as is a journeyman has took up politics and joined a Trade Union, he ain't no better than a milestone for his wife to take and talk to him."

After that Phineas went down to the Reform Club, and made one of those who were buzzing there in little crowds and uttering their prophecies as to future events. Lord de Terrier was to go out. That was certain. Whether Mr. Mildmay was to come in was uncertain. That he would go to Windsor to-morrow morning was not to be doubted; but it was thought very probable that he might plead his age, and decline to undertake the responsibility of forming a Ministry.

"And what then?" said Phineas to his friend Fitzgibbon.

"Why, then there will be a choice out of three. There is the Duke, who is the most incompetent man in England; there is Monk, who is the most unfit; and there is Gresham, who is the most unpopular. I can't conceive it possible to find a worse Prime Minister than either of the three;—but the country affords no other."

"And which would Mildmay name?"

"All of them,—one after the other, so as to make the embarrassment the greater." That was Mr. Fitzgibbon's description of the crisis; but then it was understood that Mr. Fitzgibbon was given to romancing.

CHAPTER VIII
The News about Mr. Mildmay and Sir Everard

Fitzgibbon and Phineas started together from Pall Mall for Portman Square,—as both of them had promised to call on Lady Laura,—but Fitzgibbon turned in at Brooks's as they walked up St. James's Square, and Phineas went on by himself in a cab. "You should belong here," said Fitzgibbon as his friend entered the cab, and Phineas immediately began to feel that he would have done nothing till he could get into Brooks's's. It might be very well to begin by talking politics at the Reform Club. Such talking had procured for him his seat at Loughshane. But that was done now, and something more than talking was wanted for any further progress. Nothing, as he told himself, of political import was managed at the Reform Club. No influence from thence was ever brought to bear upon the adjustment of places under the Government, or upon the arrangement of cabinets. It might be very well to count votes at the Reform Club; but after the votes had been counted,—had been counted successfully,—Brooks's was the place, as Phineas believed, to learn at the earliest moment what would be the exact result of the success. He must get into Brooks's, if it might be possible for him. Fitzgibbon was not exactly the man to propose him. Perhaps the Earl of Brentford would do it.

Lady Laura was at home, and with her was sitting—Mr. Kennedy. Phineas had intended to be triumphant as he entered Lady Laura's room. He was there with the express purpose of triumphing in the success of their great party, and of singing a pleasant paean in conjunction with Lady Laura. But his trumpet was put out of tune at once when he saw Mr. Kennedy. He said hardly a word as he gave his hand to Lady Laura,—and then afterwards to Mr. Kennedy, who chose to greet him with this show of cordiality.

"I hope you are satisfied, Mr. Finn," said Lady Laura, laughing.

"Oh yes."

"And is that all? I thought to have found your joy quite irrepressible."

"A bottle of soda-water, though it is a very lively thing when opened, won't maintain its vivacity beyond a certain period, Lady Laura."

"And you have had your gas let off already?"

"Well,—yes; at any rate, the sputtering part of it. Nineteen is very well, but the question is whether we might not have had twenty-one."

"Mr. Kennedy has just been saying that not a single available vote has been missed on our side. He has just come from Brooks's, and that seems to be what they say there."

So Mr. Kennedy also was a member of Brooks's! At the Reform Club there certainly had been an idea that the number might have been swelled to twenty-one; but then, as Phineas began to understand, nothing was correctly known at the Reform Club. For an accurate appreciation of the political balance of the day, you must go to Brooks's.

"Mr. Kennedy must of course be right," said Phineas. "I don't belong to Brooks's myself. But I was only joking, Lady Laura. There is, I suppose, no doubt that Lord de Terrier is out, and that is everything."

"He has probably tendered his resignation," said Mr. Kennedy.

"That is the same thing," said Phineas, roughly.

"Not exactly," said Lady Laura. "Should there be any difficulty about Mr. Mildmay, he might, at the Queen's request, make another attempt."

"With a majority of nineteen against him!" said Phineas. "Surely Mr. Mildmay is not the only man in the country. There is the Duke, and there is Mr. Gresham,—and there is Mr. Monk." Phineas had at his tongue's end all the lesson that he had been able to learn at the Reform Club.

"I should hardly think the Duke would venture," said Mr. Kennedy.

"Nothing venture, nothing have," said Phineas. "It is all very well to say that the Duke is incompetent, but I do not know that anything very wonderful is required in the way of genius. The Duke has held his own in both Houses successfully, and he is both honest and popular. I quite agree that a Prime Minister at the present day should be commonly honest, and more than commonly popular."

"So you are all for the Duke, are you?" said Lady Laura, again smiling as she spoke to him.

"Certainly;—if we are deserted by Mr. Mildmay. Don't you think so?"

"I don't find it quite so easy to make up my mind as you do. I am inclined to think that Mr. Mildmay will form a government; and as long as there is that prospect, I need hardly commit myself to an opinion as to his probable successor." Then the objectionable Mr. Kennedy took his leave, and Phineas was left alone with Lady Laura.

"It is glorious;—is it not?" he began, as soon as he found the field to be open for himself and his own manœuvring. But he was very young, and had not as yet learned the manner in which he might best advance his cause with such a woman as Lady Laura Standish. He was telling her too clearly that he could have no gratification in talking with her unless he could be allowed to have her all to himself. That might be very well if Lady Laura were in love with him, but would hardly be the way to reduce her to that condition.

"Mr. Finn," said she, smiling as she spoke, "I am sure that you did not mean it, but you were uncourteous to my friend Mr. Kennedy."

"Who? I? Was I? Upon my word, I didn't intend to be uncourteous."

"If I had thought you had intended it, of course I could not tell you of it. And now I take the liberty;—for it is a liberty—"

"Oh no."

"Because I feel so anxious that you should do nothing to mar your chances as a rising man."

"You are only too kind to me,—always."

"I know how clever you are, and how excellent are all your instincts; but I see that you are a little impetuous. I wonder whether you will be angry if I take upon myself the task of mentor."

"Nothing you could say would make me angry,—though you might make me very unhappy."

"I will not do that if I can help it. A mentor ought to be very old, you know, and I am infinitely older than you are."

"I should have thought it was the reverse;—indeed, I may say that I know that it is," said Phineas.

"I am not talking of years. Years have very little to do with the comparative ages of men and women. A woman at forty is quite old, whereas a man at forty is young." Phineas, remembering that he had put down Mr. Kennedy's age as forty in his own mind, frowned when he heard this, and walked about the room in displeasure. "And therefore," continued Lady Laura, "I talk to you as though I were a kind of grandmother."

"You shall be my great-grandmother if you will only be kind enough to me to say what you really think."

"You must not then be so impetuous, and you must be a little more careful to be civil to persons to whom you may not take any particular fancy. Now Mr. Kennedy is a man who may be very useful to you."

"I do not want Mr. Kennedy to be of use to me."

"That is what I call being impetuous,—being young,—being a boy. Why should not Mr. Kennedy be of use to you as well as any one else? You do not mean to conquer the world all by yourself."

"No;—but there is something mean to me in the expressed idea that I should make use of any man,—and more especially of a man whom I don't like."

"And why do you not like him, Mr. Finn?"

"Because he is one of my Dr. Fells."

"You don't like him simply because he does not talk much. That may be a good reason why you should not make of him an intimate companion,—because you like talkative people; but it should be no ground for dislike."

Phineas paused for a moment before he answered her, thinking whether or not it would be well to ask her some question which might produce from her a truth which he would not like to hear. Then he did ask it. "And do you like him?" he said.

She too paused, but only for a second. "Yes,—I think I may say that I do like him."

"No more than that?"

"Certainly no more than that;—but that I think is a great deal."

"I wonder what you would say if any one asked you whether you liked me," said Phineas, looking away from her through the window.

"Just the same;—but without the doubt, if the person who questioned me had any right to ask the question. There are not above one or two who could have such a right."

"And I was wrong, of course, to ask it about Mr. Kennedy," said Phineas, looking out into the Square.

"I did not say so."

"But I see you think it."

"You see nothing of the kind. I was quite willing to be asked the question by you, and quite willing to answer it. Mr. Kennedy is a man of great wealth."

"What can that have to do with it?"

"Wait a moment, you impetuous Irish boy, and hear me out." Phineas liked being called an impetuous Irish boy, and came close to her, sitting where he could look up into her face; and there came a smile upon his own, and he was very handsome. "I say that he is a man of great wealth," continued Lady Laura; "and as wealth gives influence, he is of great use,—politically,—to the party to which he belongs."

"Oh, politically!"

"Am I to suppose you care nothing for politics? To such men, to men who think as you think, who are to sit on the same benches with yourself, and go into the same lobby and be seen at the same club, it is your duty to be civil both for your own sake and for that of the cause. It is for the hermits of society to indulge in personal dislikings,—for men who have never been active and never mean to be active. I had been telling Mr. Kennedy how much I thought of you,—as a good Liberal."

"And I came in and spoilt it all."

"Yes, you did. You knocked down my little house, and I must build it all up again."

"Don't trouble yourself, Lady Laura."

"I shall. It will be a great deal of trouble,—a great deal, indeed; but I shall take it. I mean you to be very intimate with Mr. Kennedy, and to shoot his grouse, and to stalk his deer, and to help to keep him in progress as a liberal member of Parliament. I am quite prepared to admit, as a friend, that he would go back without some such help."

"Oh;—I understand."

"I do not believe that you do understand at all, but I must endeavour to make you do so by degrees. If you are to be my political pupil, you must at any rate be obedient. The next time you meet Mr. Kennedy, ask him his opinion instead of telling him your own. He has been in Parliament twelve years, and he was a good deal older than you when he began." At this moment a side door was opened, and the red-haired, red-bearded man whom Phineas had seen before entered the room. He hesitated a moment, as though he were going to retreat again, and then began to pull about the books and toys which lay on one of the distant tables, as though he were in quest of some article. And he would have retreated had not Lady Laura called to him.

"Oswald," she said, "let me introduce you to Mr. Finn. Mr. Finn, I do not think you have ever met my brother, Lord Chiltern." Then the two young men bowed, and each of them muttered something. "Do not be in a hurry, Oswald. You have nothing special to take you away. Here is Mr. Finn come to tell us who are all the possible new Prime Ministers. He is uncivil enough not to have named papa."

"My father is out of the question," said Lord Chiltern.

"Of course he is," said Lady Laura, "but I may be allowed my little joke."

"I suppose he will at any rate be in the Cabinet," said Phineas.

"I know nothing whatever about politics," said Lord Chiltern.

"I wish you did," said his sister,—"with all my heart."

"I never did,—and I never shall, for all your wishing. It's the meanest trade going I think, and I'm sure it's the most dishonest. They talk of legs on the turf, and of course there are legs; but what are they to the legs in the House? I don't know whether you are in Parliament, Mr. Finn."

"Yes, I am; but do not mind me."

"I beg your pardon. Of course there are honest men there, and no doubt you are one of them."

"He is indifferent honest,—as yet," said Lady Laura.

"I was speaking of men who go into Parliament to look after Government places," said Lord Chiltern.

"That is just what I'm doing," said Phineas. "Why should not a man serve the Crown? He has to work very hard for what he earns."

"I don't believe that the most of them work at all. However, I beg your pardon. I didn't mean you in particular."

"Mr. Finn is such a thorough politician that he will never forgive you," said Lady Laura.

"Yes, I will," said Phineas, "and I'll convert him some day. If he does come into the House, Lady Laura, I suppose he'll come on the right side?"

"I'll never go into the House, as you call it," said Lord Chiltern. "But, I'll tell you what; I shall be very happy if you'll dine with me to-morrow at Moroni's. They give you a capital little dinner at Moroni's, and they've the best Château Yquem in London."

"Do," said Lady Laura, in a whisper. "Oblige me."

Phineas was engaged to dine with one of the Vice-Chancellors on the day named. He had never before dined at the house of this great law luminary, whose acquaintance he had made through Mr. Low, and he had thought a great deal of the occasion. Mrs. Freemantle had sent him the invitation nearly a fortnight ago, and he understood there was to be an elaborate dinner party. He did not know it for a fact, but he was in hopes of meeting the expiring Lord Chancellor. He considered it to be his duty never to throw away such a chance. He would in all respects have preferred Mr. Freemantle's dinner in Eaton Place, dull and heavy though it might probably be, to the chance of Lord Chiltern's companions at Moroni's. Whatever might be the faults of our hero, he was not given to what is generally called dissipation by the world at large,—by which the world means self-indulgence. He cared not a brass farthing for Moroni's Château Yquem, nor for the wondrously studied repast which he would doubtless find prepared for him at that celebrated establishment in St. James's Street;—not a farthing as compared with the chance of meeting so great a man as Lord Moles. And Lord Chiltern's friends might probably be just the men whom he would not desire to know. But Lady Laura's request overrode everything with him. She had asked him to oblige her, and of course he would do so. Had he been going to dine with the incoming Prime Minister, he would have put off his engagement at her request. He was not quick enough to make an answer without hesitation; but after a moment's pause he said he should be most happy to dine with Lord Chiltern at Moroni's.

"That's right; 7.30 sharp,—only I can tell you you won't meet any other members." Then the servant announced more visitors, and Lord Chiltern escaped out of the room before he was seen by the new comers. These were Mrs. Bonteen and Laurence Fitzgibbon, and then Mr. Bonteen,—and after them Mr. Ratler, the Whip, who was in a violent hurry, and did not stay there a moment, and then Barrington Erle and young Lord James Fitz-Howard, the youngest son of the Duke of St. Bungay. In twenty or thirty minutes there was a gathering of liberal political notabilities in Lady Laura's drawing-room. There were two great pieces of news by which they were all enthralled. Mr. Mildmay would not be Prime Minister, and Sir Everard Powell was—dead. Of course nothing quite positive could be known about Mr. Mildmay. He was to be with the Queen at Windsor on the morrow at eleven o'clock, and it was improbable that he would tell his mind to any one before he told it to her Majesty. But there was no doubt that he had engaged "the Duke,"—so he was called by Lord James,—to go down to Windsor with him, that he might be in readiness if wanted. "I have learned that at home," said Lord James, who had just heard the news from his sister, who had heard it from the Duchess. Lord James was delighted with the importance given to him by his father's coming journey. From this, and from other circumstances equally well-known circumstances, it was surmised that Mr. Mildmay would decline the task proposed to him. This, nevertheless, was only a surmise,—whereas the fact with reference to Sir Everard was fully substantiated. The gout had flown to his stomach, and he was dead. "By —— yes; as dead as a herring," said Mr. Ratler, who at that moment, however, was not within hearing of either of the ladies present. And then he rubbed his hands, and looked as though he were delighted. And he was delighted,—not because his old friend Sir Everard was dead, but by the excitement of the tragedy. "Having done so good a deed in his last moments," said Laurence Fitzgibbon, "we may take it for granted that he will go straight to heaven." "I hope there will be no crowner's quest, Ratler," said Mr. Bonteen; "if there is I don't know how you'll get out of it." "I don't see anything in it so horrible," said Mr. Ratler. "If a fellow dies leading his regiment we don't think anything of it. Sir Everard's vote was of more service to his country than anything that a colonel or a captain can do." But nevertheless I think that Mr. Ratler was somewhat in dread of future newspaper paragraphs, should it be found necessary to summon a coroner's inquisition to sit upon poor Sir Everard.

While this was going on Lady Laura took Phineas apart for a moment. "I am so much obliged to you; I am indeed," she said.

"What nonsense!"

"Never mind whether it's nonsense or not;—but I am. I can't explain it all now, but I do so want you to know my brother. You may be of the greatest service to him,—of the very greatest. He is not half so bad as people say he is. In many ways he is very good,—very good. And he is very clever."

"At any rate I will think and believe no ill of him."

"Just so;—do not believe evil of him,—not more evil than you see. I am so anxious,—so very anxious to try to put him on his legs, and I find it so difficult to get any connecting link with him. Papa will not speak with him,—because of money."

27

"But he is friends with you."

"Yes; I think he loves me. I saw how distasteful it was to you to go to him;—and probably you were engaged?"

"One can always get off those sort of things if there is an object."

"Yes;—just so. And the object was to oblige me;—was it not?"

"Of course it was. But I must go now. We are to hear Daubeny's statement at four, and I would not miss it for worlds."

"I wonder whether you would go abroad with my brother in the autumn? But I have no right to think of such a thing;—have I? At any rate I will not think of it yet. Good-bye,—I shall see you perhaps on Sunday if you are in town."

Phineas walked down to Westminster with his mind very full of Lady Laura and Lord Chiltern. What did she mean by her affectionate manner to himself, and what did she mean by the continual praises which she lavished upon Mr. Kennedy? Of whom was she thinking most, of Mr. Kennedy, or of him? She had called herself his mentor. Was the description of her feelings towards himself, as conveyed in that name, of a kind to be gratifying to him? No;—he thought not. But then might it not be within his power to change the nature of those feelings? She was not in love with him at present. He could not make any boast to himself on that head. But it might be within his power to compel her to love him. The female mentor might be softened. That she could not love Mr. Kennedy, he thought that he was quite sure. There was nothing like love in her manner to Mr. Kennedy. As to Lord Chiltern, Phineas would do whatever might be in his power. All that he really knew of Lord Chiltern was that he had gambled and that he had drunk.

CHAPTER IX
The New Government

In the House of Lords that night, and in the House of Commons, the outgoing Ministers made their explanations. As our business at the present moment is with the Commons, we will confine ourselves to their chamber, and will do so the more willingly because the upshot of what was said in the two places was the same. The outgoing ministers were very grave, very self-laudatory, and very courteous. In regard to courtesy it may be declared that no stranger to the ways of the place could have understood how such soft words could be spoken by Mr. Daubeny, beaten, so quickly after the very sharp words which he had uttered when he only expected to be beaten. He announced to his fellow-commoners that his right honourable friend and colleague Lord de Terrier had thought it right to retire from the Treasury. Lord de Terrier, in constitutional obedience to the vote of the Lower House, had resigned, and the Queen had been graciously pleased to accept Lord de Terrier's resignation. Mr. Daubeny could only inform the House that her Majesty had signified her pleasure that Mr. Mildmay should wait upon her to-morrow at eleven o'clock. Mr. Mildmay,—so Mr. Daubeny understood,—would be with her Majesty to-morrow at that hour. Lord de Terrier had found it to be his duty to recommend her Majesty to send for Mr. Mildmay. Such was the real import of Mr. Daubeny's speech. That further portion of it in which he explained with blandest, most beneficent, honey-flowing words that his party would have done everything that the country could require of any party, had the House allowed it to remain on the Treasury benches for a month or two,—and explained also that his party would never recriminate, would never return evil for evil, would in no wise copy the factious opposition of their adversaries; that his party would now, as it ever had done, carry itself with the meekness of the dove, and the wisdom of the serpent,—all this, I say, was so generally felt by gentlemen on both sides of the House to be "leather and prunella" that very little attention was paid to it. The great point was that Lord de Terrier had resigned, and that Mr. Mildmay had been summoned to Windsor.

The Queen had sent for Mr. Mildmay in compliance with advice given to her by Lord de Terrier. And yet Lord de Terrier and his first lieutenant had used all the most practised efforts of their eloquence for the last three days in endeavouring to make their countrymen believe that no more unfitting Minister than Mr. Mildmay ever attempted to hold the reins of office! Nothing had been too bad for them to say of Mr. Mildmay,—and yet, in the very first moment in which they found themselves unable to carry on the Government themselves, they advised the Queen to send for that most incompetent and baneful statesman! We who are conversant with our own methods of politics, see nothing odd in this, because we are used to it; but surely in the eyes of strangers our practice must be very singular. There is nothing like it in any other country,—nothing as yet. Nowhere else is there the same good-humoured, affectionate, prize-fighting ferocity in politics. The leaders of our two great parties are to each other exactly as are the two champions of the ring who knock each other about for the belt and for five hundred pounds a side once in every two years. How they fly at each other, striking as though each blow should carry death if it were but possible! And yet there is no one whom the Birmingham Bantam respects so highly as he does Bill Burns the Brighton Bully, or with whom he has so much delight in discussing the merits of a pot of half-and-half. And so it was with Mr. Daubeny and Mr. Mildmay. In private life Mr. Daubeny almost adulated his elder rival,—and Mr. Mildmay never omitted an opportunity of taking Mr. Daubeny warmly by the hand. It is not so in the United States. There the same political enmity exists, but the political enmity produces private hatred. The leaders of parties there really mean what they say when they abuse each other, and are in earnest when they talk as though they were about to tear each other limb from limb. I doubt whether Mr. Daubeny would have injured a hair of Mr. Mildmay's venerable head, even for an assurance of six continued months in office.

When Mr. Daubeny had completed his statement, Mr. Mildmay simply told the House that he had received and would obey her Majesty's commands. The House would of course understand that he by no means meant to aver that the Queen would even commission him to form a Ministry. But if he took no such command from her Majesty it would become his duty to recommend her Majesty to impose the task upon some other person. Then everything was said that had to be said, and members returned to their clubs. A certain damp was thrown over the joy of some excitable Liberals by tidings which reached the House during Mr. Daubeny's speech. Sir Everard Powell was no more dead than was Mr. Daubeny himself. Now it is very unpleasant to find that your news is untrue, when you have been at great pains to disseminate it. "Oh, but he is dead," said Mr. Ratler. "Lady Powell assured me half an hour ago," said Mr. Ratler's opponent, "that he was at that moment a great deal better than he had been for the last three months. The journey down to the House did him a world of good." "Then we'll have him down for every division," said Mr. Ratler.

The political portion of London was in a ferment for the next five days. On the Sunday morning it was known that Mr. Mildmay had declined to put himself at the head of a liberal Government. He and the Duke of St. Bungay, and Mr. Plantagenet Palliser, had been in conference so often, and so long, that it may almost be said they lived together in conference. Then Mr. Gresham had been with Mr. Mildmay,—and Mr. Monk also. At the clubs it was said by many that Mr. Monk had been with Mr. Mildmay; but it was also said very vehemently by others that no such interview had taken place. Mr. Monk was a Radical, much admired by the people, sitting in Parliament for that most Radical of all constituencies, the Pottery Hamlets, who had never as yet been in power. It was the great question of the day whether Mr. Mildmay would or would not ask Mr. Monk to join him; and it was said by those who habitually think at every period of change that the time has now come in which the difficulties to forming a government will at last be found to be insuperable, that Mr. Mildmay could not succeed either with Mr. Monk or without him. There were at the present moment two sections of these gentlemen,—the section which declared that Mr. Mildmay had sent for Mr. Monk, and the section which declared that he had not. But there were others, who perhaps knew better what they were saying, by whom it was asserted that the whole difficulty lay with Mr. Gresham. Mr. Gresham was willing to serve with Mr. Mildmay,—with certain stipulations as to the special seat in the Cabinet which he himself was to occupy, and as to the introduction of certain friends of his own; but,—so said these gentlemen who were supposed really to understand the matter,—Mr. Gresham was not willing to serve with the Duke and with Mr. Palliser. Now, everybody who knew anything knew that the Duke and Mr. Palliser were indispensable to Mr. Mildmay. And a liberal Government, with Mr. Gresham in the opposition, could not live half through a session! All Sunday and Monday these things were discussed; and on the Monday Lord de Terrier absolutely stated to the Upper House that he had received her Majesty's commands to form another government. Mr. Daubeny, in half a dozen most modest words,—in words hardly audible, and most unlike himself,—made his statement in the Lower House to the same effect. Then Mr. Ratler, and Mr. Bonteen, and Mr. Barrington Erle, and Mr. Laurence Fitzgibbon aroused themselves and swore that such things could not be. Should the prey which they had won for themselves, the spoil of their bows and arrows, be snatched from out of their very mouths by treachery? Lord de Terrier and Mr. Daubeny could not venture even to make another attempt unless they did so in combination with Mr. Gresham. Such a combination, said Mr. Barrington Erle, would be disgraceful to both parties, but would prove Mr. Gresham to be as false as Satan himself. Early on the Tuesday morning, when it was known that Mr. Gresham had been at Lord de Terrier's house, Barrington Erle was free to confess that he had always been afraid of Mr. Gresham. "I have felt for years," said he, "that if anybody could break up the party it would be Mr. Gresham."

On that Tuesday morning Mr. Gresham certainly was with Lord de Terrier, but nothing came of it. Mr. Gresham was either not enough like Satan for the occasion, or else he was too closely like him. Lord de Terrier did not bid high enough, or else Mr. Gresham did not like biddings from that quarter. Nothing then came from this attempt, and on the Tuesday afternoon the Queen again sent for Mr. Mildmay. On the Wednesday morning the gentlemen who thought that the insuperable difficulties had at length arrived, began to wear their longest faces, and to be triumphant with melancholy forebodings. Now at last there was a dead lock. Nobody could form a government. It was asserted that Mr. Mildmay had fallen at her Majesty's feet dissolved in tears, and had implored to be relieved from further responsibility. It was well known to many at the clubs that the Queen had on that morning telegraphed to Germany for advice. There were men so gloomy as to declare that the Queen must throw herself into the arms of Mr. Monk, unless Mr. Mildmay would consent to rise from his knees and once more buckle on his ancient armour. "Even that would be better than Gresham," said Barrington Erle, in his anger. "I'll tell you what it is," said Ratler, "we shall have Gresham and Monk together, and you and I shall have to do their biddings." Mr. Barrington Erle's reply to that suggestion I may not dare to insert in these pages.

On the Wednesday night, however, it was known that everything had been arranged, and before the Houses met on the Thursday every place had been bestowed, either in reality or in imagination. The *Times*, in its second edition on the Thursday, gave a list of the Cabinet, in which four places out of fourteen were rightly filled. On the Friday it named ten places aright, and indicated the law officers, with only one mistake in reference to Ireland; and on the Saturday it gave a list of the Under Secretaries of State, and Secretaries and Vice-Presidents generally, with wonderful correctness as to the individuals, though the offices were a little jumbled. The Government was at last formed in a manner which everybody had seen to be the only possible way in which a government could be formed. Nobody was surprised, and the week's work was regarded as though the regular routine of government making had simply been followed. Mr. Mildmay was Prime Minister; Mr. Gresham was at the Foreign Office; Mr. Monk was at the Board of Trade; the Duke was President of the Council; the Earl of Brentford was Privy Seal; and Mr. Palliser was Chancellor of the Exchequer. Barrington Erle made a step up in the world, and went to the Admiralty as Secretary; Mr. Bonteen was sent again to the Admiralty; and Laurence Fitzgibbon became a junior Lord of the Treasury. Mr. Ratler was, of course, installed as Patronage Secretary to the same Board. Mr. Ratler was perhaps the only man in the party as to whose destination there could not possibly be a doubt. Mr. Ratler had really qualified himself for a position in such a way as to make all men feel that he would, as a matter of course, be called upon to fill it. I do not know whether as much could be said on behalf of any other man in the new Government.

During all this excitement, and through all these movements, Phineas Finn felt himself to be left more and more out in the cold. He had not been such a fool as to suppose that any office would be offered to him. He had never hinted at such a thing to his one dearly intimate friend, Lady Laura. He had not hitherto opened his mouth in Parliament. Indeed, when the new Government was formed he had not been sitting for above a fortnight. Of course nothing could be done for him as yet. But, nevertheless, he felt himself to be out in the cold. The very men who had discussed with him the question of the division,—who had discussed it with him because his vote was then as good as that of any other member,—did not care to talk to him about the distribution of places. He, at any rate, could not be one of them. He, at any rate, could not be a rival. He could neither mar nor assist. He could not be either a successful or a disappointed sympathiser,—because he could not himself be a candidate. The affair which perhaps disgusted him more than anything else was the offer of an office,—not in the Cabinet, indeed, but one supposed to confer high dignity,—to Mr. Kennedy. Mr. Kennedy refused the offer, and this somewhat lessened Finn's disgust, but the offer itself made him unhappy.

"I suppose it was made simply because of his money," he said to Fitzgibbon.

"I don't believe that," said Fitzgibbon. "People seem to think that he has got a head on his shoulders, though he has got no tongue in it. I wonder at his refusing it because of the Right Honourable."

"I am so glad that Mr. Kennedy refused," said Lady Laura to him.

"And why? He would have been the Right Hon. Robert Kennedy for ever and ever." Phineas when he said this did not as yet know exactly how it would have come to pass that such honour,—the honour of the enduring prefix to his name,—would have come in the way of Mr. Kennedy had Mr. Kennedy accepted the office in question; but he was very quick to learn all these things, and, in the meantime, he rarely made any mistake about them.

"What would that have been to him,—with his wealth?" said Lady Laura. "He has a position of his own and need not care for such things. There are men who should not attempt what is called independence in Parliament. By doing so they simply decline to make themselves useful. But there are a few whose special walk in life it is to be independent, and, as it were, unmoved by parties."

"Great Akinetoses! You know Orion," said Phineas.

"Mr. Kennedy is not an Akinetos," said Lady Laura.

"He holds a very proud position," said Phineas, ironically.

"A very proud position indeed," said Lady Laura, in sober earnest.

The dinner at Moroni's had been eaten, and Phineas had given an account of the entertainment to Lord Chiltern's sister. There had been only two other guests, and both of them had been men on the turf. "I was the first there," said Phineas, "and he surprised me ever so much by telling me that you had spoken to him of me before."

"Yes; I did so. I wish him to know you. I want him to know some men who think of something besides horses. He is very well educated, you know, and would certainly have taken honours if he had not quarrelled with the people at Christ Church."

"Did he take a degree?"

"No;—they sent him down. It is best always to have the truth among friends. Of course you will hear it some day. They expelled him because he was drunk." Then Lady Laura burst out into tears, and Phineas sat near her, and consoled her, and swore that if in any way he could befriend her brother he would do so.

Mr. Fitzgibbon at this time claimed a promise which he said that Phineas had made to him,—that Phineas would go over with him to Mayo to assist at his re-election. And Phineas did go. The whole affair occupied but a week, and was chiefly memorable as being the means of cementing the friendship which existed between the two Irish members.

"A thousand a year!" said Laurence Fitzgibbon, speaking of the salary of his office. "It isn't much; is it? And every fellow to whom I owe a shilling will be down upon me. If I had studied my own comfort, I should have done the same as Kennedy."

CHAPTER X
Violet Effingham

It was now the middle of May, and a month had elapsed since the terrible difficulty about the Queen's Government had been solved. A month had elapsed, and things had shaken themselves into their places with more of ease and apparent fitness than men had given them credit for possessing. Mr. Mildmay, Mr. Gresham, and Mr. Monk were the best friends in the world, swearing by each other in their own house, and supported in the other by as gallant a phalanx of Whig peers as ever were got together to fight against the instincts of their own order in compliance with the instincts of those below them. Lady Laura's father was in the Cabinet, to Lady Laura's infinite delight. It was her ambition to be brought as near to political action as was possible for a woman without surrendering any of the privileges of feminine inaction. That women should even wish to have votes at parliamentary elections was to her abominable, and the cause of the Rights of Women generally was odious to her; but, nevertheless, for herself, she delighted in hoping that she too might be useful,—in thinking that she too was perhaps, in some degree, politically powerful; and she had received considerable increase to such hopes when her father accepted the Privy Seal. The Earl himself was not an ambitious man, and, but for his daughter, would have severed himself altogether from political life before this time. He was an unhappy man;—being an obstinate man, and having in his obstinacy quarrelled with his only son. In his unhappiness he would have kept himself alone, living in the country, brooding over his wretchedness, were it not for his daughter. On her behalf, and in obedience to her requirements, he came yearly up to London, and, perhaps in compliance with her persuasion, had taken some part in the debates of the House of Lords. It is easy for a peer to be a statesman, if the trouble of the life be not too much for him. Lord Brentford was now a statesman, if a seat in the Cabinet be proof of statesmanship.

At this time, in May, there was staying with Lady Laura in Portman Square a very dear friend of hers, by name Violet Effingham. Violet Effingham was an orphan, an heiress, and a beauty; with a terrible aunt, one Lady Baldock, who was supposed to be the dragon who had Violet, as a captive maiden, in charge. But as Miss Effingham was of age, and was mistress of her own fortune, Lady Baldock was, in truth, not omnipotent as a dragon should be. The dragon, at any rate, was not now staying in Portman Square, and the captivity of the maiden was therefore not severe at the present moment. Violet Effingham was very pretty, but could hardly be said to be beautiful. She was small, with light crispy hair, which seemed to be ever on the flutter round her brows, and which yet was never a hair astray. She had sweet, soft grey eyes, which never looked at you long, hardly for a moment,—but which yet, in that half moment, nearly killed you by the power of their sweetness. Her cheek was the softest thing in nature, and the colour of it, when its colour was fixed enough to be told, was a shade of pink so faint and creamy that you would hardly dare to call it by its name. Her mouth was perfect, not small enough to give that expression of silliness which is so common, but almost divine, with the temptation of its full, rich, ruby lips. Her teeth, which she but seldom showed, were very even and very white, and there rested on her chin the dearest dimple that ever acted as a loadstar to mens's eyes. The fault of her face, if it had a fault, was in her nose,—which was a little too sharp, and perhaps too small. A woman who wanted to depreciate Violet Effingham had once called her a pug-nosed puppet; but I, as her chronicler, deny that she was pug-nosed,—and all the world who knew her soon came to understand that she was no puppet. In figure she was small, but not so small as she looked to be. Her feet and hands were delicately fine, and there was a softness about her whole person, an apparent compressibility, which seemed to indicate that she might go into very small compass. Into what compass and how compressed, there were very many men who held very different opinions. Violet Effingham was certainly no puppet. She was great at dancing,—as perhaps might be a puppet,—but she was great also at archery, great at skating,—and great, too, at hunting. With reference to that last accomplishment, she and Lady Baldock had had more than one terrible tussle, not always with advantage to the dragon. "My dear aunt," she had said once during the last winter, "I am going to the meet with George,"—George was her cousin, Lord Baldock, and was the dragon's son,—"and there, let there be an end of it." "And you will promise me that you will not go further," said the dragon. "I will promise nothing to-day to any man or to any woman," said Violet. What was to be said to a young lady who spoke in this way, and who had become of age only a fortnight since? She rode that day the famous run from Bagnall's Gorse to Foulsham Common, and was in at the death.

Violet Effingham was now sitting in conference with her friend Lady Laura, and they were discussing matters of high import,—of very high import, indeed,—to the interests of both of them. "I do not ask you to accept him," said Lady Laura.

"That is lucky," said the other, "as he has never asked me."

"He has done much the same. You know that he loves you."

"I know,—or fancy that I know,—that so many men love me! But, after all, what sort of love is it? It is just as when you and I, when we see something nice in a shop, call it a dear duck of a thing, and tell somebody to go and buy it, let the price be ever so extravagant. I know my own position, Laura. I'm a dear duck of a thing."

"You are a very dear thing to Oswald."

"But you, Laura, will some day inspire a grand passion,—or I daresay have already, for you are a great deal too close to tell;—and then there will be cutting of throats, and a mighty hubbub, and a real tragedy. I shall never go beyond genteel comedy,—unless I run away with somebody beneath me, or do something awfully improper."

"Don't do that, dear."

"I should like to, because of my aunt. I should indeed. If it were possible, without compromising myself, I should like her to be told some morning that I had gone off with the curate."

"How can you be so wicked, Violet!"

"It would serve her right, and her countenance would be so awfully comic. Mind, if it is ever to come off, I must be there to see it. I know what she would say as well as possible. She would turn to poor Gussy. 'Augusta,' she would say, 'I always expected it. I always did.' Then I should come out and curtsey to her, and say so prettily, 'Dear aunt, it was only our little joke.' That's my line. But for you,—you, if you planned it, would go off to-morrow with Lucifer himself if you liked him."

"But failing Lucifer, I shall probably be very humdrum."

"You don't mean that there is anything settled, Laura?"

"There is nothing settled,—or any beginning of anything that ever can be settled, But I am not talking about myself. He has told me that if you will accept him, he will do anything that you and I may ask him."

"Yes;—he will promise."

"Did you ever know him to break his word?"

"I know nothing about him, my dear. How should I?"

"Do not pretend to be ignorant and meek, Violet. You do know him,—much better than most girls know the men they marry. You have known him, more or less intimately, all your life."

"But am I bound to marry him because of that accident?"

"No; you are not bound to marry him,—unless you love him."

"I do not love him," said Violet, with slow, emphatic words, and a little forward motion of her face, as though she were specially eager to convince her friend that she was quite in earnest in what she said.

"I fancy, Violet, that you are nearer to loving him than any other man."

"I am not at all near to loving any man. I doubt whether I ever shall be. It does not seem to me to be possible to myself to be what girls call in love. I can like a man. I do like, perhaps, half a dozen. I like them so much that if I go to a house or to a party it is quite a matter of importance to me whether this man or that will or will not be there. And then I suppose I flirt with them. At least Augusta tells me that my aunt says that I do. But as for caring about any one of them in the way of loving him,—wanting to marry him, and have him all to myself, and that sort of thing,—I don't know what it means."

"But you intend to be married some day," said Lady Laura.

"Certainly I do. And I don't intend to wait very much longer. I am heartily tired of Lady Baldock, and though I can generally escape among my friends, that is not sufficient. I am beginning to think that it would be pleasant to have a house of my own. A girl becomes such a Bohemian when she is always going about, and doesn't quite know where any of her things are."

Then there was a silence between them for a few minutes. Violet Effingham was doubled up in a corner of a sofa, with her feet tucked under her, and her face reclining upon one of her shoulders. And as she talked she was playing with a little toy which was constructed to take various shapes as it was flung this way or that. A bystander looking at her would have thought that the toy was much more to her than the conversation. Lady Laura was sitting upright, in a common chair, at a table not far from her companion, and was manifestly devoting herself altogether to the subject that was being discussed between them. She had taken no lounging, easy attitude, she had found no employment for her fingers, and she looked steadily at Violet as she talked,—whereas Violet was looking only at the little manikin which she tossed. And now Laura got up and came to the sofa, and sat close to her friend. Violet, though she somewhat moved one foot, so as to seem to make room for the other, still went on with her play.

"If you do marry, Violet, you must choose some one man out of the lot."

"That's quite true, my dear, I certainly can't marry them all."

"And how do you mean to make the choice?"

"I don't know. I suppose I shall toss up."

"I wish you would be in earnest with me."

"Well;—I will be in earnest with me. I shall take the first that comes after I have quite made up my mind. You'll think it very horrible, but that is really what I shall do. After all, a husband is very much like a house or a horse. You don't take your house because it's the best house in the world, but because just then you want a house. You go and see a house, and if it's very nasty you don't take it. But if you think it will suit pretty well, and if you are tired of looking about for houses, you do take it. That's the way one buys one's horses,—and one's husbands."

"And you have not made up your mind yet?"

"Not quite. Lady Baldock was a little more decent than usual just before I left Baddingham. When I told her that I meant to have a pair of ponies, she merely threw up her hands and grunted. She didn't gnash her teeth, and curse and swear, and declare to me that I was a child of perdition."

"What do you mean by cursing and swearing?"

"She told me once that if I bought a certain little dog, it would lead to my being everlastingly—you know what. She isn't so squeamish as I am, and said it out."

"What did you do?"

"I bought the little dog, and it bit my aunt's heel. I was very sorry then, and gave the creature to Mary Rivers. He was such a beauty! I hope the perdition has gone with him, for I don't like Mary Rivers at all. I had to give the poor beasty to somebody, and Mary Rivers happened to be there. I told her that Puck was connected with Apollyon, but she didn't mind that. Puck was worth twenty guineas, and I daresay she has sold him."

"Oswald may have an equal chance then among the other favourites?" said Lady Laura, after another pause.

"There are no favourites, and I will not say that any man may have a chance. Why do you press me about your brother in this way?"

"Because I am so anxious. Because it would save him. Because you are the only woman for whom he has ever cared, and because he loves you with all his heart; and because his father would be reconciled to him to-morrow if he heard that you and he were engaged."

"Laura, my dear—"

"Well."

"You won't be angry if I speak out?"

"Certainly not. After what I have said, you have a right to speak out."

"It seems to me that all your reasons are reasons why he should marry me;—not reasons why I should marry him."

"Is not his love for you a reason?"

"No," said Violet, pausing,—and speaking the word in the lowest possible whisper. "If he did not love me, that, if known to me, should be a reason why I should not marry him. Ten men may love me,—I don't say that any man does—"

"He does."

"But I can't marry all the ten. And as for that business of saving him—"

"You know what I mean!"

"I don't know that I have any special mission for saving young men. I sometimes think that I shall have quite enough to do to save myself. It is strange what a propensity I feel for the wrong side of the post."

"I feel the strongest assurance that you will always keep on the right side."

"Thank you, my dear. I mean to try, but I'm quite sure that the jockey who takes me in hand ought to be very steady himself. Now, Lord Chiltern—"

"Well,—out with it. What have you to say?"

"He does not bear the best reputation in this world as a steady man. Is he altogether the sort of man that mammas of the best kind are seeking for their daughters? I like a roué myself;—and a prig who sits all night in the House, and talks about nothing but church-rates and suffrage, is to me intolerable. I prefer men who are improper, and all that sort of thing. If I were a man myself I should go in for everything I ought to leave alone. I know I should. But you see,—I'm not a man, and I must take care of myself. The wrong side of a post for a woman is so very much the wrong side. I like a fast man, but I know that I must not dare to marry the sort of man that I like."

"To be one of us, then,—the very first among us;—would that be the wrong side?"

"You mean that to be Lady Chiltern in the present tense, and Lady Brentford in the future, would be promotion for Violet Effingham in the past?"

"How hard you are, Violet!"

"Fancy,—that it should come to this,—that you should call me hard, Laura. I should like to be your sister. I should like well enough to be your father's daughter. I should like well enough to be Chiltern's friend. I am his friend. Nothing that any one has ever said of him has estranged me from him. I have fought for him till I have been black in the face. Yes, I have,—with my aunt. But I am afraid to be his wife. The risk would be so great. Suppose that I did not save him, but that he brought me to shipwreck instead?"

"That could not be!"

"Could it not? I think it might be so very well. When I was a child they used to be always telling me to mind myself. It seems to me that a child and a man need not mind themselves. Let them do what they may, they can be set right again. Let them fall as they will, you can put them on their feet. But a woman has to mind herself;—and very hard work it is when she has a dragon of her own driving her ever the wrong way."

"I want to take you from the dragon."

"Yes;—and to hand me over to a griffin."

"The truth is, Violet, that you do not know Oswald. He is not a griffin."

"I did not mean to be uncomplimentary. Take any of the dangerous wild beasts you please. I merely intend to point out that he is a dangerous wild beast. I daresay he is noble-minded, and I will call him a lion if you like it better. But even with a lion there is risk."

"Of course there will be risk. There is risk with every man,—unless you will be contented with the prig you described. Of course there would be risk with my brother. He has been a gambler."

"They say he is one still."

"He has given it up in part, and would entirely at your instance."

"And they say other things of him, Laura."

"It is true. He has had paroxysms of evil life which have well-nigh ruined him."

"And these paroxysms are so dangerous! Is he not in debt?"

"He is,—but not deeply. Every shilling that he owes would be paid;—every shilling. Mind, I know all his circumstances, and I give you my word that every shilling should be paid. He has never lied,—and he has told me everything. His father could not leave an acre away from him if he would, and would not if he could."

"I did not ask as fearing that. I spoke only of a dangerous habit. A paroxysm of spending money is apt to make one so uncomfortable. And then—"

"Well."

"I don't know why I should make a catalogue of your brother's weaknesses."

"You mean to say that he drinks too much?"

"I do not say so. People say so. The dragon says so. And as I always find her sayings to be untrue, I suppose this is like the rest of them."

"It is untrue if it be said of him as a habit."

"It is another paroxysm,—just now and then."

"Do not laugh at me, Violet, when I am taking his part, or I shall be offended."

"But you see, if I am to be his wife, it is—rather important."

"Still you need not ridicule me."

"Dear Laura, you know I do not ridicule you. You know I love you for what you are doing. Would not I do the same, and fight for him down to my nails if I had a brother?"

"And therefore I want you to be Oswald's wife;—because I know that you would fight for him. It is not true that he is a—drunkard. Look at his hand, which is as steady as yours. Look at his eye. Is there a sign of it? He has been drunk, once or twice, perhaps,—and has done fearful things."

"It might be that he would do fearful things to me."

"You never knew a man with a softer heart or with a finer spirit. I believe as I sit here that if he were married to-morrow, his vices would fall from him like old clothes."

"You will admit, Laura, that there will be some risk for the wife."

"Of course there will be a risk. Is there not always a risk?"

"The men in the city would call this double-dangerous, I think," said Violet. Then the door was opened, and the man of whom they were speaking entered the room.

CHAPTER XI
Lord Chiltern

The reader has been told that Lord Chiltern was a red man, and that peculiarity of his personal appearance was certainly the first to strike a stranger. It imparted a certain look of ferocity to him, which was apt to make men afraid of him at first sight. Women are not actuated in the same way, and are accustomed to look deeper into men at the first sight than other men will trouble themselves to do. His beard was red, and was clipped, so as to have none of the softness of waving hair. The hair on his head also was kept short, and was very red,—and the colour of his face was red. Nevertheless he was a handsome man, with well-cut features, not tall, but very strongly built, and with a certain curl in the corner of his eyelids which gave to him a look of resolution,—which perhaps he did not possess. He was known to be a clever man, and when very young had had the reputation of being a scholar. When he was three-and-twenty grey-haired votaries of the turf declared that he would make his fortune on the race-course,—so clear-headed was he as to odds, so excellent a judge of a horse's performances, and so gifted with a memory of events. When he was five-and-twenty he had lost every shilling of a fortune of his own, had squeezed from his father more than his father ever chose to name in speaking of his affairs to any one, and was known to be in debt. But he had sacrificed himself on one or two memorable occasions in conformity with turf laws of honour, and men said of him, either that he was very honest or very chivalric,—in accordance with the special views on the subject of the man who was speaking. It was reported now that he no longer owned horses on the turf;—but this was doubted by some who could name the animals which they said that he owned, and which he ran in the name of Mr. Macnab,—said some; of Mr. Pardoe,—said others; of Mr. Chickerwick,—said a third set of informants. The fact was that Lord Chiltern at this moment had no interest of his own in any horse upon the turf.

But all the world knew that he drank. He had taken by the throat a proctor's bull-dog when he had been drunk at Oxford, had nearly strangled the man, and had been expelled. He had fallen through his violence into some terrible misfortune at Paris, had been brought before a public judge, and his name and his infamy had been made notorious in every newspaper in the two capitals. After that he had fought a ruffian at Newmarket, and had really killed him with his fists. In reference to this latter affray it had been proved that the attack had been made on him, that he had not been to blame, and that he had not been drunk. After a prolonged investigation he had come forth from that affair without disgrace. He would have done so, at least, if he had not been heretofore disgraced. But we all know how the man well spoken of may steal a horse, while he who is of evil repute may not look over a hedge. It was asserted widely by many who were supposed to know all about everything that Lord Chiltern was in a fit of delirium tremens when he killed the ruffian at Newmarket. The worst of that latter affair was that it produced the total estrangement which now existed between Lord Brentford and his son. Lord Brentford would not believe that his son was in that matter more sinned against than sinning. "Such things do not happen to other men's sons," he said, when Lady Laura pleaded for her brother. Lady Laura could not induce her father to see his son, but so far prevailed that no sentence of banishment was pronounced against Lord Chiltern. There was nothing to prevent the son sitting at his father's table if he so pleased. He never did so please,—but nevertheless he continued to live in the house in Portman Square; and when he met the Earl, in the hall, perhaps, or on the staircase, would simply bow to him. Then the Earl would bow again, and shuffle on,—and look very wretched, as no doubt he was. A grown-up son must be the greatest comfort a man can have,—if he be his father's best friend; but otherwise he can hardly be a comfort. As it was in this house, the son was a constant thorn in his father's side.

"What does he do when we leave London?" Lord Brentford once said to his daughter.

"He stays here, papa."

"But he hunts still?"

"Yes, he hunts,—and he has a room somewhere at an inn,—down in Northamptonshire. But he is mostly in London. They have trains on purpose."

"What a life for my son!" said the Earl. "What a life! Of course no decent person will let him into his house." Lady Laura did not know what to say to this, for in truth Lord Chiltern was not fond of staying at the houses of persons whom the Earl would have called decent.

General Effingham, the father of Violet, and Lord Brentford had been the closest and dearest of friends. They had been young men in the same regiment, and through life each had confided in the other. When the General's only son, then a youth of seventeen, was killed in one of our grand New Zealand wars, the bereaved father and the Earl had been together for a month in their sorrow. At that time Lord Chiltern's career had still been open to hope,—and the one man had contrasted his lot with the other. General Effingham lived long enough to hear the Earl declare that his lot was the happier of the two. Now the General was dead, and Violet, the daughter of a second wife, was all that was left of the Effinghams. This second wife had been a Miss Plummer, a lady from the city with much money, whose sister had married Lord Baldock. Violet in this way had fallen to the care of the Baldock people, and not into the hands of her father's friends. But, as the reader will have surmised, she had ideas of her own of emancipating herself from Baldock thraldom.

Twice before that last terrible affair at Newmarket, before the quarrel between the father and the son had been complete, Lord Brentford had said a word to his daughter,—merely a word,—of his son in connection with Miss Effingham.

"If he thinks of it I shall be glad to see him on the subject. You may tell him so." That had been the first word. He had just then resolved that the affair in Paris should be regarded as condoned,—as among the things to be forgotten. "She is too good for him; but if he asks her let him tell her everything." That had been the second word, and had been spoken immediately subsequent to a payment of twelve thousand pounds made by the Earl towards the settlement of certain Doncaster accounts. Lady Laura in negotiating for the money had been very eloquent in describing some honest,—or shall we say chivalric,—sacrifice which had brought her brother into this special difficulty. Since that the Earl had declined to interest himself in his son's matrimonial affairs; and when Lady Laura had once again mentioned the matter, declaring her belief that it would be the means of saving her brother Oswald, the Earl had desired her to be silent. "Would you wish to destroy the poor child?" he had said. Nevertheless Lady Laura felt sure that if she were to go to her father with a positive statement that Oswald and Violet were engaged, he would relent and would accept Violet as his daughter. As for the payment of Lord Chiltern's present debts;—she had a little scheme of her own about that.

Miss Effingham, who had been already two days in Portman Square, had not as yet seen Lord Chiltern. She knew that he lived in the house, that is, that he slept there, and probably eat his breakfast in some apartment of his own;—but she knew also that the habits of the house would not by any means make it necessary that they should meet. Laura and her brother probably saw each other daily,—but they never went into society together, and did not know the same sets of people. When she had announced to Lady Baldock her intention of spending the first fortnight of her London season with her friend Lady Laura, Lady Baldock had as a matter of course—"jumped upon her," as Miss Effingham would herself call it.

"You are going to the house of the worst reprobate in all England," said Lady Baldock.

"What;—dear old Lord Brentford, whom papa loved so well!"

"I mean Lord Chiltern, who, only last year,—murdered a man!"

"That is not true, aunt."

"There is worse than that,—much worse. He is always—tipsy, and always gambling, and always— But it is quite unfit that I should speak a word more to you about such a man as Lord Chiltern. His name ought never to be mentioned."

"Then why did you mention it, aunt?"

Lady Baldock's process of jumping upon her niece,—in which I think the aunt had generally the worst of the exercise,—went on for some time, but Violet of course carried her point.

"If she marries him there will be an end of everything," said Lady Baldock to her daughter Augusta.

"She has more sense than that, mamma," said Augusta.

"I don't think she has any sense at all," said Lady Baldock;—"not in the least. I do wish my poor sister had lived;—I do indeed."

Lord Chiltern was now in the room with Violet,—immediately upon that conversation between Violet and his sister as to the expediency of Violet becoming his wife. Indeed his entrance had interrupted the conversation before it was over. "I am so glad to see you, Miss Effingham," he said. "I came in thinking that I might find you."

"Here I am, as large as life," she said, getting up from her corner on the sofa and giving him her hand. "Laura and I have been discussing the affairs of the nation for the last two days, and have nearly brought our discussion to an end." She could not help looking, first at his eye and then at his hand, not as wanting evidence to the truth of the statement which his sister had made, but because the idea of a drunkard's eye and a drunkard's hand had been brought before her mind. Lord Chiltern's hand was like the hand of any other man, but there was something in his eye that almost frightened her. It looked as though he would not hesitate to wring his wife's neck round, if ever he should be brought to threaten to do so. And then his eye, like the rest of him, was red. No;—she did not think that she could ever bring herself to marry him. Why take a venture that was double-dangerous, when there were so many ventures open to her, apparently with very little of danger attached to them? "If it should ever be said that I loved him, I would do it all the same," she said to herself.

"If I did not come and see you here, I suppose that I should never see you," said he, seating himself. "I do not often go to parties, and when I do you are not likely to be there."

"We might make our little arrangements for meeting," said she, laughing. "My aunt, Lady Baldock, is going to have an evening next week."

"The servants would be ordered to put me out of the house."

"Oh no. You can tell her that I invited you."

"I don't think that Oswald and Lady Baldock are great friends," said Lady Laura.

"Or he might come and take you and me to the Zoo on Sunday. That's the proper sort of thing for a brother and a friend to do."

"I hate that place in the Regent's Park," said Lord Chiltern.

"When were you there last?" demanded Miss Effingham.

"When I came home once from Eton. But I won't go again till I can come home from Eton again." Then he altered his tone as he continued to speak. "People would look at me as if I were the wildest beast in the whole collection."

"Then," said Violet, "if you won't go to Lady Baldock's or to the Zoo, we must confine ourselves to Laura's drawing-room;—unless, indeed, you like to take me to the top of the Monument."

"I'll take you to the top of the Monument with pleasure."

"What do you say, Laura?"

"I say that you are a foolish girl," said Lady Laura, "and that I will have nothing to do with such a scheme."

"Then there is nothing for it but that you should come here; and as you live in the house, and as I am sure to be here every morning, and as you have no possible occupation for your time, and as we have nothing particular to do with ours,—I daresay I shan't see you again before I go to my aunt's in Berkeley Square."

"Very likely not," he said.

"And why not, Oswald?" asked his sister.

He passed his hand over his face before he answered her. "Because she and I run in different grooves now, and are not such meet playfellows as we used to be once. Do you remember my taking you away right through Saulsby Wood once on the old pony, and not bringing you back till tea-time, and Miss Blink going and telling my father?"

"Do I remember it? I think it was the happiest day in my life. His pockets were crammed full of gingerbread and Everton toffy, and we had three bottles of lemonade slung on to the pony's saddlebows. I thought it was a pity that we should ever come back."

"It was a pity," said Lord Chiltern.

"But, nevertheless, substantially necessary," said Lady Laura.

"Failing our power of reproducing the toffy, I suppose it was," said Violet.

"You were not Miss Effingham then," said Lord Chiltern.

"No,—not as yet. These disagreeable realities of life grow upon one; do they not? You took off my shoes and dried them for me at a woodman's cottage. I am obliged to put up with my maid's doing those things now. And Miss Blink the mild is changed for Lady Baldock the martinet. And if I rode about with you in a wood all day I should be sent to Coventry instead of to bed. And so you see everything is changed as well as my name."

"Everything is not changed," said Lord Chiltern, getting up from his seat. "I am not changed,—at least not in this, that as I loved you better than any being in the world,—better even than Laura there,—so do I love you now infinitely the best of all. Do not look so surprised at me. You knew it before as well as you do now;—and Laura knows it. There is no secret to be kept in the matter among us three."

"But, Lord Chiltern,—" said Miss Effingham, rising also to her feet, and then pausing, not knowing how to answer him. There had been a suddenness in his mode of addressing her which had, so to say, almost taken away her breath; and then to be told by a man of his love before his sister was in itself, to her, a matter so surprising, that none of those words came at her command which will come, as though by instinct, to young ladies on such occasions.

"You have known it always," said he, as though he were angry with her.

"Lord Chiltern," she replied, "you must excuse me if I say that you are, at the least, very abrupt. I did not think when I was going back so joyfully to our childish days that you would turn the tables on me in this way."

"He has said nothing that ought to make you angry," said Lady Laura.

"Only because he has driven me to say that which will make me appear to be uncivil to himself. Lord Chiltern, I do not love you with that love of which you are speaking now. As an old friend I have always regarded you, and I hope that I may always do so." Then she got up and left the room.

"Why were you so sudden with her,—so abrupt,—so loud?" said his sister, coming up to him and taking him by the arm almost in anger.

"It would make no difference," said he. "She does not care for me."

"It makes all the difference in the world," said Lady Laura. "Such a woman as Violet cannot be had after that fashion. You must begin again."

"I have begun and ended," he said.

"That is nonsense. Of course you will persist. It was madness to speak in that way to-day. You may be sure of this, however, that there is no one she likes better than you. You must remember that you have done much to make any girl afraid of you."

"I do remember it."

"Do something now to make her fear you no longer. Speak to her softly. Tell her of the sort of life which you would live with her. Tell her that all is changed. As she comes to love you, she will believe you when she would believe no one else on that matter."

"Am I to tell her a lie?" said Lord Chiltern, looking his sister full in the face. Then he turned upon his heel and left her.

CHAPTER XII
Autumnal Prospects

The session went on very calmly after the opening battle which ousted Lord de Terrier and sent Mr. Mildmay back to the Treasury,—so calmly that Phineas Finn was unconsciously disappointed, as lacking that excitement of contest to which he had been introduced in the first days of his parliamentary career. From time to time certain waspish attacks were made by Mr. Daubeny, now on this Secretary of State and now on that; but they were felt by both parties to mean nothing; and as no great measure was brought forward, nothing which would serve by the magnitude of its interests to divide the liberal side of the House into fractions, Mr. Mildmay's Cabinet was allowed to hold its own in comparative peace and quiet. It was now July,—the middle of July,—and the member for Loughshane had not yet addressed the House. How often had he meditated doing so; how he had composed his speeches walking round the Park on his way down to the House; how he got his subjects up,—only to find on hearing them discussed that he really knew little or nothing about them; how he had his arguments and almost his very words taken out of his mouth by some other member; and lastly, how he had actually been deterred from getting upon his legs by a certain tremor of blood round his heart when the moment for rising had come,—of all this he never said a word to any man. Since that last journey to county Mayo, Laurence Fitzgibbon had been his most intimate friend, but he said nothing of all this even to Laurence Fitzgibbon. To his other friend, Lady Laura Standish, he did explain something of his feelings, not absolutely describing to her the extent of hindrance to which his modesty had subjected him, but letting her know that he had his qualms as well as his aspirations. But as Lady Laura always recommended patience, and more than once expressed her opinion that a young member would be better to sit in silence at least for one session, he was not driven to the mortification of feeling that he was incurring her contempt by his bashfulness. As regarded the men among whom he lived, I think he was almost annoyed at finding that no one seemed to expect that he should speak. Barrington Erle, when he had first talked of sending Phineas down to Loughshane, had predicted for him all manner of parliamentary successes, and had expressed the warmest admiration of the manner in which Phineas had discussed this or that subject at the Union. "We have not above one or two men in the House who can do that kind of thing," Barrington Erle had once said. But now no allusions whatever were made to his powers of speech, and Phineas in his modest moments began to be more amazed than ever that he should find himself seated in that chamber.

To the forms and technicalities of parliamentary business he did give close attention, and was unremitting in his attendance. On one or two occasions he ventured to ask a question of the Speaker, and as the words of experience fell into his ears, he would tell himself that he was going through his education,—that he was learning to be a working member, and perhaps to be a statesman. But his regrets with reference to Mr. Low and the dingy chambers in Old Square were very frequent; and had it been possible for him to undo all that he had done, he would often have abandoned to some one else the honour of representing the electors of Loughshane.

But he was supported in all his difficulties by the kindness of his friend, Lady Laura Standish. He was often in the house in Portman Square, and was always received with cordiality, and, as he thought, almost with affection. She would sit and talk to him, sometimes saying a word about her brother and sometimes about her father, as though there were more between them than the casual intimacy of London acquaintance. And in Portman Square he had been introduced to Miss Effingham, and had found Miss Effingham to be—very nice. Miss Effingham had quite taken to him, and he had danced with her at two or three parties, talking always, as he did so, about Lady Laura Standish.

"I declare, Laura, I think your friend Mr. Finn is in love with you," said Violet to Lady Laura one night.

"I don't think that. He is fond of me, and so am I of him. He is so honest, and so naïve without being awkward! And then he is undoubtedly clever."

"And so uncommonly handsome," said Violet.

"I don't know that that makes much difference," said Lady Laura.

"I think it does if a man looks like a gentleman as well."

"Mr. Finn certainly looks like a gentleman," said Lady Laura.

"And no doubt is one," said Violet. "I wonder whether he has got any money."

"Not a penny, I should say."

"How does such a man manage to live? There are so many men like that, and they are always mysteries to me. I suppose he'll have to marry an heiress."

"Whoever gets him will not have a bad husband," said Lady Laura Standish.

Phineas during the summer had very often met Mr. Kennedy. They sat on the same side of the House, they belonged to the same club, they dined together more than once in Portman Square, and on one one occasion Phineas had accepted an invitation to dinner sent to him by Mr. Kennedy himself. "A slower affair I never saw in my life," he said afterwards to Laurence Fitzgibbon. "Though there were two or three men there who talk everywhere else, they could not talk at his table." "He gave you good wine, I should say," said Fitzgibbon, "and let me tell you that that covers a multitude of sins." In spite, however, of all these opportunities for intimacy, now, nearly at the end of the session, Phineas had hardly spoken a dozen words to Mr. Kennedy, and really knew nothing whatsoever of the man, as one friend,—or even as one acquaintance knows another. Lady Laura had desired him to be on good terms with Mr. Kennedy, and for that reason he had dined with him. Nevertheless he disliked Mr. Kennedy, and felt quite sure that Mr. Kennedy disliked him. He was therefore rather surprised when he received the following note:—

Albany, Z 3, July 17, 186—.

My dear Mr. Finn,

I shall have some friends at Loughlinter next month, and should be very glad if you will join us. I will name the 16th August. I don't know whether you shoot, but there are grouse and deer.

Yours truly,

Robert Kennedy.

What was he to do? He had already begun to feel rather uncomfortable at the prospect of being separated from all his new friends as soon as the session should be over. Laurence Fitzgibbon had asked him to make another visit to county Mayo, but that he had declined. Lady Laura had said something to him about going abroad with her brother, and since that there had sprung up a sort of intimacy between him and Lord Chiltern; but nothing had been fixed about this foreign trip, and there were pecuniary objections to it which put it almost out of his power. The Christmas holidays he would of course pass with his family at Killaloe, but he hardly liked the idea of hurrying off to Killaloe immediately the session should be over. Everybody around him seemed to be looking forward to pleasant leisure doings in the country. Men talked about grouse, and of the ladies at the houses to which they were going and of the people whom they were to meet. Lady Laura had said nothing of her own movements for the early autumn, and no invitation had come to him to go to the Earl's country house. He had already felt that every one would depart and that he would be left,—and this had made him uncomfortable. What was he to do with the invitation from Mr. Kennedy? He disliked the man, and had told himself half a dozen times that he despised him. Of course he must refuse it. Even for the sake of the scenery, and the grouse, and the pleasant party, and the feeling that going to Loughlinter in August would be the proper sort of thing to do, he must refuse it! But it occurred to him at last that he would call in Portman Square before he wrote his note.

"Of course you will go," said Lady Laura, in her most decided tone.

"And why?"

"In the first place it is civil in him to ask you, and why should you be uncivil in return?"

"There is nothing uncivil in not accepting a man's invitation," said Phineas.

"We are going," said Lady Laura, "and I can only say that I shall be disappointed if you do not go too. Both Mr. Gresham and Mr. Monk will be there, and I believe they have never stayed together in the same house before. I have no doubt there are a dozen men on your side of the House who would give their eyes to be there. Of course you will go."

Of course he did go. The note accepting Mr. Kennedy's invitation was written at the Reform Club within a quarter of an hour of his leaving Portman Square. He was very careful in writing to be not more familiar or more civil than Mr. Kennedy had been to himself, and then he signed himself "Yours truly, Phineas Finn." But another proposition was made to him, and a most charming proposition, during the few minutes that he remained in Portman Square. "I am so glad," said Lady Laura, "because I can now ask you to run down to us at Saulsby for a couple of days on your way to Loughlinter. Till this was fixed I couldn't ask you to come all the way to Saulsby for two days; and there won't be room for more between our leaving London and starting to Loughlinter." Phineas swore that he would have gone if it had been but for one hour, and if Saulsby had been twice the distance. "Very well; come on the 13th and go on the 15th. You must go on the 15th, unless you choose to stay with the housekeeper. And remember, Mr. Finn, we have got no grouse at Saulsby." Phineas declared that he did not care a straw for grouse.

There was another little occurrence which happened before Phineas left London, and which was not altogether so charming as his prospects at Saulsby and Loughlinter. Early in August, when the session was still incomplete, he dined with Laurence Fitzgibbon at the Reform Club. Laurence had specially invited him to do so, and made very much of him on the occasion. "By George, my dear fellow," Laurence said to him that morning, "nothing has happened to me this session that has given me so much pleasure as your being in the House. Of course there are fellows with whom one is very intimate and of whom one is very fond,—and all that sort of thing. But most of these Englishmen on our side are such cold fellows; or else they are like Ratler and Barrington Erle, thinking of nothing but politics. And then as to our own men, there are so many of them one can hardly trust! That's the truth of it. Your being in the House has been such a comfort to me!" Phineas, who really liked his friend Laurence, expressed himself very warmly in answer to this, and became affectionate, and made sundry protestations of friendship which were perfectly sincere. Their sincerity was tested after dinner, when Fitzgibbon, as they two were seated on a sofa in the corner of the smoking-room, asked Phineas to put his name to the back of a bill for two hundred and fifty pounds at six months' date.

"But, my dear Laurence," said Phineas, "two hundred and fifty pounds is a sum of money utterly beyond my reach."

"Exactly, my dear boy, and that's why I've come to you. D'ye think I'd have asked anybody who by any impossibility might have been made to pay anything for me?"

"But what's the use of it then?"

"All the use in the world. It's for me to judge of the use, you know. Why, d'ye think I'd ask it if it wasn't any use? I'll make it of use, my boy. And take my word, you'll never hear about it again. It's just a forestalling of my salary; that's all. I wouldn't do it till I saw that we were at least safe for six months to come." Then Phineas Finn with many misgivings, with much inward hatred of himself for his own weakness, did put his name on the back of the bill which Laurence Fitzgibbon had prepared for his signature.

CHAPTER XIII
Saulsby Wood

"So you won't come to Moydrum again?" said Laurence Fitzgibbon to his friend.

"Not this autumn, Laurence. Your father would think that I want to live there."

"Bedad, it's my father would be glad to see you,—and the oftener the better."

"The fact is, my time is filled up."

"You're not going to be one of the party at Loughlinter?"

"I believe I am. Kennedy asked me, and people seem to think that everybody is to do what he bids them."

"I should think so too. I wish he had asked me. I should have thought it as good as a promise of an under-secretaryship. All the Cabinet are to be there. I don't suppose he ever had an Irishman in his house before. When do you start?"

"Well;—on the 12th or 13th. I believe I shall go to Saulsby on my way."

"The devil you will. Upon my word, Phineas, my boy, you're the luckiest fellow I know. This is your first year, and you're asked to the two most difficult houses in England. You have only to look out for an heiress now. There is little Vi Effingham;—she is sure to be at Saulsby. Good-bye, old fellow. Don't you be in the least unhappy about the bill. I'll see to making that all right."

Phineas was rather unhappy about the bill; but there was so much that was pleasant in his cup at the present moment, that he resolved, as far as possible, to ignore the bitter of that one ingredient. He was a little in the dark as to two or three matters respecting these coming visits. He would have liked to have taken a servant with him; but he had no servant, and felt ashamed to hire one for the occasion. And then he was in trouble about a gun, and the paraphernalia of shooting. He was not a bad shot at snipe in the bogs of county Clare, but he had never even seen a gun used in England. However, he bought himself a gun,—with other paraphernalia, and took a license for himself, and then groaned over the expense to which he found that his journey would subject him. And at last he hired a servant for the occasion. He was intensely ashamed of himself when he had done so, hating himself, and telling himself that he was going to the devil headlong. And why had he done it? Not that Lady Laura would like him the better, or that she would care whether he had a servant or not. She probably would know nothing of his servant. But the people about her would know, and he was foolishly anxious that the people about her should think that he was worthy of her.

Then he called on Mr. Low before he started. "I did not like to leave London without seeing you," he said; "but I know you will have nothing pleasant to say to me."

"I shall say nothing unpleasant certainly. I see your name in the divisions, and I feel a sort of envy myself."

"Any fool could go into a lobby," said Phineas.

"To tell you the truth, I have been gratified to see that you have had the patience to abstain from speaking till you had looked about you. It was more than I expected from your hot Irish blood. Going to meet Mr. Gresham and Mr. Monk,—are you? Well, I hope you may meet them in the Cabinet some day. Mind you come and see me when Parliament meets in February."

Mrs. Bunce was delighted when she found that Phineas had hired a servant; but Mr. Bunce predicted nothing but evil from so vain an expense. "Don't tell me; where is it to come from? He ain't no richer because he's in Parliament. There ain't no wages. M.P. and M.T.,"—whereby Mr. Bunce, I fear, meant empty,—"are pretty much alike when a man hasn't a fortune at his back." "But he's going to stay with all the lords in the Cabinet," said Mrs. Bunce, to whom Phineas, in his pride, had confided perhaps more than was necessary. "Cabinet, indeed," said Bunce; "if he'd stick to chambers, and let alone cabinets, he'd do a deal better. Given up his rooms, has he,—till February? He don't expect we're going to keep them empty for him!"

Phineas found that the house was full at Saulsby, although the sojourn of the visitors would necessarily be so short. There were three or four there on their way on to Loughlinter, like himself,—Mr. Bonteen and Mr. Ratler, with Mr. Palliser, the Chancellor of the Exchequer, and his wife,—and there was Violet Effingham, who, however, was not going to Loughlinter. "No, indeed," she said to our hero, who on the first evening had the pleasure of taking her in to dinner, "unfortunately I haven't a seat in Parliament, and therefore I am not asked."

"Lady Laura is going."

"Yes;—but Lady Laura has a Cabinet Minister in her keeping. I've only one comfort;—you'll be awfully dull."

"I daresay it would be very much nicer to stay here," said Phineas.

"If you want to know my real mind," said Violet, "I would give one of my little fingers to go. There will be four Cabinet Ministers in the house, and four un-Cabinet Ministers, and half a dozen other members of Parliament, and there will be Lady Glencora Palliser, who is the best fun in the world; and, in point of fact, it's the thing of the year. But I am not asked. You see I belong to the Baldock faction, and we don't sit on your side of the House. Mr. Kennedy thinks that I should tell secrets."

Why on earth had Mr. Kennedy invited him, Phineas Finn, to meet four Cabinet Ministers and Lady Glencora Palliser? He could only have done so at the instance of Lady Laura Standish. It was delightful for Phineas to think that Lady Laura cared for him so deeply; but it was not equally delightful when he remembered how very close must be the alliance between Mr. Kennedy and Lady Laura, when she was thus powerful with him.

At Saulsby Phineas did not see much of his hostess. When they were making their plans for the one entire day of this visit, she said a soft word of apology to him. "I am so busy with all these people, that I hardly know what I am doing. But we shall be able to find a quiet minute or two at Loughlinter,—unless, indeed, you intend to be on the mountains all day. I suppose you have brought a gun like everybody else?"

"Yes;—I have brought a gun. I do shoot; but I am not an inveterate sportsman."

On that one day there was a great riding party made up, and Phineas found himself mounted, after luncheon, with some dozen other equestrians. Among them were Miss Effingham and Lady Glencora, Mr. Ratler and the Earl of Brentford himself. Lady Glencora, whose husband was, as has been said, Chancellor of the Exchequer, and who was still a young woman, and a very pretty woman, had taken lately very strongly to politics, which she discussed among men and women of both parties with something more than ordinary audacity. "What a nice, happy, lazy time you've had of it since you've been in," said she to the Earl.

"I hope we have been more happy than lazy," said the Earl.

"But you've done nothing. Mr. Palliser has twenty schemes of reform, all mature; but among you you've not let him bring in one of them. The Duke and Mr. Mildmay and you will break his heart among you."

"Poor Mr. Palliser!"

"The truth is, if you don't take care he and Mr. Monk and Mr. Gresham will arise and shake themselves, and turn you all out."

"We must look to ourselves, Lady Glencora."

"Indeed, yes;—or you will be known to all posterity as the fainéant government."

"Let me tell you, Lady Glencora, that a fainéant government is not the worst government that England can have. It has been the great fault of our politicians that they have all wanted to do something."

"Mr. Mildmay is at any rate innocent of that charge," said Lady Glencora.

They were now riding through a vast wood, and Phineas found himself delightfully established by the side of Violet Effingham. "Mr. Ratler has been explaining to me that he must have nineteen next session. Now, if I were you, Mr. Finn, I would decline to be counted up in that way as one of Mr. Ratler's sheep."

"But what am I to do?"

"Do something on your own hook. You men in Parliament are so much like sheep! If one jumps at a gap, all go after him,—and then you are penned into lobbies, and then you are fed, and then you are fleeced. I wish I were in Parliament. I'd get up in the middle and make such a speech. You all seem to me to be so much afraid of one another that you don't quite dare to speak out. Do you see that cottage there?"

"What a pretty cottage it is!"

"Yes;—is it not? Twelve years ago I took off my shoes and stockings and had them dried in that cottage, and when I got back to the house I was put to bed for having been out all day in the wood."

"Were you wandering about alone?"

"No, I wasn't alone. Oswald Standish was with me. We were children then. Do you know him?"

"Lord Chiltern;—yes, I know him. He and I have been rather friends this year."

"He is very good;—is he not?"

"Good,—in what way?"

"Honest and generous!"

"I know no man whom I believe to be more so."

"And he is clever?" asked Miss Effingham.

"Very clever. That is, he talks very well if you will let him talk after his own fashion. You would always fancy that he was going to eat you;—but that is his way."

"And you like him?"

"Very much."

"I am so glad to hear you say so."

"Is he a favourite of yours, Miss Effingham?"

"Not now,—not particularly. I hardly ever see him. But his sister is the best friend I have, and I used to like him so much when he was a boy! I have not seen that cottage since that day, and I remember it as though it were yesterday. Lord Chiltern is quite changed, is he not?"

"Changed,—in what way?"

"They used to say that he was—unsteady you know."

"I think he is changed. But Chiltern is at heart a Bohemian. It is impossible not to see that at once. He hates the decencies of life."

"I suppose he does," said Violet. "He ought to marry. If he were married, that would all be cured;—don't you think so?"

"I cannot fancy him with a wife," said Phineas, "There is a savagery about him which would make him an uncomfortable companion for a woman."

"But he would love his wife?"

"Yes, as he does his horses. And he would treat her well,—as he does his horses. But he expects every horse he has to do anything that any horse can do; and he would expect the same of his wife."

Phineas had no idea how deep an injury he might be doing his friend by this description, nor did it once occur to him that his companion was thinking of herself as the possible wife of this Red Indian. Miss Effingham rode on in silence for some distance, and then she said but one word more about Lord Chiltern. "He was so good to me in that cottage."

On the following day the party at Saulsby was broken up, and there was a regular pilgrimage towards Loughlinter. Phineas resolved upon sleeping a night at Edinburgh on his way, and he found himself joined in the bands of close companionship with Mr. Ratler for the occasion. The evening was by no means thrown away, for he learned much of his trade from Mr. Ratler. And Mr. Ratler was heard to declare afterwards at Loughlinter that Mr. Finn was a pleasant young man.

It soon came to be admitted by all who knew Phineas Finn that he had a peculiar power of making himself agreeable which no one knew how to analyse or define. "I think it is because he listens so well," said one man. "But the women would not like him for that," said another. "He has studied when to listen and when to talk," said a third. The truth, however, was, that Phineas Finn had made no study in the matter at all. It was simply his nature to be pleasant.

CHAPTER XIV
Loughlinter

Phineas Finn reached Loughlinter together with Mr. Ratler in a post-chaise from the neighbouring town. Mr. Ratler, who had done this kind of thing very often before, travelled without impediments, but the new servant of our hero's was stuck outside with the driver, and was in the way. "I never bring a man with me," said Mr. Ratler to his young friend. "The servants of the house like it much better, because they get fee'd; you are just as well waited on, and it don't cost half as much." Phineas blushed as he heard all this; but there was the impediment, not to be got rid of for the nonce, and Phineas made the best of his attendant. "It's one of those points," said he, "as to which a man never quite makes up his mind. If you bring a fellow, you wish you hadn't brought him; and if you don't, you wish you had." "I'm a great deal more decided in my ways that that," said Mr. Ratler.

Loughlinter, as they approached it, seemed to Phineas to be a much finer place than Saulsby. And so it was, except that Loughlinter wanted that graceful beauty of age which Saulsby possessed. Loughlinter was all of cut stone, but the stones had been cut only yesterday. It stood on a gentle slope, with a greensward falling from the front entrance down to a mountain lake. And on the other side of the Lough there rose a mighty mountain to the skies, Ben Linter. At the foot of it, and all round to the left, there ran the woods of Linter, stretching for miles through crags and bogs and mountain lands. No better ground for deer than the side of Ben Linter was there in all those highlands. And the Linter, rushing down into the Lough through rocks which, in some places, almost met together above its waters, ran so near to the house that the pleasant noise of its cataracts could be heard from the hall door. Behind the house the expanse of drained park land seemed to be interminable; and then, again, came the mountains. There were Ben Linn and Ben Lody;—and the whole territory belonging to Mr. Kennedy. He was laird of Linn and laird of Linter, as his people used to say. And yet his father had walked into Glasgow as a little boy,—no doubt with the normal half-crown in his breeches pocket.

"Magnificent;—is it not?" said Phineas to the Treasury Secretary, as they were being driven up to the door.

"Very grand;—but the young trees show the new man. A new man may buy a forest; but he can't get park trees."

Phineas, at the moment, was thinking how far all these things which he saw, the mountains stretching everywhere around him, the castle, the lake, the river, the wealth of it all, and, more than the wealth, the nobility of the beauty, might act as temptations to Lady Laura Standish. If a woman were asked to have the half of all this, would it be possible that she should prefer to take the half of his nothing? He thought it might be possible for a girl who would confess, or seem to confess, that love should be everything. But it could hardly be possible for a woman who looked at the world almost as a man looked at it,—as an oyster to be opened with such weapon as she could find ready to her hand. Lady Laura professed to have a care for all the affairs of the world. She loved politics, and could talk of social science, and had broad ideas about religion, and was devoted to certain educational views. Such a woman would feel that wealth was necessary to her, and would be willing, for the sake of wealth, to put up with a husband without romance. Nay; might it not be that she would prefer a husband without romance? Thus Phineas was arguing to himself as he was driven up to the door of Loughlinter Castle, while Mr. Ratler was eloquent on the beauty of old park trees. "After all, a Scotch forest is a very scrubby sort of thing," said Mr. Ratler.

There was nobody in the house,—at least, they found nobody; and within half an hour Phineas was walking about the grounds by himself. Mr. Ratler had declared himself to be delighted at having an opportunity of writing letters,—and no doubt was writing them by the dozen, all dated from Loughlinter, and all detailing the facts that Mr. Gresham, and Mr. Monk, and Plantagenet Palliser, and Lord Brentford were in the same house with him. Phineas had no letters to write, and therefore rushed down across the broad lawn to the river, of which he heard the noisy tumbling waters. There was something in the air which immediately filled him with high spirits; and, in his desire to investigate the glories of the place, he forgot that he was going to dine with four Cabinet Ministers in a row. He soon reached the stream, and began to make his way up it through the ravine. There was waterfall over waterfall, and there were little bridges here and there which looked to be half natural and half artificial, and a path which required that you should climb, but which was yet a path, and all was so arranged that not a pleasant splashing rush of the waters was lost to the visitor. He went on and on, up the stream, till there was a sharp turn in the ravine, and then, looking upwards, he saw above his head a man and a woman standing together on one of the little half-made wooden bridges. His eyes were sharp, and he saw at a glance that the woman was Lady Laura Standish. He had not recognised the man, but he had very little doubt that it was Mr. Kennedy. Of course it was Mr. Kennedy, because he would prefer that it should be any other man under the sun. He would have turned back at once if he had thought that he could have done so without being observed; but he felt sure that, standing as they were, they must have observed him. He did not like to join them. He would not intrude himself. So he remained still, and began to throw stones into the river. But he had not thrown above a stone or two when he was called from above. He looked up, and then he perceived that the man who called him was his host. Of course it was Mr. Kennedy. Thereupon he ceased to throw stones, and went up the path, and joined them upon the bridge. Mr. Kennedy stepped forward, and bade him welcome to Loughlinter. His manner was less cold, and he seemed to have more words at command than was usual with him. "You have not been long," he said, "in finding out the most beautiful spot about the place."

"Is it not lovely?" said Laura. "We have not been here an hour yet, and Mr. Kennedy insisted on bringing me here."

"It is wonderfully beautiful," said Phineas.

"It is this very spot where we now stand that made me build the house where it is," said Mr. Kennedy, "and I was only eighteen when I stood here and made up my mind. That is just twenty-five years ago." "So he is forty-three," said Phineas to himself, thinking how glorious it was to be only twenty-five. "And within twelve months," continued Mr. Kennedy, "the foundations were being dug and the stone-cutters were at work."

"What a good-natured man your father must have been," said Lady Laura.

"He had nothing else to do with his money but to pour it over my head, as it were. I don't think he had any other enjoyment of it himself. Will you go a little higher, Lady Laura? We shall get a fine view over to Ben Linn just now." Lady Laura declared that she would go as much higher as he chose to take her, and Phineas was rather in doubt as to what it would become him to do. He would stay where he was, or go down, or make himself to vanish after any most acceptable fashion; but if he were to do so abruptly it would seem as though he were attributing something special to the companionship of the other two. Mr. Kennedy saw his doubt, and asked him to join them. "You may as well come on, Mr. Finn. We don't dine till eight, and it is not much past six yet. The men of business are all writing letters, and the ladies who have been travelling are in bed, I believe."

"Not all of them, Mr. Kennedy," said Lady Laura. Then they went on with their walk very pleasantly, and the lord of all that they surveyed took them from one point of vantage to another, till they both swore that of all spots upon the earth Loughlinter was surely the most lovely. "I do delight in it, I own," said the lord. "When I come up here alone, and feel that in the midst of this little bit of a crowded island I have all this to myself,—all this with which no other man's wealth can interfere,—I grow proud of my own, till I become thoroughly ashamed of myself. After all, I believe it is better to dwell in cities than in the country,—better, at any rate, for a rich man." Mr. Kennedy had now spoken more words than Phineas had heard to fall from his lips during the whole time that they had been acquainted with each other.

"I believe so too," said Laura, "if one were obliged to choose between the two. For myself, I think that a little of both is good for man and woman."

"There is no doubt about that," said Phineas.

"No doubt as far as enjoyment goes," said Mr. Kennedy.

He took them up out of the ravine on to the side of the mountain, and then down by another path through the woods to the back of the house. As they went he relapsed into his usual silence, and the conversation was kept up between the other two. At a point not very far from the castle,—just so far that one could see by the break of the ground where the castle stood, Kennedy left them. "Mr. Finn will take you back in safety, I am sure," said he, "and, as I am here, I'll go up to the farm for a moment. If I don't show myself now and again when I am here, they think I'm indifferent about the 'bestials'."

"Now, Mr. Kennedy," said Lady Laura, "you are going to pretend to understand all about sheep and oxen." Mr. Kennedy, owning that it was so, went away to his farm, and Phineas with Lady Laura returned towards the house. "I think, upon the whole," said Lady Laura, "that that is as good a man as I know."

"I should think he is an idle one," said Phineas.

"I doubt that. He is, perhaps, neither zealous nor active. But he is thoughtful and high-principled, and has a method and a purpose in the use which he makes of his money. And you see that he has poetry in his nature too, if you get him upon the right string. How fond he is of the scenery of this place!"

"Any man would be fond of that. I'm ashamed to say that it almost makes me envy him. I certainly never have wished to be Mr. Robert Kennedy in London, but I should like to be the Laird of Loughlinter."

"'Laird of Linn and Laird of Linter,—Here in summer, gone in winter.' There is some ballad about the old lairds; but that belongs to a time when Mr. Kennedy had not been heard of, when some branch of the Mackenzies lived down at that wretched old tower which you see as you first come upon the lake. When old Mr. Kennedy bought it there were hardly a hundred acres on the property under cultivation."

"And it belonged to the Mackenzies."

"Yes;—to the Mackenzie of Linn, as he was called. It was Mr. Kennedy, the old man, who was first called Loughlinter. That is Linn Castle, and they lived there for hundreds of years. But these Highlanders, with all that is said of their family pride, have forgotten the Mackenzies already, and are quite proud of their rich landlord."

"That is unpoetical," said Phineas.

"Yes;—but then poetry is so usually false. I doubt whether Scotland would not have been as prosaic a country as any under the sun but for Walter Scott;—and I have no doubt that Henry V owes the romance of his character altogether to Shakspeare."

"I sometimes think you despise poetry," said Phineas.

"When it is false I do. The difficulty is to know when it is false and when it is true. Tom Moore was always false."

"Not so false as Byron," said Phineas with energy.

"Much more so, my friend. But we will not discuss that now. Have you seen Mr. Monk since you have been here?"

"I have seen no one. I came with Mr. Ratler."

"Why with Mr. Ratler? You cannot find Mr. Ratler a companion much to your taste."

"Chance brought us together. But Mr. Ratler is a man of sense, Lady Laura, and is not to be despised."

"It always seems to me," said Lady Laura, "that nothing is to be gained in politics by sitting at the feet of the little Gamaliels."

"But the great Gamaliels will not have a novice on their footstools."

"Then sit at no man's feet. Is it not astonishing that the price generally put upon any article by the world is that which the owner puts on it?—and that this is specially true of a man's own self? If you herd with Ratler, men will take it for granted that you are a Ratlerite, and no more. If you consort with Greshams and Pallisers, you will equally be supposed to know your own place."

"I never knew a Mentor," said Phineas, "so apt as you are to fill his Telemachus with pride."

"It is because I do not think your fault lies that way. If it did, or if I thought so, my Telemachus, you may be sure that I should resign my position as Mentor. Here are Mr. Kennedy and Lady Glencora and Mrs. Gresham on the steps." Then they went up through the Ionic columns on to the broad stone terrace before the door, and there they found a crowd of men and women. For the legislators and statesmen had written their letters, and the ladies had taken their necessary rest.

Phineas, as he was dressing, considered deeply all that Lady Laura had said to him,—not so much with reference to the advice which she had given him, though that also was of importance, as to the fact that it had been given by her. She had first called herself his Mentor; but he had accepted the name and had addressed her as her Telemachus. And yet he believed himself to be older than she,—if, indeed, there was any difference in their ages. And was it possible that a female Mentor should love her Telemachus,—should love him as Phineas desired to be loved by Lady Laura? He would not say that it was impossible. Perhaps there had been mistakes between them;—a mistake in his manner of addressing her, and another in hers of addressing him. Perhaps the old bachelor of forty-three was not thinking of a wife. Had this old bachelor of forty-three been really in love with Lady Laura, would he have allowed her to walk home alone with Phineas, leaving her with some flimsy pretext of having to look at his sheep? Phineas resolved that he must at any rate play out his game,—whether he were to lose it or to win it; and in playing it he must, if possible, drop something of that Mentor and Telemachus style of conversation. As to the advice given him of herding with Greshams and Pallisers, instead of with Ratlers and Fitzgibbons,—he must use that as circumstances might direct. To him, himself, as he thought of it all, it was sufficiently astonishing that even the Ratlers and Fitzgibbons should admit him among them as one of themselves. "When I think of my father and of the old house at Killaloe, and remember that hitherto I have done nothing myself, I cannot understand how it is that I should be at Loughlinter." There was only one way of understanding it. If Lady Laura really loved him, the riddle might be read.

The rooms at Loughlinter were splendid, much larger and very much more richly furnished than those at Saulsby. But there was a certain stiffness in the movement of things, and perhaps in the manner of some of those present, which was not felt at Saulsby. Phineas at once missed the grace and prettiness and cheery audacity of Violet Effingham, and felt at the same time that Violet Effingham would be out of her element at Loughlinter. At Loughlinter they were met for business. It was at least a semi-political, or perhaps rather a semi-official gathering, and he became aware that he ought not to look simply for amusement. When he entered the drawing-room before dinner, Mr. Monk and Mr. Palliser, and Mr. Kennedy and Mr. Gresham, with sundry others, were standing in a wide group before the fireplace, and among them were Lady Glencora Palliser and Lady Laura and Mrs. Bonteen. As he approached them it seemed as though a sort of opening was made for himself; but he could see, though others did not, that the movement came from Lady Laura.

"I believe, Mr. Monk," said Lady Glencora, "that you and I are the only two in the whole party who really know what we would be at."

"If I must be divided from so many of my friends," said Mr. Monk, "I am happy to go astray in the company of Lady Glencora Palliser."

"And might I ask," said Mr. Gresham, with a peculiar smile for which he was famous, "what it is that you and Mr. Monk are really at?"

"Making men and women all equal," said Lady Glencora. "That I take to be the gist of our political theory."

"Lady Glencora, I must cry off," said Mr. Monk.

"Yes;—no doubt. If I were in the Cabinet myself I should not admit so much. There are reticences,—of course. And there is an official discretion."

"But you don't mean to say, Lady Glencora, that you would really advocate equality?" said Mrs. Bonteen.

"I do mean to say so, Mrs. Bonteen. And I mean to go further, and to tell you that you are no Liberal at heart unless you do so likewise; unless that is the basis of your political aspirations."

"Pray let me speak for myself, Lady Glencora."

"By no means,—not when you are criticising me and my politics. Do you not wish to make the lower orders comfortable?"

"Certainly," said Mrs. Bonteen.

"And educated, and happy and good?"

"Undoubtedly."

"To make them as comfortable and as good as yourself?"

"Better if possible."

"And I'm sure you wish to make yourself as good and as comfortable as anybody else,—as those above you, if anybody is above you? You will admit that?"

"Yes;—if I understand you."

"Then you have admitted everything, and are an advocate for general equality,—just as Mr. Monk is, and as I am. There is no getting out of it;—is there, Mr. Kennedy?" Then dinner was announced, and Mr. Kennedy walked off with the French Republican on his arm. As she went, she whispered into Mr. Kennedy's ear, "You will understand me. I am not saying that people are equal; but that the tendency of all law-making and of all governing should be to reduce the inequalities." In answer to which Mr. Kennedy said not a word. Lady Glencora's politics were too fast and furious for his nature.

A week passed by at Loughlinter, at the end of which Phineas found himself on terms of friendly intercourse with all the political magnates assembled in the house, but especially with Mr. Monk. He had determined that he would not follow Lady Laura's advice as to his selection of companions, if in doing so he should be driven even to a seeming of intrusion. He made no attempt to sit at the feet of anybody, and would stand aloof when bigger men than himself were talking, and was content to be less,—as indeed he was less,—than Mr. Bonteen or Mr. Ratler. But at the end of a week he found that, without any effort on his part,—almost in opposition to efforts on his part,—he had fallen into an easy pleasant way with these men which was very delightful to him. He had killed a stag in company with Mr. Palliser, and had stopped beneath a crag to discuss with him a question as to the duty on Irish malt. He had played chess with Mr. Gresham, and had been told that gentleman's opinion on the trial of Mr. Jefferson Davis. Lord Brentford had—at last—called him Finn, and had proved to him that nothing was known in Ireland about sheep. But with Mr. Monk he had had long discussions on abstract questions in politics,—and before the week was over was almost disposed to call himself a disciple, or, at least, a follower of Mr. Monk. Why not of Mr. Monk as well as of any one else? Mr. Monk was in the Cabinet, and of all the members of the Cabinet was the most advanced Liberal. "Lady Glencora was not so far wrong the other night," Mr. Monk said to him. "Equality is an ugly word and shouldn't be used. It misleads, and frightens, and is a bugbear. And she, in using it, had not perhaps a clearly defined meaning for it in her own mind. But the wish of every honest man should be to assist in lifting up those below him, till they be something nearer his own level than he finds them." To this Phineas assented,—and by degrees he found himself assenting to a great many things that Mr. Monk said to him.

Mr. Monk was a thin, tall, gaunt man, who had devoted his whole life to politics, hitherto without any personal reward beyond that which came to him from the reputation of his name, and from the honour of a seat in Parliament. He was one of four or five brothers,—and all besides him were in trade. They had prospered in trade, whereas he had prospered solely in politics; and men said that he was dependent altogether on what his relatives supplied for his support. He had now been in Parliament for more than twenty years, and had been known not only as a Radical but as a Democrat. Ten years since, when he had risen to fame, but not to repute, among the men who then governed England, nobody dreamed that Joshua Monk would ever be a paid servant of the Crown. He had inveighed against one minister after another as though they all deserved impeachment. He had advocated political doctrines which at that time seemed to be altogether at variance with any possibility of governing according to English rules of government. He had been regarded as a pestilent thorn in the sides of all ministers. But now he was a member of the Cabinet, and those whom he had terrified in the old days began to find that he was not so much unlike other men. There are but few horses which you cannot put into harness, and those of the highest spirit will generally do your work the best.

Phineas, who had his eyes about him, thought that he could perceive that Mr. Palliser did not shoot a deer with Mr. Ratler, and that Mr. Gresham played no chess with Mr. Bonteen. Bonteen, indeed, was a noisy pushing man whom nobody seemed to like, and Phineas wondered why he should be at Loughlinter, and why he should be in office. His friend Laurence Fitzgibbon had indeed once endeavoured to explain this. "A man who can vote hard, as I call it; and who will speak a few words now and then as they're wanted, without any ambition that way, may always have his price. And if he has a pretty wife into the bargain, he ought to have a pleasant time of it." Mr. Ratler no doubt was a very useful man, who thoroughly knew his business; but yet, as it seemed to Phineas, no very great distinction was shown to Mr. Ratler at

Loughlinter. "If I got as high as that," he said to himself, "I should think myself a miracle of luck. And yet nobody seems to think anything of Ratler. It is all nothing unless one can go to the very top."

"I believe I did right to accept office," Mr. Monk said to him one day, as they sat together on a rock close by one of the little bridges over the Linter. "Indeed, unless a man does so when the bonds of the office tendered to him are made compatible with his own views, he declines to proceed on the open path towards the prosecution of those views. A man who is combating one ministry after another, and striving to imbue those ministers with his convictions, can hardly decline to become a minister himself when he finds that those convictions of his own are henceforth,—or at least for some time to come,—to be the ministerial convictions of the day. Do you follow me?"

"Very clearly," said Phineas. "You would have denied your own children had you refused."

"Unless indeed a man were to feel that he was in some way unfitted for office work. I very nearly provided for myself an escape on that plea;—but when I came to sift it, I thought that it would be false. But let me tell you that the delight of political life is altogether in opposition. Why, it is freedom against slavery, fire against clay, movement against stagnation! The very inaccuracy which is permitted to opposition is in itself a charm worth more than all the patronage and all the prestige of ministerial power. You'll try them both, and then say if you do not agree with me. Give me the full swing of the benches below the gangway, where I needed to care for no one, and could always enjoy myself on my legs as long as I felt that I was true to those who sent me there! That is all over now. They have got me into harness, and my shoulders are sore. The oats, however, are of the best, and the hay is unexceptionable."

CHAPTER XV
Donald Bean's Pony

Phineas liked being told that the pleasures of opposition and the pleasures of office were both open to him,—and he liked also to be the chosen receptacle of Mr. Monk's confidence. He had come to understand that he was expected to remain ten days at Loughlinter, and that then there was to be a general movement. Since the first day he had seen but little of Mr. Kennedy, but he had found himself very frequently with Lady Laura. And then had come up the question of his projected trip to Paris with Lord Chiltern. He had received a letter from Lord Chiltern.

Dear Finn,

Are you going to Paris with me?

Yours, C.

There had been not a word beyond this, and before he answered it he made up his mind to tell Lady Laura the truth. He could not go to Paris because he had no money.

"I've just got that from your brother," said he.

"How like Oswald. He writes to me perhaps three times in the year, and his letters are just the same. You will go I hope?"

"Well;—no."

"I am sorry for that."

"I wonder whether I may tell you the real reason, Lady Laura."

"Nay;—I cannot answer that; but unless it be some political secret between you and Mr. Monk, I should think you might."

"I cannot afford to go to Paris this autumn. It seems to be a shocking admission to make,—though I don't know why it should be."

"Nor I;—but, Mr. Finn, I like you all the better for making it. I am very sorry, for Oswald's sake. It's so hard to find any companion for him whom he would like and whom we,—that is I,—should think altogether—; you know what I mean, Mr. Finn."

"Your wish that I should go with him is a great compliment, and I thoroughly wish that I could do it. As it is, I must go to Killaloe and retrieve my finances. I daresay, Lady Laura, you can hardly conceive how very poor a man I am." There was a melancholy tone about his voice as he said this, which made her think for the moment whether or no he had been right in going into Parliament, and whether she had been right in instigating him to do so. But it was too late to recur to that question now.

"You must climb into office early, and forego those pleasures of opposition which are so dear to Mr. Monk," she said, smiling. "After all, money is an accident which does not count nearly so high as do some other things. You and Mr. Kennedy have the same enjoyment of everything around you here."

"Yes; while it lasts."

"And Lady Glencora and I stand pretty much on the same footing, in spite of all her wealth,—except that she is a married woman. I do not know what she is worth,—something not to be counted; and I am worth,—just what papa chooses to give me. A ten-pound note at the present moment I should look upon as great riches." This was the first time she had ever spoken to him of her own position as regards money; but he had heard, or thought that he had heard, that she had been left a fortune altogether independent of her father.

The last of the ten days had now come, and Phineas was discontented and almost unhappy. The more he saw of Lady Laura the more he feared that it was impossible that she should become his wife. And yet from day to day his intimacy with her became more close. He had never made love to her, nor could he discover that it was possible for him to do so. She seemed to be a woman for whom all the ordinary stages of love-making were quite unsuitable, Of course he could declare his love and ask her to be his wife on any occasion on which he might find himself to be alone with her. And on this morning he had made up his mind that he would do so before the day was over. It might be possible that she would never speak to him again;—that all the pleasures and ambitious hopes to which she had introduced him might be over as soon as that rash word should have been spoken! But, nevertheless, he would speak it.

On this day there was to be a grouse-shooting party, and the shooters were to be out early. It had been talked of for some day or two past, and Phineas knew that he could not escape it. There had been some rivalry between him and Mr. Bonteen, and there was to be a sort of match as to which of the two would kill most birds before lunch. But there had also been some half promise on Lady Laura's part that she would walk with him up the Linter and come down upon the lake, taking an opposite direction from that by which they had returned with Mr. Kennedy.

"But you will be shooting all day," she said, when he proposed it to her as they were starting for the moor. The waggonet that was to take them was at the door, and she was there to see them start. Her father was one of the shooting party, and Mr. Kennedy was another.

"I will undertake to be back in time, if you will not think it too hot. I shall not see you again till we meet in town next year."

"Then I certainly will go with you,—that is to say, if you are here. But you cannot return without the rest of the party, as you are going so far."

"I'll get back somehow," said Phineas, who was resolved that a few miles more or less of mountain should not detain him from the prosecution of a task so vitally important to him. "If we start at five that will be early enough."

"Quite early enough," said Lady Laura.

Phineas went off to the mountains, and shot his grouse, and won his match, and eat his luncheon. Mr. Bonteen, however, was not beaten by much, and was in consequence somewhat ill-humoured.

"I'll tell you what I'll do," said Mr. Bonteen, "I'll back myself for the rest of the day for a ten-pound note."

Now there had been no money staked on the match at all,—but it had been simply a trial of skill, as to which would kill the most birds in a given time. And the proposition for that trial had come from Mr. Bonteen himself. "I should not think of shooting for money," said Phineas.

"And why not? A bet is the only way to decide these things."

"Partly because I'm sure I shouldn't hit a bird," said Phineas, "and partly because I haven't got any money to lose."

"I hate bets," said Mr. Kennedy to him afterwards. "I was annoyed when Bonteen offered the wager. I felt sure, however, you would not accept it."

"I suppose such bets are very common."

"I don't think men ought to propose them unless they are quite sure of their company. Maybe I'm wrong, and I often feel that I am strait-laced about such things. It is so odd to me that men cannot amuse themselves without pitting themselves against each other. When a man tells me that he can shoot better than I, I tell him that my keeper can shoot better than he."

"All the same, it's a good thing to excel," said Phineas.

"I'm not so sure of that," said Mr. Kennedy. "A man who can kill more salmon than anybody else, can rarely do anything else. Are you going on with your match?"

"No; I'm going to make my way to Loughlinter."

"Not alone?"

"Yes, alone."

"It's over nine miles. You can't walk it."

Phineas looked at his watch, and found that it was now two o'clock. It was a broiling day in August, and the way back to Loughlinter, for six or seven out of the nine miles, would be along a high road. "I must do it all the same," said he, preparing for a start. "I have an engagement with Lady Laura Standish; and as this is the last day that I shall see her, I certainly do not mean to break it."

"An engagement with Lady Laura," said Mr. Kennedy. "Why did you not tell me, that I might have a pony ready? But come along. Donald Bean has a pony. He's not much bigger than a dog, but he'll carry you to Loughlinter."

"I can walk it, Mr. Kennedy."

"Yes; and think of the state in which you'd reach Loughlinter! Come along with me."

"But I can't take you off the mountain," said Phineas.

"Then you must allow me to take you off."

So Mr. Kennedy led the way down to Donald Bean's cottage, and before three o'clock Phineas found himself mounted on a shaggy steed, which, in sober truth, was not much bigger than a large dog. "If Mr. Kennedy is really my rival," said Phineas to himself, as he trotted along, "I almost think that I am doing an unhandsome thing in taking the pony."

At five o'clock he was under the portico before the front door, and there he found Lady Laura waiting for him,—waiting for him, or at least ready for him. She had on her hat and gloves and light shawl, and her parasol was in her hand. He thought that he had never seen her look so young, so pretty, and so fit to receive a lover's vows. But at the same moment it occurred to him that she was Lady Laura Standish, the daughter of an Earl, the descendant of a line of Earls,—and that he was the son of a simple country doctor in Ireland. Was it fitting that he should ask such a woman to be his wife? But then Mr. Kennedy was the son of a man who had walked into Glasgow with half-a-crown in his pocket. Mr. Kennedy's grandfather had been,—Phineas thought that he had heard that Mr. Kennedy's grandfather had been a Scotch drover; whereas his own grandfather had been a little squire near Ennistimon, in county Clare, and his own first cousin once removed still held the paternal acres at Finn Grove. His family was supposed to be descended from kings in that part of Ireland. It certainly did not become him to fear Lady Laura on the score of rank, if it was to be allowed to Mr. Kennedy to proceed without fear on that head. As to wealth, Lady Laura had already told him that her fortune was no greater than his. Her statement to himself on that head made him feel that he should not hesitate on the score of money. They neither had any, and he was willing to work for both. If she feared the risk, let her say so.

It was thus that he argued with himself; but yet he knew,—knew as well as the reader will know,—that he was going to do that which he had no right to do. It might be very well for him to wait,—presuming him to be successful in his love,—for the opening of that oyster with his political sword, that oyster on which he proposed that they should both live; but such waiting could not well be to the taste of Lady Laura

Standish. It could hardly be pleasant to her to look forward to his being made a junior lord or an assistant secretary before she could establish herself in her home. So he told himself. And yet he told himself at the same time that it was incumbent on him to persevere.

"I did not expect you in the least," said Lady Laura.

"And yet I spoke very positively."

"But there are things as to which a man may be very positive, and yet may be allowed to fail. In the first place, how on earth did you get home?"

"Mr. Kennedy got me a pony,—Donald Bean's pony."

"You told him, then?"

"Yes; I told him why I was coming, and that I must be here. Then he took the trouble to come all the way off the mountain to persuade Donald to lend me his pony. I must acknowledge that Mr. Kennedy has conquered me at last."

"I am so glad of that," said Lady Laura. "I knew he would,—unless it were your own fault."

They went up the path by the brook, from bridge to bridge, till they found themselves out upon the open mountain at the top. Phineas had resolved that he would not speak out his mind till he found himself on that spot; that then he would ask her to sit down, and that while she was so seated he would tell her everything. At the present moment he had on his head a Scotch cap with a grouse's feather in it, and he was dressed in a velvet shooting-jacket and dark knickerbockers; and was certainly, in this costume, as handsome a man as any woman would wish to see. And there was, too, a look of breeding about him which had come to him, no doubt, from the royal Finns of old, which ever served him in great stead. He was, indeed, only Phineas Finn, and was known by the world to be no more; but he looked as though he might have been anybody,—a royal Finn himself. And then he had that special grace of appearing to be altogether unconscious of his own personal advantages. And I think that in truth he was barely conscious of them; that he depended on them very little, if at all; that there was nothing of personal vanity in his composition. He had never indulged in any hope that Lady Laura would accept him because he was a handsome man.

"After all that climbing," he said, "will you not sit down for a moment?" As he spoke to her she looked at him and told herself that he was as handsome as a god. "Do sit down for one moment," he said. "I have something that I desire to say to you, and to say it here."

"I will," she said; "but I also have something to tell you, and will say it while I am yet standing. Yesterday I accepted an offer of marriage from Mr. Kennedy."

"Then I am too late," said Phineas, and putting his hands into the pockets of his coat, he turned his back upon her, and walked away across the mountain.

What a fool he had been to let her know his secret when her knowledge of it could be of no service to him,—when her knowledge of it could only make him appear foolish in her eyes! But for his life he could not have kept his secret to himself. Nor now could he bring himself to utter a word of even decent civility. But he went on walking as though he could thus leave her there, and never see her again. What an ass he had been in supposing that she cared for him! What a fool to imagine that his poverty could stand a chance against the wealth of Loughlinter! But why had she lured him on? How he wished that he were now grinding, hard at work in Mr. Low's chambers, or sitting at home at Killaloe with the hand of that pretty little Irish girl within his own!

Presently he heard a voice behind him,—calling him gently. Then he turned and found that she was very near him. He himself had then been standing still for some moments, and she had followed him. "Mr. Finn," she said.

"Well;—yes: what is it?" And turning round he made an attempt to smile.

"Will you not wish me joy, or say a word of congratulation? Had I not thought much of your friendship, I should not have been so quick to tell you of my destiny. No one else has been told, except papa."

"Of course I hope you will be happy. Of course I do. No wonder he lent me the pony!"

"You must forget all that."

"Forget what?"

"Well,—nothing. You need forget nothing," said Lady Laura, "for nothing has been said that need be regretted. Only wish me joy, and all will be pleasant."

"Lady Laura, I do wish you joy, with all my heart,—but that will not make all things pleasant. I came up here to ask you to be my wife."

"No;—no, no; do not say it."

"But I have said it, and will say it again. I, poor, penniless, plain simple fool that I am, have been ass enough to love you, Lady Laura Standish; and I brought you up here to-day to ask you to share with me—my nothingness. And this I have done on soil that is to be all your own. Tell me that you regard me as a conceited fool,—as a bewildered idiot."

"I wish to regard you as a dear friend,—both of my own and of my husband," said she, offering him her hand.

"Should I have had a chance, I wonder, if I had spoken a week since?"

"How can I answer such a question, Mr. Finn? Or, rather, I will, answer it fully. It is not a week since we told each other, you to me and I to you, that we were both poor,—both without other means than those which come to us from our fathers. You will make your way;—will make it surely; but how at present could you marry any woman unless she had money of her own? For me,—like so many other girls, it was necessary that I should stay at home or marry some one rich enough to dispense with fortune in a wife. The man whom in all the world I think the best has asked me to share everything with him;—and I have thought it wise to accept his offer."

"And I was fool enough to think that you loved me," said Phineas. To this she made no immediate answer. "Yes, I was. I feel that I owe it you to tell you what a fool I have been. I did. I thought you loved me. At least I thought that perhaps you loved me. It was like a child wanting the moon;—was it not?"

"And why should I not have loved you?" she said slowly, laying her hand gently upon his arm.

"Why not? Because Loughlinter—"

"Stop, Mr. Finn; stop. Do not say to me any unkind word that I have not deserved, and that would make a breach between us. I have accepted the owner of Loughlinter as my husband, because I verily believe that I shall thus do my duty in that sphere of life to which it has pleased God to call me. I have always liked him, and I will love him. For you,—may I trust myself to speak openly to you?"

"You may trust me as against all others, except us two ourselves."

"For you, then, I will say also that I have always liked you since I knew you; that I have loved you as a friend;—and could have loved you otherwise had not circumstances showed me so plainly that it would be unwise."

"Oh, Lady Laura!"

"Listen a moment. And pray remember that what I say to you now must never be repeated to any ears. No one knows it but my father, my brother, and Mr. Kennedy. Early in the spring I paid my brother's debts. His affection to me is more than a return for what I have done for him. But when I did this,—when I made up my mind to do it, I made up my mind also that I could not allow myself the same freedom of choice which would otherwise have belonged to me. Will that be sufficient, Mr. Finn?"

"How can I answer you, Lady Laura? Sufficient! And you are not angry with me for what I have said?"

"No, I am not angry. But it is understood, of course, that nothing of this shall ever be repeated,—even among ourselves. Is that a bargain?"

"Oh, yes. I shall never speak of it again."

"And now you will wish me joy?"

"I have wished you joy, Lady Laura. And I will do so again. May you have every blessing which the world can give you. You cannot expect me to be very jovial for awhile myself; but there will be nobody to see my melancholy moods. I shall be hiding myself away in Ireland. When is the marriage to be?"

"Nothing has been said of that. I shall be guided by him,—but there must, of course, be delay. There will be settlements and I know not what. It may probably be in the spring,—or perhaps the summer. I shall do just what my betters tell me to do."

Phineas had now seated himself on the exact stone on which he had wished her to sit when he proposed to tell his own story, and was looking forth upon the lake. It seemed to him that everything had been changed for him while he had been up there upon the mountain, and that the change had been marvellous in its nature. When he had been coming up, there had been apparently two alternatives before him: the glory of successful love,—which, indeed, had seemed to him to be a most improbable result of the coming interview,—and the despair and utter banishment attendant on disdainful rejection. But his position was far removed from either of these alternatives. She had almost told him that she would have loved him had she not been poor,—that she was beginning to love him and had quenched her love, because it had become impossible to her to marry a poor man. In such circumstances he could not be angry with her,—he could not quarrel with her; he could not do other than swear to himself that he would be her friend. And yet he loved her better than ever;—and she was the promised wife of his rival! Why had not Donald Bean's pony broken his neck?

"Shall we go down now?" she said.

"Oh, yes."

"You will not go on by the lake?"

"What is the use? It is all the same now. You will want to be back to receive him in from shooting."

"Not that, I think. He is above those little cares. But it will be as well we should go the nearest way, as we have spent so much of our time here. I shall tell Mr. Kennedy that I have told you,—if you do not mind."

"Tell him what you please," said Phineas.

"But I won't have it taken in that way, Mr. Finn. Your brusque want of courtesy to me I have forgiven, but I shall expect you to make up for it by the alacrity of your congratulations to him. I will not have you uncourteous to Mr. Kennedy."

"If I have been uncourteous I beg your pardon."

"You need not do that. We are old friends, and may take the liberty of speaking plainly to each other;—but you will owe it to Mr. Kennedy to be gracious. Think of the pony."

They walked back to the house together, and as they went down the path very little was said. Just as they were about to come out upon the open lawn, while they were still under cover of the rocks and shrubs, Phineas stopped his companion by standing before her, and then he made his farewell speech to her.

"I must say good-bye to you. I shall be away early in the morning."

"Good-bye, and God bless you," said Lady Laura.

"Give me your hand," said he. And she gave him her hand. "I don't suppose you know what it is to love dearly."

"I hope I do."

"But to be in love! I believe you do not. And to miss your love! I think,—I am bound to think that you have never been so tormented. It is very sore;—but I will do my best, like a man, to get over it."

"Do, my friend, do. So small a trouble will never weigh heavily on shoulders such as yours."

"It will weigh very heavily, but I will struggle hard that it may not crush me. I have loved you so dearly! As we are parting give me one kiss, that I may think of it and treasure it in my memory!" What murmuring words she spoke to express her refusal of such a request, I will not quote; but the kiss had been taken before the denial was completed, and then they walked on in silence together,—and in peace, towards the house.

On the next morning six or seven men were going away, and there was an early breakfast. There were none of the ladies there, but Mr. Kennedy, the host, was among his friends. A large drag with four horses was there to take the travellers and their luggage to the station, and there was naturally a good deal of noise at the front door as the preparations for the departure were made. In the middle of them Mr. Kennedy took our hero aside. "Laura has told me," said Mr. Kennedy, "that she has acquainted you with my good fortune."

"And I congratulate you most heartily," said Phineas, grasping the other's hand. "You are indeed a lucky fellow."

46

"I feel myself to be so," said Mr. Kennedy. "Such a wife was all that was wanting to me, and such a wife is very hard to find. Will you remember, Finn, that Loughlinter will never be so full but what there will be a room for you, or so empty but what you will be made welcome? I say this on Lady Laura's part and on my own."

Phineas, as he was being carried away to the railway station, could not keep himself from speculating as to how much Kennedy knew of what had taken place during the walk up the Linter. Of one small circumstance that had occurred, he felt quite sure that Mr. Kennedy knew nothing.

CHAPTER XVI
Phineas Finn Returns to Killaloe

Phineas Finn's first session of Parliament was over,—his first session with all its adventures. When he got back to Mrs. Bunce's house,—for Mrs. Bunce received him for a night in spite of her husband's advice to the contrary,—I am afraid he almost felt that Mrs. Bunce and her rooms were beneath him. Of course he was very unhappy,—as wretched as a man can be; there were moments in which he thought that it would hardly become him to live unless he could do something to prevent the marriage of Lady Laura and Mr. Kennedy. But, nevertheless, he had his consolations. These were reflections which had in them much of melancholy satisfaction. He had not been despised by the woman to whom he had told his love. She had not shown him that she thought him to be unworthy of her. She had not regarded his love as an offence. Indeed, she had almost told him that prudence alone had forbidden her to return his passion. And he had kissed her, and had afterwards parted from her as a dear friend. I do not know why there should have been a flavour of exquisite joy in the midst of his agony as he thought of this;—but it was so. He would never kiss her again. All future delights of that kind would belong to Mr. Kennedy, and he had no real idea of interfering with that gentleman in the fruition of his privileges. But still there was the kiss,—an eternal fact. And then, in all respects except that of his love, his visit to Loughlinter had been pre-eminently successful. Mr. Monk had become his friend, and had encouraged him to speak during the next session,—setting before him various models, and prescribing for him a course of reading. Lord Brentford had become intimate with him. He was on pleasant terms with Mr. Palliser and Mr. Gresham. And as for Mr. Kennedy,—he and Mr. Kennedy were almost bosom friends. It seemed to him that he had quite surpassed the Ratlers, Fitzgibbons, and Bonteens in that politico-social success which goes so far towards downright political success, and which in itself is so pleasant. He had surpassed these men in spite of their offices and their acquired positions, and could not but think that even Mr. Low, if he knew it all, would confess that he had been right.

As to his bosom friendship with Mr. Kennedy, that of course troubled him. Ought he not to be driving a poniard into Mr. Kennedy's heart? The conventions of life forbade that; and therefore the bosom friendship was to be excused. If not an enemy to the death, then there could be no reason why he should not be a bosom friend.

He went over to Ireland, staying but one night with Mrs. Bunce, and came down upon them at Killaloe like a god out of the heavens. Even his father was well-nigh overwhelmed by admiration, and his mother and sisters thought themselves only fit to minister to his pleasures. He had learned, if he had learned nothing else, to look as though he were master of the circumstances around him, and was entirely free from internal embarrassment. When his father spoke to him about his legal studies, he did not exactly laugh at his father's ignorance, but he recapitulated to his father so much of Mr. Monk's wisdom at second hand,—showing plainly that it was his business to study the arts of speech and the technicalities of the House, and not to study law,—that his father had nothing further to say. He had become a man of such dimensions that an ordinary father could hardly dare to inquire into his proceedings; and as for an ordinary mother,—such as Mrs. Finn certainly was,—she could do no more than look after her son's linen with awe.

Mary Flood Jones,—the reader I hope will not quite have forgotten Mary Flood Jones,—was in a great tremor when first she met the hero of Loughshane after returning from the honours of his first session. She had been somewhat disappointed because the newspapers had not been full of the speeches he had made in Parliament. And indeed the ladies of the Finn household had all been ill at ease on this head. They could not imagine why Phineas had restrained himself with so much philosophy. But Miss Flood Jones in discussing the matter with the Miss Finns had never expressed the slightest doubt of his capacity or his judgment. And when tidings came,—the tidings came in a letter from Phineas to his father,—that he did not intend to speak that session, because speeches from a young member on his first session were thought to be inexpedient, Miss Flood Jones and the Miss Finns were quite willing to accept the wisdom of this decision, much as they might regret the effect of it. Mary, when she met her hero, hardly dared to look him in the face, but she remembered accurately all the circumstances of her last interview with him. Could it be that he wore that ringlet near his heart? Mary had received from Barbara Finn certain hairs supposed to have come from the head of Phineas, and these she always wore near her own. And moreover, since she had seen Phineas she had refused an offer of marriage from Mr. Elias Bodkin,—had refused it almost ignominiously,—and when doing so had told herself that she would never be false to Phineas Finn.

"We think it so good of you to come to see us again," she said.

"Good to come home to my own people?"

"Of course you might be staying with plenty of grandees if you liked it."

"No, indeed, Mary. It did happen by accident that I had to go to the house of a man whom perhaps you would call a grandee, and to meet grandees there. But it was only for a few days, and I am very glad to be taken in again here, I can assure you."

"You know how very glad we all are to have you."

"Are you glad to see me, Mary?"

"Very glad. Why should I not be glad, and Barbara the dearest friend I have in the world? Of course she talks about you,—and that makes me think of you."

"If you knew, Mary, how often I think about you." Then Mary, who was very happy at hearing such words, and who was walking in to dinner with him at the moment, could not refrain herself from pressing his arm with her little fingers. She knew that Phineas in his position could not marry at once; but she would wait for him,—oh, for ever, if he would only ask her. He of course was a wicked traitor to tell her that he was wont to think of her. But Jove smiles at lovers' perjuries;—and it is well that he should do so, as such perjuries can hardly be avoided altogether in the difficult circumstances of a successful gentleman's life. Phineas was a traitor, of course, but he was almost forced to be a traitor, by the simple fact that Lady Laura Standish was in London, and Mary Flood Jones in Killaloe.

He remained for nearly five months at Killaloe, and I doubt whether his time was altogether well spent. Some of the books recommended to him by Mr. Monk he probably did read, and was often to be found encompassed by blue books. I fear that there was a grain of pretence about his blue books and parliamentary papers, and that in these days he was, in a gentle way, something of an impostor. "You must not be angry with me for not going to you," he said once to Mary's mother when he had declined an invitation to drink tea; "but the fact is that my time is not my own." "Pray don't make any apologies. We are quite aware that we have very little to offer," said Mrs. Flood Jones, who was not altogether happy about Mary, and who perhaps knew more about members of Parliament and blue books than Phineas Finn had supposed. "Mary, you are a fool to think of that man," the mother said to her daughter the next morning. "I don't think of him, mamma; not particularly." "He is no better than anybody else that I can see, and he is beginning to give himself airs," said Mrs. Flood Jones. Mary made no answer; but she went up into her room and swore before a figure of the Virgin that she would be true to Phineas for ever and ever, in spite of her mother, in spite of all the world,—in spite, should it be necessary, even of himself.

About Christmas time there came a discussion between Phineas and his father about money. "I hope you find you get on pretty well," said the doctor, who thought that he had been liberal.

"It's a tight fit," said Phineas,—who was less afraid of his father than he had been when he last discussed these things.

"I had hoped it would have been ample," said the doctor.

"Don't think for a moment, sir, that I am complaining," said Phineas. "I know it is much more than I have a right to expect."

The doctor began to make an inquiry within his own breast as to whether his son had a right to expect anything;—whether the time had not come in which his son should be earning his own bread. "I suppose," he said, after a pause, "there is no chance of your doing anything at the bar now?"

"Not immediately. It is almost impossible to combine the two studies together." Mr. Low himself was aware of that. "But you are not to suppose that I have given the profession up."

"I hope not,—after all the money it has cost us."

"By no means, sir. And all that I am doing now will, I trust, be of assistance to me when I shall come back to work at the law. Of course it is on the cards that I may go into office,—and if so, public business will become my profession."

"And be turned out with the Ministry!"

"Yes; that is true, sir. I must run my chance. If the worst comes to the worst, I hope I might be able to secure some permanent place. I should think that I can hardly fail to do so. But I trust I may never be driven to want it. I thought, however, that we had settled all this before." Then Phineas assumed a look of injured innocence, as though his father was driving him too hard.

"And in the mean time your money has been enough?" said the doctor, after a pause.

"I had intended to ask you to advance me a hundred pounds," said Phineas. "There were expenses to which I was driven on first entering Parliament."

"A hundred pounds."

"If it be inconvenient, sir, I can do without it." He had not as yet paid for his gun, or for that velvet coat in which he had been shooting, or, most probably, for the knickerbockers. He knew he wanted the hundred pounds badly; but he felt ashamed of himself in asking for it. If he were once in office,—though the office were but a sorry junior lordship,—he would repay his father instantly.

"You shall have it, of course," said the doctor; "but do not let the necessity for asking for more hundreds come oftener than you can help." Phineas said that he would not, and then there was no further discourse about money. It need hardly be said that he told his father nothing of that bill which he had endorsed for Laurence Fitzgibbon.

At last came the time which called him again to London and the glories of London life,—to lobbies, and the clubs, and the gossip of men in office, and the chance of promotion for himself; to the glare of the gas-lamps, the mock anger of rival debaters, and the prospect of the Speaker's wig. During the idleness of the recess he had resolved at any rate upon this,—that a month of the session should not have passed by before he had been seen upon his legs in the House,—had been seen and heard. And many a time as he had wandered alone, with his gun, across the bogs which lie on the other side of the Shannon from Killaloe, he had practised the sort of address which he would make to the House. He would be short,—always short; and he would eschew all action and gesticulation; Mr. Monk had been very urgent in his instructions to him on that head; but he would be especially careful that no words should escape him which had not in them some purpose. He might be wrong in his purpose, but purpose there should be. He had been twitted more than once at Killaloe with his silence;—for it had been conceived by his fellow-townsmen that he had been sent to Parliament on the special ground of his eloquence. They should twit him no more on his next return. He would speak and would carry the House with him if a human effort might prevail.

So he packed up his things, and started again for London in the beginning of February. "Good-bye, Mary," he said with his sweetest smile. But on this occasion there was no kiss, and no culling of locks. "I know he cannot help it," said Mary to herself. "It is his position. But whether it be for good or evil, I will be true to him."

"I am afraid you are unhappy," Babara Finn said to her on the next morning.

"No; I am not unhappy,—not at all. I have a deal to make me happy and proud. I don't mean to be a bit unhappy." Then she turned away and cried heartily, and Barbara Finn cried with her for company.

CHAPTER XVII
Phineas Finn Returns to London

Phineas had received two letters during his recess at Killaloe from two women who admired him much, which, as they were both short, shall be submitted to the reader. The first was as follows:—

Saulsby, October 20, 186—.

My dear Mr. Finn,

I write a line to tell you that our marriage is to be hurried on as quickly as possible. Mr. Kennedy does not like to be absent from Parliament; nor will he be content to postpone the ceremony till the session be over. The day fixed is the 3rd of December, and we then go at once to Rome, and intend to be back in London by the opening of Parliament.

Yours most sincerely,

Laura Standish.

Our London address will be No. 52, Grosvenor Place.

To this he wrote an answer as short, expressing his ardent wishes that those winter hymeneals might produce nothing but happiness, and saying that he would not be in town many days before he knocked at the door of No. 52, Grosvenor Place.

And the second letter was as follows:—

Great Marlborough Street, December, 186—.

Dear and Honoured Sir,

Bunce is getting ever so anxious about the rooms, and says as how he has a young Equity draftsman and wife and baby as would take the whole house, and all because Miss Pouncefoot said a word about her port wine, which any lady of her age might say in her tantrums, and mean nothing after all. Me and Miss Pouncefoot's knowed each other for seven years, and what's a word or two as isn't meant after that? But, honoured sir, it's not about that as I write to trouble you, but to ask if I may say for certain that you'll take the rooms again in February. It's easy to let them for the month after Christmas, because of the pantomimes. Only say at once, because Bunce is nagging me day after day. I don't want nobody's wife and baby to have to do for, and 'd sooner have a Parliament gent like yourself than any one else.

Yours umbly and respectful,

Jane Bunce.

To this he replied that he would certainly come back to the rooms in Great Marlborough Street, should he be lucky enough to find them vacant, and he expressed his willingness to take them on and from the 1st of February. And on the 3rd of February he found himself in the old quarters, Mrs. Bunce having contrived, with much conjugal adroitness, both to keep Miss Pouncefoot and to stave off the Equity draftsman's wife and baby. Bunce, however, received Phineas very coldly, and told his wife the same evening that as far as he could see their lodger would never turn up to be a trump in the matter of the ballot. "If he means well, why did he go and stay with them lords down in Scotland? I knows all about it. I knows a man when I sees him. Mr. Low, who's looking out to be a Tory judge some of these days, is a deal better;—because he knows what he's after."

Immediately on his return to town, Phineas found himself summoned to a political meeting at Mr. Mildmay's house in St. James's Square. "We're going to begin in earnest this time," Barrington Erle said to him at the club.

"I am glad of that," said Phineas.

"I suppose you heard all about it down at Loughlinter?"

Now, in truth, Phineas had heard very little of any settled plan down at Loughlinter. He had played a game of chess with Mr. Gresham, and had shot a stag with Mr. Palliser, and had discussed sheep with Lord Brentford, but had hardly heard a word about politics from any one of those influential gentlemen. From Mr. Monk he had heard much of a coming Reform Bill; but his communications with Mr. Monk had rather been private discussions,—in which he had learned Mr. Monk's own views on certain points,—than revelations on the intention of the party to which Mr. Monk belonged. "I heard of nothing settled," said Phineas; "but I suppose we are to have a Reform Bill."

"That is a matter of course."

"And I suppose we are not to touch the question of ballot."

"That's the difficulty," said Barrington Erle. "But of course we shan't touch it as long as Mr. Mildmay is in the Cabinet. He will never consent to the ballot as First Minister of the Crown."

"Nor would Gresham, or Palliser," said Phineas, who did not choose to bring forward his greatest gun at first.

"I don't know about Gresham. It is impossible to say what Gresham might bring himself to do. Gresham is a man who may go any lengths before he has done. Planty Pall,"—for such was the name by which Mr. Plantagenet Palliser was ordinarily known among his friends,—"would of course go with Mr. Mildmay and the Duke."

"And Monk is opposed to the ballot," said Phineas.

"Ah, that's the question. No doubt he has assented to the proposition of a measure without the ballot; but if there should come a row, and men like Turnbull demand it, and the London mob kick up a shindy, I don't know how far Monk would be steady."

"Whatever he says, he'll stick to."

"He is your leader, then?" asked Barrington.

"I don't know that I have a leader. Mr. Mildmay leads our side; and if anybody leads me, he does. But I have great faith in Mr. Monk."

"There's one who would go for the ballot to-morrow, if it were brought forward stoutly," said Barrington Erle to Mr. Ratler a few minutes afterwards, pointing to Phineas as he spoke.

"I don't think much of that young man," said Ratler.

Mr. Bonteen and Mr. Ratler had put their heads together during that last evening at Loughlinter, and had agreed that they did not think much of Phineas Finn. Why did Mr. Kennedy go down off the mountain to get him a pony? And why did Mr. Gresham play chess with him? Mr. Ratler and Mr. Bonteen may have been right in making up their minds to think but little of Phineas Finn, but Barrington Erle had been quite wrong when he had said that Phineas would "go for the ballot" to-morrow. Phineas had made up his mind very strongly that he would always oppose the ballot. That he would hold the same opinion throughout his life, no one should pretend to say; but in his present mood, and under the tuition which he had received from Mr. Monk, he was prepared to demonstrate, out of the House and in it, that the ballot was, as a political measure, unmanly, ineffective, and enervating. Enervating had been a great word with Mr. Monk, and Phineas had clung to it with admiration.

The meeting took place at Mr. Mildmay's on the third day of the session. Phineas had of course heard of such meetings before, but had never attended one. Indeed, there had been no such gathering when Mr. Mildmay's party came into power early in the last session. Mr. Mildmay and his men had then made their effort in turning out their opponents, and had been well pleased to rest awhile upon their oars. Now, however, they must go again to work, and therefore the liberal party was collected at Mr. Mildmay's house, in order that the liberal party might be told what it was that Mr. Mildmay and his Cabinet intended to do.

Phineas Finn was quite in the dark as to what would be the nature of the performance on this occasion, and entertained some idea that every gentleman present would be called upon to express individually his assent or dissent in regard to the measure proposed. He walked to St. James's Square with Laurence Fitzgibbon; but even with Fitzgibbon was ashamed to show his ignorance by asking questions. "After all," said Fitzgibbon, "this kind of thing means nothing. I know as well as possible, and so do you, what Mr. Mildmay will say,—and then Gresham will say a few words; and then Turnbull will make a murmur, and then we shall all assent,—to anything or to nothing;—and then it will be over." Still Phineas did not understand whether the assent required would or would not be an individual personal assent. When the affair was over he found that he was disappointed, and that he might almost as well have stayed away from the meeting,—except that he had attended at Mr. Mildmay's bidding, and had given a silent adhesion to Mr. Mildmay's plan of reform for that session. Laurence Fitzgibbon had been very nearly correct in his description of what would occur. Mr. Mildmay made a long speech. Mr. Turnbull, the great Radical of the day,—the man who was supposed to represent what many called the Manchester school of politics,—asked half a dozen questions. In answer to these Mr. Gresham made a short speech. Then Mr. Mildmay made another speech, and then all was over. The gist of the whole thing was, that there should be a Reform Bill,—very generous in its enlargement of the franchise,—but no ballot. Mr. Turnbull expressed his doubt whether this would be satisfactory to the country; but even Mr. Turnbull was soft in his tone and complaisant in his manner. As there was no reporter present,—that plan of turning private meetings at gentlemen's houses into public assemblies not having been as yet adopted,—there could be no need for energy or violence. They went to Mr. Mildmay's house to hear Mr. Mildmay's plan,—and they heard it.

Two days after this Phineas was to dine with Mr. Monk. Mr. Monk had asked him in the lobby of the House. "I don't give dinner parties," he said, "but I should like you to come and meet Mr. Turnbull." Phineas accepted the invitation as a matter of course. There were many who said that Mr. Turnbull was the greatest man in the nation, and that the nation could be saved only by a direct obedience to Mr. Turnbull's instructions. Others said that Mr. Turnbull was a demagogue and at heart a rebel; that he was un-English, false and very dangerous. Phineas was rather inclined to believe the latter statement; and as danger and dangerous men are always more attractive than safety and safe men, he was glad to have an opportunity of meeting Mr. Turnbull at dinner.

In the meantime he went to call on Lady Laura, whom he had not seen since the last evening which he spent in her company at Loughlinter,—whom, when he was last speaking to her, he had kissed close beneath the falls of the Linter. He found her at home, and with her was her husband. "Here is a Darby and Joan meeting, is it not?" she said, getting up to welcome him. He had seen Mr. Kennedy before, and had been standing close to him during the meeting at Mr. Mildmay's.

"I am very glad to find you both together."

"But Robert is going away this instant," said Lady Laura. "Has he told you of our adventures at Rome?"

"Not a word."

"Then I must tell you;—but not now. The dear old Pope was so civil to us. I came to think it quite a pity that he should be in trouble."

"I must be off," said the husband, getting up. "But I shall meet you at dinner, I believe."

"Do you dine at Mr. Monk's?"

"Yes, and am asked expressly to hear Turnbull make a convert of you. There are only to be us four. Au revoir." Then Mr. Kennedy went, and Phineas found himself alone with Lady Laura. He hardly knew how to address her, and remained silent. He had not prepared himself for the interview as he ought to have done, and felt himself to be awkward. She evidently expected him to speak, and for a few seconds sat waiting for what he might say.

At last she found that it was incumbent on her to begin. "Were you surprised at our suddenness when you got my note?"

"A little. You had spoken of waiting."

"I had never imagined that he would have been impetuous. And he seems to think that even the business of getting himself married would not justify him staying away from Parliament. He is a rigid martinet in all matters of duty."

"I did not wonder that he should be in a hurry, but that you should submit."

"I told you that I should do just what the wise people told me. I asked papa, and he said that it would be better. So the lawyers were driven out of their minds, and the milliners out of their bodies, and the thing was done."

"Who was there at the marriage?"

"Oswald was not there. That I know is what you mean to ask. Papa said that he might come if he pleased. Oswald stipulated that he should be received as a son. Then my father spoke the hardest word that ever fell from his mouth."

"What did he say?"

"I will not repeat it,—not altogether. But he said that Oswald was not entitled to a son's treatment. He was very sore about my money, because Robert was so generous as to his settlement. So the breach between them is as wide as ever."

"And where is Chiltern now?" said Phineas.

"Down in Northamptonshire, staying at some inn from whence he hunts. He tells me that he is quite alone,—that he never dines out, never has any one to dine with him, that he hunts five or six days a week,—and reads at night."

"That is not a bad sort of life."

"Not if the reading is any good. But I cannot bear that he should be so solitary. And if he breaks down in it, then his companions will not be fit for him. Do you ever hunt?"

"Oh yes,—at home in county Clare. All Irishmen hunt."

"I wish you would go down to him and see him. He would be delighted to have you."

Phineas thought over the proposition before he answered it, and then made the reply that he had made once before. "I would do so, Lady Laura,—but that I have no money for hunting in England."

"Alas, alas!" said she, smiling. "How that hits one on every side!"

"I might manage it,—for a couple of days,—in March."

"Do not do what you think you ought not to do," said Lady Laura.

"No; certainly. But I should like it, and if I can I will."

"He could mount you, I have no doubt. He has no other expense now, and keeps a stable full of horses. I think he has seven or eight. And now tell me, Mr. Finn; when are you going to charm the House? Or is it your first intention to strike terror?"

He blushed,—he knew that he blushed as he answered. "Oh, I suppose I shall make some sort of attempt before long. I can't bear the idea of being a bore."

"I think you ought to speak, Mr. Finn."

"I do not know about that, but I certainly mean to try. There will be lots of opportunities about the new Reform Bill. Of course you know that Mr. Mildmay is going to bring it in at once. You hear all that from Mr. Kennedy."

"And papa has told me. I still see papa almost every day. You must call upon him. Mind you do." Phineas said that he certainly would. "Papa is very lonely now, and I sometimes feel that I have been almost cruel in deserting him. And I think that he has a horror of the house,—especially later in the year,—always fancying that he will meet Oswald. I am so unhappy about it all, Mr. Finn."

"Why doesn't your brother marry?" said Phineas, knowing nothing as yet of Lord Chiltern and Violet Effingham. "If he were to marry well, that would bring your father round."

"Yes,—it would."

"And why should he not?"

Lady Laura paused before she answered; and then she told the whole story. "He is violently in love, and the girl he loves has refused him twice."

"Is it with Miss Effingham?" asked Phineas, guessing the truth at once, and remembering what Miss Effingham had said to him when riding in the wood.

"Yes;—with Violet Effingham; my father's pet, his favourite, whom he loves next to myself,—almost as well as myself; whom he would really welcome as a daughter. He would gladly make her mistress of his house, and of Saulsby. Everything would then go smoothly."

"But she does not like Lord Chiltern?"

"I believe she loves him in her heart; but she is afraid of him. As she says herself, a girl is bound to be so careful of herself. With all her seeming frolic, Violet Effingham is very wise."

Phineas, though not conscious of anything akin to jealousy, was annoyed at the revelation made to him. Since he had heard that Lord Chiltern was in love with Miss Effingham, he did not like Lord Chiltern quite as well as he had done before. He himself had simply admired Miss Effingham, and had taken pleasure in her society; but, though this had been all, he did not like to hear of another man wanting to marry her, and he was almost angry with Lady Laura for saying that she believed Miss Effingham loved her brother. If Miss Effingham had twice refused Lord Chiltern, that ought to have been sufficient. It was not that Phineas was in love with Miss Effingham himself. As he was still violently in love with Lady Laura, any other love was of course impossible; but, nevertheless, there was something offensive to him in the story as it had been told. "If it be wisdom on her part," said he, answering Lady Laura's last words, "you cannot find fault with her for her decision."

"I find no fault;—but I think my brother would make her happy."

Lady Laura, when she was left alone, at once reverted to the tone in which Phineas Finn had answered her remarks about Miss Effingham. Phineas was very ill able to conceal his thoughts, and wore his heart almost upon his sleeve. "Can it be possible that he cares for her himself?" That was the nature of Lady Laura's first question to herself upon the matter. And in asking herself that question, she thought nothing of the disparity in rank or fortune between Phineas Finn and Violet Effingham. Nor did it occur to her as at all improbable that Violet might accept the love of him who had so lately been her own lover. But the idea grated against her wishes on two sides. She was most anxious that Violet should ultimately become her brother's wife,—and she could not be pleased that Phineas should be able to love any woman.

I must beg my readers not to be carried away by those last words into any erroneous conclusion. They must not suppose that Lady Laura Kennedy, the lately married bride, indulged a guilty passion for the young man who had loved her. Though she had probably thought often of Phineas Finn since her marriage, her thoughts had never been of a nature to disturb her rest. It had never occurred to her even to think that she regarded him with any feeling that was an offence to her husband. She would have hated herself had any such idea presented itself to her mind. She prided herself on being a pure high-principled woman, who had kept so strong a guard upon herself as to be nearly free from the dangers of those rocks upon which other women made shipwreck of their happiness. She took pride in this, and would then blame herself for her own pride. But though she so blamed herself, it never occurred to her to think that to her there might be danger of such shipwreck. She had put away from herself the idea of love when she had first perceived that Phineas had regarded her with more than friendship, and had accepted Mr. Kennedy's offer with an assured conviction that by doing so she was acting best for her own happiness and for that of all those concerned. She had felt the romance of the position to be sweet when Phineas had stood with her at the top of the falls of the Linter, and had told her of the hopes which he had dared to indulge. And when at the bottom of the falls he had presumed to take her in his arms, she had forgiven him without difficulty to herself, telling herself that that would be the alpha and the omega of the romance of her life. She had not felt herself bound to tell Mr. Kennedy of what had occurred,—but she had felt that he could hardly have been angry even had he been told. And she had often thought of her lover since, and of his love,—telling herself that she too had once had a lover, never regarding her husband in that light; but her thoughts had not frightened her as guilty thoughts will do. There had come a romance which had been pleasant, and it was gone. It had been soon banished,—but it had left to her a sweet flavour, of which she loved to taste the sweetness though she knew that it was gone. And the man should be her friend, but especially her husband's friend. It should be her care to see that his life was successful,—and especially her husband's care. It was a great delight to her to know that her husband liked the man. And the man would marry, and the man's wife should be her friend. All this had been very pure and very pleasant. Now an idea had flitted across her brain that the man was in love with some one else,—and she did not like it!

But she did not therefore become afraid of herself, or in the least realise at once the danger of her own position. Her immediate glance at the matter did not go beyond the falseness of men. If it were so, as she suspected,—if Phineas had in truth transferred his affections to Violet Effingham, of how little value was the love of such a man! It did not occur to her at this moment that she also had transferred hers to Robert Kennedy, or that, if not, she had done worse. But she did remember that in the autumn this young Phœbus among men had turned his back upon her out upon the mountain that he might hide from her the agony of his heart when he learned that she was to be the wife of another man; and that now, before the winter was over, he could not hide from her the fact that his heart was elsewhere! And then she speculated, and counted up facts, and satisfied herself that Phineas could not even have seen Violet Effingham since they two had stood together upon the mountain. How false are men!—how false and how weak of heart!

"Chiltern and Violet Effingham!" said Phineas to himself, as he walked away from Grosvenor Place. "Is it fair that she should be sacrificed because she is rich, and because she is so winning and so fascinating that Lord Brentford would receive even his son for the sake of receiving also such a daughter-in-law?" Phineas also liked Lord Chiltern; had seen or fancied that he had seen fine things in him; had looked forward to his regeneration, hoping, perhaps, that he might have some hand in the good work. But he did not recognise the propriety of sacrificing Violet Effingham even for work so good as this. If Miss Effingham had refused Lord Chiltern twice, surely that ought to be sufficient. It did not occur to him that the love of such a girl as Violet would be a great treasure—to himself. As regarded himself, he was still in love,—hopelessly in love, with Lady Laura Kennedy!

CHAPTER XVIII
Mr. Turnbull

It was a Wednesday evening and there was no House;—and at seven o'clock Phineas was at Mr. Monk's hall door. He was the first of the guests, and he found Mr. Monk alone in the dining-room. "I am doing butler," said Mr. Monk, who had a brace of decanters in his hands, which he proceeded to put down in the neighbourhood of the fire. "But I have finished, and now we will go up-stairs to receive the two great men properly."

"I beg your pardon for coming too early," said Finn.

"Not a minute too early. Seven is seven, and it is I who am too late. But, Lord bless you, you don't think I'm ashamed of being found in the act of decanting my own wine! I remember Lord Palmerston saying before some committee about salaries, five or six years ago now, I daresay, that it wouldn't do for an English Minister to have his hall door opened by a maid-servant. Now, I'm an English Minister, and I've got nobody but a maid-servant to open my hall door, and I'm obliged to look after my own wine. I wonder whether it's improper? I shouldn't like to be the means of injuring the British Constitution."

"Perhaps if you resign soon, and if nobody follows your example, grave evil results may be avoided."

"I sincerely hope so, for I do love the British Constitution; and I love also the respect in which members of the English Cabinet are held. Now Turnbull, who will be here in a moment, hates it all; but he is a rich man, and has more powdered footmen hanging about his house than ever Lord Palmerston had himself."

"He is still in business."

"Oh yes;—and makes his thirty thousand a year. Here he is. How are you, Turnbull? We were talking about my maid-servant. I hope she opened the door for you properly."

"Certainly,—as far as I perceived," said Mr. Turnbull, who was better at a speech than a joke. "A very respectable young woman I should say."

"There is not one more so in all London," said Mr. Monk; "but Finn seems to think that I ought to have a man in livery."

"It is a matter of perfect indifference to me," said Mr. Turnbull. "I am one of those who never think of such things."

"Nor I either," said Mr. Monk. Then the laird of Loughlinter was announced, and they all went down to dinner.

Mr. Turnbull was a good-looking robust man about sixty, with long grey hair and a red complexion, with hard eyes, a well-cut nose, and full lips. He was nearly six feet high, stood quite upright, and always wore a black swallow-tail coat, black trousers, and a black silk waistcoat. In the House, at least, he was always so dressed, and at dinner tables. What difference there might be in his costume when at home at Staleybridge few of those who saw him in London had the means of knowing. There was nothing in his face to indicate special talent. No one looking at him would take him to be a fool; but there was none of the fire of genius in his eye, nor was there in the lines of his mouth any of that play of thought or fancy which is generally to be found in the faces of men and women who have made themselves great. Mr. Turnbull had certainly made himself great, and could hardly have done so without force of intellect. He was one of the most popular, if not the most popular politician in the country. Poor men believed in him, thinking that he was their most honest public friend; and men who were not poor believed in his power, thinking that his counsels must surely prevail. He had obtained the ear of the House and the favour of the reporters, and opened his voice at no public dinner, on no public platform, without a conviction that the words spoken by him would be read by thousands.

The first necessity for good speaking is a large audience; and of this advantage Mr. Turnbull had made himself sure. And yet it could hardly be said that he was a great orator. He was gifted with a powerful voice, with strong, and I may, perhaps, call them broad convictions, with perfect self-reliance, with almost unlimited powers of endurance, with hot ambition, with no keen scruples, and with a moral skin of great thickness. Nothing said against him pained him, no attacks wounded him, no raillery touched him in the least. There was not a sore spot about him, and probably his first thoughts on waking every morning told him that he, at least, was totus teres atque rotundus. He was, of course, a thorough Radical,—and so was Mr. Monk. But Mr. Monk's first waking thoughts were probably exactly the reverse of those of his friend. Mr. Monk was a much hotter man in debate than Mr. Turnbull;—but Mr. Monk was ever doubting of himself, and never doubted of himself so much as when he had been most violent, and also most effective, in debate. When Mr. Monk jeered at himself for being a Cabinet Minister and keeping no attendant grander than a parlour-maid, there was a substratum of self-doubt under the joke.

Mr. Turnbull was certainly a great Radical, and as such enjoyed a great reputation. I do not think that high office in the State had ever been offered to him; but things had been said which justified him, or seemed to himself to justify him, in declaring that in no possible circumstances would he serve the Crown. "I serve the people," he had said, "and much as I respect the servants of the Crown, I think that my own office is the higher." He had been greatly called to task for this speech; and Mr. Mildmay, the present Premier, had asked him whether he did not recognise the so-called servants of the Crown as the most hard-worked and truest servants of the people. The House and the press had supported Mr. Mildmay, but to all that Mr. Turnbull was quite indifferent; and when an assertion made by him before three or four thousand persons at Manchester, to the effect that he,—he specially,—was the friend and servant of the people, was received with acclamation, he felt quite satisfied that he had gained his point. Progressive reform in the franchise, of which manhood suffrage should be the acknowledged and not far distant end, equal electoral districts, ballot, tenant right for England as well as Ireland, reduction of the standing army till there should be no standing army to reduce, utter disregard of all political movements in Europe, an almost idolatrous admiration for all political movements in America, free trade in everything except malt, and an absolute extinction of a State Church,—these were among the principal articles in Mr. Turnbull's political catalogue. And I think that when once he had learned the art of arranging his words as he stood upon his legs, and had so mastered his voice as to have obtained the ear of the House, the work of his life was not difficult. Having nothing to construct, he could always deal with generalities. Being free from responsibility, he was not called upon either to study details or to master even great facts. It was his business to inveigh against existing evils, and perhaps there is no easier business when once the privilege of an audience has been attained. It was his work to cut down forest-trees, and he had nothing to do with the subsequent cultivation of the land. Mr. Monk had once told Phineas Finn how great were the charms of that inaccuracy which was permitted to the Opposition. Mr. Turnbull no doubt enjoyed these charms to the full, though he would sooner have put a padlock on his mouth for a month than have owned as much. Upon the whole, Mr. Turnbull was no doubt right in resolving that he would not take office, though some reticence on that subject might have been more becoming to him.

The conversation at dinner, though it was altogether on political subjects, had in it nothing of special interest as long as the girl was there to change the plates; but when she was gone, and the door was closed, it gradually opened out, and there came on to be a pleasant sparring match between the two great Radicals,—the Radical who had joined himself to the governing powers, and the Radical who stood aloof. Mr. Kennedy barely said a word now and then, and Phineas was almost as silent as Mr. Kennedy. He had come there to hear some such discussion, and was quite willing to listen while guns of such great calibre were being fired off for his amusement.

"I think Mr. Mildmay is making a great step forward," said Mr. Turnbull.

"I think he is," said Mr. Monk.

"I did not believe that he would ever live to go so far. It will hardly suffice even for this year; but still coming from him, it is a great deal. It only shows how far a man may be made to go, if only the proper force be applied. After all, it matters very little who are the Ministers."

"That is what I have always declared," said Mr. Monk.

"Very little indeed. We don't mind whether it be Lord de Terrier, or Mr. Mildmay, or Mr. Gresham, or you yourself, if you choose to get yourself made First Lord of the Treasury."

"I have no such ambition, Turnbull."

"I should have thought you had. If I went in for that kind of thing myself, I should like to go to the top of the ladder. I should feel that if I could do any good at all by becoming a Minister, I could only do it by becoming first Minister."

"You wouldn't doubt your own fitness for such a position?"

"I doubt my fitness for the position of any Minister," said Mr. Turnbull.

"You mean that on other grounds," said Mr. Kennedy.

"I mean it on every ground," said Mr. Turnbull, rising on his legs and standing with his back to the fire. "Of course I am not fit to have diplomatic intercourse with men who would come to me simply with the desire of deceiving me. Of course I am unfit to deal with members of Parliament who would flock around me because they wanted places. Of course I am unfit to answer every man's question so as to give no information to any one."

"Could you not answer them so as to give information?" said Mr. Kennedy.

But Mr. Turnbull was so intent on his speech that it may be doubted whether he heard this interruption. He took no notice of it as he went on. "Of course I am unfit to maintain the proprieties of a seeming confidence between a Crown all-powerless and a people all-powerful. No man recognises his own unfitness for such work more clearly than I do, Mr. Monk. But if I took in hand such work at all, I should like to be the leader, and not the led. Tell us fairly, now, what are your convictions worth in Mr. Mildmay's Cabinet?"

"That is a question which a man may hardly answer himself," said Mr. Monk.

"It is a question which a man should at least answer for himself before he consents to sit there," said Mr. Turnbull, in a tone of voice which was almost angry.

"And what reason have you for supposing that I have omitted that duty?" said Mr. Monk.

"Simply this,—that I cannot reconcile your known opinions with the practices of your colleagues."

"I will not tell you what my convictions may be worth in Mr. Mildmay's Cabinet. I will not take upon myself to say that they are worth the chair on which I sit when I am there. But I will tell you what my aspirations were when I consented to fill that chair, and you shall judge of their worth. I thought that they might possibly leaven the batch of bread which we have to bake,—giving to the whole batch more of the flavour of reform than it would have possessed had I absented myself. I thought that when I was asked to join Mr. Mildmay and Mr. Gresham, the very fact of that request indicated liberal progress, and that if I refused the request I should be declining to assist in good work."

"You could have supported them, if anything were proposed worthy of support," said Mr. Turnbull.

"Yes; but I could not have been so effective in taking care that some measure be proposed worthy of support as I may possibly be now. I thought a good deal about it, and I believe that my decision was right."

"I am sure you were right," said Mr. Kennedy.

"There can be no juster object of ambition than a seat in the Cabinet," said Phineas.

"Sir, I must dispute that," said Mr. Turnbull, turning round upon our hero. "I regard the position of our high Ministers as most respectable."

"Thank you for so much," said Mr. Monk. But the orator went on again, regardless of the interruption:—

"The position of gentlemen in inferior offices,—of gentlemen who attend rather to the nods and winks of their superiors in Downing Street than to the interest of their constituents,—I do not regard as being highly respectable."

"A man cannot begin at the top," said Phineas.

"Our friend Mr. Monk has begun at what you are pleased to call the top," said Mr. Turnbull. "But I will not profess to think that even he has raised himself by going into office. To be an independent representative of a really popular commercial constituency is, in my estimation, the highest object of an Englishman's ambition."

"But why commercial, Mr. Turnbull?" said Mr. Kennedy.

"Because the commercial constituencies really do elect their own members in accordance with their own judgments, whereas the counties and the small towns are coerced either by individuals or by a combination of aristocratic influences."

"And yet," said Mr. Kennedy, "there are not half a dozen Conservatives returned by all the counties in Scotland."

"Scotland is very much to be honoured," said Mr. Turnbull.

Mr. Kennedy was the first to take his departure, and Mr. Turnbull followed him very quickly. Phineas got up to go at the same time, but stayed at his host's request, and sat for awhile smoking a cigar.

"Turnbull is a wonderful man," said Mr. Monk.

"Does he not domineer too much?"

"His fault is not arrogance, so much as ignorance that there is, or should be, a difference between public and private life. In the House of Commons a man in Mr. Turnbull's position must speak with dictatorial assurance. He is always addressing, not the House only, but the country at large, and the country will not believe in him unless he believe in himself. But he forgets that he is not always addressing the country at large. I wonder what sort of a time Mrs. Turnbull and the little Turnbulls have of it?"

Phineas, as he went home, made up his mind that Mrs. Turnbull and the little Turnbulls must probably have a bad time of it.

CHAPTER XIX
Lord Chiltern Rides His Horse Bonebreaker

It was known that whatever might be the details of Mr. Mildmay's bill, the ballot would not form a part of it; and as there was a strong party in the House of Commons, and a very numerous party out of it, who were desirous that voting by ballot should be made a part of the electoral law, it was decided that an independent motion should be brought on in anticipation of Mr. Mildmay's bill. The arrangement was probably one of Mr. Mildmay's own making; so that he might be hampered by no opposition on that subject by his own followers if,—as he did not doubt,—the motion should be lost. It was expected that the debate would not last over one night, and Phineas resolved that he would make his maiden speech on this occasion. He had very strong opinions as to the inefficacy of the ballot for any good purposes, and thought that he might be able to strike out from his convictions some sparks of that fire which used to be so plentiful with him at the old debating clubs. But even at breakfast that morning his heart began to beat quickly at the idea of having to stand on his legs before so critical an audience.

He knew that it would be well that he should if possible get the subject off his mind during the day, and therefore went out among the people who certainly would not talk to him about the ballot. He sat for nearly an hour in the morning with Mr. Low, and did not even tell Mr. Low that it was his intention to speak on that day. Then he made one or two other calls, and at about three went up to Portman Square to look for Lord Chiltern. It was now nearly the end of February, and Phineas had often seen Lady Laura. He had not seen her brother, but had learned from his sister that he had been driven up to London by the frost, He was told by the porter at Lord Brentford's that Lord Chiltern was in the house, and as he was passing through the hall he met Lord Brentford himself. He was thus driven to speak, and felt himself called upon to explain why he was there. "I am come to see Lord Chiltern," he said.

"Is Lord Chiltern in the house?" said the Earl, turning to the servant.

"Yes, my lord; his lordship arrived last night."

"You will find him upstairs, I suppose," said the Earl. "For myself I know nothing of him." He spoke in an angry tone, as though he resented the fact that any one should come to his house to call upon his son; and turned his back quickly upon Phineas. But he thought better of it before he reached the front door, and turned again. "By-the-bye," said he, "what majority shall we have to-night, Finn?"

"Pretty nearly as many as you please to name, my lord," said Phineas.

"Well;—yes; I suppose we are tolerably safe. You ought to speak upon it."

"Perhaps I may," said Phineas, feeling that he blushed as he spoke.

"Do," said the Earl. "Do. If you see Lord Chiltern will you tell him from me that I should be glad to see him before he leaves London. I shall be at home till noon to-morrow." Phineas, much astonished at the commission given to him, of course said that he would do as he was desired, and then passed on to Lord Chiltern's apartments.

He found his friend standing in the middle of the room, without coat and waistcoat, with a pair of dumb-bells in his hands. "When there's no hunting I'm driven to this kind of thing," said Lord Chiltern.

"I suppose it's good exercise," said Phineas.

"And it gives me something to do. When I'm in London I feel like a gipsy in church, till the time comes for prowling out at night. I've no occupation for my days whatever, and no place to which I can take myself. I can't stand in a club window as some men do, and I should disgrace any decent club if I did stand there. I belong to the Travellers, but I doubt whether the porter would let me go in."

"I think you pique yourself on being more of an outer Bohemian than you are," said Phineas.

"I pique myself on this, that whether Bohemian or not, I will go nowhere that I am not wanted. Though,—for the matter of that, I suppose I'm not wanted here." Then Phineas gave him the message from his father. "He wishes to see me to-morrow morning?" continued Lord Chiltern. "Let him send me word what it is he has to say to me. I do not choose to be insulted by him, though he is my father."

"I would certainly go, if I were you."

"I doubt it very much, if all the circumstances were the same. Let him tell me what he wants."

"Of course I cannot ask him, Chiltern."

"I know what he wants very well. Laura has been interfering and doing no good. You know Violet Effingham?"

"Yes; I know her," said Phineas, much surprised.

"They want her to marry me."

"And you do not wish to marry her?"

"I did not say that. But do you think that such a girl as Miss Effingham would marry such a man as I am? She would be much more likely to take you. By George, she would! Do you know that she has three thousand a year of her own?"

"I know that she has money."

"That's about the tune of it. I would take her without a shilling to-morrow, if she would have me,—because I like her. She is the only girl I ever did like. But what is the use of my liking her? They have painted me so black among them, especially my father, that no decent girl would think of marrying me."

"Your father can't be angry with you if you do your best to comply with his wishes."

"I don't care a straw whether he be angry or not. He allows me eight hundred a year, and he knows that if he stopped it I should go to the Jews the next day. I could not help myself. He can't leave an acre away from me, and yet he won't join me in raising money for the sake of paying Laura her fortune."

"Lady Laura can hardly want money now."

"That detestable prig whom she has chosen to marry, and whom I hate with all my heart, is richer than ever Crœsus was; but nevertheless Laura ought to have her own money. She shall have it some day."

"I would see Lord Brentford, if I were you."

"I will think about it. Now tell me about coming down to Willingford. Laura says you will come some day in March. I can mount you for a couple of days and should be delighted to have you. My horses all pull like the mischief, and rush like devils, and want a deal of riding; but an Irishman likes that."

"I do not dislike it particularly."

"I like it. I prefer to have something to do on horseback. When a man tells me that a horse is an armchair, I always tell him to put the brute into his bedroom. Mind you come. The house I stay at is called the Willingford Bull, and it's just four miles from Peterborough." Phineas swore that he would go down and ride the pulling horses, and then took his leave, earnestly advising Lord Chiltern, as he went, to keep the appointment proposed by his father.

When the morning came, at half-past eleven, the son, who had been standing for half an hour with his back to the fire in the large gloomy dining-room, suddenly rang the bell. "Tell the Earl," he said to the servant, "that I am here and will go to him if he wishes it." The servant came back, and said that the Earl was waiting. Then Lord Chiltern strode after the man into his father's room.

"Oswald," said the father, "I have sent for you because I think it may be as well to speak to you on some business. Will you sit down?" Lord Chiltern sat down, but did not answer a word. "I feel very unhappy about your sister's fortune," said the Earl.

"So do I,—very unhappy. We can raise the money between us, and pay her to-morrow, if you please it."

"It was in opposition to my advice that she paid your debts."

"And in opposition to mine too."

"I told her that I would not pay them, and were I to give her back to-morrow, as you say, the money that she has so used, I should be stultifying myself. But I will do so on one condition. I will join with you in raising the money for your sister, on one condition."

"What is that?"

"Laura tells me,—indeed she has told me often,—that you are attached to Violet Effingham."

"But Violet Effingham, my lord, is unhappily not attached to me."

"I do not know how that may be. Of course I cannot say. I have never taken the liberty of interrogating her upon the subject."

"Even you, my lord, could hardly have done that."

"What do you mean by that? I say that I never have," said the Earl, angrily.

"I simply mean that even you could hardly have asked Miss Effingham such a question. I have asked her, and she has refused me."

"But girls often do that, and yet accept afterwards the men whom they have refused. Laura tells me that she believes that Violet would consent if you pressed your suit."

"Laura knows nothing about it, my lord."

"There you are probably wrong. Laura and Violet are very close friends, and have no doubt discussed this matter between them. At any rate, it may be as well that you should hear what I have to say. Of course I shall not interfere myself. There is no ground on which I can do so with propriety."

"None whatever," said Lord Chiltern.

The Earl became very angry, and nearly broke down in his anger. He paused for a moment, feeling disposed to tell his son to go and never to see him again. But he gulped down his wrath, and went on with his speech. "My meaning, sir, is this;—that I have so great faith in Violet Effingham, that I would receive her acceptance of your hand as the only proof which would be convincing to me of amendment in your mode of life. If she were to do so, I would join with you in raising money to pay your sister, would make some further sacrifice with reference to an income for you and your wife, and—would make you both welcome to Saulsby,—if you chose to come." The Earl's voice hesitated much and became almost tremulous as he made the last proposition. And his eyes had fallen away from his son's gaze, and he had bent a little over the table, and was moved. But he recovered himself at once, and added, with all proper dignity, "If you have anything to say I shall be glad to hear it."

"All your offers would be nothing, my lord, if I did not like the girl."

"I should not ask you to marry a girl if you did not like her, as you call it."

"But as to Miss Effingham, it happens that our wishes jump together. I have asked her, and she has refused me. I don't even know where to find her to ask her again. If I went to Lady Baldock's house the servants would not let me in."

"And whose fault is that?"

"Yours partly, my lord. You have told everybody that I am the devil, and now all the old women believe it."

"I never told anybody so."

"I'll tell you what I'll do. I will go down to Lady Baldock's to-day. I suppose she is at Baddingham. And if I can get speech of Miss Effingham—"

"Miss Effingham is not at Baddingham. Miss Effingham is staying with your sister in Grosvenor Place. I saw her yesterday."

"She is in London?"

"I tell you that I saw her yesterday."

"Very well, my lord. Then I will do the best I can. Laura will tell you of the result."

The father would have given the son some advice as to the mode in which he should put forward his claim upon Violet's hand, but the son would not wait to hear it. Choosing to presume that the conference was over, he went back to the room in which he had kept his dumb-bells, and for a minute or two went to work at his favourite exercise. But he soon put the dumb-bells down, and began to prepare himself for his work. If this thing was to be done, it might as well be done at once. He looked out of his window, and saw that the streets were in a mess of slush. White snow was becoming black mud, as it will do in London; and the violence of frost was giving way to the horrors of thaw. All would be soft and comparatively pleasant in Northamptonshire on the following morning, and if everything went right he would breakfast at the Willingford Bull. He would go down by the hunting train, and be at the inn by ten. The meet was only six miles distant, and all would be pleasant. He would do this whatever might be the result of his work to-day;—but in the meantime he would go and do his work. He had a cab called, and within half an hour of the time at which he had left his father, he was at the door of his sister's house in Grosvenor Place. The servants told him that the ladies were at lunch. "I can't eat lunch," he said. "Tell them that I am in the drawing-room."

"He has come to see you," said Lady Laura, as soon as the servant had left the room.

"I hope not," said Violet.

"Do not say that."

"But I do say it. I hope he has not come to see me;—that is, not to see me specially. Of course I cannot pretend not to know what you mean."

"He may think it civil to call if he has heard that you are in town," said Lady Laura, after a pause.

"If it be only that, I will be civil in return;—as sweet as May to him. If it be really only that, and if I were sure of it, I should be really glad to see him." Then they finished their lunch, and Lady Laura got up and led the way to the drawing-room.

"I hope you remember," said she, gravely, "that you might be a saviour to him."

"I do not believe in girls being saviours to men. It is the man who should be the saviour to the girl. If I marry at all, I have the right to expect that protection shall be given to me,—not that I shall have to give it."

"Violet, you are determined to misrepresent what I mean."

Lord Chiltern was walking about the room, and did not sit down when they entered. The ordinary greetings took place, and Miss Effingham made some remark about the frost. "But it seems to be going," she said, "and I suppose that you will soon be at work again?"

"Yes;—I shall hunt to-morrow," said Lord Chiltern.

"And the next day, and the next, and the next," said Violet, "till about the middle of April;—and then your period of misery will begin!"

"Exactly," said Lord Chiltern. "I have nothing but hunting that I can call an occupation."

"Why don't you make one?" said his sister.

"I mean to do so, if it be possible. Laura, would you mind leaving me and Miss Effingham alone for a few minutes?"

Lady Laura got up, and so also did Miss Effingham. "For what purpose?" said the latter. "It cannot be for any good purpose."

"At any rate I wish it, and I will not harm you." Lady Laura was now going, but paused before she reached the door. "Laura, will you do as I ask you?" said the brother. Then Lady Laura went.

"It was not that I feared you would harm me, Lord Chiltern," said Violet.

"No;—I know it was not. But what I say is always said awkwardly. An hour ago I did not know that you were in town, but when I was told the news I came at once. My father told me."

"I am so glad that you see your father."

"I have not spoken to him for months before, and probably may not speak to him for months again. But there is one point, Violet, on which he and I agree."

"I hope there will soon be many."

"It is possible,—but I fear not probable. Look here, Violet,"—and he looked at her with all his eyes, till it seemed to her that he was all eyes, so great was the intensity of his gaze;—"I should scorn myself were I to permit myself to come before you with a plea for your favour founded on my father's whims. My father is unreasonable, and has been very unjust to me. He has ever believed evil of me, and has believed it often when all the world knew that he was wrong. I care little for being reconciled to a father who has been so cruel to me."

"He loves me dearly, and is my friend. I would rather that you should not speak against him to me."

"You will understand, at least, that I am asking nothing from you because he wishes it. Laura probably has told you that you may make things straight by becoming my wife."

"She has,—certainly, Lord Chiltern."

"It is an argument that she should never have used. It is an argument to which you should not listen for a moment. Make things straight indeed! Who can tell? There would be very little made straight by such a marriage, if it were not that I loved you. Violet, that is my plea, and my only one. I love you so well that I do believe that if you took me I should return to the old ways, and become as other men are, and be in time as respectable, as stupid,—and perhaps as ill-natured as old Lady Baldock herself."

"My poor aunt!"

"You know she says worse things of me than that. Now, dearest, you have heard all that I have to say to you." As he spoke he came close to her, and put out his hand,—but she did not touch it. "I have no other argument to use,—not a word more to say. As I came here in the cab I was turning it over in my mind that I might find what best I should say. But, after all, there is nothing more to be said than that."

"The words make no difference," she replied.

"Not unless they be so uttered as to force a belief. I do love you. I know no other reason but that why you should be my wife. I have no other excuse to offer for coming to you again. You are the one thing in the world that to me has any charm. Can you be surprised that I should be persistent in asking for it?" He was looking at her still with the same gaze, and there seemed to be a power in his eye from which she could not escape. He was still standing with his right hand out, as though expecting, or at least hoping, that her hand might be put into his.

"How am I to answer you?" she said.

"With your love, if you can give it to me. Do you remember how you swore once that you would love me for ever and always?"

"You should not remind me of that. I was a child then,—a naughty child," she added, smiling; "and was put to bed for what I did on that day."

"Be a child still."

"Ah, if we but could!"

"And have you no other answer to make me?"

"Of course I must answer you. You are entitled to an answer. Lord Chiltern, I am sorry that I cannot give you the love for which you ask."

"Never?"

"Never."

"Is it myself personally, or what you have heard of me, that is so hateful to you?"

"Nothing is hateful to me. I have never spoken of hate. I shall always feel the strongest regard for my old friend and playfellow. But there are many things which a woman is bound to consider before she allows herself so to love a man that she can consent to become his wife."

"Allow herself! Then it is a matter entirely of calculation."

"I suppose there should be some thought in it, Lord Chiltern."

There was now a pause, and the man's hand was at last allowed to drop, as there came no response to the proffered grasp. He walked once or twice across the room before he spoke again, and then he stopped himself closely opposite to her.

"I shall never try again," he said.

"It will be better so," she replied.

"There is something to me unmanly in a man's persecuting a girl. Just tell Laura, will you, that it is all over; and she may as well tell my father. Good-bye."

She then tendered her hand to him, but he did not take it,—probably did not see it, and at once left the room and the house.

"And yet I believe you love him," Lady Laura said to her friend in her anger, when they discussed the matter immediately on Lord Chiltern's departure.

"You have no right to say that, Laura."

"I have a right to my belief, and I do believe it. I think you love him, and that you lack the courage to risk yourself in trying to save him."

"Is a woman bound to marry a man if she love him?"

"Yes, she is," replied Lady Laura impetuously, without thinking of what she was saying; "that is, if she be convinced that she also is loved."

"Whatever be the man's character;—whatever be the circumstances? Must she do so, whatever friends may say to the contrary? Is there to be no prudence in marriage?"

"There may be a great deal too much prudence," said Lady Laura.

"That is true. There is certainly too much prudence if a woman marries prudently, but without love." Violet intended by this no attack upon her friend,—had not had present in her mind at the moment any idea of Lady Laura's special prudence in marrying Mr. Kennedy; but Lady Laura felt it keenly, and knew at once that an arrow had been shot which had wounded her.

"We shall get nothing," she said, "by descending to personalities with each other."

"I meant none, Laura."

"I suppose it is always hard," said Lady Laura, "for any one person to judge altogether of the mind of another. If I have said anything severe of your refusal of my brother, I retract it. I only wish that it could have been otherwise."

Lord Chiltern, when he left his sister's house, walked through the slush and dirt to a haunt of his in the neighbourhood of Covent Garden, and there he remained through the whole afternoon and evening. A certain Captain Clutterbuck joined him, and dined with him. He told nothing to Captain Clutterbuck of his sorrow, but Captain Clutterbuck could see that he was unhappy.

"Let's have another bottle of 'cham,'" said Captain Clutterbuck, when their dinner was nearly over. "'Cham' is the only thing to screw one up when one is down a peg."

"You can have what you like," said Lord Chiltern; "but I shall have some brandy-and-water."

"The worst of brandy-and-water is, that one gets tired of it before the night is over," said Captain Clutterbuck.

Nevertheless, Lord Chiltern did go down to Peterborough the next day by the hunting train, and rode his horse Bonebreaker so well in that famous run from Sutton springs to Gidding that after the run young Piles,—of the house of Piles, Sarsnet, and Gingham,—offered him three hundred pounds for the animal.

"He isn't worth above fifty," said Lord Chiltern.

"But I'll give you the three hundred," said Piles.

"You couldn't ride him if you'd got him," said Lord Chiltern.

"Oh, couldn't I!" said Piles. But Mr. Piles did not continue the conversation, contenting himself with telling his friend Grogram that that red devil Chiltern was as drunk as a lord.

CHAPTER XX
The Debate on the Ballot

Phineas took his seat in the House with a consciousness of much inward trepidation of heart on that night of the ballot debate. After leaving Lord Chiltern he went down to his club and dined alone. Three or four men came and spoke to him; but he could not talk to them at his ease, nor did he quite know what they were saying to him. He was going to do something which he longed to achieve, but the very idea of which, now that it was so near to him, was a terror to him. To be in the House and not to speak would, to his thinking, be a disgraceful failure. Indeed, he could not continue to keep his seat unless he spoke. He had been put there that he might speak. He would speak. Of course he would speak. Had he not already been conspicuous almost as a boy orator? And yet, at this moment he did not know whether he was eating mutton or beef, or who was standing opposite to him and talking to him, so much was he in dread of the ordeal which he had prepared for himself. As he went down to the House after dinner, he almost made up his mind that it would be a good thing to leave London by one of the night mail trains. He felt himself to be stiff and stilted as he walked, and that his clothes were uneasy to him. When he turned into Westminster Hall he regretted more keenly than ever he had done that he had seceded from the keeping of Mr. Low. He could, he thought, have spoken very well in court, and would there have learned that self-confidence which now failed him so terribly. It was, however, too late to think of that. He could only go in and take his seat.

He went in and took his seat, and the chamber seemed to him to be mysteriously large, as though benches were crowded over benches, and galleries over galleries. He had been long enough in the House to have lost the original awe inspired by the Speaker and the clerks of the House, by the row of Ministers, and by the unequalled importance of the place. On ordinary occasions he could saunter in and out, and whisper at his ease to a neighbour. But on this occasion he went direct to the bench on which he ordinarily sat, and began at once to rehearse to himself his speech. He had in truth been doing this all day, in spite of the effort that he had made to rid himself of all memory of the occasion. He had been collecting the heads of his speech while Mr. Low had been talking to him, and refreshing his quotations in the presence of Lord Chiltern and the dumb-bells. He had taxed his memory and his intellect with various tasks, which, as he feared, would not adjust themselves one with another. He had learned the headings of his speech,—so that one heading might follow the other, and nothing be forgotten. And he had learned verbatim the words which he intended to utter under each heading,—with a hope that if any one compact part should be destroyed or injured in its compactness by treachery of memory, or by the course of the debate, each other compact part might be there in its entirety, ready for use;—or at least so many of the compact parts as treachery of memory and the accidents of the debate might leave to him; so that his speech might be like a vessel, watertight in its various compartments, that would float by the buoyancy of its stern and bow, even though the hold should be waterlogged. But this use of his composed words, even though he should be able to carry it through, would not complete his work;—for it would be his duty to answer in some sort those who had gone before him, and in order to do this he must be able to insert, without any prearrangement of words or ideas, little intercalatory parts between those compact masses of argument with which he had been occupying himself for many laborious hours. As he looked round upon the House and perceived that everything was dim before him, that all his original awe of the House had returned, and with it a present quaking fear that made him feel the pulsations of his own heart, he became painfully aware that the task he had prepared for himself was too great. He should, on this the occasion of his rising to his maiden legs, have either prepared for himself a short general speech, which could indeed have done little for his credit in the House, but which might have served to carry off the novelty of the thing, and have introduced him to the sound of his own voice within those walls,—or he should have trusted to what his wit and spirit would produce for him on the spur of the moment, and not have burdened himself with a huge exercise of memory. During the presentation of a few petitions he tried to repeat to himself the first of his compact parts,—a compact part on which, as it might certainly be brought into use let the debate have gone as it might, he had expended great care. He had flattered himself that there was something of real strength in his words as he repeated them to himself in the comfortable seclusion of his own room, and he had made them so ready to his tongue that he thought it to be impossible that he should forget even an intonation. Now he found that he could not remember the first phrases without unloosing and looking at a small roll of paper which he held furtively in his hand. What was the good of looking at it? He would forget it again in the next moment. He had intended to satisfy the most eager of his friends, and to astound his opponents. As it was, no one would be satisfied,—and none astounded but they who had trusted in him.

The debate began, and if the leisure afforded by a long and tedious speech could have served him, he might have had leisure enough. He tried at first to follow all that this advocate for the ballot might say, hoping thence to acquire the impetus of strong interest; but he soon wearied of the work, and began to long that the speech might be ended, although the period of his own martyrdom would thereby be brought nearer to him. At half-past seven so many members had deserted their seats, that Phineas began to think that he might be saved all further pains by a "count out." He reckoned the members present and found that they were below the mystic forty,—first by two, then by four, by five, by seven, and at one time by eleven. It was not for him to ask the Speaker to count the House, but he wondered that no one else should do so. And yet, as the idea of this termination to the night's work came upon him, and as he thought of his lost labour, he almost took courage again,—almost dreaded rather than wished for the interference of some malicious member. But there was no malicious member then present, or else it was known that Lords of the Treasury and Lords of the Admiralty would flock in during the Speaker's ponderous counting,—and thus the slow length of the ballot-lover's verbosity was permitted to evolve itself without interruption. At eight o'clock he had completed his catalogue of illustrations, and immediately Mr. Monk rose from the Treasury bench to explain the grounds on which the Government must decline to support the motion before the House.

Phineas was aware that Mr. Monk intended to speak, and was aware also that his speech would be very short. "My idea is," he had said to Phineas, "that every man possessed of the franchise should dare to have and to express a political opinion of his own; that otherwise the franchise is not worth having; and that men will learn that when all so dare, no evil can come from such daring. As the ballot would make any courage of that kind unnecessary, I dislike the ballot. I shall confine myself to that, and leave the illustration to younger debaters." Phineas also had been informed that Mr. Turnbull would reply to Mr. Monk, with the purpose of crushing Mr. Monk into dust, and Phineas had prepared his speech with something of an intention of subsequently crushing Mr. Turnbull. He knew, however, that he could not command his opportunity. There was the chapter of accidents to which he must accommodate himself; but such had been his programme for the evening.

Mr. Monk made his speech,—and though he was short, he was very fiery and energetic. Quick as lightning words of wrath and scorn flew from him, in which he painted the cowardice, the meanness, the falsehood of the ballot. "The ballot-box," he said, "was the grave of all true political opinion." Though he spoke hardly for ten minutes, he seemed to say more than enough, ten times enough, to slaughter the argument of the former speaker. At every hot word as it fell Phineas was driven to regret that a paragraph of his own was taken away from him, and that his choicest morsels of standing ground were being cut from under his feet. When Mr. Monk sat down, Phineas felt that Mr. Monk had said all that he, Phineas Finn, had intended to say.

Then Mr. Turnbull rose slowly from the bench below the gangway. With a speaker so frequent and so famous as Mr. Turnbull no hurry is necessary. He is sure to have his opportunity. The Speaker's eye is ever travelling to the accustomed spots. Mr. Turnbull rose slowly and began his oration very mildly. "There was nothing," he said, "that he admired so much as the poetic imagery and the high-flown sentiment of his right honourable friend the member for West Bromwich,"—Mr. Monk sat for West Bromwich,—"unless it were the stubborn facts and unanswered arguments of his honourable friend who had brought forward this motion." Then Mr. Turnbull proceeded after his fashion to crush Mr. Monk. He was very prosaic, very clear both in voice and language, very harsh, and very unscrupulous. He and Mr. Monk had been joined together in politics for over twenty years;—but one would have thought, from Mr. Turnbull's words, that they had been the bitterest of enemies. Mr. Monk was taunted with his office, taunted with his desertion of the liberal party, taunted with his ambition,—and taunted with his lack of ambition. "I once thought," said Mr. Turnbull,—"nay, not long ago I thought, that he and I would have fought this battle for the people, shoulder to shoulder, and knee to knee;—but he has preferred that the knee next to his own shall wear a garter, and that the shoulder which supports him shall be decked with a blue ribbon,—as shoulders, I presume, are decked in those closet conferences which are called Cabinets."

Just after this, while Mr. Turnbull was still going on with a variety of illustrations drawn from the United States, Barrington Erle stepped across the benches up to the place where Phineas was sitting, and whispered a few words into his ear. "Bonteen is prepared to answer Turnbull, and wishes to do it. I told him that I thought you should have the opportunity, if you wish it." Phineas was not ready with a reply to Erle at the spur of the moment. "Somebody told me," continued Erle, "that you had said that you would like to speak to-night."

"So I did," said Phineas.

"Shall I tell Bonteen that you will do it?"

The chamber seemed to swim round before our hero's eyes. Mr. Turnbull was still going on with his clear, loud, unpleasant voice, but there was no knowing how long he might go on. Upon Phineas, if he should now consent, might devolve the duty, within ten minutes, within three minutes, of rising there before a full House to defend his great friend, Mr. Monk, from a gross personal attack. Was it fit that such a novice as he should undertake such a work as that? Were he to do so, all that speech which he had prepared, with its various self-floating parts, must go for nothing. The task was exactly that which, of all tasks, he would best like to have accomplished, and to have accomplished well. But if he should fail! And he felt that he would fail. For such work a man should have all his senses about him,—his full courage, perfect confidence, something almost approaching to contempt for listening opponents, and nothing of fear in regard to listening friends. He should be as a cock in his own farmyard, master of all the circumstances around him. But Phineas Finn had not even as yet heard the sound of his own voice in that room. At this moment, so confused was he, that he did not know where sat Mr. Mildmay, and where Mr. Daubeny. All was confused, and there arose as it were a sound of waters in his ears, and a feeling as of a great hell around him. "I had rather wait," he said at last. "Bonteen had better reply." Barrington Erle looked into his face, and then stepping back across the benches, told Mr. Bonteen that the opportunity was his.

Mr. Turnbull continued speaking quite long enough to give poor Phineas time for repentance; but repentance was of no use. He had decided against himself, and his decision could not be reversed. He would have left the House, only it seemed to him that had he done so every one would look at him. He drew his hat down over his eyes, and remained in his place, hating Mr. Bonteen, hating Barrington Erle, hating Mr. Turnbull,—but hating no one so much as he hated himself. He had disgraced himself for ever and could never recover the occasion which he had lost.

Mr. Bonteen's speech was in no way remarkable. Mr. Monk, he said, had done the State good service by adding his wisdom and patriotism to the Cabinet. The sort of argument which Mr. Bonteen used to prove that a man who has gained credit as a legislator should in process of time become a member of the executive, is trite and common, and was not used by Mr. Bonteen with any special force. Mr. Bonteen was glib of tongue and possessed that familiarity with the place which poor Phineas had lacked so sorely. There was one moment, however, which was terrible to Phineas. As soon as Mr. Bonteen had shown the purpose for which he was on his legs, Mr. Monk looked round at Phineas, as though in reproach. He had expected that this work should fall into the hands of one who would perform it with more warmth of heart than could be expected from Mr. Bonteen. When Mr. Bonteen ceased, two or three other short speeches were made and members fired off their little guns. Phineas having lost so great an opportunity, would not now consent to accept one that should be comparatively valueless. Then there came a division. The motion was lost by a large majority,—by any number you might choose to name, as Phineas had said to Lord Brentford; but in that there was no triumph to the poor wretch who had failed through fear, and who was now a coward in his own esteem.

He left the House alone, carefully avoiding all speech with any one. As he came out he had seen Laurence Fitzgibbon in the lobby, but he had gone on without pausing a moment, so that he might avoid his friend. And when he was out in Palace Yard, where was he to go next? He looked at his watch, and found that it was just ten. He did not dare to go to his club, and it was impossible for him to go home and to bed. He was very miserable, and nothing would comfort him but sympathy. Was there any one who would listen to his abuse of himself, and would then answer him with kindly apologies for his own weakness? Mrs. Bunce would do it if she knew how, but sympathy from Mrs. Bunce would hardly avail. There was but one person in the world to whom he could tell his own humiliation with any hope of comfort, and that person was Lady Laura Kennedy. Sympathy from any man would have been distasteful to him. He had thought for a moment of flinging himself at Mr. Monk's feet and telling all his weakness;—but he could not have endured pity even from Mr. Monk. It was not to be endured from any man.

He thought that Lady Laura Kennedy would be at home, and probably alone. He knew, at any rate, that he might be allowed to knock at her door, even at that hour. He had left Mr. Kennedy in the House, and there he would probably remain for the next hour. There was no man more constant than Mr. Kennedy in seeing the work of the day,—or of the night,—to its end. So Phineas walked up Victoria Street, and from thence into Grosvenor Place, and knocked at Lady Laura's door. "Yes; Lady Laura was at home; and alone." He was shown up into the drawing-room, and there he found Lady Laura waiting for her husband.

"So the great debate is over," she said, with as much of irony as she knew how to throw into the epithet.

"Yes; it is over."

"And what have they done,—those leviathans of the people?"

Then Phineas told her what was the majority.

"Is there anything the matter with you, Mr. Finn?" she said, looking at him suddenly. "Are you not well?"

"Yes; I am very well."

"Will you not sit down? There is something wrong, I know. What is it?"

"I have simply been the greatest idiot, the greatest coward, the most awkward ass that ever lived!"

"What do you mean?"

"I do not know why I should come to tell you of it at this hour at night, but I have come that I might tell you. Probably because there is no one else in the whole world who would not laugh at me."

"At any rate, I shall not laugh at you," said Lady Laura.

"But you will despise me."

"That I am sure I shall not do."

"You cannot help it. I despise myself. For years I have placed before myself the ambition of speaking in the House of Commons;—for years I have been thinking whether there would ever come to me an opportunity of making myself heard in that assembly, which I consider to be the first in the world. To-day the opportunity has been offered to me,—and, though the motion was nothing, the opportunity was great. The subject was one on which I was thoroughly prepared. The manner in which I was summoned was most flattering to me. I was especially called on to perform a task which was most congenial to my feelings;—and I declined because I was afraid."

"You had thought too much about it, my friend," said Lady Laura.

"Too much or too little, what does it matter?" replied Phineas, in despair. "There is the fact. I could not do it. Do you remember the story of Conachar in the 'Fair Maid of Perth;'—how his heart refused to give him blood enough to fight? He had been suckled with the milk of a timid creature, and, though he could die, there was none of the strength of manhood in him. It is about the same thing with me, I take it."

"I do not think you are at all like Conachar," said Lady Laura.

"I am equally disgraced, and I must perish after the same fashion. I shall apply for the Chiltern Hundreds in a day or two."

"You will do nothing of the kind," said Lady Laura, getting up from her chair and coming towards him. "You shall not leave this room till you have promised me that you will do nothing of the kind. I do not know as yet what has occurred to-night; but I do know that that modesty which has kept you silent is more often a grace than a disgrace."

This was the kind of sympathy which he wanted, She drew her chair nearer to him, and then he explained to her as accurately as he could what had taken place in the House on this evening,—how he had prepared his speech, how he had felt that his preparation was vain, how he perceived from the course of the debate that if he spoke at all his speech must be very different from what he had first intended; how he had declined to take upon himself a task which seemed to require so close a knowledge of the ways of the House and of the temper of the men, as the defence of such a man as Mr. Monk. In accusing himself he, unconsciously, excused himself, and his excuse, in Lady Laura's ears, was more valid than his accusation.

"And you would give it all up for that?" she said.

"Yes; I think I ought."

"I have very little doubt but that you were right in allowing Mr. Bonteen to undertake such a task. I should simply explain to Mr. Monk that you felt too keen an interest in his welfare to stand up as an untried member in his defence. It is not, I think, the work for a man who is not at home in the House. I am sure Mr. Monk will feel this, and I am quite certain that Mr. Kennedy will think that you have been right."

"I do not care what Mr. Kennedy may think."

"Why do you say that, Mr. Finn? That is not courteous."

"Simply because I care so much what Mr. Kennedy's wife may think. Your opinion is all in all to me,—only that I know you are too kind to me."

"He would not be too kind to you. He is never too kind to any one. He is justice itself."

Phineas, as he heard the tones of her voice, could not but feel that there was in Lady Laura's words something of an accusation against her husband.

"I hate justice," said Phineas. "I know that justice would condemn me. But love and friendship know nothing of justice. The value of love is that it overlooks faults, and forgives even crimes."

"I, at any rate," said Lady Laura, "will forgive the crime of your silence in the House. My strong belief in your success will not be in the least affected by what you tell me of your failure to-night. You must await another opportunity; and, if possible, you should be less anxious as to your own performance. There is Violet." As Lady Laura spoke the last words, there was a sound of a carriage stopping in the street, and the front door was immediately opened. "She is staying here, but has been dining with her uncle, Admiral Effingham." Then Violet Effingham entered the room, rolled up in pretty white furs, and silk cloaks, and lace shawls. "Here is Mr. Finn, come to tell us of the debate about the ballot."

"I don't care twopence about the ballot," said Violet, as she put out her hand to Phineas. "Are we going to have a new iron fleet built? That's the question."

"Sir Simeon has come out strong to-night," said Lady Laura.

"There is no political question of any importance except the question of the iron fleet," said Violet. "I am quite sure of that, and so, if Mr. Finn can tell me nothing about the iron fleet, I'll go to bed."

"Mr. Kennedy will tell you everything when he comes home," said Phineas.

"Oh, Mr. Kennedy! Mr. Kennedy never tells one anything. I doubt whether Mr. Kennedy thinks that any woman knows the meaning of the British Constitution."

"Do you know what it means, Violet?" asked Lady Laura.

"To be sure I do. It is liberty to growl about the iron fleet, or the ballot, or the taxes, or the peers, or the bishops,—or anything else, except the House of Commons. That's the British Constitution. Good-night, Mr. Finn."

"What a beautiful creature she is!" said Phineas.

"Yes, indeed," said Lady Laura.

"And full of wit and grace and pleasantness. I do not wonder at your brother's choice."

It will be remembered that this was said on the day before Lord Chiltern had made his offer for the third time.

"Poor Oswald! he does not know as yet that she is in town."

After that Phineas went, not wishing to await the return of Mr. Kennedy. He had felt that Violet Effingham had come into the room just in time to remedy a great difficulty. He did not wish to speak of his love to a married woman,—to the wife of the man who called him friend,—to a woman who he felt sure would have rebuked him. But he could hardly have restrained himself had not Miss Effingham been there.

But as he went home he thought more of Miss Effingham than he did of Lady Laura; and I think that the voice of Miss Effingham had done almost as much towards comforting him as had the kindness of the other.

At any rate, he had been comforted.

CHAPTER XXI
"Do be punctual"

On the very morning after his failure in the House of Commons, when Phineas was reading in the *Telegraph*,—he took the *Telegraph* not from choice but for economy,—the words of that debate which he had heard and in which he should have taken a part, a most unwelcome visit was paid to him. It was near eleven, and the breakfast things were still on the table. He was at this time on a Committee of the House with reference to the use of potted peas in the army and navy, at which he had sat once,—at a preliminary meeting,—and in reference to which he had already resolved that as he had failed so frightfully in debate, he would certainly do his duty to the utmost in the more easy but infinitely more tedious work of the Committee Room. The Committee met at twelve, and he intended to walk down to the Reform Club, and then to the House. He had just completed his reading of the debate and of the leaders in the *Telegraph* on the subject. He had told himself how little the writer of the article knew about Mr. Turnbull, how little about Mr. Monk, and how little about the people,—such being his own ideas as to the qualifications of the writer of that leading article,—and was about to start. But Mrs. Bunce arrested him by telling him that there was a man below who wanted to see him.

"What sort of a man, Mrs. Bunce?"

"He ain't a gentleman, sir."

"Did he give his name?"

"He did not, sir; but I know it's about money. I know the ways of them so well. I've seen this one's face before somewhere."

"You had better show him up," said Phineas. He knew well the business on which the man was come. The man wanted money for that bill which Laurence Fitzgibbon had sent afloat, and which Phineas had endorsed. Phineas had never as yet fallen so deeply into troubles of money as to make it necessary that he need refuse himself to any callers on that score, and he did not choose to do so now. Nevertheless he most heartily wished that he had left his lodgings for the club before the man had come. This was not the first he had heard of the bill being overdue and unpaid. The bill had been brought to him noted a month since, and then he had simply told the youth who brought it that he would see Mr. Fitzgibbon and have the matter settled. He had spoken to his friend Laurence, and Laurence had simply assured him that all should be made right in two days,—or, at furthest, by the end of a week. Since that time he had observed that his friend had been somewhat shy of speaking to him when no others were with them. Phineas would not have alluded to the bill had he and Laurence been alone together; but he had been quick enough to guess from his friend's manner that the matter was not settled. Now, no doubt, serious trouble was about to commence.

The visitor was a little man with grey hair and a white cravat, some sixty years of age, dressed in black, with a very decent hat,—which, on entering the room, he at once put down on the nearest chair,—with reference to whom, any judge on the subject would have concurred at first sight in the decision pronounced by Mrs. Bunce, though none but a judge very well used to sift the causes of his own conclusions could have given the reasons for that early decision. "He ain't a gentleman," Mrs. Bunce had said. And the man certainly was not a gentleman. The old man in the white cravat was very neatly dressed, and carried himself without any of that humility which betrays one class of uncertified aspirants to gentility, or of that assumed arrogance which is at once fatal to another class. But, nevertheless, Mrs. Bunce had seen at a glance that he was not a gentleman,—had seen, moreover, that such a man could have come only upon one mission. She was right there too. This visitor had come about money.

"About this bill, Mr. Finn," said the visitor, proceeding to take out of his breast coat-pocket a rather large leathern case, as he advanced up towards the fire. "My name is Clarkson, Mr. Finn. If I may venture so far, I'll take a chair."

"Certainly, Mr. Clarkson," said Phineas, getting up and pointing to a seat.

"Thankye, Mr. Finn, thankye. We shall be more comfortable doing business sitting, shan't we?" Whereupon the horrid little man drew himself close in to the fire, and spreading out his leathern case upon his knees, began to turn over one suspicious bit of paper after another, as though he were uncertain in what part of his portfolio lay this identical bit which he was seeking. He seemed to be quite at home, and to feel that there was no ground whatever for hurry in such comfortable quarters. Phineas hated him at once,—with a hatred altogether unconnected with the difficulty which his friend Fitzgibbon had brought upon him.

"Here it is," said Mr. Clarkson at last. "Oh, dear me, dear me! the third of November, and here we are in March! I didn't think it was so bad as this;—I didn't indeed. This is very bad,—very bad! And for Parliament gents, too, who should be more punctual than anybody, because of the privilege. Shouldn't they now, Mr. Finn?"

"All men should be punctual, I suppose," said Phineas.

"Of course they should; of course they should. I always say to my gents, 'Be punctual, and I'll do anything for you.' But, perhaps, Mr. Finn, you can hand me a cheque for this amount, and then you and I will begin square."

"Indeed I cannot, Mr. Clarkson."

"Not hand me a cheque for it!"

"Upon my word, no."

"That's very bad;—very bad indeed. Then I suppose I must take the half, and renew for the remainder, though I don't like it;—I don't indeed."

"I can pay no part of that bill, Mr. Clarkson."

"Pay no part of it!" and Mr. Clarkson, in order that he might the better express his surprise, arrested his hand in the very act of poking his host's fire.

"If you'll allow me, I'll manage the fire," said Phineas, putting out his hand for the poker.

But Mr. Clarkson was fond of poking fires, and would not surrender the poker. "Pay no part of it!" he said again, holding the poker away from Phineas in his left hand. "Don't say that, Mr. Finn. Pray don't say that. Don't drive me to be severe. I don't like to be severe with my gents. I'll do anything, Mr. Finn, if you'll only be punctual."

"The fact is, Mr. Clarkson, I have never had one penny of consideration for that bill, and—"

"Oh, Mr. Finn! oh, Mr. Finn!" and then Mr. Clarkson had his will of the fire.

"I never had one penny of consideration for that bill," continued Phineas. "Of course, I don't deny my responsibility."

"No, Mr. Finn; you can't deny that. Here it is;—Phineas Finn;—and everybody knows you, because you're a Parliament gent."

"I don't deny it. But I had no reason to suppose that I should be called upon for the money when I accommodated my friend, Mr. Fitzgibbon, and I have not got it. That is the long and the short of it. I must see him and take care that arrangements are made."

"Arrangements!"

"Yes, arrangements for settling the bill."

"He hasn't got the money, Mr. Finn. You know that as well as I do."

"I know nothing about it, Mr. Clarkson."

"Oh yes, Mr. Finn; you know; you know."

"I tell you I know nothing about it," said Phineas, waxing angry.

"As to Mr. Fitzgibbon, he's the pleasantest gent that ever lived. Isn't he now? I've know'd him these ten years. I don't suppose that for ten years I've been without his name in my pocket. But, bless you, Mr. Finn, there's an end to everything. I shouldn't have looked at this bit of paper if it hadn't been for your signature. Of course not. You're just beginning, and it's natural you should want a little help. You'll find me always ready, if you'll only be punctual."

"I tell you again, sir, that I never had a shilling out of that for myself, and do not want any such help." Here Mr. Clarkson smiled sweetly. "I gave my name to my friend simply to oblige him."

"I like you Irish gents because you do hang together so close," said Mr. Clarkson.

"Simply to oblige him," continued Phineas. "As I said before, I know that I am responsible; but, as I said before also, I have not the means of taking up that bill. I will see Mr. Fitzgibbon, and let you know what we propose to do." Then Phineas got up from his seat and took his hat. It was full time that he should go down to his Committee. But Mr. Clarkson did not get up from his seat. "I'm afraid I must ask you to leave me now, Mr. Clarkson, as I have business down at the House."

"Business at the House never presses, Mr. Finn," said Mr. Clarkson. "That's the best of Parliament. I've known Parliament gents this thirty years and more. Would you believe it—I've had a Prime Minister's name in that portfolio; that I have; and a Lord Chancellor's; that I have;—and an Archbishop's too. I know what Parliament is, Mr. Finn. Come, come; don't put me off with Parliament."

There he sat before the fire with his pouch open before him, and Phineas had no power of moving him. Could Phineas have paid him the money which was manifestly due to him on the bill, the man would of course have gone; but failing in that, Phineas could not turn him out. There was a black cloud on the young member's brow, and great anger at his heart,—against Fitzgibbon rather than against the man who was sitting there before him. "Sir," he said, "it is really imperative that I should go. I am pledged to an appointment at the House at twelve, and it wants now only a quarter. I regret that your interview with me should be so unsatisfactory, but I can only promise you that I will see Mr. Fitzgibbon."

"And when shall I call again, Mr. Finn?"

"Perhaps I had better write to you," said Phineas.

"Oh dear, no," said Mr. Clarkson. "I should much prefer to look in. Looking in is always best. We can get to understand one another in that way. Let me see. I daresay you're not particular. Suppose I say Sunday morning."

"Really, I could not see you on Sunday morning, Mr. Clarkson."

"Parliament gents ain't generally particular,—'specially not among the Catholics," pleaded Mr. Clarkson.

"I am always engaged on Sundays," said Phineas.

"Suppose we say Monday,—or Tuesday. Tuesday morning at eleven. And do be punctual, Mr. Finn. At Tuesday morning I'll come, and then no doubt I shall find you ready." Whereupon Mr. Clarkson slowly put up his bills within his portfolio, and then, before Phineas knew where he was, had warmly shaken that poor dismayed member of Parliament by the hand. "Only do be punctual, Mr. Finn," he said, as he made his way down the stairs.

It was now twelve, and Phineas rushed off to a cab. He was in such a fervour of rage and misery that he could hardly think of his position, or what he had better do, till he got into the Committee Room; and when there he could think of nothing else. He intended to go deeply into the question of potted peas, holding an equal balance between the assailed Government offices on the one hand, and the advocates of the potted peas on the other. The potters of the peas, who wanted to sell their article to the Crown, declared that an extensive,—perhaps we may say, an unlimited,—use of the article would save the whole army and navy from the scourges of scurvy, dyspepsia, and rheumatism, would be the best safeguard against typhus and other fevers, and would be an invaluable aid in all other maladies to which soldiers and sailors are peculiarly subject. The peas in question were grown on a large scale in Holstein, and their growth had been fostered with the special object of doing good to the British army and navy. The peas were so cheap that there would be a great saving in money,—and it really had seemed to many that the officials of the Horse Guards and the Admiralty had been actuated by some fiendish desire to deprive their men of salutary fresh vegetables, simply because they were of foreign growth. But the officials of the War Office and the Admiralty declared that the potted peas in question were hardly fit for swine. The motion for the Committee had been made by a gentleman of the opposition, and Phineas had been put upon it as an independent member. He had resolved to give it all his mind, and, as far as he was concerned, to reach a just decision, in which there should be no favour shown to the Government side. New brooms are proverbial for thorough work, and in this Committee work Phineas was as yet a new broom. But, unfortunately, on this day his mind was so harassed that he could hardly understand what was going on. It did not, perhaps, much signify, as the witnesses examined were altogether agricultural. They only proved the production of peas in Holstein,—a fact as to which Phineas had no doubt. The proof was naturally slow, as the evidence was given in German, and had to be translated into English. And the work of the day was much impeded by a certain member who unfortunately spoke German, who seemed to be fond of speaking German before his brethren of the Committee, and who was curious as to agriculture in Holstein generally. The chairman did not understand German, and there was a difficulty in checking this gentleman, and in making him understand that his questions were not relevant to the issue.

Phineas could not keep his mind during the whole afternoon from the subject of his misfortune. What should he do if this horrid man came to him once or twice a week? He certainly did owe the man the money. He must admit that to himself. The man no doubt was a dishonest knave who had discounted the bill probably at fifty per cent; but, nevertheless, Phineas had made himself legally responsible for the amount. The privilege of the House prohibited him from arrest. He thought of that very often, but the thought only made him the more unhappy. Would it not be said, and might it not be said truly, that he had incurred this responsibility,—a responsibility which he was altogether unequal to answer,—because he was so protected? He did feel that a certain consciousness of his privilege had been present to him when he had put his name across the paper, and there had been dishonesty in that very consciousness. And of what service would his privilege be to him, if this man could harass every hour of his life? The man was to be with him again in a day or two, and when the appointment had been proposed, he, Phineas, had not dared to negative it. And how was he to escape? As for paying the bill, that with him was altogether impossible. The man had told him,—and he had believed the man,—that payment by Fitzgibbon was out of the question. And yet Fitzgibbon was the son of a peer, whereas he was only the son of a country doctor! Of course Fitzgibbon must make some effort,—some great effort,—and have the thing settled. Alas, alas! He knew enough of the world already to feel that the hope was vain.

He went down from the Committee Room into the House, and he dined at the House, and remained there until eight or nine at night; but Fitzgibbon did not come. He then went to the Reform Club, but he was not there. Both at the club and in the House many men spoke to him about the debate of the previous night, expressing surprise that he had not spoken,—making him more and more wretched. He saw Mr. Monk, but Mr. Monk was walking arm in arm with his colleague, Mr. Palliser, and Phineas could do no more than just speak to them. He thought that Mr. Monk's nod of recognition was very cold. That might be fancy, but it certainly was a fact that Mr. Monk only nodded to him. He would tell Mr. Monk the truth, and then, if Mr. Monk chose to quarrel with him, he at any rate would take no step to renew their friendship.

From the Reform Club he went to the Shakspeare, a smaller club to which Fitzgibbon belonged,—and of which Phineas much wished to become a member,—and to which he knew that his friend resorted when he wished to enjoy himself thoroughly, and to be at ease in his inn. Men at the Shakspeare could do as they pleased. There were no politics there, no fashion, no stiffness, and no rules,—so men said; but that was hardly true. Everybody called everybody by his Christian name, and members smoked all over the house. They who did not belong to the Shakspeare thought it an Elysium upon earth; and they who did, believed it to be among Pandemoniums the most pleasant. Phineas called at the Shakspeare, and was told by the porter that Mr. Fitzgibbon was up-stairs. He was shown into the strangers room, and in five minutes his friend came down to him.

"I want you to come down to the Reform with me," said Phineas.

"By jingo, my dear fellow, I'm in the middle of a rubber of whist."

"There has been a man with me about that bill."

"What;—Clarkson?"

"Yes, Clarkson," said Phineas.

"Don't mind him," said Fitzgibbon.

"That's nonsense. How am I to help minding him? I must mind him. He is coming to me again on Tuesday morning."

"Don't see him."

"How can I help seeing him?"

"Make them say you're not at home."

"He has made an appointment. He has told me that he'll never leave me alone. He'll be the death of me if this is not settled."

"It shall be settled, my dear fellow. I'll see about it. I'll see about it and write you a line. You must excuse me now, because those fellows are waiting. I'll have it all arranged."

Again as Phineas went home he thoroughly wished that he had not seceded from Mr. Low.

CHAPTER XXII
Lady Baldock at Home

About the middle of March Lady Baldock came up from Baddingham to London, coerced into doing so, as Violet Effingham declared, in thorough opposition to all her own tastes, by the known wishes of her friends and relatives. Her friends and relatives, so Miss Effingham insinuated, were unanimous in wishing that Lady Baldock should remain at Baddingham Park, and therefore,—that wish having been indiscreetly expressed,—she had put herself to great inconvenience, and had come to London in March. "Gustavus will go mad," said Violet to Lady Laura. The Gustavus in question was the Lord Baldock of the present generation, Miss Effingham's Lady Baldock being the peer's mother. "Why does not Lord Baldock take a house himself?" asked Lady Laura. "Don't you know, my dear," Violet answered, "how much we Baddingham people think of money? We don't like being vexed and driven mad, but even that is better than keeping up two households." As regarded Violet, the injury arising from Lady Baldock's early migration was very great, for she was thus compelled to move from Grosvenor Place to Lady Baldock's house in Berkeley Square. "As you are so fond of being in London, Augusta and I have made up our minds to come up before Easter," Lady Baldock had written to her.

"I shall go to her now," Violet had said to her friend, "because I have not quite made up my mind as to what I will do for the future."

"Marry Oswald, and be your own mistress."

"I mean to be my own mistress without marrying Oswald, though I don't see my way quite clearly as yet. I think I shall set up a little house of my own, and let the world say what it pleases. I suppose they couldn't make me out to be a lunatic."

"I shouldn't wonder if they were to try," said Lady Laura.

"They could not prevent me in any other way. But I am in the dark as yet, and so I shall be obedient and go to my aunt."

Miss Effingham went to Berkeley Square, and Phineas Finn was introduced to Lady Baldock. He had been often in Grosvenor Place, and had seen Violet frequently. Mr. Kennedy gave periodical dinners,—once a week,—to which everybody went who could get an invitation; and Phineas had been a guest more than once. Indeed, in spite of his miseries he had taken to dining out a good deal, and was popular as an eater of dinners. He could talk when wanted, and did not talk too much, was pleasant in manners and appearance, and had already achieved a certain recognised position in London life. Of those who knew him intimately, not one in twenty were aware from whence he came, what was his parentage, or what his means of living. He was a member of Parliament, a friend of Mr. Kennedy's, was intimate with Mr. Monk, though an Irishman did not as a rule herd with other Irishmen, and was the right sort of person to have at your house. Some people said he was a cousin of Lord Brentford's, and others declared that he was Lord Chiltern's earliest friend. There he was, however, with a position gained, and even Lady Baldock asked him to her house.

Lady Baldock had evenings. People went to her house, and stood about the room and on the stairs, talked to each other for half an hour, and went away. In these March days there was no crowding, but still there were always enough of people there to show that Lady Baldock was successful. Why people should have gone to Lady Baldock's I cannot explain;—but there are houses to which people go without any reason. Phineas received a little card asking him to go, and he always went.

"I think you like my friend, Mr. Finn," Lady Laura said to Miss Effingham, after the first of these evenings.

"Yes, I do. I like him decidedly."

"So do I. I should hardly have thought that you would have taken a fancy to him."

"I hardly know what you call taking a fancy," said Violet. "I am not quite sure I like to be told that I have taken a fancy for a young man."

"I mean no offence, my dear."

"Of course you don't But, to speak truth, I think I have rather taken a fancy to him. There is just enough of him, but not too much. I don't mean materially,—in regard to his inches; but as to his mental belongings. I hate a stupid man who can't talk to me, and I hate a clever man who talks me down. I don't like a man who is too lazy to make any effort to shine; but I particularly dislike the man who is always striving for effect. I abominate a humble man, but yet I love to perceive that a man acknowledges the superiority of my sex, and youth, and all that kind of thing."

"You want to be flattered without plain flattery."

"Of course I do. A man who would tell me that I am pretty, unless he is over seventy, ought to be kicked out of the room. But a man who can't show me that he thinks me so without saying a word about it, is a lout. Now in all those matters, your friend, Mr. Finn, seems to know what he is about. In other words, he makes himself pleasant, and, therefore, one is glad to see him."

"I suppose you do not mean to fall in love with him?"

"Not that I know of, my dear. But when I do, I'll be sure to give you notice."

I fear that there was more of earnestness in Lady Laura's last question than Miss Effingham had supposed. She had declared to herself over and over again that she had never been in love with Phineas Finn. She had acknowledged to herself, before Mr. Kennedy had asked her hand in marriage, that there had been danger,—that she could have learned to love the man if such love would not have been ruinous to her,—that the romance of such a passion would have been pleasant to her. She had gone farther than this, and had said to herself that she would have given way to that romance, and would have been ready to accept such love if offered to her, had she not put it out of her own power to marry a poor man by her generosity to her brother. Then she had thrust the thing aside, and had clearly understood,—she thought that she had clearly understood,—that life for her must be a matter of business. Was it not the case with nine out of every ten among mankind, with nine hundred and ninety-nine out of every thousand, that life must be a matter of business and not of romance? Of course she could not marry Mr. Finn, knowing, as she did, that neither of them had a shilling. Of all men in the world she esteemed Mr. Kennedy the most, and when these thoughts were passing through her mind, she was well aware that he would ask her to be his wife. Had she not resolved that she would accept the offer, she would not have gone to Loughlinter. Having put aside all romance as unfitted to her life, she could, she thought, do her duty as Mr. Kennedy's wife. She would teach herself to love him. Nay,—she had taught herself to love him. She was at any rate so sure of her own heart that she would never give her husband cause to rue the confidence he placed in her. And yet there was something sore within her when she thought that Phineas Finn was fond of Violet Effingham.

It was Lady Baldock's second evening, and Phineas came to the house at about eleven o'clock. At this time he had encountered a second and a third interview with Mr. Clarkson, and had already failed in obtaining any word of comfort from Laurence Fitzgibbon about the bill. It was clear enough now that Laurence felt that they were both made safe by their privilege, and that Mr. Clarkson should be treated as you treat the organ-grinders. They are a nuisance and must be endured. But the nuisance is not so great but what you can live in comfort,—if only you are not too sore as to the annoyance. "My dear fellow," Laurence had said to him, "I have had Clarkson almost living in my rooms. He used to drink nearly a pint of sherry a day for me. All I looked to was that I didn't live there at the same time. If you wish it, I'll send in the sherry." This was very bad, and Phineas tried to quarrel with his friend; but he found that it was difficult to quarrel with Laurence Fitzgibbon.

But though on this side Phineas was very miserable, on another side he had obtained great comfort. Mr. Monk and he were better friends than ever. "As to what Turnbull says about me in the House," Mr. Monk had said, laughing; "he and I understand each other perfectly. I should like to see you on your legs, but it is just as well, perhaps, that you have deferred it. We shall have the real question on immediately after Easter, and then you'll have plenty of opportunities." Phineas had explained how he had attempted, how he had failed, and how he had suffered;—and Mr. Monk had been generous in his sympathy. "I know all about it," said he, "and have gone through it all myself. The more respect you feel for the House, the more satisfaction you will have in addressing it when you have mastered this difficulty."

The first person who spoke to Phineas at Lady Baldock's was Miss Fitzgibbon, Laurence's sister. Aspasia Fitzgibbon was a warm woman as regarded money, and as she was moreover a most discreet spinster, she was made welcome by Lady Baldock, in spite of the well-known iniquities of her male relatives. "Mr. Finn," said she, "how d'ye do? I want to say a word to ye. Just come here into the corner." Phineas, not knowing how to escape, did retreat into the corner with Miss Fitzgibbon. "Tell me now, Mr. Finn;—have ye been lending money to Laurence?"

"No; I have lent him no money," said Phineas, much astonished by the question.

"Don't. That's my advice to ye. Don't. On any other matter Laurence is the best creature in the world,—but he's bad to lend money to. You ain't in any hobble with him, then?"

"Well;—nothing to speak of. What makes you ask?"

"Then you are in a hobble? Dear, dear! I never saw such a man as Laurence;—never. Good-bye. I wouldn't do it again, if I were you;—that's all." Then Miss Fitzgibbon came out of the corner and made her way down-stairs.

Phineas immediately afterwards came across Miss Effingham. "I did not know," said she, "that you and the divine Aspasia were such close allies."

"We are the dearest friends in the world, but she has taken my breath away now."

"May a body be told how she has done that?" Violet asked.

"Well, no; I'm afraid not, even though the body be Miss Effingham. It was a profound secret;—really a secret concerning a third person, and she began about it just as though she were speaking about the weather!"

"How charming! I do so like her. You haven't heard, have you, that Mr. Ratler proposed to her the other day?"

"No!"

"But he did;—at least, so she tells everybody. She said she'd take him if he would promise to get her brother's salary doubled."

"Did she tell you?"

"No; not me. And of course I don't believe a word of it. I suppose Barrington Erle made up the story. Are you going out of town next week, Mr. Finn?" The week next to this was Easter-week. "I heard you were going into Northamptonshire."

"From Lady Laura?"

"Yes;—from Lady Laura."

"I intend to spend three days with Lord Chiltern at Willingford. It is an old promise. I am going to ride his horses,—that is, if I am able to ride them."

"Take care what you are about, Mr. Finn;—they say his horses are so dangerous!"

"I'm rather good at falling, I flatter myself."

"I know that Lord Chiltern rides anything he can sit, so long as it is some animal that nobody else will ride. It was always so with him. He is so odd; is he not?"

Phineas knew, of course, that Lord Chiltern had more than once asked Violet Effingham to be his wife,—and he believed that she, from her intimacy with Lady Laura, must know that he knew it. He had also heard Lady Laura express a very strong wish that, in spite of these refusals, Violet might even yet become her brother's wife. And Phineas also knew that Violet Effingham was becoming, in his own estimation, the most charming woman of his acquaintance. How was he to talk to her about Lord Chiltern?

"He is odd," said Phineas; "but he is an excellent fellow,—whom his father altogether misunderstands."

"Exactly,—just so; I am so glad to hear you say that,—you who have never had the misfortune to have anything to do with a bad set. Why don't you tell Lord Brentford? Lord Brentford would listen to you."

"To me?"

"Yes;—of course he would,—for you are just the link that is wanting. You are Chiltern's intimate friend, and you are also the friend of big-wigs and Cabinet Ministers."

"Lord Brentford would put me down at once if I spoke to him on such a subject."

"I am sure he would not. You are too big to be put down, and no man can really dislike to hear his son well spoken of by those who are well spoken of themselves. Won't you try, Mr. Finn?" Phineas said that he would think of it,—that he would try if any fit opportunity could be found. "Of course you know how intimate I have been with the Standishes," said Violet; "that Laura is to me a sister, and that Oswald used to be almost a brother."

"Why do not you speak to Lord Brentford;—you who are his favourite?"

"There are reasons, Mr. Finn. Besides, how can any girl come forward and say that she knows the disposition of any man? You can live with Lord Chiltern, and see what he is made of, and know his thoughts, and learn what is good in him, and also what is bad. After all, how is any girl really to know anything of a man's life?"

"If I can do anything, Miss Effingham, I will," said Phineas.

"And then we shall all of us be so grateful to you," said Violet, with her sweetest smile.

Phineas, retreating from this conversation, stood for a while alone, thinking of it. Had she spoken thus of Lord Chiltern because she did love him or because she did not? And the sweet commendations which had fallen from her lips upon him,—him, Phineas Finn,—were they compatible with anything like a growing partiality for himself, or were they incompatible with any such feeling? Had he most reason to be comforted or to be discomfited by what had taken place? It seemed hardly possible to his imagination that Violet Effingham should love such a nobody as he. And yet he had had fair evidence that one standing as high in the world as Violet Effingham would fain have loved him could she have followed the dictates of her heart. He had trembled when he had first resolved to declare his passion to Lady Laura,—fearing that she would scorn him as being presumptuous. But there had been no cause for such fear as that. He had declared his love, and she had not thought him to be presumptuous. That now was ages ago,—eight months since; and Lady Laura had become a married woman. Since he had become so warmly alive to the charms of Violet Effingham he had determined, with stern propriety, that a passion for a married woman was disgraceful. Such love was in itself a sin, even though it was accompanied by the severest forbearance and the most rigid propriety of conduct. No;—Lady Laura had done wisely to check the growing feeling of partiality which she had admitted; and now that she was married, he would be as wise as she. It was clear to him that, as regarded his own heart, the way was open to him for a new enterprise. But what if he were to fail again, and be told by Violet, when he declared his love, that she had just engaged herself to Lord Chiltern!

"What were you and Violet talking about so eagerly?" said Lady Laura to him, with a smile that, in its approach to laughter, almost betrayed its mistress.

"We were talking about your brother."

"You are going to him, are you not?"

"Yes; I leave London on Sunday night;—but only for a day or two."

"Has he any chance there, do you think?"

"What, with Miss Effingham?"

"Yes;—with Violet. Sometimes I think she loves him."

"How can I say? In such a matter you can judge better than I can do. One woman with reference to another can draw the line between love and friendship. She certainly likes Chiltern."

"Oh, I believe she loves him. I do indeed. But she fears him. She does not quite understand how much there is of tenderness with that assumed ferocity. And Oswald is so strange, so unwise, so impolitic, that though he loves her better than all the world beside, he will not sacrifice even a turn of a word to win her. When he asks her to marry him, he almost flies at her throat, as an angry debtor who applies for

66

instant payment. Tell him, Mr. Finn, never to give it over;—and teach him that he should be soft with her. Tell him, also, that in her heart she likes him. One woman, as you say, knows another woman; and I am certain he would win her if he would only be gentle with her." Then, again, before they parted, Lady Laura told him that this marriage was the dearest wish of her heart, and that there would be no end to her gratitude if Phineas could do anything to promote it. All which again made our hero unhappy.

CHAPTER XXIII
Sunday in Grosvenor Place

Mr. Kennedy, though he was a most scrupulously attentive member of Parliament, was a man very punctual to hours and rules in his own house,—and liked that his wife should be as punctual as himself. Lady Laura, who in marrying him had firmly resolved that she would do her duty to him in all ways, even though the ways might sometimes be painful,—and had been perhaps more punctilious in this respect than she might have been had she loved him heartily,—was not perhaps quite so fond of accurate regularity as her husband; and thus, by this time, certain habits of his had become rather bonds than habits to her. He always had prayers at nine, and breakfasted at a quarter past nine, let the hours on the night before have been as late as they might before the time for rest had come. After breakfast he would open his letters in his study, but he liked her to be with him, and desired to discuss with her every application he got from a constituent. He had his private secretary in a room apart, but he thought that everything should be filtered to his private secretary through his wife. He was very anxious that she herself should superintend the accounts of their own private expenditure, and had taken some trouble to teach her an excellent mode of book-keeping. He had recommended to her a certain course of reading,—which was pleasant enough; ladies like to receive such recommendations; but Mr. Kennedy, having drawn out the course, seemed to expect that his wife should read the books he had named, and, worse still, that she should read them in the time he had allocated for the work. This, I think, was tyranny. Then the Sundays became very wearisome to Lady Laura. Going to church twice, she had learnt, would be a part of her duty; and though in her father's household attendance at church had never been very strict, she had made up her mind to this cheerfully. But Mr. Kennedy expected also that he and she should always dine together on Sundays, that there should be no guests, and that there should be no evening company. After all, the demand was not very severe, but yet she found that it operated injuriously upon her comfort. The Sundays were very wearisome to her, and made her feel that her lord and master was—her lord and master. She made an effort or two to escape, but the efforts were all in vain. He never spoke a cross word to her. He never gave a stern command. But yet he had his way. "I won't say that reading a novel on a Sunday is a sin," he said; "but we must at any rate admit that it is a matter on which men disagree, that many of the best of men are against such occupation on Sunday, and that to abstain is to be on the safe side." So the novels were put away, and Sunday afternoon with the long evening became rather a stumbling-block to Lady Laura.

Those two hours, moreover, with her husband in the morning became very wearisome to her. At first she had declared that it would be her greatest ambition to help her husband in his work, and she had read all the letters from the MacNabs and MacFies, asking to be made gaugers and landing-waiters, with an assumed interest. But the work palled upon her very quickly. Her quick intellect discovered soon that there was nothing in it which she really did. It was all form and verbiage, and pretence at business. Her husband went through it all with the utmost patience, reading every word, giving orders as to every detail, and conscientiously doing that which he conceived he had undertaken to do. But Lady Laura wanted to meddle with high politics, to discuss reform bills, to assist in putting up Mr. This and putting down my Lord That. Why should she waste her time in doing that which the lad in the next room, who was called a private secretary, could do as well?

Still she would obey. Let the task be as hard as it might, she would obey. If he counselled her to do this or that, she would follow his counsel,—because she owed him so much. If she had accepted the half of all his wealth without loving him, she owed him the more on that account. But she knew,—she could not but know,—that her intellect was brighter than his; and might it not be possible for her to lead him? Then she made efforts to lead her husband, and found that he was as stiff-necked as an ox. Mr. Kennedy was not, perhaps, a clever man; but he was a man who knew his own way, and who intended to keep it.

"I have got a headache, Robert," she said to him one Sunday after luncheon. "I think I will not go to church this afternoon."

"It is not serious, I hope."

"Oh dear no. Don't you know how one feels sometimes that one has got a head? And when that is the case one's armchair is the best place."

"I am not sure of that," said Mr. Kennedy.

"If I went to church I should not attend," said Lady Laura.

"The fresh air would do you more good than anything else, and we could walk across the park."

"Thank you;—I won't go out again to-day." This she said with something almost of crossness in her manner, and Mr. Kennedy went to the afternoon service by himself.

Lady Laura when she was left alone began to think of her position. She was not more than four or five months married, and she was becoming very tired of her life. Was it not also true that she was becoming tired of her husband? She had twice told Phineas Finn that of all men in the world she esteemed Mr. Kennedy the most. She did not esteem him less now. She knew no point or particle in which he did not do his duty with accuracy. But no person can live happily with another,—not even with a brother or a sister or a friend,—simply upon esteem. All the virtues in the calendar, though they exist on each side, will not make a man and woman happy together, unless there be sympathy. Lady Laura was beginning to find out that there was a lack of sympathy between herself and her husband.

She thought of this till she was tired of thinking of it, and then, wishing to divert her mind, she took up the book that was lying nearest to her hand. It was a volume of a new novel which she had been reading on the previous day, and now, without much thought about it, she went on with her reading. There came to her, no doubt, some dim, half-formed idea that, as she was freed from going to church by the plea of a headache, she was also absolved by the same plea from other Sunday hindrances. A child, when it is ill, has buttered toast and a picture-book instead of bread-and-milk and lessons. In this way, Lady Laura conceived herself to be entitled to her novel.

While she was reading it, there came a knock at the door, and Barrington Erle was shown upstairs. Mr. Kennedy had given no orders against Sunday visitors, but had simply said that Sunday visiting was not to his taste. Barrington, however, was Lady Laura's cousin, and people must be very strict if they can't see their cousins on Sunday. Lady Laura soon lost her headache altogether in the animation of discussing the chances of the new Reform Bill with the Prime Minister's private secretary; and had left her chair, and was standing by the table with the novel in her hand, protesting this and denying that, expressing infinite confidence in Mr. Monk, and violently denouncing Mr. Turnbull, when her husband returned from church and came up into the drawing-room. Lady Laura had forgotten her headache altogether, and had in her composition none of that thoughtfulness of hypocrisy which would have taught her to moderate her political feeling at her husband's return.

"I do declare," she said, "that if Mr. Turnbull opposes the Government measure now, because he can't have his own way in everything, I will never again put my trust in any man who calls himself a popular leader."

"You never should," said Barrington Erle.

"That's all very well for you, Barrington, who are an aristocratic Whig of the old official school, and who call yourself a Liberal simply because Fox was a Liberal a hundred years ago. My heart's in it."

"Heart should never have anything to do with politics; should it?" said Erle, turning round to Mr. Kennedy.

Mr. Kennedy did not wish to discuss the matter on a Sunday, nor yet did he wish to say before Barrington Erle that he thought it wrong to do so. And he was desirous of treating his wife in some way as though she were an invalid,—that she thereby might be, as it were, punished; but he did not wish to do this in such a way that Barrington should be aware of the punishment.

"Laura had better not disturb herself about it now," he said.

"How is a person to help being disturbed?" said Lady Laura, laughing.

"Well, well; we won't mind all that now," said Mr. Kennedy, turning away. Then he took up the novel which Lady Laura had just laid down from her hand, and, having looked at it, carried it aside, and placed it on a book-shelf which was remote from them. Lady Laura watched him as he did this, and the whole course of her husband's thoughts on the subject was open to her at once. She regretted the novel, and she regretted also the political discussion. Soon afterwards Barrington Erle went away, and the husband and wife were alone together.

"I am glad that your head is so much better," said he. He did not intend to be severe, but he spoke with a gravity of manner which almost amounted to severity.

"Yes; it is," she said, "Barrington's coming in cheered me up."

"I am sorry that you should have wanted cheering."

"Don't you know what I mean, Robert?"

"No; I do not think that I do, exactly."

"I suppose your head is stronger. You do not get that feeling of dazed, helpless imbecility of brain, which hardly amounts to headache, but which yet—is almost as bad."

"Imbecility of brain may be worse than headache, but I don't think it can produce it."

"Well, well;—I don't know how to explain it."

"Headache comes, I think, always from the stomach, even when produced by nervous affections. But imbecility of the brain—"

"Oh, Robert, I am so sorry that I used the word."

"I see that it did not prevent your reading," he said, after a pause.

"Not such reading as that. I was up to nothing better."

Then there was another pause.

"I won't deny that it may be a prejudice," he said, "but I confess that the use of novels in my own house on Sundays is a pain to me. My mother's ideas on the subject are very strict, and I cannot think that it is bad for a son to hang on to the teaching of his mother." This he said in the most serious tone which he could command.

"I don't know why I took it up," said Lady Laura. "Simply, I believe, because it was there. I will avoid doing so for the future."

"Do, my dear," said the husband. "I shall be obliged and grateful if you will remember what I have said." Then he left her, and she sat alone, first in the dusk and then in the dark, for two hours, doing nothing. Was this to be the life which she had procured for herself by marrying Mr. Kennedy of Loughlinter? If it was harsh and unendurable in London, what would it be in the country?

CHAPTER XXIV
The Willingford Bull

Phineas left London by a night mail train on Easter Sunday, and found himself at the Willingford Bull about half an hour after midnight. Lord Chiltern was up and waiting for him, and supper was on the table. The Willingford Bull was an English inn of the old stamp, which had now, in these latter years of railway travelling, ceased to have a road business,—for there were no travellers on the road, and but little posting—but had acquired a new trade as a dépôt for hunters and hunting men. The landlord let out horses and kept hunting stables, and the house was generally filled from the beginning of November till the middle of April. Then it became a desert in the summer, and no guests were seen there, till the pink coats flocked down again into the shires.

"How many days do you mean to give us?" said Lord Chiltern, as he helped his friend to a devilled leg of turkey.

"I must go back on Wednesday," said Phineas.

"That means Wednesday night. I'll tell you what we'll do. We've the Cottesmore to-morrow. We'll get into Tailby's country on Tuesday, and Fitzwilliam will be only twelve miles off on Wednesday. We shall be rather short of horses."

"Pray don't let me put you out. I can hire something here, I suppose?"

"You won't put me out at all. There'll be three between us each day, and we'll run our luck. The horses have gone on to Empingham for to-morrow. Tailby is rather a way off,—at Somerby; but we'll manage it. If the worst comes to the worst, we can get back to Stamford by rail. On Wednesday we shall have everything very comfortable. They're out beyond Stilton and will draw home our way. I've planned it all out. I've a trap with a fast stepper, and if we start to-morrow at half-past nine, we shall be in plenty of time. You shall ride Meg Merrilies, and if she don't carry you, you may shoot her."

"Is she one of the pulling ones?"

"She is heavy in hand if you are heavy at her, but leave her mouth alone and she'll go like flowing water. You'd better not ride more in a crowd than you can help. Now what'll you drink?"

They sat up half the night smoking and talking, and Phineas learned more about Lord Chiltern then than ever he had learned before. There was brandy and water before them, but neither of them drank. Lord Chiltern, indeed, had a pint of beer by his side from which he sipped occasionally. "I've taken to beer," he said, "as being the best drink going. When a man hunts six days a week he can afford to drink beer. I'm on an allowance,—three pints a day. That's not too much."

"And you drink nothing else?"

"Nothing when I'm alone,—except a little cherry-brandy when I'm out. I never cared for drink;—never in my life. I do like excitement, and have been less careful than I ought to have been as to what it has come from. I could give up drink to-morrow, without a struggle,—if it were worth my while to make up my mind to do it. And it's the same with gambling. I never do gamble now, because I've got no money; but I own I like it better than anything in the world. While you are at it, there is life in it."

"You should take to politics, Chiltern."

"And I would have done so, but my father would not help me. Never mind, we will not talk about him. How does Laura get on with her husband?"

"Very happily, I should say."

"I don't believe it," said Lord Chiltern. "Her temper is too much like mine to allow her to be happy with such a log of wood as Robert Kennedy. It is such men as he who drive me out of the pale of decent life. If that is decency, I'd sooner be indecent. You mark my words. They'll come to grief. She'll never be able to stand it."

"I should think she had her own way in everything," said Phineas.

"No, no. Though he's a prig, he's a man; and she will not find it easy to drive him."

"But she may bend him."

"Not an inch;—that is if I understand his character. I suppose you see a good deal of them?"

"Yes,—pretty well. I'm not there so often as I used to be in the Square."

"You get sick of it, I suppose. I should. Do you see my father often?"

"Only occasionally. He is always very civil when I do see him."

"He is the very pink of civility when he pleases, but the most unjust man I ever met."

"I should not have thought that."

"Yes, he is," said the Earl's son, "and all from lack of judgment to discern the truth. He makes up his mind to a thing on insufficient proof, and then nothing will turn him. He thinks well of you,—would probably believe your word on any indifferent subject without thought of a doubt; but if you were to tell him that I didn't get drunk every night of my life and spend most of my time in thrashing policemen, he would not believe you. He would smile incredulously and make you a little bow. I can see him do it."

"You are too hard on him, Chiltern."

"He has been too hard on me, I know. Is Violet Effingham still in Grosvenor Place?"

"No; she's with Lady Baldock."

"That old grandmother of evil has come to town,—has she? Poor Violet! When we were young together we used to have such fun about that old woman."

"The old woman is an ally of mine now," said Phineas.

"You make allies everywhere. You know Violet Effingham of course?"

"Oh yes. I know her."

"Don't you think her very charming?" said Lord Chiltern.

"Exceedingly charming."

"I have asked that girl to marry me three times, and I shall never ask her again. There is a point beyond which a man shouldn't go. There are many reasons why it would be a good marriage. In the first place, her money would be serviceable. Then it would heal matters in our family, for my father is as prejudiced in her favour as he is against me. And I love her dearly. I've loved her all my life,—since I used to buy cakes for her. But I shall never ask her again."

"I would if I were you," said Phineas,—hardly knowing what it might be best for him to say.

"No; I never will. But I'll tell you what. I shall get into some desperate scrape about her. Of course she'll marry, and that soon. Then I shall make a fool of myself. When I hear that she is engaged I shall go and quarrel with the man, and kick him,—or get kicked. All the world will turn against me, and I shall be called a wild beast."

"A dog in the manger is what you should be called."

"Exactly;—but how is a man to help it? If you loved a girl, could you see another man take her?" Phineas remembered of course that he had lately come through this ordeal. "It is as though he were to come and put his hand upon me, and wanted my own heart out of me. Though I have no property in her at all, no right to her,—though she never gave me a word of encouragement, it is as though she were the most private

69

thing in the world to me. I should be half mad, and in my madness I could not master the idea that I was being robbed. I should resent it as a personal interference."

"I suppose it will come to that if you give her up yourself," said Phineas.

"It is no question of giving up. Of course I cannot make her marry me. Light another cigar, old fellow."

Phineas, as he lit the other cigar, remembered that he owed a certain duty in this matter to Lady Laura. She had commissioned him to persuade her brother that his suit with Violet Effingham would not be hopeless, if he could only restrain himself in his mode of conducting it. Phineas was disposed to do his duty, although he felt it to be very hard that he should be called upon to be eloquent against his own interest. He had been thinking for the last quarter of an hour how he must bear himself if it might turn out that he should be the man whom Lord Chiltern was resolved to kick. He looked at his friend and host, and became aware that a kicking-match with such a one would not be pleasant pastime. Nevertheless, he would be happy enough to be subject to Lord Chiltern's wrath for such a reason. He would do his duty by Lord Chiltern; and then, when that had been adequately done, he would, if occasion served, fight a battle for himself.

"You are too sudden with her, Chiltern," he said, after a pause.

"What do you mean by too sudden?" said Lord Chiltern, almost angrily.

"You frighten her by being so impetuous. You rush at her as though you wanted to conquer her by a single blow."

"So I do."

"You should be more gentle with her. You should give her time to find out whether she likes you or not."

"She has known me all her life, and has found that out long ago. Not but what you are right. I know you are right. If I were you, and had your skill in pleasing, I should drop soft words into her ear till I had caught her. But I have no gifts in that way. I am as awkward as a pig at what is called flirting. And I have an accursed pride which stands in my own light. If she were in this house this moment, and if I knew she were to be had for asking, I don't think I could bring myself to ask again. But we'll go to bed. It's half-past two, and we must be off at half-past nine, if we're to be at Exton Park gates at eleven."

Phineas, as he went up-stairs, assured himself that he had done his duty. If there ever should come to be anything between him and Violet Effingham, Lord Chiltern might quarrel with him,—might probably attempt that kicking encounter to which allusion had been made,—but nobody could justly say that he had not behaved honourably to his friend.

On the next morning there was a bustle and a scurry, as there always is on such occasions, and the two men got off about ten minutes after time. But Lord Chiltern drove hard, and they reached the meet before the master had moved off. They had a fair day's sport with the Cottesmore; and Phineas, though he found that Meg Merrilies did require a good deal of riding, went through his day's work with credit. He had been riding since he was a child, as is the custom with all boys in Munster, and had an Irishman's natural aptitude for jumping. When they got back to the Willingford Bull he felt pleased with the day and rather proud of himself. "It wasn't fast, you know," said Chiltern, "and I don't call that a stiff country. Besides, Meg is very handy when you've got her out of the crowd. You shall ride Bonebreaker to-morrow at Somerby, and you'll find that better fun."

"Bonebreaker? Haven't I heard you say he rushes like mischief?"

"Well, he does rush. But, by George! you want a horse to rush in that country. When you have to go right through four or five feet of stiff green wood, like a bullet through a target, you want a little force, or you're apt to be left up a tree."

"And what do you ride?"

"A brute I never put my leg on yet. He was sent down to Wilcox here, out of Lincolnshire, because they couldn't get anybody to ride him there. They say he goes with his head up in the air, and won't look at a fence that isn't as high as his breast. But I think he'll do here. I never saw a better made beast, or one with more power. Do you look at his shoulders. He's to be had for seventy pounds, and these are the sort of horses I like to buy."

Again they dined alone, and Lord Chiltern explained to Phineas that he rarely associated with the men of either of the hunts in which he rode. "There is a set of fellows down here who are poison to me, and there is another set, and I am poison to them. Everybody is very civil, as you see, but I have no associates. And gradually I am getting to have a reputation as though I were the devil himself. I think I shall come out next year dressed entirely in black."

"Are you not wrong to give way to that kind of thing?"

"What the deuce am I to do? I can't make civil little speeches. When once a man gets a reputation as an ogre, it is the most difficult thing in the world to drop it. I could have a score of men here every day if I liked it,—my title would do that for me;—but they would be men I should loathe, and I should be sure to tell them so, even though I did not mean it. Bonebreaker, and the new horse, and another, went on at twelve to-day. You must expect hard work to-morrow, as I daresay we shan't be home before eight."

The next day's meet was in Leicestershire, not far from Melton, and they started early. Phineas, to tell the truth of him, was rather afraid of Bonebreaker, and looked forward to the probability of an accident. He had neither wife nor child, and nobody had a better right to risk his neck. "We'll put a gag on 'im," said the groom, "and you'll ride 'im in a ring,—so that you may well-nigh break his jaw; but he is a rum un, sir." "I'll do my best," said Phineas. "He'll take all that," said the groom. "Just let him have his own way at everything," said Lord Chiltern, as they moved away from the meet to Pickwell Gorse; "and if you'll only sit on his back, he'll carry you through as safe as a church." Phineas could not help thinking that the counsels of the master and of the groom were very different. "My idea is," continued Lord Chiltern, "that in hunting you should always avoid a crowd. I don't think a horse is worth riding that will go in a crowd. It's just like yachting,—you should have plenty of sea-room. If you're to pull your horse up at every fence till somebody else is over, I think you'd better come out on a donkey." And so they went away to Pickwell Gorse.

There were over two hundred men out, and Phineas began to think that it might not be so easy to get out of the crowd. A crowd in a fast run no doubt quickly becomes small by degrees and beautifully less; but it is very difficult, especially for a stranger, to free himself from the rush at the first start. Lord Chiltern's horse plunged about so violently, as they stood on a little hill-side looking down upon the cover, that he was obliged to take him to a distance, and Phineas followed him. "If he breaks down wind," said Lord Chiltern, "we can't be better than we are here. If he goes up wind, he must turn before long, and we shall be all right." As he spoke an old hound opened true and sharp,—an old hound whom all the pack believed,—and in a moment there was no doubt that the fox had been found. "There are not above eight or nine acres in it," said Lord Chiltern, "and he can't hang long. Did you ever see such an uneasy brute as this in your life? But I feel certain he'll go well when he gets away."

Phineas was too much occupied with his own horse to think much of that on which Lord Chiltern was mounted. Bonebreaker, the very moment that he heard the old hound's note, stretched out his head, and put his mouth upon the bit, and began to tremble in every muscle. "He's a great deal more anxious for it than you and I are," said Lord Chiltern. "I see they've given you that gag. But don't you ride him on it till he wants it. Give him lots of room, and he'll go in the snaffle." All which caution made Phineas think that any insurance office would charge very dear on his life at the present moment.

The fox took two rings of the gorse, and then he went,—up wind. "It's not a vixen, I'll swear," said Lord Chiltern. "A vixen in cub never went away like that yet. Now then, Finn, my boy, keep to the right." And Lord Chiltern, with the horse out of Lincolnshire, went away across the brow of the hill, leaving the hounds to the left, and selected, as his point of exit into the next field, a stiff rail, which, had there been an accident, must have put a very wide margin of ground between the rider and his horse. "Go hard at your fences, and then you'll fall clear," he had said to Phineas. I don't think, however, that he would have ridden at the rail as he did, but that there was no help for him. "The brute began in his own way, and carried on after in the same fashion all through," he said afterwards. Phineas took the fence a little lower down, and what it was at which he rode he never knew. Bonebreaker sailed over it, whatever it was, and he soon found himself by his friend's side.

The ruck of the men were lower down than our two heroes, and there were others far away to the left, and others, again, who had been at the end of the gorse, and were now behind. Our friends were not near the hounds, not within two fields of them, but the hounds were below them, and therefore could be seen. "Don't be in a hurry, and they'll be round upon us," Lord Chiltern said. "How the deuce is one to help being in a hurry?" said Phineas, who was doing his very best to ride Bonebreaker with the snaffle, but had already began to feel that Bonebreaker cared nothing for that weak instrument. "By George, I should like to change with you," said Lord Chiltern. The Lincolnshire horse was going along with his head very low, boring as he galloped, but throwing his neck up at his fences, just when he ought to have kept himself steady. After this, though Phineas kept near Lord Chiltern throughout the run, they were not again near enough to exchange words; and, indeed, they had but little breath for such purpose.

Lord Chiltern rode still a little in advance, and Phineas, knowing his friend's partiality for solitude when taking his fences, kept a little to his left. He began to find that Bonebreaker knew pretty well what he was about. As for not using the gag rein, that was impossible. When a horse puts out what strength he has against a man's arm, a man must put out what strength he has against the horse's mouth. But Bonebreaker was cunning, and had had a gag rein on before. He contracted his lip here, and bent out his jaw there, till he had settled it to his mind, and then went away after his own fashion. He seemed to have a passion for smashing through big, high-grown ox-fences, and by degrees his rider came to feel that if there was nothing worse coming, the fun was not bad.

The fox ran up wind for a couple of miles or so, as Lord Chiltern had prophesied, and then turned,—not to the right, as would best have served him and Phineas, but to the left,—so that they were forced to make their way through the ruck of horses before they could place themselves again. Phineas found himself crossing a road, in and out of it, before he knew where he was, and for a while he lost sight of Lord Chiltern. But in truth he was leading now, whereas Lord Chiltern had led before. The two horses having been together all the morning, and on the previous day, were willing enough to remain in company, if they were allowed to do so. They both crossed the road, not very far from each other, going in and out amidst a crowd of horses, and before long were again placed well, now having the hunt on their right, whereas hitherto it had been on their left. They went over large pasture fields, and Phineas began to think that as long as Bonebreaker would be able to go through the thick grown-up hedges, all would be right. Now and again he came to a cut fence, a fence that had been cut and laid, and these were not so pleasant. Force was not sufficient for them, and they admitted of a mistake. But the horse, though he would rush at them unpleasantly, took them when they came without touching them. It might be all right yet,—unless the beast should tire with him; and then, Phineas thought, a misfortune might probably occur. He remembered, as he flew over one such impediment, that he rode a stone heavier than his friend. At the end of forty-five minutes Bonebreaker also might become aware of the fact.

The hounds were running well in sight to their right, and Phineas began to feel some of that pride which a man indulges when he becomes aware that he has taken his place comfortably, has left the squad behind, and is going well. There were men nearer the hounds than he was, but he was near enough even for ambition. There had already been enough of the run to make him sure that it would be a "good thing", and enough to make him aware also that probably it might be too good. When a run is over, men are very apt to regret the termination, who a minute or two before were anxiously longing that the hounds might pull down their game. To finish well is everything in hunting. To have led for over an hour is nothing, let the pace and country have been what they might, if you fall away during the last half mile. Therefore it is that those behind hope that the fox may make this or that cover, while the forward men long to see him turned over in every field. To ride to hounds is very glorious; but to have ridden to hounds is more glorious still. They had now crossed another road, and a larger one, and had got into a somewhat closer country. The fields were not so big, and the fences were not so high. Phineas got a moment to look about him, and saw Lord Chiltern riding without his cap. He was very red in the face, and his eyes seemed to glare, and he was tugging at his horse with all his might. But the animal seemed still to go with perfect command of strength, and Phineas had too much work on his own hands to think of offering Quixotic assistance to any one else. He saw some one, a farmer, as he thought, speak to Lord Chiltern as they rode close together; but Chiltern only shook his head and pulled at his horse.

There were brooks in those parts. The river Eye forms itself thereabouts, or some of its tributaries do so; and these tributaries, though small as rivers, are considerable to men on one side who are called by the exigencies of the occasion to place themselves quickly on the other. Phineas knew nothing of these brooks; but Bonebreaker had gone gallantly over two, and now that there came a third in the way, it was to be hoped that he might go gallantly over that also. Phineas, at any rate, had no power to decide otherwise. As long as the brute would go straight with him he could sit him; but he had long given up the idea of having a will of his own. Indeed, till he was within twenty yards of the brook, he did not see that it was larger than the others. He looked around, and there was Chiltern close to him, still fighting with his horse;—but the farmer had turned away. He thought that Chiltern nodded to him, as much as to tell him to go on. On he went at any rate. The brook, when he came to it, seemed to be a huge black hole, yawning beneath him. The banks were quite steep, and just where he was to take off there was an ugly stump. It was too late to think of anything. He stuck his knees against his saddle,—and in a moment was on the other side. The brute, who had taken off a yard before the stump, knowing well the danger of striking it with his foot, came down with a grunt, and did, I think, begin to feel the weight of that extra stone. Phineas, as soon as he was safe, looked back, and there was Lord Chiltern's horse in the very act of his spring,—higher up the rivulet, where it was even broader. At that distance Phineas could see that Lord Chiltern was wild with rage against the beast. But whether he wished to take the leap or wished to avoid it, there was no choice left to him. The animal rushed at the brook, and in a moment the horse and horseman were lost to sight. It was well then that that extra stone should tell, as it enabled Phineas to arrest his horse and to come back to his friend.

The Lincolnshire horse had chested the further bank, and of course had fallen back into the stream. When Phineas got down he found that Lord Chiltern was wedged in between the horse and the bank, which was better, at any rate, than being under the horse in the water. "All right, old fellow," he said, with a smile, when he saw Phineas. "You go on; it's too good to lose." But he was very pale, and seemed to be quite helpless where he lay. The horse did not move,—and never did move again. He had smashed his shoulder to pieces against a stump on the bank, and was afterwards shot on that very spot.

When Phineas got down he found that there was but little water where the horse lay. The depth of the stream had been on the side from which they had taken off, and the thick black mud lay within a foot of the surface, close to the bank against which Lord Chiltern was propped. "That's the worst one I ever was on," said Lord Chiltern; "but I think he's gruelled now."

"Are you hurt?"

"Well;—I fancy there is something amiss. I can't move my arms; and I catch my breath. My legs are all right if I could get away from this accursed brute."

"I told you so," said the farmer, coming and looking down upon them from the bank. "I told you so, but you wouldn't be said." Then he too got down, and between them both they extricated Lord Chiltern from his position, and got him on to the bank.

"That un's a dead un," said the farmer, pointing to the horse.

"So much the better," said his lordship. "Give us a drop of sherry, Finn."

He had broken his collar-bone and three of his ribs. They got a farmer's trap from Wissindine and took him into Oakham. When there, he insisted on being taken on through Stamford to the Willingford Bull before he would have his bones set,—picking up, however, a surgeon at Stamford. Phineas remained with him for a couple of days, losing his run with the Fitzwilliams and a day at the potted peas, and became very fond of his patient as he sat by his bedside.

"That was a good run, though, wasn't it?" said Lord Chiltern as Phineas took his leave. "And, by George, Phineas, you rode Bonebreaker so well, that you shall have him as often as you'll come down. I don't know how it is, but you Irish fellows always ride."

CHAPTER XXV
Mr. Turnbull's Carriage Stops the Way

When Phineas got back to London, a day after his time, he found that there was already a great political commotion in the metropolis. He had known that on Easter Monday and Tuesday there was to be a gathering of the people in favour of the ballot, and that on Wednesday there was to be a procession with a petition which Mr. Turnbull was to receive from the hands of the people on Primrose Hill. It had been at first intended that Mr. Turnbull should receive the petition at the door of Westminster Hall on the Thursday; but he had been requested by the Home Secretary to put aside this intention, and he had complied with the request made to him. Mr. Mildmay was to move the second reading of his Reform Bill on that day, the preliminary steps having been taken without any special notice; but the bill of course included no clause in favour of the ballot; and this petition was the consequence of that omission. Mr. Turnbull had predicted evil consequences, both in the House and out of it, and was now doing the best in his power to bring about the verification of his own prophecies. Phineas, who reached his lodgings late on the Thursday, found that the town had been in a state of ferment for three days, that on the Wednesday forty or fifty thousand persons had been collected at Primrose Hill, and that the police had been forced to interfere,—and that worse was expected on the Friday. Though Mr. Turnbull had yielded to the Government as to receiving the petition, the crowd was resolved that they would see the petition carried into the House. It was argued that the Government would have done better to have refrained from interfering as to the previously intended arrangement. It would have been easier to deal with a procession than with a mob of men gathered together without any semblance of form. Mr. Mildmay had been asked to postpone the second reading of his bill; but the request had come from his opponents, and he would not yield to it. He said that it would be a bad expedient to close Parliament from fear of the people. Phineas found at the Reform Club on the Thursday evening that members of the House of Commons were requested to enter on the Friday by the door usually used by the peers, and to make their way thence to their own House. He found that his landlord, Mr. Bunce, had been out with the people during the entire three days;—and Mrs. Bunce, with a flood of tears, begged Phineas to interfere as to the Friday. "He's that headstrong that he'll be took if anybody's took; and they say that all Westminster is to be lined with soldiers." Phineas on the Friday morning did have some conversation with his landlord; but his first work on reaching London was to see Lord Chiltern's friends, and tell them of the accident.

The potted peas Committee sat on the Thursday, and he ought to have been there. His absence, however, was unavoidable, as he could not have left his friend's bed-side so soon after the accident. On the Wednesday he had written to Lady Laura, and on the Thursday evening he went first to Portman Square and then to Grosvenor Place.

"Of course he will kill himself some day," said the Earl,—with a tear, however, in each eye.

"I hope not, my lord. He is a magnificent horseman; but accidents of course will happen."

"How many of his bones are there not broken, I wonder?" said the father. "It is useless to talk, of course. You think he is not in danger?"

"Certainly not."

"I should fear that he would be so liable to inflammation."

"The doctor says that there is none. He has been taking an enormous deal of exercise," said Phineas, "and drinking no wine. All that is in his favour."

"What does he drink, then?" asked the Earl.

"Nothing. I rather think, my lord, you are mistaken a little about his habits. I don't fancy he ever drinks unless he is provoked to do it."

"Provoked! Could anything provoke you to make a brute of yourself? But I am glad that he is in no danger. If you hear of him, let me know how he goes on."

Lady Laura was of course full of concern. "I wanted to go down to him," she said, "but Mr. Kennedy thought that there was no occasion."

"Nor is there any;—I mean in regard to danger. He is very solitary there."

"You must go to him again. Mr. Kennedy will not let me go unless I can say that there is danger. He seems to think that because Oswald has had accidents before, it is nothing. Of course I cannot leave London without his leave."

"Your brother makes very little of it, you know."

"Ah;—he would make little of anything. But if I were ill he would be in London by the first train."

"Kennedy would let you go if you asked him."

"But he advises me not to go. He says my duty does not require it, unless Oswald be in danger. Don't you know, Mr. Finn, how hard it is for a wife not to take advice when it is so given?" This she said, within six months of her marriage, to the man who had been her husband's rival!

Phineas asked her whether Violet had heard the news, and learned that she was still ignorant of it. "I got your letter only this morning, and I have not seen her," said Lady Laura. "Indeed, I am so angry with her that I hardly wish to see her." Thursday was Lady Baldock's night, and Phineas went from Grosvenor Place to Berkeley Square. There he saw Violet, and found that she had heard of the accident.

"I am so glad to see you, Mr. Finn," she said. "Do tell me;—is it much?"

"Much in inconvenience, certainly; but not much in danger."

"I think Laura was so unkind not to send me word! I only heard it just now. Did you see it?"

"I was close to him, and helped him up. The horse jumped into a river with him, and crushed him up against the bank."

"How lucky that you should be there! Had you jumped the river?"

"Yes;—almost unintentionally, for my horse was rushing so that I could not hold him. Chiltern was riding a brute that no one should have ridden. No one will again."

"Did he destroy himself?"

"He had to be killed afterwards. He broke his shoulder."

"How very lucky that you should have been near him,—and, again, how lucky that you should not have been hurt yourself!"

"It was not likely that we should both come to grief at the same fence."

"But it might have been you. And you think there is no danger?"

"None whatever,—if I may believe the doctor. His hunting is done for this year, and he will be very desolate. I shall go down again to him in a few days, and try to bring him up to town."

"Do;—do. If he is laid up in his father's house, his father must see him." Phineas had not looked at the matter in that light; but he thought that Miss Effingham might probably be right.

Early on the next morning he saw Mr. Bunce, and used all his eloquence to keep that respectable member of society at home;—but in vain. "What good do you expect to do, Mr. Bunce?" he said, with perhaps some little tone of authority in his voice.

"To carry my point," said Bunce.

"And what is your point?"

"My present point is the ballot, as a part of the Government measure."

"And you expect to carry that by going out into the streets with all the roughs of London, and putting yourself in direct opposition to the authority of the magistrates? Do you really believe that the ballot will become the law of the land any sooner because you incur this danger and inconvenience?"

"Look here, Mr. Finn; I don't believe the sea will become any fuller because the Piddle runs into it out of the Dorsetshire fields; but I do believe that the waters from all the countries is what makes the ocean. I shall help; and it's my duty to help."

"It's your duty as a respectable citizen, with a wife and family, to stay at home."

"If everybody with a wife and family was to say so, there'd be none there but roughs, and then where should we be? What would the Government people say to us then? If every man with a wife and family was to show hisself in the streets to-night, we should have the ballot before Parliament breaks up, and if none of 'em don't do it, we shall never have the ballot. Ain't that so?" Phineas, who intended to be honest, was not prepared to dispute the assertion on the spur of the moment. "If that's so," said Bunce, triumphantly, "a man's duty's clear enough. He ought to go, though he'd two wives and families." And he went.

The petition was to be presented at six o'clock, but the crowd, who collected to see it carried into Westminster Hall, began to form itself by noon. It was said afterwards that many of the houses in the neighbourhood of Palace Yard and the Bridge were filled with soldiers; but if so, the men did not show themselves. In the course of the evening three or four companies of the Guards in St. James's Park did show themselves, and had some rough work to do, for many of the people took themselves away from Westminster by that route. The police, who were very numerous in Palace Yard, had a hard time of it all the afternoon, and it was said afterwards that it would have been much better to have allowed the petition to have been brought up by the procession on Wednesday. A procession, let it be who it will that proceeds, has in it, of its own nature something of order. But now there was no order. The petition, which was said to fill fifteen cabs,—though the absolute sheets of signatures were carried into the House by four men,—was being dragged about half the day and it certainly would have been impossible for a member to have made his way into the House through Westminster Hall between the hours of four and six. To effect an entrance at all they were obliged to go round at the back of the Abbey, as all the spaces round St. Margaret's Church and Canning's monument were filled with the crowd. Parliament Street was quite impassable at five o clock, and there was no traffic across the bridge from that hour till after eight. As the evening went on, the mob extended itself to Downing Street and the front of the Treasury Chambers, and before the night was over all the hoardings round the new Government offices had been pulled down. The windows also of certain obnoxious members of Parliament were broken, when those obnoxious members lived within reach. One gentleman who unfortunately held a house in Richmond Terrace, and who was said to have said that the ballot was the resort of cowards, fared very badly;—for his windows were not only broken, but his furniture and mirrors were destroyed by the stones that were thrown. Mr. Mildmay, I say, was much blamed. But after all, it may be a doubt whether the procession on Wednesday might not have ended worse. Mr. Turnbull was heard to say afterwards that the number of people collected would have been much greater.

Mr. Mildmay moved the second reading of his bill, and made his speech. He made his speech with the knowledge that the Houses of Parliament were surrounded by a mob, and I think that the fact added to its efficacy. It certainly gave him an appropriate opportunity for a display which was not difficult. His voice faltered on two or three occasions, and faltered through real feeling; but this sort of feeling, though it be real, is at the command of orators on certain occasions, and does them yeoman's service. Mr. Mildmay was an old man, nearly worn out in the service of his country, who was known to have been true and honest, and to have loved his country well,—though there were of course they who declared that his hand had been too weak for power, and that his services had been naught;—and on this evening his virtues were remembered. Once when his voice failed him the whole House got up and cheered. The nature of a Whig Prime Minister's speech on such an occasion will be understood by most of my readers without further indication. The bill itself had been read before, and it was understood that no objection would be made to the extent of the changes provided in it by the liberal side of the House. The opposition coming from liberal members was to be confined to the subject of the ballot. And even as yet it was not known whether Mr. Turnbull and his followers would vote against the second reading, or whether they would take what was given, and declare their intention of obtaining the remainder on a separate motion. The opposition of a large party of Conservatives was a matter of certainty; but to this party Mr. Mildmay did not conceive himself bound to offer so large an amount of argument as he would have given had there been at the moment no crowd in Palace Yard. And he probably felt that that crowd would assist him with his old Tory enemies. When, in the last words of his speech, he declared that under no circumstances would he disfigure the close of his political career by voting for the ballot,—not though the people, on whose behalf he had been fighting battles all his life, should be there in any number to coerce him,—there came another round of applause from the opposition benches, and Mr. Daubeny began to fear that some young horses in his team might get loose from their traces. With great dignity Mr. Daubeny had kept aloof from Mr. Turnbull and from Mr. Turnbull's tactics; but he was not the less alive to the fact that Mr. Turnbull, with his mob and his big petition, might be of considerable assistance to him in this present duel between himself and Mr. Mildmay. I think Mr. Daubeny was in the habit of looking at these contests as duels between himself and the leader on the other side of the House,—in which assistance from any quarter might be accepted if offered.

Mr. Mildmay's speech did not occupy much over an hour, and at half-past seven Mr. Turnbull got up to reply. It was presumed that he would do so, and not a member left his place, though that time of the day is an interesting time, and though Mr. Turnbull was accustomed to be long. There soon came to be but little ground for doubting what would be the nature of Mr. Turnbull's vote on the second reading. "How may I dare," said he, "to accept so small a measure of reform as this with such a message from the country as is now conveyed to me through the presence of fifty thousand of my countrymen, who are at this moment demanding their measure of reform just beyond the frail walls of this chamber? The right honourable gentleman has told us that he will never be intimidated by a concourse of people. I do not know that there was any need that he should speak of intimidation. No one has accused the right honourable gentleman of political cowardice. But, as he has so said, I will follow in his footsteps. Neither will I be intimidated by the large majority which this House presented the other night against the wishes of the people. I will support no great measure of reform which does not include the ballot among its clauses." And so Mr. Turnbull threw down the gauntlet.

Mr. Turnbull spoke for two hours, and then the debate was adjourned till the Monday. The adjournment was moved by an independent member, who, as was known, would support the Government, and at once received Mr. Turnbull's assent. There was no great hurry with the bill, and it was felt that it would be well to let the ferment subside. Enough had been done for glory when Mr. Mildmay moved the second reading, and quite enough in the way of debate,—with such an audience almost within hearing,—when Mr. Turnbull's speech had been made. Then the House emptied itself at once. The elderly, cautious members made their exit through the peers' door. The younger men got out into the crowd through Westminster Hall, and were pushed about among the roughs for an hour or so. Phineas, who made his way through the hall with Laurence Fitzgibbon, found Mr. Turnbull's carriage waiting at the entrance with a dozen policemen round it.

"I hope he won't get home to dinner before midnight," said Phineas.

"He understands all about it," said Laurence. "He had a good meal at three, before he left home, and you'd find sandwiches and sherry in plenty if you were to search his carriage. He knows how to remedy the costs of mob popularity."

At that time poor Bunce was being hustled about in the crowd in the vicinity of Mr. Turnbull's carriage. Phineas and Fitzgibbon made their way out, and by degrees worked a passage for themselves into Parliament Street. Mr. Turnbull had been somewhat behind them in coming down the hall, and had not been without a sense of enjoyment in the ovation which was being given to him. There can be no doubt that he was wrong in what he was doing. That affair of the carriage was altogether wrong, and did Mr. Turnbull much harm for many a day afterwards. When he got outside the door, where were the twelve policemen guarding his carriage, a great number of his admirers endeavoured to shake hands with him. Among them was the devoted Bunce. But the policemen seemed to think that Mr. Turnbull was to be guarded, even from the affection of his friends, and were as careful that he should be ushered into his carriage untouched, as though he had been the favourite object of political aversion for the moment. Mr. Turnbull himself, when he began to perceive that men were crowding close upon the gates, and to hear the noise, and to feel, as it were, the breath of the mob, stepped on quickly into his carriage. He said a word or two in a loud voice. "Thank you, my friends. I trust you may obtain all your just demands." But he did not pause to speak. Indeed, he could hardly have done so, as the policemen were manifestly in a hurry. The carriage was got away at a snail's pace;—but there remained in the spot where the carriage had stood the makings of a very pretty street row.

Bunce had striven hard to shake hands with his hero,—Bunce and some other reformers as ardent and as decent as himself. The police were very determinate that there should be no such interruption to their programme for getting Mr. Turnbull off the scene. Mr. Bunce, who had his own ideas as to his right to shake hands with any gentleman at Westminster Hall who might choose to shake hands with him, became uneasy under the impediments that were placed in his way, and expressed himself warmly as to his civil rights. Now a London policeman in a political row is, I believe, the most forbearing of men. So long as he meets with no special political opposition, ordinary ill-usage does not even put him out of temper. He is paid for rough work among roughs, and takes his rubs gallantly. But he feels himself to be an instrument for the moment of despotic power as opposed to civil rights, and he won't stand what he calls "jaw." Trip up a policeman in such a scramble, and he will take it in good spirit; but mention the words "Habeas Corpus," and he'll lock you up if he can. As a rule, his instincts are right; for the man who talks about "Habeas Corpus" in a political crowd will generally do more harm than can be effected by the tripping up of any constable. But these instincts may be the means of individual injustice. I think they were so when Mr. Bunce was arrested and kept a fast prisoner. His wife had shown her knowledge of his character when she declared that he'd be "took" if any one was "took."

Bunce was taken into custody with some three or four others like himself,—decent men, who meant no harm, but who thought that as men they were bound to show their political opinions, perhaps at the expense of a little martyrdom,—and was carried into a temporary stronghold, which had been provided for the necessities of the police, under the clock-tower.

"Keep me, at your peril!" said Bunce, indignantly.

"We means it," said the sergeant who had him in custody.

"I've done no ha'porth to break the law," said Bunce.

"You was breaking the law when you was upsetting my men, as I saw you," said the sergeant.

"I've upset nobody," said Bunce.

"Very well," rejoined the sergeant; "you can say it all before the magistrate, to-morrow."

"And am I to be locked up all night?" said Bunce.

"I'm afraid you will," replied the sergeant.

Bunce, who was not by nature a very talkative man, said no more; but he swore in his heart that there should be vengeance. Between eleven and twelve he was taken to the regular police-station, and from thence he was enabled to send word to his wife.

"Bunce has been taken," said she, with something of the tragic queen, and something also of the injured wife in the tone of her voice, as soon as Phineas let himself in with the latchkey between twelve and one. And then, mingled with, and at last dominant over, those severer tones, came the voice of the loving woman whose beloved one was in trouble. "I knew how it'd be, Mr. Finn. Didn't I? And what must we do? I don't suppose he'd had a bit to eat from the moment he went out;—and as for a drop of beer, he never thinks of it, except what I puts down for him at his meals. Them nasty police always take the best. That's why I was so afeard."

Phineas said all that he could to comfort her, and promised to go to the police-office early in the morning and look after Bunce. No serious evil would, he thought, probably come of it; but still Bunce had been wrong to go.

"But you might have been took yourself," argued Mrs. Bunce, "just as well as he." Then Phineas explained that he had gone forth in the execution of a public duty. "You might have been took, all the same," said Mrs. Bunce, "for I'm sure Bunce didn't do nothing amiss."

CHAPTER XXVI

"The First Speech"

On the following morning, which was Saturday, Phineas was early at the police-office at Westminster looking after the interests of his landlord; but there had been a considerable number of men taken up during the row, and our friend could hardly procure that attention for Mr. Bunce's case to which he thought the decency of his client and his own position as a member of Parliament were entitled. The men who had been taken up were taken in batches before the magistrates; but as the soldiers in the park had been maltreated, and a considerable injury had been done in the neighbourhood of Downing Street, there was a good deal of strong feeling against the mob, and the magistrates were disposed to be severe. If decent men chose to go out among such companions, and thereby get into trouble, decent men must take the consequences. During the Saturday and Sunday a very strong feeling grew up against Mr. Turnbull. The story of the carriage was told, and he was declared to be a turbulent demagogue, only desirous of getting popularity. And together with this feeling there arose a general verdict of "Serve them right" against all who had come into contact with the police in the great Turnbull row; and thus it came to pass that Mr. Bunce had not been liberated up to the Monday morning. On the Sunday Mrs. Bunce was in hysterics, and declared her conviction that Mr. Bunce would be imprisoned for life. Poor Phineas had an unquiet time with her on the morning of that day. In every ecstasy of her grief she threw herself into his arms, either metaphorically or materially, according to the excess of her agony at the moment, and expressed repeatedly an assured conviction that all her children would die of starvation, and that she herself would be picked up under the arches of one of the bridges. Phineas, who was soft-hearted, did what he could to comfort her, and allowed himself to be worked up to strong parliamentary anger against the magistrates and police. "When they think that they have public opinion on their side, there is nothing in the way or arbitrary excess which is too great for them." This he said to Barrington Erle, who angered him and increased the warmth of his feeling by declaring that a little close confinement would be good for the Bunces of the day. "If we don't keep the mob down, the mob will keep us down," said the Whig private secretary. Phineas had no opportunity of answering this, but declared to himself that Barrington Erle was no more a Liberal at heart than was Mr. Daubeny. "He was born on that side of the question, and has been receiving Whig wages all his life. That is the history of his politics!"

On the Sunday afternoon Phineas went to Lord Brentford's in Portman Square, intending to say a word or two about Lord Chiltern, and meaning also to induce, if possible, the Cabinet Minister to take part with him against the magistrates,—having a hope also, in which he was not disappointed, that he might find Lady Laura Kennedy with her father. He had come to understand that Lady Laura was not to be visited at her own house on Sundays. So much indeed she had told him in so many words. But he had come to understand also, without any plain telling, that she rebelled in heart against this Sabbath tyranny,—and that she would escape from it when escape was possible. She had now come to talk to her father about her brother, and had brought Violet Effingham with her. They had walked together across the park after church, and intended to walk back again. Mr. Kennedy did not like to have any carriage out on a Sunday, and to this arrangement his wife made no objection.

Phineas had received a letter from the Stamford surgeon, and was able to report favourably of Lord Chiltern. "The man says that he had better not be moved for a month," said Phineas. "But that means nothing. They always say that."

"Will it not be best for him to remain where he is?" said the Earl.

"He has not a soul to speak to," said Phineas.

"I wish I were with him," said his sister.

"That is, of course, out of the question," said the Earl. "They know him at that inn, and it really seems to me best that he should stay there. I do not think he would be so much at his ease here."

"It must be dreadful for a man to be confined to his room without a creature near him, except the servants," said Violet. The Earl frowned, but said nothing further. They all perceived that as soon as he had learned that there was no real danger as to his son's life, he was determined that this accident should not work him up to any show of tenderness. "I do so hope he will come up to London," continued Violet, who was not afraid of the Earl, and was determined not to be put down.

"You don't know what you are talking about, my dear," said Lord Brentford.

After this Phineas found it very difficult to extract any sympathy from the Earl on behalf of the men who had been locked up. He was moody and cross, and could not be induced to talk on the great subject of the day. Violet Effingham declared that she did not care how many Bunces were locked up; nor for how long,—adding, however, a wish that Mr. Turnbull himself had been among the number of the prisoners. Lady Laura was somewhat softer than this, and consented to express pity in the case of Mr. Bunce himself; but Phineas perceived that the pity was awarded to him and not to the sufferer. The feeling against Mr. Turnbull was at the present moment so strong among all the upper classes, that Mr. Bunce and his brethren might have been kept in durance for a week without commiseration from them.

"It is very hard certainly on a man like Mr. Bunce," said Lady Laura.

"Why did not Mr. Bunce stay at home and mind his business?" said the Earl.

Phineas spent the remainder of that day alone, and came to a resolution that on the coming occasion he certainly would speak in the House. The debate would be resumed on the Monday, and he would rise to his legs on the very first moment that it became possible for him to do so. And he would do nothing towards preparing a speech;—nothing whatever. On this occasion he would trust entirely to such words as might come to him at the moment;—ay, and to such thoughts. He had before burdened his memory with preparations, and the very weight of the burden had been too much for his mind. He had feared to trust himself to speak, because he had felt that he was not capable of performing the double labour of saying his lesson by heart, and of facing the House for the first time. There should be nothing now for him to remember. His thoughts were full of his subject. He would support Mr. Mildmay's bill with all his eloquence, but he would implore Mr. Mildmay, and the Home Secretary, and the Government generally, to abstain from animosity against the populace of London, because they desired one special boon which Mr. Mildmay did not think that it was his duty to give them. He hoped that ideas and words would come to him. Ideas and words had been free enough with him in the old days of the Dublin debating society. If they failed him now, he must give the thing up, and go back to Mr. Low.

On the Monday morning Phineas was for two hours at the police-court in Westminster, and at about one on that day Mr. Bunce was liberated. When he was brought up before the magistrate, Mr. Bunce spoke his mind very freely as to the usage he had received, and declared his intention of bringing an action against the sergeant who had detained him. The magistrate, of course, took the part of the police, and declared that, from the evidence of two men who were examined, Bunce had certainly used such violence in the crowd as had justified his arrest.

"I used no violence," said Bunce.

"According to your own showing, you endeavoured to make your way up to Mr. Turnbull's carriage," said the magistrate.

"I was close to the carriage before the police even saw me," said Bunce.

"But you tried to force your way round to the door."

"I used no force till a man had me by the collar to push me back; and I wasn't violent, not then. I told him I was doing what I had a right to do,—and it was that as made him hang on to me."

"You were not doing what you had a right to do. You were assisting to create a riot," said the magistrate, with that indignation which a London magistrate should always know how to affect.

Phineas, however, was allowed to give evidence as to his landlord's character, and then Bunce was liberated. But before he went he again swore that that should not be the last of it, and he told the magistrate that he had been ill-used. When liberated, he was joined by a dozen sympathising friends, who escorted him home, and among them were one or two literary gentlemen, employed on those excellent penny papers, the *People's Banner* and the *Ballot-box*. It was their intention that Mr. Bunce's case should not be allowed to sleep. One of these gentlemen made a distinct offer to Phineas Finn of unbounded popularity during life and of immortality afterwards, if he, as a member of Parliament, would take up Bunce's case with vigour. Phineas, not quite understanding the nature of the offer, and not as yet knowing the profession of the gentleman, gave some general reply.

"You come out strong, Mr. Finn, and we'll see that you are properly reported. I'm on the *Banner*, sir, and I'll answer for that."

Phineas, who had been somewhat eager in expressing his sympathy with Bunce, and had not given very close attention to the gentleman who was addressing him, was still in the dark. The nature of the *Banner*, which the gentleman was on, did not at once come home to him.

"Something ought to be done, certainly," said Phineas.

"We shall take it up strong," said the gentleman, "and we shall be happy to have you among us. You'll find, Mr. Finn, that in public life there's nothing like having a horgan to back you. What is the most you can do in the 'Ouse? Nothing, if you're not reported. You're speaking to the country;—ain't you? And you can't do that without a horgan, Mr. Finn. You come among us on the *Banner*, Mr. Finn. You can't do better."

Then Phineas understood the nature of the offer made to him. As they parted, the literary gentleman gave our hero his card. "Mr. Quintus Slide." So much was printed. Then, on the corner of the card was written, "*Banner* Office, 137, Fetter Lane." Mr. Quintus Slide was a young man, under thirty, not remarkable for clean linen, and who always talked of the "'Ouse." But he was a well-known and not undistinguished member of a powerful class of men. He had been a reporter, and as such knew the "'Ouse" well, and was a writer for the press. And, though he talked of "'Ouses" and "horgans", he wrote good English with great rapidity, and was possessed of that special sort of political fervour which shows itself in a man's work rather than in his conduct. It was Mr. Slide's taste to be an advanced reformer, and in all his operations on behalf of the *People's Banner* he was a reformer very much advanced. No man could do an article on the people's indefeasible rights with more pronounced vigour than Mr. Slide. But it had never occurred to him as yet that he ought to care for anything else than the fight,—than the advantage of having a good subject on which to write slashing articles. Mr. Slide was an energetic but not a thoughtful man; but in his thoughts on politics, as far as they went with him, he regarded the wrongs of the people as being of infinitely greater value than their rights. It was not that he was insincere in all that he was daily saying;—but simply that he never thought about it. Very early in life he had fallen among "people's friends," and an opening on the liberal press had come in his way. To be a "people's friend" suited the turn of his ambition, and he was a "people's friend." It was his business to abuse Government, and to express on all occasions an opinion that as a matter of course the ruling powers were the "people's enemies." Had the ruling powers ceased to be the "people's enemies," Mr. Slide's ground would have been taken from under his feet. But such a catastrophe was out of the question. That excellent old arrangement that had gone on since demagogues were first invented was in full vigour. There were the ruling powers and there were the people,—devils on one side and angels on the other,—and as long as a people's friend had a pen in his hand all was right.

Phineas, when he left the indignant Bunce to go among his friends, walked to the House thinking a good deal of what Mr. Slide had said to him. The potted peas Committee was again on, and he had intended to be in the Committee Room by twelve punctually: but he had been unable to leave Mr. Bunce in the lurch, and it was now past one. Indeed, he had, from one unfortunate circumstance after another, failed hitherto in giving to the potted peas that resolute attention which the subject demanded. On the present occasion his mind was full of Mr. Quintus Slide and the *People's Banner*. After all, was there not something in Mr. Slide's proposition? He, Phineas, had come into Parliament as it were under the wing of a Government pack, and his friendships, which had been very successful, had been made with Ministers, and with the friends of Ministers. He had made up his mind to be Whig Ministerial, and to look for his profession in that line. He had been specially fortified in this resolution by his dislike to the ballot,—which dislike had been the result of Mr. Monk's teaching. Had Mr. Turnbull become his friend instead, it may well be that he would have liked the ballot. On such subjects men must think long, and be sure that they have thought in earnest, before they are justified in saying that their opinions are the results of their own thoughts. But now he began to reflect how far this ministerial profession would suit him. Would it be much to be a Lord of the Treasury, subject to the dominion of Mr. Ratler? Such lordship and such subjection would be the result of success. He told himself that he was at heart a true Liberal. Would it not be better for him to abandon the idea of office trammels, and go among them on the *People's Banner*? A glow of enthusiasm came over him as he thought of it. But what would Violet Effingham say to the *People's Banner* and Mr. Quintus Slide? And he would have liked the *Banner* better had not Mr. Slide talked about the 'Ouse.

From the Committee Room, in which, alas! he took no active part in reference to the potted peas, he went down to the House, and was present when the debate was resumed. Not unnaturally, one speaker after another made some allusion to the row in the streets, and the work which had fallen to the lot of the magistrates. Mr. Turnbull had declared that he would vote against the second reading of Mr. Mildmay's bill, and had explained that he would do so because he could consent to no Reform Bill which did not include the ballot as one of its measures. The debate fashioned itself after this speech of Mr. Turnbull's, and turned again very much upon the ballot,—although it had been thought that the late debate had settled that question. One or two of Mr. Turnbull's followers declared that they also would vote against the bill,—of course, as not going far enough; and one or two gentlemen from the Conservative benches extended a spoken welcome to these new colleagues. Then Mr. Palliser got up and addressed the House for an hour, struggling hard to bring back the real subject, and to make the House understand that the ballot, whether good or bad, had been knocked on the head, and that members had no right at the present moment to consider anything but the expediency or inexpediency of so much Reform as Mr. Mildmay presented to them in the present bill.

Phineas was determined to speak, and to speak on this evening if he could catch the Speaker's eye. Again the scene before him was going round before him; again things became dim, and again he felt his blood beating hard at his heart. But things were not so bad with him as they had been before, because he had nothing to remember. He hardly knew, indeed, what he intended to say. He had an idea that he was desirous of joining in earnest support of the measure, with a vehement protest against the injustice which had been done to the people in general, and to Mr. Bunce in particular. He had firmly resolved that no fear of losing favour with the Government should induce him to hold his tongue as to the Buncean cruelties. Sooner than do so he would certainly "go among them" at the *Banner* office.

He started up, wildly, when Mr. Palliser had completed his speech; but the Speaker's eye, not unnaturally, had travelled to the other side of the House, and there was a Tory of the old school upon his legs,—Mr. Western, the member for East Barsetshire, one of the gallant few who dared to vote against Sir Robert Peel's bill for repealing the Corn Laws in 1846. Mr. Western spoke with a slow, ponderous, unimpressive, but very audible voice, for some twenty minutes, disdaining to make reference to Mr. Turnbull and his politics, but pleading against any Reform, with all the old arguments. Phineas did not hear a word that he said;—did not attempt to hear. He was keen in his resolution to make another attempt at the Speaker's eye, and at the present moment was thinking of that, and of that only. He did not even give himself a moment's reflection as to what his own speech should be. He would dash at it and take his chance, resolved that at least he would not fail in courage. Twice he was on his legs before Mr. Western had finished his slow harangue, and twice he was compelled to reseat himself,—thinking that he had subjected himself to ridicule. At last the member for East Barset sat down, and Phineas was conscious that he had lost a moment or two in presenting himself again to the Speaker.

He held his ground, however, though he saw that he had various rivals for the right of speech. He held his ground, and was instantly aware that he had gained his point. There was a slight pause, and as some other urgent member did not reseat himself, Phineas heard the president of that august assembly call upon himself to address the House. The thing was now to be done. There he was with the House of Commons at his feet,—a crowded House, bound to be his auditors as long as he should think fit to address them, and reporters by tens and twenties in the gallery ready and eager to let the country know what the young member for Loughshane would say in this his maiden speech.

Phineas Finn had sundry gifts, a powerful and pleasant voice, which he had learned to modulate, a handsome presence, and a certain natural mixture of modesty and self-reliance, which would certainly protect him from the faults of arrogance and pomposity, and which, perhaps, might carry him through the perils of his new position. And he had also the great advantage of friends in the House who were anxious that he should do well. But he had not that gift of slow blood which on the former occasion would have enabled him to remember his prepared speech, and which would now have placed all his own resources within his own reach. He began with the expression of an opinion that every true reformer ought to accept Mr. Mildmay's bill, even if it were accepted only as an instalment,—but before he had got through these sentences, he became painfully conscious that he was repeating his own words.

He was cheered almost from the outset, and yet he knew as he went on that he was failing. He had certain arguments at his fingers' ends,— points with which he was, in truth, so familiar that he need hardly have troubled himself to arrange them for special use,—and he forgot even these. He found that he was going on with one platitude after another as to the benefit of reform, in a manner that would have shamed him six or seven years ago at a debating club. He pressed on, fearing that words would fail him altogether if he paused;—but he did in truth speak very much too fast, knocking his words together so that no reporter could properly catch them. But he had nothing to say for the bill except what hundreds had said before, and hundreds would say again. Still he was cheered, and still he went on; and as he became more and more conscious of his failure there grew upon him the idea,—the dangerous hope, that he might still save himself from ignominy by the eloquence of his invective against the police.

He tried it, and succeeded thoroughly in making the House understand that he was very angry,—but he succeeded in nothing else. He could not catch the words to express the thoughts of his mind. He could not explain his idea that the people out of the House had as much right to express their opinion in favour of the ballot as members in the House had to express theirs against it; and that animosity had been shown to the people by the authorities because they had so expressed their opinion. Then he attempted to tell the story of Mr. Bunce in a light and airy way, failed, and sat down in the middle of it. Again he was cheered by all around him,—cheered as a new member is usually cheered,—and in the midst of the cheer would have blown out his brains had there been a pistol there ready for such an operation.

That hour with him was very bad. He did not know how to get up and go away, or how to keep his place. For some time he sat with his hat off, forgetful of his privilege of wearing it; and then put it on hurriedly, as though the fact of his not wearing it must have been observed by everybody. At last, at about two, the debate was adjourned, and then as he was slowly leaving the House, thinking how he might creep away without companionship, Mr. Monk took him by the arm.

"Are you going to walk?" said Mr. Monk.

"Yes", said Phineas; "I shall walk."

"Then we may go together as far as Pall Mall. Come along." Phineas had no means of escape, and left the House hanging on Mr. Monk's arm, without a word. Nor did Mr. Monk speak till they were out in Palace Yard. "It was not much amiss," said Mr. Monk; "but you'll do better than that yet."

"Mr. Monk," said Phineas, "I have made an ass of myself so thoroughly, that there will at any rate be this good result, that I shall never make an ass of myself again after the same fashion."

"Ah!—I thought you had some such feeling as that, and therefore I was determined to speak to you. You may be sure, Finn, that I do not care to flatter you, and I think you ought to know that, as far as I am able, I will tell you the truth. Your speech, which was certainly nothing great, was about on a par with other maiden speeches in the House of Commons. You have done yourself neither good nor harm. Nor was it desirable that you should. My advice to you now is, never to avoid speaking on any subject that interests you, but never to speak for above three minutes till you find yourself as much at home on your legs as you are when sitting. But do not suppose that you have made an ass of yourself,—that is, in any special degree. Now, good-night."

CHAPTER XXVII
Phineas Discussed

Lady Laura Kennedy heard two accounts of her friend's speech,—and both from men who had been present. Her husband was in his place, in accordance with his constant practice, and Lord Brentford had been seated, perhaps unfortunately, in the peers' gallery.

"And you think it was a failure?" Lady Laura said to her husband.

"It certainly was not a success. There was nothing particular about it. There was a good deal of it you could hardly hear."

After that she got the morning newspapers, and turned with great interest to the report. Phineas Finn had been, as it were, adopted by her as her own political offspring,—or at any rate as her political godchild. She had made promises on his behalf to various personages of high political standing,—to her father, to Mr. Monk, to the Duke of St. Bungay, and even to Mr. Mildmay himself. She had thoroughly intended that Phineas Finn should be a political success from the first; and since her marriage, she had, I think, been more intent upon it than before. Perhaps there was a feeling on her part that having wronged him in one way, she would repay him in another. She had become so eager for his success,—for a while scorning to conceal her feeling,—that her husband had unconsciously begun to entertain a dislike to her eagerness. We know how quickly women arrive at an understanding of the feelings of those with whom they live; and now, on that very occasion, Lady Laura perceived that her husband did not take in good part her anxiety on behalf of her friend. She saw that it was so as she turned over the newspaper looking for the report of the speech. It was given in six lines, and at the end of it there was an intimation,—expressed in the shape of advice,—that the young orator had better speak more slowly if he wished to be efficacious either with the House or with the country.

"He seems to have been cheered a good deal," said Lady Laura.

"All members are cheered at their first speech," said Mr. Kennedy.

"I've no doubt he'll do well yet," said Lady Laura.

"Very likely," said Mr. Kennedy. Then he turned to his newspaper, and did not take his eyes off it as long as his wife remained with him.

Later in the day Lady Laura saw her father, and Miss Effingham was with her at the time. Lord Brentford said something which indicated that he had heard the debate on the previous evening, and Lady Laura instantly began to ask him about Phineas.

"The less said the better," was the Earl's reply.

"Do you mean that it was so bad as that?" asked Lady Laura.

"It was not very bad at first;—though indeed nobody could say it was very good. But he got himself into a mess about the police and the magistrates before he had done, and nothing but the kindly feeling always shown to a first effort saved him from being coughed down." Lady Laura had not a word more to say about Phineas to her father; but, womanlike, she resolved that she would not abandon him. How many first failures in the world had been the precursors of ultimate success! "Mildmay will lose his bill," said the Earl, sorrowfully. "There does not seem to be a doubt about that."

"And what will you all do?" asked Lady Laura.

"We must go to the country, I suppose," said the Earl.

"What's the use? You can't have a more liberal House than you have now," said Lady Laura.

"We may have one less liberal,—or rather less radical,—with fewer men to support Mr. Turnbull. I do not see what else we can do. They say that there are no less than twenty-seven men on our side of the House who will either vote with Turnbull against us, or will decline to vote at all."

"Every one of them ought to lose his seat," said Lady Laura.

"But what can we do? How is the Queen's Government to be carried on?" We all know the sad earnestness which impressed itself on the Earl's brow as he asked these momentous questions. "I don't suppose that Mr. Turnbull can form a Ministry."

"With Mr. Daubeny as whipper-in, perhaps he might," said Lady Laura.

"And will Mr. Finn lose his seat?" asked Violet Effingham. "Most probably," said the Earl. "He only got it by an accident."

"You must find him a seat somewhere in England," said Violet.

"That might be difficult," said the Earl, who then left the room.

The two women remained together for some quarter of an hour before they spoke again. Then Lady Laura said something about her brother. "If there be a dissolution, I hope Oswald will stand for Loughton." Loughton was a borough close to Saulsby, in which, as regarded its political interests, Lord Brentford was supposed to have considerable influence. To this Violet said nothing. "It is quite time," continued Lady Laura, "that old Mr. Standish should give way. He has had the seat for twenty-five years, and has never done anything, and he seldom goes to the House now."

"He is not your uncle, is he?"

"No; he is papa's cousin; but he is ever so much older than papa;—nearly eighty, I believe."

"Would not that be just the place for Mr. Finn?" said Violet.

Then Lady Laura became very serious. "Oswald would of course have a better right to it than anybody else."

"But would Lord Chiltern go into Parliament? I have heard him declare that he would not."

"If we could get papa to ask him, I think he would change his mind," said Lady Laura.

There was again silence for a few moments, after which Violet returned to the original subject of their conversation. "It would be a thousand pities that Mr. Finn should be turned out into the cold. Don't you think so?"

"I, for one, should be very sorry."

"So should I,—and the more so from what Lord Brentford says about his not speaking well last night. I don't think that it is very much of an accomplishment for a gentleman to speak well. Mr. Turnbull, I suppose, speaks well; and they say that that horrid man, Mr. Bonteen, can talk by the hour together. I don't think that it shows a man to be clever at all. But I believe Mr. Finn would do it, if he set his mind to it, and I shall think it a great shame if they turn him out."

"It would depend very much, I suppose, on Lord Tulla."

"I don't know anything about Lord Tulla," said Violet; "but I'm quite sure that he might have Loughton, if we manage it properly. Of course Lord Chiltern should have it if he wants it, but I don't think he will stand in Mr. Finn's way."

"I'm afraid it's out of the question," said Lady Laura, gravely. "Papa thinks so much about the borough." The reader will remember that both Lord Brentford and his daughter were thorough reformers! The use of a little borough of his own, however, is a convenience to a great peer.

"Those difficult things have always to be talked of for a long while, and then they become easy," said Violet. "I believe if you were to propose to Mr. Kennedy to give all his property to the Church Missionaries and emigrate to New Zealand, he'd begin to consider it seriously after a time."

"I shall not try, at any rate."

"Because you don't want to go to New Zealand;—but you might try about Loughton for poor Mr. Finn."

"Violet," said Lady Laura, after a moment's pause;—and she spoke sharply; "Violet, I believe you are in love with Mr. Finn."

"That's just like you, Laura."

"I never made such an accusation against you before, or against anybody else that I can remember. But I do begin to believe that you are in love with Mr. Finn."

"Why shouldn't I be in love with him, if I like?"

"I say nothing about that;—only he has not got a penny."

"But I have, my dear."

"And I doubt whether you have any reason for supposing that he is in love with you."

"That would be my affair, my dear."

"Then you are in love with him?"

"That is my affair also."

Lady Laura shrugged her shoulders. "Of course it is; and if you tell me to hold my tongue, of course I will do so. If you ask me whether I think it a good match, of course I must say I do not."

"I don't tell you to hold your tongue, and I don't ask you what you think about the match. You are quite welcome to talk as much about me as you please;—but as to Mr. Phineas Finn, you have no business to think anything."

"I shouldn't talk to anybody but yourself."

"I am growing to be quite indifferent as to what people say. Lady Baldock asked me the other day whether I was going to throw myself away on Mr. Laurence Fitzgibbon."

"No!"

"Indeed she did."

"And what did you answer?"

"I told her that it was not quite settled; but that as I had only spoken to him once during the last two years, and then for not more than half a minute, and as I wasn't sure whether I knew him by sight, and as I had reason to suppose he didn't know my name, there might, perhaps, be a delay of a week or two before the thing came off. Then she flounced out of the room."

"But what made her ask about Mr. Fitzgibbon?"

"Somebody had been hoaxing her. I am beginning to think that Augusta does it for her private amusement. If so, I shall think more highly of my dear cousin than I have hitherto done. But, Laura, as you have made a similar accusation against me, and as I cannot get out of it with you as I do with my aunt, I must ask you to hear my protestation. I am not in love with Mr. Phineas Finn. Heaven help me;—as far as I can tell, I am not in love with any one, and never shall be." Lady Laura looked pleased. "Do you know," continued Violet, "that I think I could be in love with Mr. Phineas Finn, if I could be in love with anybody?" Then Lady Laura looked displeased. "In the first place, he is a gentleman," continued Violet. "Then he is a man of spirit. And then he has not too much spirit;—not that kind of spirit which makes some men think that they are the finest things going. His manners are perfect;—not Chesterfieldian, and yet never offensive. He never browbeats any one, and never toadies any one. He knows how to live easily with men of all ranks, without any appearance of claiming a special status for himself. If he were made Archbishop of Canterbury to-morrow, I believe he would settle down into the place of the first subject in the land without arrogance, and without false shame."

"You are his eulogist with a vengeance."

"I am his eulogist; but I am not in love with him. If he were to ask me to be his wife to-morrow, I should be distressed, and should refuse him. If he were to marry my dearest friend in the world, I should tell him to kiss me and be my brother. As to Mr. Phineas Finn,—those are my sentiments."

"What you say is very odd."

"Why odd?"

"Simply because mine are the same."

"Are they the same? I once thought, Laura, that you did love him;—that you meant to be his wife."

Lady Laura sat for a while without making any reply to this. She sat with her elbow on the table and with her face leaning on her hand,—thinking how far it would tend to her comfort if she spoke in true confidence. Violet during the time never took her eyes from her friend's face, but remained silent as though waiting for an answer. She had been very explicit as to her feelings. Would Laura Kennedy be equally explicit? She was too clever to forget that such plainness of speech would be, must be more difficult to Lady Laura than to herself. Lady Laura was a married woman; but she felt that her friend would have been wrong to search for secrets, unless she were ready to tell her own. It was probably some such feeling which made Lady Laura speak at last.

"So I did, nearly—" said Lady Laura; "very nearly. You told me just now that you had money, and could therefore do as you pleased. I had no money, and could not do as I pleased."

"And you told me also that I had no reason for thinking that he cared for me."

"Did I? Well;—I suppose you have no reason. He did care for me. He did love me."

"He told you so?"

"Yes;—he told me so."

"And how did you answer him?"

"I had that very morning become engaged to Mr. Kennedy. That was my answer."

"And what did he say when you told him?"

"I do not know. I cannot remember. But he behaved very well."

"And now,—if he were to love me, you would grudge me his love?"

"Not for that reason,—not if I know myself. Oh no! I would not be so selfish as that."

"For what reason then?"

"Because I look upon it as written in heaven that you are to be Oswald's wife."

"Heaven's writings then are false," said Violet, getting up and walking away.

In the meantime Phineas was very wretched at home. When he reached his lodgings after leaving the House,—after his short conversation with Mr. Monk,—he tried to comfort himself with what that gentleman had said to him. For a while, while he was walking, there had been some comfort in Mr. Monk's words. Mr. Monk had much experience, and doubtless knew what he was saying,—and there might yet be hope. But all this hope faded away when Phineas was in his own rooms. There came upon him, as he looked round them, an idea that he had no business to be in Parliament, that he was an impostor, that he was going about the world under false pretences, and that he would never set himself aright, even unto himself, till he had gone through some terrible act of humiliation. He had been a cheat even to Mr. Quintus Slide of the *Banner*, in accepting an invitation to come among them. He had been a cheat to Lady Laura, in that he had induced her to think that he was fit to live with her. He was a cheat to Violet Effingham, in assuming that he was capable of making himself agreeable to her. He was a cheat to Lord Chiltern when riding his horses, and pretending to be a proper associate for a man of fortune. Why,—what was his income? What his birth? What his proper position? And now he had got the reward which all cheats deserve. Then he went to bed, and as he lay there, he thought of Mary Flood Jones. Had he plighted his troth to Mary, and then worked like a slave under Mr. Low's auspices,—he would not have been a cheat.

It seemed to him that he had hardly been asleep when the girl came into his room in the morning. "Sir," said she, "there's that gentleman there."

"What gentleman?"

"The old gentleman."

Then Phineas knew that Mr. Clarkson was in his sitting-room, and that he would not leave it till he had seen the owner of the room. Nay,—Phineas was pretty sure that Mr. Clarkson would come into the bedroom, if he were kept long waiting. "Damn the old gentleman," said Phineas in his wrath;—and the maid-servant heard him say so.

In about twenty minutes he went out into the sitting-room, with his slippers on and in his dressing-gown. Suffering under the circumstances of such an emergency, how is any man to go through the work of dressing and washing with proper exactness? As to the prayers which he said on that morning, I think that no question should be asked. He came out with a black cloud on his brow, and with his mind half made up to kick Mr. Clarkson out of the room. Mr. Clarkson, when he saw him, moved his chin round within his white cravat, as was a custom with him, and put his thumb and forefinger on his lips, and then shook his head.

"Very bad, Mr. Finn; very bad indeed; very bad, ain't it?"

"You coming here in this way at all times in the day is very bad," said Phineas.

"And where would you have me go? Would you like to see me down in the lobby of the House?"

"To tell you the truth, Mr. Clarkson, I don't want to see you anywhere."

"Ah; yes; I daresay! And that's what you call honest, being a Parliament gent! You had my money, and then you tell me you don't want to see me any more!"

"I have not had your money," said Phineas.

"But let me tell you," continued Mr. Clarkson, "that I want to see you;—and shall go on seeing you till the money is paid."

"I've not had any of your money," said Phineas.

Mr. Clarkson again twitched his chin about on the top of his cravat and smiled. "Mr. Finn," said he, showing the bill, "is that your name?"

"Yes, it is."

"Then I want my money."

"I have no money to give you."

"Do be punctual now. Why ain't you punctual? I'd do anything for you if you were punctual. I would indeed." Mr. Clarkson, as he said this, sat down in the chair which had been placed for our hero's breakfast, and cutting a slice off the loaf, began to butter it with great composure.

"Mr. Clarkson," said Phineas, "I cannot ask you to breakfast here. I am engaged."

"I'll just take a bit of bread and butter all the same," said Clarkson. "Where do you get your butter? Now I could tell you a woman who'd give it you cheaper and a deal better than this. This is all lard. Shall I send her to you?"

"No," said Phineas. There was no tea ready, and therefore Mr. Clarkson emptied the milk into a cup and drank it. "After this," said Phineas, "I must beg, Mr. Clarkson, that you will never come to my room any more. I shall not be at home to you."

"The lobby of the House is the same thing to me," said Mr. Clarkson. "They know me there well. I wish you'd be punctual, and then we'd be the best of friends." After that Mr. Clarkson, having finished his bread and butter, took his leave.

CHAPTER XXVIII
The Second Reading Is Carried

The debate on the bill was prolonged during the whole of that week. Lord Brentford, who loved his seat in the Cabinet and the glory of being a Minister, better even than he loved his borough, had taken a gloomy estimate when he spoke of twenty-seven defaulters, and of the bill as certainly lost. Men who were better able than he to make estimates,—the Bonteens and Fitzgibbons on each side of the House, and above all, the Ratlers and Robys, produced lists from day to day which varied now by three names in one direction, then by two in another, and which fluctuated at last by units only. They all concurred in declaring that it would be a very near division. A great effort was made to close the debate on the Friday, but it failed, and the full tide of speech was carried on till the following Monday. On that morning Phineas heard Mr. Ratler declare at the club that, as far as his judgment went, the division at that moment was a fair subject for a bet. "There are two men doubtful in the House," said Ratler, "and if one votes on one side and one on the other, or if neither votes at all, it will be a tie." Mr. Roby, however, the whip on the other side, was quite sure that one at least of these gentlemen would go into his lobby, and that the other would not go into Mr. Ratler's lobby. I am inclined to think that the town was generally inclined to put more confidence in the accuracy of Mr. Roby than in that of Mr. Ratler; and among betting men there certainly was a point given by those who backed the Conservatives. The odds, however, were lost, for on the division the numbers in the two lobbies were equal, and the Speaker gave his casting vote in favour of the Government. The bill was read a second time, and was lost, as a matter of course, in reference to any subsequent action. Mr. Roby declared that even Mr. Mildmay could not go on with nothing but the Speaker's vote to support him. Mr. Mildmay had no doubt felt that he could not go on with his bill from the moment in which Mr. Turnbull had declared his opposition; but he could not with propriety withdraw it in deference to Mr. Turnbull's opinion.

During the week Phineas had had his hands sufficiently full. Twice he had gone to the potted peas inquiry; but he had been at the office of the *People's Banner* more often than that. Bunce had been very resolute in his determination to bring an action against the police for false imprisonment, even though he spent every shilling of his savings in doing so. And when his wife, in the presence of Phineas, begged that bygones might be bygones, reminding him that spilt milk could not be recovered, he called her a mean-spirited woman. Then Mrs. Bunce wept a flood of tears, and told her favourite lodger that for her all comfort in this world was over. "Drat the reformers, I say. And I wish there was no Parliament; so I do. What's the use of all the voting, when it means nothing but dry bread and cross words?" Phineas by no means encouraged his landlord in his litigious spirit, advising him rather to keep his money in his pocket, and leave the fighting of the battle to the columns of the *Banner*,—which would fight it, at any rate, with economy. But Bunce, though he delighted in the *Banner*, and showed an unfortunate readiness to sit at the feet of Mr. Quintus Slide, would have his action at law;—in which resolution Mr. Slide did, I fear, encourage him behind the back of his better friend, Phineas Finn.

Phineas went with Bunce to Mr. Low's chambers,—for Mr. Low had in some way become acquainted with the law-stationer's journeyman,—and there some very good advice was given. "Have you asked yourself what is your object, Mr. Bunce?" said Mr. Low. Mr. Bunce declared he had asked himself that question, and had answered it. His object was redress. "In the shape of compensation to yourself," suggested Mr. Low. No; Mr. Bunce would not admit that he personally required any compensation. The redress wanted was punishment to the man. "Is it for vengeance?" asked Mr. Low. No; it was not for vengeance, Mr. Bunce declared. "It ought not to be," continued Mr. Low; "because, though you think that the man exceeded in his duty, you must feel that he was doing so through no personal ill-will to yourself."

"What I want is, to have the fellows kept in their proper places," said Mr. Bunce.

"Exactly;—and therefore these things, when they occur, are mentioned in the press and in Parliament,—and the attention of a Secretary of State is called to them. Thank God, we don't have very much of that kind of thing in England."

"Maybe we shall have more if we don't look to it," said Bunce stoutly.

"We always are looking to it," said Mr. Low;—"looking to it very carefully. But I don't think anything is to be done in that way by indictment against a single man, whose conduct has been already approved by the magistrates. If you want notoriety, Mr. Bunce, and don't mind what you pay for it; or have got anybody else to pay for it; then indeed—"

"There ain't nobody to pay for it," said Bunce, waxing angry.

"Then I certainly should not pay for it myself if I were you," said Mr. Low.

But Bunce was not to be counselled out of his intention. When he was out in the square with Phineas he expressed great anger against Mr. Low. "He don't know what patriotism means," said the law scrivener. "And then he talks to me about notoriety! It has always been the same way with 'em. If a man shows a spark of public feeling, it's all hambition. I don't want no notoriety. I wants to earn my bread peaceable, and to be let alone when I'm about my own business. I pays rates for the police to look after rogues, not to haul folks about and lock 'em up for days and nights, who is doing what they has a legal right to do." After that, Bunce went to his attorney, to the great detriment of the business at the stationer's shop, and Phineas visited the office of the *People's Banner*. There he wrote a leading article about Bunce's case, for which he was in due time to be paid a guinea. After all, the *People's Banner* might do more for him in this way than ever would be done by Parliament. Mr. Slide, however, and another gentleman at the *Banner* office, much older than Mr. Slide, who announced himself as the actual editor, were anxious that Phineas should rid himself of his heterodox political resolutions about the ballot. It was not that they cared much about his own opinions; and when Phineas attempted to argue with the editor on the merits of the ballot, the editor put him down very shortly. "We go in for it, Mr. Finn," he said. If Mr. Finn would go in for it too, the editor seemed to think that Mr. Finn might make himself very useful at the *Banner* Office. Phineas stoutly maintained that this was impossible,—and was therefore driven to confine his articles in the service of the people to those open subjects on which his opinions agreed with those of the *People's Banner*. This was his second article, and the editor seemed to think that, backward as he was about the ballot, he was too useful an aid to be thrown aside. A member of Parliament is not now all that he was once, but still there is a prestige in the letters affixed to his name which makes him loom larger in the eyes of the world than other men. Get into Parliament, if it be but for the borough of Loughshane, and the *People's Banners* all round will be glad of your assistance, as will also companies limited and unlimited to a very marvellous extent. Phineas wrote his article and promised to look in again, and so they went on. Mr. Quintus Slide continued to assure him that a "horgan" was indispensable to him, and Phineas began to accommodate his ears to the sound which had at first been so disagreeable. He found that his acquaintance, Mr. Slide, had ideas of his own as to getting into the 'Ouse at some future time. "I always look upon the 'Ouse as my oyster, and 'ere's my sword," said Mr. Slide, brandishing an old quill pen. "And I feel that if once there I could get along. I do indeed. What is it a man wants? It's only pluck,—that he shouldn't funk because a 'undred other men are looking at him." Then Phineas asked him whether he had any idea of a constituency, to which Mr. Slide replied that he had no absolutely formed intention. Many boroughs, however, would doubtless be set free from aristocratic influence by the redistribution of seats which must take place, as Mr. Slide declared, at any rate in the next session. Then he named the borough of Loughton; and Phineas Finn, thinking of Saulsby, thinking of the Earl, thinking of Lady Laura, and thinking of Violet, walked away disgusted. Would it not be better that the quiet town, clustering close round the walls of Saulsby, should remain as it was, than that it should be polluted by the presence of Mr. Quintus Slide?

On the last day of the debate, at a few moments before four o'clock, Phineas encountered another terrible misfortune. He had been at the potted peas since twelve, and had on this occasion targed two or three commissariat officers very tightly with questions respecting cabbages and potatoes, and had asked whether the officers on board a certain ship did not always eat preserved asparagus while the men had not even a bean. I fear that he had been put up to this business by Mr. Quintus Slide, and that he made himself nasty. There was, however, so much nastiness of the kind going, that his little effort made no great difference. The conservative members of the Committee, on whose side of the House the inquiry had originated, did not scruple to lay all manner of charges to officers whom, were they themselves in power, they would be bound to support and would support with all their energies. About a quarter before four the members of the Committee had dismissed their last witness for the day, being desirous of not losing their chance of seats on so important an occasion, and hurried down into the lobby,—so that they might enter the House before prayers. Phineas here was button-holed by Barrington Erle, who said something to him as to the approaching division. They were standing in front of the door of the House, almost in the middle of the lobby, with a crowd of members around them,—on a spot which, as frequenters know, is hallowed ground, and must not be trodden by strangers. He was in the act of answering Erle, when he was touched on the arm, and on turning round, saw Mr. Clarkson. "About that little bill, Mr. Finn," said the horrible man, turning his chin round over his white cravat. "They always tell me at your lodgings that you ain't at home." By this time a policeman was explaining to Mr. Clarkson with gentle violence that he must not stand there,—that he must go aside into one of the corners. "I know all that," said Mr. Clarkson, retreating. "Of course I do. But what is a man to do when a gent won't see him at home?" Mr. Clarkson stood aside in his corner quietly, giving the policeman no occasion for further action against him; but in retreating he spoke loud, and there was a lull of voices around, and twenty members at least had heard what had been said. Phineas Finn no doubt had his privilege, but Mr. Clarkson was determined that the privilege should avail him as little as possible.

It was very hard. The real offender, the Lord of the Treasury, the peer's son, with a thousand a year paid by the country was not treated with this cruel persecution. Phineas had in truth never taken a farthing from any one but his father; and though doubtless he owed something at this moment, he had no creditor of his own that was even angry with him. As the world goes he was a clear man,—but for this debt of his friend Fitzgibbon. He left Barrington Erle in the lobby, and hurried into the House, blushing up to the eyes. He looked for Fitzgibbon in his place, but the Lord of the Treasury was not as yet there. Doubtless he would be there for the division, and Phineas resolved that he would speak a bit of his mind before he let his friend out of his sight.

There were some great speeches made on that evening. Mr. Gresham delivered an oration of which men said that it would be known in England as long as there were any words remaining of English eloquence. In it he taunted Mr. Turnbull with being a recreant to the people, of whom he called himself so often the champion. But Mr. Turnbull was not in the least moved. Mr. Gresham knew well enough that Mr. Turnbull was not to be moved by any words;—but the words were not the less telling to the House and to the country. Men, who heard it, said that Mr. Gresham forgot himself in that speech, forgot his party, forgot his strategy, forgot his long-drawn schemes,—even his love of applause, and thought only of his cause. Mr. Daubeny replied to him with equal genius, and with equal skill,—if not with equal heart. Mr. Gresham had asked for the approbation of all present and of all future reformers. Mr. Daubeny denied him both,—the one because he would not succeed, and the other because he would not have deserved success. Then Mr. Mildmay made his reply, getting up at about three o'clock, and uttered a prayer,—a futile prayer,—that this his last work on behalf of his countrymen might be successful. His bill was read a second time, as I have said before, in obedience to the casting vote of the Speaker,—but a majority such as that was tantamount to a defeat.

There was, of course, on that night no declaration as to what ministers would do. Without a meeting of the Cabinet, and without some further consideration, though each might know that the bill would be withdrawn, they could not say in what way they would act. But late as was the hour, there were many words on the subject before members were in their beds. Mr. Turnbull and Mr. Monk left the House together, and perhaps no two gentlemen in it had in former sessions been more in the habit of walking home arm-in-arm and discussing what each had heard and what each had said in that assembly. Latterly these two men had gone strangely asunder in their paths,—very strangely for men who had for years walked so closely together. And this separation had been marked by violent words spoken against each other,—by violent words, at least, spoken against him in office by the one who had never contaminated his hands by the Queen's shilling. And yet, on such an occasion as this, they were able to walk away from the House arm-in-arm, and did not fly at each other's throat by the way.

"Singular enough, is it not," said Mr. Turnbull, "that the thing should have been so close?"

"Very odd," said Mr. Monk; "but men have said that it would be so all the week."

"Gresham was very fine," said Mr. Turnbull.

"Very fine, indeed. I never have heard anything like it before."

"Daubeny was very powerful too," said Mr. Turnbull.

"Yes;—no doubt. The occasion was great, and he answered to the spur. But Gresham's was the speech of the debate."

"Well;—yes; perhaps it was," said Mr. Turnbull, who was thinking of his own flight the other night, and who among his special friends had been much praised for what he had then done. But of course he made no allusion to his own doings,—or to those of Mr. Monk. In this way they conversed for some twenty minutes, till they parted; but neither of them interrogated the other as to what either might be called upon to do in consequence of the division which had just been effected. They might still be intimate friends, but the days of confidence between them were passed.

Phineas had seen Laurence Fitzgibbon enter the House,—which he did quite late in the night, so as to be in time for the division. No doubt he had dined in the House, and had been all the evening in the library,—or in the smoking-room. When Mr. Mildmay was on his legs making his reply, Fitzgibbon had sauntered in, not choosing to wait till he might be rung up by the bell at the last moment. Phineas was near him as they passed by the tellers, near him in the lobby, and near him again as they all passed back into the House. But at the last moment he thought that he would miss his prey. In the crowd as they left the House he failed to get his hand upon his friend's shoulder. But he hurried down the members' passage, and just at the gate leading out into Westminster Hall he overtook Fitzgibbon walking arm-in-arm with Barrington Erle.

"Laurence," he said, taking hold of his countryman's arm with a decided grasp, "I want to speak to you for a moment, if you please."

"Speak away," said Laurence. Then Phineas, looking up into his face, knew very well that he had been—what the world calls, dining.

Phineas remembered at the moment that Barrington Erle had been close to him when the odious money-lender had touched his arm and made his inquiry about that "little bill." He much wished to make Erle understand that the debt was not his own,—that he was not in the hands of usurers in reference to his own concerns. But there was a feeling within him that he still,—even still,—owed something to his friendship to Fitzgibbon. "Just give me your arm, and come on with me for a minute," said Phineas. "Erle will excuse us."

"Oh, blazes!" said Laurence, "what is it you're after? I ain't good at private conferences at three in the morning. We're all out, and isn't that enough for ye?"

"I have been dreadfully annoyed to-night," said Phineas, "and I wished to speak to you about it."

"Bedad, Finn, my boy, and there are a good many of us are annoyed;—eh, Barrington?"

Phineas perceived clearly that though Fitzgibbon had been dining, there was as much of cunning in all this as of wine, and he was determined not to submit to such unlimited ill-usage. "My annoyance comes from your friend, Mr. Clarkson, who had the impudence to address me in the lobby of the House."

"And serve you right, too, Finn, my boy. Why the devil did you sport your oak to him? He has told me all about it. There ain't such a patient little fellow as Clarkson anywhere, if you'll only let him have his own way. He'll look in, as he calls it, three times a week for a whole season, and do nothing further. Of course he don't like to be locked out."

"Is that the gentleman with whom the police interfered in the lobby?" Erle inquired.

"A confounded bill discounter to whom our friend here has introduced me,—for his own purposes," said Phineas.

"A very gentleman-like fellow," said Laurence. "Barrington knows him, I daresay. Look here, Finn, my boy, take my advice. Ask him to breakfast, and let him understand that the house will always be open to him." After this Laurence Fitzgibbon and Barrington Erle got into a cab together, and were driven away.

CHAPTER XXIX
A Cabinet Meeting

And now will the Muses assist me while I sing an altogether new song? On the Tuesday the Cabinet met at the First Lord's official residence in Downing Street, and I will attempt to describe what, according to the bewildered brain of a poor fictionist, was said or might have been said, what was done or might have been done, on so august an occasion.

The poor fictionist very frequently finds himself to have been wrong in his description of things in general, and is told so, roughly by the critics, and tenderly by the friends of his bosom. He is moved to tell of things of which he omits to learn the nature before he tells of them— as should be done by a strictly honest fictionist. He catches salmon in October; or shoots his partridges in March. His dahlias bloom in June, and his birds sing in the autumn. He opens the opera-houses before Easter, and makes Parliament sit on a Wednesday evening. And then those terrible meshes of the Law! How is a fictionist, in these excited days, to create the needed biting interest without legal difficulties; and how again is he to steer his little bark clear of so many rocks,—when the rocks and the shoals have been purposely arranged to make the taking of a pilot on board a necessity? As to those law meshes, a benevolent pilot will, indeed, now and again give a poor fictionist a helping hand,— not used, however, generally, with much discretion. But from whom is any assistance to come in the august matter of a Cabinet assembly? There can be no such assistance. No man can tell aught but they who will tell nothing. But then, again, there is this safety, that let the story be ever so mistold,—let the fiction be ever so far removed from the truth, no critic short of a Cabinet Minister himself can convict the narrator of error.

It was a large dingy room, covered with a Turkey carpet, and containing a dark polished mahogany dinner-table, on very heavy carved legs, which an old messenger was preparing at two o'clock in the day for the use of her Majesty's Ministers. The table would have been large enough for fourteen guests, and along the side further from the fire, there were placed some six heavy chairs, good comfortable chairs, stuffed at the back as well as the seat,—but on the side nearer to the fire the chairs were placed irregularly; and there were four armchairs,—two on one side and two on the other. There were four windows to the room, which looked on to St. James's Park, and the curtains of the windows were dark and heavy,—as became the gravity of the purposes to which that chamber was appropriated. In old days it had been the dining-room of one Prime Minister after another. To Pitt it had been the abode of his own familiar prandial Penates, and Lord Liverpool had been dull there among his dull friends for long year after year. The Ministers of the present day find it more convenient to live in private homes, and, indeed, not unfrequently carry their Cabinets with them. But, under Mr. Mildmay's rule, the meetings were generally held in the old room at the official residence. Thrice did the aged messenger move each armchair, now a little this way and now a little that, and then look at them as though something of the tendency of the coming meeting might depend on the comfort of its leading members. If Mr. Mildmay should find himself to be quite comfortable, so that he could hear what was said without a struggle to his ear, and see his colleagues' faces clearly, and feel the fire without burning his shins, it might be possible that he would not insist upon resigning. If this were so, how important was the work now confided to the hands of that aged messenger! When his anxious eyes had glanced round the room some half a dozen times, when he had touched each curtain, laid his hand upon every chair, and dusted certain papers which lay upon a side-table,—and which had been lying there for two years, and at which no one ever looked or would look,—he gently crept away and ensconced himself in an easy chair not far from the door of the chamber. For it might be necessary to stop the attempt of a rash intruder on those secret counsels.

Very shortly there was heard the ring of various voices in the passages,—the voices of men speaking pleasantly, the voices of men with whom it seemed, from their tone, that things were doing well in the world. And then a cluster of four or five gentlemen entered the room. At first sight they seemed to be as ordinary gentlemen as you shall meet anywhere about Pall Mall on an afternoon. There was nothing about their outward appearance of the august wiggery of statecraft, nothing of the ponderous dignity of ministerial position. That little man in the square-cut coat,—we may almost call it a shooting-coat,—swinging an umbrella and wearing no gloves, is no less a person than the Lord Chancellor,—Lord Weazeling,—who made a hundred thousand pounds as Attorney-General, and is supposed to be the best lawyer of his age. He is fifty, but he looks to be hardly over forty, and one might take him to be, from his appearance,—perhaps a clerk in the War Office, well-to-do, and popular among his brother-clerks. Immediately with him is Sir Harry Coldfoot, also a lawyer by profession, though he has never practised. He has been in the House for nearly thirty years, and is now at the Home Office. He is a stout, healthy, grey-haired gentleman, who certainly does not wear the cares of office on his face. Perhaps, however, no minister gets more bullied than he by the press, and men say that he will be very willing to give up to some political enemy the control of the police, and the onerous duty of judging in all criminal appeals. Behind these come our friend Mr. Monk, young Lord Cantrip from the colonies next door, than whom no smarter young peer now does honour to our hereditary legislature, and Sir Marmaduke Morecombe, the Chancellor of the Duchy of Lancaster. Why Sir Marmaduke has always been placed in Mr. Mildmay's Cabinets nobody ever knew. As Chancellor of the Duchy he has nothing to do,—and were there anything, he would not do it. He rarely speaks in the House, and then does not speak well. He is a handsome man, or would be but for an assumption of grandeur in the carriage of his eyes, giving to his face a character of pomposity which he himself well deserves. He was in the Guards when young, and has been in Parliament since he ceased to be young. It must be supposed that Mr. Mildmay has found something in him, for he has been included in three successive liberal Cabinets. He has probably the virtue of being true to Mr. Mildmay, and of being duly submissive to one whom he recognises as his superior.

Within two minutes afterwards the Duke followed, with Plantagenet Palliser. The Duke, as all the world knows, was the Duke of St. Bungay, the very front and head of the aristocratic old Whigs of the country,—a man who has been thrice spoken of as Prime Minister, and who really might have filled the office had he not known himself to be unfit for it. The Duke has been consulted as to the making of Cabinets for the last five-and-thirty years, and is even now not an old man in appearance;—a fussy, popular, clever, conscientious man, whose digestion has been too good to make politics a burden to him, but who has thought seriously about his country, and is one who will be sure to leave memoirs behind him. He was born in the semi-purple of ministerial influences, and men say of him that he is honester than his uncle, who was Canning's friend, but not so great a man as his grandfather, with whom Fox once quarrelled, and whom Burke loved. Plantagenet Palliser, himself the heir to a dukedom, was the young Chancellor of the Exchequer, of whom some statesmen thought much as the rising star of the age. If industry, rectitude of purpose, and a certain clearness of intellect may prevail, Planty Pall, as he is familiarly called, may become a great Minister.

Then came Viscount Thrift by himself;—the First Lord of the Admiralty, with the whole weight of a new iron-clad fleet upon his shoulders. He has undertaken the Herculean task of cleansing the dockyards,—and with it the lesser work of keeping afloat a navy that may be esteemed by his countrymen to be the best in the world. And he thinks that he will do both, if only Mr. Mildmay will not resign;—an industrious, honest, self-denying nobleman, who works without ceasing from morn to night, and who hopes to rise in time to high things,—to the translating of Homer, perhaps, and the wearing of the Garter.

Close behind him there was a ruck of Ministers, with the much-honoured grey-haired old Premier in the midst of them. There was Mr. Gresham, the Foreign Minister, said to be the greatest orator in Europe, on whose shoulders it was thought that the mantle of Mr. Mildmay would fall,—to be worn, however, quite otherwise than Mr. Mildmay had worn it. For Mr. Gresham is a man with no feelings for the past, void of historical association, hardly with memories,—living altogether for the future which he is anxious to fashion anew out of the vigour of his own brain. Whereas, with Mr. Mildmay, even his love of reform is an inherited passion for an old-world Liberalism. And there was with them Mr. Legge Wilson, the brother of a peer, Secretary at War, a great scholar and a polished gentleman, very proud of his position as a Cabinet Minister, but conscious that he has hardly earned it by political work. And Lord Plinlimmon is with them, the Comptroller of India,—of all working lords the most jaunty, the most pleasant, and the most popular, very good at taking chairs at dinners, and making becoming speeches at the shortest notice, a man apparently very free and open in his ways of life,—but cautious enough in truth as to every step, knowing well how hard it is to climb and how easy to fall. Mr. Mildmay entered the room leaning on Lord Plinlimmon's arm, and when he made his way up among the armchairs upon the rug before the fire, the others clustered around him with cheering looks and kindly questions. Then came the Privy Seal, our old friend Lord Brentford, last,—and I would say least, but that the words of no councillor could go for less in such an assemblage than will those of Sir Marmaduke Morecombe, the Chancellor of the Duchy of Lancaster.

Mr. Mildmay was soon seated in one of the armchairs, while Lord Plinlimmon leaned against the table close at his elbow. Mr. Gresham stood upright at the corner of the chimney-piece furthest from Mr. Mildmay, and Mr. Palliser at that nearest to him. The Duke took the armchair close at Mr. Mildmay's left hand. Lord Plinlimmon was, as I have said, leaning against the table, but the Lord Chancellor, who was next to him, sat upon it. Viscount Thrift and Mr. Monk occupied chairs on the further side of the table, near to Mr. Mildmay's end, and Mr. Legge Wilson placed himself at the head of the table, thus joining them as it were into a body. The Home Secretary stood before the Lord Chancellor screening him from the fire, and the Chancellor of the Duchy, after waiting for a few minutes as though in doubt, took one of the vacant armchairs. The young lord from the Colonies stood a little behind the shoulders of his great friend from the Foreign Office; and the Privy Seal, after moving about for a while uneasily, took a chair behind the Chancellor of the Duchy. One armchair was thus left vacant, but there was no other comer.

"It is not so bad as I thought it would be," said the Duke, speaking aloud, but nevertheless addressing himself specially to his chief.

"It was bad enough," said Mr. Mildmay, laughing.

"Bad enough indeed," said Sir Marmaduke Morecombe, without any laughter.

"And such a good bill lost," said Lord Plinlimmon. "The worst of these failures is, that the same identical bill can never be brought in again."

"So that if the lost bill was best, the bill that will not be lost can only be second best," said the Lord Chancellor.

"I certainly did think that after the debate before Easter we should not have come to shipwreck about the ballot," said Mr. Mildmay.

"It was brewing for us all along," said Mr. Gresham, who then with a gesture of his hand and a pressure of his lips withheld words which he was nearly uttering, and which would not, probably, have been complimentary to Mr. Turnbull. As it was, he turned half round and said something to Lord Cantrip which was not audible to any one else in the room. It was worthy of note, however, that Mr. Turnbull's name was not once mentioned aloud at that meeting.

"I am afraid it was brewing all along," said Sir Marmaduke Morecombe gravely.

"Well, gentlemen, we must take it as we get it," said Mr. Mildmay, still smiling. "And now we must consider what we shall do at once." Then he paused as though expecting that counsel would come to him first from one colleague and then from another. But no such counsel came, and probably Mr. Mildmay did not in the least expect that it would come.

"We cannot stay where we are, of course," said the Duke. The Duke was privileged to say as much as that. But though every man in the room knew that it must be so, no one but the Duke would have said it, before Mr. Mildmay had spoken plainly himself.

"No," said Mr. Mildmay; "I suppose that we can hardly stay where we are. Probably none of us wish it, gentlemen." Then he looked round upon his colleagues, and there came a sort of an assent, though there were no spoken words. The sound from Sir Marmaduke Morecombe was louder than that from the others;—but yet from him it was no more than an attesting grunt. "We have two things to consider," continued Mr. Mildmay,—and though he spoke in a very low voice, every word was heard by all present,—"two things chiefly, that is; the work of the country and the Queen's comfort. I propose to see her Majesty this afternoon at five,—that is, in something less than two hours' time, and I hope to be able to tell the House by seven what has taken place between her Majesty and me. My friend, his Grace, will do as much in the House of Lords. If you agree with me, gentlemen, I will explain to the Queen that it is not for the welfare of the country that we should retain our places, and I will place your resignations and my own in her Majesty's hands."

"You will advise her Majesty to send for Lord de Terrier," said Mr. Gresham.

"Certainly;—there will be no other course open to me."

"Or to her," said Mr. Gresham. To this remark from the rising Minister of the day, no word of reply was made; but of those present in the room three or four of the most experienced servants of the Crown felt that Mr. Gresham had been imprudent. The Duke, who had. ever been afraid of Mr. Gresham, told Mr. Palliser afterwards that such an observation should not have been made; and Sir Harry Coldfoot pondered upon it uneasily, and Sir Marmaduke Morecombe asked Mr. Mildmay what he thought about it. "Times change so much, and with the times the feelings of men," said Mr. Mildmay. But I doubt whether Sir Marmaduke quite understood him.

There was silence in the room for a moment or two after Mr. Gresham had spoken, and then Mr. Mildmay again addressed his friends. "Of course it may be possible that my Lord de Terrier may foresee difficulties, or may find difficulties which will oblige him, either at once, or after an attempt has been made, to decline the task which her Majesty will probably commit to him. All of us, no doubt, know that the arrangement of a government is not the most easy task in the world; and that it is not made the more easy by an absence of a majority in the House of Commons."

"He would dissolve, I presume," said the Duke.

"I should say so," continued Mr. Mildmay. "But it may not improbably come to pass that her Majesty will feel herself obliged to send again for some one or two of us, that we may tender to her Majesty the advice which we owe to her;—for me, for instance, or for my friend the Duke. In such a matter she would be much guided probably by what Lord de Terrier might have suggested to her. Should this be so, and should I be consulted, my present feeling is that we should resume our offices so that the necessary business of the session should be completed, and that we should then dissolve Parliament, and thus ascertain the opinion of the country. In such case, however, we should of course meet again."

"I quite think that the course proposed by Mr. Mildmay will be the best," said the Duke, who had no doubt already discussed the matter with his friend the Prime Minister in private. No one else said a word either of argument or disagreement, and the Cabinet Council was broken up. The old messenger, who had been asleep in his chair, stood up and bowed as the Ministers walked by him, and then went in and rearranged the chairs.

"He has as much idea of giving up as you or I have," said Lord Cantrip to his friend Mr. Gresham, as they walked arm-in-arm together from the Treasury Chambers across St. James's Park towards the clubs.

"I am not sure that he is not right," said Mr. Gresham.

"Do you mean for himself or for the country?" asked Lord Cantrip.

"For his future fame. They who have abdicated and have clung to their abdication have always lost by it. Cincinnatus was brought back again, and Charles V. is felt to have been foolish. The peaches of retired ministers of which we hear so often have generally been cultivated in a constrained seclusion;—or at least the world so believes." They were talking probably of Mr. Mildmay, as to whom some of his colleagues had thought it probable, knowing that he would now resign, that he would have to-day declared his intention of laying aside for ever the cares of office.

Mr. Monk walked home alone, and as he went there was something of a feeling of disappointment at heart, which made him ask himself whether Mr. Turnbull might not have been right in rebuking him for joining the Government. But this, I think, was in no way due to Mr. Mildmay's resignation, but rather to a conviction on Mr. Monk's part that that he had contributed but little to his country's welfare by sitting in Mr. Mildmay's Cabinet.

CHAPTER XXX
Mr. Kennedy's Luck

After the holding of that Cabinet Council of which the author has dared to attempt a slight sketch in the last chapter, there were various visits made to the Queen, first by Mr. Mildmay, and then by Lord de Terrier, afterwards by Mr. Mildmay and the Duke together, and then again by Lord de Terrier; and there were various explanations made to Parliament in each House, and rivals were very courteous to each other, promising assistance;—and at the end of it the old men held their seats. The only change made was effected by the retirement of Sir Marmaduke Morecombe, who was raised to the peerage, and by the selection of—Mr. Kennedy to fill his place in the Cabinet. Mr. Kennedy during the late debate had made one of those speeches, few and far between, by which he had created for himself a Parliamentary reputation; but, nevertheless, all men expressed their great surprise, and no one could quite understand why Mr. Kennedy had been made a Cabinet Minister.

"It is impossible to say whether he is pleased or not," said Lady Laura, speaking of him to Phineas. "I am pleased, of course."

"His ambition must be gratified," said Phineas.

"It would be, if he had any," said Lady Laura.

"I do not believe in a man lacking ambition."

"It is hard to say. There are men who by no means wear their hearts upon their sleeves, and my husband is one of them. He told me that it would be unbecoming in him to refuse, and that was all he said to me about it."

The old men held their seats, but they did so as it were only upon further trial. Mr. Mildmay took the course which he had indicated to his colleagues at the Cabinet meeting. Before all the explanations and journeyings were completed, April was over, and the much-needed Whitsuntide holidays were coming on. But little of the routine work of the session had been done; and, as Mr. Mildmay told the House more than once, the country would suffer were the Queen to dissolve Parliament at this period of the year. The old Ministers would go on with the business of the country, Lord de Terrier with his followers having declined to take affairs into their hands; and at the close of the session, which should be made as short as possible, writs should be issued for new elections. This was Mr. Mildmay's programme, and it was one of which no one dared to complain very loudly.

Mr. Turnbull, indeed, did speak a word of caution. He told Mr. Mildmay that he had lost his bill, good in other respects, because he had refused to introduce the ballot into his measure. Let him promise to be wiser for the future, and to obey the manifested wishes of the country, and then all would be well with him. In answer to this, Mr. Mildmay declared that to the best of his power of reading the country, his countrymen had manifested no such wish; and that if they did so, if by the fresh election it should be shown that the ballot was in truth desired, he would at once leave the execution of their wishes to abler and younger hands. Mr. Turnbull expressed himself perfectly satisfied with the Minister's answers, and said that the coming election would show whether he or Mr. Mildmay were right.

Many men, and among them some of his colleagues, thought that Mr. Mildmay had been imprudent. "No man ought ever to pledge himself to anything," said Sir Harry Coldfoot to the Duke;—"that is, to anything unnecessary." The Duke, who was very true to Mr. Mildmay, made no reply to this, but even he thought that his old friend had been betrayed into a promise too rapidly. But the pledge was given, and some people already began to make much of it. There appeared leader after leader in the *People's Banner* urging the constituencies to take advantage of the Prime Minister's words, and to show clearly at the hustings that they desired the ballot. "You had better come over to us, Mr. Finn; you had indeed," said Mr. Slide. "Now's the time to do it, and show yourself a people's friend. You'll have to do it sooner or later,—whether or no. Come to us and we'll be your horgan."

But in those days Phineas was something less in love with Mr. Quintus Slide than he had been at the time of the great debate, for he was becoming more and more closely connected with people who in their ways of living and modes of expression were very unlike Mr. Slide. This advice was given to him about the end of May, and at that time Lord Chiltern was living with him in the lodgings in Great Marlborough Street. Miss Pouncefoot had temporarily vacated her rooms on the first floor, and the Lord with the broken bones had condescended to occupy them. "I don't know that I like having a Lord," Bunce had said to his wife. "It'll soon come to you not liking anybody decent anywhere," Mrs. Bunce had replied; "but I shan't ask any questions about it. When you're wasting so much time and money at your dirty law proceedings, it's well that somebody should earn something at home."

There had been many discussions about the bringing of Lord Chiltern up to London, in all of which Phineas had been concerned. Lord Brentford had thought that his son had better remain down at the Willingford Bull; and although he said that the rooms were at his son's disposal should Lord Chiltern choose to come to London, still he said it in such a way that Phineas, who went down to Willingford, could not tell his friend that he would be made welcome in Portman Square. "I think I shall leave those diggings altogether," Lord Chiltern said to him. "My father annoys me by everything he says and does, and I annoy him by saying and doing nothing." Then there came an invitation to him from Lady Laura and Mr. Kennedy. Would he come to Grosvenor Place? Lady Laura pressed this very much, though in truth Mr. Kennedy had hardly done more than give a cold assent. But Lord Chiltern would not hear of it. "There is some reason for my going to my father's house," said he, "though he and I are not the best friends in the world; but there can be no reason for my going to the house of a man I dislike so much as I do Robert Kennedy." The matter was settled in the manner told above. Miss Pouncefoot's rooms were prepared for him at Mr. Bunce's house, and Phineas Finn went down to Willingford and brought him up. "I've sold Bonebreaker," he said,—"to a young fellow whose neck will certainly be the sacrifice if he attempts to ride him. I'd have given him to you, Phineas, only you wouldn't have known what to do with him."

Lord Chiltern when he came up to London was still in bandages, though, as the surgeon said, his bones seemed to have been made to be broken and set again; and his bandages of course were a sufficient excuse for his visiting the house neither of his father nor his brother-in-law. But Lady Laura went to him frequently, and thus became acquainted with our hero's home and with Mrs. Bunce. And there were messages taken from Violet to the man in bandages, some of which lost nothing in the carrying. Once Lady Laura tried to make Violet think that it would be right, or rather not wrong, that they two should go together to Lord Chiltern's rooms.

"And would you have me tell my aunt, or would you have me not tell her?" Violet asked.

"I would have you do just as you pleased," Lady Laura answered.

"So I shall," Violet replied, "but I will do nothing that I should be ashamed to tell any one. Your brother professes to be in love with me."

"He is in love with you," said Lady Laura. "Even you do not pretend to doubt his faith."

"Very well. In those circumstances a girl should not go to a man's rooms unless she means to consider herself as engaged to him, even with his sister;—not though he had broken every bone in his skin. I know what I may do, Laura, and I know what I mayn't; and I won't be led either by you or by my aunt."

"May I give him your love?"

"No;—because you'll give it in a wrong spirit. He knows well enough that I wish him well;—but you may tell him that from me, if you please. He has from me all those wishes which one friend owes to another."

But there were other messages sent from Violet through Phineas Finn which she worded with more show of affection,—perhaps as much for the discomfort of Phineas as for the consolation of Lord Chiltern. "Tell him to take care of himself," said Violet, "and bid him not to have any more of those wild brutes that are not fit for any Christian to ride. Tell him that I say so. It's a great thing to be brave; but what's the use of being foolhardy?"

The session was to be closed at the end of June, to the great dismay of London tradesmen and of young ladies who had not been entirely successful in the early season. But before the old Parliament was closed, and the writs for the new election were despatched, there occurred an incident which was of very much importance to Phineas Finn. Near the end of June, when the remaining days of the session were numbered by three or four, he had been dining at Lord Brentford's house in Portman Square in company with Mr. Kennedy. But Lady Laura had not been there. At this time he saw Lord Brentford not unfrequently, and there was always a word said about Lord Chiltern. The father would ask how the son occupied himself, and Phineas would hope,—though hitherto he had hoped in vain,—that he would induce the Earl to come and see Lord Chiltern. Lord Brentford could never be brought to that; but it was sufficiently evident that he would have done so, had he not been afraid to descend so far from the altitude of his paternal wrath. On this evening, at about eleven, Mr. Kennedy and Phineas left the house together, and walked from the Square through Orchard Street into Oxford Street. Here their ways parted, but Phineas crossed the road with Mr. Kennedy, as he was making some reply to a second invitation to Loughlinter. Phineas, considering what had been said before on the subject, thought that the invitation came late, and that it was not warmly worded. He had, therefore, declined it, and was in the act of declining it, when he crossed the road with Mr. Kennedy. In walking down Orchard Street from the Square he had seen two men standing in the shadow a few yards up a mews or small alley that was there, but had thought nothing of them. It was just that period of the year when there is hardly any of the darkness of night; but at this moment there were symptoms of coming rain, and heavy drops began to fall; and there were big clouds coming and going before the young moon. Mr. Kennedy had said that he would get a cab, but he had seen none as he crossed Oxford Street, and had put up his umbrella as he made his way towards Park Street. Phineas as he left him distinctly perceived the same two figures on the other side of Oxford Street, and then turning into the shadow of a butcher's porch, he saw them cross the street in the wake of Mr. Kennedy. It was now raining in earnest, and the few passengers who were out were scudding away quickly, this way and that.

It hardly occurred to Phineas to think that any danger was imminent to Mr. Kennedy from the men, but it did occur to him that he might as well take some notice of the matter. Phineas knew that Mr. Kennedy would make his way down Park Street, that being his usual route from Portman Square towards his own home, and knew also that he himself could again come across Mr. Kennedy's track by going down North Audley Street to the corner of Grosvenor Square, and thence by Brook Street into Park Street. Without much thought, therefore, he went out of his own course down to the corner of the Square, hurrying his steps till he was running, and then ran along Brook Street, thinking as he went of some special word that he might say to Mr. Kennedy as an excuse, should he again come across his late companion. He reached the corner of Park Street before that gentleman could have been there unless he also had run; but just in time to see him as he was coming on,— and also to see in the dark glimmering of the slight uncertain moonlight that the two men were behind him. He retreated a step backwards in the corner, resolving that when Mr. Kennedy came up, they two would go on together; for now it was clear that Mr. Kennedy was followed. But Mr. Kennedy did not reach the corner. When he was within two doors of it, one of the men had followed him up quickly, and had thrown something round his throat from behind him. Phineas understood well now that his friend was in the act of being garrotted, and that his instant assistance was needed. He rushed forward, and as the second ruffian had been close upon the footsteps of the first, there was almost instantaneously a concourse of the four men. But there was no fight. The man who had already nearly succeeded in putting Mr. Kennedy on to his back, made no attempt to seize his prey when he found that so unwelcome an addition had joined the party, but instantly turned to fly. His companion was turning also, but Phineas was too quick for him, and having seized on to his collar, held to him with all his power. "Dash it all," said the man, "didn't yer see as how I was a-hurrying up to help the gen'leman myself?" Phineas, however, hadn't seen this, and held on gallantly, and in a couple of minutes the first ruffian was back again upon the spot in the custody of a policeman. "You've done it uncommon neat, sir," said the policeman, complimenting Phineas upon his performance. "If the gen'leman ain't none the worst for it, it'll have been a very pretty evening's amusement." Mr. Kennedy was now leaning against the railings, and hitherto had been unable to declare whether he was really injured or not, and it was not till a second policeman came up that the hero of the night was at liberty to attend closely to his friend.

Mr. Kennedy, when he was able to speak, declared that for a minute or two he had thought that his neck had been broken; and he was not quite convinced till he found himself in his own house, that nothing more serious had really happened to him than certain bruises round his throat. The policeman was for a while anxious that at any rate Phineas should go with him to the police-office; but at last consented to take the addresses of the two gentlemen. When he found that Mr. Kennedy was a member of Parliament, and that he was designated as Right Honourable, his respect for the garrotter became more great, and he began to feel that the night was indeed a night of great importance. He expressed unbounded admiration at Mr. Finn's success in his own line, and made repeated promises that the men should be forthcoming on the morrow. Could a cab be got? Of course a cab could be got. A cab was got, and within a quarter of an hour of the making of the attack, the two members of Parliament were on their way to Grosvenor Place.

There was hardly a word spoken in the cab, for Mr. Kennedy was in pain. When, however, they reached the door in Grosvenor Place, Phineas wanted to go, and leave his friend with the servants, but this the Cabinet Minister would not allow. "Of course you must see my wife," he said. So they went up-stairs into the drawing-room, and then upon the stairs, by the lights of the house, Phineas could perceive that his companion's face was bruised and black with dirt, and that his cravat was gone.

"I have been garrotted," said the Cabinet Minister to his wife.

"What?"

"Simply that;—or should have been, if he had not been there. How he came there, God only knows."

The wife's anxiety, and then her gratitude, need hardly be described,—nor the astonishment of the husband, which by no means decreased on reflection, at the opportune re-appearance in the nick of time of the man whom three minutes before the attack he had left in the act of going in the opposite direction.

"I had seen the men, and thought it best to run round by the corner of Grosvenor Square," said Phineas.

"May God bless you," said Lady Laura.

"Amen," said the Cabinet Minister.

"I think he was born to be my friend," said Lady Laura.

The Cabinet Minister said nothing more that night. He was never given to much talking, and the little accident which had just occurred to him did not tend to make words easy to him. But he pressed our hero's hand, and Lady Laura said that of course Phineas would come to them on the morrow. Phineas remarked that his first business must be to go to the police-office, but he promised that he would come down to Grosvenor Place immediately afterwards. Then Lady Laura also pressed his hand, and looked—; she looked, I think, as though she thought that Phineas would only have done right had he repeated the offence which he had committed under the waterfall of Loughlinter.

"Garrotted!" said Lord Chiltern, when Phineas told him the story before they went to bed that night. He had been smoking, sipping brandy-and-water, and waiting for Finn's return. "Robert Kennedy garrotted!"

"The fellow was in the act of doing it."

"And you stopped him?"

"Yes;—I got there just in time. Wasn't it lucky?"

"You ought to be garrotted yourself. I should have lent the man a hand had I been there."

"How can you say anything so horrible? But you are drinking too much, old fellow, and I shall lock the bottle up."

"If there were no one in London drank more than I do, the wine merchants would have a bad time of it. And so the new Cabinet Minister has been garrotted in the street. Of course I'm sorry for poor Laura's sake."

"Luckily he's not much the worse for it;—only a little bruised."

"I wonder whether it's on the cards he should be improved by it;—worse, except in the way of being strangled, he could not be. However, as he's my brother-in-law, I'm obliged to you for rescuing him. Come, I'll go to bed. I must say, if he was to be garrotted I should like to have been there to see it." That was the manner in which Lord Chiltern received the tidings of the terrible accident which had occurred to his near relative.

CHAPTER XXXI
Finn for Loughton

By three o'clock in the day after the little accident which was told in the last chapter, all the world knew that Mr. Kennedy, the new Cabinet Minister, had been garrotted, or half garrotted, and that that child of fortune, Phineas Finn, had dropped upon the scene out of heaven at the exact moment of time, had taken the two garrotters prisoners, and saved the Cabinet Minister's neck and valuables,—if not his life. "Bedad," said Laurence Fitzgibbon, when he came to hear this, "that fellow'll marry an heiress, and be Secretary for Oireland yet." A good deal was said about it to Phineas at the clubs, but a word or two that was said to him by Violet Effingham was worth all the rest. "Why, what a Paladin you are! But you succour men in distress instead of maidens." "That's my bad luck," said Phineas. "The other will come no doubt in time," Violet replied; "and then you'll get your reward." He knew that such words from a girl mean nothing,—especially from such a girl as Violet Effingham; but nevertheless they were very pleasant to him.

"Of course you will come to us at Loughlinter when Parliament is up?" Lady Laura said the same day.

"I don't know really. You see I must go over to Ireland about my re-election."

"What has that to do with it? You are only making out excuses. We go down on the first of July, and the English elections won't begin till the middle of the month. It will be August before the men of Loughshane are ready for you."

"To tell you the truth, Lady Laura," said Phineas, "I doubt whether the men of Loughshane,—or rather the man of Loughshane, will have anything more to say to me."

"What man do you mean?"

"Lord Tulla. He was in a passion with his brother before, and I got the advantage of it. Since that he has paid his brother's debts for the fifteenth time, and of course is ready to fight any battle for the forgiven prodigal. Things are not as they were, and my father tells me that he thinks I shall be beaten."

"That is bad news."

"It is what I have a right to expect."

Every word of information that had come to Phineas about Loughshane since Mr. Mildmay had decided upon a dissolution, had gone towards making him feel at first that there was a great doubt as to his re-election, and at last that there was almost a certainty against him. And as these tidings reached him they made him very unhappy. Since he had been in Parliament he had very frequently regretted that he had left the shades of the Inns of Court for the glare of Westminster; and he had more than once made up his mind that he would desert the glare and return to the shade. But now, when the moment came in which such desertion seemed to be compulsory on him, when there would be no longer a choice, the seat in Parliament was dearer to him than ever. If he had gone of his own free will,—so he told himself,—there would have been something of nobility in such going. Mr. Low would have respected him, and even Mrs. Low might have taken him back to the friendship of her severe bosom. But he would go back now as a cur with his tail between his legs,—kicked out, as it were, from Parliament. Returning to Lincoln's Inn soiled with failure, having accomplished nothing, having broken down on the only occasion on which he had dared to show himself on his legs, not having opened a single useful book during the two years in which he had sat in Parliament, burdened with Laurence Fitzgibbon's debt, and not quite free from debt of his own, how could he start himself in any way by which he might even hope to win success? He must, he told himself, give up all thought of practising in London and betake himself to Dublin. He could not dare to face his friends in London as a young briefless barrister.

On this evening, the evening subsequent to that on which Mr. Kennedy had been attacked, the House was sitting in Committee of Ways and Means, and there came on a discussion as to a certain vote for the army. It had been known that there would be such discussion; and Mr. Monk having heard from Phineas a word or two now and again about the potted peas, had recommended him to be ready with a few remarks if he wished to support the Government in the matter of that vote. Phineas did so wish, having learned quite enough in the Committee Room up-stairs to make him believe that a large importation of the potted peas from Holstein would not be for the advantage of the army or navy,—or for that of the country at large. Mr. Monk had made his suggestion without the slightest allusion to the former failure,—just as though Phineas were a practised speaker accustomed to be on his legs three or four times a week. "If I find a chance, I will," said Phineas, taking the advice just as it was given.

Soon after prayers, a word was said in the House as to the ill-fortune which had befallen the new Cabinet Minister. Mr. Daubeny had asked Mr. Mildmay whether violent hands had not been laid in the dead of night on the sacred throat,—the throat that should have been sacred,—of the new Chancellor of the Duchy of Lancaster; and had expressed regret that the Ministry,—which was, he feared, in other respects somewhat infirm,—should now have been further weakened by this injury to that new bulwark with which it had endeavoured to support itself. The Prime Minister, answering his old rival in the same strain, said that the calamity might have been very severe, both to the country and to the Cabinet; but that fortunately for the community at large, a gallant young member of that House,—and he was proud to say a supporter of the Government,—had appeared upon the spot at the nick of time;—"As a god out of a machine," said Mr. Daubeny, interrupting him;—"By no means as a god out of a machine," continued Mr. Mildmay, "but as a real help in a very real trouble, and succeeded not only in saving my right honourable friend, the Chancellor of the Duchy, but in arresting the two malefactors who attempted to rob him in the street." Then there was a cry of "name;" and Mr. Mildmay of course named the member for Loughshane. It so happened that Phineas was not in the House, but he heard it all when he came down to attend the Committee of Ways and Means.

Then came on the discussion about provisions in the army, the subject being mooted by one of Mr. Turnbull's close allies. The gentleman on the other side of the House who had moved for the Potted Peas Committee, was silent on the occasion, having felt that the result of that committee had not been exactly what he had expected. The evidence respecting such of the Holstein potted peas as had been used in this country was not very favourable to them. But, nevertheless, the rebound from that committee,—the very fact that such a committee had been made to sit,—gave ground for a hostile attack. To attack is so easy, when a complete refutation barely suffices to save the Minister attacked,—does not suffice to save him from future dim memories of something having been wrong,—and brings down no disgrace whatsoever on the promoter of the false charge. The promoter of the false charge simply expresses his gratification at finding that he had been misled by erroneous information. It is not customary for him to express gratification at the fact, that out of all the mud which he has thrown, some will probably stick! Phineas, when the time came, did get on his legs, and spoke perhaps two or three dozen words. The doing so seemed to come to him quite naturally. He had thought very little about it beforehand,—having resolved not to think of it. And indeed the occasion was one of no great importance. The Speaker was not in the chair, and the House was thin, and he intended to make no speech,—merely to say something which he had to say. Till he had finished he hardly remembered that he was doing that, in attempting to do which he had before failed so egregiously. It was not till he sat down that he began to ask himself whether the scene was swimming before his eyes as it had done on former occasions; as it had done even when he had so much as thought of making a speech. Now he was astonished at the easiness of the thing, and as he left the House told himself that he had overcome the difficulty just when the victory could be of no avail to him. Had he been more eager, more constant in his purpose, he might at any rate have shown the world that he was fit for the place which he had presumed to take before he was cast out of it.

On the next morning he received a letter from his father. Dr. Finn had seen Lord Tulla, having been sent for to relieve his lordship in a fit of the gout, and had been informed by the Earl that he meant to fight the borough to the last man;—had he said to the last shilling he would have spoken with perhaps more accuracy. "You see, doctor, your son has had it for two years, as you may say for nothing, and I think he ought to give way. He can't expect that he's to go on there as though it were his own." And then his lordship, upon whom this touch of the gout had come somewhat sharply, expressed himself with considerable animation. The old doctor behaved with much spirit. "I told the Earl," he said, "that I could not undertake to say what you might do; but that as you had come forward at first with my sanction, I could not withdraw it now. He asked me if I should support you with money; I said that I should to a moderate extent. 'By G——,' said the Earl, 'a moderate extent will go a very little way, I can tell you.' Since that he has had Duggin with him; so, I suppose, I shall not see him any more. You can do as you please now; but, from what I hear, I fear you will have no chance." Then with much bitterness of spirit Phineas resolved that he would not interfere with Lord Tulla at Loughshane. He would go at once to the Reform Club and explain his reasons to Barrington Erle and others there who would be interested.

But he first went to Grosvenor Place. Here he was shown up into Mr. Kennedy's room. Mr. Kennedy was up and seated in an arm-chair by an open window looking over into the Queen's garden; but he was in his dressing-gown, and was to be regarded as an invalid. And indeed as he could not turn his neck, or thought that he could not do so, he was not very fit to go out about his work. Let us hope that the affairs of the Duchy of Lancaster did not suffer materially by his absence. We may take it for granted that with a man so sedulous as to all his duties there was no arrear of work when the accident took place. He put out his hand to Phineas, and said some word in a whisper,—some word or two among which Phineas caught the sound of "potted peas,"—and then continued to look out of the window. There are men who are utterly prostrated by any bodily ailment, and it seemed that Mr. Kennedy was one of them. Phineas, who was full of his own bad news, had intended to tell his sad story at once. But he perceived that the neck of the Chancellor of the Duchy was too stiff to allow of his taking any interest in external matters, and so he refrained. "What does the doctor say about it?" said Phineas, perceiving that just for the present there could be only one possible subject for remark. Mr. Kennedy was beginning to describe in a long whisper what the doctor did think about it, when Lady Laura came into the room.

Of course they began at first to talk about Mr. Kennedy. It would not have been kind to him not to have done so. And Lady Laura made much of the injury, as it behoves a wife to do in such circumstances for the sake both of the sufferer and of the hero. She declared her conviction that had Phineas been a moment later her husband's neck would have been irredeemably broken.

"I don't think they ever do kill the people," said Phineas. "At any rate they don't mean to do so."

"I thought they did," said Lady Laura.

"I fancy not," said Phineas, eager in the cause of truth.

"I think this man was very clumsy," whispered Mr. Kennedy.

"Perhaps he was a beginner," said Phineas, "and that may make a difference. If so, I'm afraid we have interfered with his education."

Then, by degrees, the conversation got away to other things, and Lady Laura asked him after Loughshane. "I've made up my mind to give it up," said he, smiling as he spoke.

"I was afraid there was but a bad chance," said Lady Laura, smiling also.

"My father has behaved so well!" said Phineas. "He has written to say he'll find the money, if I determine to contest the borough. I mean to write to him by to-night's post to decline the offer. I have no right to spend the money, and I shouldn't succeed if I did spend it. Of course it makes me a little down in the mouth." And then he smiled again.

"I've got a plan of my own," said Lady Laura.

"What plan?"

"Or rather it isn't mine, but papa's. Old Mr. Standish is going to give up Loughton, and papa wants you to come and try your luck there."

"Lady Laura!"

"It isn't quite a certainty, you know, but I suppose it's as near a certainty as anything left." And this came from a strong Radical Reformer!

"Lady Laura, I couldn't accept such a favour from your father." Then Mr. Kennedy nodded his head very slightly and whispered, "Yes, yes." "I couldn't think of it," said Phineas Finn. "I have no right to such a favour."

"That is a matter entirely for papa's consideration," said Lady Laura, with an affectation of solemnity in her voice. "I think it has always been felt that any politician may accept such an offer as that when it is made to him, but that no politician should ask for it. My father feels that he has to do the best he can with his influence in the borough, and therefore he comes to you."

"It isn't that," said Phineas, somewhat rudely.

"Of course private feelings have their weight," said Lady Laura. "It is not probable that papa would have gone to a perfect stranger. And perhaps, Mr. Finn, I may own that Mr. Kennedy and I would both be very sorry that you should not be in the House, and that that feeling on our part has had some weight with my father."

"Of course you'll stand?" whispered Mr. Kennedy, still looking straight out of the window, as though the slightest attempt to turn his neck would be fraught with danger to himself and the Duchy.

"Papa has desired me to ask you to call upon him," said Lady Laura. "I don't suppose there is very much to be said, as each of you know so well the other's way of thinking. But you had better see him to-day or to-morrow."

Of course Phineas was persuaded before he left Mr. Kennedy's room. Indeed, when he came to think of it, there appeared to him to be no valid reason why he should not sit for Loughton. The favour was of a kind that had prevailed from time out of mind in England, between the most respectable of the great land magnates, and young rising liberal politicians. Burke, Fox, and Canning had all been placed in Parliament by similar influence. Of course he, Phineas Finn, desired earnestly,—longed in his very heart of hearts,—to extinguish all such Parliamentary influence, to root out for ever the last vestige of close borough nominations; but while the thing remained it was better that the thing should contribute to the liberal than to the conservative strength of the House,—and if to the liberal, how was this to be achieved but by the acceptance of such influence by some liberal candidate? And if it were right that it should be accepted by any liberal candidate,—then, why not by him? The logic of this argument seemed to him to be perfect. He felt something like a sting of reproach as he told himself that in truth this great offer was made to him, not on account of the excellence of his politics, but because he had been instrumental in saving Lord Brentford's son-in-law from the violence of garrotters. But he crushed these qualms of conscience as being over-scrupulous, and, as he told himself, not practical. You must take the world as you find it, with a struggle to be something more honest than those around you. Phineas, as he preached to himself this sermon, declared to himself that they who attempted more than this flew too high in the clouds to be of service to men and women upon earth.

As he did not see Lord Brentford that day he postponed writing to his father for twenty-four hours. On the following morning he found the Earl at home in Portman Square, having first discussed the matter fully with Lord Chiltern. "Do not scruple about me," said Lord Chiltern; "you are quite welcome to the borough for me."

"But if I did not stand, would you do so? There are so many reasons which ought to induce you to accept a seat in Parliament!"

"Whether that be true or not, Phineas, I shall not accept my father's interest at Loughton, unless it be offered to me in a way in which it never will be offered. You know me well enough to be sure that I shall not change my mind. Nor will he. And, therefore, you may go down to Loughton with a pure conscience as far as I am concerned."

Phineas had his interview with the Earl, and in ten minutes everything was settled. On his way to Portman Square there had come across his mind the idea of a grand effort of friendship. What if he could persuade the father so to conduct himself towards his son, that the son should consent to be a member for the borough? And he did say a word or two to this effect, setting forth that Lord Chiltern would condescend to become a legislator, if only his father would condescend to acknowledge his son's fitness for such work without any comments on the son's past life. But the Earl simply waived the subject away with his hand. He could be as obstinate as his son. Lady Laura had been the Mercury between them on this subject, and Lady Laura had failed. He would not now consent to employ another Mercury. Very little,—hardly a word indeed,—was said between the Earl and Phineas about politics. Phineas was to be the Saulsby candidate at Loughton for the next election, and was to come to Saulsby with the Kennedys from Loughlinter,—either with the Kennedys or somewhat in advance of them. "I do not say that there will be no opposition," said the Earl, "but I expect none." He was very courteous,—nay, he was kind, feeling doubtless that his family owed a great debt of gratitude to the young man with whom he was conversing; but, nevertheless, there was not absent on his part a touch of that high condescension which, perhaps, might be thought to become the Earl, the Cabinet Minister, and the great borough patron. Phineas, who was sensitive, felt this and winced. He had never quite liked Lord Brentford, and could not bring himself to do so now in spite of the kindness which the Earl was showing him.

But he was very happy when he sat down to write to his father from the club. His father had told him that the money should be forthcoming for the election at Loughshane, if he resolved to stand, but that the chance of success would be very slight,—indeed that, in his opinion, there would be no chance of success. Nevertheless, his father had evidently believed, when writing, that Phineas would not abandon his seat without a useless and expensive contest. He now thanked his father with many expressions of gratitude,—declared his conviction that his father was right about Lord Tulla, and then, in the most modest language that he could use, went on to say that he had found another borough open to him in England. He was going to stand for Loughton, with the assistance of Lord Brentford, and thought that the election would probably not cost him above a couple of hundred pounds at the outside. Then he wrote a very pretty note to Lord Tulla, thanking him for his former kindness, and telling the Irish Earl that it was not his intention to interfere with the borough of Loughshane at the next election.

A few days after this Phineas was very much surprised at a visit that was made to him at his lodgings. Mr. Clarkson, after that scene in the lobby of the House, called again in Great Marlborough Street,—and was admitted. "You had better let him sit in your armchair for half an hour or so," Fitzgibbon had said; and Phineas almost believed that it would be better. The man was a terrible nuisance to him, and he was beginning to think that he had better undertake to pay the debt by degrees. It was, he knew, quite on the cards that Mr. Clarkson should have him arrested while at Saulsby. Since that scene in the lobby Mr. Clarkson had been with him twice, and there had been a preliminary conversation as to real payment. Mr. Clarkson wanted a hundred pounds down, and another bill for two hundred and twenty at three months' date. "Think of my time and trouble in coming here," Mr. Clarkson had urged when Phineas had objected to these terms. "Think of my time and trouble, and do be punctual, Mr. Finn." Phineas had offered him ten pounds a quarter, the payments to be marked on the back of the bill, a tender which Mr. Clarkson had not seemed to regard as strong evidence of punctuality. He had not been angry, but had simply expressed his intention of calling again,—giving Phineas to understand that business would probably take him to the west of Ireland in the autumn. If only business might not take him down either to Loughlinter or to Saulsby! But the strange visitor who came to Phineas in the midst of these troubles put an end to them all.

The strange visitor was Miss Aspasia Fitzgibbon. "You'll be very much surprised at my coming to your chambers, no doubt," she said, as she sat down in the chair which Phineas placed for her. Phineas could only say that he was very proud to be so highly honoured, and that he hoped she was well. "Pretty well, I thank you. I have just come about a little business, Mr. Finn, and I hope you'll excuse me."

"I'm quite sure that there is no need for excuses," said Phineas.

"Laurence, when he hears about it, will say that I've been an impertinent old fool; but I never care what Laurence says, either this way or that. I've been to that Mr. Clarkson, Mr. Finn, and I've paid him the money."

"No!" said Phineas.

"But I have, Mr. Finn. I happened to hear what occurred that night at the door of the House of Commons."

"Who told you, Miss Fitzgibbon?"

"Never mind who told me. I heard it. I knew before that you had been foolish enough to help Laurence about money, and so I put two and two together. It isn't the first time I have had to do with Mr. Clarkson. So I sent to him, and I've bought the bill. There it is." And Miss Fitzgibbon produced the document which bore the name of Phineas Finn across the front of it.

"And did you pay him two hundred and fifty pounds for it?"

"Not quite. I had a very hard tussle, and got it at last for two hundred and twenty pounds."

"And did you do it yourself?"

"All myself. If I had employed a lawyer I should have had to pay two hundred and forty pounds and five pounds for costs. And now, Mr. Finn, I hope you won't have any more money engagements with my brother Laurence." Phineas said that he thought he might promise that he would have no more. "Because, if you do, I shan't interfere. If Laurence began to find that he could get money out of me in that way, there would be no end to it. Mr. Clarkson would very soon be spending his spare time in my drawing-room. Good-bye, Mr. Finn. If Laurence says anything, just tell him that he'd better come to me." Then Phineas was left looking at the bill. It was certainly a great relief to him,—that he should be thus secured from the domiciliary visits of Mr. Clarkson; a great relief to him to be assured that Mr. Clarkson would not find him out down at Loughton; but nevertheless, he had to suffer a pang of shame as he felt that Miss Fitzgibbon had become acquainted with his poverty and had found herself obliged to satisfy his pecuniary liabilities.

CHAPTER XXXII
Lady Laura Kennedy's Headache

Phineas went down to Loughlinter early in July, taking Loughton in his way. He stayed there one night at the inn, and was introduced to sundry influential inhabitants of the borough by Mr. Grating, the ironmonger, who was known by those who knew Loughton to be a very strong supporter of the Earl's interest. Mr. Grating and about half a dozen others of the tradesmen of the town came to the inn, and met Phineas in the parlour. He told them he was a good sound Liberal and a supporter of Mr. Mildmay's Government, of which their neighbour the Earl was so conspicuous an ornament. This was almost all that was said about the Earl out loud; but each individual man of Loughton then present took an opportunity during the meeting of whispering into Mr. Finn's ear a word or two to show that he also was admitted to the secret councils of the borough,—that he too could see the inside of the arrangement. "Of course we must support the Earl," one said. "Never mind what you hear about a Tory candidate, Mr. Finn," whispered a second; "the Earl can do what he pleases here." And it seemed to Phineas that it was thought by them all to be rather a fine thing to be thus held in the hand by an English nobleman. Phineas could not but reflect much upon this as he lay in his bed at the Loughton inn. The great political question on which the political world was engrossed up in London was the enfranchisement of Englishmen,—of Englishmen down to the rank of artisans and labourers;—and yet when he found himself in contact with individual Englishmen, with men even very much above the artisan and the labourer, he found that they rather liked being bound hand and foot, and being kept as tools in the political pocket of a rich man. Every one of those Loughton tradesmen was proud of his own personal subjection to the Earl!

From Loughton he went to Loughlinter, having promised to be back in the borough for the election. Mr. Grating would propose him, and he was to be seconded by Mr. Shortribs, the butcher and grazier. Mention had been made of a Conservative candidate, and Mr. Shortribs had seemed to think that a good stand-up fight upon English principles, with a clear understanding, of course, that victory should prevail on the liberal side, would be a good thing for the borough. But the Earl's man of business saw Phineas on the morning of his departure, and told him not to regard Mr. Shortribs. "They'd all like it," said the man of business; "and I daresay they'll have enough of it when this Reform Bill is passed; but at present no one will be fool enough to come and spend his money here. We have them all in hand too well for that, Mr. Finn!"

He found the great house at Loughlinter nearly empty. Mr. Kennedy's mother was there, and Lord Brentford was there, and Lord Brentford's private secretary, and Mr. Kennedy's private secretary. At present that was the entire party. Lady Baldock was expected there, with her daughter and Violet Effingham; but, as well as Phineas could learn, they would not be at Loughlinter until after he had left it. There had come up lately a rumour that there would be an autumn session,—that the Houses would sit through October and a part of November, in order that Mr. Mildmay might try the feeling of the new Parliament. If this were to be so, Phineas had resolved that, in the event of his election at Loughton, he would not return to Ireland till after this autumn session should be over. He gave an account to the Earl, in the presence of the Earl's son-in-law, of what had taken place at Loughton, and the Earl expressed himself as satisfied. It was manifestly a great satisfaction to Lord Brentford that he should still have a borough in his pocket, and the more so because there were so very few noblemen left who had such property belonging to them. He was very careful in his speech, never saying in so many words that the privilege of returning a member was his own; but his meaning was not the less clear.

Those were dreary days at Loughlinter. There was fishing,—if Phineas chose to fish; and he was told that he could shoot a deer if he was minded to go out alone. But it seemed as though it were the intention of the host that his guests should spend their time profitably. Mr.

Kennedy himself was shut up with books and papers all the morning, and always took up a book after dinner. The Earl also would read a little,—and then would sleep a good deal. Old Mrs. Kennedy slept also, and Lady Laura looked as though she would like to sleep if it were not that her husband's eye was upon her. As it was, she administered tea, Mr. Kennedy not liking the practice of having it handed round by a servant when none were there but members of the family circle, and she read novels. Phineas got hold of a stiff bit of reading for himself, and tried to utilise his time. He took Alison in hand, and worked his way gallantly through a couple of volumes. But even he, more than once or twice, found himself on the very verge of slumber. Then he would wake up and try to think about things. Why was he, Phineas Finn, an Irishman from Killaloe, living in that great house of Loughlinter as though he were one of the family, striving to kill the hours, and feeling that he was in some way subject to the dominion of his host? Would it not be better for him to get up and go away? In his heart of hearts he did not like Mr. Kennedy, though he believed him to be a good man. And of what service to him was it to like Lady Laura, now that Lady Laura was a possession in the hands of Mr. Kennedy? Then he would tell himself that he owed his position in the world entirely to Lady Laura, and that he was ungrateful to feel himself ever dull in her society. And, moreover, there was something to be done in the world beyond making love and being merry. Mr. Kennedy could occupy himself with a blue book for hours together without wincing. So Phineas went to work again with his Alison, and read away till he nodded.

In those days he often wandered up and down the Linter and across the moor to the Linn, and so down to the lake. He would take a book with him, and would seat himself down on spots which he loved, and would pretend to read;—but I do not think that he got much advantage from his book. He was thinking of his life, and trying to calculate whether the wonderful success which he had achieved would ever be of permanent value to him. Would he be nearer to earning his bread when he should be member for Loughton than he had been when he was member for Loughshane? Or was there before him any slightest probability that he would ever earn his bread? And then he thought of Violet Effingham, and was angry with himself for remembering at that moment that Violet Effingham was the mistress of a large fortune.

Once before when he was sitting beside the Linter he had made up his mind to declare his passion to Lady Laura;—and he had done so on the very spot. Now, within a twelvemonth of that time, he made up his mind on the same spot to declare his passion to Miss Effingham, and he thought his best mode of carrying his suit would be to secure the assistance of Lady Laura. Lady Laura, no doubt, had been very anxious that her brother should marry Violet; but Lord Chiltern, as Phineas knew, had asked for Violet's hand twice in vain; and, moreover, Chiltern himself had declared to Phineas that he would never ask for it again. Lady Laura, who was always reasonable, would surely perceive that there was no hope of success for her brother. That Chiltern would quarrel with him,—would quarrel with him to the knife,—he did not doubt; but he felt that no fear of such a quarrel as that should deter him. He loved Violet Effingham, and he must indeed be pusillanimous if, loving her as he did, he was deterred from expressing his love from any fear of a suitor whom she did not favour. He would not willingly be untrue to his friendship for Lady Laura's brother. Had there been a chance for Lord Chiltern he would have abstained from putting himself forward. But what was the use of his abstaining, when by doing so he could in no wise benefit his friend,—when the result of his doing so would be that some interloper would come in and carry off the prize? He would explain all this to Lady Laura, and, if the prize would be kind to him, he would disregard the anger of Lord Chiltern, even though it might be anger to the knife.

As he was thinking of all this Lady Laura stood before him where he was sitting at the top of the falls. At this moment he remembered well all the circumstances of the scene when he had been there with her at his last visit to Loughlinter. How things had changed since then! Then he had loved Lady Laura with all his heart, and he had now already brought himself to regard her as a discreet matron whom to love would be almost as unreasonable as though he were to entertain a passion for the Lord Chancellor. The reader will understand how thorough had been the cure effected by Lady Laura's marriage and the interval of a few months, when the swain was already prepared to make this lady the depositary of his confidence in another matter of love. "You are often here, I suppose?" said Lady Laura, looking down upon him as he sat upon the rock.

"Well;—yes; not very often; I come here sometimes because the view down upon the lake is so fine."

"It is the prettiest spot about the place. I hardly ever get here now. Indeed this is only the second time that I have been up since we have been at home, and then I came to bring papa here." There was a little wooden seat near to the rock upon which Phineas had been lying, and upon this Lady Laura sat down. Phineas, with his eyes turned upon the lake, was considering how he might introduce the subject of his love for Violet Effingham; but he did not find the matter very easy. He had just resolved to begin by saying that Violet would certainly never accept Lord Chiltern, when Lady Laura spoke a word or two which stopped him altogether. "How well I remember," she said, "the day when you and I were here last autumn!"

"So do I. You told me then that you were going to marry Mr. Kennedy. How much has happened since then!"

"Much indeed! Enough for a whole lifetime. And yet how slow the time has gone!"

"I do not think it has been slow with me," said Phineas.

"No; you have been active. You have had your hands full of work. I am beginning to think that it is a great curse to have been born a woman."

"And yet I have heard you say that a woman may do as much as a man."

"That was before I had learned my lesson properly. I know better than that now. Oh dear! I have no doubt it is all for the best as it is, but I have a kind of wish that I might be allowed to go out and milk the cows."

"And may you not milk the cows if you wish it, Lady Laura?"

"By no means;—not only not milk them, but hardly look at them. At any rate, I must not talk about them." Phineas of course understood that she was complaining of her husband, and hardly knew how to reply to her. He had been sharp enough to perceive already that Mr. Kennedy was an autocrat in his own house, and he knew Lady Laura well enough to be sure that such masterdom would be very irksome to her. But he had not imagined that she would complain to him. "It was so different at Saulsby," Lady Laura continued. "Everything there seemed to be my own."

"And everything here is your own."

"Yes,—according to the prayer-book. And everything in truth is my own,—as all the dainties at the banquet belonged to Sancho the Governor."

"You mean," said he,—and then he hesitated; "you mean that Mr. Kennedy stands over you, guarding you for your own welfare, as the doctor stood over Sancho and guarded him?"

There was a pause before she answered,—a long pause, during which he was looking away over the lake, and thinking how he might introduce the subject of his love. But long as was the pause, he had not begun when Lady Laura was again speaking. "The truth is, my friend," she said, "that I have made a mistake."

"A mistake?"

"Yes, Phineas, a mistake. I have blundered as fools blunder, thinking that I was clever enough to pick my footsteps aright without asking counsel from any one. I have blundered and stumbled and fallen, and now I am so bruised that I am not able to stand upon my feet." The word that struck him most in all this was his own Christian name. She had never called him Phineas before. He was aware that the circle of his acquaintance had fallen into a way of miscalling him by his Christian name, as one observes to be done now and again in reference to some special young man. Most of the men whom he called his friends called him Phineas. Even the Earl had done so more than once on occasions in which the greatness of his position had dropped for a moment out of his mind. Mrs. Low had called him Phineas when she regarded him as her husband's most cherished pupil; and Mrs. Bunce had called him Mr. Phineas. He had always been Phineas to everybody at Killaloe. But still he was quite sure that Lady Laura had never so called him before. Nor would she have done so now in her husband's presence. He was sure of that also.

"You mean that you are unhappy?" he said, still looking away from her towards the lake.

"Yes, I do mean that. Though I do not know why I should come and tell you so,—except that I am still blundering and stumbling, and have fallen into a way of hurting myself at every step."

"You can tell no one who is more anxious for your happiness," said Phineas.

"That is a very pretty speech, but what would you do for my happiness? Indeed, what is it possible that you should do? I mean it as no rebuke when I say that my happiness or unhappiness is a matter as to which you will soon become perfectly indifferent."

"Why should you say so, Lady Laura?"

"Because it is natural that it should be so. You and Mr. Kennedy might have been friends. Not that you will be, because you are unlike each other in all your ways. But it might have been so."

"And are not you and I to be friends?" he asked.

"No. In a very few months you will not think of telling me what are your desires or what your sorrows;—and as for me, it will be out of the question that I should tell mine to you. How can you be my friend?"

"If you were not quite sure of my friendship, Lady Laura, you would not speak to me as you are speaking now." Still he did not look at her, but lay with his face supported on his hands, and his eyes turned away upon the lake. But she, where she was sitting, could see him, and was aided by her sight in making comparisons in her mind between the two men who had been her lovers,—between him whom she had taken and him whom she had left. There was something in the hard, dry, unsympathising, unchanging virtues of her husband which almost revolted her. He had not a fault, but she had tried him at every point and had been able to strike no spark of fire from him. Even by disobeying she could produce no heat,—only an access of firmness. How would it have been with her had she thrown all ideas of fortune to the winds, and linked her lot to that of the young Phœbus who was lying at her feet? If she had ever loved any one she had loved him. And she had not thrown away her love for money. So she swore to herself over and over again, trying to console herself in her cold unhappiness. She had married a rich man in order that she might be able to do something in the world;—and now that she was this rich man's wife she found that she could do nothing. The rich man thought it to be quite enough for her to sit at home and look after his welfare. In the meantime young Phœbus,—her Phœbus as he had been once,—was thinking altogether of some one else.

"Phineas," she said, slowly, "I have in you such perfect confidence that I will tell you the truth;—as one man may tell it to another. I wish you would go from here."

"What, at once?"

"Not to-day, or to-morrow. Stay here now till the election; but do not return. He will ask you to come, and press you hard, and will be hurt;—for, strange to say, with all his coldness, he really likes you. He has a pleasure in seeing you here. But he must not have that pleasure at the expense of trouble to me."

"And why is it a trouble to you?" he asked. Men are such fools;—so awkward, so unready, with their wits ever behind the occasion by a dozen seconds or so! As soon as the words were uttered, he knew that they should not have been spoken.

"Because I am a fool," she said. "Why else? Is not that enough for you?"

"Laura—," he said.

"No,—no; I will have none of that. I am a fool, but not such a fool as to suppose that any cure is to be found there."

"Only say what I can do for you, though it be with my entire life, and I will do it."

"You can do nothing,—except to keep away from me."

"Are you earnest in telling me that?" Now at last he had turned himself round and was looking at her, and as he looked he saw the hat of a man appearing up the path, and immediately afterwards the face. It was the hat and face of the laird of Loughlinter. "Here is Mr. Kennedy," said Phineas, in a tone of voice not devoid of dismay and trouble.

"So I perceive," said Lady Laura. But there was no dismay or trouble in the tone of her voice.

In the countenance of Mr. Kennedy, as he approached closer, there was not much to be read,—only, perhaps, some slight addition of gloom, or rather, perhaps, of that frigid propriety of moral demeanour for which he had always been conspicuous, which had grown upon him at his marriage, and which had been greatly increased by the double action of being made a Cabinet Minister and being garrotted. "I am glad that your headache is better," he said to his wife, who had risen from her seat to meet him. Phineas also had risen, and was now looking somewhat sheepish where he stood.

"I came out because it was worse," she said. "It irritated me so that I could not stand the house any longer."

94

"I will send to Callender for Dr. Macnuthrie."

"Pray do nothing of the kind, Robert. I do not want Dr. Macnuthrie at all."

"Where there is illness, medical advice is always expedient."

"I am not ill. A headache is not illness."

"I had thought it was," said Mr. Kennedy, very drily.

"At any rate, I would rather not have Dr. Macnuthrie."

"I am sure it cannot do you any good to climb up here in the heat of the sun. Had you been here long, Finn?"

"All the morning;—here, or hereabouts. I clambered up from the lake and had a book in my pocket."

"And you happened to come across him by accident?" Mr. Kennedy asked. There was something so simple in the question that its very simplicity proved that there was no suspicion.

"Yes;—by chance," said Lady Laura. "But every one at Loughlinter always comes up here. If any one ever were missing whom I wanted to find, this is where I should look."

"I am going on towards Linter forest to meet Blane," said Mr. Kennedy. Blane was the gamekeeper. "If you don't mind the trouble, Finn, I wish you'd take Lady Laura down to the house. Do not let her stay out in the heat. I will take care that somebody goes over to Callender for Dr. Macnuthrie." Then Mr. Kennedy went on, and Phineas was left with the charge of taking Lady Laura back to the house. When Mr. Kennedy's hat had first appeared coming up the walk, Phineas had been ready to proclaim himself prepared for any devotion in the service of Lady Laura. Indeed, he had begun to reply with criminal tenderness to the indiscreet avowal which Lady Laura had made to him. But he felt now, after what had just occurred in the husband's presence, that any show of tenderness,—of criminal tenderness,—was impossible. The absence of all suspicion on the part of Mr. Kennedy had made Phineas feel that he was bound by all social laws to refrain from such tenderness. Lady Laura began to descend the path before him without a word;—and went on, and on, as though she would have reached the house without speaking, had he not addressed her. "Does your head still pain you?" he asked.

"Of course it does."

"I suppose he is right in saying that you should not be out in the heat."

"I do not know. It is not worth while to think about that. He sends me in, and so of course I must go. And he tells you to take me, and so of course you must take me."

"Would you wish that I should let you go alone?"

"Yes, I would. Only he will be sure to find it out; and you must not tell him that you left me at my request."

"Do you think that I am afraid of him?" said Phineas.

"Yes;—I think you are. I know that I am, and that papa is; and that his mother hardly dares to call her soul her own. I do not know why you should escape."

"Mr. Kennedy is nothing to me."

"He is something to me, and so I suppose I had better go on. And now I shall have that horrid man from the little town pawing me and covering everything with snuff, and bidding me take Scotch physic,—which seems to increase in quantity and nastiness as doses in England decrease. And he will stand over me to see that I take it."

"What;—the doctor from Callender?"

"No;—but Mr. Kennedy will. If he advised me to have a hole in my glove mended, he would ask me before he went to bed whether it was done. He never forgot anything in his life, and was never unmindful of anything. That I think will do, Mr. Finn. You have brought me out from the trees, and that may be taken as bringing me home. We shall hardly get scolded if we part here. Remember what I told you up above. And remember also that it is in your power to do nothing else for me. Good-bye." So he turned away towards the lake, and let Lady Laura go across the wide lawn to the house by herself.

He had failed altogether in his intention of telling his friend of his love for Violet, and had come to perceive that he could not for the present carry out that intention. After what had passed it would be impossible for him to go to Lady Laura with a passionate tale of his longing for Violet Effingham. If he were even to speak to her of love at all, it must be quite of another love than that. But he never would speak to her of love; nor,—as he felt quite sure,—would she allow him to do so. But what astounded him most as he thought of the interview which had just passed, was the fact that the Lady Laura whom he had known,—whom he had thought he had known,—should have become so subject to such a man as Mr. Kennedy, a man whom he had despised as being weak, irresolute, and without a purpose! For the day or two that he remained at Loughlinter, he watched the family closely, and became aware that Lady Laura had been right when she declared that her father was afraid of Mr. Kennedy.

"I shall follow you almost immediately," said the Earl confidentially to Phineas, when the candidate for the borough took his departure from Loughlinter. "I don't like to be there just when the election is going on, but I'll be at Saulsby to receive you the day afterwards."

Phineas took his leave from Mr. Kennedy, with a warm expression of friendship on the part of his host, and from Lady Laura with a mere touch of the hand. He tried to say a word; but she was sullen, or, if not, she put on some mood like to sullenness, and said never a word to him.

On the day after the departure of Phineas Finn for Loughton Lady Laura Kennedy still had a headache. She had complained of a headache ever since she had been at Loughlinter, and Dr. Macnuthrie had been over more than once. "I wonder what it is that ails you," said her husband, standing over her in her own sitting-room up-stairs. It was a pretty room, looking away to the mountains, with just a glimpse of the lake to be caught from the window, and it had been prepared for her with all the skill and taste of an accomplished upholsterer. She had selected the room for herself soon after her engagement, and had thanked her future husband with her sweetest smile for giving her the choice. She had thanked him and told him that she always meant to be happy,—so happy in that room! He was a man not much given to romance, but he thought of this promise as he stood over her and asked after her health. As far as he could see she had never been even comfortable since she had been at Loughlinter. A shadow of the truth came across his mind. Perhaps his wife was bored. If so, what was to be the future of his life and of hers? He went up to London every year, and to Parliament, as a duty; and then, during some period of the recess, would have his house full of guests,—as another duty. But his happiness was to consist in such hours as these which seemed to inflict upon his wife the penalty of a continual headache. A shadow of the truth came upon him. What if his wife did not like living quietly at home as the mistress of her husband's house? What if a headache was always to be the result of a simple performance of domestic duties?

More than a shadow of truth had come upon Lady Laura herself. The dark cloud created by the entire truth was upon her, making everything black and wretched around her. She had asked herself a question or two, and had discovered that she had no love for her husband, that the kind of life which he intended to exact from her was insupportable to her, and that she had blundered and fallen in her entrance upon life. She perceived that her father had already become weary of Mr. Kennedy, and that, lonely and sad as he would be at Saulsby by himself, it was his intention to repudiate the idea of making a home at Loughlinter. Yes;—she would be deserted by everyone, except of course by her husband; and then— Then she would throw herself on some early morning into the lake, for life would be insupportable.

"I wonder what it is that ails you," said Mr. Kennedy.

"Nothing serious. One can't always help having a headache, you know."

"I don't think you take enough exercise, Laura. I would propose that you should walk four miles every day after breakfast. I will always be ready to accompany you. I have spoken to Dr. Macnuthrie—"

"I hate Dr. Macnuthrie."

"Why should you hate Dr. Macnuthrie, Laura?"

"How can I tell why? I do. That is quite reason enough why you should not send for him to me."

"You are unreasonable, Laura. One chooses a doctor on account of his reputation in his profession, and that of Dr. Macnuthrie stands high."

"I do not want any doctor."

"But if you are ill, my dear—"

"I am not ill."

"But you said you had a headache. You have said so for the last ten days."

"Having a headache is not being ill. I only wish you would not talk of it, and then perhaps I should get rid of it."

"I cannot believe that. Headache in nine cases out of ten comes from the stomach." Though he said this,—saying it because it was the common-place common-sense sort of thing to say, still at the very moment there was the shadow of the truth before his eyes. What if this headache meant simple dislike to him, and to his modes of life?

"It is nothing of that sort," said Lady Laura, impatient at having her ailment inquired into with so much accuracy.

"Then what is it? You cannot think that I can be happy to hear you complaining of headache every day,—making it an excuse for absolute idleness."

"What is it that you want me to do?" she said, jumping up from her seat. "Set me a task, and if I don't go mad over it, I'll get through it. There are the account books. Give them to me. I don't suppose I can see the figures, but I'll try to see them."

"Laura, this is unkind of you,—and ungrateful."

"Of course;—it is everything that is bad. What a pity that you did not find it out last year! Oh dear, oh dear! what am I to do?" Then she threw herself down upon the sofa, and put both her hands up to her temples.

"I will send for Dr. Macnuthrie at once," said Mr. Kennedy, walking towards the door very slowly, and speaking as slowly as he walked.

"No;—do no such thing," she said, springing to her feet again and intercepting him before he reached the door. "If he comes I will not see him. I give you my word that I will not speak to him if he comes. You do not understand," she said; "you do not understand at all."

"What is it that I ought to understand?" he asked.

"That a woman does not like to be bothered."

He made no reply at once, but stood there twisting the handle of the door, and collecting his thoughts. "Yes," said he at last; "I am beginning to find that out;—and to find out also what it is that bothers a woman, as you call it. I can see now what it is that makes your head ache. It is not the stomach. You are quite right there. It is the prospect of a quiet decent life, to which would be attached the performance of certain homely duties. Dr. Macnuthrie is a learned man, but I doubt whether he can do anything for such a malady."

"You are quite right, Robert; he can do nothing."

"It is a malady you must cure for yourself, Laura;—and which is to be cured by perseverance. If you can bring yourself to try—"

"But I cannot bring myself to try at all," she said.

"Do you mean to tell me, Laura, that you will make no effort to do your duty as my wife?"

"I mean to tell you that I will not try to cure a headache by doing sums. That is all that I mean to say at this moment. If you will leave me for awhile, so that I may lie down, perhaps I shall be able to come to dinner." He still hesitated, standing with the door in his hand. "But if you go on scolding me," she continued, "what I shall do is to go to bed directly you go away." He hesitated for a moment longer, and then left the room without another word.

CHAPTER XXXIII
Mr. Slide's Grievance

Our hero was elected member for Loughton without any trouble to him or, as far as he could see, to any one else. He made one speech from a small raised booth that was called a platform, and that was all that he was called upon to do. Mr. Grating made a speech in proposing him, and Mr. Shortribs another in seconding him; and these were all the speeches that were required. The thing seemed to be so very easy that he was afterwards almost offended when he was told that the bill for so insignificant a piece of work came to £247 13s. 9d. He had seen no occasion for spending even the odd forty-seven pounds. But then he was member for Loughton; and as he passed the evening alone at the inn, having dined in company with Messrs. Grating, Shortribs, and sundry other influential electors, he began to reflect that, after all, it was not so very great a thing to be a member of Parliament. It almost seemed that that which had come to him so easily could not be of much value.

On the following day he went to the castle, and was there when the Earl arrived. They two were alone together, and the Earl was very kind to him. "So you had no opponent after all," said the great man of Loughton, with a slight smile.

"Not the ghost of another candidate."

"I did not think there would be. They have tried it once or twice and have always failed. There are only one or two in the place who like to go one way just because their neighbours go the other. But, in truth, there is no conservative feeling in the place!"

Phineas, although he was at the present moment the member for Loughton himself, could not but enjoy the joke of this. Could there be any liberal feeling in such a place, or, indeed, any political feeling whatsoever? Would not Messrs. Grating and Shortribs have done just the same had it happened that Lord Brentford had been a Tory peer? "They all seemed to be very obliging," said Phineas, in answer to the Earl.

"Yes, they are. There isn't a house in the town, you know, let for longer than seven years, and most of them merely from year to year. And, do you know, I haven't a farmer on the property with a lease,—not one; and they don't want leases. They know they're safe. But I do like the people round me to be of the same way of thinking as myself about politics."

On the second day after dinner,—the last evening of Finn's visit to Saulsby,—the Earl fell suddenly into a confidential conversation about his daughter and his son, and about Violet Effingham. So sudden, indeed, and so confidential was the conversation, that Phineas was almost silenced for awhile. A word or two had been said about Loughlinter, of the beauty of the place and of the vastness of the property. "I am almost afraid," said Lord Brentford, "that Laura is not happy there."

"I hope she is," said Phineas.

"He is so hard and dry, and what I call exacting. That is just the word for it. Now Laura has never been used to that. With me she always had her own way in everything, and I always found her fit to have it. I do not understand why her husband should treat her differently."

"Perhaps it is the temper of the man."

"Temper, yes; but what a bad prospect is that for her! And she, too, has a temper, and so he will find if he tries her too far. I cannot stand Loughlinter. I told Laura so fairly. It is one of those houses in which a man cannot call his hours his own. I told Laura that I could not undertake to remain there for above a day or two."

"It is very sad," said Phineas.

"Yes, indeed; it is sad for her, poor girl; and very sad for me too. I have no one else but Laura,—literally no one; and now I am divided from her! It seems that she has been taken as much away from me as though her husband lived in China. I have lost them both now!"

"I hope not, my lord."

"I say I have. As to Chiltern, I can perceive that he becomes more and more indifferent to me every day. He thinks of me only as a man in his way who must die some day and may die soon."

"You wrong him, Lord Brentford."

"I do not wrong him at all. Why has he answered every offer I have made him with so much insolence as to make it impossible for me to put myself into further communion with him?"

"He thinks that you have wronged him."

"Yes;—because I have been unable to shut my eyes to his mode of living. I was to go on paying his debts, and taking no other notice whatsoever of his conduct!"

"I do not think he is in debt now."

"Because his sister the other day spent every shilling of her fortune in paying them. She gave him £40,000! Do you think she would have married Kennedy but for that? I don't. I could not prevent her. I had said that I would not cripple my remaining years of life by raising the money, and I could not go back from my word."

"You and Chiltern might raise the money between you."

"It would do no good now. She has married Mr. Kennedy, and the money is nothing to her or to him. Chiltern might have put things right by marrying Miss Effingham if he pleased."

"I think he did his best there."

"No;—he did his worst. He asked her to be his wife as a man asks for a railway-ticket or a pair of gloves, which he buys with a price; and because she would not jump into his mouth he gave it up. I don't believe he even really wanted to marry her. I suppose he has some disreputable connection to prevent it."

"Nothing of the kind. He would marry her to-morrow if he could. My belief is that Miss Effingham is sincere in refusing him."

"I don't doubt her sincerity."

"And that she will never change."

"Ah, well; I don't agree with you, and I daresay I know them both better than you do. But everything goes against me. I had set my heart upon it, and therefore of course I shall be disappointed. What is he going to do this autumn?"

"He is yachting now."

"And who are with him?"

"I think the boat belongs to Captain Colepepper."

"The greatest blackguard in all England! A man who shoots pigeons and rides steeple-chases! And the worst of Chiltern is this, that even if he didn't like the man, and if he were tired of this sort of life, he would go on just the same because he thinks it a fine thing not to give way."

This was so true that Phineas did not dare to contradict the statement, and therefore said nothing. "I had some faint hope," continued the Earl, "while Laura could always watch him; because, in his way, he was fond of his sister. But that is all over now. She will have enough to do to watch herself!"

Phineas had felt that the Earl had put him down rather sharply when he had said that Violet would never accept Lord Chiltern, and he was therefore not a little surprised when Lord Brentford spoke again of Miss Effingham the following morning, holding in his hand a letter which he had just received from her. "They are to be at Loughlinter on the tenth," he said, "and she purposes to come here for a couple of nights on her way."

"Lady Baldock and all?"

"Well, yes; Lady Baldock and all. I am not very fond of Lady Baldock, but I will put up with her for a couple of days for the sake of having Violet. She is more like a child of my own now than anybody else. I shall not see her all the autumn afterwards. I cannot stand Loughlinter."

"It will be better when the house is full."

"You will be there, I suppose?"

"Well, no; I think not," said Phineas.

"You have had enough of it, have you?" Phineas made no reply to this, but smiled slightly. "By Jove, I don't wonder at it," said the Earl. Phineas, who would have given all he had in the world to be staying in the same country house with Violet Effingham, could not explain how it had come to pass that he was obliged to absent himself. "I suppose you were asked?" said the Earl.

"Oh, yes, I was asked. Nothing can be kinder than they are."

"Kennedy told me that you were coming as a matter of course."

"I explained to him after that," said Phineas, "that I should not return. I shall go over to Ireland. I have a deal of hard reading to do, and I can get through it there without interruption."

He went up from Saulsby to London on that day, and found himself quite alone in Mrs. Bunce's lodgings. I mean not only that he was alone at his lodgings, but that he was alone at his club, and alone in the streets. July was not quite over, and yet all the birds of passage had migrated. Mr. Mildmay, by his short session, had half ruined the London tradesmen, and had changed the summer mode of life of all those who account themselves to be anybody. Phineas, as he sat alone in his room, felt himself to be nobody. He had told the Earl that he was going to Ireland, and to Ireland he must go;—because he had nothing else to do. He had been asked indeed to join one or two parties in their autumn plans. Mr. Monk had wanted him to go to the Pyrenees, and Lord Chiltern had suggested that he should join the yacht;—but neither plan suited him. It would have suited him to be at Loughlinter with Violet Effingham, but Loughlinter was a barred house to him. His old friend, Lady Laura, had told him not to come thither, explaining, with sufficient clearness, her reasons for excluding him from the number of her husband's guests. As he thought of it the past scenes of his life became very marvellous to him. Twelve months since he would have given all the world for a word of love from Lady Laura, and had barely dared to hope that such a word, at some future day, might possibly be spoken. Now such a word had in truth been spoken, and it had come to be simply a trouble to him. She had owned to him,—for, in truth, such had been the meaning of her warning to him,—that, though she had married another man, she had loved and did love him. But in thinking of this he took no pride in it. It was not till he had thought of it long that he began to ask himself whether he might not be justified in gathering from what happened some hope that Violet also might learn to love him. He had thought so little of himself as to have been afraid at first to press his suit with Lady Laura. Might he not venture to think more of himself, having learned how far he had succeeded?

But how was he to get at Violet Effingham? From the moment at which he had left Saulsby he had been angry with himself for not having asked Lord Brentford to allow him to remain there till after the Baldock party should have gone on to Loughlinter. The Earl, who was very lonely in his house, would have consented at once. Phineas, indeed, was driven to confess to himself that success with Violet would at once have put an end to all his friendship with Lord Brentford;—as also to all his friendship with Lord Chiltern. He would, in such case, be bound in honour to vacate his seat and give back Loughton to his offended patron. But he would have given up much more than his seat for Violet Effingham! At present, however, he had no means of getting at her to ask her the question. He could hardly go to Loughlinter in opposition to the wishes of Lady Laura.

A little adventure happened to him in London which somewhat relieved the dulness of the days of the first week in August. He remained in London till the middle of August, half resolving to rush down to Saulsby when Violet Effingham should be there,—endeavouring to find some excuse for such a proceeding, but racking his brains in vain,—and then there came about his little adventure. The adventure was commenced by the receipt of the following letter:—

Banner of the People Office,
3rd August, 186—.

My dear Finn,

I must say I think you have treated me badly, and without that sort of brotherly fairness which we on the public press expect from one another. However, perhaps we can come to an understanding, and if so, things may yet go smoothly. Give me a turn and I am not at all adverse to give you one. Will you come to me here, or shall I call upon you?

Yours always, Q. S.

Phineas was not only surprised, but disgusted also, at the receipt of this letter. He could not imagine what was the deed by which he had offended Mr. Slide. He thought over all the circumstances of his short connection with the *People's Banner*, but could remember nothing which might have created offence. But his disgust was greater than his surprise. He thought that he had done nothing and said nothing to justify Quintus Slide in calling him "dear Finn." He, who had Lady Laura's secret in his keeping; he who hoped to be the possessor of Violet Effingham's affections,—he to be called "dear Finn" by such a one as Quintus Slide! He soon made up his mind that he would not answer the note, but would go at once to the *People's Banner* office at the hour at which Quintus Slide was always there. He certainly would not write to "dear Slide;" and, until he had heard something more of this cause of offence, he would not make an enemy for ever by calling the man "dear

Sir." He went to the office of the *People's Banner*, and found Mr. Slide ensconced in a little glass cupboard, writing an article for the next day's copy.

"I suppose you're very busy," said Phineas, inserting himself with some difficulty on to a little stool in the corner of the cupboard.

"Not so particular but what I'm glad to see you. You shoot, don't you?"

"Shoot!" said Phineas. It could not be possible that Mr. Slide was intending, after this abrupt fashion, to propose a duel with pistols.

"Grouse and pheasants, and them sort of things?" asked Mr. Slide.

"Oh, ah; I understand. Yes, I shoot sometimes."

"Is it the 12th or 20th for grouse in Scotland?"

"The 12th," said Phineas. "What makes you ask that just now?"

"I'm doing a letter about it,—advising men not to shoot too many of the young birds, and showing that they'll have none next year if they do. I had a fellow here just now who knew all about it, and he put down a lot; but I forgot to make him tell me the day of beginning. What's a good place to date from?"

Phineas suggested Callender or Stirling.

"Stirling's too much of a town, isn't it? Callender sounds better for game, I think."

So the letter which was to save the young grouse was dated from Callender; and Mr. Quintus Slide having written the word, threw down his pen, came off his stool, and rushed at once at his subject.

"Well, now, Finn," he said, "don't you know that you've treated me badly about Loughton?"

"Treated you badly about Loughton!" Phineas, as he repeated the words, was quite in the dark as to Mr. Slide's meaning. Did Mr. Slide intend to convey a reproach because Phineas had not personally sent some tidings of the election to the *People's Banner*?

"Very badly," said Mr. Slide, with his arms akimbo,—"very badly indeed! Men on the press together do expect that they're to be stuck by, and not thrown over. Damn it, I say; what's the good of a brotherhood if it ain't to be brotherhood?"

"Upon my word, I don't know what you mean," said Phineas.

"Didn't I tell you that I had Loughton in my heye?" said Quintus.

"Oh—h!"

"It's very well to say ho, and look guilty, but didn't I tell you?"

"I never heard such nonsense in my life."

"Nonsense?"

"How on earth could you have stood for Loughton? What interest would you have there? You could not even have found an elector to propose you."

"Now, I'll tell you what I'll do, Finn. I think you have thrown me over most shabby, but I won't stand about that. You shall have Loughton this session if you'll promise to make way for me after the next election. If you'll agree to that, we'll have a special leader to say how well Lord What's-his-name has done with the borough; and we'll be your horgan through the whole session."

"I never heard such nonsense in my life. In the first place, Loughton is safe to be in the schedule of reduced boroughs. It will be thrown into the county, or joined with a group."

"I'll stand the chance of that. Will you agree?"

"Agree! No! It's the most absurd proposal that was ever made. You might as well ask me whether I would agree that you should go to heaven. Go to heaven if you can, I should say. I have not the slightest objection. But it's nothing to me."

"Very well," said Quintus Slide. "Very well! Now we understand each other, and that's all that I desire. I think that I can show you what it is to come among gentlemen of the press, and then to throw them over. Good morning."

Phineas, quite satisfied at the result of the interview as regarded himself, and by no means sorry that there should have arisen a cause of separation between Mr. Quintus Slide and his "dear Finn," shook off a little dust from his foot as he left the office of the *People's Banner*, and resolved that in future he would attempt to make no connection in that direction. As he returned home he told himself that a member of Parliament should be altogether independent of the press. On the second morning after his meeting with his late friend, he saw the result of his independence. There was a startling article, a tremendous article, showing the pressing necessity of immediate reform, and proving the necessity by an illustration of the borough-mongering rottenness of the present system. When such a patron as Lord Brentford,—himself a Cabinet Minister with a sinecure,—could by his mere word put into the House such a stick as Phineas Finn,—a man who had struggled to stand on his legs before the Speaker, but had wanted both the courage and the capacity, nothing further could surely be wanted to prove that the Reform Bill of 1832 required to be supplemented by some more energetic measure.

Phineas laughed as he read the article, and declared to himself that the joke was a good joke. But, nevertheless, he suffered. Mr. Quintus Slide, when he was really anxious to use his thong earnestly, could generally raise a wale.

CHAPTER XXXIV

Was He Honest?

On the 10th of August, Phineas Finn did return to Loughton. He went down by the mail train on the night of the 10th, having telegraphed to the inn for a bed, and was up eating his breakfast in that hospitable house at nine o'clock. The landlord and landlady with all their staff were at a loss to imagine what had brought down their member again so quickly to his borough; but the reader, who will remember that Lady Baldock with her daughter and Violet Effingham were to pass the 11th of the month at Saulsby, may perhaps be able to make a guess on the subject.

Phineas had been thinking of making this sudden visit to Loughton ever since he had been up in town, but he could suggest to himself no reason to be given to Lord Brentford for his sudden reappearance. The Earl had been very kind to him, but he had said nothing which could justify his young friend in running in and out of Saulsby Castle at pleasure, without invitation and without notice. Phineas was so well aware of this himself that often as he had half resolved during the last ten days to return to Saulsby, so often had he determined that he could not do so. He could think of no excuse. Then the heavens favoured him, and he received a letter from Lord Chiltern, in which there was a message for Lord Brentford. "If you see my father, tell him that I am ready at any moment to do what is necessary for raising the money for Laura." Taking this as his excuse he returned to Loughton.

As chance arranged it, he met the Earl standing on the great steps before his own castle doors. "What, Finn; is this you? I thought you were in Ireland."

"Not yet, my lord, as you see." Then he opened his budget at once, and blushed at his own hypocrisy as he went on with his story. He had, he said, felt the message from Chiltern to be so all-important that he could not bring himself to go over to Ireland without delivering it. He urged upon the Earl that he might learn from this how anxious Lord Chiltern was to effect a reconciliation. When it occurred to him, he said, that there might be a hope of doing anything towards such an object, he could not go to Ireland leaving the good work behind him. In love and war all things are fair. So he declared to himself; but as he did so he felt that his story was so weak that it would hardly gain for him an admittance into the Castle. In this he was completely wrong. The Earl, swallowing the bait, put his arm through that of the intruder, and, walking with him through the paths of the shrubbery, at length confessed that he would be glad to be reconciled to his son if it were possible. "Let him come here, and she shall be here also," said the Earl, speaking of Violet. To this Phineas could say nothing out loud, but he told himself that all should be fair between them. He would take no dishonest advantage of Lord Chiltern. He would give Lord Chiltern the whole message as it was given to him by Lord Brentford. But should it so turn out that he himself got an opportunity of saying to Violet all that he had come to say, and should it also turn out,—an event which he acknowledged to himself to be most unlikely,—that Violet did not reject him, then how could he write his letter to Lord Chiltern? So he resolved that the letter should be written before he saw Violet. But how could he write such a letter and instantly afterwards do that which would be false to the spirit of a letter so written? Could he bid Lord Chiltern come home to woo Violet Effingham, and instantly go forth to woo her for himself? He found that he could not do so,—unless he told the whole truth to Lord Chiltern. In no other way could he carry out his project and satisfy his own idea of what was honest.

The Earl bade him send to the hotel for his things. "The Baldock people are all here, you know, but they go very early to-morrow." Then Phineas declared that he also must return to London very early on the morrow;—but in the meantime he would go to the inn and fetch his things. The Earl thanked him again and again for his generous kindness; and Phineas, blushing as he received the thanks, went back and wrote his letter to Lord Chiltern. It was an elaborate letter, written, as regards the first and larger portion of it, with words intended to bring the prodigal son back to the father's home. And everything was said about Miss Effingham that could or should have been said. Then, on the last page, he told his own story. "Now," he said, "I must speak of myself:"—and he went on to explain to his friend, in the plainest language that he could use, his own position. "I have loved her," he said, "for six months, and I am here with the express intention of asking her to take me. The chances are ten to one that she refuses me. I do not deprecate your anger,—if you choose to be angry. But I am endeavouring to treat you well, and I ask you to do the same by me. I must convey to you your father's message, and after doing so I cannot address myself to Miss Effingham without telling you. I should feel myself to be false were I to do so. In the event,—the probable, nay, almost certain event of my being refused,—I shall trust you to keep my secret. Do not quarrel with me if you can help it;—but if you must I will be ready." Then he posted the letter and went up to the Castle.

He had only the one day for his action, and he knew that Violet was watched by Lady Baldock as by a dragon. He was told that the Earl was out with the young ladies, and was shown to his room. On going to the drawing-room he found Lady Baldock, with whom he had been, to a certain degree, a favourite, and was soon deeply engaged in a conversation as to the practicability of shutting up all the breweries and distilleries by Act of Parliament. But lunch relieved him, and brought the young ladies in at two. Miss Effingham seemed to be really glad to see him, and even Miss Boreham, Lady Baldock's daughter, was very gracious to him. For the Earl had been speaking well of his young member, and Phineas had in a way grown into the good graces of sober and discreet people. After lunch they were to ride;—the Earl, that is, and Violet. Lady Baldock and her daughter were to have the carriage. "I can mount you, Finn, if you would like it," said the Earl. "Of course he'll like it," said Violet; "do you suppose Mr. Finn will object to ride with me in Saulsby Woods? It won't be the first time, will it?" "Violet," said Lady Baldock, "you have the most singular way of talking." "I suppose I have," said Violet; "but I don't think I can change it now. Mr. Finn knows me too well to mind it much."

It was past five before they were on horseback, and up to that time Phineas had not found himself alone with Violet Effingham for a moment. They had sat together after lunch in the dining-room for nearly an hour, and had sauntered into the hall and knocked about the billiard balls, and then stood together at the open doors of a conservatory. But Lady Baldock or Miss Boreham had always been there. Nothing could be more pleasant than Miss Effingham's words, or more familiar than her manner to Phineas. She had expressed strong delight at his success in getting a seat in Parliament, and had talked to him about the Kennedys as though they had created some special bond of union between her and Phineas which ought to make them intimate. But, for all that, she could not be got to separate herself from Lady Baldock;—and when she was told that if she meant to ride she must go and dress herself, she went at once.

But he thought that he might have a chance on horseback; and after they had been out about half an hour, chance did favour him. For awhile he rode behind with the carriage, calculating that by his so doing the Earl would be put off his guard, and would be disposed after awhile to change places with him. And so it fell out. At a certain fall of ground in the park, where the road turned round and crossed a bridge over the little river, the carriage came up with the first two horses, and Lady Baldock spoke a word to the Earl. Then Violet pulled up, allowing the vehicle to pass the bridge first, and in this way she and Phineas were brought together,—and in this way they rode on. But he was aware that he must greatly increase the distance between them and the others of their party before he could dare to plead his suit, and even were that done he felt that he would not know how to plead it on horseback.

They had gone on some half mile in this way when they reached a spot on which a green ride led away from the main road through the trees to the left. "You remember this place, do you not?" said Violet. Phineas declared that he remembered it well. "I must go round by the woodman's cottage. You won't mind coming?" Phineas said that he would not mind, and trotted on to tell them in the carriage.

"Where is she going?" asked Lady Baldock; and then, when Phineas explained, she begged the Earl to go back to Violet. The Earl, feeling the absurdity of this, declared that Violet knew her way very well herself, and thus Phineas got his opportunity.

They rode on almost without speaking for nearly a mile, cantering through the trees, and then they took another turn to the right, and came upon the cottage. They rode to the door, and spoke a word or two to the woman there, and then passed on. "I always come here when I am at Saulsby," said Violet, "that I may teach myself to think kindly of Lord Chiltern."

"I understand it all," said Phineas.

"He used to be so nice;—and is so still, I believe, only that he has taught himself to be so rough. Will he ever change, do you think?"

Phineas knew that in this emergency it was his especial duty to be honest. "I think he would be changed altogether if we could bring him here,—so that he should live among his friends."

"Do you think he would? We must put our heads together, and do it. Don't you think that it is to be done?"

Phineas replied that he thought it was to be done. "I'll tell you the truth at once, Miss Effingham," he said. "You can do it by a single word."

"Yes;—yes;" she said; "but I do not mean that;—without that. It is absurd, you know, that a father should make such a condition as that." Phineas said that he thought it was absurd; and then they rode on again, cantering through the wood. He had been bold to speak to her about Lord Chiltern as he had done, and she had answered just as he would have wished to be answered. But how could he press his suit for himself while she was cantering by his side?

Presently they came to rough ground over which they were forced to walk, and he was close by her side. "Mr. Finn," she said, "I wonder whether I may ask a question?"

"Any question," he replied.

"Is there any quarrel between you and Lady Laura?"

"None."

"Or between you and him?"

"No;—none. We are greater allies than ever."

"Then why are you not going to be at Loughlinter? She has written to me expressly saying you would not be there."

He paused a moment before he replied. "It did not suit," he said at last.

"It is a secret then?"

"Yes;—it is a secret. You are not angry with me?"

"Angry; no."

"It is not a secret of my own, or I should not keep it from you."

"Perhaps I can guess it," she said. "But I will not try. I will not even think of it."

"The cause, whatever it be, has been full of sorrow to me. I would have given my left hand to have been at Loughlinter this autumn."

"Are you so fond of it?"

"I should have been staying there with you," he said. He paused, and for a moment there was no word spoken by either of them; but he could perceive that the hand in which she held her whip was playing with her horse's mane with a nervous movement. "When I found how it must be, and that I must miss you, I rushed down here that I might see you for a moment. And now I am here I do not dare to speak to you of myself." They were now beyond the rocks, and Violet, without speaking a word, again put her horse into a trot. He was by her side in a moment, but he could not see her face. "Have you not a word to say to me?" he asked.

"No;—no;—no;" she replied, "not a word when you speak to me like that. There is the carriage. Come;—we will join them." Then she cantered on, and he followed her till they reached the Earl and Lady Baldock and Miss Boreham. "I have done my devotions now," said Miss Effingham, "and am ready to return to ordinary life."

Phineas could not find another moment in which to speak to her. Though he spent the evening with her, and stood over her as she sang at the Earl's request, and pressed her hand as she went to bed, and was up to see her start in the morning, he could not draw from her either a word or a look.

CHAPTER XXXV
Mr. Monk upon Reform

Phineas Finn went to Ireland immediately after his return from Saulsby, having said nothing further to Violet Effingham, and having heard nothing further from her than what is recorded in the last chapter. He felt very keenly that his position was unsatisfactory, and brooded over it all the autumn and early winter; but he could form no plan for improving it. A dozen times he thought of writing to Miss Effingham, and asking for an explicit answer. He could not, however, bring himself to write the letter, thinking that written expressions of love are always weak and vapid,—and deterred also by a conviction that Violet, if driven to reply in writing, would undoubtedly reply by a refusal. Fifty times he rode again in his imagination his ride in Saulsby Wood, and he told himself as often that the syren's answer to him,—her no, no, no,—had been, of all possible answers, the most indefinite and provoking. The tone of her voice as she galloped away from him, the bearing of her countenance when he rejoined her, her manner to him when he saw her start from the Castle in the morning, all forbade him to believe that his words to her had been taken as an offence. She had replied to him with a direct negative, simply with the word "no;" but she had so said it that there had hardly been any sting in the no; and he had known at the moment that whatever might be the result of his suit, he need not regard Violet Effingham as his enemy.

But the doubt made his sojourn in Ireland very wearisome to him. And there were other matters which tended also to his discomfort, though he was not left even at this period of his life without a continuation of success which seemed to be very wonderful. And, first, I will say a word of his discomfort. He heard not a line from Lord Chiltern in answer to the letter which he had written to his lordship. From Lady Laura he did hear frequently. Lady Laura wrote to him exactly as though she had never warned him away from Loughlinter, and as though there had been no occasion for such warning. She sent him letters filled chiefly with politics, saying something also of the guests at Loughlinter, something of the game, and just a word or two here and there of her husband. The letters were very good letters, and he preserved them carefully. It was manifest to him that they were intended to be good letters, and, as such, to be preserved. In one of these, which he received about the end of November, she told him that her brother was again in his old haunt, at the Willingford Bull, and that he had sent to Portman Square for all property of his own that had been left there. But there was no word in that letter of Violet Effingham; and though Lady Laura did speak more than once of Violet, she always did so as though Violet were simply a joint acquaintance of herself and her correspondent. There was no allusion to the existence of any special regard on his part for Miss Effingham. He had thought that Violet might probably tell her friend what had occurred at Saulsby;—but if she did so, Lady Laura was happy in her powers of reticence. Our hero was disturbed also when he reached home by finding that Mrs. Flood Jones and Miss Flood Jones had retired from Killaloe for the winter. I do not know whether he might not have been more disturbed by the presence of the young lady, for he would have found himself constrained to exhibit towards her some tenderness of manner; and any such tenderness of manner would, in his existing circumstances, have been dangerous. But he was made to understand that Mary Flood Jones had been taken away from Killaloe because it was thought that he had ill-treated the lady, and the accusation made him unhappy. In the middle of the heat of the last session he had received a letter from his sister, in which some pushing question had been asked as to his then existing feeling about poor Mary. This he had answered petulantly. Nothing more had been written to him about Miss Jones, and nothing was said to him when he reached home. He could not, however, but ask after Mary, and when he did ask, the accusation was made again in that quietly severe manner with which, perhaps, most of us have been made acquainted at some period of our lives. "I think, Phineas," said his sister, "we had better say nothing about dear Mary. She is not here at present, and probably you may not see her while you remain with us." "What's all that about?" Phineas had demanded,—understanding the whole matter thoroughly. Then his sister had demurely refused to say a word further on the subject, and not a word further was said about Miss Mary Flood Jones. They were at Floodborough, living, he did not doubt, in a very desolate way,—and quite willing, he did not doubt also, to abandon their desolation if he would go over there in the manner that would become him after what had passed on one or two occasions between him and the young lady. But how was he to do this with such work on his hands as he had undertaken? Now that he was in Ireland, he thought that he did love dear Mary very dearly. He felt that he had two identities,—that he was, as it were, two separate persons,—and that he could, without any real faithlessness, be very much in love with Violet Effingham in his position of man of fashion and member of Parliament in England, and also warmly attached to dear little Mary Flood Jones as an Irishman of Killaloe. He was aware, however, that there was a prejudice against such fulness of heart, and, therefore, resolved sternly that it was his duty to be constant to Miss Effingham. How was it possible that he should marry dear Mary,—he, with such extensive jobs of work on his hands! It was not possible. He must abandon all thought of making dear Mary his own. No doubt they had been right to remove her. But, still, as he took his solitary walks along the Shannon, and up on the hills that overhung the lake above the town, he felt somewhat ashamed of himself, and dreamed of giving up Parliament, of leaving Violet to some noble suitor,—to Lord Chiltern, if she would take him,—and of going to Floodborough with an honest proposal that he should be allowed to press Mary to his heart. Miss Effingham would probably reject him at last; whereas Mary, dear Mary, would come to his heart without a scruple of doubt. Dear Mary! In these days of dreaming, he told himself that, after all, dear Mary was his real love. But, of course, such days were days of dreaming only. He had letters in his pocket from Lady Laura Kennedy which made it impossible for him to think in earnest of giving up Parliament.

And then there came a wonderful piece of luck in his way. There lived, or had lived, in the town of Galway a very eccentric old lady, one Miss Marian Persse, who was the aunt of Mrs. Finn, the mother of our hero. With this lady Dr. Finn had quarrelled persistently ever since his marriage, because the lady had expressed her wish to interfere in the management of his family,—offering to purchase such right by favourable arrangements in reference to her will. This the doctor had resented, and there had been quarrels. Miss Persse was not a very rich old lady, but she thought a good deal of her own money. And now she died, leaving £3,000 to her nephew Phineas Finn. Another sum of about equal amount she bequeathed to a Roman Catholic seminary; and thus was her worldly wealth divided. "She couldn't have done better with it," said the old doctor; "and as far as we are concerned, the windfall is the more pleasant as being wholly unexpected." In these days the doctor was undoubtedly gratified by his son's success in life, and never said much about the law. Phineas in truth did do some work during the autumn, reading blue-books, reading law books, reading perhaps a novel or two at the same time,—but shutting himself up very carefully as he studied, so that his sisters were made to understand that for a certain four hours in the day not a sound was to be allowed to disturb him.

On the receipt of his legacy he at once offered to repay his father all money that had been advanced him over and above his original allowance; but this the doctor refused to take. "It comes to the same thing, Phineas," he said. "What you have of your share now you can't have hereafter. As regards my present income, it has only made me work a little longer than I had intended; and I believe that the later in life a man works, the more likely he is to live." Phineas, therefore, when he returned to London, had his £3,000 in his pocket. He owed some £500; and the remainder he would, of course, invest.

There had been some talk of an autumnal session, but Mr. Mildmay's decision had at last been against it. Who cannot understand that such would be the decision of any Minister to whom was left the slightest fraction of free will in the matter? Why should any Minister court the danger of unnecessary attack, submit himself to unnecessary work, and incur the odium of summoning all his friends from their rest? In the midst of the doubts as to the new and old Ministry, when the political needle was vacillating so tremulously on its pivot, pointing now to one set of men as the coming Government and then to another, vague suggestions as to an autumn session might be useful. And they were thrown out in all good faith. Mr. Mildmay, when he spoke on the subject to the Duke, was earnest in thinking that the question of Reform should not be postponed even for six months. "Don't pledge yourself," said the Duke;—and Mr. Mildmay did not pledge himself. Afterwards, when Mr. Mildmay found that he was once more assuredly Prime Minister, he changed his mind, and felt himself to be under a fresh obligation to the Duke. Lord de Terrier had altogether failed, and the country might very well wait till February. The country did wait till February, somewhat to the disappointment of Phineas Finn, who had become tired of blue-books at Killaloe. The difference between his English life and his life at home was so great, that it was hardly possible that he should not become weary of the latter. He did become weary of it, but strove gallantly to hide his weariness from his father and mother.

At this time the world was talking much about Reform, though Mr. Mildmay had become placidly patient. The feeling was growing, and Mr. Turnbull, with his friends, was doing all he could to make it grow fast. There was a certain amount of excitement on the subject; but the excitement had grown downwards, from the leaders to the people,—from the self-instituted leaders of popular politics down, by means of the press, to the ranks of working men, instead of growing upwards, from the dissatisfaction of the masses, till it expressed itself by this mouthpiece and that, chosen by the people themselves. There was no strong throb through the country, making men feel that safety was to be had by Reform, and could not be had without Reform. But there was an understanding that the press and the orators were too strong to be ignored, and that some new measure of Reform must be conceded to them. The sooner the concession was made, the less it might be necessary to concede. And all men of all parties were agreed on this point. That Reform was in itself odious to many of those who spoke of it freely, who offered themselves willingly to be its promoters, was acknowledged. It was not only odious to Lord de Terrier and to most of those who worked with him, but was equally so to many of Mr. Mildmay's most constant supporters. The Duke had no wish for Reform. Indeed it is hard to suppose that such a Duke can wish for any change in a state of things that must seem to him to be so salutary. Workmen were getting full wages. Farmers were paying their rent. Capitalists by the dozen were creating capitalists by the hundreds. Nothing was wrong in the country, but the over-dominant spirit of speculative commerce;—and there was nothing in Reform to check that. Why should the Duke want Reform? As for such men as Lord Brentford, Sir Harry Coldfoot, Lord Plinlimmon, and Mr. Legge Wilson, it was known to all men that they advocated Reform as we all of us advocate doctors. Some amount of doctoring is necessary for us. We may hardly hope to avoid it. But let us have as little of the doctor as possible. Mr. Turnbull, and the cheap press, and the rising spirit of the loudest among the people, made it manifest that something must be conceded. Let us be generous in our concession. That was now the doctrine of many,— perhaps of most of the leading politicians of the day. Let us be generous. Let us at any rate seem to be generous. Let us give with an open hand,—but still with a hand which, though open, shall not bestow too much. The coach must be allowed to run down the hill. Indeed, unless the coach goes on running no journey will be made. But let us have the drag on both the hind wheels. And we must remember that coaches running down hill without drags are apt to come to serious misfortune.

But there were men, even in the Cabinet, who had other ideas of public service than that of dragging the wheels of the coach. Mr. Gresham was in earnest. Plantagenet Palliser was in earnest. That exceedingly intelligent young nobleman Lord Cantrip was in earnest. Mr. Mildmay threw, perhaps, as much of earnestness into the matter as was compatible with his age and his full appreciation of the manner in which the present cry for Reform had been aroused. He was thoroughly honest, thoroughly patriotic, and thoroughly ambitious that he should be written of hereafter as one who to the end of a long life had worked sedulously for the welfare of the people;—but he disbelieved in Mr. Turnbull, and in the bottom of his heart indulged an aristocratic contempt for the penny press. And there was no man in England more in earnest, more truly desirous of Reform, than Mr. Monk. It was his great political idea that political advantages should be extended to the people, whether the people clamoured for them or did not clamour for them,—even whether they desired them or did not desire them. "You do not ask a child whether he would like to learn his lesson," he would say. "At any rate, you do not wait till he cries for his book." When, therefore, men said to him that there was no earnestness in the cry for Reform, that the cry was a false cry, got up for factious purposes by interested persons, he would reply that the thing to be done should not be done in obedience to any cry, but because it was demanded by justice, and was a debt due to the people.

Our hero in the autumn had written to Mr. Monk on the politics of the moment, and the following had been Mr. Monk's reply:—

Longroyston, October 12, 186—.

My dear Finn,

I am staying here with the Duke and Duchess of St. Bungay. The house is very full, and Mr. Mildmay was here last week; but as I don't shoot, and can't play billiards, and have no taste for charades, I am becoming tired of the gaieties, and shall leave them to-morrow. Of course you know that we are not to have the autumn session. I think that Mr. Mildmay is right. Could we have been sure of passing our measure, it would have been very well; but we could not have been sure, and failure with our bill in a session convened for the express purpose of passing it would have injured the cause greatly. We could hardly have gone on with it again in the spring. Indeed, we must have resigned. And though I may truly say that I would as lief have a good measure from Lord de Terrier as from Mr. Mildmay, and that I am indifferent to my own present personal position, still I think that we should endeavour to keep our seats as long as we honestly believe ourselves to be more capable of passing a good measure than are our opponents.

I am astonished by the difference of opinion which exists about Reform,—not only as to the difference in the extent and exact tendency of the measure that is needed,—but that there should be such a divergence of ideas as to the grand thing to be done and the grand reason for doing it. We are all agreed that we want Reform in order that the House of Commons may be returned by a larger proportion of the people than is at present employed upon that work, and that each member when returned should represent a somewhat more equal section of the whole constituencies of the country than our members generally do at present. All men confess that a £50 county franchise must be too high, and that a borough with less than two hundred registered voters must be wrong. But it seems to me that but few among us perceive, or at any rate acknowledge, the real reasons for changing these things and reforming what is wrong without delay. One great authority told us the other day that the sole object of legislation on this subject should be to get together the best possible 658 members of Parliament. That to me would be a most repulsive idea if it were not that by its very vagueness it becomes inoperative. Who shall say what is best; or what characteristic constitutes excellence in a member of Parliament? If the gentleman means excellence in general wisdom, or in statecraft, or in skill in talking, or in private character, or even excellence in patriotism, then I say that he is utterly wrong, and has never touched with his intellect the true theory of representation. One only excellence may be acknowledged, and that is the excellence of likeness. As a portrait should be like the person portrayed, so should a representative House be like the people whom it represents. Nor in arranging a franchise does it seem to me that we have a right to regard any other view. If a country be unfit for representative government,—and it may be that there are still peoples unable to use properly that greatest of all blessings,—the question as to what state policy may be best for them is a different question. But if we do have representation, let the representative assembly be like the people, whatever else may be its virtues,—and whatever else its vices.

Another great authority has told us that our House of Commons should be the mirror of the people. I say, not its mirror, but its miniature. And let the artist be careful to put in every line of the expression of that ever-moving face. To do this is a great work, and the artist must know his trade well. In America the work has been done with so coarse a hand that nothing is shown in the picture but the broad, plain, unspeaking outline of the face. As you look from the represented to the representation you cannot but acknowledge the likeness;—but there is in that portrait more of the body than of the mind. The true portrait should represent more than the body. With us, hitherto, there have been snatches of the countenance of the nation which have been inimitable,—a turn of the eye here and a curl of the lip there, which have seemed to denote a power almost divine. There have been marvels on the canvas so beautiful that one approaches the work of remodelling it with awe. But not only is the picture imperfect,—a thing of snatches,—but with years it becomes less and still less like its original.

The necessity for remodelling it is imperative, and we shall be cowards if we decline the work. But let us be specially careful to retain as much as possible of those lines which we all acknowledge to be so faithfully representative of our nation. To give to a bare numerical majority of the people that power which the numerical majority has in the United States, would not be to achieve representation. The nation as it now exists would not be known by such a portrait;—but neither can it now be known by that which exists. It seems to me that they who are adverse to change, looking back with an unmeasured respect on what our old Parliaments have done for us, ignore the majestic growth of the English people, and forget the present in their worship of the past. They think that we must be what we were,—at any rate, what we were thirty years since. They have not, perhaps, gone into the houses of artisans, or, if there, they have not looked into the breasts of the men. With population vice has increased, and these politicians, with ears but no eyes, hear of drunkenness and sin and ignorance. And then they declare to themselves that this wicked, half-barbarous, idle people should be controlled and not represented. A wicked, half-barbarous, idle people may be controlled;—but not a people thoughtful, educated, and industrious. We must look to it that we do not endeavour to carry our control beyond the wickedness and the barbarity, and that we be ready to submit to control from thoughtfulness and industry.

I hope we shall find you helping at the good work early in the spring.

Yours, always faithfully,

Joshua Monk.

Phineas was up in London before the end of January, but did not find there many of those whom he wished to see. Mr. Low was there, and to him he showed Mr. Monk's letter, thinking that it must be convincing even to Mr. Low. This he did in Mrs. Low's drawing-room, knowing that Mrs. Low would also condescend to discuss politics on an occasion. He had dined with them, and they had been glad to see him, and Mrs. Low had been less severe than hitherto against the great sin of her husband's late pupil. She had condescended to congratulate him on becoming member for an English borough instead of an Irish one, and had asked him questions about Saulsby Castle. But, nevertheless, Mr. Monk's letter was not received with that respectful admiration which Phineas thought that it deserved. Phineas, foolishly, had read it out loud, so that the attack came upon him simultaneously from the husband and from the wife.

"It is just the usual claptrap," said Mr. Low, "only put into language somewhat more grandiloquent than usual."

"Claptrap!" said Phineas.

"It's what I call downright Radical nonsense," said Mrs. Low, nodding her head energetically. "Portrait indeed! Why should we want to have a portrait of ignorance and ugliness? What we all want is to have things quiet and orderly."

"Then you'd better have a paternal government at once," said Phineas.

"Just so," said Mr. Low,—"only that what you call a paternal government is not always quiet and orderly. National order I take to be submission to the law. I should not think it quiet and orderly if I were sent to Cayenne without being brought before a jury."

"But such a man as you would not be sent to Cayenne," said Phineas,

"My next-door neighbour might be,—which would be almost as bad. Let him be sent to Cayenne if he deserves it, but let a jury say that he has deserved it. My idea of government is this,—that we want to be governed by law and not by caprice, and that we must have a legislature to make our laws. If I thought that Parliament as at present established made the laws badly, I would desire a change; but I doubt whether we shall have them better from any change in Parliament which Reform will give us."

"Of course not," said Mrs. Low. "But we shall have a lot of beggars put on horseback, and we all know where they ride to."

Then Phineas became aware that it is not easy to convince any man or any woman on a point of politics,—not even though he who argues may have an eloquent letter from a philosophical Cabinet Minister in his pocket to assist him.

CHAPTER XXXVI
Phineas Finn Makes Progress

February was far advanced and the new Reform Bill had already been brought forward, before Lady Laura Kennedy came up to town. Phineas had of course seen Mr. Kennedy and had heard from him tidings of his wife. She was at Saulsby with Lady Baldock and Miss Boreham and Violet Effingham, but was to be in London soon. Mr. Kennedy, as it appeared, did not quite know when he was to expect his wife; and Phineas thought that he could perceive from the tone of the husband's voice that something was amiss. He could not however ask any questions excepting such as referred to the expected arrival. Was Miss Effingham to come to London with Lady Laura? Mr. Kennedy believed that Miss Effingham would be up before Easter, but he did not know whether she would come with his wife. "Women," he said, "are so fond of mystery that one can never quite know what they intend to do." He corrected himself at once however, perceiving that he had seemed to say something against his wife, and explained that his general accusation against the sex was not intended to apply to Lady Laura. This, however, he did so awkwardly as to strengthen the feeling with Phineas that something assuredly was wrong. "Miss Effingham," said Mr. Kennedy, "never seems to know her own mind." "I suppose she is like other beautiful girls who are petted on all sides," said Phineas. "As for her beauty, I don't think much of it," said Mr. Kennedy; "and as for petting, I do not understand it in reference to grown persons. Children may be petted, and dogs,—though that too is bad; but what you call petting for grown persons is I think frivolous and almost indecent." Phineas could not help thinking of Lord Chiltern's opinion that it would have been wise to have left Mr. Kennedy in the hands of the garrotters.

The debate on the second reading of the bill was to be commenced on the 1st of March, and two days before that Lady Laura arrived in Grosvenor Place. Phineas got a note from her in three words to say that she was at home and would see him if he called on Sunday afternoon. The Sunday to which she alluded was the last day of February. Phineas was now more certain than ever that something was wrong. Had there been nothing wrong between Lady Laura and her husband, she would not have rebelled against him by asking visitors to the house on a Sunday. He had nothing to do with that, however, and of course he did as he was desired. He called on the Sunday, and found Mrs. Bonteen sitting with Lady Laura. "I am just in time for the debate," said Lady Laura, when the first greeting was over.

"You don't mean to say that you intend to sit it out," said Mrs. Bonteen.

"Every word of it,—unless I lose my seat. What else is there to be done at present?"

"But the place they give us is so unpleasant," said Mrs. Bonteen.

"There are worse places even than the Ladies' Gallery," said Lady Laura. "And perhaps it is as well to make oneself used to inconveniences of all kinds. You will speak, Mr. Finn?"

"I intend to do so."

"Of course you will. The great speeches will be Mr. Gresham's, Mr. Daubeny's, and Mr. Monk's."

"Mr. Palliser intends to be very strong," said Mrs. Bonteen.

"A man cannot be strong or not as he likes it," said Lady Laura. "Mr. Palliser I believe to be a most useful man, but he never can become an orator. He is of the same class as Mr. Kennedy,—only of course higher in the class."

"We all look for a great speech from Mr. Kennedy," said Mrs. Bonteen.

"I have not the slightest idea whether he will open his lips," said Lady Laura. Immediately after that Mrs. Bonteen took her leave. "I hate that woman like poison," continued Lady Laura. "She is always playing a game, and it is such a small game that she plays! And she contributes so little to society. She is not witty nor well-informed,—not even sufficiently ignorant or ridiculous to be a laughing-stock. One gets nothing from her, and yet she has made her footing good in the world."

"I thought she was a friend of yours."

"You did not think so! You could not have thought so! How can you bring such an accusation against me, knowing me as you do? But never mind Mrs. Bonteen now. On what day shall you speak?"

"On Tuesday if I can."

"I suppose you can arrange it?"

"I shall endeavour to do so, as far as any arrangement can go."

"We shall carry the second reading," said Lady Laura.

"Yes," said Phineas; "I think we shall; but by the votes of men who are determined so to pull the bill to pieces in committee, that its own parents will not know it. I doubt whether Mr. Mildmay will have the temper to stand it."

"They tell me that Mr. Mildmay will abandon the custody of the bill to Mr. Gresham after his first speech."

"I don't know that Mr. Gresham's temper is more enduring than Mr. Mildmay's," said Phineas.

"Well;—we shall see. My own impression is that nothing would save the country so effectually at the present moment as the removal of Mr. Turnbull to a higher and a better sphere."

"Let us say the House of Lords," said Phineas.

"God forbid!" said Lady Laura.

Phineas sat there for half an hour and then got up to go, having spoken no word on any other subject than that of politics. He longed to ask after Violet. He longed to make some inquiry respecting Lord Chiltern. And, to tell the truth, he felt painfully curious to hear Lady Laura say something about her own self. He could not but remember what had been said between them up over the waterfall, and how he had been warned not to return to Loughlinter. And then again, did Lady Laura know anything of what had passed between him and Violet? "Where is your brother?" he said, as he rose from his chair.

"Oswald is in London. He was here not an hour before you came in."

"Where is he staying?"

"At Moroni's. He goes down on Tuesday, I think. He is to see his father to-morrow morning."

"By agreement?"

"Yes;—by agreement. There is a new trouble,—about money that they think to be due to me. But I cannot tell you all now. There have been some words between Mr. Kennedy and papa. But I won't talk about it. You would find Oswald at Moroni's at any hour before eleven to-morrow."

"Did he say anything about me?" asked Phineas.

"We mentioned your name certainly."

"I do not ask from vanity, but I want to know whether he is angry with me."

"Angry with you! Not in the least. I'll tell you just what he said. He said he should not wish to live even with you, but that he would sooner try it with you than with any man he ever knew."

"He had got a letter from me?"

"He did not say so;—but he did not say he had not."

"I will see him to-morrow if I can." And then Phineas prepared to go.

"One word, Mr. Finn," said Lady Laura, hardly looking him in the face and yet making an effort to do so. "I wish you to forget what I said to you at Loughlinter."

"It shall be as though it were forgotten," said Phineas.

"Let it be absolutely forgotten. In such a case a man is bound to do all that a woman asks him, and no man has a truer spirit of chivalry than yourself. That is all. Look in when you can. I will not ask you to dine here as yet, because we are so frightfully dull. Do your best on Tuesday, and then let us see you on Wednesday. Good-bye."

Phineas as he walked across the park towards his club made up his mind that he would forget the scene by the waterfall. He had never quite known what it had meant, and he would wipe it away from his mind altogether. He acknowledged to himself that chivalry did demand of him that he should never allow himself to think of Lady Laura's rash words to him. That she was not happy with her husband was very clear to him;—but that was altogether another affair. She might be unhappy with her husband without indulging any guilty love. He had never thought it possible that she could be happy living with such a husband as Mr. Kennedy. All that, however, was now past remedy, and she must simply endure the mode of life which she had prepared for herself. There were other men and women in London tied together for better and worse, in reference to whose union their friends knew that there would be no better;—that it must be all worse. Lady Laura must bear it, as it was borne by many another married woman.

On the Monday morning Phineas called at Moroni's Hotel at ten o'clock, but in spite of Lady Laura's assurance to the contrary, he found that Lord Chiltern was out. He had felt some palpitation at the heart as he made his inquiry, knowing well the fiery nature of the man he expected to see. It might be that there would be some actual personal conflict between him and this half-mad lord before he got back again into the street. What Lady Laura had said about her brother did not in the estimation of Phineas make this at all the less probable. The half-mad lord was so singular in his ways that it might well be that he should speak handsomely of a rival behind his back and yet take him by the throat as soon as they were together, face to face. And yet, as Phineas thought, it was necessary that he should see the half-mad lord. He had written a letter to which he had received no reply, and he considered it to be incumbent on him to ask whether it had been received and whether any answer to it was intended to be given. He went therefore to Lord Chiltern at once,—as I have said, with some feeling at his heart that there might be violence, at any rate of words, before he should find himself again in the street. But Lord Chiltern was not there. All that the porter knew was that Lord Chiltern intended to leave the house on the following morning. Then Phineas wrote a note and left it with the porter.

Dear Chiltern,

I particularly want to see you with reference to a letter I wrote to you last summer. I must be in the House to-day from four till the debate is over. I will be at the Reform Club from two till half-past three, and will come if you will send for me, or I will meet you anywhere at any hour to-morrow morning.

Yours, always, P. F.

No message came to him at the Reform Club, and he was in his seat in the House by four o'clock. During the debate a note was brought to him, which ran as follows:—

I have got your letter this moment. Of course we must meet. I hunt on Tuesday, and go down by the early train; but I will come to town on Wednesday. We shall require to be private, and I will therefore be at your rooms at one o'clock on that day.—C.

Phineas at once perceived that the note was a hostile note, written in an angry spirit,—written to one whom the writer did not at the moment acknowledge to be his friend. This was certainly the case, whatever Lord Chiltern may have said to his sister as to his friendship for Phineas. Phineas crushed the note into his pocket, and of course determined that he would be in his rooms at the hour named.

The debate was opened by a speech from Mr. Mildmay, in which that gentleman at great length and with much perspicuity explained his notion of that measure of Parliamentary Reform which he thought to be necessary. He was listened to with the greatest attention to the close,—and perhaps, at the end of his speech, with more attention than usual, as there had gone abroad a rumour that the Prime Minister intended to declare that this would be the last effort of his life in that course. But, if he ever intended to utter such a pledge, his heart misgave him when the time came for uttering it. He merely said that as the management of the bill in committee would be an affair of much labour, and probably spread over many nights, he would be assisted in his work by his colleagues, and especially by his right honourable friend the Secretary of State for Foreign Affairs. It was then understood that Mr. Gresham would take the lead should the bill go into committee;—but it was understood also that no resignation of leadership had been made by Mr. Mildmay.

The measure now proposed to the House was very much the same as that which had been brought forward in the last session. The existing theory of British representation was not to be changed, but the actual practice was to be brought nearer to the ideal theory. The ideas of manhood suffrage, and of electoral districts, were to be as for ever removed from the bulwarks of the British Constitution. There were to be counties with agricultural constituencies, purposely arranged to be purely agricultural, whenever the nature of the counties would admit of its being so. No artificer at Reform, let him be Conservative or Liberal, can make Middlesex or Lancashire agricultural; but Wiltshire and Suffolk were to be preserved inviolable to the plough,—and the apples of Devonshire were still to have their sway. Every town in the three kingdoms with a certain population was to have two members. But here there was much room for cavil,—as all men knew would be the case. Who shall say what is a town, or where shall be its limits? Bits of counties might be borrowed, so as to lessen the Conservatism of the county without endangering the Liberalism of the borough. And then there were the boroughs with one member,—and then the groups of little boroughs. In the discussion of any such arrangement how easy is the picking of holes; how impossible the fabrication of a garment that shall be impervious to such picking! Then again there was that great question of the ballot. On that there was to be no mistake. Mr. Mildmay again pledged himself to disappear from the Treasury bench should any motion, clause, or resolution be carried by that House in favour of the ballot. He spoke for three hours, and then left the carcass of his bill to be fought for by the opposing armies.

No reader of these pages will desire that the speeches in the debate should be even indicated. It soon became known that the Conservatives would not divide the House against the second reading of the bill. They declared, however, very plainly their intention of so altering the clauses of the bill in committee,—or at least of attempting so to do,—as to make the bill their bill, rather than the bill of their opponents. To this Mr. Palliser replied that as long as nothing vital was touched, the Government would only be too happy to oblige their friends opposite. If anything vital were touched, the Government could only fall back upon their friends on that side. And in this way men were very civil to each other. But Mr. Turnbull, who opened the debate on the Tuesday, thundered out an assurance to gods and men that he would divide the House on the second reading of the bill itself. He did not doubt but that there were many good men and true to go with him into the lobby, but into the lobby he would go if he had no more than a single friend to support him. And he warned the Sovereign, and he warned the House, and he warned the people of England, that the measure of Reform now proposed by a so-called liberal Minister was a measure prepared in concert with the ancient enemies of the people. He was very loud, very angry, and quite successful in hallooing down sundry attempts which were made to interrupt him. "I find," he said, "that there are many members here who do not know me yet,—young members, probably, who are green from the waste lands and road-sides of private life. They will know me soon, and then, may be, there will be less of this foolish noise, less of this elongation of unnecessary necks. Our Rome must be aroused to a sense of its danger by other voices than these." He was called to order, but it was ruled that he had not been out of order,—and he was very triumphant. Mr. Monk answered him, and it was declared afterwards that Mr. Monk's speech was one of the finest pieces of oratory that had ever been uttered in that House. He made one remark personal to Mr. Turnbull. "I quite agreed with the right honourable gentleman in the chair," he said, "when he declared that the honourable member was not out of order just now. We all of us agree with him always on such points. The rules of our House have been laid down with the utmost latitude, so that the course of our debates may not be frivolously or too easily interrupted. But a member may be so in order as to incur the displeasure of the House, and to merit the reproaches of his countrymen." This little duel gave great life to the debate; but it was said that those two great Reformers, Mr. Turnbull and Mr. Monk, could never again meet as friends.

In the course of the debate on Tuesday, Phineas got upon his legs. The reader, I trust, will remember that hitherto he had failed altogether as a speaker. On one occasion he had lacked even the spirit to use and deliver an oration which he had prepared. On a second occasion he had broken down,—woefully, and past all redemption, as said those who were not his friends,—unfortunately, but not past redemption, as said those who were his true friends. After that once again he had arisen and said a few words which had called for no remark, and had been spoken as though he were in the habit of addressing the House daily. It may be doubted whether there were half-a-dozen men now present who recognised the fact that this man, who was so well known to so many of them, was now about to make another attempt at a first speech. Phineas himself diligently attempted to forget that such was the case. He had prepared for himself a few headings of what he intended to say, and on one or two points had arranged his words. His hope was that even though he should forget the words, he might still be able to cling to the thread of his discourse. When he found himself again upon his legs amidst those crowded seats, for a few moments there came upon him that old sensation of awe. Again things grew dim before his eyes, and again he hardly knew at which end of that long chamber the Speaker was sitting. But there arose within him a sudden courage, as soon as the sound of his own voice in that room had made itself intimate to his ear; and after the first few sentences, all fear, all awe, was gone from him. When he read his speech in the report afterwards, he found that he had strayed very wide of his intended course, but he had strayed without tumbling into ditches, or falling into sunken pits. He had spoken much from Mr. Monk's letter, but had had the grace to acknowledge whence had come his inspiration. He hardly knew, however, whether he had failed again or not, till Barrington Erle came up to him as they were leaving the House, with his old easy pressing manner. "So you have got into form at last," he said. "I always thought that it would come. I never for a moment believed but that it would come sooner or later." Phineas Finn answered not a word; but he went home and lay awake all night triumphant. The verdict of Barrington Erle sufficed to assure him that he had succeeded.

CHAPTER XXXVII
A Rough Encounter

Phineas, when he woke, had two matters to occupy his mind,—his success of the previous night, and his coming interview with Lord Chiltern. He stayed at home the whole morning, knowing that nothing could be done before the hour Lord Chiltern had named for his visit. He read every word of the debate, studiously postponing the perusal of his own speech till he should come to it in due order. And then he wrote to his father, commencing his letter as though his writing had no reference to the affairs of the previous night. But he soon found himself compelled to break into some mention of it. "I send you a *Times*," he said, "in order that you may see that I have had my finger in the pie. I have hitherto abstained from putting myself forward in the House, partly through a base fear for which I despise myself, and partly through a feeling of prudence that a man of my age should not be in a hurry to gather laurels. This is literally true. There has been the fear, and there has been the prudence. My wonder is, that I have not incurred more contempt from others because I have been a coward. People have been so kind to me that I must suppose them to have judged me more leniently than I have judged myself." Then, as he was putting up the paper, he looked again at his own speech, and of course read every word of it once more. As he did so it occurred to him that the reporters had been more than courteous to him. The man who had followed him had been, he thought, at any rate as long-winded as himself; but to this orator less than half a column had been granted. To him had been granted ten lines in big type, and after that a whole column and a half. Let Lord Chiltern come and do his worst!

When it wanted but twenty minutes to one, and he was beginning to think in what way he had better answer the half-mad lord, should the lord in his wrath be very mad, there came to him a note by the hand of some messenger. He knew at once that it was from Lady Laura, and opened it in hot haste It was as follows:—

Dear Mr. Finn,

We are all talking about your speech. My father was in the gallery and heard it,—and said that he had to thank me for sending you to Loughton. That made me very happy. Mr. Kennedy declares that you were eloquent, but too short. That coming from him is praise indeed. I have seen Barrington, who takes pride to himself that you are his political child. Violet says that it is the only speech she ever read. I was there, and was delighted. I was sure that it was in you to do it.

Yours, L. K.

I suppose we shall see you after the House is up, but I write this as I shall barely have an opportunity of speaking to you then. I shall be in Portman Square, not at home, from six till seven.

The moment in which Phineas refolded this note and put it into his breast coat-pocket was, I think, the happiest of his life. Then, before he had withdrawn his hand from his breast, he remembered that what was now about to take place between him and Lord Chiltern would probably be the means of separating him altogether from Lady Laura and her family. Nay, might it not render it necessary that he should abandon the seat in Parliament which had been conferred upon him by the personal kindness of Lord Brentford? Let that be as it might. One thing was clear to him. He would not abandon Violet Effingham till he should be desired to do so in the plainest language by Violet Effingham herself. Looking at his watch he saw that it was one o'clock, and at that moment Lord Chiltern was announced.

Phineas went forward immediately with his hand out to meet his visitor. "Chiltern," he said, "I am very glad to see you." But Lord Chiltern did not take his hand. Passing on to the table, with his hat still on his head, and with a dark scowl upon his brow, the young lord stood for a few moments perfectly silent. Then he chucked a letter across the table to the spot at which Phineas was standing. Phineas, taking up the letter, perceived that it was that which he, in his great attempt to be honest, had written from the inn at Loughton. "It is my own letter to you," he said.

"Yes; it is your letter to me. I received it oddly enough together with your own note at Moroni's,—on Monday morning. It has been round the world, I suppose, and reached me only then. You must withdraw it."

"Withdraw it?"

"Yes, sir, withdraw it. As far as I can learn, without asking any question which would have committed myself or the young lady, you have not acted upon it. You have not yet done what you there threaten to do. In that you have been very wise, and there can be no difficulty in your withdrawing the letter."

"I certainly shall not withdraw it, Lord Chiltern."

"Do you remember—what—I once—told you,—about myself and Miss Effingham?" This question he asked very slowly, pausing between the words, and looking full into the face of his rival, towards whom he had gradually come nearer. And his countenance, as he did so, was by no means pleasant. The redness of his complexion had become more ruddy than usual; he still wore his hat as though with studied insolence; his right hand was clenched; and there was that look of angry purpose in his eye which no man likes to see in the eye of an antagonist. Phineas was afraid of no violence, personal to himself; but he was afraid of,—of what I may, perhaps, best call "a row." To be tumbling over the chairs and tables with his late friend and present enemy in Mrs. Bunce's room would be most unpleasant to him. If there were to be blows he, too, must strike;—and he was very averse to strike Lady Laura's brother, Lord Brentford's son, Violet Effingham's friend. If need be, however, he would strike.

"I suppose I remember what you mean," said Phineas. "I think you declared that you would quarrel with any man who might presume to address Miss Effingham. Is it that to which you allude?"

"It is that," said Lord Chiltern.

"I remember what you said very well. If nothing else was to deter me from asking Miss Effingham to be my wife, you will hardly think that that ought to have any weight. The threat had no weight."

"It was not spoken as a threat, sir, and that you know as well as I do. It was said from a friend to a friend,—as I thought then. But it is not the less true. I wonder what you can think of faith and truth and honesty of purpose when you took advantage of my absence,—you, whom I had told a thousand times that I loved her better than my own soul! You stand before the world as a rising man, and I stand before the world as a man—damned. You have been chosen by my father to sit for our family borough, while I am an outcast from his house. You have Cabinet Ministers for your friends, while I have hardly a decent associate left to me in the world. But I can say of myself that I have never done anything unworthy of a gentleman, while this thing that you are doing is unworthy of the lowest man."

"I have done nothing unworthy," said Phineas. "I wrote to you instantly when I had resolved,—though it was painful to me to have to tell such a secret to any one."

"You wrote! Yes; when I was miles distant; weeks, months away. But I did not come here to bullyrag like an old woman. I got your letter only on Monday, and know nothing of what has occurred. Is Miss Effingham to be—your wife?" Lord Chiltern had now come quite close to Phineas, and Phineas felt that that clenched fist might be in his face in half a moment. Miss Effingham of course was not engaged to him, but it seemed to him that if he were now so to declare, such declaration would appear to have been drawn from him by fear. "I ask you," said Lord Chiltern, "in what position you now stand towards Miss Effingham. If you are not a coward you will tell me."

"Whether I tell you or not, you know that I am not a coward," said Phineas.

"I shall have to try," said Lord Chiltern. "But if you please I will ask you for an answer to my question."

Phineas paused for a moment, thinking what honesty of purpose and a high spirit would, when combined together, demand of him, and together with these requirements he felt that he was bound to join some feeling of duty towards Miss Effingham. Lord Chiltern was standing there, fiery red, with his hand still clenched, and his hat still on, waiting for his answer. "Let me have your question again," said Phineas, "and I will answer it if I find that I can do so without loss of self-respect."

"I ask you in what position you stand towards Miss Effingham. Mind, I do not doubt at all, but I choose to have a reply from yourself."

"You will remember, of course, that I can only answer to the best of my belief."

"Answer to the best of your belief."

"I think she regards me as an intimate friend."

"Had you said as an indifferent acquaintance, you would, I think, have been nearer the mark. But we will let that be. I presume I may understand that you have given up any idea of changing that position?"

"You may understand nothing of the kind, Lord Chiltern."

"Why;—what hope have you?"

108

"That is another thing. I shall not speak of that;—at any rate not to you."

"Then, sir,—" and now Lord Chiltern advanced another step and raised his hand as though he were about to put it with some form of violence on the person of his rival.

"Stop, Chiltern," said Phineas, stepping back, so that there was some article of furniture between him and his adversary. "I do not choose that there should be a riot here."

"What do you call a riot, sir? I believe that after all you are a poltroon. What I require of you is that you shall meet me. Will you do that?"

"You mean,—to fight?"

"Yes,—to fight; to fight; to fight. For what other purpose do you suppose that I can wish to meet you?" Phineas felt at the moment that the fighting of a duel would be destructive to all his political hopes. Few Englishmen fight duels in these days. They who do so are always reckoned to be fools. And a duel between him and Lord Brentford's son must, as he thought, separate him from Violet, from Lady Laura, from Lord Brentford, and from his borough. But yet how could he refuse? "What have you to think of, sir, when such an offer as that is made to you?" said the fiery-red lord.

"I have to think whether I have courage enough to refuse to make myself an ass."

"You say that you do not wish to have a riot. That is your way to escape what you call—a riot."

"You want to bully me, Chiltern."

"No, sir;—I simply want this, that you should leave me where you found me, and not interfere with that which you have long known I claim as my own."

"But it is not your own."

"Then you can only fight me."

"You had better send some friend to me, and I will name some one, whom he shall meet."

"Of course I will do that if I have your promise to meet me. We can be in Belgium in an hour or two, and back again in a few more hours;—that is, any one of us who may chance to be alive.

"I will select a friend, and will tell him everything, and will then do as he bids me."

"Yes;—some old steady-going buffer. Mr. Kennedy, perhaps."

"It will certainly not be Mr. Kennedy. I shall probably ask Laurence Fitzgibbon to manage for me in such an affair."

"Perhaps you will see him at once, then, so that Colepepper may arrange with him this afternoon. And let me assure you, Mr. Finn, that there will be a meeting between us after some fashion, let the ideas of your friend Mr. Fitzgibbon be what they may." Then Lord Chiltern purposed to go, but turned again as he was going. "And remember this," he said, "my complaint is that you have been false to me,—damnably false; not that you have fallen in love with this young lady or with that." Then the fiery-red lord opened the door for himself and took his departure.

Phineas, as soon as he was alone, walked down to the House, at which there was an early sitting. As he went there was one great question which he had to settle with himself,—Was there any justice in the charge made against him that he had been false to his friend? When he had thought over the matter at Saulsby, after rushing down there that he might throw himself at Violet's feet, he had assured himself that such a letter as that which he resolved to write to Lord Chiltern, would be even chivalrous in its absolute honesty. He would tell his purpose to Lord Chiltern the moment that his purpose was formed;—and would afterwards speak of Lord Chiltern behind his back as one dear friend should speak of another. Had Miss Effingham shown the slightest intention of accepting Lord Chiltern's offer, he would have acknowledged to himself that the circumstances of his position made it impossible that he should, with honour, become his friend's rival. But was he to be debarred for ever from getting that which he wanted because Lord Chiltern wanted it also,—knowing, as he did so well, that Lord Chiltern could not get the thing which he wanted? All this had been quite sufficient for him at Saulsby. But now the charge against him that he had been false to his friend rang in his ears and made him unhappy. It certainly was true that Lord Chiltern had not given up his hopes, and that he had spoken probably more openly to Phineas respecting them than he had done to any other human being. If it was true that he had been false, then he must comply with any requisition which Lord Chiltern might make,—short of voluntarily giving up the lady. He must fight if he were asked to do so, even though fighting were his ruin.

When again in the House yesterday's scene came back upon him, and more than one man came to him congratulating him. Mr. Monk took his hand and spoke a word to him. The old Premier nodded to him. Mr. Gresham greeted him; and Plantagenet Palliser openly told him that he had made a good speech. How sweet would all this have been had there not been ever at his heart the remembrance of his terrible difficulty,—the consciousness that he was about to be forced into an absurdity which would put an end to all this sweetness! Why was the world in England so severe against duelling? After all, as he regarded the matter now, a duel might be the best way, nay, the only way out of a difficulty. If he might only be allowed to go out with Lord Chiltern the whole thing might be arranged. If he were not shot he might carry on his suit with Miss Effingham unfettered by any impediment on that side. And if he were shot, what matter was that to any one but himself? Why should the world be so thin-skinned,—so foolishly chary of human life?

Laurence Fitzgibbon did not come to the House, and Phineas looked for him at both the clubs which he frequented,—leaving a note at each as he did not find him. He also left a note for him at his lodgings in Duke Street. "I must see you this evening. I shall dine at the Reform Club,—pray come there." After that, Phineas went up to Portman Square, in accordance with the instructions received from Lady Laura.

There he saw Violet Effingham, meeting her for the first time since he had parted from her on the great steps at Saulsby. Of course he spoke to her, and of course she was gracious to him. But her graciousness was only a smile and his speech was only a word. There were many in the room, but not enough to make privacy possible,—as it becomes possible at a crowded evening meeting. Lord Brentford was there, and the Bonteens, and Barrington Erle, and Lady Glencora Palliser, and Lord Cantrip with his young wife. It was manifestly a meeting of Liberals, semi-social and semi-political;—so arranged that ladies might feel that some interest in politics was allowed to them, and perhaps some influence also. Afterwards Mr. Palliser himself came in. Phineas, however, was most struck by finding that Laurence Fitzgibbon was there, and that Mr. Kennedy was not. In regard to Mr. Kennedy, he was quite sure that had such a meeting taken place before Lady Laura's marriage, Mr. Kennedy would have been present. "I must speak to you as we go away," said Phineas, whispering a word into Fitzgibbon's ear. "I have been leaving notes for you all about the town." "Not a duel, I hope," said Fitzgibbon.

How pleasant it was,—that meeting; or would have been had there not been that nightmare on his breast! They all talked as though there were perfect accord between them and perfect confidence. There were there great men,—Cabinet Ministers, and beautiful women,—the wives and daughters of some of England's highest nobles. And Phineas Finn, throwing back, now and again, a thought to Killaloe, found himself among them as one of themselves. How could any Mr. Low say that he was wrong?

On a sofa near to him, so that he could almost touch her foot with his, was sitting Violet Effingham, and as he leaned over from his chair discussing some point in Mr. Mildmay's bill with that most inveterate politician, Lady Glencora, Violet looked into his face and smiled. Oh heavens! If Lord Chiltern and he might only toss up as to which of them should go to Patagonia and remain there for the next ten years, and which should have Violet Effingham for a wife in London!

"Come along, Phineas, if you mean to come," said Laurence Fitzgibbon. Phineas was of course bound to go, though Lady Glencora was still talking Radicalism, and Violet Effingham was still smiling ineffably.

VOLUME II

CHAPTER XXXVIII
The Duel

"I knew it was a duel;—bedad I did," said Laurence Fitzgibbon, standing at the corner of Orchard Street and Oxford Street, when Phineas had half told his story. "I was sure of it from the tone of your voice, my boy. We mustn't let it come off, that's all;—not if we can help it." Then Phineas was allowed to proceed and finish his story. "I don't see any way out of it; I don't, indeed," said Laurence. By this time Phineas had come to think that the duel was in very truth the best way out of the difficulty. It was a bad way out, but then it was a way;—and he could not see any other. "As for ill treating him, that's nonsense," said Laurence. "What are the girls to do, if one fellow mayn't come on as soon as another fellow is down? But then, you see, a fellow never knows when he's down himself, and therefore he thinks that he's ill used. I'll tell you what now. I shouldn't wonder if we couldn't do it on the sly,—unless one of you is stupid enough to hit the other in an awkward place. If you are certain of your hand now, the right shoulder is the best spot." Phineas felt very certain that he would not hit Lord Chiltern in an awkward place, although he was by no means sure of his hand. Let come what might, he would not aim at his adversary. But of this he had thought it proper to say nothing to Laurence Fitzgibbon.

And the duel did come off on the sly. The meeting in the drawing-room in Portman Square, of which mention was made in the last chapter, took place on a Wednesday afternoon. On the Thursday, Friday, Monday, and Tuesday following, the great debate on Mr. Mildmay's bill was continued, and at three on the Tuesday night the House divided. There was a majority in favour of the Ministers, not large enough to permit them to claim a triumph for their party, or even an ovation for themselves; but still sufficient to enable them to send their bill into committee. Mr. Daubeny and Mr. Turnbull had again joined their forces together in opposition to the ministerial measure. On the Thursday Phineas had shown himself in the House, but during the remainder of this interesting period he was absent from his place, nor was he seen at the clubs, nor did any man know of his whereabouts. I think that Lady Laura Kennedy was the first to miss him with any real sense of his absence. She would now go to Portman Square on the afternoon of every Sunday,—at which time her husband was attending the second service of his church,—and there she would receive those whom she called her father's guests. But as her father was never there on the Sundays, and as these gatherings had been created by herself, the reader will probably think that she was obeying her husband's behests in regard to the Sabbath after a very indifferent fashion. The reader may be quite sure, however, that Mr. Kennedy knew well what was being done in Portman Square. Whatever might be Lady Laura's faults, she did not commit the fault of disobeying her husband in secret. There were, probably, a few words on the subject; but we need not go very closely into that matter at the present moment.

On the Sunday which afforded some rest in the middle of the great Reform debate Lady Laura asked for Mr. Finn, and no one could answer her question. And then it was remembered that Laurence Fitzgibbon was also absent. Barrington Erle knew nothing of Phineas,—had heard nothing; but was able to say that Fitzgibbon had been with Mr. Ratler, the patronage secretary and liberal whip, early on Thursday, expressing his intention of absenting himself for two days. Mr. Ratler had been wroth, bidding him remain at his duty, and pointing out to him the great importance of the moment. Then Barrington Erle quoted Laurence Fitzgibbon's reply. "My boy," said Laurence to poor Ratler, "the path of duty leads but to the grave. All the same; I'll be in at the death, Ratler, my boy, as sure as the sun's in heaven." Not ten minutes after the telling of this little story, Fitzgibbon entered the room in Portman Square, and Lady Laura at once asked him after Phineas. "Bedad, Lady Laura, I have been out of town myself for two days, and I know nothing."

"Mr. Finn has not been with you, then?"

"With me! No,—not with me. I had a job of business of my own which took me over to Paris. And has Phinny fled too? Poor Ratler! I shouldn't wonder if it isn't an asylum he's in before the session is over."

Laurence Fitzgibbon certainly possessed the rare accomplishment of telling a lie with a good grace. Had any man called him a liar he would have considered himself to be not only insulted, but injured also. He believed himself to be a man of truth. There were, however, in his estimation certain subjects on which a man might depart as wide as the poles are asunder from truth without subjecting himself to any ignominy for falsehood. In dealing with a tradesman as to his debts, or with a rival as to a lady, or with any man or woman in defence of a lady's character, or in any such matter as that of a duel, Laurence believed that a gentleman was bound to lie, and that he would be no gentleman if he hesitated to do so. Not the slightest prick of conscience disturbed him when he told Lady Laura that he had been in Paris, and that he knew nothing of Phineas Finn. But, in truth, during the last day or two he had been in Flanders, and not in Paris, and had stood as second with his friend Phineas on the sands at Blankenberg, a little fishing-town some twelve miles distant from Bruges, and had left his friend since that at an hotel at Ostend,—with a wound just under the shoulder, from which a bullet had been extracted.

The manner of the meeting had been in this wise. Captain Colepepper and Laurence Fitzgibbon had held their meeting, and at this meeting Laurence had taken certain standing-ground on behalf of his friend, and in obedience to his friend's positive instruction;—which was this, that his friend could not abandon his right of addressing the young lady, should he hereafter ever think fit to do so. Let that be granted, and Laurence would do anything. But then that could not be granted, and Laurence could only shrug his shoulders. Nor would Laurence admit that his friend had been false. "The question lies in a nutshell," said Laurence, with that sweet Connaught brogue which always came to him when he desired to be effective;—"here it is. One gentleman tells another that he's sweet upon a young lady, but that the young lady has refused him, and always will refuse him, for ever and ever. That's the truth anyhow. Is the second gentleman bound by that not to address the young lady? I say he is not bound. It'd be a d——d hard tratement, Captain Colepepper, if a man's mouth and all the ardent affections of his heart were to be stopped in that manner! By Jases, I don't know who'd like to be the friend of any man if that's to be the way of it."

Captain Colepepper was not very good at an argument. "I think they'd better see each other," said Colepepper, pulling his thick grey moustache.

"If you choose to have it so, so be it. But I think it the hardest thing in the world;—I do indeed." Then they put their heads together in the most friendly way, and declared that the affair should, if possible, be kept private.

On the Thursday night Lord Chiltern and Captain Colepepper went over by Calais and Lille to Bruges. Laurence Fitzgibbon, with his friend Dr. O'Shaughnessy, crossed by the direct boat from Dover to Ostend. Phineas went to Ostend by Dover and Calais, but he took the day route on Friday. It had all been arranged among them, so that there might be no suspicion as to the job in hand. Even O'Shaughnessy and Laurence Fitzgibbon had left London by separate trains. They met on the sands at Blankenberg about nine o'clock on the Saturday morning, having reached that village in different vehicles from Ostend and Bruges, and had met quite unobserved amidst the sand-heaps. But one shot had been exchanged, and Phineas had been wounded in the right shoulder. He had proposed to exchange another shot with his left hand, declaring his capability of shooting quite as well with the left as with the right; but to this both Colepepper and Fitzgibbon had objected. Lord Chiltern had offered to shake hands with his late friend in a true spirit of friendship, if only his late friend would say that he did not intend to prosecute his suit with the young lady. In all these disputes the young lady's name was never mentioned. Phineas indeed had not once named Violet to Fitzgibbon, speaking of her always as the lady in question; and though Laurence correctly surmised the identity of the young lady, he never hinted that he had even guessed her name. I doubt whether Lord Chiltern had been so wary when alone with Captain Colepepper; but then Lord Chiltern was, when he spoke at all, a very plain-spoken man. Of course his lordship's late friend Phineas would give no such pledge, and therefore Lord Chiltern moved off the ground and back to Blankenberg and Bruges, and into Brussels, in still living enmity with our hero. Laurence and the doctor took Phineas back to Ostend, and though the bullet was then in his shoulder, Phineas made his way through Blankenberg after such a fashion that no one there knew what had occurred. Not a living soul, except the five concerned, was at that time aware that a duel had been fought among the sand-hills.

Laurence Fitzgibbon made his way to Dover by the Saturday night's boat, and was able to show himself in Portman Square on the Sunday. "Know anything about Phinny Finn?" he said afterwards to Barrington Erle, in answer to an inquiry from that anxious gentleman. "Not a word! I think you'd better send the town-crier round after him." Barrington, however, did not feel quite so well assured of Fitzgibbon's truth as Lady Laura had done.

Dr. O'Shaughnessy remained during the Sunday and Monday at Ostend with his patient, and the people at the inn only knew that Mr. Finn had sprained his shoulder badly; and on the Tuesday they came back to London again, via Calais and Dover. No bone had been broken, and Phineas, though his shoulder was very painful, bore the journey well. O'Shaughnessy had received a telegram on the Monday, telling him that the division would certainly take place on the Tuesday,—and on the Tuesday, at about ten in the evening, Phineas went down to the House. "By ——, you're here," said Ratler, taking hold of him with an affection that was too warm. "Yes; I'm here," said Phineas, wincing in agony; "but be a little careful, there's a good fellow. I've been down in Kent and put my arm out."

"Put your arm out, have you?" said Ratler, observing the sling for the first time. "I'm sorry for that. But you'll stop and vote?"

"Yes;—I'll stop and vote. I've come up for the purpose. But I hope it won't be very late."

"There are both Daubeny and Gresham to speak yet, and at least three others. I don't suppose it will be much before three. But you're all right now. You can go down and smoke if you like!" In this way Phineas Finn spoke in the debate, and heard the end of it, voting for his party, and fought his duel with Lord Chiltern in the middle of it.

He did go and sit on a well-cushioned bench in the smoking-room, and then was interrogated by many of his friends as to his mysterious absence. He had, he said, been down in Kent, and had had an accident with his arm, by which he had been confined. When this questioner and that perceived that there was some little mystery in the matter, the questioners did not push their questions, but simply entertained their own surmises. One indiscreet questioner, however, did trouble Phineas sorely, declaring that there must have been some affair in which a woman had had a part, and asking after the young lady of Kent. This indiscreet questioner was Laurence Fitzgibbon, who, as Phineas thought, carried his spirit of intrigue a little too far. Phineas stayed and voted, and then he went painfully home to his lodgings.

How singular would it be if this affair of the duel should pass away, and no one be a bit the wiser but those four men who had been with him on the sands at Blankenberg! Again he wondered at his own luck. He had told himself that a duel with Lord Chiltern must create a quarrel between him and Lord Chiltern's relations, and also between him and Violet Effingham; that it must banish him from his comfortable seat for Loughton, and ruin him in regard to his political prospects. And now he had fought his duel, and was back in town,—and the thing seemed to have been a thing of nothing. He had not as yet seen Lady Laura or Violet, but he had no doubt but they both were as much in the dark as other people. The day might arrive, he thought, on which it would be pleasant for him to tell Violet Effingham what had occurred, but that day had not come as yet. Whither Lord Chiltern had gone, or what Lord Chiltern intended to do, he had not any idea; but he imagined that he should soon hear something of her brother from Lady Laura. That Lord Chiltern should say a word to Lady Laura of what had occurred,—or to any other person in the world,—he did not in the least suspect. There could be no man more likely to be reticent in such matters than Lord Chiltern,—or more sure to be guided by an almost exaggerated sense of what honour required of him. Nor did he doubt the discretion of his friend Fitzgibbon;—if only his friend might not damage the secret by being too discreet. Of the silence of the doctor and the captain he was by no means equally sure; but even though they should gossip, the gossiping would take so long a time in oozing out and becoming recognised information, as to have lost much of its power for injuring him. Were Lady Laura to hear at this moment that he had been over to Belgium, and had fought a duel with Lord Chiltern respecting Violet, she would probably feel herself obliged to quarrel with him; but no such obligation would rest on her, if in the course of six or nine months she should gradually have become aware that such an encounter had taken place.

Lord Chiltern, during their interview at the rooms in Great Marlborough Street, had said a word to him about the seat in Parliament;—had expressed some opinion that as he, Phineas Finn, was interfering with the views of the Standish family in regard to Miss Effingham, he ought not to keep the Standish seat, which had been conferred upon him in ignorance of any such intended interference. Phineas, as he thought of this, could not remember Lord Chiltern's words, but there was present to him an idea that such had been their purport. Was he bound, in circumstances as they now existed, to give up Loughton? He made up his mind that he was not so bound unless Lord Chiltern should demand from him that he should do so; but, nevertheless, he was uneasy in his position. It was quite true that the seat now was his for this session by all parliamentary law, even though the electors themselves might wish to be rid of him, and that Lord Brentford could not even open his mouth upon the matter in a tone more loud than that of a whisper. But Phineas, feeling that he had consented to accept the favour of a corrupt seat from Lord Brentford, felt also that he was bound to give up the spoil if it were demanded from him. If it were demanded from him, either by the father or the son, it should be given up at once.

On the following morning he found a leading article in the *People's Banner* devoted solely to himself. "During the late debate,"—so ran a passage in the leading article,—"Mr. Finn, Lord Brentford's Irish nominee for his pocket-borough at Loughton, did at last manage to stand on his legs and open his mouth. If we are not mistaken, this is Mr. Finn's third session in Parliament, and hitherto he has been unable to articulate three sentences, though he has on more than one occasion made the attempt. For what special merit this young man has been selected for aristocratic patronage we do not know,—but that there must be some merit recognisable by aristocratic eyes, we surmise. Three years ago he was a raw young Irishman, living in London as Irishmen only know how to live, earning nothing, and apparently without means; and then suddenly he bursts out as a member of Parliament and as the friend of Cabinet Ministers. The possession of one good gift must be acceded to the honourable member for Loughton,—he is a handsome young man, and looks to be as strong as a coal-porter. Can it be that his promotion has sprung from this? Be this as it may, we should like to know where he has been during his late mysterious absence from Parliament, and in what way he came by the wound in his arm. Even handsome young members of Parliament, fêted by titled ladies and their rich lords, are amenable to the laws,—to the laws of this country, and to the laws of any other which it may suit them to visit for a while!"

"Infamous scoundrel!" said Phineas to himself, as he read this. "Vile, low, disreputable blackguard!" It was clear enough, however, that Quintus Slide had found out something of his secret. If so, his only hope would rest on the fact that his friends were not likely to see the columns of the *People's Banner*.

CHAPTER XXXIX
Lady Laura Is Told

By the time that Mr. Mildmay's great bill was going into committee Phineas was able to move about London in comfort,—with his arm, however, still in a sling. There had been nothing more about him and his wound in the *People's Banner*, and he was beginning to hope that that nuisance would also be allowed to die away. He had seen Lady Laura,—having dined in Grosvenor Place, where he had been petted to his heart's content. His dinner had been cut up for him, and his wound had been treated with the tenderest sympathy. And, singular to say, no questions were asked. He had been to Kent and had come by an accident. No more than that was told, and his dear sympathising friends were content to receive so much information, and to ask for no more. But he had not as yet seen Violet Effingham, and he was beginning to think that this romance about Violet might as well be brought to a close. He had not, however, as yet been able to go into crowded rooms, and unless he went out to large parties he could not be sure that he would meet Miss Effingham.

At last he resolved that he would tell Lady Laura the whole truth,—not the truth about the duel, but the truth about Violet Effingham, and ask for her assistance. When making this resolution, I think that he must have forgotten much that he had learned of his friend's character; and by making it, I think that he showed also that he had not learned as much as his opportunities might have taught him. He knew Lady Laura's obstinacy of purpose, he knew her devotion to her brother, and he knew also how desirous she had been that her brother should win Violet Effingham for himself. This knowledge should, I think, have sufficed to show him how improbable it was that Lady Laura should assist him in his enterprise. But beyond all this was the fact,—a fact as to the consequences of which Phineas himself was entirely blind, beautifully ignorant,—that Lady Laura had once condescended to love himself. Nay;—she had gone farther than this, and had ventured to tell him, even after her marriage, that the remembrance of some feeling that had once dwelt in her heart in regard to him was still a danger to her. She had warned him from Loughlinter, and then had received him in London;—and now he selected her as his confidante in this love affair! Had he not been beautifully ignorant and most modestly blind, he would surely have placed his confidence elsewhere.

It was not that Lady Laura Kennedy ever confessed to herself the existence of a vicious passion. She had, indeed, learned to tell herself that she could not love her husband; and once, in the excitement of such silent announcements to herself, she had asked herself whether her heart was quite a blank, and had answered herself by desiring Phineas Finn to absent himself from Loughlinter. During all the subsequent winter she had scourged herself inwardly for her own imprudence, her quite unnecessary folly in so doing. What! could not she, Laura Standish, who from her earliest years of girlish womanhood had resolved that she would use the world as men use it, and not as women do,—could not she have felt the slight shock of a passing tenderness for a handsome youth without allowing the feeling to be a rock before her big enough and sharp enough for the destruction of her entire barque? Could not she command, if not her heart, at any rate her mind, so that she might safely assure herself that, whether this man or any man was here or there, her course would be unaltered? What though Phineas Finn had been in the same house with her throughout all the winter, could not she have so lived with him on terms of friendship, that every deed and word and look of her friendship might have been open to her husband,—or open to all the world? She could have done so. She told herself that that was not,—need not have been her great calamity. Whether she could endure the dull, monotonous control of her slow but imperious lord,—or whether she must not rather tell him that it was not to be endured,—that was her trouble. So she told herself, and again admitted Phineas to her intimacy in London. But, nevertheless, Phineas, had he not been beautifully ignorant and most blind to his own achievements, would not have expected from Lady Laura Kennedy assistance with Miss Violet Effingham.

Phineas knew when to find Lady Laura alone, and he came upon her one day at the favourable hour. The two first clauses of the bill had been passed after twenty fights and endless divisions. Two points had been settled, as to which, however, Mr. Gresham had been driven to give way so far and to yield so much, that men declared that such a bill as the Government could consent to call its own could never be passed by that Parliament in that session. Immediately on his entrance into her room Lady Laura began about the third clause. Would the House let Mr. Gresham have his way about the—? Phineas stopped her at once. "My dear friend," he said, "I have come to you in a private trouble, and I want you to drop politics for half an hour. I have come to you for help."

"A private trouble, Mr. Finn! Is it serious?"

"It is very serious,—but it is no trouble of the kind of which you are thinking. But it is serious enough to take up every thought."

"Can I help you?"

"Indeed you can. Whether you will or no is a different thing."

"I would help you in anything in my power, Mr. Finn. Do you not know it?"

"You have been very kind to me!"

"And so would Mr. Kennedy."

"Mr. Kennedy cannot help me here."

"What is it, Mr. Finn?"

"I suppose I may as well tell you at once,—in plain language, I do not know how to put my story into words that shall fit it. I love Violet Effingham. Will you help me to win her to be my wife?"

"You love Violet Effingham!" said Lady Laura. And as she spoke the look of her countenance towards him was so changed that he became at once aware that from her no assistance might be expected. His eyes were not opened in any degree to the second reason above given for Lady Laura's opposition to his wishes, but he instantly perceived that she would still cling to that destination of Violet's hand which had for years past been the favourite scheme of her life. "Have you not always known, Mr. Finn, what have been our hopes for Violet?"

Phineas, though he had perceived his mistake, felt that he must go on with his cause. Lady Laura must know his wishes sooner or later, and it was as well that she should learn them in this way as in any other. "Yes;—but I have known also, from your brother's own lips,—and indeed from yours also, Lady Laura,—that Chiltern has been three times refused by Miss Effingham."

"What does that matter? Do men never ask more than three times?"

"And must I be debarred for ever while he prosecutes a hopeless suit?"

"Yes;—you of all men."

"Why so, Lady Laura?"

"Because in this matter you have been his chosen friend,—and mine. We have told you everything, trusting to you. We have believed in your honour. We have thought that with you, at any rate, we were safe." These words were very bitter to Phineas, and yet when he had written his letter at Loughton, he had intended to be so perfectly honest, chivalrously honest! Now Lady Laura spoke to him and looked at him as though he had been most basely false—most untrue to that noble friendship which had been lavished upon him by all her family. He felt that he would become the prey of her most injurious thoughts unless he could fully explain his ideas, and he felt, also, that the circumstances did not admit of his explaining them. He could not take up the argument on Violet's side, and show how unfair it would be to her that she should be debarred from the homage due to her by any man who really loved her, because Lord Chiltern chose to think that he still had a claim,—or at any rate a chance. And Phineas knew well of himself,—or thought that he knew well,—that he would not have interfered had there been any chance for Lord Chiltern. Lord Chiltern had himself told him more than once that there was no such chance. How was he to explain all this to Lady Laura? "Mr. Finn," said Lady Laura, "I can hardly believe this of you, even when you tell it me yourself."

"Listen to me, Lady Laura, for a moment."

"Certainly, I will listen. But that you should come to me for assistance! I cannot understand it. Men sometimes become harder than stones."

"I do not think that I am hard." Poor blind fool! He was still thinking only of Violet, and of the accusation made against him that he was untrue to his friendship for Lord Chiltern. Of that other accusation which could not be expressed in open words he understood nothing,—nothing at all as yet.

"Hard and false,—capable of receiving no impression beyond the outside husk of the heart."

"Oh, Lady Laura, do not say that. If you could only know how true I am in my affection for you all."

"And how do you show it?—by coming in between Oswald and the only means that are open to us of reconciling him to his father;—means that have been explained to you exactly as though you had been one of ourselves. Oswald has treated you as a brother in the matter, telling you everything, and this is the way you would repay him for his confidence!"

"Can I help it, that I have learnt to love this girl?"

"Yes, sir,—you can help it. What if she had been Oswald's wife;—would you have loved her then? Do you speak of loving a woman as if it were an affair of fate, over which you have no control? I doubt whether your passions are so strong as that. You had better put aside your love for Miss Effingham. I feel assured that it will never hurt you." Then some remembrance of what had passed between him and Lady Laura Standish near the falls of the Linter, when he first visited Scotland, came across his mind. "Believe me," she said with a smile, "this little wound in your heart will soon be cured."

He stood silent before her, looking away from her, thinking over it all. He certainly had believed himself to be violently in love with Lady Laura, and yet when he had just now entered her drawing-room, he had almost forgotten that there had been such a passage in his life. And he had believed that she had forgotten it,—even though she had counselled him not to come to Loughlinter within the last nine months! He had been a boy then, and had not known himself;—but now he was a man, and was proud of the intensity of his love. There came upon him some passing throb of pain from his shoulder, reminding him of the duel, and he was proud also of that. He had been willing to risk everything,—life, prospects, and position,—sooner than abandon the slight hope which was his of possessing Violet Effingham. And now he was told that this wound in his heart would soon be cured, and was told so by a woman to whom he had once sung a song of another passion. It is very hard to answer a woman in such circumstances, because her womanhood gives her so strong a ground of vantage! Lady Laura might venture to throw in his teeth the fickleness of his heart, but he could not in reply tell her that to change a love was better than to marry without love,—that to be capable of such a change showed no such inferiority of nature as did the capacity for such a marriage. She could hit him with her argument; but he could only remember his, and think how violent might be the blow he could inflict,—if it were not that she were a woman, and therefore guarded. "You will not help me then?" he said, when they had both been silent for a while.

"Help you? How should I help you?"

"I wanted no other help than this,—that I might have had an opportunity of meeting Violet here, and of getting from her some answer."

"Has the question then never been asked already?" said Lady Laura. To this Phineas made no immediate reply. There was no reason why he should show his whole hand to an adversary. "Why do you not go to Lady Baldock's house?" continued Lady Laura. "You are admitted there. You know Lady Baldock. Go and ask her to stand your friend with her niece. See what she will say to you. As far as I understand these matters, that is the fair, honourable, open way in which gentlemen are wont to make their overtures."

"I would make mine to none but to herself," said Phineas.

"Then why have you made it to me, sir?" demanded Lady Laura.

"I have come to you as I would to my sister."

"Your sister? Psha! I am not your sister, Mr. Finn. Nor, were I so, should I fail to remember that I have a dearer brother to whom my faith is pledged. Look here. Within the last three weeks Oswald has sacrificed everything to his father, because he was determined that Mr. Kennedy should have the money which he thought was due to my husband. He has enabled my father to do what he will with Saulsby. Papa will never hurt him;—I know that. Hard as papa is with him, he will never hurt Oswald's future position. Papa is too proud to do that. Violet has heard what Oswald has done; and now that he has nothing of his own to offer her for the future but his bare title, now that he has given papa power to do what he will with the property, I believe that she would accept him instantly. That is her disposition."

Phineas again paused a moment before he replied. "Let him try," he said.

"He is away,—in Brussels."

"Send to him, and bid him return. I will be patient, Lady Laura. Let him come and try, and I will bide my time. I confess that I have no right to interfere with him if there be a chance for him. If there is no chance, my right is as good as that of any other."

There was something in this which made Lady Laura feel that she could not maintain her hostility against this man on behalf of her brother;—and yet she could not force herself to be other than hostile to him. Her heart was sore, and it was he that had made it sore. She had lectured herself, schooling herself with mental sackcloth and ashes, rebuking herself with heaviest censures from day to day, because she had found herself to be in danger of regarding this man with a perilous love; and she had been constant in this work of penance till she had been able to assure herself that the sackcloth and ashes had done their work, and that the danger was past. "I like him still and love him well," she had said to herself with something almost of triumph, "but I have ceased to think of him as one who might have been my lover." And yet she was now sick and sore, almost beside herself with the agony of the wound, because this man whom she had been able to throw aside from her heart had also been able so to throw her aside. And she felt herself constrained to rebuke him with what bitterest words she might use. She had felt it easy to do this at first, on her brother's score. She had accused him of treachery to his friendship,—both as to Oswald and as to herself. On that she could say cutting words without subjecting herself to suspicion even from herself. But now this power was taken away from her, and still she wished to wound him. She desired to taunt him with his old fickleness, and yet to subject herself to no imputation. "Your right!" she said. "What gives you any right in the matter?"

"Simply the right of a fair field, and no favour."

"And yet you come to me for favour,—to me, because I am her friend. You cannot win her yourself, and think I may help you! I do not believe in your love for her. There! If there were no other reason, and I could help you, I would not, because I think your heart is a sham heart. She is pretty, and has money—"

"Lady Laura!"

"She is pretty, and has money, and is the fashion. I do not wonder that you should wish to have her. But, Mr. Finn, I believe that Oswald really loves her;—and that you do not. His nature is deeper than yours."

He understood it all now as he listened to the tone of her voice, and looked into the lines of her face. There was written there plainly enough that spretæ injuria formæ of which she herself was conscious, but only conscious. Even his eyes, blind as he had been, were opened,—and he knew that he had been a fool.

"I am sorry that I came to you," he said.

"It would have been better that you should not have done so," she replied.

"And yet perhaps it is well that there should be no misunderstanding between us."

"Of course I must tell my brother."

He paused but for a moment, and then he answered her with a sharp voice, "He has been told."

"And who told him?"

"I did. I wrote to him the moment that I knew my own mind. I owed it to him to do so. But my letter missed him, and he only learned it the other day."

"Have you seen him since?"

"Yes;—I have seen him."

"And what did he say? How did he take it? Did he bear it from you quietly?"

"No, indeed;" and Phineas smiled as he spoke.

"Tell me, Mr. Finn; what happened? What is to be done?"

"Nothing is to be done. Everything has been done. I may as well tell you all. I am sure that for the sake of me, as well as of your brother, you will keep our secret. He required that I should either give up my suit, or that I should,—fight him. As I could not comply with the one request, I found myself bound to comply with the other."

"And there has been a duel?"

"Yes;—there has been a duel. We went over to Belgium, and it was soon settled. He wounded me here in the arm."

"Suppose you had killed him, Mr. Finn?"

"That, Lady Laura, would have been a misfortune so terrible that I was bound to prevent it." Then he paused again, regretting what he had said. "You have surprised me, Lady Laura, into an answer that I should not have made. I may be sure,—may I not,—that my words will not go beyond yourself?"

"Yes;—you may be sure of that." This she said plaintively, with a tone of voice and demeanour of body altogether different from that which she lately bore. Neither of them knew what was taking place between them; but she was, in truth, gradually submitting herself again to this man's influence. Though she rebuked him at every turn for what he said, for what he had done, for what he proposed to do, still she could not teach herself to despise him, or even to cease to love him for any part of it. She knew it all now,—except that word or two which had passed between Violet and Phineas in the rides of Saulsby Park. But she suspected something even of that, feeling sure that the only matter on which Phineas would say nothing would be that of his own success,—if success there had been. "And so you and Oswald have quarrelled, and there has been a duel. That is why you were away?"

"That is why I was away."

"How wrong of you,—how very wrong! Had he been,—killed, how could you have looked us in the face again?"

"I could not have looked you in the face again."

"But that is over now. And were you friends afterwards?"

"No;—we did not part as friends. Having gone there to fight with him,—most unwillingly,—I could not afterwards promise him that I would give up Miss Effingham. You say she will accept him now. Let him come and try." She had nothing further to say,—no other argument to use. There was the soreness at her heart still present to her, making her wretched, instigating her to hurt him if she knew how to do so, in spite of her regard for him. But she felt that she was weak and powerless. She had shot her arrows at him,—all but one,—and if she used that, its poisoned point would wound herself far more surely than it would touch him. "The duel was very silly," he said. "You will not speak of it."

"No; certainly not."

"I am glad at least that I have told you everything."

"I do not know why you should be glad. I cannot help you."

"And you will say nothing to Violet?"

"Everything that I can say in Oswald's favour. I will say nothing of the duel; but beyond that you have no right to demand my secrecy with her. Yes; you had better go, Mr. Finn, for I am hardly well. And remember this,—If you can forget this little episode about Miss Effingham, so will I forget it also; and so will Oswald. I can promise for him." Then she smiled and gave him her hand, and he went.

She rose from her chair as he left the room, and waited till she heard the sound of the great door closing behind him before she again sat down. Then, when he was gone,—when she was sure that he was no longer there with her in the same house,—she laid her head down upon the arm of the sofa, and burst into a flood of tears. She was no longer angry with Phineas. There was no further longing in her heart for revenge. She did not now desire to injure him, though she had done so as long as he was with her. Nay,—she resolved instantly, almost instinctively, that Lord Brentford must know nothing of all this, lest the political prospects of the young member for Loughton should be injured. To have rebuked him, to rebuke him again and again, would be only fair,—would at least be womanly; but she would protect him from all material injury as far as her power of protection might avail. And why was she weeping now so bitterly? Of course she asked herself, as she rubbed away the tears with her hands,—Why should she weep? She was not weak enough to tell herself that she was weeping for any injury that had been done to Oswald. She got up suddenly from the sofa, and pushed away her hair from her face, and pushed away the tears from her cheeks, and then clenched her fists as she held them out at full length from her body, and stood, looking up with her eyes fixed upon the wall. "Ass!" she exclaimed. "Fool! Idiot! That I should not be able to crush it into nothing and have done with it! Why should he not have her? After all, he is better than Oswald. Oh,—is that you?" The door of the room had been opened while she was standing thus, and her husband had entered.

"Yes,—it is I. Is anything wrong?"

"Very much is wrong."

"What is it, Laura?"

"You cannot help me."

"If you are in trouble you should tell me what it is, and leave it to me to try to help you."

"Nonsense!" she said, shaking her head.

"Laura, that is uncourteous,—not to say undutiful also."

"I suppose it was,—both. I beg your pardon, but I could not help it."

"Laura, you should help such words to me."

"There are moments, Robert, when even a married woman must be herself rather than her husband's wife. It is so, though you cannot understand it."

"I certainly do not understand it."

"You cannot make a woman subject to you as a dog is so. You may have all the outside and as much of the inside as you can master. With a dog you may be sure of both."

"I suppose this means that you have secrets in which I am not to share."

"I have troubles about my father and my brother which you cannot share. My brother is a ruined man."

"Who ruined him?"

"I will not talk about it any more. I will not speak to you of him or of papa. I only want you to understand that there is a subject which must be secret to myself, and on which I may be allowed to shed tears,—if I am so weak. I will not trouble you on a matter in which I have not your sympathy." Then she left him, standing in the middle of the room, depressed by what had occurred,—but not thinking of it as of a trouble which would do more than make him uncomfortable for that day.

CHAPTER XL
Madame Max Goesler

Day after day, and clause after clause, the bill was fought in committee, and few men fought with more constancy on the side of the Ministers than did the member for Loughton. Troubled though he was by his quarrel with Lord Chiltern, by his love for Violet Effingham, by the silence of his friend Lady Laura,—for since he had told her of the duel she had become silent to him, never writing to him, and hardly speaking to him when she met him in society,—nevertheless Phineas was not so troubled but what he could work at his vocation. Now, when he would find himself upon his legs in the House, he would wonder at the hesitation which had lately troubled him so sorely. He would sit sometimes and speculate upon that dimness of eye, upon that tendency of things to go round, upon that obtrusive palpitation of heart, which had afflicted him so seriously for so long a time. The House now was no more to him than any other chamber, and the members no more than other men. He guarded himself from orations, speaking always very shortly,—because he believed that policy and good judgment required that he should be short. But words were very easy to him, and he would feel as though he could talk for ever. And there quickly came to him a reputation for practical usefulness. He was a man with strong opinions, who could yet be submissive. And no man seemed to know how his reputation had come. He had made one good speech after two or three failures. All who knew him, his whole party, had been aware of his failure; and his one good speech had been regarded by many as no very wonderful effort. But he was a man who was pleasant to other men,—not combative, not self-asserting beyond the point at which self-assertion ceases to be a necessity of manliness. Nature had been very good to him, making him comely inside and out,—and with this comeliness he had crept into popularity.

The secret of the duel was, I think, at this time, known to a great many men and women. So Phineas perceived; but it was not, he thought, known either to Lord Brentford or to Violet Effingham. And in this he was right. No rumour of it had yet reached the ears of either of these persons;—and rumour, though she flies so fast and so far, is often slow in reaching those ears which would be most interested in her tidings. Some dim report of the duel reached even Mr. Kennedy, and he asked his wife. "Who told you?" said she, sharply.

"Bonteen told me that it was certainly so."

"Mr. Bonteen always knows more than anybody else about everything except his own business."

"Then it is not true?"

Lady Laura paused,—and then she lied. "Of course it is not true. I should be very sorry to ask either of them, but to me it seems to be the most improbable thing in life." Then Mr. Kennedy believed that there had been no duel. In his wife's word he put absolute faith, and he thought that she would certainly know anything that her brother had done. As he was a man given to but little discourse, he asked no further questions about the duel either in the House or at the Clubs.

At first, Phineas had been greatly dismayed when men had asked him questions tending to elicit from him some explanation of the mystery;—but by degrees he became used to it, and as the tidings which had got abroad did not seem to injure him, and as the questionings were not pushed very closely, he became indifferent. There came out another article in the *People's Banner* in which Lord C——n and Mr. P——s F——n were spoken of as glaring examples of that aristocratic snobility,—that was the expressive word coined, evidently with great delight, for the occasion,—which the rotten state of London society in high quarters now produced. Here was a young lord, infamously notorious, quarrelling with one of his boon-companions, whom he had appointed to a private seat in the House of Commons, fighting duels, breaking the laws, scandalising the public,—and all this was done without punishment to the guilty! There were old stories afloat,—so said the article—of what in a former century had been done by Lord Mohuns and Mr. Bests; but now, in 186—, &c. &c. &c. And so the article went on. Any reader may fill in without difficulty the concluding indignation and virtuous appeal for reform in social morals as well as Parliament. But Phineas had so far progressed that he had almost come to like this kind of thing.

Certainly I think that the duel did him no harm in society. Otherwise he would hardly have been asked to a semi-political dinner at Lady Glencora Palliser's, even though he might have been invited to make one of the five hundred guests who were crowded into her saloons and staircases after the dinner was over. To have been one of the five hundred was nothing; but to be one of the sixteen was a great deal,—was indeed so much that Phineas, not understanding as yet the advantage of his own comeliness, was at a loss to conceive why so pleasant an honour was conferred upon him. There was no man among the eight men at the dinner-party not in Parliament,—and the only other except Phineas not attached to the Government was Mr. Palliser's great friend, John Grey, the member for Silverbridge. There were four Cabinet Ministers in the room,—the Duke, Lord Cantrip, Mr. Gresham, and the owner of the mansion. There was also Barrington Erle and young Lord Fawn, an Under-Secretary of State. But the wit and grace of the ladies present lent more of character to the party than even the position of the men. Lady Glencora Palliser herself was a host. There was no woman then in London better able to talk to a dozen people on a dozen subjects; and then, moreover, she was still in the flush of her beauty and the bloom of her youth. Lady Laura was there;—by what means divided from her husband Phineas could not imagine; but Lady Glencora was good at such divisions. Lady Cantrip had been allowed to come with her lord;—but, as was well understood, Lord Cantrip was not so manifestly a husband as was Mr. Kennedy. There are men who cannot guard themselves from the assertion of marital rights at most inappropriate moments. Now Lord Cantrip lived with his wife most happily; yet you should pass hours with him and her together, and hardly know that they knew each other. One of the Duke's daughters was there,—but not the Duchess, who was known to be heavy;—and there was the beauteous Marchioness of Hartletop. Violet Effingham was in the room also,—giving Phineas a blow at the heart as he saw her smile. Might it be that he could speak a word to her on this occasion? Mr. Grey had also brought his wife;—and then there was Madame Max Goesler. Phineas found that it was his fortune to take down to dinner,—not Violet Effingham, but Madame Max Goesler. And, when he was placed at dinner, on the other side of him there sat Lady Hartletop, who addressed the few words which she spoke exclusively to Mr. Palliser. There had been in former days matters difficult of arrangement between those two; but I think that those old passages had now been forgotten by them both. Phineas was, therefore, driven to depend exclusively on Madame Max Goesler for conversation, and he found that he was not called upon to cast his seed into barren ground.

Up to that moment he had never heard of Madame Max Goesler. Lady Glencora, in introducing them, had pronounced the lady's name so clearly that he had caught it with accuracy, but he could not surmise whence she had come, or why she was there. She was a woman probably something over thirty years of age. She had thick black hair, which she wore in curls,—unlike anybody else in the world,—in curls which hung down low beneath her face, covering, and perhaps intended to cover, a certain thinness in her cheeks which would otherwise have taken something from the charm of her countenance. Her eyes were large, of a dark blue colour, and very bright,—and she used them in a manner which is as yet hardly common with Englishwomen. She seemed to intend that you should know that she employed them to conquer you, looking as a knight may have looked in olden days who entered a chamber with his sword drawn from the scabbard and in his hand. Her forehead was broad and somewhat low. Her nose was not classically beautiful, being broader at the nostrils than beauty required, and, moreover, not perfectly straight in its line. Her lips were thin. Her teeth, which she endeavoured to show as little as possible, were perfect in form and colour. They who criticised her severely said, however, that they were too large. Her chin was well formed, and divided by a dimple which gave to her face a softness of grace which would otherwise have been much missed. But perhaps her great beauty was in the brilliant clearness of her dark complexion. You might almost fancy that you could see into it so as to read the different lines beneath the skin. She was somewhat tall, though by no means tall to a fault, and was so thin as to be almost meagre in her proportions. She always wore her dress close up to her neck, and never showed the bareness of her arms. Though she was the only woman so clad now present in the room, this singularity did not specially strike one, because in other respects her apparel was so rich and quaint as to make inattention to it impossible. The observer who did not observe very closely would perceive that Madame Max Goesler's dress was unlike the dress of other women, but seeing that it was unlike in make, unlike in colour, and unlike in material, the ordinary observer would not see also that it was unlike in form for any other purpose than that of maintaining its general peculiarity of character. In colour she was abundant, and yet the fabric of her garment was always black. My pen may not dare to describe the traceries of yellow and ruby silk which went in and out through the black lace, across her bosom, and round her neck, and over her shoulders, and along her arms, and down to the very ground at her feet, robbing the black stuff of all its sombre solemnity, and producing a brightness in which there was nothing gaudy. She wore no vestige of crinoline, and hardly anything that could be called a train. And the lace sleeves of her dress, with their bright traceries of silk, were fitted close to her arms; and round her neck she wore the smallest possible collar of lace, above which there was a short chain of Roman gold with a ruby pendant. And she had rubies in her ears, and a ruby brooch, and rubies in the bracelets on her arms. Such, as regarded the outward woman, was Madame Max Goesler; and Phineas, as he took his place by her side, thought that fortune for the nonce had done well with him,—only that he should have liked it so much better could he have been seated next to Violet Effingham!

I have said that in the matter of conversation his morsel of seed was not thrown into barren ground. I do not know that he can truly be said to have produced even a morsel. The subjects were all mooted by the lady, and so great was her fertility in discoursing that all conversational grasses seemed to grow with her spontaneously. "Mr. Finn," she said, "what would I not give to be a member of the British Parliament at such a moment as this!"

"Why at such a moment as this particularly?"

"Because there is something to be done, which, let me tell you, senator though you are, is not always the case with you."

"My experience is short, but it sometimes seems to me that there is too much to be done."

"Too much of nothingness, Mr. Finn. Is not that the case? But now there is a real fight in the lists. The one great drawback to the life of women is that they cannot act in politics."

"And which side would you take?"

"What, here in England?" said Madame Max Goesler,—from which expression, and from one or two others of a similar nature, Phineas was led into a doubt whether the lady were a countrywoman of his or not. "Indeed, it is hard to say. Politically I should want to out-Turnbull Mr. Turnbull, to vote for everything that could be voted for,—ballot, manhood suffrage, womanhood suffrage, unlimited right of striking, tenant right, education of everybody, annual parliaments, and the abolition of at least the bench of bishops."

"That is a strong programme," said Phineas.

"It is strong, Mr. Finn, but that's what I should like. I think, however, that I should be tempted to feel a dastard security in the conviction that I might advocate my views without any danger of seeing them carried out. For, to tell you the truth, I don't at all want to put down ladies and gentlemen."

"You think that they would go with the bench of bishops?"

"I don't want anything to go,—that is, as far as real life is concerned. There's that dear good Bishop of Abingdon is the best friend I have in the world,—and as for the Bishop of Dorchester, I'd walk from here to there to hear him preach. And I'd sooner hem aprons for them all myself than that they should want those pretty decorations. But then, Mr. Finn, there is such a difference between life and theory;—is there not?"

"And it is so comfortable to have theories that one is not bound to carry out," said Phineas.

"Isn't it? Mr. Palliser, do you live up to your political theories?" At this moment Mr. Palliser was sitting perfectly silent between Lady Hartletop and the Duke's daughter, and he gave a little spring in his chair as this sudden address was made to him. "Your House of Commons theories, I mean, Mr. Palliser. Mr. Finn is saying that it is very well to have far advanced ideas,—it does not matter how far advanced,—because one is never called upon to act upon them practically."

"That is a dangerous doctrine, I think," said Mr. Palliser.

"But pleasant,—so at least Mr. Finn says."

"It is at least very common," said Phineas, not caring to protect himself by a contradiction.

"For myself," said Mr. Palliser gravely, "I think I may say that I always am really anxious to carry into practice all those doctrines of policy which I advocate in theory."

During this conversation Lady Hartletop sat as though no word of it reached her ears. She did not understand Madame Max Goesler, and by no means loved her. Mr. Palliser, when he had made his little speech, turned to the Duke's daughter and asked some question about the conservatories at Longroyston.

"I have called forth a word of wisdom," said Madame Max Goesler, almost in a whisper.

"Yes," said Phineas, "and taught a Cabinet Minister to believe that I am a most unsound politician. You may have ruined my prospects for life, Madame Max Goesler."

"Let me hope not. As far as I can understand the way of things in your Government, the aspirants to office succeed chiefly by making themselves uncommonly unpleasant to those who are in power. If a man can hit hard enough he is sure to be taken into the elysium of the Treasury bench,—not that he may hit others, but that he may cease to hit those who are there. I don't think men are chosen because they are useful."

"You are very severe upon us all."

"Indeed, as far as I can see, one man is as useful as another. But to put aside joking,—they tell me that you are sure to become a minister."

Phineas felt that he blushed. Could it be that people said of him behind his back that he was a man likely to rise high in political position? "Your informants are very kind," he replied awkwardly, "but I do not know who they are. I shall never get up in the way you describe,—that is, by abusing the men I support."

After that Madame Max Goesler turned round to Mr. Grey, who was sitting on the other side of her, and Phineas was left for a moment in silence. He tried to say a word to Lady Hartletop, but Lady Hartletop only bowed her head gracefully in recognition of the truth of the statement he made. So he applied himself for a while to his dinner.

"What do you think of Miss Effingham?" said Madame Max Goesler, again addressing him suddenly.

"What do I think about her?"

"You know her, I suppose."

"Oh yes, I know her. She is closely connected with the Kennedys, who are friends of mine."

"So I have heard. They tell me that scores of men are raving about her. Are you one of them?"

"Oh yes;—I don't mind being one of sundry scores. There is nothing particular in owning to that."

"But you admire her?"

"Of course I do," said Phineas.

"Ah, I see you are joking. I do amazingly. They say women never do admire women, but I most sincerely do admire Miss Effingham."

"Is she a friend of yours?"

"Oh no;—I must not dare to say so much as that. I was with her last winter for a week at Matching, and of course I meet her about at people's houses. She seems to me to be the most independent girl I ever knew in my life. I do believe that nothing would make her marry a man unless she loved him and honoured him, and I think it is so very seldom that you can say that of a girl."

"I believe so also," said Phineas. Then he paused a moment before he continued to speak. "I cannot say that I know Miss Effingham very intimately, but from what I have seen of her, I should think it very probable that she may not marry at all."

"Very probably," said Madame Max Goesler, who then again turned away to Mr. Grey.

Ten minutes after this, when the moment was just at hand in which the ladies were to retreat, Madame Max Goesler again addressed Phineas, looking very full into his face as she did so. "I wonder whether the time will ever come, Mr. Finn, in which you will give me an account of that day's journey to Blankenberg?"

"To Blankenberg!"

"Yes;—to Blankenberg. I am not asking for it now. But I shall look for it some day." Then Lady Glencora rose from her seat, and Madame Max Goesler went out with the others.

CHAPTER XLI
Lord Fawn

What had Madame Max Goesler to do with his journey to Blankenberg? thought Phineas, as he sat for a while in silence between Mr. Palliser and Mr. Grey; and why should she, who was a perfect stranger to him, have dared to ask him such a question? But as the conversation round the table, after the ladies had gone, soon drifted into politics and became general, Phineas, for a while, forgot Madame Max Goesler and the Blankenberg journey, and listened to the eager words of Cabinet Ministers, now and again uttering a word of his own, and showing that he, too, was as eager as others. But the session in Mr. Palliser's dining-room was not long, and Phineas soon found himself making his way amidst a throng of coming guests into the rooms above. His object was to meet Violet Effingham, but, failing that, he would not be unwilling to say a few more words to Madame Max Goesler.

He first encountered Lady Laura, to whom he had not spoken as yet, and, finding himself standing close to her for a while, he asked her after his late neighbour. "Do tell me one thing, Lady Laura;—who is Madame Max Goesler, and why have I never met her before?"

"That will be two things, Mr. Finn; but I will answer both questions as well as I can. You have not met her before, because she was in Germany last spring and summer, and in the year before that you were not about so much as you have been since. Still you must have seen her, I think. She is the widow of an Austrian banker, and has lived the greater part of her life at Vienna. She is very rich, and has a small house in Park Lane, where she receives people so exclusively that it has come to be thought an honour to be invited by Madame Max Goesler. Her enemies say that her father was a German Jew, living in England, in the employment of the Viennese bankers, and they say also that she has been married a second time to an Austrian Count, to whom she allows ever so much a year to stay away from her. But of all this, nobody, I fancy, knows anything. What they do know is that Madame Max Goesler spends seven or eight thousand a year, and that she will give no man an opportunity of even asking her to marry him. People used to be shy of her, but she goes almost everywhere now."

"She has not been at Portman Square?"

"Oh no; but then Lady Glencora is so much more advanced than we are! After all, we are but humdrum people, as the world goes now."

Then Phineas began to roam about the rooms, striving to find an opportunity of engrossing five minutes of Miss Effingham's attention. During the time that Lady Laura was giving him the history of Madame Max Goesler his eyes had wandered round, and he had perceived that Violet was standing in the further corner of a large lobby on to which the stairs opened,—so situated, indeed, that she could hardly escape, because of the increasing crowd, but on that very account almost impossible to be reached. He could see, also, that she was talking to Lord Fawn, an unmarried peer of something over thirty years of age, with an unrivalled pair of whiskers, a small estate, and a rising political reputation. Lord Fawn had been talking to Violet through the whole dinner, and Phineas was beginning to think that he should like to make another journey to Blankenberg, with the object of meeting his lordship on the sands. When Lady Laura had done speaking, his eyes were turned through a large open doorway towards the spot on which his idol was standing. "It is of no use, my friend," she said, touching his arm. "I wish I could make you know that it is of no use, because then I think you would be happier." To this Phineas made no answer, but went and roamed about the rooms. Why should it be of no use? Would Violet Effingham marry any man merely because he was a lord?

Some half-hour after this he had succeeded in making his way up to the place in which Violet was still standing, with Lord Fawn beside her. "I have been making such a struggle to get to you," he said.

"And now you are here, you will have to stay, for it is impossible to get out," she answered. "Lord Fawn has made the attempt half-a-dozen times, but has failed grievously."

"I have been quite contented," said Lord Fawn;—"more than contented."

Phineas felt that he ought to give some special reason to Miss Effingham to account for his efforts to reach her, but yet he had nothing special to say. Had Lord Fawn not been there, he would immediately have told her that he was waiting for an answer to the question he had asked her in Saulsby Park, but he could hardly do this in presence of the noble Under-Secretary of State. She received him with her pleasant genial smile, looking exactly as she had looked when he had parted from her on the morning after their ride. She did not show any sign of anger, or even of indifference at his approach. But still it was almost necessary that he should account for his search of her. "I have so longed to hear from you how you got on at Loughlinter," he said.

"Yes,—yes; and I will tell you something of it some day, perhaps. Why do you not come to Lady Baldock's?"

"I did not even know that Lady Baldock was in town."

"You ought to have known. Of course she is in town. Where did you suppose I was living? Lord Fawn was there yesterday, and can tell you that my aunt is quite blooming."

"Lady Baldock is blooming," said Lord Fawn; "certainly blooming;—that is, if evergreens may be said to bloom."

"Evergreens do bloom, as well as spring plants, Lord Fawn. You come and see her, Mr. Finn;—only you must bring a little money with you for the Female Protestant Unmarried Women's Emigration Society. That is my aunt's present hobby, as Lord Fawn knows to his cost."

"I wish I may never spend half-a-sovereign worse."

"But it is a perilous affair for me, as my aunt wants me to go out as a sort of leading Protestant unmarried female emigrant pioneer myself."

"You don't mean that," said Lord Fawn, with much anxiety.

"Of course you'll go," said Phineas. "I should, if I were you."

"I am in doubt," said Violet.

"It is such a grand prospect," said he. "Such an opening in life. So much excitement, you know; and such a useful career."

"As if there were not plenty of opening here for Miss Effingham," said Lord Fawn, "and plenty of excitement."

"Do you think there is?" said Violet. "You are much more civil than Mr. Finn, I must say." Then Phineas began to hope that he need not be afraid of Lord Fawn. "What a happy man you were at dinner!" continued Violet, addressing herself to Phineas.

"I thought Lord Fawn was the happy man."

"You had Madame Max Goesler all to yourself for nearly two hours, and I suppose there was not a creature in the room who did not envy you. I don't doubt that ever so much interest was made with Lady Glencora as to taking Madame Max down to dinner. Lord Fawn, I know, intrigued."

"Miss Effingham, really I must—contradict you."

"And Barrington Erle begged for it as a particular favour. The Duke, with a sigh, owned that it was impossible, because of his cumbrous rank; and Mr. Gresham, when it was offered to him, declared that he was fatigued with the business of the House, and not up to the occasion. How much did she say to you; and what did she talk about?"

"The ballot chiefly,—that, and manhood suffrage."

"Ah! she said something more than that, I am sure. Madame Max Goesler never lets any man go without entrancing him. If you have anything near your heart, Mr. Finn, Madame Max Goesler touched it, I am sure." Now Phineas had two things near his heart,—political promotion and Violet Effingham,—and Madame Max Goesler had managed to touch them both. She had asked him respecting his journey to Blankenberg, and had touched him very nearly in reference to Miss Effingham. "You know Madame Max Goesler, of course?" said Violet to Lord Fawn.

"Oh yes, I know the lady;—that is, as well as other people do. No one, I take it, knows much of her; and it seems to me that the world is becoming tired of her. A mystery is good for nothing if it remains always a mystery."

"And it is good for nothing at all when it is found out," said Violet.

"And therefore it is that Madame Max Goesler is a bore," said Lord Fawn.

"You did not find her a bore?" said Violet. Then Phineas, choosing to oppose Lord Fawn as well as he could on that matter, as on every other, declared that he had found Madame Max Goesler most delightful. "And beautiful,—is she not?" said Violet.

"Beautiful!" exclaimed Lord Fawn.

"I think her very beautiful," said Phineas.

"So do I," said Violet. "And she is a dear ally of mine. We were a week together last winter, and swore an undying friendship. She told me ever so much about Mr. Goesler."

"But she told you nothing of her second husband?" said Lord Fawn.

"Now that you have run into scandal, I shall have done," said Violet.

Half an hour after this, when Phineas was preparing to fight his way out of the house, he was again close to Madame Max Goesler. He had not found a single moment in which to ask Violet for an answer to his old question, and was retiring from the field discomfited, but not dispirited. Lord Fawn, he thought, was not a serious obstacle in his way. Lady Laura had told him that there was no hope for him; but then Lady Laura's mind on that subject was, he thought, prejudiced. Violet Effingham certainly knew what were his wishes, and knowing them, smiled on him and was gracious to him. Would she do so if his pretensions were thoroughly objectionable to her?

"I saw that you were successful this evening," said Madame Max Goesler to him.

"I was not aware of any success."

"I call it great success to be able to make your way where you will through such a crowd as there is here. You seem to me to be so stout a cavalier that I shall ask you to find my servant, and bid him get my carriage. Will you mind?" Phineas, of course, declared that he would be delighted. "He is a German, and not in livery. But if somebody will call out, he will hear. He is very sharp, and much more attentive than your English footmen. An Englishman hardly ever makes a good servant."

"Is that a compliment to us Britons?"

"No, certainly not. If a man is a servant, he should be clever enough to be a good one." Phineas had now given the order for the carriage, and, having returned, was standing with Madame Max Goesler in the cloak-room. "After all, we are surely the most awkward people in the world," she said. "You know Lord Fawn, who was talking to Miss Effingham just now. You should have heard him trying to pay me a compliment before dinner. It was like a donkey walking a minuet, and yet they say he is a clever man and can make speeches." Could it be possible that Madame Max Goesler's ears were so sharp that she had heard the things which Lord Fawn had said of her?

"He is a well-informed man," said Phineas.

"For a lord, you mean," said Madame Max Goesler. "But he is an oaf, is he not? And yet they say he is to marry that girl."

"I do not think he will," said Phineas, stoutly.

"I hope not, with all my heart; and I hope that somebody else may,—unless somebody else should change his mind. Thank you; I am so much obliged to you. Mind you come and call on me,—193, Park Lane. I dare say you know the little cottage." Then he put Madame Max Goesler into her carriage, and walked away to his club.

CHAPTER XLII
Lady Baldock Does Not Send a Card to Phineas Finn

Lady Baldock's house in Berkeley Square was very stately,—a large house with five front windows in a row, and a big door, and a huge square hall, and a fat porter in a round-topped chair;—but it was dingy and dull, and could not have been painted for the last ten years, or furnished for the last twenty. Nevertheless, Lady Baldock had "evenings," and people went to them,—though not such a crowd of people as would go to the evenings of Lady Glencora. Now Mr. Phineas Finn had not been asked to the evenings of Lady Baldock for the present season, and the reason was after this wise.

"Yes, Mr. Finn," Lady Baldock had said to her daughter, who, early in the spring, was preparing the cards. "You may send one to Mr. Finn, certainly."

"I don't know that he is very nice," said Augusta Boreham, whose eyes at Saulsby had been sharper perhaps than her mother's, and who had her suspicions.

But Lady Baldock did not like interference from her daughter. "Mr. Finn, certainly," she continued. "They tell me that he is a very rising young man, and he sits for Lord Brentford's borough. Of course he is a Radical, but we cannot help that. All the rising young men are Radicals now. I thought him very civil at Saulsby."

"But, mamma—"

"Well!"

"Don't you think that he is a little free with Violet?"

"What on earth do you mean, Augusta?"

"Have you not fancied that he is—fond of her?"

"Good gracious, no!"

"I think he is. And I have sometimes fancied that she is fond of him, too."

"I don't believe a word of it, Augusta,—not a word. I should have seen it if it was so. I am very sharp in seeing such things. They never escape me. Even Violet would not be such a fool as that. Send him a card, and if he comes I shall soon see." Miss Boreham quite understood her mother, though she could never master her,—and the card was prepared. Miss Boreham could never master her mother by her own efforts; but it was, I think, by a little intrigue on her part that Lady Baldock was mastered, and, indeed, altogether cowed, in reference to our hero, and that this victory was gained on that very afternoon in time to prevent the sending of the card.

When the mother and daughter were at tea, before dinner, Lord Baldock came into the room, and, after having been patted and petted and praised by his mother, he took up all the cards out of a china bowl and ran his eyes over them. "Lord Fawn!" he said, "the greatest ass in all London! Lady Hartletop! you know she won't come." "I don't see why she shouldn't come," said Lady Baldock;—"a mere country clergyman's daughter!" "Julius Cæsar Conway;—a great friend of mine, and therefore he always blackballs my other friends at the club. Lord Chiltern; I thought you were at daggers drawn with Chiltern." "They say he is going to be reconciled to his father, Gustavus, and I do it for Lord Brentford's sake. And he won't come, so it does not signify. And I do believe that Violet has really refused him." "You are quite right about his not coming," said Lord Baldock, continuing to read the cards; "Chiltern certainly won't come. Count Sparrowsky;—I wonder what you know about Sparrowsky that you should ask him here." "He is asked about, Gustavus; he is indeed," pleaded Lady Baldock. "I believe that Sparrowsky is a penniless adventurer. Mr. Monk; well, he is a Cabinet Minister. Sir Gregory Greeswing; you mix your people nicely at any rate. Sir Gregory Greeswing is the most old-fashioned Tory in England." "Of course we are not political, Gustavus." "Phineas Finn. They come alternately,—one and one.

"Mr. Finn is asked everywhere, Gustavus."

"I don't doubt it. They say he is a very good sort of fellow. They say also that Violet has found that out as well as other people."

"What do you mean, Gustavus?"

"I mean that everybody is saying that this Phineas Finn is going to set himself up in the world by marrying your niece. He is quite right to try it on, if he has a chance."

"I don't think he would be right at all," said Lady Baldock, with much energy. "I think he would be wrong,—shamefully wrong. They say he is the son of an Irish doctor, and that he hasn't a shilling in the world."

"That is just why he would be right. What is such a man to do, but to marry money? He's a deuced good-looking fellow, too, and will be sure to do it."

"He should work for his money in the city, then, or somewhere there. But I don't believe it, Gustavus; I don't, indeed."

"Very well. I only tell you what I hear. The fact is that he and Chiltern have already quarrelled about her. If I were to tell you that they have been over to Holland together and fought a duel about her, you wouldn't believe that."

"Fought a duel about Violet! People don't fight duels now, and I should not believe it."

"Very well. Then send your card to Mr. Finn." And, so saying, Lord Baldock left the room.

Lady Baldock sat in silence for some time toasting her toes at the fire, and Augusta Boreham sat by, waiting for orders. She felt pretty nearly sure that new orders would be given if she did not herself interfere. "You had better put by that card for the present, my dear," said Lady Baldock at last. "I will make inquiries. I don't believe a word of what Gustavus has said. I don't think that even Violet is such a fool as that. But if rash and ill-natured people have spoken of it, it may be as well to be careful."

"It is always well to be careful;—is it not, mamma?"

"Not but what I think it very improper that these things should be said about a young woman; and as for the story of the duel, I don't believe a word of it. It is absurd. I dare say that Gustavus invented it at the moment, just to amuse himself."

The card of course was not sent, and Lady Baldock at any rate put so much faith in her son's story as to make her feel it to be her duty to interrogate her niece on the subject. Lady Baldock at this period of her life was certainly not free from fear of Violet Effingham. In the numerous encounters which take place between them, the aunt seldom gained that amount of victory which would have completely satisfied her spirit. She longed to be dominant over her niece as she was dominant over her daughter; and when she found that she missed such supremacy, she longed to tell Violet to depart from out her borders, and be no longer niece of hers. But had she ever done so, Violet would have gone at the instant, and then terrible things would have followed. There is a satisfaction in turning out of doors a nephew or niece who is pecuniarily dependent, but when the youthful relative is richly endowed, the satisfaction is much diminished. It is the duty of a guardian, no doubt, to look after the ward; but if this cannot be done, the ward's money should at least be held with as close a fist as possible. But Lady Baldock, though she knew that she would be sorely wounded, poked about on her old body with the sharp lances of disobedience, and struck with the cruel swords of satire, if she took upon herself to scold or even to question Violet, nevertheless would not abandon the pleasure of lecturing and teaching. "It is my duty," she would say to herself, "and though it be taken in a bad spirit, I will always perform my duty." So she performed her duty, and asked Violet Effingham some few questions respecting Phineas Finn. "My dear," she said, "do you remember meeting a Mr. Finn at Saulsby?"

"A Mr. Finn, aunt! Why, he is a particular friend of mine. Of course I do, and he was at Saulsby. I have met him there more than once. Don't you remember that we were riding about together?"

"I remember that he was there, certainly; but I did not know that he was a special—friend."

"Most especial, aunt. A 1, I may say;—among young men, I mean."

Lady Baldock was certainly the most indiscreet of old women in such a matter as this, and Violet the most provoking of young ladies. Lady Baldock, believing that there was something to fear,—as, indeed, there was, much to fear,—should have been content to destroy the card, and to keep the young lady away from the young gentleman, if such keeping away was possible to her. But Miss Effingham was certainly very wrong to speak of any young man as being A 1. Fond as I am of Miss Effingham, I cannot justify her, and must acknowledge that she used the most offensive phrase she could find, on purpose to annoy her aunt.

"Violet," said Lady Baldock, bridling up, "I never heard such a word before from the lips of a young lady."

"Not as A 1? I thought it simply meant very good."

121

"A 1 is a nobleman," said Lady Baldock.

"No, aunt;—A 1 is a ship,—a ship that is very good," said Violet.

"And do you mean to say that Mr. Finn is,—is,—is,—very good?"

"Yes, indeed. You ask Lord Brentford, and Mr. Kennedy. You know he saved poor Mr. Kennedy from being throttled in the streets."

"That has nothing to do with it. A policeman might have done that."

"Then he would have been A 1 of policemen,—though A 1 does not mean a policeman."

"He would have done his duty, and so perhaps did Mr. Finn."

"Of course he did, aunt. It couldn't have been his duty to stand by and see Mr. Kennedy throttled. And he nearly killed one of the men, and took the other prisoner with his own hands. And he made a beautiful speech the other day. I read every word of it. I am so glad he's a Liberal. I do like young men to be Liberals." Now Lord Baldock was a Tory, as had been all the Lord Baldocks,—since the first who had been bought over from the Whigs in the time of George III at the cost of a barony.

"You have nothing to do with politics, Violet."

"Why shouldn't I have something to do with politics, aunt?"

"And I must tell you that your name is being very unpleasantly mentioned in connection with that of this young man because of your indiscretion."

"What indiscretion?" Violet, as she made her demand for a more direct accusation, stood quite upright before her aunt, looking the old woman full in the face,—almost with her arms akimbo.

"Calling him A 1, Violet."

"People have been talking about me and Mr. Finn, because I just now, at this very moment, called him A 1 to you! If you want to scold me about anything, aunt, do find out something less ridiculous than that."

"It was most improper language,—and if you used it to me, I am sure you would to others."

"To what others?"

"To Mr. Finn,—and those sort of people."

"Call Mr. Finn A 1 to his face! Well,—upon my honour I don't know why I should not. Lord Chiltern says he rides beautifully, and if we were talking about riding I might do so."

"You have no business to talk to Lord Chiltern about Mr. Finn at all."

"Have I not? I thought that perhaps the one sin might palliate the other. You know, aunt, no young lady, let her be ever so ill-disposed, can marry two objectionable young men,—at the same time."

"I said nothing about your marrying Mr. Finn."

"Then, aunt, what did you mean?"

"I meant that you should not allow yourself to be talked of with an adventurer, a young man without a shilling, a person who has come from nobody knows where in the bogs of Ireland."

"But you used to ask him here."

"Yes,—as long as he knew his place. But I shall not do so again. And I must beg you to be circumspect."

"My dear aunt, we may as well understand each other. I will not be circumspect, as you call it. And if Mr. Finn asked me to marry him to-morrow, and if I liked him well enough, I would take him,—even though he had been dug right out of a bog. Not only because I liked him,—mind! If I were unfortunate enough to like a man who was nothing, I would refuse him in spite of my liking,—because he was nothing. But this young man is not nothing. Mr. Finn is a fine fellow, and if there were no other reason to prevent my marrying him than his being the son of a doctor, and coming out of the bogs, that would not do so. Now I have made a clean breast to you as regards Mr. Finn; and if you do not like what I've said, aunt, you must acknowledge that you have brought it on yourself."

Lady Baldock was left for a time speechless. But no card was sent to Phineas Finn.

CHAPTER XLIII
Promotion

Phineas got no card from Lady Baldock, but one morning he received a note from Lord Brentford which was of more importance to him than any card could have been. At this time, bit by bit, the Reform Bill of the day had nearly made its way through the committee, but had been so mutilated as to be almost impossible of recognition by its progenitors. And there was still a clause or two as to the rearrangement of seats, respecting which it was known that there would be a combat,—probably combats,—carried on after the internecine fashion. There was a certain clipping of counties to be done, as to which it was said that Mr. Daubeny had declared that he would not yield till he was made to do so by the brute force of majorities;—and there was another clause for the drafting of certain superfluous members from little boroughs, and bestowing them on populous towns at which they were much wanted, respecting which Mr. Turnbull had proclaimed that the clause as it now stood was a fainéant clause, capable of doing, and intended to do, no good in the proper direction; a clause put into the bill to gull ignorant folk who had not eyes enough to recognise the fact that it was fainéant; a make-believe clause,—so said Mr. Turnbull,—to be detested on that account by every true reformer worse than the old Philistine bonds and Tory figments of representation, as to which there was at least no hypocritical pretence of popular fitness. Mr. Turnbull had been very loud and very angry,—had talked much of demonstrations among the people, and had almost threatened the House. The House in its present mood did not fear any demonstrations,—but it did fear that Mr. Turnbull might help Mr. Daubeny, and that Mr. Daubeny might help Mr. Turnbull. It was now May,—the middle of May,—and ministers, who had been at work on their Reform Bill ever since the beginning of the session, were becoming weary of it. And then, should these odious clauses escape the threatened Turnbull-Daubeny alliance,—then there was the House of Lords! "What a pity we can't pass our bills at the Treasury, and have done with them!" said Laurence Fitzgibbon. "Yes, indeed," replied Mr. Ratler. "For myself, I was never so tired of a session in my life. I wouldn't go through it again to be made,—no, not to be made Chancellor of the Exchequer."

Lord Brentford's note to Phineas Finn was as follows:—

House of Lords, 16th May, 186—.

My dear Mr. Finn,

You are no doubt aware that Lord Bosanquet's death has taken Mr. Mottram into the Upper House, and that as he was Under-Secretary for the Colonies, and as the Under-Secretary must be in the Lower House, the vacancy must be filled up.

The heart of Phineas Finn at this moment was almost in his mouth. Not only to be selected for political employment, but to be selected at once for an office so singularly desirable! Under-Secretaries, he fancied, were paid two thousand a year. What would Mr. Low say now? But his great triumph soon received a check. "Mr. Mildmay has spoken to me on the subject," continued the letter, "and informs me that he has offered the place at the colonies to his old supporter, Mr. Laurence Fitzgibbon." Laurence Fitzgibbon!

I am inclined to think that he could not have done better, as Mr. Fitzgibbon has shown great zeal for his party. This will vacate the Irish seat at the Treasury Board, and I am commissioned by Mr. Mildmay to offer it to you. Perhaps you will do me the pleasure of calling on me to-morrow between the hours of eleven and twelve.

Yours very sincerely,

Brentford.

Phineas was himself surprised to find that his first feeling on reading this letter was one of dissatisfaction. Here were his golden hopes about to be realised,—hopes as to the realisation of which he had been quite despondent twelve months ago,—and yet he was uncomfortable because he was to be postponed to Laurence Fitzgibbon. Had the new Under-Secretary been a man whom he had not known, whom he had not learned to look down upon as inferior to himself, he would not have minded it,—would have been full of joy at the promotion proposed for himself. But Laurence Fitzgibbon was such a poor creature, that the idea of filling a place from which Laurence had risen was distasteful to him. "It seems to be all a matter of favour and convenience," he said to himself, "without any reference to the service." His triumph would have been so complete had Mr. Mildmay allowed him to go into the higher place at one leap. Other men who had made themselves useful had done so. In the first hour after receiving Lord Brentford's letter, the idea of becoming a Lord of the Treasury was almost displeasing to him. He had an idea that junior lordships of the Treasury were generally bestowed on young members whom it was convenient to secure, but who were not good at doing anything. There was a moment in which he thought that he would refuse to be made a junior lord.

But during the night cooler reflections told him that he had been very wrong. He had taken up politics with the express desire of getting his foot upon a rung of the ladder of promotion, and now, in his third session, he was about to be successful. Even as a junior lord he would have a thousand a year; and how long might he have sat in chambers, and have wandered about Lincoln's Inn, and have loitered in the courts striving to look as though he had business, before he would have earned a thousand a year! Even as a junior lord he could make himself useful, and when once he should be known to be a good working man, promotion would come to him. No ladder can be mounted without labour; but this ladder was now open above his head, and he already had his foot upon it.

At half-past eleven he was with Lord Brentford, who received him with the blandest smile and a pressure of the hand which was quite cordial. "My dear Finn," he said, "this gives me the most sincere pleasure,—the greatest pleasure in the world. Our connection together at Loughton of course makes it doubly agreeable to me."

"I cannot be too grateful to you, Lord Brentford."

"No, no; no, no. It is all your own doing. When Mr. Mildmay asked me whether I did not think you the most promising of the young members on our side in your House, I certainly did say that I quite concurred. But I should be taking too much on myself, I should be acting dishonestly, if I were to allow you to imagine that it was my proposition. Had he asked me to recommend, I should have named you; that I say frankly. But he did not. He did not. Mr. Mildmay named you himself. 'Do you think,' he said, 'that your friend Finn would join us at the Treasury?' I told him that I did think so. 'And do you not think,' said he, 'that it would be a useful appointment?' Then I ventured to say that I had no doubt whatever on that point;—that I knew you well enough to feel confident that you would lend a strength to the Liberal Government. Then there were a few words said about your seat, and I was commissioned to write to you. That was all."

Phineas was grateful, but not too grateful, and bore himself very well in the interview. He explained to Lord Brentford that of course it was his object to serve the country,—and to be paid for his services,—and that he considered himself to be very fortunate to be selected so early in his career for parliamentary place. He would endeavour to do his duty, and could safely say of himself that he did not wish to eat the bread of idleness. As he made this assertion, he thought of Laurence Fitzgibbon. Laurence Fitzgibbon had eaten the bread of idleness, and yet he was promoted. But Phineas said nothing to Lord Brentford about his idle friend. When he had made his little speech he asked a question about the borough.

"I have already ventured to write a letter to my agent at Loughton, telling him that you have accepted office, and that you will be shortly there again. He will see Shortribs and arrange it. But if I were you I should write to Shortribs and to Grating,—after I had seen Mr. Mildmay. Of course you will not mention my name," And the Earl looked very grave as he uttered this caution.

"Of course I will not," said Phineas.

"I do not think you'll find any difficulty about the seat," said the peer. "There never has been any difficulty at Loughton yet. I must say that for them. And if we can scrape through with Clause 72 we shall be all right;—shall we not?" This was the clause as to which so violent an opposition was expected from Mr. Turnbull,—a clause as to which Phineas himself had felt that he would hardly know how to support the Government, in the event of the committee being pressed to a division upon it. Could he, an ardent reformer, a reformer at heart,—could he say that such a borough as Loughton should be spared;—that the arrangement by which Shortribs and Grating had sent him to Parliament, in obedience to Lord Brentford's orders, was in due accord with the theory of a representative legislature? In what respect had Gatton and Old Sarum been worse than Loughton? Was he not himself false to his principle in sitting for such a borough as Loughton? He had spoken to Mr. Monk, and Mr. Monk had told him that Rome was not built in a day,—and had told him also that good things were most valued and were more valuable when they came by instalments. But then Mr. Monk himself enjoyed the satisfaction of sitting for a popular Constituency. He was not personally pricked in the conscience by his own parliamentary position. Now, however,—now that Phineas had consented to join the Government, any such considerations as these must be laid aside. He could no longer be a free agent, or even a free thinker. He had been quite aware of this, and had taught himself to understand that members of Parliament in the direct service of the Government were absolved from the necessity of free-thinking. Individual free-thinking was incompatible with the position of a member of the Government, and unless such abnegation were practised, no government would be possible. It was of course a man's duty to bind himself together with no other men but those with whom, on matters of general policy, he could agree heartily;—but having found that he could so agree, he knew that it would be his duty as a subaltern to vote as he was directed. It would trouble his conscience less to sit for Loughton and vote for an objectionable clause as a member of the Government, than it would have done to give such a vote as an independent member. In so resolving, he thought that he was simply acting in accordance with the acknowledged rules of parliamentary government. And therefore, when Lord Brentford spoke of Clause 72, he could answer pleasantly, "I think we shall carry it; and, you see, in getting it through committee, if we can carry it by one, that is as good as a hundred. That's the comfort of close-fighting in committee. In the open House we are almost as much beaten by a narrow majority as by a vote against us."

"Just so; just so," said Lord Brentford, delighted to see that his young pupil,—as he regarded him,—understood so well the system of parliamentary management. "By-the-bye, Finn, have you seen Chiltern lately?"

"Not quite lately," said Phineas, blushing up to his eyes.

"Or heard from him?"

"No;—nor heard from him. When last I heard of him he was in Brussels."

"Ah,—yes; he is somewhere on the Rhine now. I thought that as you were so intimate, perhaps you corresponded with him. Have you heard that we have arranged about Lady Laura's money?"

"I have heard. Lady Laura has told me."

"I wish he would return," said Lord Brentford sadly,—almost solemnly. "As that great difficulty is over, I would receive him willingly, and make my house pleasant to him, if I can do so. I am most anxious that he should settle, and marry. Could you not write to him?" Phineas, not daring to tell Lord Brentford that he had quarrelled with Lord Chiltern,—feeling that if he did so everything would go wrong,—said that he would write to Lord Chiltern.

As he went away he felt that he was bound to get an answer from Violet Effingham. If it should be necessary, he was willing to break with Lord Brentford on that matter,—even though such breaking should lose him his borough and his place;—but not on any other matter.

CHAPTER XLIV
Phineas and His Friends

Our hero's friends were, I think, almost more elated by our hero's promotion than was our hero himself. He never told himself that it was a great thing to be a junior lord of the Treasury, though he acknowledged to himself that to have made a successful beginning was a very great thing. But his friends were loud in their congratulations,—or condolements as the case might be.

He had his interview with Mr. Mildmay, and, after that, one of his first steps was to inform Mrs. Bunce that he must change his lodgings. "The truth is, Mrs. Bunce, not that I want anything better; but that a better position will be advantageous to me, and that I can afford to pay for it." Mrs. Bunce acknowledged the truth of the argument, with her apron up to her eyes. "I've got to be so fond of looking after you, Mr. Finn! I have indeed," said Mrs. Bunce. "It is not just what you pays like, because another party will pay as much. But we've got so used to you, Mr. Finn,—haven't we?" Mrs. Bunce was probably not aware herself that the comeliness of her lodger had pleased her feminine eye, and touched her feminine heart. Had anybody said that Mrs. Bunce was in love with Phineas, the scandal would have been monstrous. And yet it was so,—after a fashion. And Bunce knew it,—after his fashion. "Don't be such an old fool," he said, "crying after him because he's six foot high." "I ain't crying after him because he's six foot high," whined the poor woman;—"but one does like old faces better than new, and a gentleman about one's place is pleasant." "Gentleman be d——d," said Bunce. But his anger was excited, not by his wife's love for Phineas, but by the use of an objectionable word.

Bunce himself had been on very friendly terms with Phineas, and they two had had many discussions on matters of politics, Bunce taking up the cudgels always for Mr. Turnbull, and generally slipping away gradually into some account of his own martyrdom. For he had been a martyr, having failed in obtaining any redress against the policeman who had imprisoned him so wrongfully. The *People's Banner* had fought for him manfully, and therefore there was a little disagreement between him and Phineas on the subject of that great organ of public opinion. And as Mr. Bunce thought that his lodger was very wrong to sit for Lord Brentford's borough, subjects were sometimes touched which were a little galling to Phineas.

Touching this promotion, Bunce had nothing but condolement to offer to the new junior lord. "Oh yes," said he, in answer to an argument from Phineas, "I suppose there must be lords, as you call 'em; though for the matter of that I can't see as they is of any mortal use."

"Wouldn't you have the Government carried on?"

"Government! Well; I suppose there must be government. But the less of it the better. I'm not against government;—nor yet against laws, Mr. Finn; though the less of them, too, the better. But what does these lords do in the Government? Lords indeed! I'll tell you what they do, Mr. Finn. They wotes; that's what they do! They wotes hard; black or white, white or black. Ain't that true? When you're a 'lord,' will you be able to wote against Mr. Mildmay to save your very soul?"

"If it comes to be a question of soul-saving, Mr. Bunce, I shan't save my place at the expense of my conscience."

"Not if you knows it, you mean. But the worst of it is that a man gets so thick into the mud that he don't know whether he's dirty or clean. You'll have to wote as you're told, and of course you'll think it's right enough. Ain't you been among Parliament gents long enough to know that that's the way it goes?"

"You think no honest man can be a member of the Government?"

"I don't say that, but I think honesty's a deal easier away from 'em. The fact is, Mr. Finn, it's all wrong with us yet, and will be till we get it nigher to the great American model. If a poor man gets into Parliament,—you'll excuse me, Mr. Finn, but I calls you a poor man."

"Certainly,—as a member of Parliament I am a very poor man."

"Just so,—and therefore what do you do? You goes and lays yourself out for government! I'm not saying as how you're anyways wrong. A man has to live. You has winning ways, and a good physiognomy of your own, and are as big as a life-guardsman." Phineas as he heard this doubtful praise laughed and blushed. "Very well; you makes your way with the big wigs, lords and earls and them like, and you gets returned for a rotten borough;—you'll excuse me, but that's about it, ain't it?—and then you goes in for government! A man may have a mission to govern, such as Washington and Cromwell and the like o' them. But when I hears of Mr. Fitzgibbon a-governing, why then I says,—d——n it all."

"There must be good and bad you know."

"We've got to change a deal yet, Mr. Finn, and we'll do it. When a young man as has liberal feelings gets into Parliament, he shouldn't be snapped up and brought into the governing business just because he's poor and wants a salary. They don't do it that way in the States; and they won't do it that way here long. It's the system as I hates, and not you, Mr. Finn. Well, good-bye, sir. I hope you'll like the governing business, and find it suits your health."

These condolements from Mr. Bunce were not pleasant, but they set him thinking. He felt assured that Bunce and Quintus Slide and Mr. Turnbull were wrong. Bunce was ignorant. Quintus Slide was dishonest. Turnbull was greedy of popularity. For himself, he thought that as a young man he was fairly well informed. He knew that he meant to be true in his vocation. And he was quite sure that the object nearest to his heart in politics was not self-aggrandisement, but the welfare of the people in general. And yet he could not but agree with Bunce that there was something wrong. When such men as Laurence Fitzgibbon were called upon to act as governors, was it not to be expected that the ignorant but still intelligent Bunces of the population should—"d——n it all"?

On the evening of that day he went up to Mrs. Low's, very sure that he should receive some encouragement from her and from her husband. She had been angry with him because he had put himself into a position in which money must be spent and none could be made. The Lows, especially Mrs. Low, had refused to believe that any success was within his reach. Now that he had succeeded, now that he was in receipt of a salary on which he could live and save money, he would be sure of sympathy from his old friends the Lows!

But Mrs. Low was as severe upon him as Mr. Bunce had been, and even from Mr. Low he could extract no real comfort. "Of course I congratulate you," said Mr. Low coldly.

"And you, Mrs. Low?"

"Well, you know, Mr. Finn, I think you have begun at the wrong end. I thought so before, and I think so still. I suppose I ought not to say so to a Lord of the Treasury, but if you ask me, what can I do?"

"Speak the truth out, of course."

"Exactly. That's what I must do. Well, the truth is, Mr. Finn, that I do not think it is a very good opening for a young man to be made what they call a Lord of the Treasury,—unless he has got a private fortune, you know, to support that kind of life."

"You see, Phineas, a ministry is such an uncertain thing," said Mr. Low.

"Of course it's uncertain;—but as I did go into the House, it's something to have succeeded."

"If you call that success," said Mrs. Low.

"You did intend to go on with your profession," said Mr. Low. He could not tell them that he had changed his mind, and that he meant to marry Violet Effingham, who would much prefer a parliamentary life for her husband to that of a working barrister. "I suppose that is all given up now," continued Mr. Low.

"Just for the present," said Phineas.

"Yes;—and for ever I fear," said Mrs. Low, "You'll never go back to real work after frittering away your time as a Lord of the Treasury. What sort of work must it be when just anybody can do it that it suits them to lay hold of? But of course a thousand a year is something, though a man may have it for only six months."

It came out in the course of the evening that Mr. Low was going to stand for the borough vacated by Mr. Mottram, at which it was considered that the Conservatives might possibly prevail. "You see, after all, Phineas," said Mr. Low, "that I am following your steps."

"Ah; you are going into the House in the course of your profession."

"Just so," said Mrs. Low.

"And are taking the first step towards being a Tory Attorney-General."

"That's as may be," said Mr. Low. "But it's the kind of thing a man does after twenty years of hard work. For myself, I really don't care much whether I succeed or fail. I should like to live to be a Vice-Chancellor. I don't mind saying as much as that to you. But I'm not at all sure that Parliament is the best way to the Equity Bench."

"But it is a grand thing to get into Parliament when you do it by means of your profession," said Mrs. Low.

Soon after that Phineas took his departure from the house, feeling sore and unhappy. But on the next morning he was received in Grosvenor Place with an amount of triumph which went far to compensate him. Lady Laura had written to him to call there, and on his arrival he found both Violet Effingham and Madame Max Goesler with his friend. When Phineas entered the room his first feeling was one of intense joy at seeing that Violet Effingham was present there. Then there was one of surprise that Madame Max Goesler should make one of the little party.

Lady Laura had told him at Mr. Palliser's dinner-party that they, in Portman Square, had not as yet advanced far enough to receive Madame Max Goesler,—and yet here was the lady in Mr. Kennedy's drawing-room. Now Phineas would have thought it more likely that he should find her in Portman Square than in Grosvenor Place. The truth was that Madame Goesler had been brought by Miss Effingham,—with the consent, indeed, of Lady Laura, but with a consent given with much of hesitation. "What are you afraid of?" Violet had asked. "I am afraid of nothing," Lady Laura had answered; "but one has to choose one's acquaintance in accordance with rules which one doesn't lay down very strictly." "She is a clever woman," said Violet, "and everybody likes her; but if you think Mr. Kennedy would object, of course you are right." Then Lady Laura had consented, telling herself that it was not necessary that she should ask her husband's approval as to every new acquaintance she might form. At the same time Violet had been told that Phineas would be there, and so the party had been made up.

"'See the conquering hero comes,' said Violet in her cheeriest voice.

"I am so glad that Mr. Finn has been made a lord of something," said Madame Max Goesler. "I had the pleasure of a long political discussion with him the other night, and I quite approve of him."

"We are so much gratified, Mr. Finn," said Lady Laura. "Mr. Kennedy says that it is the best appointment they could have made, and papa is quite proud about it."

"You are Lord Brentford's member; are you not?" asked Madame Max Goesler. This was a question which Phineas did not quite like, and which he was obliged to excuse by remembering that the questioner had lived so long out of England as to be probably ignorant of the myths, and theories, and system, and working of the British Constitution. Violet Effingham, little as she knew of politics, would never have asked a question so imprudent.

But the question was turned off, and Phineas, with an easy grace, submitted himself to be petted, and congratulated, and purred over, and almost caressed by the three ladies, Their good-natured enthusiasm was at any rate better than the satire of Bunce, or the wisdom of Mrs. Low. Lady Laura had no misgivings as to Phineas being fit for governing, and Violet Effingham said nothing as to the short-lived tenure of ministers. Madame Max Goesler, though she had asked an indiscreet question, thoroughly appreciated the advantage of Government pay, and the prestige of Government power. "You are a lord now," she said, speaking, as was customary with her, with the slightest possible foreign accent, "and you will be a president soon, and then perhaps a secretary. The order of promotion seems odd, but I am told it is very pleasant."

"It is pleasant to succeed, of course," said Phineas, "let the success be ever so little."

"We knew you would succeed," said Lady Laura. "We were quite sure of it. Were we not, Violet?"

"You always said so, my dear. For myself I do not venture to have an opinion on such matters. Will you always have to go to that big building in the corner, Mr. Finn, and stay there from ten till four? Won't that be a bore?"

"We have a half-holiday on Saturday, you know," said Phineas.

"And do the Lords of the Treasury have to take care of the money?" asked Madame Max Goesler.

"Only their own; and they generally fail in doing that," said Phineas.

He sat there for a considerable time, wondering whether Mr. Kennedy would come in, and wondering also as to what Mr. Kennedy would say to Madame Max Goesler when he did come in. He knew that it was useless for him to expect any opportunity, then or there, of being alone for a moment with Violet Effingham. His only chance in that direction would be in some crowded room, at some ball at which he might ask her to dance with him; but it seemed that fate was very unkind to him, and that no such chance came in his way. Mr. Kennedy did not appear, and Madame Max Goesler with Violet went away, leaving Phineas still sitting with Lady Laura. Each of them said a kind word to him as they went. "I don't know whether I may dare to expect that a Lord of the Treasury will come and see me?" said Madame Max Goesler. Then Phineas made a second promise that he would call in Park Lane. Violet blushed as she remembered that she could not ask him to call at Lady Baldock's. "Good-bye, Mr. Finn," she said, giving him her hand. "I'm so very glad that they have chosen you; and I do hope that, as Madame Max says, they'll make you a secretary and a president, and everything else very quickly,—till it will come to your turn to be making other people." "He is very nice," said Madame Goesler to Violet as she took her place in the carriage. "He bears being petted and spoilt without being either awkward or conceited." "On the whole, he is rather nice," said Violet; "only he has not got a shilling in the world, and has to make himself before he will be anybody." "He must marry money, of course," said Madame Max Goesler.

"I hope you are contented?" said Lady Laura, rising from her chair and coming opposite to him as soon as they were alone.

"Of course I am contented."

"I was not,—when I first heard of it. Why did they promote that empty-headed countryman of yours to a place for which he was quite unfit? I was not contented. But then I am more ambitious for you than you are for yourself." He sat without answering her for awhile, and she stood waiting for his reply. "Have you nothing to say to me?" she asked.

"I do not know what to say. When I think of it all, I am lost in amazement. You tell me that you are not contented;—that you are ambitious for me. Why is it that you should feel any interest in the matter?"

"Is it not reasonable that we should be interested for our friends?"

"But when you and I last parted here in this room you were hardly my friend."

"Was I not? You wrong me there;—very deeply."

"I told you what was my ambition, and you resented it," said Phineas.

"I think I said that I could not help you, and I think I said also that I thought you would fail. I do not know that I showed much resentment. You see, I told her that you were here, that she might come and meet you. You know that I wished my brother should succeed. I wished it before I ever knew you. You cannot expect that I should change my wishes."

"But if he cannot succeed," pleaded Phineas.

"Who is to say that? Has a woman never been won by devotion and perseverance? Besides, how can I wish to see you go on with a suit which must sever you from my father, and injure your political prospects;—perhaps fatally injure them? It seems to me now that my father is almost the only man in London who has not heard of this duel."

"Of course he will hear of it. I have half made up my mind to tell him myself."

"Do not do that, Mr. Finn. There can be no reason for it. But I did not ask you to come here to-day to talk to you about Oswald or Violet. I have given you my advice about that, and I can do no more."

"Lady Laura, I cannot take it. It is out of my power to take it."

"Very well. The matter shall be what you members of Parliament call an open question between us. When papa asked you to accept this place at the Treasury, did it ever occur to you to refuse it?"

"It did;—for half an hour or so."

"I hoped you would,—and yet I knew that I was wrong. I thought that you should count yourself to be worth more than that, and that you should, as it were, assert yourself. But then it is so difficult to draw the line between proper self-assertion and proper self-denial;—to know how high to go up the table, and how low to go down. I do not doubt that you have been right,—only make them understand that you are not as other junior lords;—that you have been willing to be a junior lord, or anything else for a purpose; but that the purpose is something higher than that of fetching and carrying in Parliament for Mr. Mildmay and Mr. Palliser."

"I hope in time to get beyond fetching and carrying," said Phineas.

"Of course you will; and knowing that, I am glad that you are in office. I suppose there will be no difficulty about Loughton."

Then Phineas laughed. "I hear," said he, "that Mr. Quintus Slide, of the *People's Banner*, has already gone down to canvass the electors."

"Mr. Quintus Slide! To canvass the electors of Loughton!" and Lady Laura drew herself up and spoke of this unseemly intrusion on her father's borough, as though the vulgar man who had been named had forced his way into the very drawing-room in Portman Square. At that moment Mr. Kennedy came in. "Do you hear what Mr. Finn tells me?" she said. "He has heard that Mr. Quintus Slide has gone down to Loughton to stand against him."

"And why not?" said Mr. Kennedy.

"My dear!" ejaculated Lady Laura.

"Mr. Quintus Slide will no doubt lose his time and his money;—but he will gain the prestige of having stood for a borough, which will be something for him on the staff of the *People's Banner*," said Mr. Kennedy.

"He will get that horrid man Vellum to propose him," said Lady Laura.

"Very likely," said Mr. Kennedy. "And the less any of us say about it the better. Finn, my dear fellow, I congratulate you heartily. Nothing for a long time has given me greater pleasure than hearing of your appointment. It is equally honourable to yourself and to Mr. Mildmay. It is a great step to have gained so early."

Phineas, as he thanked his friend, could not help asking himself what his friend had done to be made a Cabinet Minister. Little as he, Phineas, himself had done in the House in his two sessions and a half, Mr. Kennedy had hardly done more in his fifteen or twenty. But then Mr. Kennedy was possessed of almost miraculous wealth, and owned half a county, whereas he, Phineas, owned almost nothing at all. Of course no Prime Minister would offer a junior lordship at the Treasury to a man with £30,000 a year. Soon after this Phineas took his leave. "I think he will do well," said Mr. Kennedy to his wife.

"I am sure he will do well," replied Lady Laura, almost scornfully.

"He is not quite such a black swan with me as he is with you; but still I think he will succeed, if he takes care of himself. It is astonishing how that absurd story of his duel with Chiltern has got about."

"It is impossible to prevent people talking," said Lady Laura.

"I suppose there was some quarrel, though neither of them will tell you. They say it was about Miss Effingham. I should hardly think that Finn could have any hopes in that direction."

"Why should he not have hopes?"

"Because he has neither position, nor money, nor birth," said Mr. Kennedy.

"He is a gentleman." said Lady Laura; "and I think he has position. I do not see why he should not ask any girl to marry him."

"There is no understanding you, Laura," said Mr. Kennedy, angrily. "I thought you had quite other hopes about Miss Effingham."

"So I have; but that has nothing to do with it. You spoke of Mr. Finn as though he would be guilty of some crime were he to ask Violet Effingham to be his wife. In that I disagree with you. Mr. Finn is—"

"You will make me sick of the name of Mr. Finn."

"I am sorry that I offend you by my gratitude to a man who saved your life." Mr. Kennedy shook his head. He knew that the argument used against him was false, but he did not know how to show that he knew that it was false. "Perhaps I had better not mention his name any more," continued Lady Laura.

"Nonsense!"

"I quite agree with you that it is nonsense, Robert."

"All I mean to say is, that if you go on as you do, you will turn his head and spoil him. Do you think I do not know what is going on among you?"

"And what is going on among us,—as you call it?"

"You are taking this young man up and putting him on a pedestal and worshipping him, just because he is well-looking, and rather clever and decently behaved. It's always the way with women who have nothing to do, and who cannot be made to understand that they should have duties. They cannot live without some kind of idolatry."

"Have I neglected my duty to you, Robert?"

"Yes,—you know you have;—in going to those receptions at your father's house on Sundays."

"What has that to do with Mr. Finn?"

"Psha!"

"I begin to think I had better tell Mr. Finn not to come here any more, since his presence is disagreeable to you. All the world knows how great is the service he did you, and it will seem to be very ridiculous. People will say all manner of things; but anything will be better than that you should go on as you have done,—accusing your wife of idolatry towards—a young man, because—he is—well-looking."

"I never said anything of the kind."

"You did, Robert."

"I did not. I did not speak more of you than of a lot of others."

"You accused me personally, saying that because of my idolatry I had neglected my duty; but really you made such a jumble of it all, with papa's visitors, and Sunday afternoons, that I cannot follow what was in your mind."

Then Mr. Kennedy stood for awhile, collecting his thoughts, so that he might unravel the jumble, if that were possible to him; but finding that it was not possible, he left the room, and closed the door behind him.

Then Lady Laura was left alone to consider the nature of the accusation which her husband had brought against her; or the nature rather of the accusation which she had chosen to assert that her husband had implied. For in her heart she knew that he had made no such accusation, and had intended to make none such. The idolatry of which he had spoken was the idolatry which a woman might show to her cat, her dog, her picture, her china, her furniture, her carriage and horses, or her pet maid-servant. Such was the idolatry of which Mr. Kennedy had spoken;—but was there no other worship in her heart, worse, more pernicious than that, in reference to this young man?

She had schooled herself about him very severely, and had come to various resolutions. She had found out and confessed to herself that she did not, and could not, love her husband. She had found out and confessed to herself that she did love, and could not help loving, Phineas Finn. Then she had resolved to banish him from her presence, and had gone the length of telling him so. After that she had perceived that she had been wrong, and had determined to meet him as she met other men,—and to conquer her love. Then, when this could not be done, when something almost like idolatry grew upon her, she determined that it should be the idolatry of friendship, that she would not sin even in thought, that there should be nothing in her heart of which she need be ashamed;—but that the one great object and purport of her life should be the promotion of this friend's welfare. She had just begun to love after this fashion, had taught herself to believe that she might combine something of the pleasure of idolatry towards her friend with a full complement of duty towards her husband, when Phineas came to her with his tale of love for Violet Effingham. The lesson which she got then was a very rough one,—so hard that at first she could not bear it. Her anger at his love for her brother's wished-for bride was lost in her dismay that Phineas should love any one after having once loved her. But by sheer force of mind she had conquered that dismay, that feeling of desolation at her heart, and had almost taught herself to hope that Phineas might succeed with Violet. He wished it,—and why should he not have what he wished,—he, whom she so fondly idolised? It was not his fault that he and she were not man and wife. She had chosen to arrange it otherwise, and was she not bound to assist him now in the present object of his reasonable wishes? She had got over in her heart that difficulty about her brother, but she could not quite conquer the other difficulty. She could not bring herself to plead his cause with Violet. She had not brought herself as yet to do it.

And now she was accused of idolatry for Phineas by her husband,—she with "a lot of others," in which lot Violet was of course included. Would it not be better that they two should be brought together? Would not her friend's husband still be her friend? Would she not then forget to love him? Would she not then be safer than she was now?

As she sat alone struggling with her difficulties, she had not as yet forgotten to love him,—nor was she as yet safe.

CHAPTER XLV
Miss Effingham's Four Lovers

One morning early in June Lady Laura called at Lady Baldock's house and asked for Miss Effingham. The servant was showing her into the large drawing-room, when she again asked specially for Miss Effingham. "I think Miss Effingham is there," said the man, opening the door. Miss Effingham was not there. Lady Baldock was sitting all alone, and Lady Laura perceived that she had been caught in the net which she specially wished to avoid. Now Lady Baldock had not actually or openly quarrelled with Lady Laura Kennedy or with Lord Brentford, but she had conceived a strong idea that her niece Violet was countenanced in all improprieties by the Standish family generally, and that therefore the Standish family was to be regarded as a family of enemies. There was doubtless in her mind considerable confusion on the subject, for she did not know whether Lord Chiltern or Mr. Finn was the suitor whom she most feared,—and she was aware, after a sort of muddled fashion, that the claims of these two wicked young men were antagonistic to each other. But they were both regarded by her as emanations from the same source of iniquity, and, therefore, without going deeply into the machinations of Lady Laura,—without resolving whether Lady Laura was injuring her by pressing her brother as a suitor upon Miss Effingham, or by pressing a rival of her brother,—still she became aware that it was her duty to turn a cold shoulder on those two houses in Portman Square and Grosvenor Place. But her difficulties in doing this were very great, and it may be said that Lady Baldock was placed in an unjust and cruel position. Before the end of May she had proposed to leave London, and to take her daughter and Violet down to Baddingham,—or to Brighton, if they preferred it, or to Switzerland. "Brighton in June!" Violet had exclaimed. "Would not a month among the glaciers be delightful!" Miss Boreham had said. "Don't let me keep you in town, aunt," Violet replied; "but I do not think I shall go till other people go. I can have a room at Laura Kennedy's house." Then Lady Baldock, whose position was hard and cruel, resolved that she would stay in town. Here she had in her hands a ward over whom she had no positive power, and yet in respect to whom her duty was imperative! Her duty was imperative, and Lady Baldock was not the woman to neglect her duty;—and yet she knew that the doing of her duty would all be in vain. Violet would marry a shoe-black out of the streets if she were so minded. It was of no use that the poor lady had provided herself with two strings, two most excellent strings, to her bow,—two strings either one of which should have contented Miss Effingham. There was Lord Fawn, a young peer, not very rich indeed,—but still with means sufficient for a wife, a rising man, and in every way respectable, although a Whig. And there was Mr. Appledom, one of the richest commoners in England, a fine Conservative too, with a seat in the House, and everything appropriate. He was fifty, but looked hardly more than thirty-five, and was,—so at least Lady Baldock frequently asserted,—violently in love with Violet Effingham. Why had not the law, or the executors, or the Lord Chancellor, or some power levied for the protection of the proprieties, made Violet absolutely subject to her guardian till she should be made subject to a husband?

"Yes, I think she is at home," said Lady Baldock, in answer to Lady Laura's inquiry for Violet. "At least, I hardly know. She seldom tells me what she means to do,—and sometimes she will walk out quite alone!" A most imprudent old woman was Lady Baldock, always opening her hand to her adversaries, unable to control herself in the scolding of people, either before their faces or behind their backs, even at moments in which such scolding was most injurious to her own cause. "However, we will see," she continued. Then the bell was rung, and in a few minutes Violet was in the room. In a few minutes more they were up-stairs together in Violet's own room, in spite of the openly-displayed wrath of Lady Baldock. "I almost wish she had never been born," said Lady Baldock to her daughter. "Oh, mamma, don't say that." "I certainly do wish that I had never seen her." "Indeed she has been a grievous trouble to you, mamma," said Miss Boreham, sympathetically.

"Brighton! What nonsense!" said Lady Laura.

"Of course it's nonsense. Fancy going to Brighton! And then they have proposed Switzerland. If you could only hear Augusta talking in rapture of a month among the glaciers! And I feel so ungrateful. I believe they would spend three months with me at any horrible place that I could suggest,—at Hong Kong if I were to ask it,—so intent are they on taking me away from metropolitan danger."

"But you will not go?"

"No!—I won't go. I know I am very naughty; but I can't help feeling that I cannot be good without being a fool at the same time. I must either fight my aunt, or give way to her. If I were to yield, what a life I should have;—and I should despise myself after all."

"And what is the special danger to be feared now?"

"I don't know;—you, I fancy. I told her that if she went, I should go to you. I knew that would make her stay."

"I wish you would come to me," said Lady Laura.

"I shouldn't think of it really,—not for any length of time."

"Why not?"

"Because I should be in Mr. Kennedy's way."

"You wouldn't be in his way in the least. If you would only be down punctually for morning prayers, and go to church with him on Sunday afternoon, he would be delighted to have you."

"What did he say about Madame Max coming?"

"Not a word. I don't think he quite knew who she was then. I fancy he has inquired since, by something he said yesterday."

"What did he say?"

"Nothing that matters;—only a word. I haven't come here to talk about Madame Max Goesler,—nor yet about Mr. Kennedy."

"Whom have you come to talk about?" asked Violet, laughing a little, with something of increased colour in her cheeks, though she could not be said to blush.

"A lover of course," said Lady Laura.

"I wish you would leave me alone with my lovers. You are as bad or worse than my aunt. She, at any rate, varies her prescription. She has become sick of poor Lord Fawn because he's a Whig."

"And who is her favourite now?"

"Old Mr. Appledom,—who is really a most unexceptionable old party, and whom I like of all things. I really think I could consent to be Mrs. Appledom, to get rid of my troubles,—if he did not dye his whiskers and have his coats padded."

"He'd give up those little things if you asked him."

"I shouldn't have the heart to do it. Besides, this isn't his time of the year for making proposals. His love fever, which is of a very low kind, and intermits annually, never comes on till the autumn. It is a rural malady, against which he is proof while among his clubs!"

"Well, Violet,—I am like your aunt."

"Like Lady Baldock?"

"In one respect. I, too, will vary my prescription."

"What do you mean, Laura?"

"Just this,—that if you like to marry Phineas Finn, I will say that you are right."

"Heaven and earth! And why am I to marry Phineas Finn?"

"Only for two reasons; because he loves you, and because—"

"No,—I deny it. I do not."

"I had come to fancy that you did."

"Keep your fancy more under control then. But upon my word I can't understand this. He was your great friend."

"What has that to do with it?" demanded Lady Laura.

"And you have thrown over your brother, Laura?"

"You have thrown him over. Is he to go on for ever asking and being refused?"

"I do not know why he should not," said Violet, "seeing how very little trouble it gives him. Half an hour once in six months does it all for him, allowing him time for coming and going in a cab."

"Violet, I do not understand you. Have you refused Oswald so often because he does not pass hours on his knees before you?"

"No, indeed! His nature would be altered very much for the worse before he could do that."

"Why do you throw it in his teeth then that he does not give you more of his time?"

"Why have you come to tell me to marry Mr. Phineas Finn? That is what I want to know. Mr. Phineas Finn, as far as I am aware, has not a shilling in the world,—except a month's salary now due to him from the Government. Mr. Phineas Finn I believe to be the son of a country doctor in Ireland,—with about seven sisters. Mr. Phineas Finn is a Roman Catholic. Mr. Phineas Finn is,—or was a short time ago,—in love with another lady; and Mr. Phineas Finn is not so much in love at this moment but what he is able to intrust his cause to an ambassador. None short of a royal suitor should ever do that with success."

"Has he never pleaded his cause to you himself?"

"My dear, I never tell gentlemen's secrets. It seems that if he has, his success was so trifling that he has thought he had better trust some one else for the future."

"He has not trusted me. He has not given me any commission."

"Then why have you come?"

"Because,—I hardly know how to tell his story. There have been things about Oswald which made it almost necessary that Mr. Finn should explain himself to me."

"I know it all;—about their fighting. Foolish young men! I am not a bit obliged to either of them,—not a bit. Only fancy, if my aunt knew it, what a life she would lead me! Gustavus knows all about it, and I feel that I am living at his mercy. Why were they so wrong-headed?"

"I cannot answer that,—though I know them well enough to be sure that Chiltern was the one in fault."

"It is so odd that you should have thrown your brother over."

"I have not thrown my brother over. Will you accept Oswald if he asks you again?"

"No," almost shouted Violet.

"Then I hope that Mr. Finn may succeed. I want him to succeed in everything. There;—you may know it all. He is my Phœbus Apollo."

"That is flattering to me,—looking at the position in which you desire to place your Phœbus at the present moment."

"Come, Violet, I am true to you, and let me have a little truth from you. This man loves you, and I think is worthy of you. He does not love me, but he is my friend. As his friend, and believing in his worth, I wish for his success beyond almost anything else in the world. Listen to me, Violet. I don't believe in those reasons which you gave me just now for not becoming this man's wife."

"Nor do I."

"I know you do not. Look at me. I, who have less of real heart than you, I who thought that I could trust myself to satisfy my mind and my ambition without caring for my heart, I have married for what you call position. My husband is very rich, and a Cabinet Minister, and will probably be a peer. And he was willing to marry me at a time when I had not a shilling of my own."

"He was very generous."

"He has asked for it since," said Lady Laura. "But never mind. I have not come to talk about myself;—otherwise than to bid you not do what I have done. All that you have said about this man's want of money and of family is nothing."

"Nothing at all," said Violet. "Mere words,—fit only for such people as my aunt."

"Well then?"

"Well?"

"If you love him—!"

"Ah! but if I do not? You are very close in inquiring into my secrets. Tell me, Laura;—was not this young Crichton once a lover of your own?"

"Psha! And do you think I cannot keep a gentleman's secret as well as you?"

"What is the good of any secret, Laura, when we have been already so open? He tried his 'prentice hand on you; and then he came to me. Let us watch him, and see who'll be the third. I too like him well enough to hope that he'll land himself safely at last."

CHAPTER XLVI
The Mousetrap

Phineas had certainly no desire to make love by an ambassador,—at second-hand. He had given no commission to Lady Laura, and was, as the reader is aware, quite ignorant of what was being done and said on his behalf. He had asked no more from Lady Laura than an opportunity of speaking for himself, and that he had asked almost with a conviction that by so asking he would turn his friend into an enemy. He had read but little of the workings of Lady Laura's heart towards himself, and had no idea of the assistance she was anxious to give him. She had never told him that she was willing to sacrifice her brother on his behalf, and, of course, had not told him that she was willing also to sacrifice herself. Nor, when she wrote to him one June morning and told him that Violet would be found in Portman Square, alone, that afternoon,—naming an hour, and explaining that Miss Effingham would be there to meet herself and her father, but that at such an hour she would be certainly alone,—did he even then know how much she was prepared to do for him. The short note was signed "L.," and then there came a long postscript. "Ask for me," she said in a postscript. "I shall be there later, and I have told them to bid you wait. I can give you no hope of success, but if you choose to try,—you can do so. If you do not come, I shall know that you have changed your mind. I shall not think the worse of you, and your secret will be safe with me. I do that which you have asked me to do,—simply because you have asked it. Burn this at once,—because I ask it." Phineas destroyed the note, tearing it into atoms, the moment that he had read it and re-read it. Of course he would go to Portman Square at the hour named. Of course he would take his chance. He was not buoyed up by much of hope;—but even though there were no hope, he would take his chance.

When Lord Brentford had first told Phineas of his promotion, he had also asked the new Lord of the Treasury to make a certain communication on his behalf to his son. This Phineas had found himself obliged to promise to do;—and he had done it. The letter had been difficult enough to write,—but he had written it. After having made the promise, he had found himself bound to keep it.

"Dear Lord Chiltern," he had commenced, "I will not think that there was anything in our late encounter to prevent my so addressing you. I now write at the instance of your father, who has heard nothing of our little affair." Then he explained at length Lord Brentford's wishes as he understood them. "Pray come home," he said, finishing his letter. "Touching V. E., I feel that I am bound to tell you that I still mean to try my fortune, but that I have no ground for hoping that my fortune will be good. Since the day on the sands, I have never met her but in society. I know you will be glad to hear that my wound was nothing; and I think you will be glad to hear that I have got my foot on to the ladder of promotion.—Yours always,

"Phineas Finn."

Now he had to try his fortune,—that fortune of which he had told Lord Chiltern that he had no reason for hoping that it would be good. He went direct from his office at the Treasury to Portman Square, resolving that he would take no trouble as to his dress, simply washing his hands and brushing his hair as though he were going down to the House, and he knocked at the Earl's door exactly at the hour named by Lady Laura.

"Miss Effingham," he said, "I am so glad to find you alone."

"Yes," she said, laughing. "I am alone,—a poor unprotected female. But I fear nothing. I have strong reason for believing that Lord Brentford is somewhere about. And Pomfret the butler, who has known me since I was a baby, is a host in himself."

"With such allies you can have nothing to fear," he replied, attempting to carry on her little jest.

"Nor even without them, Mr. Finn. We unprotected females in these days are so self-reliant that our natural protectors fall off from us, finding themselves to be no longer wanted. Now with you,—what can I fear?"

"Nothing,—as I hope."

"There used to be a time, and that not so long ago either, when young gentlemen and ladies were thought to be very dangerous to each other if they were left alone. But propriety is less rampant now, and upon the whole virtue and morals, with discretion and all that kind of thing, have been the gainers. Don't you think so?"

"I am sure of it."

"All the same, but I don't like to be caught in a trap, Mr. Finn."

"In a trap?"

"Yes;—in a trap. Is there no trap here? If you will say so, I will acknowledge myself to be a dolt, and will beg your pardon."

"I hardly know what you call a trap."

"You were told that I was here?"

He paused a moment before he replied. "Yes, I was told."

"I call that a trap."

"Am I to blame?"

"I don't say that you set it,—but you use it."

"Miss Effingham, of course I have used it. You must know,—I think you must know that I have that to say to you which has made me long for such an opportunity as this."

"And therefore you have called in the assistance of your friend."

"It is true."

"In such matters you should never talk to any one, Mr. Finn. If you cannot fight your own battle, no one can fight it for you."

"Miss Effingham, do you remember our ride at Saulsby?"

"Very well;—as if it were yesterday."

"And do you remember that I asked you a question which you have never answered?"

"I did answer it,—as well as I knew how, so that I might tell you a truth without hurting you."

"It was necessary,—is necessary that I should be hurt sorely, or made perfectly happy. Violet Effingham, I have come to you to ask you to be my wife;—to tell you that I love you, and to ask for your love in return. Whatever may be my fate, the question must be asked, and an answer must be given. I have not hoped that you should tell me that you loved me—"

"For what then have you hoped?"

"For not much, indeed;—but if for anything, then for some chance that you might tell me so hereafter."

"If I loved you, I would tell you so now,—instantly. I give you my word of that."

"Can you never love me?"

"What is a woman to answer to such a question? No;—I believe never. I do not think I shall ever wish you to be my husband. You ask me to be plain, and I must be plain."

"Is it because—?" He paused, hardly knowing what the question was which he proposed to himself to ask.

"It is for no because,—for no cause except that simple one which should make any girl refuse any man whom she did not love. Mr. Finn, I could say pleasant things to you on any other subject than this,—because I like you."

"I know that I have nothing to justify my suit."

"You have everything to justify it;—at least I am bound to presume that you have. If you love me,—you are justified."

"You know that I love you."

"I am sorry that it should ever have been so,—very sorry. I can only hope that I have not been in fault."

"Will you try to love me?"

"No;—why should I try? If any trying were necessary, I would try rather not to love you. Why should I try to do that which would displease everybody belonging to me? For yourself, I admit your right to address me,—and tell you frankly that it would not be in vain, if I loved you. But I tell you as frankly that such a marriage would not please those whom I am bound to try to please."

He paused a moment before he spoke further. "I shall wait," he said, "and come again."

"What am I to say to that? Do not tease me, so that I be driven to treat you with lack of courtesy. Lady Laura is so much attached to you, and Mr. Kennedy, and Lord Brentford,—and indeed I may say, I myself also, that I trust there may be nothing to mar our good fellowship. Come, Mr. Finn,—say that you will take an answer, and I will give you my hand."

"Give it me," said he. She gave him her hand, and he put it up to his lips and pressed it. "I will wait and come again," he said. "I will assuredly come again." Then he turned from her and went out of the house. At the corner of the square he saw Lady Laura's carriage, but did not stop to speak to her. And she also saw him.

"So you have had a visitor here," said Lady Laura to Violet.

"Yes;—I have been caught in the trap."

"Poor mouse! And has the cat made a meal of you?"

"I fancy he has, after his fashion. There be cats that eat their mice without playing,—and cats that play with their mice, and then eat them; and cats again which only play with their mice, and don't care to eat them. Mr. Finn is a cat of the latter kind, and has had his afternoon's diversion."

"You wrong him there."

"I think not, Laura. I do not mean to say that he would not have liked me to accept him. But, if I can see inside his bosom, such a little job as that he has now done will be looked back upon as one of the past pleasures of his life;—not as a pain."

CHAPTER XLVII
Mr. Mildmay's Bill

It will be necessary that we should go back in our story for a very short period in order that the reader may be told that Phineas Finn was duly re-elected at Loughton after his appointment at the Treasury Board. There was some little trouble at Loughton, and something more of expense than he had before encountered. Mr. Quintus Slide absolutely came down, and was proposed by Mr. Vellum for the borough. Mr. Vellum being a gentleman learned in the law, and hostile to the interests of the noble owner of Saulsby, was able to raise a little trouble against our hero. Mr. Slide was proposed by Mr. Vellum, and seconded by Mr. Vellum's clerk,—though, as it afterwards appeared, Mr. Vellum's clerk was not in truth an elector,—and went to the poll like a man. He received three votes, and at twelve o'clock withdrew. This in itself could hardly have afforded compensation for the expense which Mr. Slide or his backers must have encountered;—but he had an opportunity of making a speech, every word of which was reported in the *People's Banner*; and if the speech was made in the language given in the report, Mr. Slide was really possessed of some oratorical power. Most of those who read the speech in the columns of the *People's Banner* were probably not aware how favourable an opportunity of retouching his sentences in type had been given to Mr. Slide by the fact of his connection with the newspaper. The speech had been very severe upon our hero; and though the speaker had been so hooted and pelted at Loughton as to have been altogether inaudible,—so maltreated that in point of fact he had not been able to speak above a tenth part of his speech at all,—nevertheless the speech did give Phineas a certain amount of pain. Why Phineas should have read it who can tell? But who is there that abstains from reading that which is printed in abuse of himself?

In the speech as it was printed Mr. Slide declared that he had no thought of being returned for the borough. He knew too well how the borough was managed, what slaves the electors were;—how they groaned under a tyranny from which hitherto they had been unable to release themselves. Of course the Earl's nominee, his lacquey, as the honourable gentleman might be called, would be returned. The Earl could order them to return whichever of his lacqueys he pleased.—There is something peculiarly pleasing to the democratic ear in the word lacquey! Any one serving a big man, whatever the service may be, is the big man's lacquey in the *People's Banner*.—The speech throughout was very bitter. Mr. Phineas Finn, who had previously served in Parliament as the lacquey of an Irish earl, and had been turned off by him, had now fallen into the service of the English earl, and was the lacquey chosen for the present occasion. But he, Quintus Slide, who boasted himself to be a man of the people,—he could tell them that the days of their thraldom were coming to an end, and that their enfranchisement was near at hand. That friend of the people, Mr. Turnbull, had a clause in his breeches-pocket which he would either force down the unwilling throat of Mr. Mildmay, or else drive the imbecile Premier from office by carrying it in his teeth. Loughton, as Loughton, must be destroyed, but it should be born again in a better birth as a part of a real electoral district, sending a real member, chosen by a real constituency, to a real Parliament. In those days,—and they would come soon,—Mr. Quintus Slide rather thought that Mr. Phineas Finn would be found "nowhere," and he rather thought also that when he showed himself again, as he certainly should do, in the midst of that democratic electoral district as the popular candidate for the honour of representing it in Parliament, that democratic electoral district would accord to him a reception very different from that which he was now receiving from the Earl's lacqueys in the parliamentary village of Loughton. A prettier bit of fiction than these sentences as composing a part of any speech delivered, or proposed to be delivered, at Loughton, Phineas thought he had never seen. And when he read at the close of the speech that though the Earl's hired bullies did their worst, the remarks of Mr. Slide were received by the people with reiterated cheering, he threw himself back in his chair at the Treasury and roared. The poor fellow had been three minutes on his legs, had received three rotten eggs, and one dead dog, and had retired. But not the half of the speech as printed in the *People's Banner* has been quoted. The sins of Phineas, who in spite of his inability to open his mouth in public had been made a Treasury hack by the aristocratic influence,—"by aristocratic influence not confined to the male sex,"—were described at great length, and in such language that

Phineas for a while was fool enough to think that it would be his duty to belabour Mr. Slide with a horsewhip. This notion, however, did not endure long with him, and when Mr. Monk told him that things of that kind came as a matter of course, he was comforted.

But he found it much more difficult to obtain comfort when he weighed the arguments brought forward against the abominations of such a borough as that for which he sat, and reflected that if Mr. Turnbull brought forward his clause, he, Phineas Finn, would be bound to vote against the clause, knowing the clause to be right, because he was a servant of the Government. The arguments, even though they appeared in the *People's Banner*, were true arguments; and he had on one occasion admitted their truth to his friend Lady Laura,—in the presence of that great Cabinet Minister, her husband. "What business has such a man as that down there? Is there a single creature who wants him?" Lady Laura had said. "I don't suppose anybody does want Mr. Quintus Slide," Phineas had replied; "but I am disposed to think the electors should choose the man they do want, and that at present they have no choice left to them." "They are quite satisfied," said Lady Laura, angrily. "Then, Lady Laura," continued Phineas, "that alone should be sufficient to prove that their privilege of returning a member to Parliament is too much for them. We can't defend it." "It is defended by tradition," said Mr. Kennedy. "And by its great utility," said Lady Laura, bowing to the young member who was present, and forgetting that very useless old gentleman, her cousin, who had sat for the borough for many years. "In this country it doesn't do to go too fast," said Mr. Kennedy. "And then the mixture of vulgarity, falsehood, and pretence!" said Lady Laura, shuddering as her mind recurred to the fact that Mr. Quintus Slide had contaminated Loughton by his presence. "I am told that they hardly let him leave the place alive."

Whatever Mr. Kennedy and Lady Laura might think about Loughton and the general question of small boroughs, it was found by the Government, to their great cost, that Mr. Turnbull's clause was a reality. After two months of hard work, all questions of franchise had been settled, rating and renting, new and newfangled, fancy franchises and those which no one fancied, franchises for boroughs and franchises for counties, franchises single, dual, three-cornered, and four-sided,—by various clauses to which the Committee of the whole House had agreed after some score of divisions,—the matter of the franchise had been settled. No doubt there was the House of Lords, and there might yet be shipwreck. But it was generally believed that the Lords would hardly look at the bill,—that they would not even venture on an amendment. The Lords would only be too happy to let the matter be settled by the Commons themselves. But then, after the franchise, came redistribution. How sick of the subject were all members of the Government, no one could tell who did not see their weary faces. The whole House was sick, having been whipped into various lobbies, night after night, during the heat of the summer, for weeks past. Redistribution! Why should there be any redistribution? They had got, or would get, a beautiful franchise. Could they not see what that would do for them? Why redistribute anything? But, alas, it was too late to go back to so blessed an idea as that! Redistribution they must have. But there should be as little redistribution as possible. Men were sick of it all, and would not be exigeant. Something should be done for overgrown counties;—something for new towns which had prospered in brick and mortar. It would be easy to crush up a peccant borough or two,—a borough that had been discovered in its sin. And a few boroughs now blessed with two members might consent to be blessed only with one. Fifteen small clauses might settle the redistribution, in spite of Mr. Turnbull,—if only Mr. Daubeny would be good-natured.

Neither the weather, which was very hot, nor the tedium of the session, which had been very great, nor the anxiety of Ministers, which was very pressing, had any effect in impairing the energy of Mr. Turnbull. He was as instant, as oratorical, as hostile, as indignant about redistribution as he had been about the franchise. He had been sure then, and he was sure now, that Ministers desired to burke the question, to deceive the people, to produce a bill that should be no bill. He brought out his clause,—and made Loughton his instance. "Would the honourable gentleman who sat lowest on the Treasury bench,—who at this moment was in sweet confidential intercourse with the right honourable gentleman now President of the Board of Trade, who had once been a friend of the people,—would the young Lord of the Treasury get up in his place and tell them that no peer of Parliament had at present a voice in sending a member to their House of Commons,—that no peer would have a voice if this bill, as proposed by the Government, were passed in its present useless, ineffectual, conservative, and most dishonest form?"

Phineas, who replied to this, and who told Mr. Turnbull that he himself could not answer for any peers,—but that he thought it probable that most peers would, by their opinions, somewhat influence the opinions of some electors,—was thought to have got out of his difficulty very well. But there was the clause of Mr. Turnbull to be dealt with,—a clause directly disfranchising seven single-winged boroughs, of which Loughton was of course one,—a clause to which the Government must either submit or object. Submission would be certain defeat in one way, and objection would be as certain defeat in another,—if the gentlemen on the other side were not disposed to assist the ministers. It was said that the Cabinet was divided. Mr. Gresham and Mr. Monk were for letting the seven boroughs go. Mr. Mildmay could not bring himself to obey Mr. Turnbull, and Mr. Palliser supported him. When Mr. Mildmay was told that Mr. Daubeny would certainly go into the same lobby with Mr. Turnbull respecting the seven boroughs, he was reported to have said that in that case Mr. Daubeny must be prepared with a Government. Mr. Daubeny made a beautiful speech about the seven boroughs;—the seven sins, and seven stars, and seven churches, and seven lamps. He would make no party question of this. Gentlemen who usually acted with him would vote as their own sense of right or wrong directed them;—from which expression of a special sanction it was considered that these gentlemen were not accustomed to exercise the privilege now accorded to them. But in regarding the question as one of right and wrong, and in looking at what he believed to be both the wish of the country and its interests, he, Mr. Daubeny,—he, himself, being simply a humble member of that House,—must support the clause of the honourable gentleman. Almost all those to whom had been surrendered the privilege of using their own judgment for that occasion only, used it discreetly,—as their chief had used it himself,—and Mr. Turnbull carried his clause by a majority of fifteen. It was then 3 a.m., and Mr. Gresham, rising after the division, said that his right honourable friend the First Lord of the Treasury was too tired to return to the House, and had requested him to state that the Government would declare their purpose at 6 p.m. on the following evening.

Phineas, though he had made his little speech in answer to Mr. Turnbull with good-humoured flippancy, had recorded his vote in favour of the seven boroughs with a sore heart. Much as he disliked Mr. Turnbull, he knew that Mr. Turnbull was right in this. He had spoken to Mr. Monk on the subject, as it were asking Mr. Monk's permission to throw up his office, and vote against Mr. Mildmay. But Mr. Monk was angry with him, telling him that his conscience was of that restless, uneasy sort which is neither useful nor manly. "We all know," said Mr. Monk, "and none better than Mr. Mildmay, that we cannot justify such a borough as Loughton by the theory of our parliamentary representation,—any more than we can justify the fact that Huntingdonshire should return as many members as the East Riding. There must be compromises, and you should trust to others who have studied the matter more thoroughly than you, to say how far the compromise should go at the present moment."

"It is the influence of the peer, not the paucity of the electors," said Phineas.

"And has no peer any influence in a county? Would you disfranchise Westmoreland? Believe me, Finn, if you want to be useful, you must submit yourself in such matters to those with whom you act."

Phineas had no answer to make, but he was not happy in his mind. And he was the less happy, perhaps, because he was very sure that Mr. Mildmay would be beaten. Mr. Low in these days harassed him sorely. Mr. Low was very keen against such boroughs as Loughton, declaring that Mr. Daubeny was quite right to join his standard to that of Mr. Turnbull on such an issue. Mr. Low was the reformer now, and Phineas found himself obliged to fight a losing battle on behalf of an acknowledged abuse. He never went near Bunce; but, unfortunately for him, Bunce caught him once in the street and showed him no mercy. "Slide was a little 'eavy on you in the *Banner* the other day,—eh, Mr. Finn?— too 'eavy, as I told him."

"Mr. Slide can be just as heavy as he pleases, Bunce."

"That's in course. The press is free, thank God,—as yet. But it wasn't any good rattling away at the Earl's little borough when it's sure to go. Of course it'll go, Mr. Finn."

"I think it will."

"The whole seven on 'em. The 'ouse couldn't but do it. They tell me it's all Mr. Mildmay's own work, sticking out for keeping on 'em. He's very old, and so we'll forgive him. But he must go, Mr. Finn."

"We shall know all about that soon, Bunce."

"If you don't get another seat, Mr. Finn, I suppose we shall see you back at the Inn. I hope we may. It's better than being member for Loughton, Mr. Finn;—you may be sure of that." And then Mr. Bunce passed on.

Mr. Turnbull carried his clause, and Loughton was doomed. Loughton and the other six deadly sins were anathematized, exorcised, and finally got rid of out of the world by the voices of the gentlemen who had been proclaiming the beauty of such pleasant vices all their lives, and who in their hearts hated all changes that tended towards popular representation. But not the less was Mr. Mildmay beaten; and, in accordance with the promise made by his first lieutenant immediately after the vote was taken, the Prime Minister came forward on the next evening and made his statement. He had already put his resignation into the hands of Her Majesty, and Her Majesty had graciously accepted it. He was very old, and felt that the time had come in which it behoved him to retire into that leisure which he thought he had, perhaps, earned. He had hoped to carry this bill as the last act of his political life; but he was too old, too stiff, as he said, in his prejudices, to bend further than he had bent already, and he must leave the completion of the matter in other hands. Her Majesty had sent for Mr. Gresham, and Mr. Gresham had already seen Her Majesty. Mr. Gresham and his other colleagues, though they dissented from the clause which had been carried by the united efforts of gentlemen opposite to him, and of gentlemen below him on his own side of the House, were younger men than he, and would, for the country's sake,—and for the sake of Her Majesty,—endeavour to carry the bill through. There would then, of course, be a dissolution, and the future Government would, no doubt, depend on the choice of the country. From all which it was understood that Mr. Gresham was to go on with the bill to a conclusion, whatever might be the divisions carried against him, and that a new Secretary of State for Foreign Affairs must be chosen. Phineas understood, also, that he had lost his seat at Loughton. For the borough of Loughton there would never again be an election. "If I had been Mr. Mildmay, I would have thrown the bill up altogether," Lord Brentford said afterwards; "but of course it was not for me to interfere."

The session was protracted for two months after that,—beyond the time at which grouse should have been shot,—and by the 23rd of August became the law of the land. "I shall never get over it," said Mr. Ratler to Mr. Finn, seated one terribly hot evening on a bench behind the Cabinet Ministers,—"never. I don't suppose such a session for work was ever known before. Think what it is to have to keep men together in August, with the thermometer at 81°, and the river stinking like,—like the very mischief." Mr. Ratler, however, did not die.

On the last day of the session Laurence Fitzgibbon resigned. Rumours reached the ears of Phineas as to the cause of this, but no certain cause was told him. It was said that Lord Cantrip had insisted upon it, Laurence having by mischance been called upon for some official statement during an unfortunate period of absence. There was, however, a mystery about it;—but the mystery was not half so wonderful as the triumph to Phineas, when Mr. Gresham offered him the place.

"But I shall have no seat," said Phineas.

"We shall none of us have seats to-morrow," said Mr. Gresham.

"But I shall be at a loss to find a place to stand for."

"The election will not come on till November, and you must look about you. Both Mr. Monk and Lord Brentford seem to think you will be in the House."

And so the bill was carried, and the session was ended.

CHAPTER XLVIII
"The Duke"

By the middle of September there was assembled a large party at Matching Priory, a country mansion belonging to Mr. Plantagenet Palliser. The men had certainly been chosen in reference to their political feelings and position,—for there was not a guest in the house who had voted for Mr. Turnbull's clause, or the wife or daughter, or sister of any one who had so voted. Indeed, in these days politics ran so high that among politicians all social gatherings were brought together with some reference to the state of parties. Phineas was invited, and when he arrived at Matching he found that half the Cabinet was there. Mr. Kennedy was not there, nor was Lady Laura. Mr. Monk was there, and the Duke,—with the Duchess, and Mr. Gresham, and Lord Thrift; Mrs. Max Goesler was there also, and Mrs. Bonteen,—Mr. Bonteen being detained somewhere out of the way; and Violet Effingham was expected in two days, and Lord Chiltern at the end of the week. Lady Glencora took an opportunity of imparting this latter information to Phineas very soon after his arrival; and Phineas, as he watched her eye and her mouth while she spoke, was quite sure that Lady Glencora knew the story of the duel. "I shall be delighted to see him again," said Phineas. "That is all right," said Lady Glencora. There were also there Mr. and Mrs. Grey, who were great friends of the Pallisers,—and on the very day on which Phineas reached Matching, at half an hour before the time for dressing, the Duke of Omnium arrived. Now, Mr. Palliser was the Duke's nephew and heir,—and the Duke of Omnium was a very great person indeed. I hardly know why it should have been so, but the Duke of Omnium was certainly a greater man in public estimation than the other duke then present,—the Duke of St. Bungay. The Duke of St. Bungay was a useful man, and had been so all his life, sitting in Cabinets and serving his country, constant as any peer in the House of Lords, always ready to take on his own shoulders any troublesome work required of him, than whom Mr. Mildmay, and Mr. Mildmay's predecessor at the head of the liberal party, had had no more devoted adherent. But the Duke of Omnium had never yet done a day's work on behalf of his country. They both wore the Garter, the Duke of St. Bungay having earned it by service, the Duke of Omnium having been decorated with the blue ribbon,—because he was Duke of Omnium. The one was a moral, good man, a good husband, a good father, and a good friend. The other,—did not bear quite so high a reputation. But men and women thought but little of the Duke of St. Bungay, while the other duke was regarded with an almost reverential awe. I think the secret lay in the simple fact that the Duke of Omnium had not been common in the eyes of the people. He had contrived to envelope himself in something of the ancient mystery of wealth and rank. Within three minutes of the Duke's arrival Mrs. Bonteen, with an air of great importance, whispered a word to Phineas. "He has come. He arrived exactly at seven!"

"Who has come?" Phineas asked.

"The Duke of Omnium!" she said, almost reprimanding him by her tone of voice for his indifference. "There has been a great doubt whether or no he would show himself at last. Lady Glencora told me that he never will pledge himself. I am so glad he has come."

"I don't think I ever saw him," said Phineas.

"Oh, I have seen him,—a magnificent-looking man! I think it is so very nice of Lady Glencora getting him to meet us. It is very rarely that he will join in a great party, but they say Lady Glencora can do anything with him since the heir was born. I suppose you have heard all about that."

"No," said Phineas; "I have heard nothing of the heir, but I know that there are three or four babies."

"There was no heir, you know, for a year and a half, and they were all au désespoir; and the Duke was very nearly quarrelling with his nephew; and Mr. Palliser—; you know it had very nearly come to a separation."

"I don't know anything at all about it," said Phineas, who was not very fond of the lady who was giving him the information.

"It is so, I can assure you; but since the boy was born Lady Glencora can do anything with the Duke. She made him go to Ascot last spring, and he presented her with the favourite for one of the races on the very morning the horse ran. They say he gave three thousand pounds for him."

"And did Lady Glencora win?"

"No;—the horse lost; and Mr. Palliser has never known what to do with him since. But it was very pretty of the Duke;—was it not?"

Phineas, though he had intended to show to Mrs. Bonteen how little he thought about the Duke of Omnium,—how small was his respect for a great peer who took no part in politics,—could not protect himself from a certain feeling of anxiety as to the aspect and gait and words of the man of whom people thought so much, of whom he had heard so often, and of whom he had seen so little. He told himself that the Duke of Omnium should be no more to him than any other man, but yet the Duke of Omnium was more to him than other men. When he came down into the drawing-room he was angry with himself, and stood apart;—and was then angry with himself again because he stood apart. Why should he make a difference in his own bearing because there was such a man in the company? And yet he could not avoid it. When he entered the room the Duke was standing in a large bow-window, and two or three ladies and two or three men were standing round him. Phineas would not go near the group, telling himself that he would not approach a man so grand as was the Duke of Omnium. He saw Madame Max Goesler among the party, and after a while he saw her retreat. As she retreated, Phineas knew that some words from Madame Max Goesler had not been received with the graciousness which she had expected. There was the prettiest smile in the world on the lady's face, and she took a corner on a sofa with an air of perfect satisfaction. But yet Phineas knew that she had received a wound.

"I called twice on you in London," said Phineas, coming up close to her, "but was not fortunate enough to find you!"

"Yes;—but you came so late in the season as to make it impossible that there should be any arrangements for our meeting. What can any woman do when a gentleman calls on her in August?"

"I came in July."

"Yes, you did; on the 31st. I keep the most accurate record of all such things, Mr. Finn. But let us hope that we may have better luck next year. In the meantime, we can only enjoy the good things that are going."

"Socially, or politically, Madame Goesler?"

"Oh, socially. How can I mean anything else when the Duke of Omnium is here? I feel so much taller at being in the same house with him. Do not you? But you are a spoilt child of fortune, and perhaps you have met him before."

"I think I once saw the back of a hat in the park, and somebody told me that the Duke's head was inside it."

"And you have never seen him but that once?"

"Never but that once,—till now."

"And do not you feel elated?"

"Of course I do. For what do you take me, Madame Goesler?"

"I do,—immensely. I believe him to be a fool, and I never heard of his doing a kind act to anybody in my life."

"Not when he gave the racehorse to Lady Glencora?"

"I wonder whether that was true. Did you ever hear of such an absurdity? As I was saying, I don't think he ever did anything for anybody;—but then, you know, to be Duke of Omnium! It isn't necessary,—is it,—that a Duke of Omnium should do anything except be Duke of Omnium?"

At this moment Lady Glencora came up to Phineas, and took him across to the Duke. The Duke had expressed a desire to be introduced to him. Phineas, half-pleased and half-disgusted, had no alternative, and followed Lady Glencora. The Duke shook hands with him, and made a little bow, and said something about the garrotters, which Phineas, in his confusion, did not quite understand. He tried to reply as he would have replied to anybody else, but the weight of the Duke's majesty was too much for him, and he bungled. The Duke made another little bow, and in a moment was speaking a word of condescension to some other favoured individual. Phineas retreated altogether disgusted,—hating the Duke, but hating himself worse; but he would not retreat in the direction of Madame Max Goesler. It might suit that lady to take an instant little revenge for her discomfiture, but it did not suit him to do so. The question with him would be, whether in some future part of his career it might not be his duty to assist in putting down Dukes of Omnium.

At dinner Phineas sat between Mrs. Bonteen and the Duchess of St. Bungay, and did not find himself very happy. At the other end of the table the Duke,—the great Duke, was seated at Lady Glencora's right hand, and on his other side Fortune had placed Madame Max Goesler. The greatest interest which Phineas had during the dinner was in watching the operations,—the triumphantly successful operations of that lady. Before dinner she had been wounded by the Duke. The Duke had not condescended to accord the honour of his little bow of graciousness to some little flattering morsel of wit which the lady had uttered on his behoof. She had said a sharp word or two in her momentary anger to Phineas; but when Fortune was so good to her in that matter of her place at dinner, she was not fool enough to throw away her chance. Throughout the soup and fish she was very quiet. She said a word or two after her first glass of champagne. The Duke refused two dishes, one after another, and then she glided into conversation. By the time that he had his roast mutton before him she was in full play, and as she eat her peach, the Duke was bending over her with his most gracious smile.

"Didn't you think the session was very long, Mr. Finn?" said the Duchess to Phineas.

"Very long indeed, Duchess," said Phineas, with his attention still fixed on Madame Max Goesler.

"The Duke found it very troublesome."

"I daresay he did," said Phineas. That duke and that duchess were no more than any other man and any other man's wife. The session had not been longer to the Duke of St. Bungay than to all the public servants. Phineas had the greatest possible respect for the Duke of St. Bungay, but he could not take much interest in the wailings of the Duchess on her husband's behalf.

"And things do seem to be so very uncomfortable now," said the Duchess,—thinking partly of the resignation of Mr. Mildmay, and partly of the fact that her own old peculiar maid who had lived with her for thirty years had retired into private life.

"Not so very bad, Duchess, I hope," said Phineas, observing that at this moment Madame Max Goesler's eyes were brilliant with triumph. Then there came upon him a sudden ambition,—that he would like to "cut out" the Duke of Omnium in the estimation of Madame Max Goesler. The brightness of Madame Max Goesler's eyes had not been thrown away upon our hero.

Violet Effingham came at the appointed time, and, to the surprise of Phineas, was brought to Matching by Lord Brentford. Phineas at first thought that it was intended that the Earl and his son should meet and make up their quarrel at Mr. Palliser's house. But Lord Brentford stayed only one night, and Phineas on the next morning heard the whole history of his coming and going from Violet. "I have almost been on my knees to him to stay," she said. "Indeed, I did go on my knees,—actually on my knees."

"And what did he say?"

"He put his arm round me and kissed me, and,—and,—I cannot tell you all that he said. But it ended in this,—that if Chiltern can be made to go to Saulsby, fatted calves without stint will be killed. I shall do all I can to make him go; and so must you, Mr. Finn. Of course that silly affair in foreign parts is not to make any difference between you two."

Phineas smiled, and said he would do his best, and looked up into her face, and was just able to talk to her as though things were going comfortably with him. But his heart was very cold. As Violet had spoken to him about Lord Chiltern there had come upon him, for the first time,—for the first time since he had known that Lord Chiltern had been refused,—an idea, a doubt, whether even yet Violet might not become Lord Chiltern's wife. His heart was very sad, but he struggled on,—declaring that it was incumbent on them both to bring together the father and son.

"I am so glad to hear you say so, Mr. Finn," said Violet. "I really do believe that you can do more towards it than any one else. Lord Chiltern would think nothing of my advice,—would hardly speak to me on such a subject. But he respects you as well as likes you, and not the less because of what has occurred."

How was it that Violet should know aught of the respect or liking felt by this rejected suitor for that other suitor,—who had also been rejected? And how was it that she was thus able to talk of one of them to the other, as though neither of them had ever come forward with such a suit? Phineas felt his position to be so strange as to be almost burdensome. He had told Violet, when she had refused him, very plainly, that he should come again to her, and ask once more for the great gift which he coveted. But he could not ask again now. In the first place, there was that in her manner which made him sure that were he to do so, he would ask in vain; and then he felt that she was placing a special confidence in him, against which he would commit a sin were he to use her present intimacy with him for the purposes of making love. They two were to put their shoulders together to help Lord Chiltern, and while doing so he could not continue a suit which would be felt by both of them to be hostile to Lord Chiltern. There might be opportunity for a chance word, and if so the chance word should be spoken; but he could not make a deliberate attack, such as he had made in Portman Square. Violet also probably understood that she had not now been caught in a mousetrap.

The Duke was to spend four days at Matching, and on the third day,—the day before Lord Chiltern was expected,—he was to be seen riding with Madame Max Goesler by his side. Madame Max Goesler was known as a perfect horsewoman,—one indeed who was rather fond of going a little fast on horseback, and who rode well to hounds. But the Duke seldom moved out of a walk, and on this occasion Madame Max was as steady in her seat and almost as slow as the mounted ghost in *Don Juan*. But it was said by some there, especially by Mrs. Bonteen, that the conversation between them was not slow. And on the next morning the Duke and Madame Max Goesler were together again before luncheon, standing on a terrace at the back of the house, looking down on a party who were playing croquet on the lawn.

"Do you never play?" said the Duke.

"Oh yes;—one does everything a little."

"I am sure you would play well. Why do you not play now?"

"No;—I shall not play now."

"I should like to see you with your mallet."

"I am sorry your Grace cannot be gratified. I have played croquet till I am tired of it, and have come to think it is only fit for boys and girls. The great thing is to give them opportunities for flirting, and it does that."

"And do you never flirt, Madame Goesler?"

"Never at croquet, Duke."

"And what with you is the choicest time?"

"That depends on so many things,—and so much on the chosen person. What do you recommend?"

"Ah,—I am so ignorant. I can recommend nothing."

"What do you say to a mountain-top at dawn on a summer day?" asked Madame Max Goesler.

"You make me shiver," said the Duke.

"Or a boat on a lake on a summer evening, or a good lead after hounds with nobody else within three fields, or the bottom of a salt-mine, or the deck of an ocean steamer, or a military hospital in time of war, or a railway journey from Paris to Marseilles?"

"Madame Max Goesler, you have the most uncomfortable ideas."

"I have no doubt your Grace has tried each of them,—successfully. But perhaps, after all, a comfortable chair over a good fire, in a pretty room, beats everything."

"I think it does,—certainly," said the Duke. Then he whispered something at which Madame Max Goesler blushed and smiled, and immediately after that she followed those who had already gone in to lunch.

Mrs. Bonteen had been hovering round the spot on the terrace on which the Duke and Madame Max Goesler had been standing, looking on with envious eyes, meditating some attack, some interruption, some excuse for an interpolation, but her courage had failed her and she had not dared to approach. The Duke had known nothing of the hovering propinquity of Mrs. Bonteen, but Madame Goesler had seen and had understood it all.

"Dear Mrs. Bonteen," she said afterwards, "why did you not come and join us? The Duke was so pleasant."

"Two is company, and three is none," said Mrs. Bonteen, who in her anger was hardly able to choose her words quite as well as she might have done had she been more cool.

"Our friend Madame Max has made quite a new conquest," said Mrs. Bonteen to Lady Glencora.

"I am so pleased," said Lady Glencora, with apparently unaffected delight. "It is such a great thing to get anybody to amuse my uncle. You see everybody cannot talk to him, and he will not talk to everybody."

"He talked enough to her in all conscience," said Mrs. Bonteen, who was now more angry than ever.

CHAPTER XLIX
The Duellists Meet

Lord Chiltern arrived, and Phineas was a little nervous as to their meeting. He came back from shooting on the day in question, and was told by the servant that Lord Chiltern was in the house. Phineas went into the billiard-room in his knickerbockers, thinking probably that he might be there, and then into the drawing-room, and at last into the library,—but Lord Chiltern was not to be found. At last he came across Violet.

"Have you seen him?" he asked.

"Yes;—he was with me half an hour since, walking round the gardens."

"And how is he? Come;—tell me something about him."

"I never knew him to be more pleasant. He would give no promise about Saulsby, but he did not say that he would not go."

"Does he know that I am here?"

"Yes;—I told him so. I told him how much pleasure I should have in seeing you two together,—as friends."

"And what did he say?"

"He laughed, and said you were the best fellow in the world. You see I am obliged to be explicit."

"But why did he laugh?" Phineas asked.

"He did not tell me, but I suppose it was because he was thinking of a little trip he once took to Belgium, and he perceived that I knew all about it."

"I wonder who told you. But never mind. I do not mean to ask any questions. As I do not like that our first meeting should be before all the people in the drawing-room, I will go to him in his own room."

"Do, do;—that will be so nice of you."

Phineas sent his card up by a servant, and in a few minutes was standing with his hand on the lock of Lord Chiltern's door. The last time he had seen this man, they had met with pistols in their hands to shoot at each other, and Lord Chiltern had in truth done his very best to shoot his opponent. The cause of quarrel was the same between them as ever. Phineas had not given up Violet, and had no intention of giving her up. And he had received no intimation whatever from his rival that there was to be a truce between them. Phineas had indeed written in friendship to Lord Chiltern, but he had received no answer;—and nothing of certainty was to be gathered from the report which Violet had just made. It might well be that Lord Chiltern would turn upon him now in his wrath, and that there would be some scene which in a strange house would be obviously objectionable. Nevertheless he had resolved that even that would be better than a chance encounter among strangers in a drawing-room. So the door was opened and the two men met.

"Well, old fellow," said Lord Chiltern, laughing. Then all doubt was over, and in a moment Phineas was shaking his former,—and present friend, warmly by the hand. "So we've come to be an Under-Secretary have we?—and all that kind of thing."

"I had to get into harness,—when the harness offered itself," said Phineas.

"I suppose so. It's a deuce of a bore, isn't it?"

"I always liked work, you know."

"I thought you liked hunting better. You used to ride as if you did. There's Bonebreaker back again in the stable for you. That poor fool who bought him could do nothing with him, and I let him have his money back."

"I don't see why you should have done that."

"Because I was the biggest fool of the two. Do you remember when that brute got me down under the bank in the river? That was about the nearest touch I ever had. Lord bless me;—how he did squeeze me! So here you are;—staying with the Pallisers,—one of a Government party I suppose. But what are you going to do for a seat, my friend?"

"Don't talk about that yet, Chiltern."

"A sore subject,—isn't it? I think they have been quite right, you know, to put Loughton into the melting-pot,—though I'm sorry enough for your sake."

"Quite right," said Phineas.

"And yet you voted against it, old chap? But, come; I'm not going to be down upon you. So my father has been here?"

"Yes;—he was here for a day or two."

"Violet has just been telling me. You and he are as good friends as ever?"

"I trust we are."

"He never heard of that little affair?" And Lord Chiltern nodded his head, intending to indicate the direction of Blankenberg.

"I do not think he has yet."

"So Violet tells me. Of course you know that she has heard all about it."

"I have reason to suppose as much."

"And so does Laura."

"I told her myself," said Phineas.

"The deuce you did! But I daresay it was for the best. It's a pity you had not proclaimed it at Charing Cross, and then nobody would have believed a word about it. Of course my father will hear it some day."

"You are going to Saulsby, I hope, Chiltern?"

"That question is easier asked than answered. It is quite true that the great difficulty has been got over. Laura has had her money. And if my father will only acknowledge that he has wronged me throughout, from beginning to end, I will go to Saulsby to-morrow;—and would cut you out at Loughton the next day, only that Loughton is not Loughton any longer."

"You cannot expect your father to do that."

"No;—and therefore there is a difficulty. So you've had that awfully ponderous Duke here. How did you get on with him?"

"Admirably. He condescended to do something which he called shaking hands with me."

"He is the greatest old dust out," said Lord Chiltern, disrespectfully. "Did he take any notice of Violet?"

"Not that I observed."

"He ought not to be allowed into the same room with her." After that there was a short pause, and Phineas felt some hesitation in speaking of Miss Effingham to Lord Chiltern. "And how do you get on with her?" asked Lord Chiltern. Here was a question for a man to answer. The question was so hard to be answered, that Phineas did not at first make any attempt to answer it. "You know exactly the ground that I stand on," continued Lord Chiltern. "She has refused me three times. Have you been more fortunate?"

Lord Chiltern, as he asked his question, looked full into Finn's face in a manner that was irresistible. His look was not one of anger nor even of pride. It was not, indeed, without a strong dash of fun. But such as it was it showed Phineas that Lord Chiltern intended to have an answer. "No," said he at last, "I have not been more fortunate."

"Perhaps you have changed your mind," said his host.

"No;—I have not changed my mind," said Phineas, quickly.

"How stands it then? Come;—let us be honest to each other. I told you down at Willingford that I would quarrel with any man who attempted to cut me out with Violet Effingham. You made up your mind that you would do so, and therefore I quarrelled with you. But we can't always be fighting duels."

"I hope we may not have to fight another."

"No;—it would be absurd," said Lord Chiltern. "I rather think that what we did was absurd. But upon my life I did not see any other way out of it. However, that is over. How is it to be now?"

"What am I to say in answer to that?" asked Phineas.

"Just the truth. You have asked her, I suppose?"

"Yes;—I have asked her."

"And she has refused you?"

"Yes;—she has refused me."

"And you mean to ask her again?"

"I shall;—if I ever think that there is a chance. Indeed, Chiltern, I believe I shall whether I think that I have any chance or not."

"Then we start fairly, Finn. I certainly shall do so. I believe I once told you that I never would;—but that was long before I suspected that you would enter for the same plate. What a man says on such a matter when he is down in the mouth goes for nothing. Now we understand each other, and you had better go and dress. The bell rang nearly half an hour ago, and my fellow is hanging about outside the door."

The interview had in one respect been very pleasant to Phineas, and in another it had been very bitter. It was pleasant to him to know that he and Lord Chiltern were again friends. It was a delight to him to feel that this half-savage but high-spirited young nobleman, who had been so anxious to fight with him and to shoot him, was nevertheless ready to own that he had behaved well. Lord Chiltern had in fact acknowledged that though he had been anxious to blow out our hero's brains, he was aware all the time that our hero was a good sort of fellow. Phineas understood this, and felt that it was pleasant. But with this understanding, and accompanying this pleasure, there was a conviction in his heart that the distance between Lord Chiltern and Violet would daily grow to be less and still less,—and that Lord Chiltern could afford to be generous. If Miss Effingham could teach herself to be fond of Lord Chiltern, what had he, Phineas Finn, to offer in opposition to the claims of such a suitor?

That evening Lord Chiltern took Miss Effingham out to dinner. Phineas told himself that this was of course so arranged by Lady Glencora, with the express view of serving the Saulsby interest. It was almost nothing to him at the moment that Madame Max Goesler was intrusted to him. He had his ambition respecting Madame Max Goesler; but that for the time was in abeyance. He could hardly keep his eyes off Miss Effingham. And yet, as he well knew, his observation of her must be quite useless. He knew beforehand, with absolute accuracy, the manner in which she would treat her lover. She would be kind, genial, friendly, confidential, nay, affectionate; and yet her manner would mean nothing, would give no clue to her future decision either for or against Lord Chiltern. It was, as Phineas thought, a peculiarity with Violet Effingham that she could treat her rejected lovers as dear familiar friends immediately after her rejection of them.

"Mr. Finn," said Madame Max Goesler, "your eyes and ears are tell-tales of your passion."

"I hope not," said Phineas, "as I certainly do not wish that any one should guess how strong is my regard for you."

"That is prettily turned,—very prettily turned; and shows more readiness of wit than I gave you credit for under your present suffering. But of course we all know where your heart is. Men do not undertake perilous journeys to Belgium for nothing."

"That unfortunate journey to Belgium! But, dear Madame Max, really nobody knows why I went."

"You met Lord Chiltern there?"

"Oh yes;—I met Lord Chiltern there."

"And there was a duel?"

"Madame Max,—you must not ask me to criminate myself!"

"Of course there was, and of course it was about Miss Effingham, and of course the lady thinks herself bound to refuse both the gentlemen who were so very wicked, and of course—"

"Well,—what follows?"

"Ah! if you have not wit enough to see, I do not think it can be my duty to tell you. But I wished to caution you as a friend that your eyes and ears should be more under your command."

"You will go to Saulsby?" Violet said to Lord Chiltern.

"I cannot possibly tell as yet," said he, frowning.

"Then I can tell you that you ought to go. I do not care a bit for your frowns. What does the fifth commandment say?"

"If you have no better arguments than the commandments, Violet—"

"There can be none better. Do you mean to say that the commandments are nothing to you?"

"I mean to say that I shan't go to Saulsby because I am told in the twentieth chapter of Exodus to honour my father and mother,—and that I shouldn't believe anybody who told me that he did anything because of the commandments."

"Oh, Lord Chiltern!"

"People are so prejudiced and so used to humbug that for the most part they do not in the least know their own motives for what they do. I will go to Saulsby to-morrow,—for a reward."

"For what reward?" said Violet, blushing.

"For the only one in the world that could tempt me to do anything."

"You should go for the sake of duty. I should not even care to see you go, much as I long for it, if that feeling did not take you there."

It was arranged that Phineas and Lord Chiltern were to leave Matching together. Phineas was to remain at his office all October, and in November the general election was to take place. What he had hitherto heard about a future seat was most vague, but he was to meet Ratler and Barrington Erle in London, and it had been understood that Barrington Erle, who was now at Saulsby, was to make some inquiry as to that group of boroughs of which Loughton at this moment formed one. But as Loughton was the smallest of four boroughs, and as one of the four had for many years had a representative of its own, Phineas feared that no success would be found there. In his present agony he began to think that there might be a strong plea made for a few private seats in the House of Commons, and that the propriety of throwing Loughton into the melting-pot was, after all, open to question. He and Lord Chiltern were to return to London together, and Lord Chiltern, according to his present scheme, was to proceed at once to Willingford to look after the cub-hunting. Nothing that either Violet or Phineas could say to him would induce him to promise to go to Saulsby. When Phineas pressed it, he was told by Lord Chiltern that he was a fool for his pains,—by which Phineas understood perfectly well that when Lord Chiltern did go to Saulsby, he, Phineas, was to take that as strong evidence that everything was over for him as regarded Violet Effingham. When Violet expressed her eagerness that the visit should be made, she was stopped with an assurance that she could have it done at once if she pleased. Let him only be enabled to carry with him the tidings of his betrothal, and he would start for his father's house without an hour's delay. But this authority Violet would not give him. When he answered her after this fashion she could only tell him that he was ungenerous. "At any rate I am not false," he replied on one occasion. "What I say is the truth."

There was a very tender parting between Phineas and Madame Max Goesler. She had learned from him pretty nearly all his history, and certainly knew more of the reality of his affairs than any of those in London who had been his most staunch friends. "Of course you'll get a seat," she said as he took his leave of her. "If I understand it at all, they never throw over an ally so useful as you are."

"But the intention is that in this matter nobody shall any longer have the power of throwing over, or of not throwing over, anybody."

"That is all very well, my friend; but cakes will still be hot in the mouth, even though Mr. Daubeny turn purist, with Mr. Turnbull to help him. If you want any assistance in finding a seat you will not go to the *People's Banner*,—even yet."

"Certainly not to the *People's Banner*."

"I don't quite understand what the franchise is," continued Madame Max Goesler.

"Household in boroughs," said Phineas with some energy.

"Very well;—household in boroughs. I daresay that is very fine and very liberal, though I don't comprehend it in the least. And you want a borough. Very well. You won't go to the households. I don't think you will;—not at first, that is."

"Where shall I go then?"

"Oh,—to some great patron of a borough;—or to a club;—or perhaps to some great firm. The households will know nothing about it till they are told. Is not that it?"

"The truth is, Madame Max, I do not know where I shall go. I am like a child lost in a wood. And you may understand this;—if you do not see me in Park Lane before the end of January, I shall have perished in the wood."

"Then I will come and find you,—with a troop of householders. You will come. You will be there. I do not believe in death coming without signs. You are full of life." As she spoke, she had hold of his hand, and there was nobody near them. They were in a little book-room inside the library at Matching, and the door, though not latched, was nearly closed. Phineas had flattered himself that Madame Goesler had retreated there in order that this farewell might be spoken without interruption. "And, Mr. Finn;—I wonder whether I may say one thing," she continued.

"You may say anything to me," he replied.

"No,—not in this country, in this England. There are things one may not say here,—that are tabooed by a sort of consent,—and that without any reason." She paused again, and Phineas was at a loss to think what was the subject on which she was about to speak. Could she mean—? No; she could not mean to give him any outward plain-spoken sign that she was attached to him. It was the peculiar merit of this man that he was not vain, though much was done to him to fill him with vanity; and as the idea crossed his brain, he hated himself because it had been there.

"To me you may say anything, Madame Goesler," he said,—"here in England, as plainly as though we were in Vienna."

"But I cannot say it in English," she said. Then in French, blushing and laughing as she spoke,—almost stammering in spite of her usual self-confidence,—she told him that accident had made her rich, full of money. Money was a drug with her. Money she knew was wanted, even for householders. Would he not understand her, and come to her, and learn from her how faithful a woman could be?

He still was holding her by the hand, and he now raised it to his lips and kissed it. "The offer from you," he said, "is as high-minded, as generous, and as honourable as its acceptance by me would be mean-spirited, vile, and ignoble. But whether I fail or whether I succeed, you shall see me before the winter is over."

CHAPTER L
Again Successful

Phineas also said a word of farewell to Violet before he left Matching, but there was nothing peculiar in her little speech to him, or in his to her. "Of course we shall see each other in London. Don't talk of not being in the House. Of course you will be in the House." Then Phineas had shaken his head and smiled. Where was he to find a requisite number of householders prepared to return him? But as he went up to London he told himself that the air of the House of Commons was now the very breath of his nostrils. Life to him without it would be no life. To have come within the reach of the good things of political life, to have made his mark so as to have almost insured future success, to have been the petted young official aspirant of the day,—and then to sink down into the miserable platitudes of private life, to undergo daily attendance in law-courts without a brief, to listen to men who had come to be much below him in estimation and social intercourse, to sit in a wretched chamber up three pairs of stairs at Lincoln's Inn, whereas he was now at this moment provided with a gorgeous apartment looking out into the Park from the Colonial Office in Downing Street, to be attended by a mongrel between a clerk and an errand boy at 17s. 6d. a week instead of by a private secretary who was the son of an earl's sister, and was petted by countesses' daughters innumerable,—all this would surely break his heart. He could have done it, so he told himself, and could have taken glory in doing it, had not these other things come in his way. But the other things had come. He had run the risk, and had thrown the dice. And now when the game was so nearly won, must it be that everything should be lost at last?

He knew that nothing was to be gained by melancholy looks at his club, or by show of wretchedness at his office. London was very empty; but the approaching elections still kept some there who otherwise would have been looking after the first flush of pheasants. Barrington Erle was there, and was not long in asking Phineas what were his views.

"Ah;—that is so hard to say. Ratler told me that he would be looking about."

"Ratler is very well in the House," said Barrington, "but he is of no use for anything beyond it. I suppose you were not brought up at the London University?"

"Oh no," said Phineas, remembering the glories of Trinity.

"Because there would have been an opening. What do you say to Stratford,—the new Essex borough?"

"Broadbury the brewer is there already!"

"Yes;—and ready to spend any money you like to name. Let me see. Loughton is grouped with Smotherem, and Walker is a deal too strong at Smotherem to hear of any other claim. I don't think we could dare to propose it. There are the Chelsea hamlets, but it will take a wack of money."

"I have not got a wack of money," said Phineas, laughing.

"That's the devil of it. I think, if I were you, I should hark back upon some place in Ireland. Couldn't you get Laurence to give you up his seat?"

"What! Fitzgibbon?"

"Yes. He has not a ghost of a chance of getting into office again. Nothing on earth would induce him to look at a paper during all those weeks he was at the Colonial Office; and when Cantrip spoke to him, all he said was, 'Ah, bother!' Cantrip did not like it, I can tell you."

"But that wouldn't make him give up his seat."

"Of course you'd have to arrange it." By which Phineas understood Barrington Erle to mean that he, Phineas, was in some way to give to Laurence Fitzgibbon some adequate compensation for the surrender of his position as a county member.

"I'm afraid that's out of the question," said Phineas. "If he were to go, I should not get it."

"Would you have a chance at Loughshane?"

"I was thinking of trying it," said Phineas.

"Of course you know that Morris is very ill." This Mr. Morris was the brother of Lord Tulla, and was the sitting member of Loughshane. "Upon my word I think I should try that. I don't see where we're to put our hands on a seat in England. I don't indeed." Phineas, as he listened to this, could not help thinking that Barrington Erle, though he had certainly expressed a great deal of solicitude, was not as true a friend as he used to be. Perhaps he, Phineas, had risen too fast, and Barrington Erle was beginning to think that he might as well be out of the way.

He wrote to his father, asking after the borough, and asking after the health of Mr. Morris. And in his letter he told his own story very plainly,—almost pathetically. He perhaps had been wrong to make the attempt which he had made. He began to believe that he had been wrong. But at any rate he had made it so far successfully, and failure now would be doubly bitter. He thought that the party to which he belonged must now remain in office. It would hardly be possible that a new election would produce a House of Commons favourable to a conservative ministry. And with a liberal ministry he, Phineas, would be sure of his place, and sure of an official income,—if only he could find a seat. It was all very true, and was almost pathetic. The old doctor, who was inclined to be proud of his son, was not unwilling to make a sacrifice. Mrs. Finn declared before her daughters that if there was a seat in all Ireland, Phineas ought to have it. And Mary Flood Jones stood by listening, and wondering what Phineas would do if he lost his seat. Would he come back and live in County Clare, and be like any other girl's lover? Poor Mary had come to lose her ambition, and to think that girls whose lovers stayed at home were the happiest. Nevertheless, she would have walked all the way to Lord Tulla's house and back again, might that have availed to get the seat for Phineas. Then there came an express over from Castlemorris. The doctor was wanted at once to see Mr. Morris. Mr. Morris was very bad with gout in his stomach. According to the messenger it was supposed that Mr. Morris was dying. Before Dr. Finn had had an opportunity of answering his son's letter, Mr. Morris, the late member for Loughshane, had been gathered to his fathers.

Dr. Finn understood enough of elections for Parliament, and of the nature of boroughs, to be aware that a candidate's chance of success is very much improved by being early in the field; and he was aware, also, that the death of Mr. Morris would probably create various aspirants for the honour of representing Loughshane. But he could hardly address the Earl on the subject while the dead body of the late member was lying in the house at Castlemorris. The bill which had passed in the late session for reforming the constitution of the House of Commons had not touched Ireland, a future measure having been promised to the Irish for their comfort; and Loughshane therefore was, as to Lord Tulla's influence, the same as it had ever been. He had not there the plenary power which the other lord had held in his hands in regard to Loughton;—but still the Castlemorris interest would go a long way. It might be possible to stand against it, but it would be much more desirable that the candidate should have it at his back. Dr. Finn was fully alive to this as he sat opposite to the old lord, saying now a word about the old lord's gout in his legs and arms, and then about the gout in the stomach, which had carried away to another world the lamented late member for the borough.

"Poor Jack!" said Lord Tulla, piteously. "If I'd known it, I needn't have paid over two thousand pounds for him last year;—need I, doctor?"

"No, indeed," said Dr. Finn, feeling that his patient might perhaps approach the subject of the borough himself.

"He never would live by any rule, you know," said the desolate brother.

"Very hard to guide;—was he not, my lord?"

"The very devil. Now, you see, I do do what I'm told pretty well,—don't I, doctor?"

"Sometimes."

"By George, I do nearly always. I don't know what you mean by sometimes. I've been drinking brandy-and-water till I'm sick of it, to oblige you, and you tell me about—sometimes. You doctors expect a man to be a slave. Haven't I kept it out of my stomach?"

"Thank God, yes."

"It's all very well thanking God, but I should have gone as poor Jack has gone, if I hadn't been the most careful man in the world. He was drinking champagne ten days ago;—would do it, you know." Lord Tulla could talk about himself and his own ailments by the hour together, and Dr. Finn, who had thought that his noble patient was approaching the subject of the borough, was beginning again to feel that the double interest of the gout that was present, and the gout that had passed away, would be too absorbing. He, however, could say but little to direct the conversation.

"Mr. Morris, you see, lived more in London than you do, and was subject to temptation."

"I don't know what you call temptation. Haven't I the temptation of a bottle of wine under my nose every day of my life?"

"No doubt you have."

"And I don't drink it. I hardly ever take above a glass or two of brown sherry. By George! when I think of it, I wonder at my own courage. I do, indeed."

"But a man in London, my lord—"

"Why the deuce would he go to London? By-the-bye, what am I to do about the borough now?"

"Let my son stand for it, if you will, my lord."

"They've clean swept away Brentford's seat at Loughton, haven't they? Ha, ha, ha! What a nice game for him,—to have been forced to help to do it himself! There's nobody on earth I pity so much as a radical peer who is obliged to work like a nigger with a spade to shovel away the ground from under his own feet. As for me, I don't care who sits for Loughshane. I did care for poor Jack while he was alive. I don't think I shall interfere any longer. I am glad it lasted Jack's time." Lord Tulla had probably already forgotten that he himself had thrown Jack over for the last session but one.

"Phineas, my lord," began the father, "is now Under-Secretary of State."

"Oh, I've no doubt he's a very fine fellow;—but you see, he's an out-and-out Radical."

"No, my lord."

"Then how can he serve with such men as Mr. Gresham and Mr. Monk? They've turned out poor old Mildmay among them, because he's not fast enough for them. Don't tell me."

"My anxiety, of course, is for my boy's prospects. He seems to have done so well in Parliament."

"Why don't he stand for Marylebone or Finsbury?"

"The money, you know, my lord!"

"I shan't interfere here, doctor. If he comes, and the people then choose to return him, I shall say nothing. They may do just as they please. They tell me Lambert St. George, of Mockrath, is going to stand. If he does, it's the d—— piece of impudence I ever heard of. He's a tenant of my own, though he has a lease for ever; and his father never owned an acre of land in the county till his uncle died." Then the doctor knew that, with a little management, the lord's interest might be secured for his son.

Phineas came over and stood for the borough against Mr. Lambert St. George, and the contest was sharp enough. The gentry of the neighbourhood could not understand why such a man as Lord Tulla should admit a liberal candidate to succeed his brother. No one canvassed for the young Under-Secretary with more persistent zeal than did his father, who, when Phineas first spoke of going into Parliament, had produced so many good arguments against that perilous step. Lord Tulla's agent stood aloof,—desolate with grief at the death of the late member. At such a moment of family affliction, Lord Tulla, he declared, could not think of such a matter as the borough. But it was known that Lord Tulla was dreadfully jealous of Mr. Lambert St. George, whose property in that part of the county was now nearly equal to his own, and who saw much more company at Mockrath than was ever entertained at Castlemorris. A word from Lord Tulla,—so said the Conservatives of the county,—would have put Mr. St. George into the seat; but that word was not spoken, and the Conservatives of the neighbourhood swore that Lord Tulla was a renegade. The contest was very sharp, but our hero was returned by a majority of seventeen votes.

Again successful! As he thought of it he remembered stories of great generals who were said to have chained Fortune to the wheels of their chariots, but it seemed to him that the goddess had never served any general with such staunch obedience as she had displayed in his cause. Had not everything gone well with him;—so well, as almost to justify him in expecting that even yet Violet Effingham would become his wife? Dear, dearest Violet! If he could only achieve that, no general, who ever led an army across the Alps, would be his equal either in success or in the reward of success. Then he questioned himself as to what he would say to Miss Flood Jones on that very night. He was to meet dear little Mary Flood Jones that evening at a neighbour's house. His sister Barbara had so told him in a tone of voice which he quite understood to imply a caution. "I shall be so glad to see her," Phineas had replied.

"If there ever was an angel on earth, it is Mary," said Barbara Finn.

"I know that she is as good as gold," said Phineas.

"Gold!" replied Barbara,—"gold indeed! She is more precious than refined gold. But, Phineas, perhaps you had better not single her out for any special attention. She has thought it wisest to meet you."

"Of course," said Phineas. "Why not?"

"That is all, Phineas. I have nothing more to say. Men of course are different from girls."

"That's true, Barbara, at any rate."

"Don't laugh at me, Phineas, when I am thinking of nothing but of you and your interests, and when I am making all manner of excuses for you because I know what must be the distractions of the world in which you live." Barbara made more than one attempt to renew the conversation before the evening came, but Phineas thought that he had had enough of it. He did not like being told that excuses were made for him. After all, what had he done? He had once kissed Mary Flood Jones behind the door.

"I am so glad to see you, Mary," he said, coming and taking a chair by her side. He had been specially warned not to single Mary out for his attention, and yet there was the chair left vacant as though it were expected that he would fall into it.

"Thank you. We did not happen to meet last year, did we,—Mr. Finn?"

"Do not call me Mr. Finn, Mary."

"You are such a great man now!"

"Not at all a great man. If you only knew what little men we understrappers are in London you would hardly speak to me."

"But you are something—of State now;—are you not?"

"Well;—yes. That's the name they give me. It simply means that if any member wants to badger some one in the House about the Colonies, I am the man to be badgered. But if there is any credit to be had, I am not the man who is to have it."

"But it is a great thing to be in Parliament and in the Government too."

"It is a great thing for me, Mary, to have a salary, though it may only be for a year or two. However, I will not deny that it is pleasant to have been successful."

"It has been very pleasant to us, Phineas. Mamma has been so much rejoiced."

"I am so sorry not to see her. She is at Floodborough, I suppose."

"Oh, yes;—she is at home. She does not like coming out at night in winter. I have been staying here you know for two days, but I go home to-morrow."

"I will ride over and call on your mother." Then there was a pause in the conversation for a moment. "Does it not seem odd, Mary, that we should see so little of each other?"

"You are so much away, of course."

"Yes;—that is the reason. But still it seems almost unnatural. I often wonder when the time will come that I shall be quietly at home again. I have to be back in my office in London this day week, and yet I have not had a single hour to myself since I have been at Killaloe. But I will certainly ride over and see your mother. You will be at home on Wednesday I suppose."

"Yes,—I shall be at home."

Upon that he got up and went away, but again in the evening he found himself near her. Perhaps there is no position more perilous to a man's honesty than that in which Phineas now found himself;—that, namely, of knowing himself to be quite loved by a girl whom he almost loves himself. Of course he loved Violet Effingham; and they who talk best of love protest that no man or woman can be in love with two persons at once. Phineas was not in love with Mary Flood Jones; but he would have liked to take her in his arms and kiss her;—he would have liked to gratify her by swearing that she was dearer to him than all the world; he would have liked to have an episode,—and did, at the moment, think that it might be possible to have one life in London and another life altogether different at Killaloe. "Dear Mary," he said as he pressed her hand that night, "things will get themselves settled at last, I suppose." He was behaving very ill to her, but he did not mean to behave ill.

He rode over to Floodborough, and saw Mrs. Flood Jones. Mrs. Flood Jones, however, received him very coldly; and Mary did not appear. Mary had communicated to her mother her resolutions as to her future life. "The fact is, mamma, I love him. I cannot help it. If he ever chooses to come for me, here I am. If he does not, I will bear it as well as I can. It may be very mean of me, but it's true."

CHAPTER LI
Troubles at Loughlinter

There was a dull house at Loughlinter during the greater part of this autumn. A few men went down for the grouse shooting late in the season; but they stayed but a short time, and when they went Lady Laura was left alone with her husband. Mr. Kennedy had explained to his wife, more than once, that though he understood the duties of hospitality and enjoyed the performance of them, he had not married with the intention of living in a whirlwind. He was disposed to think that the whirlwind had hitherto been too predominant, and had said so very plainly with a good deal of marital authority. This autumn and winter were to be devoted to the cultivation of proper relations between him and his wife. "Does that mean Darby and Joan?" his wife had asked him, when the proposition was made to her. "It means mutual regard and esteem," replied Mr. Kennedy in his most solemn tone, "and I trust that such mutual regard and esteem between us may yet be possible." When Lady Laura showed him a letter from her brother, received some weeks after this conversation, in which Lord Chiltern expressed his intention of coming to Loughlinter for Christmas, he returned the note to his wife without a word. He suspected that she had made the arrangement without asking him, and was angry; but he would not tell her that her brother would not be welcome at his house. "It is not my doing," she said, when she saw the frown on his brow.

"I said nothing about anybody's doing," he replied.

"I will write to Oswald and bid him not come, if you wish it. Of course you can understand why he is coming."

"Not to see me, I am sure," said Mr. Kennedy.

"Nor me," replied Lady Laura. "He is coming because my friend Violet Effingham will be here."

"Miss Effingham! Why was I not told of this? I knew nothing of Miss Effingham's coming."

"Robert, it was settled in your own presence last July."

"I deny it."

Then Lady Laura rose up, very haughty in her gait and with something of fire in her eye, and silently left the room. Mr. Kennedy, when he found himself alone, was very unhappy. Looking back in his mind to the summer weeks in London, he remembered that his wife had told Violet that she was to spend her Christmas at Loughlinter, that he himself had given a muttered assent and that Violet,—as far as he could remember,—had made no reply. It had been one of those things which are so often mentioned, but not settled. He felt that he had been strictly right in denying that it had been "settled" in his presence;—but yet he felt that he had been wrong in contradicting his wife so peremptorily. He was a just man, and he would apologise for his fault; but he was an austere man, and would take back the value of his apology in additional austerity. He did not see his wife for some hours after the conversation which has been narrated, but when he did meet her his mind was still full of the subject. "Laura", he said, "I am sorry that I contradicted you."

"I am quite used to it, Robert."

"No;—you are not used to it." She smiled and bowed her head. "You wrong me by saying that you are used to it." Then he paused a moment, but she said not a word,—only smiled and bowed her head again. "I remember," he continued, "that something was said in my presence to Miss Effingham about her coming here at Christmas. It was so slight, however, that it had passed out of my memory till recalled by an effort. I beg your pardon."

"That is unnecessary, Robert."

"It is, dear."

"And do you wish that I should put her off,—or put Oswald off,—or both? My brother never yet has seen me in your house."

"And whose fault has that been?"

"I have said nothing about anybody's fault, Robert. I merely mentioned a fact. Will you let me know whether I shall bid him stay away?"

"He is welcome to come,—only I do not like assignations for love-making."

"Assignations!"

"Clandestine meetings. Lady Baldock would not wish it."

"Lady Baldock! Do you think that Violet would exercise any secrecy in the matter,—or that she will not tell Lady Baldock that Oswald will be here,—as soon as she knows it herself?"

"That has nothing to do with it."

"Surely, Robert, it must have much to do with it. And why should not these two young people meet? The acknowledged wish of all the family is that they should marry each other. And in this matter, at any rate, my brother has behaved extremely well." Mr. Kennedy said nothing further at the time, and it became an understanding that Violet Effingham was to be a month at Loughlinter, staying from the 20th of December to the 20th of January, and that Lord Chiltern was to come there for Christmas,—which with him would probably mean three days.

Before Christmas came, however, there were various other sources of uneasiness at Loughlinter. There had been, as a matter of course, great anxiety as to the elections. With Lady Laura this anxiety had been very strong, and even Mr. Kennedy had been warmed with some amount of fire as the announcements reached him of the successes and of the failures. The English returns came first,—and then the Scotch, which were quite as interesting to Mr. Kennedy as the English. His own seat was quite safe,—was not contested; but some neighbouring seats were sources of great solicitude. Then, when this was over, there were the tidings from Ireland to be received; and respecting one special borough in Ireland, Lady Laura evinced more solicitude than her husband approved. There was much danger for the domestic bliss of the house of Loughlinter, when things came to such a pass, and such words were spoken, as the election at Loughshane produced.

"He is in," said Lady Laura, opening a telegram.

"Who is in?" said Mr. Kennedy, with that frown on his brow to which his wife was now well accustomed. Though he asked the question, he knew very well who was the hero to whom the telegram referred.

"Our friend Phineas Finn," said Lady Laura, speaking still with an excited voice,—with a voice that was intended to display excitement. If there was to be a battle on this matter, there should be a battle. She would display all her anxiety for her young friend, and fling it in her husband's face if he chose to take it as an injury. What,—should she endure reproach from her husband because she regarded the interests of the man who had saved his life, of the man respecting whom she had suffered so many heart-struggles, and as to whom she had at last come to the conclusion that he should ever be regarded as a second brother, loved equally with the elder brother? She had done her duty by her husband,—so at least she had assured herself;—and should he dare to reproach her on this subject, she would be ready for the battle. And now the battle came. "I am glad of this," she said, with all the eagerness she could throw into her voice. "I am, indeed,—and so ought you to be." The husband's brow grew blacker and blacker, but still he said nothing. He had long been too proud to be jealous, and was now too proud to express his jealousy,—if only he could keep the expression back. But his wife would not leave the subject. "I am so thankful for this," she said, pressing the telegram between her hands. "I was so afraid he would fail!"

"You over-do your anxiety on such a subject," at last he said, speaking very slowly.

"What do you mean, Robert? How can I be over-anxious? If it concerned any other dear friend that I have in the world, it would not be an affair of life and death. To him it is almost so. I would have walked from here to London to get him his election." And as she spoke she held up the clenched fist of her left hand, and shook it, while she still held the telegram in her right hand.

"Laura, I must tell you that it is improper that you should speak of any man in those terms;—of any man that is a stranger to your blood."

"A stranger to my blood! What has that to do with it? This man is my friend, is your friend;—saved your life, has been my brother's best friend, is loved by my father,—and is loved by me, very dearly. Tell me what you mean by improper!"

"I will not have you love any man,—very dearly."

"Robert!"

"I tell you that I will have no such expressions from you. They are unseemly, and are used only to provoke me."

"Am I to understand that I am insulted by an accusation? If so, let me beg at once that I may be allowed to go to Saulsby. I would rather accept your apology and retractation there than here."

"You will not go to Saulsby, and there has been no accusation, and there will be no apology. If you please there will be no more mention of Mr. Finn's name between us, for the present. If you will take my advice you will cease to think of him extravagantly;—and I must desire you to hold no further direct communication with him."

"I have held no communication with him," said Lady Laura, advancing a step towards him. But Mr. Kennedy simply pointed to the telegram in her hand, and left the room. Now in respect to this telegram there had been an unfortunate mistake. I am not prepared to say that there was any reason why Phineas himself should not have sent the news of his success to Lady Laura; but he had not done so. The piece of paper which she still held crushed in her hand was in itself very innocent. "Hurrah for the Loughshanes. Finny has done the trick." Such were the words written on the slip, and they had been sent to Lady Laura by her young cousin, the clerk in the office who acted as private secretary to the Under-Secretary of State. Lady Laura resolved that her husband should never see those innocent but rather undignified words. The occasion had become one of importance, and such words were unworthy of it. Besides, she would not condescend to defend herself by bringing forward a telegram as evidence in her favour. So she burned the morsel of paper.

Lady Laura and Mr. Kennedy did not meet again till late that evening. She was ill, she said, and would not come down to dinner. After dinner she wrote him a note. "Dear Robert, I think you must regret what you said to me. If so, pray let me have a line from you to that effect. Yours affectionately, L." When the servant handed it to him, and he had read it, he smiled and thanked the girl who had brought it, and said he would see her mistress just now. Anything would be better than that the servants should know that there was a quarrel. But every servant in the house had known all about it for the last three hours. When the door was closed and he was alone, he sat fingering the note, thinking deeply how he should answer it, or whether he would answer it at all. No; he would not answer it;—not in writing. He would give his wife no written record of his humiliation. He had not acted wrongly. He had said nothing more than now, upon mature consideration, he thought that the circumstances demanded. But yet he felt that he must in some sort withdraw the accusation which he had made. If he did not withdraw it, there was no knowing what his wife might do. About ten in the evening he went up to her and made his little speech. "My dear, I have come to answer your note."

"I thought you would have written to me a line."

"I have come instead, Laura. Now, if you will listen to me for one moment, I think everything will be made smooth."

"Of course I will listen," said Lady Laura, knowing very well that her husband's moment would be rather tedious, and resolving that she also would have her moment afterwards.

"I think you will acknowledge that if there be a difference of opinion between you and me as to any question of social intercourse, it will be better that you should consent to adopt my opinion."

"You have the law on your side."

"I am not speaking of the law."

"Well;—go on, Robert. I will not interrupt you if I can help it."

"I am not speaking of the law. I am speaking simply of convenience, and of that which you must feel to be right. If I wish that your intercourse with any person should be of such or such a nature it must be best that you should comply with my wishes." He paused for her assent, but she neither assented nor dissented. "As far as I can understand the position of a man and wife in this country, there is no other way in which life can be made harmonious."

"Life will not run in harmonies."

"I expect that ours shall be made to do so, Laura. I need hardly say to you that I intend to accuse you of no impropriety of feeling in reference to this young man."

"No, Robert; you need hardly say that. Indeed, to speak my own mind, I think that you need hardly have alluded to it. I might go further, and say that such an allusion is in itself an insult,—an insult now repeated after hours of deliberation,—an insult which I will not endure to have repeated again. If you say another word in any way suggesting the possibility of improper relations between me and Mr. Finn, either as to deeds or thoughts, as God is above me, I will write to both my father and my brother, and desire them to take me from your house. If you wish me to remain here, you had better be careful!" As she was making this speech, her temper seemed to rise, and to become hot, and then hotter, till it glowed with a red heat. She had been cool till the word insult, used by herself, had conveyed back to her a strong impression of her own wrong,—or perhaps I should rather say a strong feeling of the necessity of becoming indignant. She was standing as she spoke, and the fire flashed from her eyes, and he quailed before her. The threat which she had held out to him was very dreadful to him. He was a man terribly in fear of the world's good opinion, who lacked the courage to go through a great and harassing trial in order that something better might come afterwards. His married life had been unhappy. His wife had not submitted either to his will or to his ways. He had that great desire to enjoy his full rights, so strong in the minds of weak, ambitious men, and he had told himself that a wife's obedience was one of those rights which he could not abandon without injury to his self-esteem. He had thought about the matter, slowly, as was his wont, and had resolved that he would assert himself. He had asserted himself, and his wife told him to his face that she would go away and leave him. He could detain her legally, but he could not do even that without the fact of such forcible detention being known to all the world. How was he to answer her now at this moment, so that she might not write to her father, and so that his self-assertion might still be maintained?

"Passion, Laura, can never be right."

"Would you have a woman submit to insult without passion? I at any rate am not such a woman." Then there was a pause for a moment. "If you have nothing else to say to me, you had better leave me. I am far from well, and my head is throbbing."

He came up and took her hand, but she snatched it away from him. "Laura," he said, "do not let us quarrel."

"I certainly shall quarrel if such insinuations are repeated."

"I made no insinuation."

"Do not repeat them. That is all."

He was cowed and left her, having first attempted to get out of the difficulty of his position by making much of her alleged illness, and by offering to send for Dr. Macnuthrie. She positively refused to see Dr. Macnuthrie, and at last succeeded in inducing him to quit the room.

This had occurred about the end of November, and on the 20th of December Violet Effingham reached Loughlinter. Life in Mr. Kennedy's house had gone quietly during the intervening three weeks, but not very pleasantly. The name of Phineas Finn had not been mentioned. Lady Laura had triumphed; but she had no desire to acerbate her husband by any unpalatable allusion to her victory. And he was quite willing to let the subject die away, if only it would die. On some other matters he continued to assert himself, taking his wife to church twice every Sunday, using longer family prayers than she approved, reading an additional sermon himself every Sunday evening, calling upon her for weekly attention to elaborate household accounts, asking for her personal assistance in much local visiting, initiating her into his favourite methods of family life in the country, till sometimes she almost longed to talk again about Phineas Finn, so that there might be a rupture, and she might escape. But her husband asserted himself within bounds, and she submitted, longing for the coming of Violet Effingham. She could not write to her father and beg to be taken away, because her husband would read a sermon to her on Sunday evening.

To Violet, very shortly after her arrival, she told her whole story. "This is terrible," said Violet. "This makes me feel that I never will be married."

"And yet what can a woman become if she remain single? The curse is to be a woman at all."

"I have always felt so proud of the privileges of my sex," said Violet.

"I never have found them," said the other; "never. I have tried to make the best of its weaknesses, and this is what I have come to! I suppose I ought to have loved some man."

"And did you never love any man?"

"No;—I think I never did,—not as people mean when they speak of love. I have felt that I would consent to be cut in little pieces for my brother,—because of my regard for him."

"Ah, that is nothing."

"And I have felt something of the same thing for another,—a longing for his welfare, a delight to hear him praised, a charm in his presence,—so strong a feeling for his interest, that were he to go to wrack and ruin, I too, should, after a fashion, be wracked and ruined. But it has not been love either."

"Do I know whom you mean? May I name him? It is Phineas Finn."

"Of course it is Phineas Finn."

"Did he ever ask you,—to love him?"

"I feared he would do so, and therefore accepted Mr. Kennedy's offer almost at the first word."

"I do not quite understand your reasoning, Laura."

"I understand it. I could have refused him nothing in my power to give him, but I did not wish to be his wife."

"And he never asked you?"

Lady Laura paused a moment, thinking what reply she should make;—and then she told a fib. "No; he never asked me." But Violet did not believe the fib. Violet was quite sure that Phineas had asked Lady Laura Standish to be his wife. "As far as I can see," said Violet, "Madame Max Goesler is his present passion."

"I do not believe it in the least," said Lady Laura, firing up.

"It does not much matter," said Violet.

"It would matter very much. You know, you,—you; you know whom he loves. And I do believe that sooner or later you will be his wife."

"Never."

"Yes, you will. Had you not loved him you would never have condescended to accuse him about that woman."

"I have not accused him. Why should he not marry Madame Max Goesler? It would be just the thing for him. She is very rich."

"Never. You will be his wife."

"Laura, you are the most capricious of women. You have two dear friends, and you insist that I shall marry them both. Which shall I take first?"

"Oswald will be here in a day or two, and you can take him if you like it. No doubt he will ask you. But I do not think you will."

"No; I do not think I shall. I shall knock under to Mr. Mill, and go in for women's rights, and look forward to stand for some female borough. Matrimony never seemed to me to be very charming, and upon my word it does not become more alluring by what I find at Loughlinter."

It was thus that Violet and Lady Laura discussed these matters together, but Violet had never showed to her friend the cards in her hand, as Lady Laura had shown those which she held. Lady Laura had in fact told almost everything that there was to tell,—had spoken either plainly with true words, or equally plainly with words that were not true. Violet Effingham had almost come to love Phineas Finn;—but she never told her friend that it was so. At one time she had almost made up her mind to give herself and all her wealth to this adventurer. He was a better man, she thought, than Lord Chiltern; and she had come to persuade herself that it was almost imperative on her to take the one or the other. Though she could talk about remaining unmarried, she knew that that was practically impossible. All those around her,—those of the Baldock as well as those of the Brentford faction,—would make such a life impossible to her. Besides, in such a case what could she do? It was all very well to talk of disregarding the world and of setting up a house for herself;—but she was quite aware that that project could not be used further than for the purpose of scaring her amiable aunt. And if not that,—then could she content herself to look forward to a joint life with Lady Baldock and Augusta Boreham? She might, of course, oblige her aunt by taking Lord Fawn, or oblige her aunt equally by taking Mr. Appledom; but she was strongly of opinion that either Lord Chiltern or Phineas would be preferable to these. Thinking over it always she had come to feel that it must be either Lord Chiltern or Phineas; but she had never whispered her thought to man or woman. On her journey to Loughlinter, where she then knew that she was to meet Lord Chiltern, she endeavoured to persuade herself that it should be Phineas. But Lady Laura had marred it all by that ill-told fib. There had been a moment before in which Violet had felt that Phineas had sacrificed something of that truth of love for which she gave him credit to the glances of Madame Goesler's eyes; but she had rebuked herself for the idea, accusing herself not only of a little jealousy, but of foolish vanity. Was he, whom she had rejected, not to speak to another woman? Then came the blow from Lady Laura, and Violet knew that it was a blow. This gallant lover, this young Crichton, this unassuming but ardent lover, had simply taken up with her as soon as he had failed with her friend. Lady Laura had been most enthusiastic in her expressions of friendship. Such platonic regards might be all very well. It was for Mr. Kennedy to look to that. But, for herself, she felt that such expressions were hardly compatible with her ideas of having her lover all to herself. And then she again remembered Madame Goesler's bright blue eyes.

Lord Chiltern came on Christmas eve, and was received with open arms by his sister, and with that painful, irritating affection which such a girl as Violet can show to such a man as Lord Chiltern, when she will not give him that other affection for which his heart is panting. The two men were civil to each other,—but very cold. They called each other Kennedy and Chiltern, but even that was not done without an effort. On the Christmas morning Mr. Kennedy asked his brother-in-law to go to church. "It's a kind of thing I never do," said Lord Chiltern. Mr. Kennedy gave a little start, and looked a look of horror. Lady Laura showed that she was unhappy. Violet Effingham turned away her face, and smiled.

As they walked across the park Violet took Lord Chiltern's part. "He only means that he does not go to church on Christmas day."

"I don't know what he means," said Mr. Kennedy.

"We need not speak of it," said Lady Laura.

"Certainly not," said Mr. Kennedy.

"I have been to church with him on Sundays myself," said Violet, perhaps not reflecting that the practices of early years had little to do with the young man's life at present.

Christmas day and the next day passed without any sign from Lord Chiltern, and on the day after that he was to go away. But he was not to leave till one or two in the afternoon. Not a word had been said between the two women, since he had been in the house, on the subject of which both of them were thinking. Very much had been said of the expediency of his going to Saulsby, but on this matter he had declined to make any promise. Sitting in Lady Laura's room, in the presence of both of them, he had refused to do so. "I am bad to drive," he said, turning to Violet, "and you had better not try to drive me."

"Why should not you be driven as well as another?" she answered, laughing.

CHAPTER LII
The First Blow

Lord Chiltern, though he had passed two entire days in the house with Violet without renewing his suit, had come to Loughlinter for the express purpose of doing so, and had his plans perfectly fixed in his own mind. After breakfast on that last morning he was up-stairs with his sister in her own room, and immediately made his request to her. "Laura," he said, "go down like a good girl, and make Violet come up here." She stood a moment looking at him and smiled. "And, mind," he continued, "you are not to come back yourself. I must have Violet alone."

"But suppose Violet will not come? Young ladies do not generally wait upon young men on such occasions."

"No;—but I rank her so high among young women, that I think she will have common sense enough to teach her that, after what has passed between us, I have a right to ask for an interview, and that it may be more conveniently had here than in the wilderness of the house below."

Whatever may have been the arguments used by her friend, Violet did come. She reached the door all alone, and opened it bravely. She had promised herself, as she came along the passages, that she would not pause with her hand on the lock for a moment. She had first gone to her own room, and as she left it she had looked into the glass with a hurried glance, and had then rested for a moment,—thinking that something should be done, that her hair might be smoothed, or a ribbon set straight, or the chain arranged under her brooch. A girl would wish to look well before her lover, even when she means to refuse him. But her pause was but for an instant, and then she went on, having touched nothing. She shook her head and pressed her hands together, and went on quick and opened the door,—almost with a little start. "Violet, this is very good of you," said Lord Chiltern, standing with his back to the fire, and not moving from the spot.

"Laura has told me that you thought I would do as much as this for you, and therefore I have done it."

"Thanks, dearest. It is the old story, Violet, and I am so bad at words!"

"I must have been bad at words too, as I have not been able to make you understand."

"I think I have understood. You are always clear-spoken, and I, though I cannot talk, am not muddle-pated. I have understood. But while you are single there must be yet hope;—unless, indeed, you will tell me that you have already given yourself to another man."

"I have not done that."

"Then how can I not hope? Violet, I would if I could tell you all my feelings plainly. Once, twice, thrice, I have said to myself that I would think of you no more. I have tried to persuade myself that I am better single than married."

"But I am not the only woman."

"To me you are,—absolutely, as though there were none other on the face of God's earth. I live much alone; but you are always with me. Should you marry any other man, it will be the same with me still. If you refuse me now I shall go away,—and live wildly."

"Oswald, what do you mean?"

"I mean that I will go to some distant part of the world, where I may be killed or live a life of adventure. But I shall do so simply in despair. It will not be that I do not know how much better and greater should be the life at home of a man in my position."

"Then do not talk of going."

"I cannot stay. You will acknowledge, Violet, that I have never lied to you. I am thinking of you day and night. The more indifferent you show yourself to me, the more I love you. Violet, try to love me." He came up to her, and took her by both her hands, and tears were in his eyes. "Say you will try to love me."

"It is not that," said Violet, looking away, but still leaving her hands with him.

"It is not what, dear?"

"What you call,—trying."

"It is that you do not wish to try?"

"Oswald, you are so violent, so headstrong. I am afraid of you,—as is everybody. Why have you not written to your father, as we have asked you?"

"I will write to him instantly, now, before I leave the room, and you shall dictate the letter to him. By heavens, you shall!" He had dropped her hands when she called him violent; but now he took them again, and still she permitted it. "I have postponed it only till I had spoken to you once again."

"No, Lord Chiltern, I will not dictate to you."

"But will you love me?" She paused and looked down, having even now not withdrawn her hands from him. But I do not think he knew how much he had gained. "You used to love me,—a little," he said.

"Indeed,—indeed, I did."

"And now? Is it all changed now?"

"No," she said, retreating from him.

"How is it, then? Violet, speak to me honestly. Will you be my wife?" She did not answer him, and he stood for a moment looking at her. Then he rushed at her, and, seizing her in his arms, kissed her all over,—her forehead, her lips, her cheeks, then both her hands, and then her lips again. "By G——, she is my own!" he said. Then he went back to the rug before the fire, and stood there with his back turned to her. Violet, when she found herself thus deserted, retreated to a sofa, and sat herself down. She had no negative to produce now in answer to the violent assertion which he had pronounced as to his own success. It was true. She had doubted, and doubted,—and still doubted. But now she must doubt no longer. Of one thing she was quite sure. She could love him. As things had now gone, she would make him quite happy with assurances on that subject. As to that other question,—that fearful question, whether or not she could trust him,—on that matter she had better at present say nothing, and think as little, perhaps, as might be. She had taken the jump, and therefore why should she not be gracious to him? But how was she to be gracious to a lover who stood there with his back turned to her?

After the interval of a minute or two he remembered himself, and turned round. Seeing her seated, he approached her, and went down on both knees close at her feet. Then he took her hands again, for the third time, and looked up into her eyes.

"Oswald, you on your knees!" she said.

"I would not bend to a princess," he said, "to ask for half her throne; but I will kneel here all day, if you will let me, in thanks for the gift of your love. I never kneeled to beg for it."

"This is the man who cannot make speeches."

"I think I could talk now by the hour, with you for a listener."

"Oh, but I must talk too."

"What will you say to me?"

"Nothing while you are kneeling. It is not natural that you should kneel. You are like Samson with his locks shorn, or Hercules with a distaff."

"Is that better?" he said, as he got up and put his arm round her waist.

"You are in earnest?" she asked.

"In earnest. I hardly thought that that would be doubted. Do you not believe me?"

"I do believe you. And you will be good?"

"Ah,—I do not know that."

"Try, and I will love you so dearly. Nay, I do love you dearly. I do. I do."

"Say it again."

"I will say it fifty times,—till your ears are weary with it";—and she did say it to him, after her own fashion, fifty times.

"This is a great change," he said, getting up after a while and walking about the room.

"But a change for the better;—is it not, Oswald?"

"So much for the better that I hardly know myself in my new joy. But, Violet, we'll have no delay,—will we? No shilly-shallying. What is the use of waiting now that it's settled?"

"None in the least, Lord Chiltern. Let us say,—this day twelvemonth."

"You are laughing at me, Violet."

"Remember, sir, that the first thing you have to do is to write to your father."

He instantly went to the writing-table and took up paper and pen. "Come along," he said. "You are to dictate it." But this she refused to do, telling him that he must write his letter to his father out of his own head, and out of his own heart. "I cannot write it," he said, throwing down the pen. "My blood is in such a tumult that I cannot steady my hand."

"You must not be so tumultuous, Oswald, or I shall have to live in a whirlwind."

"Oh, I shall shake down. I shall become as steady as an old stager. I'll go as quiet in harness by-and-by as though I had been broken to it a four-year-old. I wonder whether Laura could not write this letter."

"I think you should write it yourself, Oswald."

"If you bid me I will."

"Bid you indeed! As if it was for me to bid you. Do you not know that in these new troubles you are undertaking you will have to bid me in everything, and that I shall be bound to do your bidding? Does it not seem to be dreadful? My wonder is that any girl can ever accept any man."

"But you have accepted me now."

"Yes, indeed."

"And you repent?"

"No, indeed, and I will try to do your biddings;—but you must not be rough to me, and outrageous, and fierce,—will you, Oswald?"

"I will not at any rate be like Kennedy is with poor Laura."

"No;—that is not your nature."

"I will do my best, dearest. And you may at any rate be sure of this, that I will love you always. So much good of myself, if it be good, I can say."

"It is very good," she answered; "the best of all good words. And now I must go. And as you are leaving Loughlinter I will say good-bye. When am I to have the honour and felicity of beholding your lordship again?"

"Say a nice word to me before I am off, Violet."

"I,—love,—you,—better,—than all the world beside; and I mean,—to be your wife,—some day. Are not those twenty nice words?"

He would not prolong his stay at Loughlinter, though he was asked to do so both by Violet and his sister, and though, as he confessed himself, he had no special business elsewhere. "It is no use mincing the matter. I don't like Kennedy, and I don't like being in his house," he said to Violet. And then he promised that there should be a party got up at Saulsby before the winter was over. His plan was to stop that night at Carlisle, and write to his father from thence. "Your blood, perhaps, won't be so tumultuous at Carlisle," said Violet. He shook his head and went on with his plans. He would then go on to London and down to Willingford, and there wait for his father's answer. "There is no reason why I should lose more of the hunting than necessary." "Pray don't lose a day for me," said Violet. As soon as he heard from his father, he would do his father's bidding. "You will go to Saulsby," said Violet; "you can hunt at Saulsby, you know."

"I will go to Jericho if he asks me, only you will have to go with me." "I thought we were to go to,—Belgium," said Violet.

"And so that is settled at last," said Violet to Laura that night.

"I hope you do not regret it."

"On the contrary, I am as happy as the moments are long."

"My fine girl!"

"I am happy because I love him. I have always loved him. You have known that."

"Indeed, no."

"But I have, after my fashion. I am not tumultuous, as he calls himself. Since he began to make eyes at me when he was nineteen—"

"Fancy Oswald making eyes!"

"Oh, he did, and mouths too. But from the beginning, when I was a child, I have known that he was dangerous, and I have thought that he would pass on and forget me after a while. And I could have lived without him. Nay, there have been moments when I thought I could learn to love some one else."

"Poor Phineas, for instance."

"We will mention no names. Mr. Appledom, perhaps, more likely. He has been my most constant lover, and then he would be so safe! Your brother, Laura, is dangerous. He is like the bad ice in the parks where they stick up the poles. He has had a pole stuck upon him ever since he was a boy."

"Yes;—give a dog a bad name and hang him."

"Remember that I do not love him a bit the less on that account;—perhaps the better. A sense of danger does not make me unhappy, though the threatened evil may be fatal. I have entered myself for my forlorn hope, and I mean to stick to it. Now I must go and write to his worship. Only think,—I never wrote a love-letter yet!"

Nothing more shall be said about Miss Effingham's first love-letter, which was, no doubt, creditable to her head and heart; but there were two other letters sent by the same post from Loughlinter which shall be submitted to the reader, as they will assist the telling of the story. One was from Lady Laura Kennedy to her friend Phineas Finn, and the other from Violet to her aunt, Lady Baldock. No letter was written to Lord Brentford, as it was thought desirable that he should receive the first intimation of what had been done from his son.

Respecting the letter to Phineas, which shall be first given, Lady Laura thought it right to say a word to her husband. He had been of course told of the engagement, and had replied that he could have wished that the arrangement could have been made elsewhere than at his house, knowing as he did that Lady Baldock would not approve of it. To this Lady Laura had made no reply, and Mr. Kennedy had condescended to congratulate the bride-elect. When Lady Laura's letter to Phineas was completed she took care to put it into the letter-box in the presence of her husband. "I have written to Mr. Finn," she said, "to tell him of this marriage."

"Why was it necessary that he should be told?"

"I think it was due to him,—from certain circumstances."

"I wonder whether there was any truth in what everybody was saying about their fighting a duel?" asked Mr. Kennedy. His wife made no answer, and then he continued—"You told me of your own knowledge that it was untrue."

"Not of my own knowledge, Robert."

"Yes;—of your own knowledge." Then Mr. Kennedy walked away, and was certain that his wife had deceived him about the duel. There had been a duel, and she had known it; and yet she had told him that the report was a ridiculous fabrication. He never forgot anything. He remembered at this moment the words of the falsehood, and the look of her face as she told it. He had believed her implicitly, but he would never believe her again. He was one of those men who, in spite of their experience of the world, of their experience of their own lives, imagine that lips that have once lied can never tell the truth.

Lady Laura's letter to Phineas was as follows:

Loughlinter, December 28th, 186—.

My dear Friend,

Violet Effingham is here, and Oswald has just left us. It is possible that you may see him as he passes through London. But, at any rate, I think it best to let you know immediately that she has accepted him,—at last. If there be any pang in this to you, be sure that I will grieve for you. You will not wish me to say that I regret that which was the dearest wish of my heart before I knew you. Lately, indeed, I have been torn in two ways. You will understand what I mean, and I believe I need say nothing more;—except this, that it shall be among my prayers that you may obtain all things that may tend to make you happy, honourable, and of high esteem.

Your most sincere friend

Laura Kennedy.

Even though her husband should read the letter, there was nothing in that of which she need be ashamed. But he did not read the letter. He simply speculated as to its contents, and inquired within himself whether it would not be for the welfare of the world in general, and for the welfare of himself in particular, that husbands should demand to read their wives' letters.

And this was Violet's letter to her aunt:—

My dear Aunt,

The thing has come at last, and all your troubles will be soon over;—for I do believe that all your troubles have come from your unfortunate niece. At last I am going to be married, and thus take myself off your hands. Lord Chiltern has just been here, and I have accepted him. I am afraid you hardly think so well of Lord Chiltern as I do; but then, perhaps, you have not known him so long. You do know, however, that there has been some difference between him and his father. I think I may take upon myself to say that now, upon his engagement, this will be settled. I have the inexpressible pleasure of feeling sure that Lord Brentford will welcome me as his daughter-in-law. Tell the news to Augusta with my best love. I will write to her in a day or two. I hope my cousin Gustavus will condescend to give me away. Of course there is nothing fixed about time;—but I should say, perhaps, in nine years.

Your affectionate niece,

Violet Effingham.

Loughlinter, Friday.

"What does she mean about nine years?" said Lady Baldock in her wrath.

"She is joking," said the mild Augusta.

"I believe she would—joke, if I were going to be buried," said Lady Baldock.

CHAPTER LIII
Showing How Phineas Bore the Blow

When Phineas received Lady Laura Kennedy's letter, he was sitting in his gorgeous apartment in the Colonial Office. It was gorgeous in comparison with the very dingy room at Mr. Low's to which he had been accustomed in his early days,—and somewhat gorgeous also as compared with the lodgings he had so long inhabited in Mr. Bunce's house. The room was large and square, and looked out from three windows on to St. James's Park. There were in it two very comfortable arm-chairs and a comfortable sofa. And the office table at which he sat was of old mahogany, shining brightly, and seemed to be fitted up with every possible appliance for official comfort. This stood near one of the windows, so that he could sit and look down upon the park. And there was a large round table covered with books and newspapers. And the walls of the room were bright with maps of all the colonies. And there was one very interesting map,—but not very bright,—showing the American colonies, as they used to be. And there was a little inner closet in which he could brush his hair and wash his hands; and in the room adjoining there sat,—or ought to have sat, for he was often absent, vexing the mind of Phineas,—the Earl's nephew, his private secretary. And it was all very gorgeous. Often as he looked round upon it, thinking of his old bedroom at Killaloe, of his little garrets at Trinity, of the dingy chambers in Lincoln's Inn, he would tell himself that it was very gorgeous. He would wonder that anything so grand had fallen to his lot.

The letter from Scotland was brought to him in the afternoon, having reached London by some day-mail from Glasgow. He was sitting at his desk with a heap of papers before him referring to a contemplated railway from Halifax, in Nova Scotia, to the foot of the Rocky Mountains. It had become his business to get up the subject, and then discuss with his principal, Lord Cantrip, the expediency of advising the Government to lend a company five million of money, in order that this railway might be made. It was a big subject, and the contemplation of it gratified him. It required that he should look forward to great events, and exercise the wisdom of a statesman. What was the chance of these colonies being swallowed up by those other regions,—once colonies,—of which the map that hung in the corner told so eloquent a tale? And if so, would the five million ever be repaid? And if not swallowed up, were the colonies worth so great an adventure of national money? Could they repay it? Would they do so? Should they be made to do so? Mr. Low, who was now a Q.C. and in Parliament, would not have greater subjects than this before him, even if he should come to be Solicitor General. Lord Cantrip had specially asked him to get up this matter,—and he was getting it up sedulously. Once in nine years the harbour of Halifax was blocked up by ice. He had just jotted down the fact, which was material, when Lady Laura's letter was brought to him. He read it, and putting it down by his side very gently, went back to his maps as though the thing would not so trouble his mind as to disturb his work. He absolutely wrote, automatically, certain words of a note about the harbour, after he had received the information. A horse will gallop for some scores of yards, after his back has been broken, before he knows of his great ruin;—and so it was with Phineas Finn. His back was broken, but, nevertheless, he galloped, for a yard or two. "Closed in 1860-61 for thirteen days." Then he began to be aware that his back was broken, and that the writing of any more notes about the ice in Halifax harbour was for the present out of the question. "I think it best to let you know immediately that she has accepted him." These were the words which he read the oftenest. Then it was all over! The game was played out, and all his victories were as nothing to him. He sat for an hour in his gorgeous room thinking of it, and various were the answers which he gave during the time to various messages;—but he would see nobody. As for the colonies, he did not care if they revolted to-morrow. He would have parted with every colony belonging to Great Britain to have gotten the hand of Violet Effingham for himself. Now,—now at this moment, he told himself with oaths that he had never loved any one but Violet Effingham.

There had been so much to make such a marriage desirable! I should wrong my hero deeply were I to say that the weight of his sorrow was occasioned by the fact that he had lost an heiress. He would never have thought of looking for Violet Effingham had he not first learned to love her. But as the idea opened itself out to him, everything had seemed to be so suitable. Had Miss Effingham become his wife, the mouths of the Lows and of the Bunces would have been stopped altogether. Mr. Monk would have come to his house as his familiar guest, and he would have been connected with half a score of peers. A seat in Parliament would be simply his proper place, and even Under-Secretaryships of State might soon come to be below him. He was playing a great game, but hitherto he had played it with so much success,—with such wonderful luck! that it had seemed to him that all things were within his reach. Nothing more had been wanting to him than Violet's hand for his own comfort, and Violet's fortune to support his position; and these, too, had almost seemed to be within his grasp. His goddess had indeed refused him,—but not with disdain. Even Lady Laura had talked of his marriage as not improbable. All the world, almost, had heard of the duel; and all the world had smiled, and seemed to think that in the real fight Phineas Finn would be the victor,—that the lucky pistol was in his hands. It had never occurred to any one to suppose,—as far as he could see,—that he was presuming at all, or pushing himself out of his own sphere, in asking Violet Effingham to be his wife. No;—he would trust his luck, would persevere, and would succeed. Such had been his resolution on that very morning,—and now there had come this letter to dash him to the ground.

There were moments in which he declared to himself that he would not believe the letter,—not that there was any moment in which there was in his mind the slightest spark of real hope. But he would tell himself that he would still persevere. Violet might have been driven to accept that violent man by violent influence,—or it might be that she had not in truth accepted him, that Chiltern had simply so asserted. Or, even if it were so, did women never change their minds? The manly thing would be to persevere to the end. Had he not before been successful, when success seemed to be as far from him? But he could buoy himself up with no real hope. Even when these ideas were present to his mind, he knew,—he knew well,—at those very moments, that his back was broken.

Some one had come in and lighted the candles and drawn down the blinds while he was sitting there, and now, as he looked at his watch, he found that it was past five o'clock. He was engaged to dine with Madame Max Goesler at eight, and in his agony he half-resolved that he would send an excuse. Madame Max would be full of wrath, as she was very particular about her little dinner-parties;—but, what did he care now about the wrath of Madame Max Goesler? And yet only this morning he had been congratulating himself, among his other successes, upon her favour, and had laughed inwardly at his own falseness,—his falseness to Violet Effingham,—as he did so. He had said something to himself jocosely about lovers' perjuries, the remembrance of which was now very bitter to him. He took up a sheet of note-paper and scrawled an excuse to Madame Goesler. News from the country, he said, made it impossible that he should go out to-night. But he did not send the note. At about half-past five he opened the door of his private secretary's room and found the young man fast asleep, with a cigar in his mouth. "Halloa, Charles," he said.

"All right!" Charles Standish was a first cousin of Lady Laura's, and, having been in the office before Phineas had joined it, and being a great favourite with his cousin, had of course become the Under-Secretary's private secretary. "I'm all here," said Charles Standish, getting up and shaking himself.

"I am going. Just tie up those papers,—exactly as they are. I shall be here early to-morrow, but I shan't want you before twelve. Good night, Charles."

"Ta, ta," said his private secretary, who was very fond of his master, but not very respectful,—unless upon express occasions.

Then Phineas went out and walked across the park; but as he went he became quite aware that his back was broken. It was not the less broken because he sang to himself little songs to prove to himself that it was whole and sound. It was broken, and it seemed to him now that he never could become an Atlas again, to bear the weight of the world upon his shoulders. What did anything signify? All that he had done had been part of a game which he had been playing throughout, and now he had been beaten in his game. He absolutely ignored his old passion for Lady Laura as though it had never been, and regarded himself as a model of constancy,—as a man who had loved, not wisely perhaps, but much too well,—and who must now therefore suffer a living death. He hated Parliament. He hated the Colonial Office. He hated his friend Mr. Monk; and he especially hated Madame Max Goesler. As to Lord Chiltern,—he believed that Lord Chiltern had obtained his object by violence. He would see to that! Yes;—let the consequences be what they might, he would see to that!

He went up by the Duke of York's column, and as he passed the Athenæum he saw his chief, Lord Cantrip, standing under the portico talking to a bishop. He would have gone on unnoticed, had it been possible; but Lord Cantrip came down to him at once. "I have put your name down here," said his lordship.

"What's the use?" said Phineas, who was profoundly indifferent at this moment to all the clubs in London.

"It can't do any harm, you know. You'll come up in time. And if you should get into the ministry, they'll let you in at once."

"Ministry!" ejaculated Phineas. But Lord Cantrip took the tone of voice as simply suggestive of humility, and suspected nothing of that profound indifference to all ministers and ministerial honours which Phineas had intended to express. "By-the-bye," said Lord Cantrip, putting his arm through that of the Under-Secretary, "I wanted to speak to you about the guarantees. We shall be in the devil's own mess, you know—" And so the Secretary of State went on about the Rocky Mountain Railroad, and Phineas strove hard to bear his burden with his broken back. He was obliged to say something about the guarantees, and the railway, and the frozen harbour,—and something especially about the difficulties which would be found, not in the measures themselves, but in the natural pugnacity of the Opposition. In the fabrication of garments for the national wear, the great thing is to produce garments that shall, as far as possible, defy hole-picking. It may be, and sometimes is, the case, that garments so fabricated will be good also for wear. Lord Cantrip, at the present moment, was very anxious and very ingenious in the stopping of holes; and he thought that perhaps his Under-Secretary was too much prone to the indulgence of large philanthropical views without sufficient thought of the hole-pickers. But on this occasion, by the time that he reached Brooks's, he had been enabled to convince his Under-Secretary, and though he had always thought well of his Under-Secretary, he thought better of him now than ever he had done. Phineas during the whole time had been meditating what he could do to Lord Chiltern when they two should meet. Could he take him by the throat and smite him? "I happen to know that Broderick is working as hard at the matter as we are," said Lord Cantrip, stopping opposite to the club. "He moved for papers, you know, at the end of last session." Now Mr. Broderick was a gentleman in the House looking for promotion in a Conservative Government, and of course would oppose any measure that could be brought forward by the Cantrip-Finn Colonial Administration. Then Lord Cantrip slipped into the club, and Phineas went on alone.

A spark of his old ambition with reference to Brooks's was the first thing to make him forget his misery for a moment. He had asked Lord Brentford to put his name down, and was not sure whether it had been done. The threat of Mr. Broderick's opposition had been of no use towards the strengthening of his broken back, but the sight of Lord Cantrip hurrying in at the coveted door did do something. "A man can't cut his throat or blow his brains out," he said to himself; "after all, he must go on and do his work. For hearts will break, yet brokenly live on."

Thereupon he went home, and after sitting for an hour over his own fire, and looking wistfully at a little treasure which he had,—a treasure obtained by some slight fraud at Saulsby, and which he now chucked into the fire, and then instantly again pulled out of it, soiled but unscorched,—he dressed himself for dinner, and went out to Madame Max Goesler's. Upon the whole, he was glad that he had not sent the note of excuse. A man must live, even though his heart be broken, and living he must dine.

Madame Max Goesler was fond of giving little dinners at this period of the year, before London was crowded, and when her guests might probably not be called away by subsequent social arrangements. Her number seldom exceeded six or eight, and she always spoke of these entertainments as being of the humblest kind. She sent out no big cards. She preferred to catch her people as though by chance, when that was possible. "Dear Mr. Jones. Mr. Smith is coming to tell me about some sherry on Tuesday. Will you come and tell me too? I daresay you know as much about it." And then there was a studious absence of parade. The dishes were not very numerous. The bill of fare was simply written out once, for the mistress, and so circulated round the table. Not a word about the things to be eaten or the things to be drunk was ever spoken at the table,—or at least no such word was ever spoken by Madame Goesler. But, nevertheless, they who knew anything about dinners were aware that Madame Goesler gave very good dinners indeed. Phineas Finn was beginning to flatter himself that he knew something about dinners, and had been heard to assert that the soups at the cottage in Park Lane were not to be beaten in London. But he cared for no soup to-day, as he slowly made his way up Madame Goesler's staircase.

There had been one difficulty in the way of Madame Goesler's dinner-parties which had required some patience and great ingenuity in its management. She must either have ladies, or she must not have them. There was a great allurement in the latter alternative; but she knew well that if she gave way to it, all prospect of general society would for her be closed,—and for ever. This had been in the early days of her widowhood in Park Lane. She cared but little for women's society; but she knew well that the society of gentlemen without women would not be that which she desired. She knew also that she might as effectually crush herself and all her aspirations by bringing to her house indifferent women,—women lacking something either in character, or in position, or in talent,—as by having none at all. Thus there had been a great difficulty, and sometimes she had thought that the thing could not be done at all. "These English are so stiff, so hard, so heavy!" And yet she would not have cared to succeed elsewhere than among the English. By degrees, however, the thing was done. Her prudence equalled her wit, and even suspicious people had come to acknowledge that they could not put their fingers on anything wrong. When Lady Glencora Palliser had once dined at the cottage in Park Lane, Madame Max Goesler had told herself that henceforth she did not care what the suspicious people said. Since that the Duke of Omnium had almost promised that he would come. If she could only entertain the Duke of Omnium she would have done everything.

But there was no Duke of Omnium there to-night. At this time the Duke of Omnium was, of course, not in London. But Lord Fawn was there; and our old friend Laurence Fitzgibbon, who had—resigned his place at the Colonial Office; and there were Mr. and Mrs. Bonteen. They, with our hero, made up the party. No one doubted for a moment to what source Mr. Bonteen owed his dinner. Mrs. Bonteen was good-looking, could talk, was sufficiently proper, and all that kind of thing,—and did as well as any other woman at this time of year to keep Madame Max Goesler in countenance. There was never any sitting after dinner at the cottage; or, I should rather say, there was never any sitting after Madame Goesler went; so that the two ladies could not weary each other by being alone together. Mrs. Bonteen understood quite well that she was not required there to talk to her hostess, and was as willing as any woman to make herself agreeable to the gentlemen she might meet at Madame Goesler's table. And thus Mr. and Mrs. Bonteen not unfrequently dined in Park Lane.

"Now we have only to wait for that horrible man, Mr. Fitzgibbon," said Madame Max Goesler, as she welcomed Phineas. "He is always late."

"What a blow for me!" said Phineas.

"No,—you are always in good time. But there is a limit beyond which good time ends, and being shamefully late at once begins. But here he is." And then, as Laurence Fitzgibbon entered the room, Madame Goesler rang the bell for dinner.

Phineas found himself placed between his hostess and Mr. Bonteen, and Lord Fawn was on the other side of Madame Goesler. They were hardly seated at the table before some one stated it as a fact that Lord Brentford and his son were reconciled. Now Phineas knew, or thought that he knew, that this could not as yet be the case; and indeed such was not the case, though the father had already received the son's letter. But Phineas did not choose to say anything at present about Lord Chiltern.

"How odd it is," said Madame Goesler; "how often you English fathers quarrel with your sons!"

"How often we English sons quarrel with our fathers rather," said Lord Fawn, who was known for the respect he had always paid to the fifth commandment.

"It all comes from entail and primogeniture, and old-fashioned English prejudices of that kind," said Madame Goesler. "Lord Chiltern is a friend of yours, Mr. Finn, I think."

"They are both friends of mine," said Phineas.

"Ah, yes; but you,—you,—you and Lord Chiltern once did something odd together. There was a little mystery, was there not?"

"It is very little of a mystery now," said Fitzgibbon.

"It was about a lady;—was it not?" said Mrs. Bonteen, affecting to whisper to her neighbour.

"I am not at liberty to say anything on the subject," said Fitzgibbon; "but I have no doubt Phineas will tell you."

"I don't believe this about Lord Brentford," said Mr. Bonteen. "I happen to know that Chiltern was down at Loughlinter three days ago, and that he passed through London yesterday on his way to the place where he hunts. The Earl is at Saulsby. He would have gone to Saulsby if it were true."

"It all depends upon whether Miss Effingham will accept him," said Mrs. Bonteen, looking over at Phineas as she spoke.

As there were two of Violet Effingham's suitors at table, the subject was becoming disagreeably personal; and the more so, as every one of the party knew or surmised something of the facts of the case. The cause of the duel at Blankenberg had become almost as public as the duel, and Lord Fawn's courtship had not been altogether hidden from the public eye. He on the present occasion might probably be able to carry himself better than Phineas, even presuming him to be equally eager in his love,—for he knew nothing of the fatal truth. But he was unable to hear Mrs. Bonteen's statement with indifference, and showed his concern in the matter by his reply. "Any lady will be much to be pitied," he said, "who does that. Chiltern is the last man in the world to whom I would wish to trust the happiness of a woman for whom I cared."

"Chiltern is a very good fellow," said Laurence Fitzgibbon.

"Just a little wild," said Mrs. Bonteen.

"And never had a shilling in his pocket in his life," said her husband.

"I regard him as simply a madman," said Lord Fawn.

"I do so wish I knew him," said Madame Max Goesler. "I am fond of madmen, and men who haven't shillings, and who are a little wild, Could you not bring him here, Mr. Finn?"

Phineas did not know what to say, or how to open his mouth without showing his deep concern. "I shall be happy to ask him if you wish it," he replied, as though the question had been put to him in earnest; "but I do not see so much of Lord Chiltern as I used to do."

"You do not believe that Violet Effingham will accept him?" asked Mrs. Bonteen.

He paused a moment before he spoke, and then made his answer in a deep solemn voice,—with a seriousness which he was unable to repress. "She has accepted him," he said.

"Do you mean that you know it?" said Madame Goesler.

"Yes;—I mean that I know it."

Had anybody told him beforehand that he would openly make this declaration at Madame Goesler's table, he would have said that of all things it was the most impossible. He would have declared that nothing would have induced him to speak of Violet Effingham in his existing frame of mind, and that he would have had his tongue cut out before he spoke of her as the promised bride of his rival. And now he had declared the whole truth of his own wretchedness and discomfiture. He was well aware that all of them there knew why he had fought the duel at Blankenberg;—all, that is, except perhaps Lord Fawn. And he felt as he made the statement as to Lord Chiltern that he blushed up to his forehead, and that his voice was strange, and that he was telling the tale of his own disgrace. But when the direct question had been asked him he had been unable to refrain from answering it directly. He had thought of turning it off with some jest or affectation of drollery, but had failed. At the moment he had been unable not to speak the truth.

"I don't believe a word of it," said Lord Fawn,—who also forgot himself.

"I do believe it, if Mr. Finn says so," said Mrs. Bonteen, who rather liked the confusion she had caused.

"But who could have told you, Finn?" asked Mr. Bonteen.

"His sister, Lady Laura, told me so," said Phineas.

"Then it must be true," said Madame Goesler.

"It is quite impossible," said Lord Fawn. "I think I may say that I know that it is impossible. If it were so, it would be a most shameful arrangement. Every shilling she has in the world would be swallowed up." Now, Lord Fawn in making his proposals had been magnanimous in his offers as to settlements and pecuniary provisions generally.

For some minutes after that Phineas did not speak another word, and the conversation generally was not so brisk and bright as it was expected to be at Madame Goesler's. Madame Max Goesler herself thoroughly understood our hero's position, and felt for him. She would have encouraged no questionings about Violet Effingham had she thought that they would have led to such a result, and now she exerted herself to turn the minds of her guests to other subjects. At last she succeeded; and after a while, too, Phineas himself was able to talk. He drank two or three glasses of wine, and dashed away into politics, taking the earliest opportunity in his power of contradicting Lord Fawn very plainly on one or two matters. Laurence Fitzgibbon was of course of opinion that the ministry could not stay in long. Since he had left the Government the ministers had made wonderful mistakes, and he spoke of them quite as an enemy might speak. "And yet, Fitz," said Mr. Bonteen, "you used to be so staunch a supporter."

"I have seen the error of my way, I can assure you," said Laurence.

"I always observe," said Madame Max Goesler, "that when any of you gentlemen resign,—which you usually do on some very trivial matter,—the resigning gentleman becomes of all foes the bitterest. Somebody goes on very well with his friends, agreeing most cordially about everything, till he finds that his public virtue cannot swallow some little detail, and then he resigns. Or some one, perhaps, on the other side has attacked him, and in the mêlée he is hurt, and so he resigns. But when he has resigned, and made his parting speech full of love and gratitude, I know well after that where to look for the bitterest hostility to his late friends. Yes, I am beginning to understand the way in which politics are done in England."

All this was rather severe upon Laurence Fitzgibbon; but he was a man of the world, and bore it better than Phineas had borne his defeat.

The dinner, taken altogether, was not a success, and so Madame Goesler understood. Lord Fawn, after he had been contradicted by Phineas, hardly opened his mouth. Phineas himself talked rather too much and rather too loudly; and Mrs. Bonteen, who was well enough inclined to flatter Lord Fawn, contradicted him. "I made a mistake," said Madame Goesler afterwards, "in having four members of Parliament who all of them were or had been in office. I never will have two men in office together again." This she said to Mrs. Bonteen. "My dear Madame Max," said Mrs. Bonteen, "your resolution ought to be that you will never again have two claimants for the same young lady."

In the drawing-room up-stairs Madame Goesler managed to be alone for three minutes with Phineas Finn. "And it is as you say, my friend?" she asked. Her voice was plaintive and soft, and there was a look of real sympathy in her eyes. Phineas almost felt that if they two had been quite alone he could have told her everything, and have wept at her feet.

"Yes," he said, "it is so."

"I never doubted it when you had declared it. May I venture to say that I wish it had been otherwise?"

"It is too late now, Madame Goesler. A man of course is a fool to show that he has any feelings in such a matter. The fact is, I heard it just before I came here, and had made up my mind to send you an excuse. I wish I had now."

"Do not say that, Mr. Finn."

"I have made such an ass of myself."

"In my estimation you have done yourself honour. But if I may venture to give you counsel, do not speak of this affair again as though you had been personally concerned in it. In the world now-a-days the only thing disgraceful is to admit a failure."

"And I have failed."

"But you need not admit it, Mr. Finn. I know I ought not to say as much to you."

"I, rather, am deeply indebted to you. I will go now, Madame Goesler, as I do not wish to leave the house with Lord Fawn."

"But you will come and see me soon." Then Phineas promised that he would come soon; and felt as he made the promise that he would have an opportunity of talking over his love with his new friend at any rate without fresh shame as to his failure.

Laurence Fitzgibbon went away with Phineas, and Mr. Bonteen, having sent his wife away by herself, walked off towards the clubs with Lord Fawn. He was very anxious to have a few words with Lord Fawn. Lord Fawn had evidently been annoyed by Phineas, and Mr. Bonteen did not at all love the young Under-Secretary. "That fellow has become the most consummate puppy I ever met," said he, as he linked himself on to the lord, "Monk, and one or two others among them, have contrived to spoil him altogether."

"I don't believe a word of what he said about Lord Chiltern," said Lord Fawn.

"About his marriage with Miss Effingham?"

"It would be such an abominable shame to sacrifice the girl," said Lord Fawn. "Only think of it. Everything is gone. The man is a drunkard, and I don't believe he is any more reconciled to his father than you are. Lady Laura Kennedy must have had some object in saying so."

"Perhaps an invention of Finn's altogether," said Mr. Bonteen. "Those Irish fellows are just the men for that kind of thing."

"A man, you know, so violent that nobody can hold him," said Lord Fawn, thinking of Chiltern.

"And so absurdly conceited," said Mr. Bonteen, thinking of Phineas.

"A man who has never done anything, with all his advantages in the world,—and never will."

"He won't hold his place long," said Mr. Bonteen.

"Whom do you mean?"

"Phineas Finn."

"Oh, Mr. Finn. I was talking of Lord Chiltern. I believe Finn to be a very good sort of a fellow, and he is undoubtedly clever. They say Cantrip likes him amazingly. He'll do very well. But I don't believe a word of this about Lord Chiltern." Then Mr. Bonteen felt himself to be snubbed, and soon afterwards left Lord Fawn alone.

CHAPTER LIV
Consolation

On the day following Madame Goesler's dinner party, Phineas, though he was early at his office, was not able to do much work, still feeling that as regarded the realities of the world, his back was broken. He might no doubt go on learning, and, after a time, might be able to exert himself in a perhaps useful, but altogether uninteresting kind of way, doing his work simply because it was there to be done,—as the carter or the tailor does his;—and from the same cause, knowing that a man must have bread to live. But as for ambition, and the idea of doing good, and the love of work for work's sake,—as for the elastic springs of delicious and beneficent labour,—all that was over for him. He would have worked from day till night, and from night till day, and from month till month throughout the year to have secured for Violet Effingham the assurance that her husband's position was worthy of her own. But now he had no motive for such work as this. As long as he took the public pay, he would earn it; and that was all.

On the next day things were a little better with him. He received a note in the morning from Lord Cantrip saying that they two were to see the Prime Minister that evening, in order that the whole question of the railway to the Rocky Mountains might be understood, and Phineas was driven to his work. Before the time of the meeting came he had once more lost his own identity in great ideas of colonial welfare, and had planned and peopled a mighty region on the Red River, which should have no sympathy with American democracy. When he waited upon Mr. Gresham in the afternoon he said nothing about the mighty region; indeed, he left it to Lord Cantrip to explain most of the proposed arrangements,—speaking only a word or two here and there as occasion required. But he was aware that he had so far recovered as to be able to save himself from losing ground during the interview.

"He's about the first Irishman we've had that has been worth his salt," said Mr. Gresham to his colleague afterwards.

"That other Irishman was a terrible fellow," said Lord Cantrip, shaking his head.

On the fourth day after his sorrow had befallen him, Phineas went again to the cottage in Park Lane. And in order that he might not be balked in his search for sympathy he wrote a line to Madame Goesler to ask if she would be at home. "I will be at home from five to six,—and alone.—M. M. G." That was the answer from Marie Max Goesler, and Phineas was of course at the cottage a few minutes after five. It is not, I think, surprising that a man when he wants sympathy in such a calamity as that which had now befallen Phineas Finn, should seek it from a woman. Women sympathise most effectually with men, as men do with women. But it is, perhaps, a little odd that a man when he wants consolation because his heart has been broken, always likes to receive it from a pretty woman. One would be disposed to think that at such a moment he would be profoundly indifferent to such a matter, that no delight could come to him from female beauty, and that all he would want would be the softness of a simply sympathetic soul. But he generally wants a soft hand as well, and an eye that can be bright behind the mutual tear, and lips that shall be young and fresh as they express their concern for his sorrow. All these things were added to Phineas when he went to Madame Goesler in his grief.

"I am so glad to see you," said Madame Max.

"You are very good-natured to let me come."

"No;—but it is so good of you to trust me. But I was sure you would come after what took place the other night. I saw that you were pained, and I was so sorry for it."

"I made such a fool of myself."

"Not at all. And I thought that you were right to tell them when the question had been asked. If the thing was not to be kept a secret, it was better to speak it out. You will get over it quicker in that way than in any other. I have never seen the young lord, myself."

"Oh, there is nothing amiss about him. As to what Lord Fawn said, the half of it is simply exaggeration, and the other half is misunderstood."

"In this country it is so much to be a lord," said Madame Goesler.

Phineas thought a moment of that matter before he replied. All the Standish family had been very good to him, and Violet Effingham had been very good. It was not the fault of any of them that he was now wretched and back-broken. He had meditated much on this, and had resolved that he would not even think evil of them. "I do not in my heart believe that that has had anything to do with it," he said.

"But it has, my friend,—always. I do not know your Violet Effingham."

"She is not mine."

"Well;—I do not know this Violet that is not yours. I have met her, and did not specially admire her. But then the tastes of men and women about beauty are never the same. But I know she is one that always lives with lords and countesses. A girl who always lived with countesses feels it to be hard to settle down as a plain Mistress."

"She has had plenty of choice among all sorts of men. It was not the title. She would not have accepted Chiltern unless she had—. But what is the use of talking of it?"

"They had known each other long?"

"Oh, yes,—as children. And the Earl desired it of all things."

"Ah;—then he arranged it."

"Not exactly. Nobody could arrange anything for Chiltern,—nor, as far as that goes, for Miss Effingham. They arranged it themselves, I fancy."

"You had asked her?"

"Yes;—twice. And she had refused him more than twice. I have nothing for which to blame her; but yet I had thought,—I had thought—"

"She is a jilt then?"

"No;—I will not let you say that of her. She is no jilt. But I think she has been strangely ignorant of her own mind. What is the use of talking of it, Madame Goesler?"

"None;—only sometimes it is better to speak a word, than to keep one's sorrow to oneself."

"So it is;—and there is not one in the world to whom I can speak such a word, except yourself. Is not that odd? I have sisters, but they have never heard of Miss Effingham, and would be quite indifferent."

"Perhaps they have some other favourites."

"Ah;—well. That does not matter, And my best friend here in London is Lord Chiltern's own sister."

"She knew of your attachment?"

"Oh, yes."

"And she told you of Miss Effingham's engagement. Was she glad of it?"

"She has always desired the marriage. And yet I think she would have been satisfied had it been otherwise. But of course her heart must be with her brother. I need not have troubled myself to go to Blankenberg after all."

"It was for the best, perhaps. Everybody says you behaved so well."

"I could not but go, as things were then."

"What if you had—shot him?"

"There would have been an end of everything. She would never have seen me after that. Indeed I should have shot myself next, feeling that there was nothing else left for me to do."

"Ah;—you English are so peculiar. But I suppose it is best not to shoot a man. And, Mr. Finn, there are other ladies in the world prettier than Miss Violet Effingham. No;—of course you will not admit that now. Just at this moment, and for a month or two, she is peerless, and you will feel yourself to be of all men the most unfortunate. But you have the ball at your feet. I know no one so young who has got the ball at his feet so well. I call it nothing to have the ball at your feet if you are born with it there. It is so easy to be a lord if your father is one before you,—and so easy to marry a pretty girl if you can make her a countess. But to make yourself a lord, or to be as good as a lord, when nothing has been born to you,—that I call very much. And there are women, and pretty women too, Mr. Finn, who have spirit enough to understand this, and to think that the man, after all, is more important than the lord." Then she sang the old well-worn verse of the Scotch song with wonderful spirit, and with a clearness of voice and knowledge of music for which he had hitherto never given her credit.

"A prince can mak' a belted knight,
A marquis, duke, and a' that;
But an honest man's aboon his might,
Guid faith he mauna fa' that."

"I did not know that you sung, Madame Goesler."

"Only now and then when something specially requires it. And I am very fond of Scotch songs. I will sing to you now if you like it." Then she sang the whole song,—"A man's a man for a' that," she said as she finished. "Even though he cannot get the special bit of painted Eve's flesh for which his heart has had a craving." Then she sang again:—

"There are maidens in Scotland more lovely by far,
Who would gladly be bride to the young Lochinvar."

"But young Lochinvar got his bride," said Phineas.

"Take the spirit of the lines, Mr. Finn, which is true; and not the tale as it is told, which is probably false. I often think that Jock of Hazledean, and young Lochinvar too, probably lived to repent their bargains. We will hope that Lord Chiltern may not do so."

"I am sure he never will."

"That is all right. And as for you, do you for a while think of your politics, and your speeches, and your colonies, rather than of your love. You are at home there, and no Lord Chiltern can rob you of your success. And if you are down in the mouth, come to me, and I will sing you a Scotch song. And, look you, the next time I ask you to dinner I will promise you that Mrs. Bonteen shall not be here. Good-bye." She gave him her hand, which was very soft, and left it for a moment in his, and he was consoled.

Madame Goesler, when she was alone, threw herself on to her chair and began to think of things. In these days she would often ask herself what in truth was the object of her ambition, and the aim of her life. Now at this moment she had in her hand a note from the Duke of Omnium. The Duke had allowed himself to say something about a photograph, which had justified her in writing to him,—or which she had taken for such justification. And the Duke had replied. "He would not," he said, "lose the opportunity of waiting upon her in person which the presentation of the little gift might afford him." It would be a great success to have the Duke of Omnium at her house,—but to what would the success reach? What was her definite object,—or had she any? In what way could she make herself happy? She could not say that she was happy yet. The hours with her were too long and the days too many.

The Duke of Omnium should come,—if he would. And she was quite resolved as to this,—that if the Duke did come she would not be afraid of him. Heavens and earth! What would be the feelings of such a woman as her, were the world to greet her some fine morning as Duchess of Omnium! Then she made up her mind very resolutely on one subject. Should the Duke give her any opportunity she would take a very short time in letting him know what was the extent of her ambition.

CHAPTER LV
Lord Chiltern at Saulsby

Lord Chiltern did exactly as he said he would do. He wrote to his father as he passed through Carlisle, and at once went on to his hunting at Willingford. But his letter was very stiff and ungainly, and it may be doubted whether Miss Effingham was not wrong in refusing the offer which he had made to her as to the dictation of it. He began his letter, "My Lord," and did not much improve the style as he went on with it. The reader may as well see the whole letter;—

Railway Hotel, Carlisle,
December 27, 186—.

My Lord,

I am now on my way from Loughlinter to London, and write this letter to you in compliance with a promise made by me to my sister and to Miss Effingham. I have asked Violet to be my wife, and she has accepted me, and they think that you will be pleased to hear that this has been done. I shall be, of course, obliged, if you will instruct Mr. Edwards to let me know what you would propose to do in regard to settlements. Laura thinks that you will wish to see both Violet and myself at Saulsby. For myself, I can only say that, should you desire me to come, I will do so on receiving your assurance that I shall be treated neither with fatted calves nor with reproaches. I am not aware that I have deserved either.

I am, my lord, yours affect.,

Chiltern.

P.S.—My address will be "The Bull, Willingford."

That last word, in which he half-declared himself to be joined in affectionate relations to his father, caused him a world of trouble. But he could find no term for expressing, without a circumlocution which was disagreeable to him, exactly that position of feeling towards his father which really belonged to him. He would have written "yours with affection," or "yours with deadly enmity," or "yours with respect," or "yours with most profound indifference," exactly in accordance with the state of his father's mind, if he had only known what was that state. He was afraid of going beyond his father in any offer of reconciliation, and was firmly fixed in his resolution that he would never be either repentant or submissive in regard to the past. If his father had wishes for the future, he would comply with them if he could do so without unreasonable inconvenience, but he would not give way a single point as to things done and gone. If his father should choose to make any reference to them, his father must prepare for battle.

The Earl was of course disgusted by the pertinacious obstinacy of his son's letter, and for an hour or two swore to himself that he would not answer it. But it is natural that the father should yearn for the son, while the son's feeling for the father is of a very much weaker nature. Here, at any rate, was that engagement made which he had ever desired. And his son had made a step, though it was so very unsatisfactory a step, towards reconciliation. When the old man read the letter a second time, he skipped that reference to fatted calves which had been so peculiarly distasteful to him, and before the evening had passed he had answered his son as follows:—

Saulsby, December 29, 186—.

My dear Chiltern,

I have received your letter, and am truly delighted to hear that dear Violet has accepted you as her husband. Her fortune will be very material to you, but she herself is better than any fortune. You have long known my opinion of her. I shall be proud to welcome her as a daughter to my house.

I shall of course write to her immediately, and will endeavour to settle some early day for her coming here. When I have done so, I will write to you again, and can only say that I will endeavour to make Saulsby comfortable to you.

Your affectionate father,

Brentford.

Richards, the groom, is still here. You had perhaps better write to him direct about your horses.

By the middle of February arrangements had all been made, and Violet met her lover at his father's house. She in the meantime had been with her aunt, and had undergone a good deal of mild unceasing persecution. "My dear Violet," said her aunt to her on her arrival at Baddingham, speaking with a solemnity that ought to have been terrible to the young lady, "I do not know what to say to you."

"Say 'how d'you do?' aunt," said Violet.

"I mean about this engagement," said Lady Baldock, with an increase of awe-inspiring severity in her voice.

"Say nothing about it at all, if you don't like it," said Violet.

"How can I say nothing about it? How can I be silent? Or how am I to congratulate you?"

"The least said, perhaps, the soonest mended," and Violet smiled as she spoke.

"That is very well, and if I had no duty to perform, I would be silent. But, Violet, you have been left in my charge. If I see you shipwrecked in life, I shall ever tell myself that the fault has been partly mine."

"Nay, aunt, that will be quite unnecessary. I will always admit that you did everything in your power to—to—to—make me run straight, as the sporting men say."

"Sporting men! Oh, Violet."

"And you know, aunt, I still hope that I shall be found to have kept on the right side of the posts. You will find that poor Lord Chiltern is not so black as he is painted."

"But why take anybody that is black at all?"

"I like a little shade in the picture, aunt."

"Look at Lord Fawn."

"I have looked at him."

"A young nobleman beginning a career of useful official life, that will end in—; there is no knowing what it may end in."

"I daresay not;—but it never could have begun or ended in my being Lady Fawn."

"And Mr. Appledom!"

"Poor Mr. Appledom. I do like Mr. Appledom. But, you see, aunt, I like Lord Chiltern so much better. A young woman will go by her feelings."

"And yet you refused him a dozen times."

"I never counted the times, aunt; but not quite so many as that."

The same thing was repeated over and over again during the month that Miss Effingham remained at Baddingham, but Lady Baldock had no power of interfering, and Violet bore her persecution bravely. Her future husband was generally spoken of as "that violent young man," and hints were thrown out as to the personal injuries to which his wife might be possibly subjected. But the threatened bride only laughed, and spoke of these coming dangers as part of the general lot of married women. "I daresay, if the truth were known, my uncle Baldock did not always keep his temper," she once said. Now, the truth was, as Violet well knew, that "my uncle Baldock" had been dumb as a sheep before the shearers in the hands of his wife, and had never been known to do anything improper by those who had been most intimate with him even in his earlier days. "Your uncle Baldock, miss," said the outraged aunt, "was a nobleman as different in his manner of life from Lord Chiltern as chalk from cheese." "But then comes the question, which is the cheese?" said Violet. Lady Baldock would not argue the question any further, but stalked out of the room.

Lady Laura Kennedy met them at Saulsby, having had something of a battle with her husband before she left her home to do so. When she told him of her desire to assist at this reconciliation between her father and brother, he replied by pointing out that her first duty was at Loughlinter, and before the interview was ended had come to express an opinion that that duty was very much neglected. She in the meantime had declared that she would go to Saulsby, or that she would explain to her father that she was forbidden by her husband to do so. "And I also forbid any such communication," said Mr. Kennedy. In answer to which, Lady Laura told him that there were some marital commands which she should not consider it to be her duty to obey. When matters had come to this pass, it may be conceived that both Mr. Kennedy and his wife were very unhappy. She had almost resolved that she would take steps to enable her to live apart from her husband; and he had begun to consider what course he would pursue if such steps were taken. The wife was subject to her husband by the laws both of God and man; and Mr. Kennedy was one who thought much of such laws. In the meantime, Lady Laura carried her point and went to Saulsby, leaving her husband to go up to London and begin the session by himself.

Lady Laura and Violet were both at Saulsby before Lord Chiltern arrived, and many were the consultations which were held between them as to the best mode in which things might be arranged. Violet was of opinion that there had better be no arrangement, that Lord Chiltern should be allowed to come in and take his father's hand, and sit down to dinner,—and that so things should fall into their places. Lady Laura was rather in favour of some scene. But the interview had taken place before either of them were able to say a word. Lord Chiltern, on his arrival, had gone immediately to his father, taking the Earl very much by surprise, and had come off best in the encounter.

"My lord," said he, walking up to his father with his hand out, "I am very glad to come back to Saulsby." He had written to his sister to say that he would be at Saulsby on that day, but had named no hour. He now appeared between ten and eleven in the morning, and his father had as yet made no preparation for him,—had arranged no appropriate words. He had walked in at the front door, and had asked for the Earl. The Earl was in his own morning-room,—a gloomy room, full of dark books and darker furniture, and thither Lord Chiltern had at once gone. The two women still were sitting together over the fire in the breakfast-room, and knew nothing of his arrival.

"Oswald!" said his father, "I hardly expected you so early."

"I have come early. I came across country, and slept at Birmingham. I suppose Violet is here."

"Yes, she is here,—and Laura. They will be very glad to see you. So am I." And the father took the son's hand for the second time.

"Thank you, sir," said Lord Chiltern, looking his father full in the face.

"I have been very much pleased by this engagement," continued the Earl.

"What do you think I must be, then?" said the son, laughing. "I have been at it, you know, off and on, ever so many years; and have sometimes thought I was quite a fool not to get it out of my head. But I couldn't get it out of my head. And now she talks as though it were she who had been in love with me all the time!"

"Perhaps she was," said the father.

"I don't believe it in the least. She may be a little so now."

"I hope you mean that she always shall be so."

"I shan't be the worst husband in the world, I hope; and I am quite sure I shan't be the best. I will go and see her now. I suppose I shall find her somewhere in the house. I thought it best to see you first."

"Stop half a moment, Oswald," said the Earl. And then Lord Brentford did make something of a shambling speech, in which he expressed a hope that they two might for the future live together on friendly terms, forgetting the past. He ought to have been prepared for the occasion, and the speech was poor and shambling. But I think that it was more useful than it might have been, had it been uttered roundly and with that paternal and almost majestic effect which he would have achieved had he been thoroughly prepared. But the roundness and the majesty would have gone against the grain with his son, and there would have been a danger of some outbreak. As it was, Lord Chiltern smiled, and muttered some word about things being "all right," and then made his way out of the room. "That's a great deal better than I had hoped," he said to himself; "and it has all come from my going in without being announced." But there was still a fear upon him that his father even yet might prepare a speech, and speak it, to the great peril of their mutual comfort.

His meeting with Violet was of course pleasant enough. Now that she had succumbed, and had told herself and had told him that she loved him, she did not scruple to be as generous as a maiden should be who has acknowledged herself to be conquered, and has rendered herself to the conqueror. She would walk with him and ride with him, and take a lively interest in the performances of all his horses, and listen to hunting stories as long as he chose to tell them. In all this, she was so good and so loving that Lady Laura was more than once tempted to throw in her teeth her old, often-repeated assertions, that she was not prone to be in love,—that it was not her nature to feel any ardent affection for a man, and that, therefore, she would probably remain unmarried. "You begrudge me my little bits of pleasure," Violet said, in answer to one such attack. "No;—but it is so odd to see you, of all women, become so love-lorn," "I am not love-lorn," said Violet, "but I like the freedom of telling him everything and of hearing everything from him, and of having him for my own best friend. He might go away for twelve months, and I should not be unhappy, believing, as I do, that he would be true to me." All of which set Lady Laura thinking whether her friend had not been wiser than she had been. She had never known anything of that sort of friendship with her husband which already seemed to be quite established between these two.

In her misery one day Lady Laura told the whole story of her own unhappiness to her brother, saying nothing of Phineas Finn,—thinking nothing of him as she told her story, but speaking more strongly perhaps than she should have done, of the terrible dreariness of her life at Loughlinter, and of her inability to induce her husband to alter it for her sake.

"Do you mean that he,—ill-treats you?" said the brother, with a scowl on his face which seemed to indicate that he would like no task better than that of resenting such ill-treatment.

"He does not beat me, if you mean that."

"Is he cruel to you? Does he use harsh language?"

"He never said a word in his life either to me or, as I believe, to any other human being, that he would think himself bound to regret."

"What is it then?"

"He simply chooses to have his own way, and his way cannot be my way. He is hard, and dry, and just, and dispassionate, and he wishes me to be the same. That is all."

"I tell you fairly, Laura, as far as I am concerned, I never could speak to him. He is antipathetic to me. But then I am not his wife."

"I am;—and I suppose I must bear it."

"Have you spoken to my father?"

"No."

"Or to Violet?"

"Yes."

"And what does she say?"

"What can she say? She has nothing to say. Nor have you. Nor, if I am driven to leave him, can I make the world understand why I do so. To be simply miserable, as I am, is nothing to the world."

"I could never understand why you married him."

"Do not be cruel to me, Oswald."

"Cruel! I will stick by you in any way that you wish. If you think well of it, I will go off to Loughlinter to-morrow, and tell him that you will never return to him. And if you are not safe from him here at Saulsby, you shall go abroad with us. I am sure Violet would not object. I will not be cruel to you."

But in truth neither of Lady Laura's councillors was able to give her advice that could serve her. She felt that she could not leave her husband without other cause than now existed, although she felt, also, that to go back to him was to go back to utter wretchedness. And when she saw Violet and her brother together there came to her dreams of what might have been her own happiness had she kept herself free from those terrible bonds in which she was now held a prisoner. She could not get out of her heart the remembrance of that young man who would have been her lover, if she would have let him,—of whose love for herself she had been aware before she had handed herself over as a bale of goods to her unloved, unloving husband. She had married Mr. Kennedy because she was afraid that otherwise she might find herself forced to own that she loved that other man who was then a nobody;—almost nobody. It was not Mr. Kennedy's money that had bought her. This woman in regard to money had shown herself to be as generous as the sun. But in marrying Mr. Kennedy she had maintained herself in her high position, among the first of her own people,—among the first socially and among the first politically. But had she married Phineas,—had she become Lady Laura Finn,—there would have been a great descent. She could not have entertained the leading men of her party. She would not have been on a level with the wives and daughters of Cabinet Ministers. She might, indeed, have remained unmarried! But she knew that had she done so,—had she so resolved,—that which she called her fancy would have been too strong for her. She would not have remained unmarried. At that time it was her fate to be either Lady Laura Kennedy or Lady Laura Finn. And she had chosen to be Lady Laura Kennedy. To neither Violet Effingham nor to her brother could she tell one half of the sorrow which afflicted her.

"I shall go back to Loughlinter," she said to her brother.

"Do not, unless you wish it," he answered.

"I do not wish it. But I shall do it. Mr. Kennedy is in London now, and has been there since Parliament met, but he will be in Scotland again in March, and I will go and meet him there. I told him that I would do so when I left."

"But you will go up to London?"

"I suppose so. I must do as he tells me, of course. What I mean is, I will try it for another year."

"If it does not succeed, come to us."

"I cannot say what I will do. I would die if I knew how. Never be a tyrant, Oswald; or at any rate, not a cold tyrant. And remember this, there is no tyranny to a woman like telling her of her duty. Talk of beating a woman! Beating might often be a mercy."

Lord Chiltern remained ten days at Saulsby, and at last did not get away without a few unpleasant words with his father,—or without a few words that were almost unpleasant with his mistress. On his first arrival he had told his sister that he should go on a certain day, and some intimation to this effect had probably been conveyed to the Earl. But when his son told him one evening that the post-chaise had been ordered for seven o'clock the next morning, he felt that his son was ungracious and abrupt. There were many things still to be said, and indeed there had been no speech of any account made at all as yet.

"That is very sudden," said the Earl.

"I thought Laura had told you."

"She has not told me a word lately. She may have said something before you came here. What is there to hurry you?"

"I thought ten days would be as long as you would care to have me here, and as I said that I would be back by the first, I would rather not change my plans."

"You are going to hunt?"

"Yes;—I shall hunt till the end of March."

"You might have hunted here, Oswald." But the son made no sign of changing his plans; and the father, seeing that he would not change them, became solemn and severe. There were a few words which he must say to his son,—something of a speech that he must make;—so he led the way into the room with the dark books and the dark furniture, and pointed to a great deep arm-chair for his son's accommodation. But as he did not sit down himself, neither did Lord Chiltern. Lord Chiltern understood very well how great is the advantage of a standing orator over a sitting recipient of his oratory, and that advantage he would not give to his father. "I had hoped to have an opportunity of saying a few words to you about the future," said the Earl.

"I think we shall be married in July," said Lord Chiltern.

"So I have heard;—but after that. Now I do not want to interfere, Oswald, and of course the less so, because Violet's money will to a great degree restore the inroads which have been made upon the property."

"It will more than restore them altogether."

"Not if her estate be settled on a second son, Oswald, and I hear from Lady Baldock that that is the wish of her relations."

"She shall have her own way,—as she ought. What that way is I do not know. I have not even asked about it. She asked me, and I told her to speak to you."

"Of course I should wish it to go with the family property. Of course that would be best."

"She shall have her own way,—as far as I am concerned."

"But it is not about that, Oswald, that I would speak. What are your plans of life when you are married?"

"Plans of life?"

"Yes;—plans of life. I suppose you have some plans. I suppose you mean to apply yourself to some useful occupation?"

"I don't know really, sir, that I am of much use for any purpose." Lord Chiltern laughed as he said this, but did not laugh pleasantly.

"You would not be a drone in the hive always?"

"As far as I can see, sir, we who call ourselves lords generally are drones."

"I deny it," said the Earl, becoming quite energetic as he defended his order. "I deny it utterly. I know no class of men who do work more useful or more honest. Am I a drone? Have I been so from my youth upwards? I have always worked, either in the one House or in the other, and those of my fellows with whom I have been most intimate have worked also. The same career is open to you."

"You mean politics?"

"Of course I mean politics."

"I don't care for politics. I see no difference in parties."

"But you should care for politics, and you should see a difference in parties. It is your duty to do so. My wish is that you should go into Parliament."

"I can't do that, sir."

"And why not?"

"In the first place, sir, you have not got a seat to offer me. You have managed matters among you in such a way that poor little Loughton has been swallowed up. If I were to canvass the electors of Smotherem, I don't think that many would look very sweet on me."

"There is the county, Oswald."

"And whom am I to turn out? I should spend four or five thousand pounds, and have nothing but vexation in return for it. I had rather not begin that game, and indeed I am too old for Parliament. I did not take it up early enough to believe in it."

All this made the Earl very angry, and from these things they went on to worse things. When questioned again as to the future, Lord Chiltern scowled, and at last declared that it was his idea to live abroad in the summer for his wife's recreation, and somewhere down in the shires during the winter for his own. He would admit of no purpose higher than recreation, and when his father again talked to him of a nobleman's duty, he said that he knew of no other special duty than that of not exceeding his income. Then his father made a longer speech than before, and at the end of it Lord Chiltern simply wished him good night. "It's getting late, and I've promised to see Violet before I go to bed. Good-bye." Then he was off, and Lord Brentford was left there, standing with his back to the fire.

After that Lord Chiltern had a discussion with Violet, which lasted nearly half the night; and during the discussion she told him more than once that he was wrong. "Such as I am you must take me, or leave me," he said, in anger. "Nay; there is no choice now," she answered. "I have taken you, and I will stick by you,—whether you are right or wrong. But when I think you wrong, I shall say so." He swore to her as he pressed her to his heart that she was the finest, grandest, sweetest woman that ever the world had produced. But still there was present on his palate, when he left her, the bitter taste of her reprimand.

CHAPTER LVI
What the People in Marylebone Thought

Phineas Finn, when the session began, was still hard at work upon his Canada bill, and in his work found some relief for his broken back. He went into the matter with all his energy, and before the debate came on, knew much more about the seven thousand inhabitants of some hundreds of thousands of square miles at the back of Canada, than he did of the people of London or of County Clare. And he found some consolation also in the good-nature of Madame Goesler, whose drawing-room was always open to him. He could talk freely now to Madame Goesler about Violet, and had even ventured to tell her that once, in old days, he had thought of loving Lady Laura Standish. He spoke of those days as being very old; and then he perhaps said some word to her about dear little Mary Flood Jones. I think that there was not much in his career of which he did not say something to Madame Goesler, and that he received from her a good deal of excellent advice and encouragement in the direction of his political ambition. "A man should work," she said,—"and you do work. A woman can only look on, and admire and long. What is there that I can do? I can learn to care for these Canadians, just because you care for them. If it was the beavers that you told me of, I should have to care for the beavers." Then Phineas of course told her that such sympathy from her was all and all to him. But the reader must not on this account suppose that he was untrue in his love to Violet Effingham. His back was altogether broken by his fall, and he was quite aware that such was the fact. Not as yet, at least, had come to him any remotest idea that a cure was possible.

Early in March he heard that Lady Laura was up in town, and of course he was bound to go to her. The information was given to him by Mr. Kennedy himself, who told him that he had been to Scotland to fetch her. In these days there was an acknowledged friendship between these two, but there was no intimacy. Indeed, Mr. Kennedy was a man who was hardly intimate with any other man. With Phineas he now and then exchanged a few words in the lobby of the House, and when they chanced to meet each other, they met as friends. Mr. Kennedy had no strong wish to see again in his house the man respecting whom he had ventured to caution his wife; but he was thoughtful; and thinking over it all, he found it better to ask him there. No one must know that there was any reason why Phineas should not come to his house; especially as all the world knew that Phineas had protected him from the garrotters. "Lady Laura is in town now," he said; "you must go and see her before long." Phineas of course promised that he would go.

In these days Phineas was beginning to be aware that he had enemies,—though he could not understand why anybody should be his enemy now that Violet Effingham had decided against him. There was poor Laurence Fitzgibbon, indeed, whom he had superseded at the Colonial Office, but Laurence Fitzgibbon, to give merit where merit was due, felt no animosity against him at all. "You're welcome, me boy; you're welcome,—as far as yourself goes. But as for the party, bedad, it's rotten to the core, and won't stand another session. Mind, it's I who tell you so." And the poor idle Irishman, in so speaking, spoke the truth as well as he knew it. But the Ratlers and the Bonteens were Finn's bitter foes, and did not scruple to let him know that such was the case. Barrington Erle had scruples on the subject, and in a certain mildly apologetic way still spoke well of the young man, whom he had himself first introduced into political life only four years since;—but there was no earnestness or cordiality in Barrington Erle's manner, and Phineas knew that his first staunch friend could no longer be regarded as a pillar of support. But there was a set of men, quite as influential,—so Phineas thought,—as the busy politicians of the club, who were very friendly to him. These were men, generally of high position, of steady character,—hard workers,—who thought quite as much of what a man did in his office as what he said in the House. Lords Cantrip, Thrift, and Fawn were of this class,—and they were all very courteous to Phineas. Envious men began to say of him that he cared little now for any one of the party who had not a handle to his name, and that he preferred to live with lords and lordlings. This was hard upon him, as the great political ambition of his life was to call Mr. Monk his friend; and he would sooner have acted with Mr. Monk than with any other man in the Cabinet. But though Mr. Monk had not deserted him, there had come to be little of late in common between the two. His life was becoming that of a parliamentary official rather than that of a politician;—whereas, though Mr. Monk was in office, his public life was purely political. Mr. Monk had great ideas of his own which he intended to hold, whether by holding them he might remain in office or be forced out of office; and he was indifferent as to the direction which things in this respect might take with him. But Phineas, who had achieved his declared object in getting into place, felt that he was almost constrained to adopt the views of others, let them be what they might. Men spoke to him, as though his parliamentary career were wholly at the disposal of the Government,—as though he were like a proxy in Mr. Gresham's pocket,—with this difference, that when directed to get up and speak on a subject he was bound to do so. This annoyed him, and he complained to Mr. Monk; but Mr. Monk only shrugged his shoulders and told him that he must make his choice. He soon discovered Mr. Monk's meaning. "If you choose to make Parliament a profession,—as you have chosen,—you can have no right even to think of independence. If the country finds you out when you are in Parliament, and then invites you to office, of course the thing is different. But the latter is a slow career, and probably would not have suited you." That was the meaning of what Mr. Monk said to him. After all, these official and parliamentary honours were greater when seen at a distance than he found them to be now that he possessed them. Mr. Low worked ten hours a day, and could rarely call a day his own; but, after all, with all this work, Mr. Low was less of a slave, and more independent, than was he, Phineas Finn, Under-Secretary of State, the friend of Cabinet Ministers, and Member of Parliament since his twenty-fifth year! He began to dislike the House, and to think it a bore to sit on the Treasury bench;—he, who a few years since had regarded Parliament as the British heaven on earth, and who, since he had been in Parliament, had looked at that bench with longing envious eyes. Laurence Fitzgibbon, who seemed to have as much to eat and drink as ever, and a bed also to lie on, could come and go in the House as he pleased, since his—resignation.

And there was a new trouble coming. The Reform Bill for England had passed; but now there was to be another Reform Bill for Ireland. Let them pass what bill they might, this would not render necessary a new Irish election till the entire House should be dissolved. But he feared that he would be called upon to vote for the abolition of his own borough,—and for other points almost equally distasteful to him. He knew that he would not be consulted,—but would be called upon to vote, and perhaps to speak; and was certain that if he did so, there would be war between him and his constituents. Lord Tulla had already communicated to him his ideas that, for certain excellent reasons, Loughshane ought to be spared. But this evil was, he hoped, a distant one. It was generally thought that, as the English Reform Bill had been passed last year, and as the Irish bill, if carried, could not be immediately operative, the doing of the thing might probably be postponed to the next session.

When he first saw Lady Laura he was struck by the great change in her look and manner. She seemed to him to be old and worn, and he judged her to be wretched,—as she was. She had written to him to say that she would be at her father's house on such and such a morning, and he had gone to her there. "It is of no use your coming to Grosvenor Place," she said. "I see nobody there, and the house is like a prison." Later in the interview she told him not to come and dine there, even though Mr. Kennedy should ask him.

"And why not?" he demanded.

"Because everything would be stiff, and cold, and uncomfortable. I suppose you do not wish to make your way into a lady's house if she asks you not." There was a sort of smile on her face as she said this, but he could perceive that it was a very bitter smile. "You can easily excuse yourself."

"Yes, I can excuse myself."

"Then do so. If you are particularly anxious to dine with Mr. Kennedy, you can easily do so at your club." In the tone of her voice, and the words she used, she hardly attempted to conceal her dislike of her husband.

"And now tell me about Miss Effingham," he said.

"There is nothing for me to tell."

"Yes there is;—much to tell. You need not spare me. I do not pretend to deny to you that I have been hit hard,—so hard, that I have been nearly knocked down; but it will not hurt me now to hear of it all. Did she always love him?"

"I cannot say. I think she did after her own fashion."

"I sometimes think women would be less cruel," he said, "if they knew how great is the anguish they can cause."

"Has she been cruel to you?"

"I have nothing to complain of. But if she loved Chiltern, why did she not tell him so at once? And why—"

"This is complaining, Mr. Finn."

"I will not complain. I would not even think of it, if I could help it. Are they to be married soon?"

"In July;—so they now say."

"And where will they live?"

"Ah! no one can tell. I do not think that they agree as yet as to that. But if she has a strong wish Oswald will yield to it. He was always generous."

"I would not even have had a wish,—except to have her with me."

There was a pause for a moment, and then Lady Laura answered him with a touch of scorn in her voice,—and with some scorn, too, in her eye:—"That is all very well, Mr. Finn; but the season will not be over before there is some one else."

"There you wrong me."

"They tell me that you are already at Madame Goesler's feet."

"Madame Goesler!"

"What matters who it is as long as she is young and pretty, and has the interest attached to her of something more than ordinary position? When men tell me of the cruelty of women, I think that no woman can be really cruel because no man is capable of suffering. A woman, if she is thrown aside, does suffer."

"Do you mean to tell me, then, that I am indifferent to Miss Effingham?" When he thus spoke, I wonder whether he had forgotten that he had ever declared to this very woman to whom he was speaking, a passion for herself.

"Psha!"

"It suits you, Lady Laura, to be harsh to me, but you are not speaking your thoughts."

Then she lost all control of herself, and poured out to him the real truth that was in her. "And whose thoughts did you speak when you and I were on the braes of Loughlinter? Am I wrong in saying that change is easy to you, or have I grown to be so old that you can talk to me as though those far-away follies ought to be forgotten? Was it so long ago? Talk of love! I tell you, sir, that your heart is one in which love can have no durable hold. Violet Effingham! There may be a dozen Violets after her, and you will be none the worse." Then she walked away from him to the window, and he stood still, dumb, on the spot that he had occupied. "You had better go now," she said, "and forget what has passed between us. I know that you are a gentleman, and that you will forget it." The strong idea of his mind when he heard all this was the injustice of her attack,—of the attack as coming from her, who had all but openly acknowledged that she had married a man whom she had not loved because it suited her to escape from a man whom she did love. She was reproaching him now for his fickleness in having ventured to set his heart upon another woman, when she herself had been so much worse than fickle,—so profoundly false! And yet he could not defend himself by accusing her. What would she have had of him? What would she have proposed to him, had he questioned her as to his future, when they were together on the braes of Loughlinter? Would she not have bid him to find some one else whom he could love? Would she then have suggested to him the propriety of nursing his love for herself,—for her who was about to become another man's wife,—for her after she should have become another man's wife? And yet because he had not done so, and because she had made herself wretched by marrying a man whom she did not love, she reproached him!

He could not tell her of all this, so he fell back for his defence on words which had passed between them since the day when they had met on the braes. "Lady Laura," he said, "it is only a month or two since you spoke to me as though you wished that Violet Effingham might be my wife."

"I never wished it. I never said that I wished it. There are moments in which we try to give a child any brick on the chimney top for which it may whimper." Then there was another silence which she was the first to break. "You had better go," she said. "I know that I have committed myself, and of course I would rather be alone."

"And what would you wish that I should do?"

"Do?" she said. "What you do can be nothing to me."

"Must we be strangers, you and I, because there was a time in which we were almost more than friends?"

"I have spoken nothing about myself, sir,—only as I have been drawn to do so by your pretence of being love-sick. You can do nothing for me,—nothing,—nothing. What is it possible that you should do for me? You are not my father, or my brother." It is not to be supposed that she wanted him to fall at her feet. It is to be supposed that had he done so her reproaches would have been hot and heavy on him; but yet it almost seemed to him as though he had no other alternative. No!—He was not her father or her brother;—nor could he be her husband. And at this very moment, as she knew, his heart was sore with love for another woman. And yet he hardly knew how not to throw himself at her feet, and swear, that he would return now and for ever to his old passion, hopeless, sinful, degraded as it would be.

"I wish it were possible for me to do something," he said, drawing near to her.

"There is nothing to be done," she said, clasping her hands together. "For me nothing. I have before me no escape, no hope, no prospect of relief, no place of consolation. You have everything before you. You complain of a wound! You have at least shown that such wounds with you are capable of cure. You cannot but feel that when I hear your wailings, I must be impatient. You had better leave me now, if you please."

"And are we to be no longer friends?" he asked.

"As far as friendship can go without intercourse, I shall always be your friend."

Then he went, and as he walked down to his office, so intent was he on that which had just passed that he hardly saw the people as he met them, or was aware of the streets through which his way led him. There had been something in the later words which Lady Laura had spoken that had made him feel almost unconsciously that the injustice of her reproaches was not so great as he had at first felt it to be, and that she had some cause for her scorn. If her case was such as she had so plainly described it, what was his plight as compared with hers? He had lost his Violet, and was in pain. There must be much of suffering before him. But though Violet were lost, the world was not all blank before his eyes. He had not told himself, even in his dreariest moments, that there was before him "no escape, no hope, no prospect of relief, no place of consolation." And then he began to think whether this must in truth be the case with Lady Laura. What if Mr. Kennedy were to die? What in such case as that would he do? In ten or perhaps in five years time might it not be possible for him to go through the ceremony of falling upon his knees, with stiffened joints indeed, but still with something left of the ardour of his old love, of his oldest love of all?

As he was thinking of this he was brought up short in his walk as he was entering the Green Park beneath the Duke's figure, by Laurence Fitzgibbon. "How dare you not be in your office at such an hour as this, Finn, me boy,—or, at least, not in the House,—or serving your masters after some fashion?" said the late Under-Secretary.

"So I am. I've been on a message to Marylebone, to find what the people there think about the Canadas."

"And what do they think about the Canadas in Marylebone?"

"Not one man in a thousand cares whether the Canadians prosper or fail to prosper. They care that Canada should not go to the States, because,—though they don't love the Canadians, they do hate the Americans. That's about the feeling in Marylebone,—and it's astonishing how like the Maryleboners are to the rest of the world."

"Dear me, what a fellow you are for an Under-Secretary! You've heard the news about little Violet."

"What news?"

"She has quarrelled with Chiltern, you know."

"Who says so?"

"Never mind who says so, but they tell me it's true. Take an old friend's advice, and strike while the iron's hot."

Phineas did not believe what he had heard, but though he did not believe it, still the tidings set his heart beating. He would have believed it less perhaps had he known that Laurence had just received the news from Mrs. Bonteen.

CHAPTER LVII
The Top Brick of the Chimney

Madame Max Goesler was a lady who knew that in fighting the battles which fell to her lot, in arranging the social difficulties which she found in her way, in doing the work of the world which came to her share, very much more care was necessary,—and care too about things apparently trifling,—than was demanded by the affairs of people in general. And this was not the case so much on account of any special disadvantage under which she laboured, as because she was ambitious of doing the very uttermost with those advantages which she possessed. Her own birth had not been high, and that of her husband, we may perhaps say, had been very low. He had been old when she had married him, and she had had little power of making any progress till he had left her a widow. Then she found herself possessed of money, certainly; of wit,—as she believed; and of a something in her personal appearance which, as she plainly told herself, she might perhaps palm off upon the world as beauty. She was a woman who did not flatter herself, who did not strongly believe in herself, who could even bring herself to wonder that men and women in high position should condescend to notice such a one as her. With all her ambition, there was a something of genuine humility about her; and with all the hardness she had learned there was a touch of womanly softness which would sometimes obtrude itself upon her heart. When she found a woman really kind to her, she would be very kind in return. And though she prized wealth, and knew that her money was her only rock of strength, she could be lavish with it, as though it were dirt.

But she was highly ambitious, and she played her game with great skill and great caution. Her doors were not open to all callers;—were shut even to some who find but few doors closed against them;—were shut occasionally to those whom she most specially wished to see within them. She knew how to allure by denying, and to make the gift rich by delaying it. We are told by the Latin proverb that he who gives quickly gives twice; but I say that she who gives quickly seldom gives more than half. When in the early spring the Duke of Omnium first knocked at Madame Max Goesler's door, he was informed that she was not at home. The Duke felt very cross as he handed his card out from his dark green brougham,—on the panel of which there was no blazon to tell the owner's rank. He was very cross. She had told him that she was always at home between four and six on a Thursday. He had condescended to remember the information, and had acted upon it,—and now she was not at home! She was not at home, though he had come on a Thursday at the very hour she had named to him. Any duke would have been cross, but the Duke of Omnium was particularly cross. No;—he certainly would give himself no further trouble by going to the cottage in Park Lane. And yet Madame Max Goesler had been in her own drawing-room, while the Duke was handing out his card from the brougham below.

On the next morning there came to him a note from the cottage,—such a pretty note!—so penitent, so full of remorse,—and, which was better still, so laden with disappointment, that he forgave her.

My dear Duke,

I hardly know how to apologise to you, after having told you that I am always at home on Thursdays; and I was at home yesterday when you called. But I was unwell, and I had told the servant to deny me, not thinking how much I might be losing. Indeed, indeed, I would not have given way to a silly headache, had I thought that your Grace would have been here. I suppose that now I must not even hope for the photograph.

Yours penitently,

Marie M. G.

The note-paper was very pretty note-paper, hardly scented, and yet conveying a sense of something sweet, and the monogram was small and new, and fantastic without being grotesque, and the writing was of that sort which the Duke, having much experience, had learned to like,—and there was something in the signature which pleased him. So he wrote a reply,—

Dear Madame Max Goesler,

I will call again next Thursday, or, if prevented, will let you know.

Yours faithfully,

O.

When the green brougham drew up at the door of the cottage on the next Thursday, Madame Goesler was at home, and had no headache.

She was not at all penitent now. She had probably studied the subject, and had resolved that penitence was more alluring in a letter than when acted in person. She received her guest with perfect ease, and apologised for the injury done to him in the preceding week, with much self-complacency. "I was so sorry when I got your card," she said; "and yet I am so glad now that you were refused."

"If you were ill," said the Duke, "it was better."

"I was horribly ill, to tell the truth;—as pale as a death's head, and without a word to say for myself. I was fit to see no one."

"Then of course you were right."

"But it flashed upon me immediately that I had named a day, and that you had been kind enough to remember it. But I did not think you came to London till the March winds were over."

"The March winds blow everywhere in this wretched island, Madame Goesler, and there is no escaping them. Youth may prevail against them; but on me they are so potent that I think they will succeed in driving me out of my country. I doubt whether an old man should ever live in England if he can help it."

The Duke certainly was an old man, if a man turned of seventy be old;—and he was a man too who did not bear his years with hearty strength. He moved slowly, and turned his limbs, when he did turn them, as though the joints were stiff in their sockets. But there was nevertheless about him a dignity of demeanour, a majesty of person, and an upright carriage which did not leave an idea of old age as the first impress on the minds of those who encountered the Duke of Omnium. He was tall and moved without a stoop; and though he moved slowly, he had learned to seem so to do because it was the proper kind of movement for one so high up in the world as himself. And perhaps his tailor did something for him. He had not been long under Madame Max Goesler's eyes before she perceived that his tailor had done a good deal for him. When he alluded to his own age and to her youth, she said some pleasant little word as to the difference between oak-trees and currant-bushes; and by that time she was seated comfortably on her sofa, and the Duke was on a chair before her,—just as might have been any man who was not a Duke.

After a little time the photograph was brought forth from his Grace's pocket. That bringing out and giving of photographs, with the demand for counter photographs, is the most absurd practice of the day. "I don't think I look very nice, do I?" "Oh yes,—very nice, but a little too old; and certainly you haven't got those spots all over your forehead. These are the remarks which on such occasions are the most common. It may be said that to give a photograph or to take a photograph without the utterance of some words which would be felt by a bystander to be absurd, is almost an impossibility. At this moment there was no bystander, and therefore the Duke and the lady had no need for caution. Words were spoken that were very absurd. Madame Goesler protested that the Duke's photograph was more to her than the photographs of all the world beside; and the Duke declared that he would carry the lady's picture next to his heart,—I am afraid he said for ever and ever. Then he took her hand and pressed it, and was conscious that for a man over seventy years of age he did that kind of thing very well.

"You will come and dine with me, Duke?" she said, when he began to talk of going.

"I never dine out."

"That is just the reason you should dine with me. You shall meet nobody you do not wish to meet."

"I would so much rather see you in this way,—I would indeed. I do dine out occasionally, but it is at big formal parties, which I cannot escape without giving offence."

"And you cannot escape my little not formal party,—without giving offence." She looked into his face as she spoke, and he knew that she meant it. And he looked into hers, and thought that her eyes were brighter than any he was in the habit of seeing in these latter days. "Name your own day, Duke. Will a Sunday suit you?"

"If I must come—"

"You must come." As she spoke her eyes sparkled more and more, and her colour went and came, and she shook her curls till they emitted through the air the same soft feeling of a perfume that her note had produced. Then her foot peeped out from beneath the black and yellow drapery of her dress, and the Duke saw that it was perfect. And she put out her finger and touched his arm as she spoke. Her hand was very fair, and her fingers were bright with rich gems. To men such as the Duke, a hand, to be quite fair, should be bright with rich gems. "You must come," she said,—not imploring him now but commanding him.

"Then I will come," he answered, and a certain Sunday was fixed.

The arranging of the guests was a little difficulty, till Madame Goesler begged the Duke to bring with him Lady Glencora Palliser, his nephew's wife. This at last he agreed to do. As the wife of his nephew and heir, Lady Glencora was to the Duke all that a woman could be. She was everything that was proper as to her own conduct, and not obtrusive as to his. She did not bore him, and yet she was attentive. Although in her husband's house she was a fierce politician, in his house she was simply an attractive woman. "Ah; she is very clever," the Duke once said, "she adapts herself. If she were to go from any one place to any other, she would be at home in both." And the movement of his Grace's hand as he spoke seemed to indicate the widest possible sphere for travelling and the widest possible scope for adaptation. The dinner was arranged, and went off very pleasantly. Madame Goesler's eyes were not quite so bright as they were during that morning visit, nor did she touch her guest's arm in a manner so alluring. She was very quiet, allowing her guests to do most of the talking. But the dinner and the flowers and the wine were excellent, and the whole thing was so quiet that the Duke liked it. "And now you must come and dine with me," the Duke said as he took his leave. "A command to that effect will be one which I certainly shall not disobey," whispered Madame Goesler.

"I am afraid he is going to get fond of that woman." These words were spoken early on the following morning by Lady Glencora to her husband, Mr. Palliser.

"He is always getting fond of some woman, and he will to the end," said Mr. Palliser.

"But this Madame Max Goesler is very clever."

"So they tell me. I have generally thought that my uncle likes talking to a fool the best."

"Every man likes a clever woman the best," said Lady Glencora, "if the clever woman only knows how to use her cleverness."

"I'm sure I hope he'll be amused," said Mr. Palliser innocently. "A little amusement is all that he cares for now."

"Suppose you were told some day that he was going—to be married?" said Lady Glencora.

"My uncle married!"

"Why not he as well as another?"

"And to Madame Goesler?"

"If he be ever married it will be to some such woman."

"There is not a man in all England who thinks more of his own position than my uncle," said Mr. Palliser somewhat proudly,—almost with a touch of anger.

"That is all very well, Plantagenet, and true enough in a kind of way. But a child will sacrifice all that it has for the top brick of the chimney, and old men sometimes become children. You would not like to be told some morning that there was a little Lord Silverbridge in the world." Now the eldest son of the Duke of Omnium, when the Duke of Omnium had a son, was called the Earl of Silverbridge; and Mr. Palliser, when this question was asked him, became very pale. Mr. Palliser knew well how thoroughly the cunning of the serpent was joined to the purity of the dove in the person of his wife, and he was sure that there was cause for fear when she hinted at danger.

"Perhaps you had better keep your eye upon him," he said to his wife.

"And upon her," said Lady Glencora.

When Madame Goesler dined at the Duke's house in St. James's Square there was a large party, and Lady Glencora knew that there was no need for apprehension then. Indeed Madame Goesler was no more than any other guest, and the Duke hardly spoke to her. There was a Duchess there,—the Duchess of St. Bungay, and old Lady Hartletop, who was a dowager marchioness,—an old lady who pestered the Duke very sorely,—and Madame Max Goesler received her reward, and knew that she was receiving it, in being asked to meet these people. Would not all these names, including her own, be blazoned to the world in the columns of the next day's *Morning Post*? There was no absolute danger here, as Lady Glencora knew; and Lady Glencora, who was tolerant and begrudged nothing to Madame Max except the one thing, was quite willing to meet the lady at such a grand affair as this. But the Duke, even should he become ever so childish a child in his old age, still would have that plain green brougham at his command, and could go anywhere in that at any hour in the day. And then Madame Goesler was so manifestly a clever woman. A Duchess of Omnium might be said to fill,—in the estimation, at any rate, of English people,—the highest position in the world short of royalty. And the reader will remember that Lady Glencora intended to be a Duchess of Omnium herself,—unless some very unexpected event should intrude itself. She intended also that her little boy, her fair-haired, curly-pated, bold-faced little boy, should be Earl of Silverbridge when the sand of the old man should have run itself out. Heavens, what a blow would it be, should some little wizen-cheeked half-monkey baby, with black brows, and yellow skin, be brought forward and shown to her some day as the heir! What a blow to herself;—and what a blow to all England! "We can't prevent it if he chooses to do it," said her husband, who had his budget to bring forward that very night, and who in truth cared more for his budget than he did for his heirship at that moment. "But we must prevent it," said Lady Glencora. "If I stick to him by the tail of his coat, I'll prevent it." At the time when she thus spoke, the dark green brougham had been twice again brought up at the door in Park Lane.

And the brougham was standing there a third time. It was May now, the latter end of May, and the park opposite was beautiful with green things, and the air was soft and balmy, as it will be sometimes even in May, and the flowers in the balcony were full of perfume, and the charm of London,—what London can be to the rich,—was at its height. The Duke was sitting in Madame Goesler's drawing-room, at some distance from her, for she had retreated. The Duke had a habit of taking her hand, which she never would permit for above a few seconds. At such times she would show no anger, but would retreat.

"Marie," said the Duke, "you will go abroad when the summer is over." As an old man he had taken the privilege of calling her Marie, and she had not forbidden it.

Yes, probably; to Vienna. I have property in Vienna you know, which must be looked after.

"Do not mind Vienna this year. Come to Italy."

"What; in summer, Duke?"

"The lakes are charming in August. I have a villa on Como which is empty now, and I think I shall go there. If you do not know the Italian lakes, I shall be so happy to show them to you."

"I know them well, my lord. When I was young I was on the Maggiore almost alone. Some day I will tell you a history of what I was in those days."

"You shall tell it me there."

"No, my lord, I fear not. I have no villa there."

"Will you not accept the loan of mine? It shall be all your own while you use it."

"My own,—to deny the right of entrance to its owner?"

"If it so pleases you."

"It would not please me. It would so far from please me that I will never put myself in a position that might make it possible for me to require to do so. No, Duke; it behoves me to live in houses of my own. Women of whom more is known can afford to be your guests."

"Marie, I would have no other guest than you."

"It cannot be so, Duke."

"And why not?"

"Why not? Am I to be put to the blush by being made to answer such a question as that? Because the world would say that the Duke of Omnium had a new mistress, and that Madame Goesler was the woman. Do you think that I would be any man's mistress;—even yours? Or do you believe that for the sake of the softness of a summer evening on an Italian lake, I would give cause to the tongues of the women here to say that I was such a thing? You would have me lose all that I have gained by steady years of sober work for the sake of a week or two of dalliance such as that! No, Duke; not for your dukedom!"

How his Grace might have got through his difficulty had they been left alone, cannot be told. For at this moment the door was opened, and Lady Glencora Palliser was announced.

CHAPTER LVIII

"Come and see the country and judge for yourself," said Phineas.

"I should like nothing better," said Mr. Monk.

"It has often seemed to me that men in Parliament know less about Ireland than they do of the interior of Africa," said Phineas.

"It is seldom that we know anything accurately on any subject that we have not made matter of careful study," said Mr. Monk, "and very often do not do so even then. We are very apt to think that we men and women understand one another; but most probably you know nothing even of the modes of thought of the man who lives next door to you."

"I suppose not."

"There are general laws current in the world as to morality. 'Thou shalt not steal,' for instance. That has necessarily been current as a law through all nations. But the first man you meet in the street will have ideas about theft so different from yours, that, if you knew them as you know your own, you would say that this law and yours were not even founded on the same principle. It is compatible with this man's honesty to cheat you in a matter of horseflesh, with that man's in a traffic of railway shares, with that other man's as to a woman's fortune; with a fourth's anything may be done for a seat in Parliament, while the fifth man, who stands high among us, and who implores his God every Sunday to write that law on his heart, spends every hour of his daily toil in a system of fraud, and is regarded as a pattern of the national commerce!"

Mr. Monk and Phineas were dining together at Mr. Monk's house, and the elder politician of the two in this little speech had recurred to certain matters which had already been discussed between them. Mr. Monk was becoming somewhat sick of his place in the Cabinet, though he had not as yet whispered a word of his sickness to any living ears; and he had begun to pine for the lost freedom of a seat below the gangway. He had been discussing political honesty with Phineas, and hence had come the sermon of which I have ventured to reproduce the concluding denunciations.

Phineas was fond of such discussions and fond of holding them with Mr. Monk,—in this matter fluttering like a moth round a candle. He would not perceive that as he had made up his mind to be a servant of the public in Parliament, he must abandon all idea of independent action; and unless he did so he could be neither successful as regarded himself, or useful to the public whom he served. Could a man be honest in Parliament, and yet abandon all idea of independence? When he put such questions to Mr. Monk he did not get a direct answer. And indeed the question was never put directly. But the teaching which he received was ever of a nature to make him uneasy. It was always to this effect: "You have taken up the trade now, and seem to be fit for success in it. You had better give up thinking about its special honesty." And yet Mr. Monk would on an occasion preach to him such a sermon as that which he had just uttered! Perhaps there is no question more difficult to a man's mind than that of the expediency or inexpediency of scruples in political life. Whether would a candidate for office be more liable to rejection from a leader because he was known to be scrupulous, or because he was known to be the reverse?

"But putting aside the fourth commandment and all the theories, you will come to Ireland?" said Phineas.

"I shall be delighted."

"I don't live in a castle, you know."

"I thought everybody did live in a castle in Ireland," said Mr. Monk. "They seemed to do when I was there twenty years ago. But for myself, I prefer a cottage."

This trip to Ireland had been proposed in consequence of certain ideas respecting tenant-right which Mr. Monk was beginning to adopt, and as to which the minds of politicians were becoming moved. It had been all very well to put down Fenianism, and Ribandmen, and Repeal,— and everything that had been put down in Ireland in the way of rebellion for the last seventy-five years. England and Ireland had been apparently joined together by laws of nature so fixed, that even politicians liberal as was Mr. Monk,—liberal as was Mr. Turnbull,—could not trust themselves to think that disunion could be for the good of the Irish. They had taught themselves that it certainly could not be good for the English. But if it was incumbent on England to force upon Ireland the maintenance of the Union for her own sake, and for England's sake, because England could not afford independence established so close against her own ribs,—it was at any rate necessary to England's character that the bride thus bound in a compulsory wedlock should be endowed with all the best privileges that a wife can enjoy. Let her at least not be a kept mistress. Let it be bone of my bone and flesh of my flesh, if we are to live together in the married state. Between husband and wife a warm word now and then matters but little, if there be a thoroughly good understanding at bottom. But let there be that good understanding at bottom. What about this Protestant Church; and what about this tenant-right? Mr. Monk had been asking himself these questions for some time past. In regard to the Church, he had long made up his mind that the Establishment in Ireland was a crying sin. A man had married a woman whom he knew to be of a religion different from his own, and then insisted that his wife should say that she believed those things which he knew very well that she did not believe. But, as Mr. Monk well knew, the subject of the Protestant Endowments in Ireland was so difficult that it would require almost more than human wisdom to adjust it. It was one of those matters which almost seemed to require the interposition of some higher power,—the coming of some apparently chance event,—to clear away the evil; as a fire comes, and pestilential alleys are removed; as a famine comes, and men are driven from want and ignorance and dirt to seek new homes and new thoughts across the broad waters; as a war comes, and slavery is banished from the face of the earth. But in regard to tenant-right, to some arrangement by which a tenant in Ireland might be at least encouraged to lay out what little capital he might have in labour or money without being at once called upon to pay rent for that outlay which was his own, as well as for the land which was not his own,—Mr. Monk thought that it was possible that if a man would look hard enough he might perhaps be able to see his way as to that. He had spoken to two of his colleagues on the subject, the two men in the Cabinet whom he believed to be the most thoroughly honest in their ideas as public servants, the Duke and Mr. Gresham. There was so much to be done;—and then so little was known upon the subject! "I will endeavour to study it," said Mr. Monk. "If you can see your way, do;" said Mr. Gresham,—"but of course we cannot bind ourselves." "I should be glad to see it named in the Queen's speech at the beginning of the next session," said Mr. Monk. "That is a long way off as yet," said Mr. Gresham, laughing. "Who will be in then, and who will be out?" So the matter was disposed of at the time, but Mr. Monk did not abandon his idea. He rather felt himself the more bound to cling to it because he received so little encouragement. What was a seat in the Cabinet to him that he should on that account omit a duty? He had not taken up politics as a trade. He had sat far behind the Treasury bench or below the gangway for many a year, without owing any man a shilling,—and could afford to do so again.

But it was different with Phineas Finn, as Mr. Monk himself understood;—and, understanding this, he felt himself bound to caution his young friend. But it may be a question whether his cautions did not do more harm than good. "I shall be delighted," he said, "to go over with you in August, but I do not think that if I were you, I would take up this matter."

"And why not? You don't want to fight the battle singlehanded?"

"No; I desire no such glory, and would wish to have no better lieutenant than you. But you have a subject of which you are really fond, which you are beginning to understand, and in regard to which you can make yourself useful."

"You mean this Canada business?"

"Yes;—and that will grow to other matters as regards the colonies. There is nothing so important to a public man as that he should have his own subject;—the thing which he understands, and in respect of which he can make himself really useful."

"Then there comes a change."

"Yes;—and the man who has half learned how to have a ship built without waste is sent into opposition, and is then brought back to look after regiments, or perhaps has to take up that beautiful subject, a study of the career of India. But, nevertheless, if you have a subject, stick to it at any rate as long as it will stick to you."

"But," said Phineas, "if a man takes up his own subject, independent of the Government, no man can drive him from it."

"And how often does he do anything? Look at the annual motions which come forward in the hands of private men,—Maynooth and the ballot for instance. It is becoming more and more apparent every day that all legislation must be carried by the Government, and must be carried in obedience to the expressed wish of the people. The truest democracy that ever had a chance of living is that which we are now establishing in Great Britain."

"Then leave tenant-right to the people and the Cabinet. Why should you take it up?"

Mr. Monk paused a moment or two before he replied. "If I choose to run a-muck, there is no reason why you should follow me. I am old and you are young. I want nothing from politics as a profession, and you do. Moreover, you have a congenial subject where you are, and need not disturb yourself. For myself, I tell you, in confidence, that I cannot speak so comfortably of my own position."

"We will go and see, at any rate," said Phineas.

"Yes," said Mr. Monk, "we will go and see." And thus, in the month of May, it was settled between them that, as soon as the session should be over, and the incidental work of his office should allow Phineas to pack up and be off, they two should start together for Ireland. Phineas felt rather proud as he wrote to his father and asked permission to bring home with him a Cabinet Minister as a visitor. At this time the reputation of Phineas at Killaloe, as well in the minds of the Killaloeians generally as in those of the inhabitants of the paternal house, stood very high indeed. How could a father think that a son had done badly when before he was thirty years of age he was earning £2,000 a year? And how could a father not think well of a son who had absolutely paid back certain moneys into the paternal coffers? The moneys so repaid had not been much; but the repayment of any such money at Killaloe had been regarded as little short of miraculous. The news of Mr. Monk's coming flew about the town, about the county, about the diocese, and all people began to say all good things about the old doctor's only son. Mrs. Finn had long since been quite sure that a real black swan had been sent forth out of her nest. And the sisters Finn, for some time past, had felt in all social gatherings they stood quite on a different footing than formerly because of their brother. They were asked about in the county, and two of them had been staying only last Easter with the Molonys,—the Molonys of Poldoodie! How should a father and a mother and sisters not be grateful to such a son, to such a brother, to such a veritable black swan out of the nest! And as for dear little Mary Flood Jones, her eyes became suffused with tears as in her solitude she thought how much out of her reach this swan was flying. And yet she took joy in his swanhood, and swore that she would love him still;—that she would love him always. Might he bring home with him to Killaloe, Mr. Monk, the Cabinet Minister! Of course he might. When Mrs. Finn first heard of this august arrival, she felt as though she would like to expend herself in entertaining, though but an hour, the whole cabinet.

Phineas, during the spring, had, of course, met Mr. Kennedy frequently in and about the House, and had become aware that Lady Laura's husband, from time to time, made little overtures of civility to him,—taking him now and again by the button-hole, walking home with him as far as their joint paths allowed, and asking him once or twice to come and dine in Grosvenor Place. These little advances towards a repetition of the old friendship Phineas would have avoided altogether, had it been possible. The invitation to Mr. Kennedy's house he did refuse, feeling himself positively bound to do so by Lady Laura's command, let the consequences be what they might. When he did refuse, Mr. Kennedy would assume a look of displeasure and leave him, and Phineas would hope that the work was done. Then there would come another encounter, and the invitation would be repeated. At last, about the middle of May, there came another note. "Dear Finn, will you dine with us on Wednesday, the 28th? I give you a long notice, because you seem to have so many appointments. Yours always, Robert Kennedy." He had no alternative. He must refuse, even though double the notice had been given. He could only think that Mr. Kennedy was a very obtuse man and one who would not take a hint, and hope that he might succeed at last. So he wrote an answer, not intended to be conciliatory. "My dear Kennedy, I am sorry to say that I am engaged on the 28th. Yours always, Phineas Finn." At this period he did his best to keep out of Mr. Kennedy's way, and would be very cunning in his manœuvres that they should not be alone together. It was difficult, as they sat on the same bench in the House, and consequently saw each other almost every day of their lives. Nevertheless, he thought that with a little cunning he might prevail, especially as he was not unwilling to give so much of offence as might assist his own object. But when Mr. Kennedy called upon him at his office the day after he had written the above note, he had no means of escape.

"I am sorry you cannot come to us on the 28th," Mr. Kennedy said, as soon as he was seated.

Phineas was taken so much by surprise that all his cunning failed him. "Well, yes," said he; "I was very sorry;—very sorry indeed."

"It seems to me, Finn, that you have had some reason for avoiding me of late. I do not know that I have done anything to offend you."

"Nothing on earth," said Phineas.

"I am wrong, then, in supposing that anything beyond mere chance has prevented you from coming to my house?" Phineas felt that he was in a terrible difficulty, and he felt also that he was being rather ill-used in being thus cross-examined as to his reasons for not going to a gentleman's dinner. He thought that a man ought to be allowed to choose where he would go and where he would not go, and that questions such as these were very uncommon. Mr. Kennedy was sitting opposite to him, looking more grave and more sour than usual;—and now his own countenance also became a little solemn. It was impossible that he should use Lady Laura's name, and yet he must, in some way, let his persecuting friend know that no further invitation would be of any use;—that there was something beyond mere chance in his not going to Grosvenor Place. But how was he to do this? The difficulty was so great that he could not see his way out of it. So he sat silent with a solemn face. Mr. Kennedy then asked him another question, which made the difficulty ten times greater. "Has my wife asked you not to come to our house?"

It was necessary now that he should make a rush and get out of his trouble in some way. "To tell you the truth, Kennedy, I don't think she wants to see me there."

"That does not answer my question. Has she asked you not to come?"

"She said that which left on my mind an impression that she would sooner that I did not come."

"What did she say?"

"How can I answer such a question as that, Kennedy? Is it fair to ask it?"

"Quite fair,—I think."

"I think it quite unfair, and I must decline to answer it. I cannot imagine what you expect to gain by cross-questioning me in this way. Of course no man likes to go to a house if he does not believe that everybody there will make him welcome."

"You and Lady Laura used to be great friends."

"I hope we are not enemies now. But things will occur that cause friendships to grow cool."

"Have you quarrelled with her father?"

"With Lord Brentford?—no."

"Or with her brother,—since the duel I mean?"

"Upon my word and honour I cannot stand this, and I will not. I have not as yet quarrelled with anybody; but I must quarrel with you, if you go on in this way. It is quite unusual that a man should be put through his facings after such a fashion, and I must beg that there may be an end of it."

"Then I must ask Lady Laura."

"You can say what you like to your own wife of course. I cannot hinder you."

Upon that Mr. Kennedy formally shook hands with him, in token that there was no positive breach between them,—as two nations may still maintain their alliance, though they have made up their minds to hate each other, and thwart each other at every turn,—and took his leave. Phineas, as he sat at his window, looking out into the park, and thinking of what had passed, could not but reflect that, disagreeable as Mr. Kennedy had been to him, he would probably make himself much more disagreeable to his wife. And, for himself, he thought that he had got out of the scrape very well by the exhibition of a little mock anger.

CHAPTER LIX
The Earl's Wrath

The reader may remember that a rumour had been conveyed to Phineas,—a rumour indeed which reached him from a source which he regarded as very untrustworthy,—that Violet Effingham had quarrelled with her lover. He would probably have paid no attention to the rumour, beyond that which necessarily attached itself to any tidings as to a matter so full of interest to him, had it not been repeated to him in another quarter. "A bird has told me that your Violet Effingham has broken with her lover," Madame Goesler said to him one day. "What bird?" he asked. "Ah, that I cannot tell you. But this I will confess to you, that these birds which tell us news are seldom very credible,—and are often not very creditable, You must take a bird's word for what it may be worth. It is said that they have quarrelled. I daresay, if the truth were known, they are billing and cooing in each other's arms at this moment."

Phineas did not like to be told of their billing and cooing,—did not like to be told even of their quarrelling. Though they were to quarrel, it would do him no good. He would rather that nobody should mention their names to him;—so that his back, which had been so utterly broken, might in process of time get itself cured. From what he knew of Violet he thought it very improbable that, even were she to quarrel with one lover, she would at once throw herself into the arms of another. And he did feel, too, that there would be some meanness in taking her, were she willing to be so taken. But, nevertheless, these rumours, coming to him in this way from different sources, almost made it incumbent on him to find out the truth. He began to think that his broken back was not cured;—that perhaps, after all, it was not in the way of being cured, And was it not possible that there might be explanations? Then he went to work and built castles in the air, so constructed as to admit of the possibility of Violet Effingham becoming his wife.

This had been in April, and at that time all that he knew of Violet was, that she was not yet in London. And he thought that he knew the same as to Lord Chiltern. The Earl had told him that Chiltern was not in town, nor expected in town as yet; and in saying so had seemed to express displeasure against his son. Phineas had met Lady Baldock at some house which he frequented, and had been quite surprised to find himself graciously received by the old woman. She had said not a word of Violet, but had spoken of Lord Chiltern,—mentioning his name in bitter wrath. "But he is a friend of mine," said Phineas, smiling. "A friend indeed! Mr. Finn. I know what sort of a friend. I don't believe that you are his friend. I am afraid he is not worthy of having any friend." Phineas did not quite understand from this that Lady Baldock was signifying to him that, badly as she had thought of him as a suitor for her niece, she would have preferred him,—especially now when people were beginning to speak well of him,—to that terrible young man, who, from his youth upwards, had been to her a cause of fear and trembling. Of course it was desirable that Violet should marry an elder son, and a peer's heir. All that kind of thing, in Lady Baldock's eyes, was most desirable. But, nevertheless, anything was better than Lord Chiltern. If Violet would not take Mr. Appledom or Lord Fawn, in heaven's name let her take this young man, who was kind, worthy, and steady, who was civilised in his manners, and would no doubt be amenable in regard to settlements. Lady Baldock had so far fallen in the world that she would have consented to make a bargain with her niece,—almost any bargain, so long as Lord Chiltern was excluded. Phineas did not quite understand all this; but when Lady Baldock asked him to come to Berkeley Square, he perceived that help was being proffered to him where he certainly had not looked for help.

He was frequently with Lord Brentford, who talked to him constantly on matters connected with his parliamentary life. After having been the intimate friend of the daughter and of the son, it now seemed to be his lot to be the intimate friend of the father. The Earl had constantly discussed with him his arrangements with his son, and had lately expressed himself as only half satisfied with such reconciliation as had taken place. And Phineas could perceive that from day to day the Earl was less and less satisfied. He would complain bitterly of his son,—complain of his silence, complain of his not coming to London, complain of his conduct to Violet, complain of his idle indifference to anything like proper occupation; but he had never as yet said a word to show that there had been any quarrel between Violet and her lover, and Phineas had felt that he could not ask the question. "Mr. Finn," said the Earl to him one morning, as soon as he entered the room, "I have just heard a story which has almost seemed to me to be incredible." The nobleman's manner was very stern, and the fact that he called his young friend "Mr. Finn", showed at once that something was wrong.

"What is it you have heard, my lord?" said Phineas.

"That you and Chiltern went over,—last year to,—Belgium, and fought,—a duel there!"

Now it must have been the case that, in the set among which they all lived,—Lord Brentford and his son and daughter and Phineas Finn,—the old lord was the only man who had not heard of the duel before this. It had even penetrated to the dull ears of Mr. Kennedy, reminding him, as it did so, that his wife had,—told him a lie! But it was the fact that no rumour of the duel had reached the Earl till this morning.

"It is true," said Phineas.

"I have never been so much shocked in my life;—never. I had no idea that you had any thought of aspiring to the hand of Miss Effingham." The lord's voice as he said this was very stern.

"As I aspired in vain, and as Chiltern has been successful, that need not now be made a reproach against me."

"I do not know what to think of it, Mr. Finn. I am so much surprised that I hardly know what to say. I must declare my opinion at once, that you behaved,—very badly."

"I do not know how much you know, my lord, and how much you do not know; and the circumstances of the little affair do not permit me to be explicit about them; but, as you have expressed your opinion so openly you must allow me to express mine, and to say that, as far as I can judge of my own actions, I did not behave badly at all."

"Do you intend to defend duelling, sir?"

"No. If you mean to tell me that a duel is of itself sinful, I have nothing to say. I suppose it is. My defence of myself merely goes to the manner in which this duel was fought, and the fact that I fought it with your son."

"I cannot conceive how you can have come to my house as my guest, and stood upon my interest for my borough, when you at the time were doing your very best to interpose yourself between Chiltern and the lady whom you so well knew I wished to become his wife." Phineas was aware that the Earl must have been very much moved indeed when he thus permitted himself to speak of "his" borough. He said nothing now, however, though the Earl paused;—and then the angry lord went on. "I must say that there was something,—something almost approaching to duplicity in such conduct."

"If I were to defend myself by evidence, Lord Brentford, I should have to go back to exact dates,—and dates not of facts which I could verify, but dates as to my feelings which could not be verified,—and that would be useless. I can only say that I believe I know what the honour and truth of a gentleman demand,—even to the verge of self-sacrifice, and that I have done nothing that ought to place my character as a gentleman in jeopardy. If you will ask your son, I think he will tell you the same."

"I have asked him. It was he who told me of the duel."

"When did he tell you, my lord?"

"Just now; this morning." Thus Phineas learned that Lord Chiltern was at this moment in the house,—or at least in London.

"And did he complain of my conduct?"

"I complain of it, sir. I complain of it very bitterly. I placed the greatest confidence in you, especially in regard to my son's affairs, and you deceived me." The Earl was very angry, and was more angry from the fact that this young man who had offended him, to whom he had given such vital assistance when assistance was needed, had used that assistance to its utmost before his sin was found out. Had Phineas still been sitting for Loughton, so that the Earl could have said to him, "You are now bound to retreat from this borough because you have offended me, your patron," I think that he would have forgiven the offender and allowed him to remain in his seat. There would have been a scene, and the Earl would have been pacified. But now the offender was beyond his reach altogether, having used the borough as a most convenient stepping-stone over his difficulties, and having so used it just at the time when he was committing this sin. There was a good fortune about Phineas which added greatly to the lord's wrath. And then, to tell the truth, he had not that rich consolation for which Phineas gave him credit. Lord Chiltern had told him that morning that the engagement between him and Violet was at an end. "You have so preached to her, my lord, about my duties," the son had said to his father, "that she finds herself obliged to give me your sermons at second hand, till I can bear them no longer." But of this Phineas knew nothing as yet. The Earl, however, was so imprudent in his anger that before this interview was over he had told the whole story. "Yes;—you deceived me," he continued; "and I can never trust you again."

"Was it for me, my lord, to tell you of that which would have increased your anger against your own son? When he wanted me to fight was I to come, like a sneak at school, and tell you the story? I know what you would have thought of me had I done so. And when it was over was I to come and tell you then? Think what you yourself would have done when you were young, and you may be quite sure that I did the same. What have I gained? He has got all that he wanted; and you have also got all that you wanted,—and I have helped you both. Lord Brentford, I can put my hand on my heart and say that I have been honest to you."

"I have got nothing that I wanted," said the Earl in his despair.

"Lord Chiltern and Miss Effingham will be man and wife."

"No;—they will not. He has quarrelled with her. He is so obstinate that she will not bear with him."

Then it was all true, even though the rumours had reached him through Laurence Fitzgibbon and Madame Max Goesler. "At any rate, my lord, that has not been my fault," he said, after a moment's hesitation. The Earl was walking up and down the room, angry with himself at his own mistake in having told the story, and not knowing what further to say to his visitor. He had been in the habit of talking so freely to Phineas about his son that he could hardly resist the temptation of doing so still; and yet it was impossible that he could swallow his anger and continue in the same strain. "My lord," said Phineas, after a while, "I can assure you that I grieve that you should be grieved. I have received so much undeserved favour from your family, that I owe you a debt which I can never pay. I am sorry that you should be angry with me now; but I hope that a time may come when you will think less severely of my conduct."

He was about to leave the room when the Earl stopped him. "Will you give me your word," said the Earl, "that you will think no more of Miss Effingham?" Phineas stood silent, considering how he might answer this proposal, resolving that nothing should bring him to such a pledge as that suggested while there was yet a ledge for hope to stand on. "Say that, Mr. Finn, and I will forgive everything."

"I cannot acknowledge that I have done anything to be forgiven."

"Say that," repeated the Earl, "and everything shall be forgotten."

"There need be no cause for alarm, my lord," said Phineas. "You may be sure that Miss Effingham will not think of me."

"Will you give me your word?"

"No, my lord;—certainly not. You have no right to ask it, and the pursuit is open to me as to any other man who may choose to follow it. I have hardly a vestige of a hope of success. It is barely possible that I should succeed. But if it be true that Miss Effingham be disengaged, I shall endeavour to find an opportunity of urging my suit. I would give up everything that I have, my seat in Parliament, all the ambition of my life, for the barest chance of success. When she had accepted your son, I desisted,—of course. I have now heard, from more sources than one, that she or he or both of them have changed their minds. If this be so, I am free to try again." The Earl stood opposite to him, scowling at him, but said nothing. "Good morning, my lord."

"Good morning, sir."

"I am afraid it must be good-bye, for some long days to come."

"Good morning, sir," And the Earl as he spoke rang the bell. Then Phineas took up his hat and departed.

As he walked away his mind filled itself gradually with various ideas, all springing from the words which Lord Brentford had spoken. What account had Lord Chiltern given to his father of the duel? Our hero was a man very sensitive as to the good opinion of others, and in spite of his bold assertion of his own knowledge of what became a gentleman, was beyond measure solicitous that others should acknowledge his claim at any rate to that title. He thought that he had been generous to Lord Chiltern; and as he went back in his memory over almost every word that had been spoken in the interview that had just passed, he fancied that he was able to collect evidence that his antagonist at Blankenberg had not spoken ill of him. As to the charge of deceit which the Earl had made against him, he told himself that the Earl had made it in anger. He would not even think hardly of the Earl who had been so good a friend to him, but he believed in his heart that the Earl had made the accusation out of his wrath and not out of his judgment. "He cannot think that I have been false to him," Phineas said to himself. But it was very sad to him that he should have to quarrel with all the family of the Standishes, as he could not but feel that it was they who had put him on his feet. It seemed as though he were never to see Lady Laura again except when they chanced to meet in company,—on which occasions he simply bowed to her. Now the Earl had almost turned him out of his house. And though there had been to a certain extent a reconciliation between him and Lord Chiltern, he in these days never saw the friend who had once put him upon Bonebreaker; and now,— now that Violet Effingham was again free,—how was it possible to avoid some renewal of enmity between them? He would, however, endeavour to see Lord Chiltern at once.

And then he thought of Violet,—of Violet again free, of Violet as again a possible wife for himself, of Violet to whom he might address himself at any rate without any scruple as to his own unworthiness. Everybody concerned, and many who were not concerned at all, were aware that he had been among her lovers, and he thought that he could perceive that those who interested themselves on the subject, had regarded him as the only horse in the race likely to run with success against Lord Chiltern. She herself had received his offers without scorn, and had always treated him as though he were a favoured friend, though not favoured as a lover. And now even Lady Baldock was smiling upon him, and asking him to her house as though the red-faced porter in the hall in Berkeley Square had never been ordered to refuse him a moment's admission inside the doors. He had been very humble in speaking of his own hopes to the Earl, but surely there might be a chance. What if after all the little strain which he had had in his back was to be cured after such a fashion as this! When he got to his lodgings, he found a card from Lady Baldock, informing him that Lady Baldock would be at home on a certain night, and that there would be music. He could not go to Lady Baldock's on the night named, as it would be necessary that he should be in the House;—nor did he much care to go there, as Violet Effingham was not in town. But he would call and explain, and endeavour to curry favour in that way.

He at once wrote a note to Lord Chiltern, which he addressed to Portman Square. "As you are in town, can we not meet? Come and dine with me at the —— Club on Saturday." That was the note. After a few days he received the following answer, dated from the Bull at Willingford. Why on earth should Chiltern be staying at the Bull at Willingford in May?

The old Shop at W——, Friday.

Dear Phineas,

I can't dine with you, because I am down here, looking after the cripples, and writing a sporting novel. They tell me I ought to do something, so I am going to do that. I hope you don't think I turned informer against you in telling the Earl of our pleasant little meeting on the sands. It had become necessary, and you are too much of a man to care much for any truth being told. He was terribly angry both with me and with you; but the fact is, he is so blindly unreasonable that one cannot regard his anger. I endeavoured to tell the story truly, and, so told, it certainly should not have injured you in his estimation. But it did. Very sorry, old fellow, and I hope you'll get over it. It is a good deal more important to me than to you.

Yours,

C.

There was not a word about Violet. But then it was hardly to be expected that there should be words about Violet. It was not likely that a man should write to his rival of his own failure. But yet there was a flavour of Violet in the letter which would not have been there, so Phineas thought, if the writer had been despondent. The pleasant little meeting on the sands had been convened altogether in respect of Violet. And the telling of the story to the Earl must have arisen from discussions about Violet. Lord Chiltern must have told his father that Phineas was his rival. Could the rejected suitor have written on such a subject in such a strain to such a correspondent if he had believed his own rejection to be certain? But then Lord Chiltern was not like anybody else in the world, and it was impossible to judge of him by one's experience of the motives of others.

Shortly afterwards Phineas did call in Berkeley Square, and was shown up at once into Lady Baldock's drawing-room. The whole aspect of the porter's countenance was changed towards him, and from this, too, he gathered good auguries This had surprised him; but his surprise was far greater, when, on entering the room, he found Violet Effingham there alone. A little fresh colour came to her face as she greeted him, though it cannot be said that she blushed. She behaved herself admirably, not endeavouring to conceal some little emotion at thus meeting him, but betraying none that was injurious to her composure. "I am so glad to see you, Mr. Finn," she said. "My aunt has just left me, and will be back directly."

He was by no means her equal in his management of himself on the occasion; but perhaps it may be acknowledged that his position was the more difficult of the two. He had not seen her since her engagement had been proclaimed to the world, and now he had heard from a source which was not to be doubted, that it had been broken off. Of course there was nothing to be said on that matter. He could not have congratulated her in the one case, nor could he either congratulate her or condole with her on the other. And yet he did not know how to speak to her as though no such events had occurred. "I did not know that you were in town," he said.

"I only came yesterday. I have been, you know, at Rome with the Effinghams; and since that I have been—; but, indeed, I have been such a vagrant that I cannot tell you of all my comings and goings. And you,—you are hard at work!"

"Oh yes;—always."

"That is right. I wish I could be something, if it were only a stick in waiting, or a door-keeper. It is so good to be something." Was it some such teaching as this that had jarred against Lord Chiltern's susceptibilities, and had seemed to him to be a repetition of his father's sermons?

"A man should try to be something," said Phineas.

"And a woman must be content to be nothing,—unless Mr. Mill can pull us through! And now, tell me,—have you seen Lady Laura?"

"Not lately."

"Nor Mr. Kennedy?"

"I sometimes see him in the House." The visit to the Colonial Office of which the reader has been made aware had not at that time as yet been made.

"I am sorry for all that," she said. Upon which Phineas smiled and shook his head. "I am very sorry that there should be a quarrel between you two."

"There is no quarrel."

"I used to think that you and he might do so much for each other,—that is, of course, if you could make a friend of him."

"He is a man of whom it is very hard to make a friend," said Phineas, feeling that he was dishonest to Mr. Kennedy in saying so, but thinking that such dishonesty was justified by what he owed to Lady Laura.

"Yes;—he is hard, and what I call ungenial. We won't say anything about him,—will we? Have you seen much of the Earl?" This she asked as though such a question had no reference whatever to Lord Chiltern.

"Oh dear,—alas, alas!"

"You have not quarrelled with him too?"

"He has quarrelled with me. He has heard, Miss Effingham, of what happened last year, and he thinks that I was wrong."

"Of course you were wrong, Mr. Finn."

"Very likely. To him I chose to defend myself, but I certainly shall not do so to you. At any rate, you did not think it necessary to quarrel with me."

"I ought to have done so. I wonder why my aunt does not come." Then she rang the bell.

"Now I have told you all about myself," said he; "you should tell me something of yourself."

"About me? I am like the knife-grinder, who had no story to tell,—none at least to be told. We have all, no doubt, got our little stories, interesting enough to ourselves."

"But your story, Miss Effingham," he said, "is of such intense interest to me." At that moment, luckily, Lady Baldock came into the room, and Phineas was saved from the necessity of making a declaration at a moment which would have been most inopportune.

Lady Baldock was exceedingly gracious to him, bidding Violet use her influence to persuade him to come to the gathering. "Persuade him to desert his work to come and hear some fiddlers!" said Miss Effingham. "Indeed I shall not, aunt. Who can tell but what the colonies might suffer from it through centuries, and that such a lapse of duty might drive a province or two into the arms of our mortal enemies?"

"Herr Moll is coming," said Lady Baldock, "and so is Signor Scrubi, and Pjinskt, who, they say, is the greatest man living on the flageolet. Have you ever heard Pjinskt, Mr. Finn?" Phineas never had heard Pjinskt. "And as for Herr Moll, there is nothing equal to him, this year, at least." Lady Baldock had taken up music this season, but all her enthusiasm was unable to shake the conscientious zeal of the young Under-Secretary of State. At such a gathering he would have been unable to say a word in private to Violet Effingham.

CHAPTER LX
Madame Goesler's Politics

It may be remembered that when Lady Glencora Palliser was shown into Madame Goesler's room, Madame Goesler had just explained somewhat forcibly to the Duke of Omnium her reasons for refusing the loan of his Grace's villa at Como. She had told the Duke in so many words that she did not mean to give the world an opportunity of maligning her, and it would then have been left to the Duke to decide whether any other arrangements might have been made for taking Madame Goesler to Como, had he not been interrupted. That he was very anxious to take her was certain. The green brougham had already been often enough at the door in Park Lane to make his Grace feel that Madame Goesler's company was very desirable,—was, perhaps, of all things left for his enjoyment, the one thing the most desirable. Lady Glencora had spoken to her husband of children crying for the top brick of the chimney. Now it had come to this, that in the eyes of the Duke of Omnium Marie Max Goesler was the top brick of the chimney. She had more wit for him than other women,—more of that sort of wit which he was capable of enjoying. She had a beauty which he had learned to think more alluring than other beauty. He was sick of fair faces, and fat arms, and free necks. Madame Goesler's eyes sparkled as other eyes did not sparkle, and there was something of the vagueness of mystery in the very blackness and gloss and abundance of her hair,—as though her beauty was the beauty of some world which he had not yet known. And there was a quickness and yet a grace of motion about her which was quite new to him. The ladies upon whom the Duke had of late most often smiled had been somewhat slow,—perhaps almost heavy,—though, no doubt, graceful withal. In his early youth he remembered to have seen, somewhere in Greece, such a houri as was this Madame Goesler. The houri in that case had run off with the captain of a Russian vessel engaged in the tallow trade; but not the less was there left on his Grace's mind some dreamy memory of charms which had impressed him very strongly when he was simply a young Mr. Palliser, and had had at his command not so convenient a mode of sudden abduction as the Russian captain's tallow ship. Pressed hard by such circumstances as these, there is no knowing how the Duke might have got out of his difficulties had not Lady Glencora appeared upon the scene.

Since the future little Lord Silverbridge had been born, the Duke had been very constant in his worship of Lady Glencora, and as, from year to year, a little brother was added, thus making the family very strong and stable, his acts of worship had increased; but with his worship there had come of late something almost of dread,—something almost of obedience, which had made those who were immediately about the Duke declare that his Grace was a good deal changed. For, hitherto, whatever may have been the Duke's weaknesses, he certainly had known no master. His heir, Plantagenet Palliser, had been always subject to him. His other relations had been kept at such a distance as hardly to be more than recognised; and though his Grace no doubt had had his intimacies, they who had been intimate with him had either never tried to obtain ascendancy, or had failed. Lady Glencora, whether with or without a struggle, had succeeded, and people about the Duke said that the Duke was much changed. Mr. Fothergill,—who was his Grace's man of business, and who was not a favourite with Lady Glencora,—said that he was very much changed indeed. Finding his Grace so much changed, Mr. Fothergill had made a little attempt at dictation himself, but had receded with fingers very much scorched in the attempt. It was indeed possible that the Duke was becoming in the slightest degree weary of Lady Glencora's thraldom, and that he thought that Madame Max Goesler might be more tender with him. Madame Max Goesler, however, intended to be tender only on one condition.

When Lady Glencora entered the room, Madame Goesler received her beautifully. "How lucky that you should have come just when his Grace is here!" she said.

"I saw my uncle's carriage, and of course I knew it," said Lady Glencora.

"Then the favour is to him," said Madame Goesler, smiling.

"No, indeed; I was coming. If my word is to be doubted in that point, I must insist on having the servant up; I must, certainly. I told him to drive to this door, as far back as Grosvenor Street. Did I not, Planty?" Planty was the little Lord Silverbridge as was to be, if nothing unfortunate intervened, who was now sitting on his granduncle's knee.

"Dou said to the little house in Park Lane," said the boy.

"Yes,—because I forgot the number."

"And it is the smallest house in Park Lane, so the evidence is complete," said Madame Goesler. Lady Glencora had not cared much for evidence to convince Madame Goesler, but she had not wished her uncle to think that he was watched and hunted down. It might be necessary that he should know that he was watched, but things had not come to that as yet.

"How is Plantagenet?" asked the Duke.

"Answer for papa," said Lady Glencora to her child.

"Papa is very well, but he almost never comes home."

"He is working for his country," said the Duke. "Your papa is a busy, useful man, and can't afford time to play with a little boy as I can."

"But papa is not a duke."

"He will be some day, and that probably before long, my boy. He will be a duke quite as soon as he wants to be a duke. He likes the House of Commons better than the strawberry leaves, I fancy. There is not a man in England less in a hurry than he is."

"No, indeed," said Lady Glencora.

"How nice that is," said Madame Goesler.

"And I ain't in a hurry either,—am I, mamma?" said the little future Lord Silverbridge.

"You are a wicked little monkey," said his grand-uncle, kissing him. At this moment Lady Glencora was, no doubt, thinking how necessary it was that she should be careful to see that things did turn out in the manner proposed,—so that people who had waited should not be disappointed; and the Duke was perhaps thinking that he was not absolutely bound to his nephew by any law of God or man; and Madame Max Goesler,—I wonder whether her thoughts were injurious to the prospects of that handsome bold-faced little boy.

Lady Glencora rose to take her leave first. It was not for her to show any anxiety to force the Duke out of the lady's presence. If the Duke were resolved to make a fool of himself, nothing that she could do would prevent it. But she thought that this little inspection might possibly be of service, and that her uncle's ardour would be cooled by the interruption to which he had been subjected. So she went, and immediately afterwards the Duke followed her. The interruption had, at any rate, saved him on that occasion from making the highest bid for the pleasure of Madame Goesler's company at Como. The Duke went down with the little boy in his hand, so that there was not an opportunity for a single word of interest between the gentleman and the lady.

Madame Goesler, when she was alone, seated herself on her sofa, tucking her feet up under her as though she were seated somewhere in the East, pushed her ringlets back roughly from her face, and then placed her two hands to her sides so that her thumbs rested lightly on her girdle. When alone with something weighty on her mind she would sit in this form for the hour together, resolving, or trying to resolve, what should be her conduct. She did few things without much thinking, and though she walked very boldly, she walked warily. She often told herself that such success as she had achieved could not have been achieved without much caution. And yet she was ever discontented with herself, telling herself that all that she had done was nothing, or worse than nothing. What was it all, to have a duke and to have lords dining with her, to dine with lords or with a duke itself, if life were dull with her, and the hours hung heavy! Life with her was dull, and the hours did hang heavy. And what if she caught this old man, and became herself a duchess,—caught him by means of his weakness, to the inexpressible dismay of all those who were bound to him by ties of blood,—would that make her life happier, or her hours less tedious? That prospect of a life on the Italian lakes with an old man tied to her side was not so charming in her eyes as it was in those of the Duke. Were she to succeed, and to be blazoned forth to the world as Duchess of Omnium, what would she have gained?

She perfectly understood the motive of Lady Glencora's visit, and thought that she would at any rate gain something in the very triumph of baffling the manœuvres of so clever a woman. Let Lady Glencora throw her ægis before the Duke, and it would be something to carry off his Grace from beneath the protection of so thick a shield. The very flavour of the contest was pleasing to Madame Goesler. But, the victory gained, what then would remain to her? Money she had already; position, too, she had of her own. She was free as air, and should it suit her at any time to go off to some lake of Como in society that would personally be more agreeable to her than that of the Duke of Omnium, there was nothing to hinder her for a moment. And then came a smile over her face,—but the saddest smile,—as she thought of one with whom it might be pleasant to look at the colour of Italian skies and feel the softness of Italian breezes. In feigning to like to do this with an old man, in acting the raptures of love on behalf of a worn-out duke who at the best would scarce believe in her acting, there would not be much delight for her. She had never yet known what it was to have anything of the pleasure of love. She had grown, as she often told herself, to be a hard, cautious, selfish, successful woman, without any interference or assistance from such pleasure. Might there not be yet time left for her to try it without selfishness,—with an absolute devotion of self,—if only she could find the right companion? There was one who might be such a companion, but the Duke of Omnium certainly could not be such a one.

But to be Duchess of Omnium! After all, success in this world is everything;—is at any rate the only thing the pleasure of which will endure. There was the name of many a woman written in a black list within Madame Goesler's breast,—written there because of scorn, because of rejected overtures, because of deep social injury; and Madame Goesler told herself often that it would be a pleasure to her to use the list, and to be revenged on those who had ill-used and scornfully treated her. She did not readily forgive those who had injured her. As Duchess of Omnium she thought that probably she might use that list with efficacy. Lady Glencora had treated her well, and she had no such feeling against Lady Glencora. As Duchess of Omnium she would accept Lady Glencora as her dearest friend, if Lady Glencora would admit it. But if it should be necessary that there should be a little duel between them, as to which of them should take the Duke in hand, the duel must of course be fought. In a matter so important, one woman would of course expect no false sentiment from another. She and Lady Glencora would understand each other;—and no doubt, respect each other.

I have said that she would sit there resolving, or trying to resolve. There is nothing in the world so difficult as that task of making up one's mind. Who is there that has not longed that the power and privilege of selection among alternatives should be taken away from him in some important crisis of his life, and that his conduct should be arranged for him, either this way or that, by some divine power if it were possible,—by some patriarchal power in the absence of divinity,—or by chance even, if nothing better than chance could be found to do it? But no one dares to cast the die, and to go honestly by the hazard. There must be the actual necessity of obeying the die, before even the die can be of any use. As it was, when Madame Goesler had sat there for an hour, till her legs were tired beneath her, she had not resolved. It must be as her impulse should direct her when the important moment came. There was not a soul on earth to whom she could go for counsel, and when she asked herself for counsel, the counsel would not come.

Two days afterwards the Duke called again. He would come generally on a Thursday,—early, so that he might be there before other visitors; and he had already quite learned that when he was there other visitors would probably be refused admittance. How Lady Glencora had made her way in, telling the servant that her uncle was there, he had not understood. That visit had been made on the Thursday, but now he came on the Saturday,—having, I regret to say, sent down some early fruit from his own hot-houses,—or from Covent Garden,—with a little note on the previous day. The grapes might have been pretty well, but the note was injudicious. There were three lines about the grapes, as to which there was some special history, the vine having been brought from the garden of some villa in which some ill-used queen had lived and died; and then there was a postscript in one line to say that the Duke would call on the following morning. I do not think that he had meant to add this when he began his note; but then children, who want the top brick, want it so badly, and cry for it so perversely!

Of course Madame Goesler was at home. But even then she had not made up her mind. She had made up her mind only to this,—that he should be made to speak plainly, and that she would take time for her reply. Not even with such a gem as the Duke's coronet before her eyes, would she jump at it. Where there was so much doubt, there need at least be no impatience.

"You ran away the other day, Duke, because you could not resist the charm of that little boy," she said, laughing.

"He is a dear little boy,—but it was not that," he answered.

"Then what was it? Your niece carried you off in a whirl-wind. She was come and gone, taking you with her, in half a minute."

"She had disturbed me when I was thinking of something," said the Duke.

"Things shouldn't be thought of,—not so deeply as that." Madame Goesler was playing with a bunch of his grapes now, eating one or two from a small china plate which had stood upon the table, and he thought that he had never seen a woman so graceful and yet so natural. "Will you not eat your own grapes with me? They are delicious;—flavoured with the poor queen's sorrows." He shook his head, knowing that it did not suit his gastric juices to have to deal with fruit eaten at odd times. "Never think, Duke. I am convinced that it does no good. It simply means doubting, and doubt always leads to error. The safest way in the world is to do nothing."

173

"I believe so," said the Duke.

"Much the safest. But if you have not sufficient command over yourself to enable you to sit in repose, always quiet, never committing yourself to the chance of any danger,—then take a leap in the dark; or rather many leaps. A stumbling horse regains his footing by persevering in his onward course. As for moving cautiously, that I detest."

"And yet one must think;—for instance, whether one will succeed or not."

"Take that for granted always. Remember, I do not recommend motion at all. Repose is my idea of life;—repose and grapes."

The Duke sat for a while silent, taking his repose as far as the outer man was concerned, looking at his top brick of the chimney, as from time to time she ate one of his grapes. Probably she did not eat above half-a-dozen of them altogether, but he thought that the grapes must have been made for the woman, she was so pretty in the eating of them. But it was necessary that he should speak at last. "Have you been thinking of coming to Como?" he said.

"I told you that I never think."

"But I want an answer to my proposition."

"I thought I had answered your Grace on that question." Then she put down the grapes, and moved herself on her chair, so that she sat with her face turned away from him.

"But a request to a lady may be made twice."

"Oh, yes. And I am grateful, knowing how far it is from your intention to do me any harm. And I am somewhat ashamed of my warmth on the other day. But still there can be but one answer. There are delights which a woman must deny herself, let them be ever so delightful."

"I had thought,—" the Duke began, and then he stopped himself.

"Your Grace was saying that you thought,—"

"Marie, a man at my age does not like to be denied."

"What man likes to be denied anything by a woman at any age? A woman who denies anything is called cruel at once,—even though it be her very soul." She had turned round upon him now, and was leaning forward towards him from her chair, so that he could touch her if he put out his hand.

He put out his hand and touched her. "Marie," he said, "will you deny me if I ask?"

"Nay, my lord; how shall I say? There is many a trifle I would deny you. There is many a great gift I would give you willingly."

"But the greatest gift of all?"

"My lord, if you have anything to say, you must say it plainly. There never was a woman worse than I am at the reading of riddles."

"Could you endure to live in the quietude of an Italian lake with an old man?" Now he touched her again, and had taken her hand.

"No, my lord;—nor with a young one,—for all my days. But I do not know that age would guide me."

Then the Duke rose and made his proposition in form. "Marie, you know that I love you. Why it is that I at my age should feel so sore a love, I cannot say."

"So sore a love!"

"So sore, if it be not gratified. Marie, I ask you to be my wife."

"Duke of Omnium, this from you!"

"Yes, from me. My coronet is at your feet. If you will allow me to raise it, I will place it on your brow."

Then she went away from him, and seated herself at a distance. After a moment or two he followed her, and stood with his arm upon her shoulder. "You will give me an answer, Marie?"

"You cannot have thought of this, my lord."

"Nay; I have thought of it much."

"And your friends?"

"My dear, I may venture to please myself in this,—as in everything. Will you not answer me?"

"Certainly not on the spur of the moment, my lord. Think how high is the position you offer me, and how immense is the change you propose to me. Allow me two days, and I will answer you by letter. I am so fluttered now that I must leave you." Then he came to her, took her hand, kissed her brow, and opened the door for her.

CHAPTER LXI
Another Duel

It happened that there were at this time certain matters of business to be settled between the Duke of Omnium and his nephew Mr. Palliser, respecting which the latter called upon his uncle on the morning after the Duke had committed himself by his offer. Mr. Palliser had come by appointment made with Mr. Fothergill, the Duke's man of business, and had expected to meet Mr. Fothergill. Mr. Fothergill, however, was not with the Duke, and the uncle told the nephew that the business had been postponed. Then Mr. Palliser asked some question as to the reason of such postponement, not meaning much by his question,—and the Duke, after a moment's hesitation, answered him, meaning very much by his answer. "The truth is, Plantagenet, that it is possible that I may marry, and if so this arrangement would not suit me."

"Are you going to be married?" asked the astonished nephew.

"It is not exactly that,—but it is possible that I may do so. Since I proposed this matter to Fothergill, I have been thinking over it, and I have changed my mind. It will make but little difference to you; and after all you are a far richer man than I am."

"I am not thinking of money, Duke," said Plantagenet Palliser.

"Of what then were you thinking?"

"Simply of what you told me. I do not in the least mean to interfere."

"I hope not, Plantagenet."

"But I could not hear such a statement from you without some surprise. Whatever you do I hope will tend to make you happy."

So much passed between the uncle and the nephew, and what the uncle told to the nephew, the nephew of course told to his wife. "He was with her again, yesterday," said Lady Glencora, "for more than an hour. And he had been half the morning dressing himself before he went to her."

"He is not engaged to her, or he would have told me," said Plantagenet Palliser.

"I think he would, but there is no knowing. At the present moment I have only one doubt,—whether to act upon him or upon her."

"I do not see that you can do good by going to either."

"Well, we will see. If she be the woman I take her to be, I think I could do something with her. I have never supposed her to be a bad woman,—never. I will think of it." Then Lady Glencora left her husband, and did not consult him afterwards as to the course she would pursue. He had his budget to manage, and his speeches to make. The little affair of the Duke and Madame Goesler, she thought it best to take into her own hands without any assistance from him. "What a fool I was," she said to herself, "to have her down there when the Duke was at Matching!"

Madame Goesler, when she was left alone, felt that now indeed she must make up her mind. She had asked for two days. The intervening day was a Sunday, and on the Monday she must send her answer. She might doubt at any rate for this one night,—the Saturday night,—and sit playing, as it were, with the coronet of a duchess in her lap. She had been born the daughter of a small country attorney, and now a duke had asked her to be his wife,—and a duke who was acknowledged to stand above other dukes! Nothing at any rate could rob her of that satisfaction. Whatever resolution she might form at last, she had by her own resources reached a point of success in remembering which there would always be a keen gratification. It would be much to be Duchess of Omnium; but it would be something also to have refused to be a Duchess of Omnium. During that evening, that night, and the next morning, she remained playing with the coronet in her lap. She would not go to church. What good could any sermon do her while that bauble was dangling before her eyes? After church-time, about two o'clock, Phineas Finn came to her. Just at this period Phineas would come to her often;—sometimes full of a new decision to forget Violet Effingham altogether, at others minded to continue his siege let the hope of success be ever so small. He had now heard that Violet and Lord Chiltern had in truth quarrelled, and was of course anxious to be advised to continue the siege. When he first came in and spoke a word or two, in which there was no reference to Violet Effingham, there came upon Madame Goesler a strong wish to decide at once that she would play no longer with the coronet, that the gem was not worth the cost she would be called upon to pay for it. There was something in the world better for her than the coronet,—if only it might be had. But within ten minutes he had told her the whole tale about Lord Chiltern, and how he had seen Violet at Lady Baldock's,—and how there might yet be hope for him. What would she advise him to do? "Go home, Mr. Finn," she said, "and write a sonnet to her eyebrow. See if that will have any effect."

"Ah, well! It is natural that you should laugh at me; but somehow, I did not expect it from you."

"Do not be angry with me. What I mean is that such little things seem to influence this Violet of yours."

"Do they? I have not found that they do so."

"If she had loved Lord Chiltern she would not have quarrelled with him for a few words. If she had loved you, she would not have accepted Lord Chiltern. If she loves neither of you, she should say so. I am losing my respect for her."

"Do not say that, Madame Goesler. I respect her as strongly as I love her." Then Madame Goesler almost made up her mind that she would have the coronet. There was a substance about the coronet that would not elude her grasp.

Late that afternoon, while she was still hesitating, there came another caller to the cottage in Park Lane. She was still hesitating, feeling that she had as yet another night before her. Should she be Duchess of Omnium or not? All that she wished to be, she could not be;—but to be Duchess of Omnium was within her reach. Then she began to ask herself various questions. Would the Queen refuse to accept her in her new rank? Refuse! How could any Queen refuse to accept her? She had not done aught amiss in life. There was no slur on her name; no stain on her character. What though her father had been a small attorney, and her first husband a Jew banker! She had broken no law of God or man, had been accused of breaking no law, which breaking or which accusation need stand in the way of her being as good a duchess as any other woman! She was sitting thinking of this, almost angry with herself at the awe with which the proposed rank inspired her, when Lady Glencora was announced to her.

"Madame Goesler," said Lady Glencora, "I am very glad to find you."

"And I more than equally so, to be found," said Madame Goesler, smiling with all her grace.

"My uncle has been with you since I saw you last?"

"Oh yes;—more than once if I remember right. He was here yesterday at any rate."

"He comes often to you then?"

"Not so often as I would wish, Lady Glencora. The Duke is one of my dearest friends."

"It has been a quick friendship."

"Yes;—a quick friendship," said Madame Goesler. Then there was a pause for some moments which Madame Goesler was determined that she would not break. It was clear to her now on what ground Lady Glencora had come to her, and she was fully minded that if she could bear the full light of the god himself in all his glory, she would not allow herself to be scorched by any reflected heat coming from the god's niece. She thought she could endure anything that Lady Glencora might say; but she would wait and hear what might be said.

"I think, Madame Goesler, that I had better hurry on to my subject at once," said Lady Glencora, almost hesitating as she spoke, and feeling that the colour was rushing up to her cheeks and covering her brow. "Of course what I have to say will be disagreeable. Of course I shall offend you. And yet I do not mean it."

"I shall be offended at nothing, Lady Glencora, unless I think that you mean to offend me."

"I protest that I do not. You have seen my little boy."

"Yes, indeed. The sweetest child! God never gave me anything half so precious as that."

"He is the Duke's heir."

"So I understand."

"For myself, by my honour as a woman, I care nothing. I am rich and have all that the world can give me. For my husband, in this matter, I care nothing. His career he will make for himself, and it will depend on no title."

"Why all this to me, Lady Glencora? What have I to do with your husband's titles?"

"Much;—if it be true that there is an idea of marriage between you and the Duke of Omnium."

"Psha!" said Madame Goesler, with all the scorn of which she was mistress.

"It is untrue, then?" asked Lady Glencora.

"No;—it is not untrue. There is an idea of such a marriage."

"And you are engaged to him?"

"No;—I am not engaged to him."

"Has he asked you?"

"Lady Glencora, I really must say that such a cross-questioning from one lady to another is very unusual. I have promised not to be offended, unless I thought that you wished to offend me. But do not drive me too far."

"Madame Goesler, if you will tell me that I am mistaken, I will beg your pardon, and offer to you the most sincere friendship which one woman can give another."

"Lady Glencora, I can tell you nothing of the kind."

"Then it is to be so! And have you thought what you would gain?"

"I have thought much of what I should gain:—and something also of what I should lose."

"You have money."

"Yes, indeed; plenty,—for wants so moderate as mine."

"And position."

"Well, yes; a sort of position. Not such as yours, Lady Glencora. That, if it be not born to a woman, can only come to her from a husband. She cannot win it for herself."

"You are free as air, going where you like, and doing what you like."

"Too free, sometimes," said Madame Goesler.

"And what will you gain by changing all this simply for a title?"

"But for such a title, Lady Glencora! It may be little to you to be Duchess of Omnium, but think what it must be to me!"

"And for this you will not hesitate to rob him of all his friends, to embitter his future life, to degrade him among his peers,—"

"Degrade him! Who dares say that I shall degrade him? He will exalt me, but I shall no whit degrade him. You forget yourself, Lady Glencora."

"Ask any one. It is not that I despise you. If I did, would I offer you my hand in friendship? But an old man, over seventy, carrying the weight and burden of such rank as his, will degrade himself in the eyes of his fellows, if he marries a young woman without rank, let her be ever so clever, ever so beautiful. A Duke of Omnium may not do as he pleases, as may another man."

"It may be well, Lady Glencora, for other dukes, and for the daughters and heirs and cousins of other dukes, that his Grace should try that question. I will, if you wish it, argue this matter with you on many points, but I will not allow you to say that I should degrade any man whom I might marry. My name is as unstained as your own."

"I meant nothing of that," said Lady Glencora.

"For him;—I certainly would not willingly injure him. Who wishes to injure a friend? And, in truth, I have so little to gain, that the temptation to do him an injury, if I thought it one, is not strong. For your little boy, Lady Glencora, I think your fears are premature." As she said this, there came a smile over her face, which threatened to break from control and almost become laughter. "But, if you will allow me to say so, my mind will not be turned against this marriage half so strongly by any arguments you can use as by those which I can adduce myself. You have nearly driven me into it by telling me I should degrade his house. It is almost incumbent on me to prove that you are wrong. But you had better leave me to settle the matter in my own bosom. You had indeed."

After a while Lady Glencora did leave her,—to settle the matter within her own bosom,—having no other alternative.

CHAPTER LXII
The Letter That Was Sent to Brighton

Monday morning came and Madame Goesler had as yet written no answer to the Duke of Omnium. Had not Lady Glencora gone to Park Lane on the Sunday afternoon, I think the letter would have been written on that day; but, whatever may have been the effect of Lady Glencora's visit, it so far disturbed Madame Goesler as to keep her from her writing-table. There was yet another night for thought, and then the letter should be written on the Monday morning.

When Lady Glencora left Madame Goesler she went at once to the Duke's house. It was her custom to see her husband's uncle on a Sunday, and she would most frequently find him just at this hour,—before he went up-stairs to dress for dinner. She usually took her boy with her, but on this occasion she went alone. She had tried what she could do with Madame Goesler, and she found that she had failed. She must now make her attempt upon the Duke. But the Duke, perhaps anticipating some attack of the kind, had fled. "Where is his Grace, Barker?" said Lady Glencora to the porter. "We do not know, your ladyship. His Grace went away yesterday evening with nobody but Lapoule." Lapoule was the Duke's French valet. Lady Glencora could only return home and consider in her own mind what batteries might yet be brought to bear upon the Duke, towards stopping the marriage, even after the engagement should have been made,—if it were to be made. Lady Glencora felt that such batteries might still be brought up as would not improbably have an effect on a proud, weak old man. If all other resources failed, royalty in some of its branches might be induced to make a request, and every august relation in the peerage should interfere. The Duke no doubt might persevere and marry whom he pleased,—if he were strong enough. But it requires much personal strength,—that standing alone against the well-armed batteries of all one's friends. Lady Glencora had once tried such a battle on her own behalf, and had failed. She had wished to be imprudent when she was young; but her friends had been too strong for her. She had been reduced, and kept in order, and made to run in a groove,—and was now, when she sat looking at her little boy with his bold face, almost inclined to think that the world was right, and that grooves were best. But if she had been controlled when she was young, so ought the Duke to be controlled now that he was old. It is all very well for a man or woman to boast that he,—or she,—may do what he likes with his own,—or with her own. But there are circumstances in which such self-action is ruinous to so many that coercion from the outside becomes absolutely needed. Nobody had felt the injustice of such coercion when applied to herself more sharply than had Lady Glencora. But she had lived to acknowledge that such coercion might be proper, and was now prepared to use it in any shape in which it might be made available. It was all very well for Madame Goesler to laugh and exclaim, "Psha!" when Lady Glencora declared her real trouble. But should it ever come to pass that a black-browed baby with a yellow skin should be shown to the world as Lord Silverbridge, Lady Glencora knew that her peace of mind would be gone for ever. She had begun the world desiring one thing, and had missed it. She had suffered much, and had then reconciled herself to other hopes. If those other hopes were also to be cut away from her, the world would not be worth a pinch of snuff to her. The Duke had fled, and she could do nothing to-day; but to-morrow she would begin with her batteries. And she herself had done the mischief! She had invited this woman down to Matching! Heaven and earth!—that such a man as the Duke should be such a fool!—The widow of a Jew banker! He, the Duke of Omnium,—and thus to cut away from himself, for the rest of his life, all honour, all peace of mind, all the grace of a noble end to a career which, if not very noble in itself, had received the praise of nobility! And to do this for a thin, black-browed, yellow-visaged woman with ringlets and devil's eyes, and a beard on her upper lip,—a Jewess,—a creature of whose habits of life and manners of thought they all were absolutely ignorant; who drank, possibly; who might have been a forger, for what any one knew; an adventuress who had found her way into society by her art and perseverance,—and who did not even pretend to have a relation in the world! That such a one should have influence enough to intrude herself into the house of Omnium, and blot the scutcheon, and,—what was worst of all,—perhaps be the mother of future dukes! Lady Glencora, in her anger, was very unjust to Madame Goesler, thinking all evil of her, accusing her in her mind of every crime, denying her all charm, all beauty. Had the Duke forgotten himself and his position for the sake of some fair girl with a pink complexion and grey eyes, and smooth hair, and a father, Lady Glencora thought that she would have forgiven it better. It might be that Madame Goesler would win her way to the coronet; but when she came to put it on, she should find that there were sharp thorns inside the lining of it. Not a woman worth the knowing in all London should speak to her;—nor a man either of those men with whom a Duchess of Omnium would wish to hold converse. She should find her husband rated as a doting fool, and herself rated as a scheming female adventuress. And it should go hard with Lady Glencora, if the Duke were not separated from his new Duchess before the end of the first year! In her anger Lady Glencora was very unjust.

The Duke, when he left his house without telling his household whither he was going, did send his address to,—the top brick of the chimney. His note, which was delivered at Madame Goesler's house late on the Sunday evening, was as follows:—"I am to have your answer on Monday. I shall be at Brighton. Send it by a private messenger to the Bedford Hotel there. I need not tell you with what expectation, with what hope, with what fear I shall await it.—O." Poor old man! He had run through all the pleasures of life too quickly, and had not much left with which to amuse himself. At length he had set his eyes on a top brick, and being tired of everything else, wanted it very sorely. Poor old man! How should it do him any good, even if he got it? Madame Goesler, when she received the note, sat with it in her hand, thinking of his great want. "And he would be tired of his new plaything after a month," she said to herself. But she had given herself to the next morning, and she would not make up her mind that night. She would sleep once more with the coronet of a duchess within her reach. She did do so; and woke in the morning with her mind absolutely in doubt. When she walked down to breakfast, all doubt was at an end. The time had come when it was necessary that she should resolve, and while her maid was brushing her hair for her she did make her resolution.

"What a thing it is to be a great lady," said the maid, who may probably have reflected that the Duke of Omnium did not come here so often for nothing.

"What do you mean by that, Lotta?"

"The women I know, madame, talk so much of their countesses, and ladyships, and duchesses. I would never rest till I had a title in this country, if I were a lady,—and rich and beautiful."

"And can the countesses, and the ladyships, and the duchesses do as they please?"

"Ah, madame;—I know not that."

"But I know. That will do, Lotta. Now leave me." Then Madame Goesler had made up her mind; but I do not know whether that doubt as to having her own way had much to do with it. As the wife of an old man she would probably have had much of her own way. Immediately after breakfast she wrote her answer to the Duke, which was as follows:—

Park Lane, Monday.

My dear Duke of Omnium,

I find so great a difficulty in expressing myself to your Grace in a written letter, that since you left me I have never ceased to wish that I had been less nervous, less doubting, and less foolish when you were present with me here in my room. I might then have said in one word what will take so many awkward words to explain.

Great as is the honour you propose to confer on me, rich as is the gift you offer me, I cannot accept it. I cannot be your Grace's wife. I may almost say that I knew it was so when you parted from me; but the surprise of the situation took away from me a part of my judgment, and made me unable to answer you as I should have done. My lord, the truth is, that I am not fit to be the wife of the Duke of Omnium. I should injure you; and though I should raise myself in name, I should injure myself in character. But you must not think, because I say this, that there is any reason why I should not be an honest man's wife. There is none. I have nothing on my conscience which I could not tell you,—or to another man; nothing that I need fear to tell to all the world. Indeed, my lord, there is nothing to tell but this,—that I am not fitted by birth and position to be the wife of the Duke of Omnium. You would have to blush for me, and that no man shall ever have to do on my account.

I will own that I have been ambitious, too ambitious, and have been pleased to think that one so exalted as you are, one whose high position is so rife in the eyes of all men, should have taken pleasure in my company. I will confess to a foolish woman's silly vanity in having wished to be known to be the friend of the Duke of Omnium. I am like the other moths that flutter near the light and have their wings burned. But I am wiser than they in this, that having been scorched, I know that I must keep my distance. You will easily believe that a woman, such as I am, does not refuse to ride in a carriage with your Grace's arms on the panels without a regret. I am no philosopher. I do not pretend to despise the rich things of the world, or the high things. According to my way of thinking a woman ought to wish to be Duchess of Omnium;—but she ought to wish also to be able to carry her coronet with a proper grace. As Madame Goesler I can live, even among my superiors, at my ease. As your Grace's wife, I should be easy no longer;—nor would your Grace.

You will think perhaps that what I write is heartless, that I speak altogether of your rank, and not at all of the affection you have shown me, or of that which I might possibly bear towards you. I think that when the first flush of passion is over in early youth men and women should strive to regulate their love, as they do their other desires, by their reason. I could love your Grace, fondly, as your wife, if I thought it well for your Grace or for myself that we should be man and wife. As I think it would be ill for both of us, I will restrain that feeling, and remember your Grace ever with the purest feeling of true friendship.

Before I close this letter, I must utter a word of gratitude. In the kind of life which I have led as a widow, a life which has been very isolated as regards true fellowship, it has been my greatest effort to obtain the good opinion of those among whom I have attempted to make my way. I may, perhaps, own to you now that I have had many difficulties. A woman who is alone in the world is ever regarded with suspicion. In this country a woman with a foreign name, with means derived from foreign sources, with a foreign history, is specially suspected. I have striven to live that down, and I have succeeded. But in my wildest dreams I never dreamed of such success as this,—that the Duke of Omnium should think me the worthiest of the worthy. You may be sure that I am not ungrateful,—that I never will be ungrateful. And I trust it will not derogate from your opinion of my worth, that I have known what was due to your Grace's highness.

I have the honour to be,
My Lord Duke,
Your most obliged and faithful servant,
Marie Max Goesler.

"How many unmarried women in England are there would do the same?" she said to herself, as she folded the paper, and put it into an envelope, and sealed the cover. The moment that the letter was completed she sent it off, as she was directed to send it, so that there might be no possibility of repentance and subsequent hesitation. She had at last made up her mind, and she would stand by the making. She knew that there would come moments in which she would deeply regret the opportunity that she had lost,—the chance of greatness that she had flung away from her. But so would she have often regretted it, also, had she accepted the greatness. Her position was one in which there must be regret, let her decision have been what it might. But she had decided, and the thing was done. She would still be free,—Marie Max Goesler,—unless in abandoning her freedom she would obtain something that she might in truth prefer to it. When the letter was gone she sat disconsolate, at the window of an up-stairs room in which she had written, thinking much of the coronet, much of the name, much of the rank, much of that position in society which she had flattered herself she might have won for herself as Duchess of Omnium by her beauty, her grace, and her wit. It had not been simply her ambition to be a duchess, without further aim or object. She had fancied that she might have been such a duchess as there is never another, so that her fame might have been great throughout Europe, as a woman charming at all points. And she would have had friends, then,—real friends, and would not have lived alone as it was now her fate to do. And she would have loved her ducal husband, old though he was, and stiff with pomp and ceremony. She would have loved him, and done her best to add something of brightness to his life. It was indeed true that there was one whom she loved better; but of what avail was it to love a man who, when he came to her, would speak to her of nothing but of the charms which he found in another woman!

She had been sitting thus at her window, with a book in her hand, at which she never looked, gazing over the park which was now beautiful with its May verdure, when on a sudden a thought struck her. Lady Glencora Palliser had come to her, trying to enlist her sympathy for the little heir, behaving, indeed, not very well, as Madame Goesler had thought, but still with an earnest purpose which was in itself good. She would write to Lady Glencora and put her out of her misery. Perhaps there was some feeling of triumph in her mind as she returned to the desk from which her epistle had been sent to the Duke;—not of that triumph which would have found its gratification in boasting of the offer that had been made to her, but arising from a feeling that she could now show the proud mother of the bold-faced boy that though she would not pledge herself to any woman as to what she might do or not do, she was nevertheless capable of resisting such a temptation as would have been irresistible to many. Of the Duke's offer to her she would have spoken to no human being, had not this woman shown that the Duke's purpose was known at least to her, and now, in her letter, she would write no plain word of that offer. She would not state, in words intelligible to any one who might read, that the Duke had offered her his hand and his coronet. But she would write so that Lady Glencora should understand her. And she would be careful that there should be no word in the letter to make Lady Glencora think that she supposed herself to be unfit for the rank offered to her. She had been very humble in what she had written to the Duke, but she would not be at all humble in what she was about to write to the mother of the bold-faced boy. And this was the letter when it was written:—

My dear Lady Glencora,

I venture to send you a line to put you out of your misery;—for you were very miserable when you were so good as to come here yesterday. Your dear little boy is safe from me;—and, what is more to the purpose, so are you and your husband,—and your uncle, whom, in truth, I love. You asked me a downright question which I did not then choose to answer by a downright answer. The downright answer was not at that time due to you. It has since been given, and as I like you too well to wish you to be in torment, I send you a line to say that I shall never be in the way of you or your boy.

And now, dear Lady Glencora, one word more. Should it ever again appear to you to be necessary to use your zeal for the protection of your husband or your child, do not endeavour to dissuade a woman by trying to make her think that she, by her alliance, would bring degradation into any house, or to any man. If there could have been an argument powerful with me, to make me do that which you wished to prevent, it was the argument which you used. But my own comfort, and the happiness of another person whom I value almost as much as myself, were too important to be sacrificed even to a woman's revenge. I take mine by writing to you and telling you that I am better and more rational and wiser than you took me to be.

If, after this, you choose to be on good terms with me, I shall be happy to be your friend. I shall want no further revenge. You owe me some little apology; but whether you make it or not, I will be contented, and will never do more than ask whether your darling's prospects are still safe. There are more women than one in the world, you know, and you must not consider yourself to be out of the wood because you have escaped from a single danger. If there arise another, come to me, and we will consult together.

Dear Lady Glencora, yours always sincerely,

Marie M. G.

There was a thing or two besides which she longed to say, laughing as she thought of them. But she refrained, and her letter, when finished, was as it is given above.

On the day following, Lady Glencora was again in Park Lane. When she first read Madame Goesler's letter, she felt herself to be annoyed and angry, but her anger was with herself rather than with her correspondent. Ever since her last interview with the woman whom she had feared, she had been conscious of having been indiscreet. All her feelings had been too violent, and it might well have been that she should have driven this woman to do the very thing that she was so anxious to avoid. "You owe me some little apology," Madame Goesler had said. It was true,—and she would apologise. Undue pride was not a part of Lady Glencora's character. Indeed, there was not enough of pride in her composition. She had been quite ready to hate this woman, and to fight her on every point as long as the danger existed; but she was equally willing to take the woman to her heart now that the danger was over. Apologise! Of course she would apologise. And she would make a friend of the woman if the woman wished it. But she would not have the woman and the Duke at Matching together again, lest, after all, there might be a mistake. She did not show Madame Goesler's letter to her husband, or tell him anything of the relief she had received. He had cared but little for the danger, thinking more of his budget than of the danger; and would be sufficiently at his ease if he heard no more rumours of his uncle's marriage. Lady Glencora went to Park Lane early on the Tuesday morning, but she did not take her boy with her. She understood that Madame Goesler might perhaps indulge in a little gentle raillery at the child's expense, and the mother felt that this might be borne the more easily if the child were not present.

"I have come to thank you for your letter, Madame Goesler," said Lady Glencora, before she sat down.

"Oh, come ye in peace here, or come ye in war, or to dance at our bridal?" said Madame Goesler, standing up from her chair and laughing, as she sang the lines.

"Certainly not to dance at your bridal," said Lady Glencora.

"Alas! no. You have forbidden the banns too effectually for that, and I sit here wearing the willow all alone. Why shouldn't I be allowed to get married as well as another woman, I wonder? I think you have been very hard upon me among you. But sit down, Lady Glencora. At any rate you come in peace."

"Certainly in peace, and with much admiration,—and a great deal of love and affection, and all that kind of thing, if you will only accept it."

"I shall be too proud, Lady Glencora;—for the Duke's sake, if for no other reason."

"And I have to make my apology."

"It was made as soon as your carriage stopped at my door with friendly wheels. Of course I understand. I can know how terrible it all was to you,—even though the dear little Plantagenet might not have been in much danger. Fancy what it would be to disturb the career of a Plantagenet! I am far too well read in history, I can assure you."

"I said a word for which I am sorry, and which I should not have said."

"Never mind the word. After all, it was a true word. I do not hesitate to say so now myself, though I will allow no other woman to say it,—and no man either. I should have degraded him,—and disgraced him." Madame Goesler now had dropped the bantering tone which she had assumed, and was speaking in sober earnest. "I, for myself, have nothing about me of which I am ashamed. I have no history to hide, no story to be brought to light to my discredit. But I have not been so born, or so placed by circumstances, as make me fit to be the wife of the Duke of Omnium. I should not have been happy, you know."

"You want nothing, dear Madame Goesler. You have all that society can give you."

"I do not know about that. I have much given to me by society, but there are many things that I want;—a bright-faced little boy, for instance, to go about with me in my carriage. Why did you not bring him, Lady Glencora?"

"I came out in my penitential sheet, and when one goes in that guise, one goes alone. I had half a mind to walk."

"You will bring him soon?"

"Oh, yes. He was very anxious to know the other day who was the beautiful lady with the black hair."

"You did not tell him that the beautiful lady with the black hair was a possible aunt, was a possible—? But we will not think any more of things so horrible."

"I told him nothing of my fears, you may be sure."

"Some day, when I am a very old woman, and when his father is quite an old duke, and when he has a dozen little boys and girls of his own, you will tell him the story. Then he will reflect what a madman his great-uncle must have been, to have thought of making a duchess out of such a wizened old woman as that."

They parted the best of friends, but Lady Glencora was still of opinion that if the lady and the Duke were to be brought together at Matching, or elsewhere, there might still be danger.

CHAPTER LXIII
Showing How the Duke Stood His Ground

Mr. Low the barrister, who had given so many lectures to our friend Phineas Finn, lectures that ought to have been useful, was now himself in the House of Commons, having reached it in the legitimate course of his profession. At a certain point of his career, supposing his career to have been sufficiently prosperous, it becomes natural to a barrister to stand for some constituency, and natural for him also to form his politics at that period of his life with a view to his further advancement, looking, as he does so, carefully at the age and standing of the various candidates for high legal office. When a man has worked as Mr. Low had worked, he begins to regard the bench wistfully, and to calculate the profits of a two years' run in the Attorney-Generalship. It is the way of the profession, and thus a proper and sufficient number of real barristers finds its way into the House. Mr. Low had been angry with Phineas because he, being a barrister, had climbed into it after another fashion, having taken up politics, not in the proper way as an assistance to his great profession, but as a profession in itself. Mr. Low had been quite sure that his pupil had been wrong in this, and that the error would at last show itself, to his pupil's cost. And Mrs. Low had been more sure than Mr. Low, having not unnaturally been jealous that a young whipper-snapper of a pupil,—as she had once called Phineas,—should become a Parliament man before her husband, who had worked his way up gallantly, in the usual course. She would not give way a jot even now,—not even when she heard that Phineas was going to marry this and that heiress. For at this period of his life such rumours were afloat about him, originating probably in his hopes as to Violet Effingham and his intimacy with Madame Goesler. "Oh, heiresses!" said Mrs. Low. "I don't believe in heiresses' money till I see it. Three or four hundred a year is a great fortune for a woman, but it don't go far in keeping a house in London. And when a woman has got a little money she generally knows how to spend it. He has begun at the wrong end, and they who do that never get themselves right at the last."

At this time Phineas had become somewhat of a fine gentleman, which made Mrs. Low the more angry with him. He showed himself willing enough to go to Mrs. Low's house, but when there he seemed to her to give himself airs. I think that she was unjust to him, and that it was natural that he should not bear himself beneath her remarks exactly as he had done when he was nobody. He had certainly been very successful. He was always listened to in the House, and rarely spoke except on subjects which belonged to him, or had been allotted to him as part of his business. He lived quite at his ease with people of the highest rank,—and those of his own mode of life who disliked him did so simply because they regarded with envy his too rapid rise. He rode upon a pretty horse in the park, and was careful in his dress, and had about him an air of comfortable wealth which Mrs. Low thought he had not earned. When her husband told her of his sufficient salary, she would shake her head and express her opinion that a good time was coming. By which she perhaps meant to imply a belief that a time was coming in which her husband would have a salary much better than that now enjoyed by Phineas, and much more likely to be permanent. The Radicals were not to have office for ever, and when they were gone, what then? "I don't suppose he saves a shilling," said Mrs. Low. "How can he, keeping a horse in the park, and hunting down in the country, and living with lords? I shouldn't wonder if he isn't found to be over head and ears in debt when things come to be looked into." Mrs. Low was fond of an assured prosperity, of money in the funds, and was proud to think that her husband lived in a house of his own. "£19 10s. ground-rent to the Portman estate is what we pay, Mr. Bunce," she once said to that gallant Radical, "and that comes of beginning at the right end. Mr. Low had nothing when he began the world, and I had just what made us decent the day we married. But he began at the right end, and let things go as they may he can't get a fall." Mr. Bunce and Mrs. Low, though they differed much in politics, sympathised in reference to Phineas.

"I never believes, ma'am, in nobody doing any good by getting a place," said Mr. Bunce. "Of course I don't mean judges and them like, which must be. But when a young man has ever so much a year for sitting in a big room down at Whitehall, and reading a newspaper with his feet up on a chair, I don't think it honest, whether he's a Parliament man or whether he ain't." Whence Mr. Bunce had got his notions as to the way in which officials at Whitehall pass their time, I cannot say; but his notions are very common notions. The British world at large is slow to believe that the great British housekeeper keeps no more cats than what kill mice.

Mr. Low, who was now frequently in the habit of seeing Phineas at the House, had somewhat changed his opinions, and was not so eager in condemning Phineas as was his wife. He had begun to think that perhaps Phineas had shown some knowledge of his own aptitudes in the career which he had sought, and was aware, at any rate, that his late pupil was somebody in the House of Commons. A man will almost always respect him whom those around him respect, and will generally look up to one who is evidently above himself in his own daily avocation. Now Phineas was certainly above Mr. Low in parliamentary reputation. He sat on a front bench. He knew the leaders of parties. He was at home amidst the forms of the House. He enjoyed something of the prestige of Government power. And he walked about familiarly with the sons of dukes and the brothers of earls in a manner which had its effect even on Mr. Low. Seeing these things Mr. Low could not maintain his old opinion as stoutly as did his wife. It was almost a privilege to Mr. Low to be intimate with Phineas Finn. How then could he look down upon him?

He was surprised, therefore, one day when Phineas discussed the matter with him fully. Phineas had asked him what would be his chance of success if even now he were to give up politics and take to the Bar as the means of earning his livelihood. "You would have uphill work at first, as a matter of course," said Mr. Low.

"But it might be done, I suppose. To have been in office would not be fatal to me?"

"No, not fatal, Nothing of the kind need be fatal. Men have succeeded, and have sat on the bench afterwards, who did not begin till they were past forty. You would have to live down a prejudice created against yourself; that is all. The attorneys do not like barristers who are anything else but barristers."

"The attorneys are very arbitrary, I know," said Phineas.

"Yes;—and there would be this against you—that it is so difficult for a man to go back to the verdure and malleability of pupildom, who has once escaped from the necessary humility of its conditions. You will find it difficult to sit and wait for business in a Vice-Chancellor's Court, after having had Vice-Chancellors, or men as big as Vice-Chancellors, to wait upon you."

"I do not think much of that."

"But others would think of it, and you would find that there were difficulties. But you are not thinking of it in earnest?"

"Yes, in earnest."

"Why so? I should have thought that every day had removed you further and further from any such idea."

"The ground I'm on at present is so slippery."

"Well, yes. I can understand that. But yet it is less slippery than it used to be."

"Ah;—you do not exactly see. What if I were to lose my seat?"

"You are safe at least for the next four years, I should say."

"Ah;—no one can tell. And suppose I took it into my head to differ from the Government?"

"You must not do that. You have put yourself into a boat with these men, and you must remain in the boat. I should have thought all that was easy to you."

"It is not so easy as it seems. The very necessity of sitting still in the boat is in itself irksome,—very irksome. And then there comes some crisis in which a man cannot sit still."

"Is there any such crisis at hand now?"

"I cannot say that;—but I am beginning to find that sitting still is very disagreeable to me. When I hear those fellows below having their own way, and saying just what they like, it makes me furious. There is Robson. He tried office for a couple of years, and has broken away; and now, by George, there is no man they think so much of as they do of Robson. He is twice the man he was when he sat on the Treasury Bench."

"He is a man of fortune;—is he not?"

"I suppose so. Of course he is, because he lives. He never earns anything. His wife had money."

"My dear Finn, that makes all the difference. When a man has means of his own he can please himself. Do you marry a wife with money, and then you may kick up your heels, and do as you like about the Colonial Office. When a man hasn't money, of course he must fit himself to the circumstances of a profession."

"Though his profession may require him to be dishonest."

"I did not say that."

"But I say it, my dear Low. A man who is ready to vote black white because somebody tells him, is dishonest. Never mind, old fellow. I shall pull through, I daresay. Don't go and tell your wife all this, or she'll be harder upon me than ever when she sees me." After that Mr. Low began to think that his wife's judgment in this matter had been better than his own.

Robson could do as he liked because he had married a woman with money. Phineas told himself that that game was also open to him. He, too, might marry money. Violet Effingham had money;—quite enough to make him independent were he married to her. And Madame Goesler had money;—plenty of money. And an idea had begun to creep upon him that Madame Goesler would take him were he to offer himself. But he would sooner go back to the Bar as the lowest pupil, sooner clean boots for barristers,—so he told himself,—than marry a woman simply because she had money, than marry any other woman as long as there was a chance that Violet might be won. But it was very desirable that he should know whether Violet might be won or not. It was now July, and everybody would be gone in another month. Before August would be over he was to start for Ireland with Mr. Monk, and he knew that words would be spoken in Ireland which might make it indispensable for him to be, at any rate, able to throw up his office. In these days he became more anxious than he used to be about Miss Effingham's fortune.

He had never spoken as yet to Lord Brentford since the day on which the Earl had quarrelled with him, nor had he ever been at the house in Portman Square. Lady Laura he met occasionally, and had always spoken to her. She was gracious to him, but there had been no renewal of their intimacy. Rumours had reached him that things were going badly with her and her husband; but when men repeated such rumours in his presence, he said little or nothing on the subject. It was not for him, at any rate, to speak of Lady Laura's unhappiness. Lord Chiltern he had seen once or twice during the last month, and they had met cordially as friends. Of course he could ask no question from Lord Chiltern as to Violet; but he did learn that his friend had again patched up some reconciliation with his father. "He has quarrelled with me, you know," said Phineas.

"I am very sorry, but what could I do? As things went, I was obliged to tell him."

"Do not suppose for a moment that I am blaming you. It is, no doubt, much better that he should know it all."

"And it cannot make much difference to you, I should say."

"One doesn't like to quarrel with those who have been kind to one," said Phineas.

"But it isn't your doing. He'll come right again after a time. When I can get my own affairs settled, you may be sure I'll do my best to bring him round. But what's the reason you never see Laura now?"

"What's the reason that everything goes awry?" said Phineas, bitterly.

"When I mentioned your name to Kennedy the other day, he looked as black as thunder. But it is not odd that any one should quarrel with him. I can't stand him. Do you know, I sometimes think that Laura will have to give it up. Then there will be another mess in the family!"

This was all very well as coming from Lord Chiltern; but there was no word about Violet, and Phineas did not know how to get a word from any one. Lady Laura could have told him everything, but he could not go to Lady Laura. He did go to Lady Baldock's house as often as he thought he could with propriety, and occasionally he saw Violet. But he could do no more than see her, and the days and weeks were passing by, and the time was coming in which he would have to go away, and be with her no more. The end of the season, which was always to other men,—to other working men such as our hero,—a period of pleasurable anticipation, to him was a time of sadness, in which he felt that he was not exactly like to, or even equal to, the men with whom he lived in London. In the old days, in which he was allowed to go to Loughlinter or to Saulsby, when all men and women were going to their Loughlinters and their Saulsbys, it was very well with him; but there was something melancholy to him in his yearly journey to Ireland. He loved his father and mother and sisters as well as do other men; but there was a falling off in the manner of his life which made him feel that he had been in some sort out of his own element in London. He would have liked to have shot grouse at Loughlinter, or pheasants at Saulsby, or to have hunted down at Willingford,—or better still, to have made love to Violet Effingham wherever Violet Effingham might have placed herself. But all this was closed to him now; and there would be nothing for him but to remain at Killaloe, or to return to his work in Downing Street, from August to February. Mr. Monk, indeed, was going with him for a few weeks; but even this association did not make up for that sort of society which he would have preferred.

The session went on very quietly. The question of the Irish Reform Bill was postponed till the next year, which was a great thing gained. He carried his bill about the Canada Railway, with sundry other small bills appertaining to it, through the House in a manner which redounded infinitely to his credit. There was just enough of opposition to give a zest to the work, and to make the affair conspicuous among the affairs of the year. As his chief was in the other house, the work fell altogether into his hands, so that he came to be conspicuous among Under-Secretaries. It was only when he said a word to any leaders of his party about other matters,—about Irish Tenant-right, for instance, which was beginning to loom very large, that he found himself to be snubbed. But there was no room for action this year in reference to Irish Tenant-right, and therefore any deep consideration of that discomfort might be legitimately postponed. If he did by chance open his mouth on the subject to Mr. Monk, even Mr. Monk discouraged him.

In the early days of July, when the weather was very hot, and people were beginning to complain of the Thames, and members were becoming thirsty after grouse, and the remaining days of parliamentary work were being counted up, there came to him news,—news that was soon known throughout the fashionable world,—that the Duke of Omnium was going to give a garden party at a certain villa residence on the banks of the Thames above Richmond. It was to be such a garden party as had never been seen before. And it would be the more remarkable because the Duke had never been known to do such a thing. The villa was called The Horns, and had, indeed, been given by the Duke to Lady Glencora on her marriage; but the party was to be the Duke's party, and The Horns, with all its gardens, conservatories, lawns, shrubberies, paddocks, boat-houses, and boats, was to be made bright and beautiful for the occasion. Scores of workmen were about the place through the three first weeks of July. The world at large did not at all know why the Duke was doing so unwonted a thing,—why he should undertake so new a trouble. But Lady Glencora knew, and Madame Goesler shrewdly guessed, the riddle. When Madame Goesler's unexpected refusal had reached his Grace, he felt that he must either accept the lady's refusal, or persevere. After a day's consideration, he resolved that he would accept it. The top brick of the chimney was very desirable; but perhaps it might be well that he should endeavour to live without it. Then, accepting this refusal, he must either stand his ground and bear the blow,—or he must run away to that villa at Como, or elsewhere. The running away seemed to him at first to be the better, or at least the more pleasant, course; but at last he determined that he would stand his ground and bear the blow. Therefore he gave his garden party at The Horns.

Who was to be invited? Before the first week in July was over, many a bosom in London was fluttering with anxiety on that subject. The Duke, in giving his short word of instruction to Lady Glencora, made her understand that he would wish her to be particular in her invitations. Her Royal Highness the Princess, and his Royal Highness the Prince, had both been so gracious as to say that they would honour his fête. The Duke himself had made out a short list, with not more than a dozen names. Lady Glencora was employed to select the real crowd,—the five hundred out of the ten thousand who were to be blessed. On the Duke's own private list was the name of Madame Goesler. Lady Glencora understood it all. When Madame Goesler got her card, she thought that she understood it too. And she thought also that the Duke was behaving in a gallant way.

There was, no doubt, much difficulty about the invitations, and a considerable amount of ill-will was created. And they who considered themselves entitled to be asked, and were not asked, were full of wrath against their more fortunate friends, instead of being angry with the Duke or with Lady Glencora, who had neglected them. It was soon known that Lady Glencora was the real dispenser of the favours, and I fancy that her ladyship was tired of her task before it was completed. The party was to take place on Wednesday, the 27th of July, and before the day had come, men and women had become so hardy in the combat that personal applications were made with unflinching importunity; and letters were written to Lady Glencora putting forward this claim and that claim with a piteous clamour. "No, that is too bad," Lady Glencora said to her particular friend, Mrs. Grey, when a letter came from Mrs. Bonteen, stating all that her husband had ever done towards supporting Mr. Palliser in Parliament,—and all that he ever would do. "She shan't have it, even though she could put Plantagenet into a minority to-morrow."

Mrs. Bonteen did not get a card; and when she heard that Phineas Finn had received one, her wrath against Phineas was very great. He was "an Irish adventurer," and she regretted deeply that Mr. Bonteen had ever interested himself in bringing such an upstart forward in the world of politics. But as Mr. Bonteen never had done anything towards bringing Phineas forward, there was not much cause for regret on this head. Phineas, however, got his card, and, of course, accepted the invitation.

The grounds were opened at four. There was to be an early dinner out in tents at five; and after dinner men and women were to walk about, or dance, or make love—or hay, as suited them. The haycocks, however, were ready prepared, while it was expected that they should bring the love with them. Phineas, knowing that he should meet Violet Effingham, took a great deal with him ready made.

For an hour and a half Lady Glencora kept her position in a saloon through which the guests passed to the grounds, and to every comer she imparted the information that the Duke was on the lawn;—to every comer but one. To Madame Goesler she said no such word. "So glad to see you, my dear," she said, as she pressed her friend's hand: "if I am not killed by this work, I'll make you out again by-and-by." Then Madame Goesler passed on, and soon found herself amidst a throng of acquaintance. After a few minutes she saw the Duke seated in an arm-chair, close to the river-bank, and she bravely went up to him, and thanked him for the invitation. "The thanks are due to you for gracing our entertainment," said the Duke, rising to greet her. There were a dozen people standing round, and so the thing was done without difficulty. At that moment there came a notice that their royal highnesses were on the ground, and the Duke, of course, went off to meet them. There was not a word more spoken between the Duke and Madame Goesler on that afternoon.

Phineas did not come till late,—till seven, when the banquet was over. I think he was right in this, as the banqueting in tents loses in comfort almost more than it gains in romance. A small picnic may be very well, and the distance previously travelled may give to a dinner on the ground the seeming excuse of necessity. Frail human nature must be supported,—and human nature, having gone so far in pursuit of the beautiful, is entitled to what best support the unaccustomed circumstances will allow. Therefore, out with the cold pies, out with the salads, and the chickens, and the champagne. Since no better may be, let us recruit human nature sitting upon this moss, and forget our discomforts in the glory of the verdure around us. And dear Mary, seeing that the cushion from the waggonet is small, and not wishing to accept the too generous offer that she should take it all for her own use, will admit a contact somewhat closer than the ordinary chairs of a dining-room render necessary. That in its way is very well;—but I hold that a banquet on narrow tables in a tent is displeasing.

Phineas strolled into the grounds when the tent was nearly empty, and when Lady Glencora, almost sinking beneath her exertions, was taking rest in an inner room. The Duke at this time was dining with their royal highnesses, and three or four others, specially selected, very comfortably within doors. Out of doors the world had begun to dance,—and the world was beginning to say that it would be much nicer to go and dance upon the boards inside as soon as possible. For, though of all parties a garden party is the nicest, everybody is always anxious to get out of the garden as quick as may be. A few ardent lovers of suburban picturesque effect were sitting beneath the haycocks, and four forlorn damsels were vainly endeavouring to excite the sympathy of manly youth by playing croquet in a corner. I am not sure, however, that the lovers beneath the haycocks and the players at croquet were not actors hired by Lady Glencora for the occasion.

Phineas had not been long on the lawn before he saw Lady Laura Kennedy. She was standing with another lady, and Barrington Erle was with them. "So you have been successful?" said Barrington, greeting him.

"Successful in what?"

"In what? In getting a ticket. I have had to promise three tide-waiterships, and to give deep hints about a bishopric expected to be vacant, before I got in. But what matters? Success pays for everything. My only trouble now is how I'm to get back to London."

Lady Laura shook hands with Phineas, and then as he was passing on, followed him for a step and whispered a word to him. "Mr. Finn," she said, "if you are not going yet, come back to me presently. I have something to say to you. I shall not be far from the river, and shall stay here for about an hour."

Phineas said that he would, and then went on, not knowing exactly where he was going. He had one desire,—to find Violet Effingham, but when he should find her he could not carry her off, and sit with her beneath a haycock.

CHAPTER LXIV
The Horns

While looking for Violet Effingham, Phineas encountered Madame Goesler, among a crowd of people who were watching the adventurous embarkation of certain daring spirits in a pleasure-boat. There were watermen there in the Duke's livery, ready to take such spirits down to Richmond or up to Teddington lock, and many daring spirits did take such trips,—to the great peril of muslins, ribbons, and starch, to the peril also of ornamental summer white garments, so that when the thing was over, the boats were voted to have been a bore.

"Are you going to venture?" said Phineas to the lady.

"I should like it of all things if I were not afraid for my clothes. Will you come?"

"I was never good upon the water. I should be sea-sick to a certainty. They are going down beneath the bridge too, and we should be splashed by the steamers. I don't think my courage is high enough." Thus Phineas excused himself, being still intent on prosecuting his search for Violet.

"Then neither will I," said Madame Goesler. "One dash from a peccant oar would destroy the whole symmetry of my dress. Look. That green young lady has already been sprinkled."

"But the blue young gentleman has been sprinkled also," said Phineas, "and they will be happy in a joint baptism." Then they strolled along the river path together, and were soon alone. "You will be leaving town soon, Madame Goesler?"

"Almost immediately."

"And where do you go?"

"Oh,—to Vienna. I am there for a couple of months every year, minding my business. I wonder whether you would know me, if you saw me;—sometimes sitting on a stool in a counting-house, sometimes going about among old houses, settling what must be done to save them from tumbling down. I dress so differently at such times, and talk so differently, and look so much older, that I almost fancy myself to be another person."

"Is it a great trouble to you?"

"No,—I rather like it. It makes me feel that I do something in the world."

"Do you go alone?"

"Quite alone. I take a German maid with me, and never speak a word to any one else on the journey."

"That must be very bad," said Phineas.

"Yes; it is the worst of it. But then I am so much accustomed to be alone. You see me in society, and in society only, and therefore naturally look upon me as one of a gregarious herd; but I am in truth an animal that feeds alone and lives alone. Take the hours of the year all through, and I am a solitary during four-fifths of them. And what do you intend to do?"

"I go to Ireland."

"Home to your own people. How nice! I have no people to go to. I have one sister, who lives with her husband at Riga. She is my only relation, and I never see her."

"But you have thousands of friends in England."

"Yes,—as you see them,"—and she turned and spread out her hands towards the crowded lawn, which was behind them. "What are such friends worth? What would they do for me?"

"I do not know that the Duke would do much," said Phineas laughing.

Madame Goesler laughed also. "The Duke is not so bad," she said. "The Duke would do as much as any one else. I won't have the Duke abused."

"He may be your particular friend, for what I know," said Phineas.

"Ah;—no. I have no particular friend. And were I to wish to choose one, I should think the Duke a little above me."

"Oh, yes;—and too stiff, and too old, and too pompous, and too cold, and too make-believe, and too gingerbread."

"Mr. Finn!"

"The Duke is all buckram, you know."

"Then why do you come to his house?"

"To see you, Madame Goesler."

"Is that true, Mr. Finn?"

"Yes;—it is true in its way. One goes about to meet those whom one likes, not always for the pleasure of the host's society. I hope I am not wrong because I go to houses at which I like neither the host nor the hostess." Phineas as he said this was thinking of Lady Baldock, to whom of late he had been exceedingly civil,—but he certainly did not like Lady Baldock.

"I think you have been too hard upon the Duke of Omnium. Do you know him well?"

"Personally? certainly not. Do you? Does anybody?"

"I think he is a gracious gentleman," said Madame Goesler, "and though I cannot boast of knowing him well, I do not like to hear him called buckram. I do not think he is buckram. It is not very easy for a man in his position to live so as to please all people. He has to maintain the prestige of the highest aristocracy in Europe."

"Look at his nephew, who will be the next Duke, and who works as hard as any man in the country. Will he not maintain it better? What good did the present man ever do?"

"You believe only in motion, Mr. Finn;—and not at all in quiescence. An express train at full speed is grander to you than a mountain with heaps of snow. I own that to me there is something glorious in the dignity of a man too high to do anything,—if only he knows how to carry that dignity with a proper grace. I think that there should be breasts made to carry stars."

"Stars which they have never earned," said Phineas.

"Ah;—well; we will not fight about it. Go and earn your star, and I will say that it becomes you better than any glitter on the coat of the Duke of Omnium." This she said with an earnestness which he could not pretend not to notice or not to understand. "I too may be able to see that the express train is really greater than the mountain."

"Though, for your own life, you would prefer to sit and gaze upon the snowy peaks?"

"No;—that is not so. For myself, I would prefer to be of use somewhere,—to some one, if it were possible. I strive sometimes."

"And I am sure successfully."

"Never mind. I hate to talk about myself. You and the Duke are fair subjects for conversation; you as the express train, who will probably do your sixty miles an hour in safety, but may possibly go down a bank with a crash."

"Certainly I may," said Phineas.

"And the Duke, as the mountain, which is fixed in its stateliness, short of the power of some earthquake, which shall be grander and more terrible than any earthquake yet known. Here we are at the house again. I will go in and sit down for a while."

"If I leave you, Madame Goesler, I will say good-bye till next winter."

"I shall be in town again before Christmas, you know. You will come and see me?"

"Of course I will."

"And then this love trouble of course will be over,—one way or the other;—will it not?"

"Ah!—who can say?"

"Faint heart never won fair lady. But your heart is never faint. Farewell."

Then he left her. Up to this moment he had not seen Violet, and yet he knew that she was to be there. She had herself told him that she was to accompany Lady Laura, whom he had already met. Lady Baldock had not been invited, and had expressed great animosity against the Duke in consequence. She had gone so far as to say that the Duke was a man at whose house a young lady such as her niece ought not to be seen. But Violet had laughed at this, and declared her intention of accepting the invitation. "Go," she had said; "of course I shall go. I should have broken my heart if I could not have got there." Phineas therefore was sure that she must be in the place. He had kept his eyes ever on the alert, and yet he had not found her. And now he must keep his appointment with Lady Laura Kennedy. So he went down to the path by the river, and there he found her seated close by the water's edge. Her cousin Barrington Erle was still with her, but as soon as Phineas joined them, Erle went away. "I had told him," said Lady Laura, "that I wished to speak to you, and he stayed with me till you came. There are worse men than Barrington a great deal."

"I am sure of that."

"Are you and he still friends, Mr. Finn?"

"I hope so. I do not see so much of him as I did when I had less to do."

"He says that you have got into altogether a different set."

"I don't know that. I have gone as circumstances have directed me, but I have certainly not intended to throw over so old and good a friend as Barrington Erle."

"Oh,—he does not blame you. He tells me that you have found your way among what he calls the working men of the party, and he thinks you will do very well,—if you can only be patient enough. We all expected a different line from you, you know,—more of words and less of deeds, if I may say so;—more of liberal oratory and less of government action; but I do not doubt that you are right."

"I think that I have been wrong," said Phineas. "I am becoming heartily sick of officialities."

"That comes from the fickleness about which papa is so fond of quoting his Latin. The ox desires the saddle. The charger wants to plough."

"And which am I?"

"Your career may combine the dignity of the one with the utility of the other. At any rate you must not think of changing now. Have you seen Mr. Kennedy lately?" She asked the question abruptly, showing that she was anxious to get to the matter respecting which she had summoned him to her side, and that all that she had said hitherto had been uttered as it were in preparation of that subject.

"Seen him? yes; I see him daily. But we hardly do more than speak,"

"Why not?" Phineas stood for a moment in silence, hesitating. "Why is it that he and you do not speak?"

"How can I answer that question, Lady Laura?"

"Do you know any reason? Sit down, or, if you please, I will get up and walk with you. He tells me that you have chosen to quarrel with him, and that I have made you do so. He says that you have confessed to him that I have asked you to quarrel with him."

"He can hardly have said that."

"But he has said it,—in so many words. Do you think that I would tell you such a story falsely?"

"Is he here now?"

"No;—he is not here. He would not come. I came alone."

"Is not Miss Effingham with you?"

"No;—she is to come with my father later. She is here no doubt, now. But answer my question, Mr. Finn;—unless you find that you cannot answer it. What was it that you did say to my husband?"

"Nothing to justify what he has told you."

"Do you mean to say that he has spoken falsely?"

"I mean to use no harsh word,—but I think that Mr. Kennedy when troubled in his spirit looks at things gloomily, and puts meaning upon words which they should not bear."

"And what has troubled his spirit?"

"You must know that better than I can do, Lady Laura. I will tell you all that I can tell you. He invited me to his house and I would not go, because you had forbidden me. Then he asked me some questions about you. Did I refuse because of you,—or of anything that you had said? If I remember right, I told him that I did fancy that you would not be glad to see me,—and that therefore I would rather stay away. What was I to say?"

"You should have said nothing."

"Nothing with him would have been worse than what I did say. Remember that he asked me the question point-blank, and that no reply would have been equal to an affirmation. I should have confessed that his suggestion was true."

"He could not then have twitted me with your words."

"If I have erred, Lady Laura, and brought any sorrow on you, I am indeed grieved."

"It is all sorrow. There is nothing but sorrow. I have made up my mind to leave him."

"Oh, Lady Laura!"

"It is very bad,—but not so bad, I think, as the life I am now leading. He has accused me—, of what do you think? He says that you are my lover!"

"He did not say that,—in those words?"

"He said it in words which made me feel that I must part from him."

"And how did you answer him?"

"I would not answer him at all. If he had come to me like a man,—not accusing me, but asking me,—I would have told him everything. And what was there to tell? I should have broken my faith to you, in speaking of that scene at Loughlinter, but women always tell such stories to their husbands when their husbands are good to them, and true, and just. And it is well that they should be told. But to Mr. Kennedy I can tell nothing. He does not believe my word."

"Not believe you, Lady Laura?"

"No! Because I did not blurt out to him all that story about your foolish duel,—because I thought it best to keep my brother's secret, as long as there was a secret to be kept, he told me that I had,—lied to him!"

"What!—with that word?"

"Yes,—with that very word. He is not particular about his words, when he thinks it necessary to express himself strongly. And he has told me since that because of that he could never believe me again. How is it possible that a woman should live with such a man?" But why did she come to him with this story,—to him whom she had been accused of entertaining as a lover;—to him who of all her friends was the last whom she should have chosen as the recipient for such a tale? Phineas as he thought how he might best answer her, with what words he might try to comfort her, could not but ask himself this question. "The moment that the word was out of his mouth," she went on to say, "I resolved that I would tell you. The accusation is against you as it is against me, and is equally false to both. I have written to him, and there is my letter."

185

"But you will see him again?"

"No;—I will go to my father's house. I have already arranged it. Mr. Kennedy has my letter by this time, and I go from hence home with my father."

"Do you wish that I should read the letter?"

"Yes,—certainly. I wish that you should read it. Should I ever meet him again, I shall tell him that you saw it."

They were now standing close upon the river's bank, at a corner of the grounds, and, though the voices of people sounded near to them, they were alone. Phineas had no alternative but to read the letter, which was as follows:—

After what you have said to me it is impossible that I should return to your house. I shall meet my father at the Duke of Omnium's, and have already asked him to give me an asylum. It is my wish to remain wherever he may be, either in town or in the country. Should I change my purpose in this, and change my residence, I will not fail to let you know where I go and what I propose to do. You I think must have forgotten that I was your wife; but I will never forget it.

You have accused me of having a lover. You cannot have expected that I should continue to live with you after such an accusation. For myself I cannot understand how any man can have brought himself to bring such a charge against his wife. Even had it been true the accusation should not have been made by your mouth to my ears.

That it is untrue I believe you must be as well aware as I am myself. How intimate I was with. Mr. Finn, and what were the limits of my intimacy with him you knew before I married you. After our marriage I encouraged his friendship till I found that there was something in it that displeased you,—and, after learning that, I discouraged it. You have said that he is my lover, but you have probably not defined for yourself that word very clearly. You have felt yourself slighted because his name has been mentioned with praise;—and your jealousy has been wounded because you have thought that I have regarded him as in some way superior to yourself. You have never really thought that he was my lover,—that he spoke words to me which others might not hear, that he claimed from me aught that a wife may not give, that he received aught which a friend should not receive. The accusation has been a coward's accusation.

I shall be at my father's to-night, and to-morrow I will get you to let my servant bring to me such things as are my own,—my clothes, namely, and desk, and a few books. She will know what I want. I trust you may be happier without a wife, than ever you have been with me. I have felt almost daily since we were married that you were a man who would have been happier without a wife than with one.

Yours affectionately,

Laura Kennedy.

"It is at any rate true," she said, when Phineas had read the letter.

"True! Doubtless it is true," said Phineas, "except that I do not suppose he was ever really angry with me, or jealous, or anything of the sort,—because I got on well. It seems absurd even to think it."

"There is nothing too absurd for some men. I remember your telling me that he was weak, and poor, and unworthy. I remember your saying so when I first thought that he might become my husband. I wish I had believed you when you told me so. I should not have made such a shipwreck of myself as I have done. That is all I had to say to you. After what has passed between us I did not choose that you should hear how I was separated from my husband from any lips but my own. I will go now and find papa. Do not come with me. I prefer being alone." Then he was left standing by himself, looking down upon the river as it glided by. How would it have been with both of them if Lady Laura had accepted him three years ago, when she consented to join her lot with that of Mr. Kennedy, and had rejected him? As he stood he heard the sound of music from the house, and remembered that he had come there with the one sole object of seeing Violet Effingham. He had known that he would meet Lady Laura, and it had been in his mind to break through that law of silence which she had imposed upon him, and once more to ask her to assist him,—to implore her for the sake of their old friendship to tell him whether there might yet be for him any chance of success. But in the interview which had just taken place it had been impossible for him to speak a word of himself or of Violet. To her, in her great desolation, he could address himself on no other subject than that of her own misery. But not the less when she was talking to him of her own sorrow, of her regret that she had not listened to him when in years past he had spoken slightingly of Mr. Kennedy, was he thinking of Violet Effingham. Mr. Kennedy had certainly mistaken the signs of things when he had accused his wife by saying that Phineas was her lover. Phineas had soon got over that early feeling; and as far as he himself was concerned had never regretted Lady Laura's marriage.

He remained down by the water for a few minutes, giving Lady Laura time to escape, and then he wandered across the grounds towards the house. It was now about nine o'clock, and though there were still many walking about the grounds, the crowd of people were in the rooms. The musicians were ranged out on a verandah, so that their music might have been available for dancing within or without; but the dancers had found the boards pleasanter than the lawn, and the Duke's garden party was becoming a mere ball, with privilege for the dancers to stroll about the lawn between the dances. And in this respect the fun was better than at a ball,—that let the engagements made for partners be what they might, they could always be broken with ease. No lady felt herself bound to dance with a cavalier who was displeasing to her; and some gentlemen were left sadly in the lurch. Phineas felt himself to be very much in the lurch, even after he had discovered Violet Effingham standing up to dance with Lord Fawn.

He bided his time patiently, and at last he found his opportunity. "Would she dance with him?" She declared that she intended to dance no more, and that she had promised to be ready to return home with Lord Brentford before ten o'clock. "I have pledged myself not to be after ten," she said, laughing. Then she put her hand upon his arm, and they stepped out upon the terrace together. "Have you heard anything?" she asked him, almost in a whisper.

"Yes," he said. "I have heard what you mean. I have heard it all."

"Is it not dreadful?"

"I fear it is the best thing she can do. She has never been happy with him."

"But to be accused after that fashion,—by her husband!" said Violet. "One can hardly believe it in these days. And of all women she is the last to deserve such accusation."

"The very last," said Phineas, feeling that the subject was one upon which it was not easy for him to speak.

"I cannot conceive to whom he can have alluded," said Violet. Then Phineas began to understand that Violet had not heard the whole story; but the difficulty of speaking was still very great.

"It has been the result of ungovernable temper," he said.

"But a man does not usually strive to dishonour himself because he is in a rage. And this man is incapable of rage. He must be cursed with one of those dark gloomy minds in which love always leads to jealousy. She will never return to him."

"One cannot say. In many respects it would be better that she should," said Phineas.

"She will never return to him," repeated Violet,—"never. Would you advise her to do so?"

"How can I say? If one were called upon for advice, one would think so much before one spoke."

"I would not,—not for a minute. What! to be accused of that! How are a man and woman to live together after there have been such words between them? Poor Laura! What a terrible end to all her high hopes! Do you not grieve for her?"

They were now at some distance from the house, and Phineas could not but feel that chance had been very good to him in giving him his opportunity. She was leaning on his arm, and they were alone, and she was speaking to him with all the familiarity of old friendship. "I wonder whether I may change the subject," said he, "and ask you a word about yourself?"

"What word?" she said sharply.

"I have heard—"

"What have you heard?"

"Simply this,—that you are not now as you were six months ago. Your marriage was then fixed for June."

"It has been unfixed since then," she said.

"Yes;—it has been unfixed. I know it. Miss Effingham, you will not be angry with me if I say that when I heard it was so, something of a hope,—no, I must not call it a hope,—something that longed to form itself into hope returned to my breast, and from that hour to this has been the only subject on which I have cared to think."

"Lord Chiltern is your friend, Mr. Finn?"

"He is so, and I do not think that I have ever been untrue to my friendship for him."

"He says that no man has ever had a truer friend. He will swear to that in all companies. And I, when it was allowed to me to swear with him, swore it too. As his friend, let me tell you one thing,—one thing which I would never tell to any other man,—one thing which I know I may tell you in confidence. You are a gentleman, and will not break my confidence?"

"I think I will not."

"I know you will not, because you are a gentleman. I told Lord Chiltern in the autumn of last year that I loved him. And I did love him. I shall never have the same confession to make to another man. That he and I are not now,—on those loving terms,—which once existed, can make no difference in that. A woman cannot transfer her heart. There have been things which have made me feel,—that I was perhaps mistaken,—in saying that I would be,—his wife. But I said so, and cannot now give myself to another. Here is Lord Brentford, and we will join him." There was Lord Brentford with Lady Laura on his arm, very gloomy,—resolving on what way he might be avenged on the man who had insulted his daughter. He took but little notice of Phineas as he resumed his charge of Miss Effingham; but the two ladies wished him good night.

"Good night, Lady Laura," said Phineas, standing with his hat in his hand,—"good night, Miss Effingham." Then he was alone,—quite alone. Would it not be well for him to go down to the bottom of the garden, and fling himself into the quiet river, so that there might be an end of him? Or would it not be better still that he should create for himself some quiet river of life, away from London, away from politics, away from lords, and titled ladies, and fashionable squares, and the parties given by dukes, and the disappointments incident to a small man in attempting to make for himself a career among big men? There had frequently been in the mind of this young man an idea that there was something almost false in his own position,—that his life was a pretence, and that he would ultimately be subject to that ruin which always comes, sooner or later, on things which are false; and now as he wandered alone about Lady Glencora's gardens, this feeling was very strong within his bosom, and robbed him altogether of the honour and glory of having been one of the Duke of Omnium's guests.

CHAPTER LXV
The Cabinet Minister at Killaloe

Phineas did not throw himself into the river from the Duke's garden; and was ready, in spite of Violet Effingham, to start for Ireland with Mr. Monk at the end of the first week in August. The close of that season in London certainly was not a happy period of his life. Violet had spoken to him after such a fashion that he could not bring himself not to believe her. She had given him no hint whether it was likely or unlikely that she and Lord Chiltern would be reconciled; but she had convinced him that he could not be allowed to take Lord Chiltern's place. "A woman cannot transfer her heart," she had said. Phineas was well aware that many women do transfer their hearts; but he had gone to this woman too soon after the wrench which her love had received; he had been too sudden with his proposal for a transfer; and the punishment for such ill judgment must be that success would now be impossible to him. And yet how could he have waited, feeling that Miss Effingham, if she were at all like other girls whom he had known, might have promised herself to some other lover before she would return within his reach in the succeeding spring? But she was not like some other girls. Ah;—he knew that now, and repented him of his haste.

But he was ready for Mr. Monk on the 7th of August, and they started together. Something less than twenty hours took them from London to Killaloe, and during four or five of those twenty hours Mr. Monk was unfitted for any conversation by the uncomfortable feelings incidental to the passage from Holyhead to Kingstown. Nevertheless, there was a great deal of conversation between them during the journey. Mr. Monk had almost made up his mind to leave the Cabinet. "It is sad to me to have to confess it," he said, "but the truth is that my old rival, Turnbull, is right. A man who begins his political life as I began mine, is not the man of whom a Minister should be formed. I am inclined to think that Ministers of Government require almost as much education in their trade as shoemakers or tallow-chandlers. I doubt whether you can make a good public servant of a man simply because he has got the ear of the House of Commons."

"Then you mean to say," said Phineas, "that we are altogether wrong from beginning to end, in our way of arranging these things?"

"I do not say that at all. Look at the men who have been leading statesmen since our present mode of government was formed,—from the days in which it was forming itself, say from Walpole down, and you will find that all who have been of real use had early training as public servants."

"Are we never to get out of the old groove?"

"Not if the groove is good," said Mr. Monk, "Those who have been efficient as ministers sucked in their efficacy with their mother's milk. Lord Brock did so, and Lord de Terrier, and Mr. Mildmay. They seated themselves in office chairs the moment they left college. Mr. Gresham was in office before he was eight-and-twenty. The Duke of St. Bungay was at work as a Private Secretary when he was three-and-twenty. You, luckily for yourself, have done the same."

"And regret it every hour of my life."

"You have no cause for regret, but it is not so with me. If there be any man unfitted by his previous career for office, it is he who has become, or who has endeavoured to become, a popular politician,—an exponent, if I may say so, of public opinion. As far as I can see, office is offered to such men with one view only,—that of clipping their wings."

"And of obtaining their help."

"It is the same thing. Help from Turnbull would mean the withdrawal of all power of opposition from him. He could not give other help for any long term, as the very fact of his accepting power and patronage would take from him his popular leadership. The masses outside require to have their minister as the Queen has hers; but the same man cannot be minister to both. If the people's minister chooses to change his master, and to take the Queen's shilling, something of temporary relief may be gained by government in the fact that the other place will for a time be vacant. But there are candidates enough for such places, and the vacancy is not a vacancy long. Of course the Crown has this pull, that it pays wages, and the people do not."

"I do not think that that influenced you," said Phineas.

"It did not influence me. To you I will make bold to state so much positively, though it would be foolish, perhaps, to do so to others. I did not go for the shilling, though I am so poor a man that the shilling is more to me than it would be to almost any man in the House. I took the shilling, much doubting, but guided in part by this, that I was ashamed of being afraid to take it. They told me,—Mr. Mildmay and the Duke,—that I could earn it to the benefit of the country. I have not earned it, and the country has not been benefited,—unless it be for the good of the country that my voice in the House should be silenced. If I believe that, I ought to hold my tongue without taking a salary for holding it. I have made a mistake, my friend. Such mistakes made at my time of life cannot be wholly rectified; but, being convinced of my error, I must do the best in my power to put myself right again."

There was a bitterness in all this to Phineas himself of which he could not but make plaint to his companion. "The truth is," he said, "that a man in office must be a slave, and that slavery is distasteful."

"There I think you are wrong. If you mean that you cannot do joint work with other men altogether after your own fashion the same may be said of all work. If you had stuck to the Bar you must have pleaded your causes in conformity with instructions from the attorneys."

"I should have been guided by my own lights in advising those attorneys."

"I cannot see that you suffer anything that ought to go against the grain with you. You are beginning young, and it is your first adopted career. With me it is otherwise. If by my telling you this I shall have led you astray, I shall regret my openness with you. Could I begin again, I would willingly begin as you began."

It was a great day in Killaloe, that on which Mr. Monk arrived with Phineas at the doctor's house. In London, perhaps, a bishop inspires more awe than a Cabinet Minister. In Killaloe, where a bishop might be seen walking about every day, the mitred dignitary of the Church, though much loved, was thought of, I fear, but lightly; whereas a Cabinet Minister coming to stay in the house of a townsman was a thing to be wondered at, to be talked about, to be afraid of, to be a fruitful source of conversation for a year to come. There were many in Killaloe, especially among the elder ladies, who had shaken their heads and expressed the saddest doubts when young Phineas Finn had first become a Parliament man. And though by degrees they had been half brought round, having been driven to acknowledge that he had been wonderfully successful as a Parliament man, still they had continued to shake their heads among themselves, and to fear something in the future,—until he appeared at his old home leading a Cabinet Minister by the hand. There was such assurance in this that even old Mrs. Callaghan, at the brewery, gave way, and began to say all manner of good things, and to praise the doctor's luck in that he had a son gifted with parts so excellent. There was a great desire to see the Cabinet Minister in the flesh, to be with him when he ate and drank, to watch the gait and countenance of the man, and to drink water from this fountain of state lore which had been so wonderfully brought among them by their young townsman. Mrs. Finn was aware that it behoved her to be chary of her invitations, but the lady from the brewery had said such good things of Mrs. Finn's black swan, that she carried her point, and was invited to meet the Cabinet Minister at dinner on the day after his arrival.

Mrs. Flood Jones and her daughter were invited also to be of the party. When Phineas had been last at Killaloe, Mrs. Flood Jones, as the reader may remember, had remained with her daughter at Floodborough,—feeling it to be her duty to keep her daughter away from the danger of an unrequited attachment. But it seemed that her purpose was changed now, or that she no longer feared the danger,—for both Mary and her mother were now again living in Killaloe, and Mary was at the doctor's house as much as ever.

A day or two before the coming of the god and the demigod to the little town, Barbara Finn and her friend had thus come to understand each other as they walked along the Shannon side. "I am sure, my dear, that he is engaged to nobody," said Barbara Finn.

"And I am sure, my dear," said Mary, "that I do not care whether he is or is not."

"What do you mean, Mary?"

"I mean what I say. Why should I care? Five years ago I had a foolish dream, and now I am awake again. Think how old I have got to be!"

"Yes;—you are twenty-three. What has that to do with it?"

"It has this to do with it;—that I am old enough to know better. Mamma and I quite understand each other. She used to be angry with him, but she has got over all that foolishness now. It always made me so vexed;—the idea of being angry with a man because,—because—! You know one can't talk about it, it is so foolish. But that is all over now."

"Do you mean to say you don't care for him, Mary? Do you remember what you used to swear to me less than two years ago?"

"I remember it all very well, and I remember what a goose I was. As for caring for him, of course I do,—because he is your brother, and because I have known him all my life. But if he were going to be married to-morrow, you would see that it would make no difference to me."

Barbara Finn walked on for a couple of minutes in silence before she replied. "Mary," she said at last, "I don't believe a word of it."

"Very well;—then all that I shall ask of you is, that we may not talk about him any more. Mamma believes it, and that is enough for me." Nevertheless, they did talk about Phineas during the whole of that day, and very often talked about him afterwards, as long as Mary remained at Killaloe.

There was a large dinner party at the doctor's on the day after Mr. Monk's arrival. The bishop was not there, though he was on terms sufficiently friendly with the doctor's family to have been invited on so grand an occasion; but he was not there, because Mrs. Finn was determined that she would be taken out to dinner by a Cabinet Minister in the face of all her friends. She was aware that had the bishop been there, she must have taken the bishop's arm. And though there would have been glory in that, the other glory was more to her taste. It was the first time in her life that she had ever seen a Cabinet Minister, and I think that she was a little disappointed at finding him so like other middle-aged gentlemen. She had hoped that Mr. Monk would have assumed something of the dignity of his position; but he assumed nothing. Now the bishop, though he was a very mild man, did assume something by the very facts of his apron and knee-breeches.

"I am sure, sir, it is very good of you to come and put up with our humble way of living," said Mrs. Finn to her guest, as they sat down at table. And yet she had resolved that she would not make any speech of the kind,—that she would condescend to no apology,—that she would bear herself as though a Cabinet Minister dined with her at least once a year. But when the moment came, she broke down, and made this apology with almost abject meekness, and then hated herself because she had done so.

"My dear madam," said Mr. Monk, "I live myself so much like a hermit that your house is a palace of luxury to me." Then he felt that he had made a foolish speech, and he also hated himself. He found it very difficult to talk to his hostess upon any subject, until by chance he mentioned his young friend Phineas. Then her tongue was unloosed. "Your son, madam," he said, "is going with me to Limerick and back to Dublin. It is a shame, I know, taking him so soon away from home, but I should not know how to get on without him."

"Oh, Mr. Monk, it is such a blessing for him, and such an honour for us, that you should be so good to him." Then the mother spoke out all her past fears and all her present hopes, and acknowledged the great glory which it was to her to have a son sitting in Parliament, holding an office with a stately name and a great salary, and blessed with the friendship of such a man as Mr. Monk. After that Mr. Monk got on better with her.

"I don't know any young man," said he, "in whose career I have taken so strong an interest."

"He was always good," said Mrs. Finn, with a tear forcing itself into the corner of each eye. "I am his mother, and of course I ought not to say so,—not in this way; but it is true, Mr. Monk." And then the poor lady was obliged to raise her handkerchief and wipe away the drops.

Phineas on this occasion had taken out to dinner the mother of his devoted Mary, Mrs. Flood Jones. "What a pleasure it must be to the doctor and Mrs. Finn to see you come back in this way," said Mrs. Flood Jones.

"With all my bones unbroken?" said he, laughing.

"Yes; with all your bones unbroken. You know, Phineas, when we first heard that you were to sit in Parliament, we were afraid that you might break a rib or two,—since you choose to talk about the breaking of bones."

"Yes, I know. Everybody thought I should come to grief; but nobody felt so sure of it as I did myself."

"But you have not come to grief."

"I am not out of the wood yet, you know, Mrs. Flood Jones. There is plenty of possibility for grief in my way still."

"As far as I can understand it, you are out of the wood. All that your friends here want to see now is, that you should marry some nice English girl, with a little money, if possible. Rumours have reached us, you know."

"Rumours always lie," said Phineas.

"Sometimes they do, of course; and I am not going to ask any indiscreet questions. But that is what we all hope. Mary was saying, only the other day, that if you were once married, we should all feel quite safe about you. And you know we all take the most lively interest in your welfare. It is not every day that a man from County Clare gets on as you have done, and therefore we are bound to think of you." Thus Mrs. Flood Jones signified to Phineas Finn that she had forgiven him the thoughtlessness of his early youth,—even though there had been something of treachery in that thoughtlessness to her own daughter; and showed him, also, that whatever Mary's feelings might have been once, they were not now of a nature to trouble her. "Of course you will marry?" said Mrs. Flood Jones.

"I should think very likely not," said Phineas, who perhaps looked farther into the mind of the lady than the lady intended.

"Oh, do," said the lady. "Every man should marry as soon as he can, and especially a man in your position."

When the ladies met together in the drawing-room after dinner, it was impossible but that they should discuss Mr. Monk. There was Mrs. Callaghan from the brewery there, and old Lady Blood, of Bloodstone,—who on ordinary occasions would hardly admit that she was on dining-out terms with any one in Killaloe except the bishop, but who had found it impossible to decline to meet a Cabinet Minister,—and there was Mrs. Stackpoole from Sixmiletown, a far-away cousin of the Finns, who hated Lady Blood with a true provincial hatred.

"I don't see anything particularly uncommon in him, after all," said Lady Blood.

"I think he is very nice indeed," said Mrs. Flood Jones.

"So very quiet, my dear, and just like other people," said Mrs. Callaghan, meaning to pronounce a strong eulogium on the Cabinet Minister.

"Very like other people indeed," said Lady Blood.

"And what would you expect, Lady Blood?" said Mrs. Stackpoole. "Men and women in London walk upon two legs, just as they do in Ennis." Now Lady Blood herself had been born and bred in Ennis, whereas Mrs. Stackpoole had come from Limerick, which is a much more considerable town, and therefore there was a satire in this allusion to the habits of the men of Ennis which Lady Blood understood thoroughly.

"My dear Mrs. Stackpoole, I know how the people walk in London quite as well as you do." Lady Blood had once passed three months in London while Sir Patrick had been alive, whereas Mrs. Stackpoole had never done more than visit the metropolis for a day or two.

"Oh, no doubt," said Mrs. Stackpoole; "but I never can understand what it is that people expect. I suppose Mr. Monk ought to have come with his stars on the breast of his coat, to have pleased Lady Blood."

"My dear Mrs. Stackpoole, Cabinet Ministers don't have stars," said Lady Blood.

"I never said they did," said Mrs. Stackpoole.

"He is so nice and gentle to talk to," said Mrs. Finn. "You may say what you will, but men who are high up do very often give themselves airs. Now I must say that this friend of my son's does not do anything of that kind."

"Not the least," said Mrs. Callaghan.

"Quite the contrary," said Mrs. Stackpoole.

"I dare say he is a wonderful man," said Lady Blood. "All I say is, that I didn't hear anything wonderful come out of his mouth; and as for people in Ennis walking on two legs, I have seen donkeys in Limerick doing just the same thing." Now it was well known that Mrs. Stackpoole had two sons living in Limerick, as to neither of whom was it expected that he would set the Shannon on fire. After this little speech there was no further mention of Mr. Monk, as it became necessary that all the good-nature of Mrs. Finn and all the tact of Mrs. Flood Jones and all the energy of Mrs. Callaghan should be used, to prevent the raging of an internecine battle between Mrs. Stackpoole and Lady Blood.

CHAPTER LXVI
Victrix

Mr. Monk's holiday programme allowed him a week at Killaloe, and from thence he was to go to Limerick, and from Limerick to Dublin, in order that, at both places, he might be entertained at a public dinner and make a speech about tenant-right. Foreseeing that Phineas might commit himself if he attended these meetings, Mr. Monk had counselled him to remain at Killaloe. But Phineas had refused to subject himself to such cautious abstinence. Mr. Monk had come to Ireland as his friend, and he would see him through his travels. "I shall not, probably, be asked to speak," said Phineas, "and if I am asked, I need not say more than a few words. And what if I did speak out?"

"You might find it disadvantageous to you in London."

"I must take my chance of that. I am not going to tie myself down for ever and ever for the sake of being Under-Secretary to the Colonies." Mr. Monk said very much to him on the subject,—was constantly saying very much to him about it; but in spite of all that Mr. Monk said, Phineas did make the journey to Limerick and Dublin.

He had not, since his arrival at Killaloe, been a moment alone with Mary Flood Jones till the evening before he started with Mr. Monk. She had kept out of his way successfully, though she had constantly been with him in company, and was beginning to plume herself on the strength and valour of her conduct. But her self-praise had in it nothing of joy, and her glory was very sad. Of course she would care for him no more,—more especially as it was so very evident that he cared not at all for her. But the very fact of her keeping out of his way, made her acknowledge to herself that her position was very miserable. She had declared to her mother that she might certainly go to Killaloe with safety,—that it would be better for her to put herself in the way of meeting him as an old friend,—that the idea of the necessity of shutting herself up because of his approach, was the one thing that gave her real pain. Therefore her mother had brought her to Killaloe and she had met him; but her fancied security had deserted her, and she found herself to be miserable, hoping for something she did not know what, still dreaming of possibilities, feeling during every moment of his presence with her that some special conduct was necessary on her part. She could not make further confession to her mother and ask to be carried back to Floodborough; but she knew that she was very wretched at Killaloe.

As for Phineas, he had felt that his old friend was very cold to him. He was in that humour with reference to Violet Effingham which seemed especially to require consolation. He knew now that all hope was over there. Violet Effingham could never be his wife. Even were she not to marry Lord Chiltern for the next five years, she would not, during those five years, marry any other man. Such was our hero's conviction; and, suffering under this conviction, he was in want of the comfort of feminine sympathy. Had Mary known all this, and had it suited her to play such a part, I think she might have had Phineas at her feet before he had been a week at home. But she had kept aloof from him and had heard nothing of his sorrows. As a natural consequence of this, Phineas was more in love with her than ever.

On the evening before he started with Mr. Monk for Limerick, he managed to be alone with her for a few minutes. Barbara may probably have assisted in bringing about this arrangement, and had, perhaps, been guilty of some treachery,—sisters in such circumstances will sometimes be very treacherous to their friends. I feel sure, however, that Mary herself was quite innocent of any guile in the matter. "Mary," Phineas said to her suddenly, "it seems to me that you have avoided me purposely ever since I have been at home." She smiled and blushed, and stammered and said nothing. "Has there been any reason for it, Mary?"

"No reason at all that I know of," she said.

"We used to be such great friends."

"That was before you were a great man, Phineas. It must necessarily be different now. You know so many people now, and people of such a different sort, that of course I fall a little into the background."

"When you talk in that way, Mary, I know that you are laughing at me."

"Indeed, indeed I am not."

"I believe there is no one in the whole world," he said, after a pause, "whose friendship is more to me than yours is. I think of it so often, Mary. Say that when we come back it shall be between us as it used to be." Then he put out his hand for hers, and she could not help giving it to him. "Of course there will be people," he said, "who talk nonsense, and one cannot help it; but I will not put up with it from you."

"I did not mean to talk nonsense, Phineas!" Then there came some one across them, and the conversation was ended; but the sound of his voice remained on her ears, and she could not help but remember that he had declared that her friendship was dearer to him than the friendship of any one else.

Phineas went with Mr. Monk first to Limerick and then to Dublin, and found himself at both places to be regarded as a hero only second to the great hero. At both places the one subject of debate was tenant-right;—could anything be done to make it profitable for men with capital to put their capital into Irish land? The fertility of the soil was questioned by no one,—nor the sufficiency of external circumstances, such as railroads and the like;—nor the abundance of labour;—nor even security for the wealth to be produced. The only difficulty was in this, that the men who were to produce the wealth had no guarantee that it would be theirs when it was created. In England and elsewhere such guarantees were in existence. Might it not be possible to introduce them into Ireland? That was the question which Mr. Monk had in hand; and in various speeches which he made both before and after the dinners given to him, he pledged himself to keep it well in hand when Parliament should meet. Of course Phineas spoke also. It was impossible that he should be silent when his friend and leader was pouring out his eloquence. Of course he spoke, and of course he pledged himself. Something like the old pleasures of the debating society returned to him, as standing upon a platform before a listening multitude, he gave full vent to his words. In the House of Commons, of late he had been so cabined, cribbed, and confined by office as to have enjoyed nothing of this. Indeed, from the commencement of his career, he had fallen so thoroughly into the decorum of Government ways, as to have missed altogether the delights of that wild irresponsible oratory of which Mr. Monk had spoken to him so often. He had envied men below the gangway, who, though supporting the Government on main questions, could get up on their legs whenever the House was full enough to make it worth their while, and say almost whatever they pleased. There was that Mr. Robson, who literally did say just what came uppermost; and the thing that came uppermost was often ill-natured, often unbecoming the gravity of the House, was always startling; but men listened to him and liked him to speak. But Mr. Robson had—married a woman with money. Oh, why,—why, had not Violet Effingham been kinder to him? He might even yet, perhaps, marry a woman with money. But he could not bring himself to do so unless he loved her.

The upshot of the Dublin meeting was that he also positively pledged himself to support during the next session of Parliament a bill advocating tenant-right. "I am sorry you went so far as that," Mr. Monk said to him almost as soon as the meeting was over. They were standing on the pier at Kingstown, and Mr. Monk was preparing to return to England.

"And why not I as far as you?"

"Because I had thought about it, and I do not think that you have. I am prepared to resign my office to-morrow; and directly that I can see Mr. Gresham and explain to him what I have done, I shall offer to do so."

"He won't accept your resignation."

"He must accept it, unless he is prepared to instruct the Irish Secretary to bring in such a bill as I can support."

"I shall be exactly in the same boat."

"But you ought not to be in the same boat;—nor need you. My advice to you is to say nothing about it till you get back to London, and then speak to Lord Cantrip. Tell him that you will not say anything on the subject in the House, but that in the event of there being a division you hope to be allowed to vote as on an open question. It may be that I shall get Gresham's assent, and if so we shall be all right. If I do not, and if they choose to make it a point with you, you must resign also."

"Of course I shall," said Phineas.

"But I do not think they will. You have been too useful, and they will wish to avoid the weakness which comes to a ministry from changing its team. Good-bye, my dear fellow; and remember this,—my last word of advice to you is to stick by the ship. I am quite sure it is a career which will suit you. I did not begin it soon enough."

Phineas was rather melancholy as he returned alone to Killaloe. It was all very well to bid him stick to the ship, and he knew as well as any one could tell him how material the ship was to him; but there are circumstances in which a man cannot stick to his ship,—cannot stick, at least, to this special Government ship. He knew that whither Mr. Monk went, in this session, he must follow. He had considerable hope that when Mr. Monk explained his purpose to the Prime Minister, the Prime Minister would feel himself obliged to give way. In that case Phineas would not only be able to keep his office, but would have such an opportunity of making a speech in Parliament as circumstances had never yet given to him. When he was again at home he said nothing to his father or to the Killaloeians as to the danger of his position. Of what use would it be to make his mother and sisters miserable, or to incur the useless counsels of the doctor? They seemed to think his speech at Dublin very fine, and were never tired of talking of what Mr. Monk and Phineas were going to do; but the idea had not come home to them that if Mr. Monk or Phineas chose to do anything on their own account, they must give up the places which they held under the Crown.

It was September when Phineas found himself back at Killaloe, and he was due to be at his office in London in November. The excitement of Mr. Monk's company was now over, and he had nothing to do but to receive pouches full of official papers from the Colonial Office, and study all the statistics which came within his reach in reference to the proposed new law for tenant-right. In the meantime Mary was still living with her mother at Killaloe, and still kept herself somewhat aloof from the man she loved. How could it be possible for him not to give way in such circumstances as those?

One day he found himself talking to her about himself, and speaking to her of his own position with more frankness than he ever used with his own family. He had begun by reminding her of that conversation which they had had before he went away with Mr. Monk, and by reminding her also that she had promised to return to her old friendly ways with him.

"Nay, Phineas; there was no promise," she said.

"And are we not to be friends?"

"I only say that I made no particular promise. Of course we are friends. We have always been friends."

"What would you say if you heard that I had resigned my office and given up my seat?" he asked. Of course she expressed her surprise, almost her horror, at such an idea, and then he told her everything. It took long in the telling, because it was necessary that he should explain to her the working of the system which made it impossible for him, as a member of the Government, to entertain an opinion of his own.

"And do you mean that you would lose your salary?" she asked.

"Certainly I should."

"Would not that be very dreadful?"

He laughed as he acknowledged that it would be dreadful. "It is very dreadful, Mary, to have nothing to eat and drink. But what is a man to do? Would you recommend me to say that black is white?"

"I am sure you will never do that."

"You see, Mary, it is very nice to be called by a big name and to have a salary, and it is very comfortable to be envied by one's friends and enemies;—but there are drawbacks. There is this especial drawback." Then he paused for a moment before he went on.

"What especial drawback, Phineas?"

"A man cannot do what he pleases with himself. How can a man marry, so circumstanced as I am?"

She hesitated for a moment, and then she answered him,—"A man may be very happy without marrying, I suppose."

He also paused for many moments before he spoke again, and she then made a faint attempt to escape from him. But before she succeeded he had asked her a question which arrested her. "I wonder whether you would listen to me if I were to tell you a history?" Of course she listened, and the history he told her was the tale of his love for Violet Effingham.

"And she has money of her own?" Mary asked.

"Yes;—she is rich. She has a large fortune."

"Then, Mr. Finn, you must seek some one else who is equally blessed."

"Mary, that is untrue,—that is ill-natured. You do not mean that. Say that you do not mean it. You have not believed that I loved Miss Effingham because she was rich."

"But you have told me that you could love no one who is not rich."

"I have said nothing of the kind. Love is involuntary. It does not often run in a yoke with prudence. I have told you my history as far as it is concerned with Violet Effingham. I did love her very dearly."

"Did love her, Mr. Finn?"

"Yes;—did love her. Is there any inconstancy in ceasing to love when one is not loved? Is there inconstancy in changing one's love, and in loving again?"

"I do not know," said Mary, to whom the occasion was becoming so embarrassing that she no longer was able to reply with words that had a meaning in them.

"If there be, dear, I am inconstant." He paused, but of course she had not a syllable to say. "I have changed my love. But I could not speak of a new passion till I had told the story of that which has passed away. You have heard it all now, Mary. Can you try to love me, after that?" It had come at last,—the thing for which she had been ever wishing. It had come in spite of her imprudence, and in spite of her prudence. When she had heard him to the end she was not a whit angry with him,—she was not in the least aggrieved,—because he had been lost to her in his love for this Miss Effingham, while she had been so nearly lost by her love for him. For women such episodes in the lives of their lovers have an excitement which is almost pleasurable, whereas each man is anxious to hear his lady swear that until he appeared upon the scene her heart had been fancy free. Mary, upon the whole, had liked the story,—had thought that it had been finely told, and was well pleased with the final catastrophe. But, nevertheless, she was not prepared with her reply. "Have you no answer to give me, Mary?" he said, looking up into her eyes. I am afraid that he did not doubt what would be her answer,—as it would be good that all lovers should do. "You must vouchsafe me some word, Mary."

When she essayed to speak she found that she was dumb. She could not get her voice to give her the assistance of a single word. She did not cry, but there was a motion as of sobbing in her throat which impeded all utterance. She was as happy as earth,—as heaven could make her; but she did not know how to tell him that she was happy. And yet she longed to tell it, that he might know how thankful she was to him for his goodness. He still sat looking at her, and now by degrees he had got her hand in his. "Mary," he said, "will you be my wife,—my own wife?"

When half an hour had passed, they were still together, and now she had found the use of her tongue. "Do whatever you like best," she said. "I do not care which you do. If you came to me to-morrow and told me you had no income, it would make no difference. Though to love you and to have your love is all the world to me,—though it makes all the difference between misery and happiness,—I would sooner give up that than be a clog on you." Then he took her in his arms and kissed her. "Oh, Phineas!" she said, "I do love you so entirely!"

"My own one!"

"Yes; your own one. But if you had known it always! Never mind. Now you are my own,—are you not?"

"Indeed yes, dearest."

"Oh, what a thing it is to be victorious at last."

"What on earth are you two doing here these two hours together?" said Barbara, bursting into the room.

"What are we doing?" said Phineas.

"Yes;—what are you doing?"

"Nothing in particular," said Mary.

"Nothing at all in particular," said Phineas. "Only this,—that we have engaged ourselves to marry each other. It is quite a trifle,—is it not, Mary?"

"Oh, Barbara!" said the joyful girl, springing forward into her friend's arms; "I do believe I am the happiest creature on the face of this earth!"

CHAPTER LXVII
Job's Comforters

Before Phineas had returned to London his engagement with Mary Flood Jones was known to all his family, was known to Mrs. Flood Jones, and was indeed known generally to all Killaloe. That other secret of his, which had reference to the probability of his being obliged to throw up his office, was known only to Mary herself. He thought that he had done all that honour required of him in telling her of his position before he had proposed;—so that she might on that ground refuse him if she were so minded. And yet he had known very well that such prudence on her part was not to be expected. If she loved him, of course she would say so when she was asked. And he had known that she loved him. "There may be delay, Mary," he said to her as he was going; "nay, there must be delay, if I am obliged to resign."

"I do not care a straw for delay if you will be true to me," she said.

"Do you doubt my truth, dearest?"

"Not in the least. I will swear by it as the one thing that is truest in the world."

"You may, dearest. And if this should come to pass I must go to work and put my shoulder to the wheel, and earn an income for you by my old profession before I can make you my wife. With such a motive before me I know that I shall earn an income." And thus they parted. Mary, though of course she would have preferred that her future husband should remain in his high office, that he should be a member of Parliament and an Under-Secretary of State, admitted no doubt into her mind to disturb her happiness; and Phineas, though he had many misgivings as to the prudence of what he had done, was not the less strong in his resolution of constancy and endurance. He would throw up his position, resign his seat, and go to work at the Bar instantly, if he found that his independence as a man required him to do so. And, above all, let come what might, he would be true to Mary Flood Jones.

December was half over before he saw Lord Cantrip. "Yes,—yes;" said Lord Cantrip, when the Under-Secretary began to tell his story; "I saw what you were about. I wish I had been at your elbow."

"If you knew the country as I know it, you would be as eager about it as I am."

"Then I can only say that I am very glad that I do not know the country as you know it. You see, Finn, it's my idea that if a man wants to make himself useful he should stick to some special kind of work. With you it's a thousand pities that you should not do so."

"You think, then, I ought to resign?"

"I don't say anything about that. As you wish it, of course I'll speak to Gresham. Monk, I believe, has resigned already."

"He has written to me, and told me so," said Phineas.

"I always felt afraid of him for your sake, Finn. Mr. Monk is a clever man, and as honest a man as any in the House, but I always thought that he was a dangerous friend for you. However, we will see. I will speak to Gresham after Christmas. There is no hurry about it."

When Parliament met the first great subject of interest was the desertion of Mr. Monk from the Ministry. He at once took his place below the gangway, sitting as it happened exactly in front of Mr. Turnbull, and there he made his explanation. Some one opposite asked a question whether a certain right honourable gentleman had not left the Cabinet. Then Mr. Gresham replied that to his infinite regret his right honourable friend, who lately presided at the Board of Trade, had resigned; and he went on to explain that this resignation had, according to his ideas, been quite unnecessary. His right honourable friend entertained certain ideas about Irish tenant-right, as to which he himself and his right honourable friend the Secretary for Ireland could not exactly pledge themselves to be in unison with him; but he had thought that the motion might have rested at any rate over this session. Then Mr. Monk explained, making his first great speech on Irish tenant-right. He found himself obliged to advocate some immediate measure for giving security to the Irish farmer; and as he could not do so as a member of the Cabinet, he was forced to resign the honour of that position. He said something also as to the great doubt which had ever weighed on his own mind as to the inexpediency of a man at his time of life submitting himself for the first time to the trammels of office. This called up Mr. Turnbull, who took the opportunity of saying that he now agreed cordially with his old friend for the first time since that old friend had listened to the blandishments of the ministerial seducer, and that he welcomed his old friend back to those independent benches with great satisfaction. In this way the debate was very exciting. Nothing was said which made it then necessary for Phineas to get upon his legs or to declare himself; but he perceived that the time would rapidly come in which he must do so. Mr. Gresham, though he strove to speak with gentle words, was evidently very angry with the late President of the Board of Trade; and, moreover, it was quite clear that a bill would be introduced by Mr. Monk himself, which Mr. Gresham was determined to oppose. If all this came to pass and there should be a close division, Phineas felt that his fate would be sealed. When he again spoke to Lord Cantrip on the subject, the Secretary of State shrugged his shoulders and shook his head. "I can only advise you," said Lord Cantrip, "to forget all that took place in Ireland. If you will do so, nobody else will remember it." "As if it were possible to forget such things," he said in the letter which he wrote to Mary that night. "Of course I shall go now. If it were not for your sake, I should not in the least regret it."

He had been with Madame Goesler frequently in the winter, and had discussed with her so often the question of his official position that she had declared that she was coming at last to understand the mysteries of an English Cabinet. "I think you are quite right, my friend," she said,—"quite right. What—you are to be in Parliament and say that this black thing is white, or that this white thing is black, because you like to take your salary! That cannot be honest!" Then, when he came to talk to her of money,—that he must give up Parliament itself, if he gave up his place,—she offered to lend him money. "Why should you not treat me as a friend?" she said. When he pointed out to her that there would never come a time in which he could pay such money back, she stamped her foot and told him that he had better leave her. "You have high principle," she said, "but not principle sufficiently high to understand that this thing could be done between you and me without disgrace to either of us." Then Phineas assured her with tears in his eyes that such an arrangement was impossible without disgrace to him.

But he whispered to this new friend no word of the engagement with his dear Irish Mary. His Irish life, he would tell himself, was a thing quite apart and separate from his life in England. He said not a word about Mary Flood Jones to any of those with whom he lived in London. Why should he, feeling as he did that it would so soon be necessary that he should disappear from among them? About Miss Effingham he had said much to Madame Goesler. She had asked him whether he had abandoned all hope. "That affair, then, is over?" she had said.

"Yes;—it is all over now."

"And she will marry the red-headed, violent lord?"

"Heaven knows. I think she will. But she is exactly the girl to remain unmarried if she takes it into her head that the man she likes is in any way unfitted for her."

"Does she love this lord?"

"Oh yes;—there is no doubt of that." And Phineas, as he made this acknowledgment, seemed to do so without much inward agony of soul. When he had been last in London he could not speak of Violet and Lord Chiltern together without showing that his misery was almost too much for him.

At this time he received some counsel from two friends. One was Laurence Fitzgibbon, and the other was Barrington Erle. Laurence had always been true to him after a fashion, and had never resented his intrusion at the Colonial Office. "Phineas, me boy," he said, "if all this is thrue, you're about up a tree."

"It is true that I shall support Monk's motion."

"Then, me boy, you're up a tree as far as office goes. A place like that niver suited me, because, you see, that poker of a young lord expected so much of a man; but you don't mind that kind of thing, and I thought you were as snug as snug."

"Troubles will come, you see, Laurence."

"Bedad, yes. It's all throubles, I think, sometimes. But you've a way out of all your throubles."

"What way?"

"Pop the question to Madame Max. The money's all thrue, you know."

"I don't doubt the money in the least," said Phineas.

"And it's my belief she'll take you without a second word. Anyways, thry it, Phinny, my boy. That's my advice." Phineas so far agreed with his friend Laurence that he thought it possible that Madame Goesler might accept him were he to propose marriage to her. He knew, of course, that that mode of escape from his difficulties was out of the question for him, but he could not explain this to Laurence Fitzgibbon.

"I am sorry to hear that you have taken up a bad cause," said Barrington Erle to him.

"It is a pity;—is it not?"

"And the worst of it is that you'll sacrifice yourself and do no good to the cause. I never knew a man break away in this fashion, and not feel afterwards that he had done it all for nothing."

"But what is a man to do, Barrington? He can't smother his convictions."

"Convictions! There is nothing on earth that I'm so much afraid of in a young member of Parliament as convictions. There are ever so many rocks against which men get broken. One man can't keep his temper. Another can't hold his tongue. A third can't say a word unless he has been priming himself half a session. A fourth is always thinking of himself, and wanting more than he can get. A fifth is idle, and won't be there when he's wanted. A sixth is always in the way. A seventh lies so that you never can trust him. I've had to do with them all, but a fellow with convictions is the worst of all."

"I don't see how a fellow is to help himself," said Phineas. "When a fellow begins to meddle with politics they will come."

"Why can't you grow into them gradually as your betters and elders have done before you? It ought to be enough for any man, when he begins, to know that he's a Liberal. He understands which side of the House he's to vote, and who is to lead him. What's the meaning of having a leader to a party, if it's not that? Do you think that you and Mr. Monk can go and make a government between you?"

"Whatever I think, I'm sure he doesn't."

"I'm not so sure of that. But look here, Phineas, I don't care two straws about Monk's going. I always thought that Mildmay and the Duke were wrong when they asked him to join. I knew he'd go over the traces,—unless, indeed, he took his money and did nothing for it, which is the way with some of those Radicals. I look upon him as gone."

"He has gone."

"The devil go along with him, as you say in Ireland. But don't you be such a fool as to ruin yourself for a crotchet of Monk's. It isn't too late yet for you to hold back. To tell you the truth, Gresham has said a word to me about it already. He is most anxious that you should stay, but of course you can't stay and vote against us."

"Of course I cannot."

"I look upon you, you know, as in some sort my own child. I've tried to bring other fellows forward who seemed to have something in them, but I have never succeeded as I have with you. You've hit the thing off, and have got the ball at your foot. Upon my honour, in the whole course of my experience I have never known such good fortune as yours."

"And I shall always remember how it began, Barrington," said Phineas, who was greatly moved by the energy and solicitude of his friend.

"But, for God's sake, don't go and destroy it all by such mad perversity as this. They mean to do something next session. Morrison is going to take it up." Sir Walter Morrison was at this time Secretary for Ireland. "But of course we can't let a fellow like Monk take the matter into his own hands just when he pleases. I call it d——d treachery."

"Monk is no traitor, Barrington."

"Men will have their own opinions about that. It's generally understood that when a man is asked to take a seat in the Cabinet he is expected to conform with his colleagues, unless something very special turns up. But I am speaking of you now, and not of Monk. You are not a man of fortune. You cannot afford to make ducks and drakes. You are excellently placed, and you have plenty of time to hark back, if you'll only listen to reason. All that Irish stump balderdash will never be thrown in your teeth by us, if you will just go on as though it had never been uttered."

Phineas could only thank his friend for his advice, which was at least disinterested, and was good of its kind, and tell him that he would think of it. He did think of it very much. He almost thought that, were it to do again, he would allow Mr. Monk to go upon his tour alone, and keep himself from the utterance of anything that so good a judge as Erle could call stump balderdash. As he sat in his arm-chair in his room at the Colonial Office, with despatch-boxes around him, and official papers spread before him,—feeling himself to be one of those who in truth managed and governed the affairs of this great nation, feeling also that if he relinquished his post now he could never regain it,—he did wish that he had been a little less in love with independence, a little quieter in his boastings that no official considerations should ever silence his tongue. But all this was too late now. He knew that his skin was not thick enough to bear the arrows of those archers who would bend their bows against him if he should now dare to vote against Mr. Monk's motion. His own party might be willing to forgive and forget; but there would be others who would read those reports, and would appear in the House with the odious tell-tale newspapers in their hands.

Then he received a letter from his father. Some good-natured person had enlightened the doctor as to the danger in which his son was placing himself. Dr. Finn, who in his own profession was a very excellent and well-instructed man, had been so ignorant of Parliamentary tactics, as to have been proud at his son's success at the Irish meetings. He had thought that Phineas was carrying on his trade as a public speaker with proper energy and continued success. He had cared nothing himself for tenant-right, and had acknowledged to Mr. Monk that he could not understand in what it was that the farmers were wronged. But he knew that Mr. Monk was a Cabinet Minister, and he thought that Phineas was earning his salary. Then there came some one who undeceived him, and the paternal bosom of the doctor was dismayed. "I don't mean to interfere," he said in his letter, "but I can hardly believe that you really intend to resign your place. Yet I am told that you must do so if you go on with this matter. My dear boy, pray think about it. I cannot imagine you are disposed to lose all that you have won for nothing." Mary also wrote to him. Mrs. Finn had been talking to her, and Mary had taught herself to believe that after the many sweet conversations she had had with a man so high in office as Phineas, she really did understand something about the British Government. Mrs. Finn had interrogated Mary, and Mary had been obliged to own that it was quite possible that Phineas would be called upon to resign.

"But why, my dear? Heaven and earth! Resign two thousand a year!"

"That he may maintain his independence," said Mary proudly.

"Fiddlestick!" said Mrs. Finn. "How is he to maintain you, or himself either, if he goes on in that way? I shouldn't wonder if he didn't get himself all wrong, even now." Then Mrs. Finn began to cry; and Mary could only write to her lover, pointing out to him how very anxious all his friends were that he should do nothing in a hurry. But what if the thing were done already! Phineas in his great discomfort went to seek further counsel from Madame Goesler. Of all his counsellors, Madame Goesler was the only one who applauded him for what he was about to do.

"But, after all, what is it you give up? Mr. Gresham may be out to-morrow, and then where will be your place?"

"There does not seem to be much chance of that at present."

"Who can tell? Of course I do not understand,—but it was only the other day when Mr. Mildmay was there, and only the day before that when Lord de Terrier was there, and again only the day before that when Lord Brock was there." Phineas endeavoured to make her understand that of the four Prime Ministers whom she had named, three were men of the same party as himself, under whom it would have suited him to serve. "I would not serve under any man if I were an English gentleman in Parliament," said Madame Goesler.

"What is a poor fellow to do?" said Phineas, laughing.

"A poor fellow need not be a poor fellow unless he likes," said Madame Goesler. Immediately after this Phineas left her, and as he went along the street he began to question himself whether the prospects of his own darling Mary were at all endangered by his visits to Park Lane; and to reflect what sort of a blackguard he would be,—a blackguard of how deep a dye,—were he to desert Mary and marry Madame Max Goesler. Then he also asked himself as to the nature and quality of his own political honesty if he were to abandon Mary in order that he might maintain his parliamentary independence. After all, if it should ever come to pass that his biography should be written, his biographer would say very much more about the manner in which he kept his seat in Parliament than of the manner in which he kept his engagement with Miss Mary Flood Jones. Half a dozen people who knew him and her might think ill of him for his conduct to Mary, but the world would not condemn him! And when he thundered forth his liberal eloquence from below the gangway as an independent member, having the fortune of his charming wife to back him, giving excellent dinners at the same time in Park Lane, would not the world praise him very loudly?

When he got to his office he found a note from Lord Brentford inviting him to dine in Portman Square.

CHAPTER LXVIII
The Joint Attack

The note from Lord Brentford surprised our hero not a little. He had had no communication with the Earl since the day on which he had been so savagely scolded about the duel, when the Earl had plainly told him that his conduct had been as bad as it could be. Phineas had not on that account become at all ashamed of his conduct in reference to the duel, but he had conceived that any reconciliation between him and the Earl had been out of the question. Now there had come a civilly-worded invitation, asking him to dine with the offended nobleman. The note had been written by Lady Laura, but it had purported to come from Lord Brentford himself. He sent back word to say that he should be happy to have the honour of dining with Lord Brentford.

Parliament at this time had been sitting nearly a month, and it was already March. Phineas had heard nothing of Lady Laura, and did not even know that she was in London till he saw her handwriting. He did not know that she had not gone back to her husband, and that she had remained with her father all the winter at Saulsby. He had also heard that Lord Chiltern had been at Saulsby. All the world had been talking of the separation of Mr. Kennedy from his wife, one half of the world declaring that his wife, if not absolutely false to him, had neglected all her duties; and the other half asserting that Mr. Kennedy's treatment of his wife had been so bad that no woman could possibly have lived with him. There had even been a rumour that Lady Laura had gone off with a lover from the Duke of Omnium's garden party, and some indiscreet tongue had hinted that a certain unmarried Under-Secretary of State was missing at the same time. But Lord Chiltern upon this had shown his teeth with so strong a propensity to do some real biting, that no one had ventured to repeat that rumour. Its untruth was soon established by the fact that Lady Laura Kennedy was living with her father at Saulsby. Of Mr. Kennedy, Phineas had as yet seen nothing since he had been up in town. That gentleman, though a member of the Cabinet, had not been in London at the opening of the session, nor had he attended the Cabinet meetings during the recess. It had been stated in the newspapers that he was ill, and stated in private that he could not bear to show himself since his wife had left him. At last, however, he came to London, and Phineas saw him in the House. Then, when the first meeting of the Cabinet was summoned after his return, it became known that he also had resigned his office. There was nothing said about his resignation in the House. He had resigned on the score of ill-health, and that very worthy peer, Lord Mount Thistle, formerly Sir Marmaduke Morecombe, came back to the Duchy of Lancaster in his place. A Prime Minister sometimes finds great relief in the possession of a serviceable stick who can be made to go in and out as occasion may require; only it generally happens that the stick will expect some reward when he is made to go out. Lord Mount Thistle immediately saw his way to a viscount's coronet, when he was once more summoned to the august councils of the Ministers.

A few days after this had been arranged, in the interval between Lord Brentford's invitation and Lord Brentford's dinner, Phineas encountered Mr. Kennedy so closely in one of the passages of the House that it was impossible that they should not speak to each other, unless they were to avoid each other as people do who have palpably quarrelled. Phineas saw that Mr. Kennedy was hesitating, and therefore took the bull by the horns. He greeted his former friend in a friendly fashion, shaking him by the hand, and then prepared to pass on. But Mr. Kennedy, though he had hesitated at first, now detained his brother member. "Finn," he said, "if you are not engaged I should like to speak to you for a moment." Phineas was not engaged, and allowed himself to be led out arm-in-arm by the late Chancellor of the Duchy into Westminster Hall. "Of course you know what a terrible thing has happened to me," said Mr. Kennedy.

"Yes;—I have heard of it," said Phineas.

"Everybody has heard of it. That is one of the terrible cruelties of such a blow."

"All those things are very bad of course. I was very much grieved,—because you have both been intimate friends of mine."

"Yes,—yes; we were. Do you ever see her now?"

"Not since last July,—at the Duke's party, you know."

"Ah, yes; the morning of that day was the last on which I spoke to her. It was then she left me."

"I am going to dine with Lord Brentford to-morrow, and I dare say she will be there."

"Yes;—she is in town. I saw her yesterday in her father's carriage. I think that she had no cause to leave me."

"Of course I cannot say anything about that."

"I think she had no cause to leave me." Phineas as he heard this could not but remember all that Lady Laura had told himself, and thought that no woman had ever had a better reason for leaving her husband. "There were things I did not like, and I said so."

"I suppose that is generally the way," replied Phineas.

"But surely a wife should listen to a word of caution from her husband."

"I fancy they never like it," said Phineas.

"But are we all of us to have all that we like? I have not found it so. Or would it be good for us if we had?" Then he paused; but as Phineas had no further remark to make, he continued speaking after they had walked about a third of the length of the hall. "It is not of my own comfort I am thinking now so much as of her name and her future conduct. Of course it will in every sense be best for her that she should come back to her husband's roof."

"Well; yes;—perhaps it would," said Phineas.

"Has she not accepted that lot for better or for worse?" said Mr. Kennedy, solemnly.

"But incompatibility of temper, you know, is always,—always supposed—. You understand me?"

"It is my intention that she should come back to me. I do not wish to make any legal demand;—at any rate, not as yet. Will you consent to be the bearer of a message from me both to herself and to the Earl?"

Now it seemed to Phineas that of all the messengers whom Mr. Kennedy could have chosen he was the most unsuited to be a Mercury in this cause,—not perceiving that he had been so selected with some craft, in order that Lady Laura might understand that the accusation against her was, at any rate, withdrawn, which had named Phineas as her lover. He paused again before he answered. "Of course," he said, "I should be most willing to be of service, if it were possible. But I do not see how I can speak to the Earl about it. Though I am going to dine with him I don't know why he has asked me;—for he and I are on very bad terms. He heard that stupid story about the duel, and has not spoken to me since."

"I heard that, too," said Mr. Kennedy, frowning blackly as he remembered his wife's duplicity.

"Everybody heard of it. But it has made such a difference between him and me, that I don't think I can meddle. Send for Lord Chiltern, and speak to him."

"Speak to Chiltern! Never! He would probably strike me on the head with his club."

"Call on the Earl yourself."

"I did, and he would not see me."

"Write to him."

"I did, and he sent back my letter unopened."

"Write to her."

"I did;—and she answered me, saying only thus; 'Indeed, indeed, it cannot be so.' But it must be so. The laws of God require it, and the laws of man permit it. I want some one to point out that to them more softly than I could do if I were simply to write to that effect. To the Earl, of course, I cannot write again." The conference ended by a promise from Phineas that he would, if possible, say a word to Lady Laura.

When he was shown into Lord Brentford's drawing-room he found not only Lady Laura there, but her brother. Lord Brentford was not in the room. Barrington Erle was there, and so also were Lord and Lady Cantrip.

"Is not your father going to be here?" he said to Lady Laura, after their first greeting.

"We live in that hope," said she, "and do not at all know why he should be late. What has become of him, Oswald?"

"He came in with me half an hour ago, and I suppose he does not dress as quickly as I do," said Lord Chiltern; upon which Phineas immediately understood that the father and the son were reconciled, and he rushed to the conclusion that Violet and her lover would also soon be reconciled, if such were not already the case. He felt some remnant of a soreness that it should be so, as a man feels where his headache has been when the real ache itself has left him. Then the host came in and made his apologies. "Chiltern kept me standing about," he said, "till the east wind had chilled me through and through. The only charm I recognise in youth is that it is impervious to the east wind." Phineas felt quite sure now that Violet and her lover were reconciled, and he had a distinct feeling of the place where the ache had been. Dear Violet! But, after all, Violet lacked that sweet, clinging, feminine softness which made Mary Flood Jones so pre-eminently the most charming of her sex. The Earl, when he had repeated his general apology, especially to Lady Cantrip, who was the only lady present except his daughter, came up to our hero and shook him kindly by the hand. He took him up to one of the windows and then addressed him in a voice of mock solemnity.

"Stick to the colonies, young man," he said, "and never meddle with foreign affairs;—especially not at Blankenberg."

"Never again, my Lord;—never again."

"And leave all questions of fire-arms to be arranged between the Horse Guards and the War Office. I have heard a good deal about it since I saw you, and I retract a part of what I said. But a duel is a foolish thing,—a very foolish thing. Come;—here is dinner." And the Earl walked off with Lady Cantrip, and Lord Cantrip walked off with Lady Laura. Barrington Erle followed, and Phineas had an opportunity of saying a word to his friend, Lord Chiltern, as they went down together.

"It's all right between you and your father?"

"Yes;—after a fashion. There is no knowing how long it will last. He wants me to do three things, and I won't do any one of them."

"What are the three?"

"To go into Parliament, to be an owner of sheep and oxen, and to hunt in his own county. I should never attend the first, I should ruin myself with the second, and I should never get a run in the third." But there was not a word said about his marriage.

There were only seven who sat down to dinner, and the six were all people with whom Phineas was or had been on most intimate terms. Lord Cantrip was his official chief, and, since that connection had existed between them, Lady Cantrip had been very gracious to him. She quite understood the comfort which it was to her husband to have under him, as his representative in the House of Commons, a man whom he could thoroughly trust and like, and therefore she had used her woman's arts to bind Phineas to her lord in more than mere official bondage. She had tried her skill also upon Laurence Fitzgibbon,—but altogether in vain. He had eaten her dinners and accepted her courtesies, and had given for them no return whatever. But Phineas had possessed a more grateful mind, and had done all that had been required of him;—had done all that had been required of him till there had come that terrible absurdity in Ireland. "I knew very well what sort of things would happen when they brought such a man as Mr. Monk into the Cabinet," Lady Cantrip had said to her husband.

But though the party was very small, and though the guests were all his intimate friends, Phineas suspected nothing special till an attack was made upon him as soon as the servants had left the room. This was done in the presence of the two ladies, and, no doubt, had been preconcerted. There was Lord Cantrip there, who had already said much to him, and Barrington Erle who had said more even than Lord Cantrip. Lord Brentford, himself a member of the Cabinet, opened the attack by asking whether it was actually true that Mr. Monk meant to go on with his motion. Barrington Erle asserted that Mr. Monk positively would do so. "And Gresham will oppose it?" asked the Earl. "Of course he will," said Barrington. "Of course he will," said Lord Cantrip. "I know what I should think of him if he did not," said Lady Cantrip. "He is the last man in the world to be forced into a thing," said Lady Laura. Then Phineas knew pretty well what was coming on him.

Lord Brentford began again by asking how many supporters Mr. Monk would have in the House. "That depends upon the amount of courage which the Conservatives may have," said Barrington Erle. "If they dare to vote for a thoroughly democratic measure, simply for the sake of turning us out, it is quite on the cards that they may succeed." "But of our own people?" asked Lord Cantrip. "You had better inquire that of Phineas Finn," said Barrington. And then the attack was made.

Our hero had a bad half hour of it, though many words were said which must have gratified him much. They all wanted to keep him,—so Lord Cantrip declared, "except one or two whom I could name, and who are particularly anxious to wear his shoes," said Barrington, thinking that certain reminiscences of Phineas with regard to Mr. Bonteen and others might operate as strongly as any other consideration to make him love his place. Lord Brentford declared that he could not understand it,—that he should find himself lost in amazement if such a man as his young friend allowed himself to be led into the outer wilderness by such an ignis-fatuus of light as this. Lord Cantrip laid down the unwritten traditional law of Government officials very plainly. A man in office,—in an office which really imposed upon him as much work as he could possibly do with credit to himself or his cause,—was dispensed from the necessity of a conscience with reference to other matters. It was for Sir Walter Morrison to have a conscience about Irish tenant-right, as no doubt he had,—just as Phineas Finn had a conscience about Canada, and Jamaica, and the Cape. Barrington Erle was very strong about parties in general, and painted the comforts of official position in glowing colours. But I think that the two ladies were more efficacious than even their male relatives in the arguments which they used. "We have been so happy to have you among us," said Lady Cantrip, looking at him with beseeching, almost loving eyes. "Mr. Finn knows," said Lady Laura, "that since he first came into Parliament I have always believed in his success, and I have been very proud to see it." "We shall weep over him, as over a fallen angel, if he leaves us," said Lady Cantrip. "I won't say that I will weep," said Lady Laura, "but I do not know anything of the kind that would so truly make me unhappy."

What was he to say in answer to applications so flattering and so pressing? He would have said nothing, had that been possible, but he felt himself obliged to reply. He replied very weakly,—of course, not justifying himself, but declaring that as he had gone so far he must go further. He must vote for the measure now. Both his chief and Barrington Erle proved, or attempted to prove, that he was wrong in this. Of course he would not speak on the measure, and his vote for his party would probably be allowed to pass without notice. One or two newspapers might perhaps attack him; but what public man cared for such attacks as those? His whole party would hang by him, and in that he would find ample consolation. Phineas could only say that he would think of it;—and this he said in so irresolute a tone of voice that all the men then present believed that he was gained. The two ladies, however, were of a different opinion. "In spite of anything that anybody may say, he will do what he thinks right when the time comes," said Laura to her father afterwards. But then Lady Laura had been in love with him,—was perhaps almost in love with him still. "I'm afraid he is a mule," said Lady Cantrip to her husband. "He's a good mule up a hill with a load on his back," said his lordship. "But with a mule there always comes a time when you can't manage him," said Lady Cantrip. But Lady Cantrip had never been in love with Phineas.

Phineas found a moment, before he left Lord Brentford's house, to say a word to Lady Laura as to the commission that had been given to him. "It can never be," said Lady Laura, shuddering;—"never, never, never!"

"You are not angry with me for speaking?"

"Oh, no—not if he told you."

"He made me promise that I would."

"Tell him it cannot be. Tell him that if he has any instruction to send me as to what he considers to be my duty, I will endeavour to comply, if that duty can be done apart. I will recognize him so far, because of my vow. But not even for the sake of my vow, will I endeavour to live with him. His presence would kill me!"

When Phineas repeated this, or as much of this as he judged to be necessary, to Mr. Kennedy a day or two afterwards, that gentleman replied that in such case he would have no alternative but to seek redress at law. "I have done nothing to my wife," said he, "of which I need be ashamed. It will be sad, no doubt, to have all our affairs bandied about in court, and made the subject of comment in newspapers, but a man must go through that, or worse than that, in the vindication of his rights, and for the performance of his duty to his Maker." That very day Mr. Kennedy went to his lawyer, and desired that steps might be taken for the restitution to him of his conjugal rights.

CHAPTER LXIX
The Temptress

Mr. Monk's bill was read the first time before Easter, and Phineas Finn still held his office. He had spoken to the Prime Minister once on the subject, and had been surprised at that gentleman's courtesy;—for Mr. Gresham had the reputation of being unconciliatory in his manners, and very prone to resent anything like desertion from that allegiance which was due to himself as the leader of his party. "You had better stay where you are and take no step that may be irretrievable, till you have quite made up your mind," said Mr. Gresham.

"I fear I have made up my mind," said Phineas.

"Nothing can be done till after Easter," replied the great man, "and there is no knowing how things may go then. I strongly recommend you to stay with us. If you can do this it will be only necessary that you shall put your resignation in Lord Cantrip's hands before you speak or vote against us. See Monk and talk it over with him." Mr. Gresham possibly imagined that Mr. Monk might be moved to abandon his bill, when he saw what injury he was about to do.

At this time Phineas received the following letter from his darling Mary:—

Floodborough, Thursday.
Dearest Phineas,

We have just got home from Killaloe, and mean to remain here all through the summer. After leaving your sisters this house seems so desolate; but I shall have the more time to think of you. I have been reading Tennyson, as you told me, and I fancy that I could in truth be a Mariana here, if it were not that I am so quite certain that you will come;—and that makes all the difference in the world in a moated grange. Last night I sat at the window and tried to realise what I should feel if you were to tell me that you did not want me; and I got myself into such an ecstatic state of mock melancholy that I cried for half an hour. But when one has such a real living joy at the back of one's romantic melancholy, tears are very pleasant;—they water and do not burn.

I must tell you about them all at Killaloe. They certainly are very unhappy at the idea of your resigning. Your father says very little, but I made him own that to act as you are acting for the sake of principle is very grand. I would not leave him till he had said so, and he did say it. Dear Mrs. Finn does not understand it as well, but she will do so. She complains mostly for my sake, and when I tell her that I will wait twenty years if it is necessary, she tells me I do not know what waiting means. But I will,—and will be happy, and will never really think myself a Mariana. Dear, dear, dear Phineas, indeed I won't. The girls are half sad and half proud. But I am wholly proud, and know that you are doing just what you ought to do. I shall think more of you as a man who might have been a Prime Minister than if you were really sitting in the Cabinet like Lord Cantrip. As for mamma, I cannot make her quite understand it. She merely says that no young man who is going to be married ought to resign anything. Dear mamma;—sometimes she does say such odd things.

You told me to tell you everything, and so I have. I talk to some of the people here, and tell them what they might do if they had tenant-right. One old fellow, Mike Dufferty,—I don't know whether you remember him,—asked if he would have to pay the rent all the same. When I said certainly he would, then he shook his head. But as you said once, when we want to do good to people one has no right to expect that they should understand it. It is like baptizing little infants.

I got both your notes;—seven words in one, Mr. Under-Secretary, and nine in the other! But the one little word at the end was worth a whole sheet full of common words. How nice it is to write letters without paying postage, and to send them about the world with a grand name in the corner. When Barney brings me one he always looks as if he didn't know whether it was a love letter or an order to go to Botany Bay. If he saw the inside of them, how short they are, I don't think he'd think much of you as a lover nor yet as an Under-Secretary.

But I think ever so much of you as both;—I do, indeed; and I am not scolding you a bit. As long as I can have two or three dear, sweet, loving words, I shall be as happy as a queen. Ah, if you knew it all! But you never can know it all. A man has so many other things to learn that he cannot understand it.

Good-bye, dear, dear, dearest man. Whatever you do I shall be quite sure you have done the best.

Ever your own, with all the love of her heart,

Mary F. Jones.

This was very nice. Such a man as was Phineas Finn always takes a delight which he cannot express even to himself in the receipt of such a letter as this. There is nothing so flattering as the warm expression of the confidence of a woman's love, and Phineas thought that no woman ever expressed this more completely than did his Mary. Dear, dearest Mary. As for giving her up, as for treachery to one so trusting, so sweet, so well beloved, that was out of the question. But nevertheless the truth came home to him more clearly day by day, that he of all men was the last who ought to have given himself up to such a passion. For her sake he ought to have abstained. So he told himself now. For her sake he ought to have kept aloof from her;—and for his own sake he ought to have kept aloof from Mr. Monk. That very day, with Mary's letter in his pocket, he went to the livery stables and explained that he would not keep his horse any longer. There was no difficulty about the horse. Mr. Howard Macleod of the Treasury would take him from that very hour. Phineas, as he walked away, uttered a curse upon Mr. Howard Macleod. Mr. Howard Macleod was just beginning the glory of his life in London, and he, Phineas Finn, was bringing his to an end.

With Mary's letter in his pocket he went up to Portman Square. He had again got into the habit of seeing Lady Laura frequently, and was often with her brother, who now again lived at his father's house. A letter had reached Lord Brentford, through his lawyer, in which a demand was made by Mr. Kennedy for the return of his wife. She was quite determined that she would never go back to him; and there had come to her a doubt whether it would not be expedient that she should live abroad so as to be out of the way of persecution from her husband. Lord Brentford was in great wrath, and Lord Chiltern had once or twice hinted that perhaps he had better "see" Mr. Kennedy. The amenities of such an interview, as this would be, had up to the present day been postponed; and, in a certain way, Phineas had been used as a messenger between Mr. Kennedy and his wife's family.

"I think it will end," she said, "in my going to Dresden, and settling myself there. Papa will come to me when Parliament is not sitting."

"It will be very dull."

"Dull! What does dulness amount to when one has come to such a pass as this? When one is in the ruck of fortune, to be dull is very bad; but when misfortune comes, simple dulness is nothing. It sounds almost like relief."

"It is so hard that you should be driven away." She did not answer him for a while, and he was beginning to think of his own case also. Was it not hard that he too should be driven away? "It is odd enough that we should both be going at the same time."

"But you will not go?"

"I think I shall. I have resolved upon this,—that if I give up my place, I will give up my seat too. I went into Parliament with the hope of office, and how can I remain there when I shall have gained it and then have lost it?"

"But you will stay in London, Mr. Finn?"

"I think not. After all that has come and gone I should not be happy here, and I should make my way easier and on cheaper terms in Dublin. My present idea is that I shall endeavour to make a practice over in my own country. It will be hard work beginning at the bottom;—will it not?"

"And so unnecessary."

"Ah, Lady Laura,—if it only could be avoided! But it is of no use going through all that again."

"How much we would both of us avoid if we could only have another chance!" said Lady Laura. "If I could only be as I was before I persuaded myself to marry a man whom I never loved, what a paradise the earth would be to me! With me all regrets are too late."

"And with me as much so."

"No, Mr. Finn. Even should you resign your office, there is no reason why you should give up your seat."

"Simply that I have no income to maintain me in London."

She was silent for a few moments, during which she changed her seat so as to come nearer to him, placing herself on a corner of a sofa close to the chair on which he was seated. "I wonder whether I may speak to you plainly," she said.

"Indeed you may."

"On any subject?"

"Yes;—on any subject."

"I trust you have been able to rid your bosom of all remembrances of Violet Effingham."

"Certainly not of all remembrances, Lady Laura."

"Of all hope, then?"

"I have no such hope."

"And of all lingering desires?"

"Well, yes;—and of all lingering desires. I know now that it cannot be. Your brother is welcome to her."

"Ah;—of that I know nothing. He, with his perversity, has estranged her. But I am sure of this,—that if she do not marry him, she will marry no one. But it is not on account of him that I speak. He must fight his own battles now."

"I shall not interfere with him, Lady Laura."

"Then why should you not establish yourself by a marriage that will make place a matter of indifference to you? I know that it is within your power to do so." Phineas put his hand up to his breastcoat pocket, and felt that Mary's letter,—her precious letter,—was there safe. It certainly was not in his power to do this thing which Lady Laura recommended to him, but he hardly thought that the present was a moment suitable for explaining to her the nature of the impediment which stood in the way of such an arrangement. He had so lately spoken to Lady Laura with an assurance of undying constancy of his love for Miss Effingham, that he could not as yet acknowledge the force of another passion. He shook his head by way of reply. "I tell you that it is so," she said with energy.

"I am afraid not."

"Go to Madame Goesler, and ask her. Hear what she will say."

"Madame Goesler would laugh at me, no doubt."

"Psha! You do not think so. You know that she would not laugh. And are you the man to be afraid of a woman's laughter? I think not."

Again he did not answer her at once, and when he did speak the tone of his voice was altered. "What was it you said of yourself, just now?"

"What did I say of myself?"

"You regretted that you had consented to marry a man,—whom you did not love."

"Why should you not love her? And it is so different with a man! A woman is wretched if she does not love her husband, but I fancy that a man gets on very well without any such feeling. She cannot domineer over you. She cannot expect you to pluck yourself out of your own soil, and begin a new growth altogether in accordance with the laws of her own. It was that which Mr. Kennedy did."

"I do not for a moment think that she would take me, if I were to offer myself."

"Try her," said Lady Laura energetically. "Such trials cost you but little;—we both of us know that!" Still he said nothing of the letter in his pocket. "It is everything that you should go on now that you have once begun. I do not believe in you working at the Bar. You cannot do it. A man who has commenced life as you have done with the excitement of politics, who has known what it is to take a prominent part in the control of public affairs, cannot give it up and be happy at other work. Make her your wife, and you may resign or remain in office just as you choose. Office will be much easier to you than it is now, because it will not be a necessity. Let me at any rate have the pleasure of thinking that one of us can remain here,—that we need not both fall together."

Still he did not tell her of the letter in his pocket. He felt that she moved him,—that she made him acknowledge to himself how great would be the pity of such a failure as would be his. He was quite as much alive as she could be to the fact that work at the Bar, either in London or in Dublin, would have no charms for him now. The prospect of such a life was very dreary to him. Even with the comfort of Mary's love such a life would be very dreary to him. And then he knew,—he thought that he knew,—that were he to offer himself to Madame Goesler he would not in truth be rejected. She had told him that if poverty was a trouble to him he need be no longer poor. Of course he had understood this. Her money was at his service if he should choose to stoop and pick it up. And it was not only money that such a marriage would give him. He had acknowledged to himself more than once that Madame Goesler was very lovely, that she was clever, attractive in every way, and as far as he could see, blessed with a sweet temper. She had a position, too, in the world that would help him rather than mar him. What might he not do with an independent seat in the House of Commons, and as joint owner of the little house in Park Lane? Of all careers which the world could offer to a man the pleasantest would then be within his reach. "You appear to me as a tempter," he said at last to Lady Laura.

"It is unkind of you to say that, and ungrateful. I would do anything on earth in my power to help you."

"Nevertheless you are a tempter."

"I know how it ought to have been," she said, in a low voice. "I know very well how it ought to have been. I should have kept myself free till that time when we met on the braes of Loughlinter, and then all would have been well with us."

"I do not know how that might have been," said Phineas, hoarsely.

"You do not know! But I know. Of course you have stabbed me with a thousand daggers when you have told me from time to time of your love for Violet. You have been very cruel,—needlessly cruel. Men are so cruel! But for all that I have known that I could have kept you,—had it not been too late when you spoke to me. Will you not own as much as that?"

"Of course you would have been everything to me. I should never have thought of Violet then."

"That is the only kind word you have said to me from that day to this. I try to comfort myself in thinking that it would have been so. But all that is past and gone, and done. I have had my romance and you have had yours. As you are a man, it is natural that you should have been disturbed by a double image;—it is not so with me."

"And yet you can advise me to offer marriage to a woman,—a woman whom I am to seek merely because she is rich?"

"Yes;—I do so advise you. You have had your romance and must now put up with reality. Why should I so advise you but for the interest that I have in you? Your prosperity will do me no good. I shall not even be here to see it. I shall hear of it only as so many a woman banished out of England hears a distant misunderstood report of what is going on in the country she has left. But I still have regard enough,—I will be bold, and, knowing that you will not take it amiss, will say love enough for you,—to feel a desire that you should not be shipwrecked. Since we first took you in hand between us, Barrington and I, I have never swerved in my anxiety on your behalf. When I resolved that it would be better for us both that we should be only friends, I did not swerve. When you would talk to me so cruelly of your love for Violet, I did not swerve. When I warned you from Loughlinter because I thought there was danger, I did not swerve. When I bade you not to come to me in London because of my husband, I did not swerve. When my father was hard upon you, I did not swerve then. I would not leave him till he was softened. When you tried to rob Oswald of his love, and I thought you would succeed,—for I did think so,—I did not swerve. I have ever been true to you. And now that I must hide myself and go away, and be seen no more, I am true still."

"Laura,—dearest Laura!" he exclaimed.

"Ah, no!" she said, speaking with no touch of anger, but all in sorrow;—"it must not be like that. There is no room for that. Nor do you mean it. I do not think so ill of you. But there may not be even words of affection between us—only such as I may speak to make you know that I am your friend."

"You are my friend," he said, stretching out his hand to her as he turned away his face. "You are my friend, indeed."

"Then do as I would have you do."

He put his hand into his pocket, and had the letter between his fingers with the purport of showing it to her. But at the moment the thought occurred to him that were he to do so, then, indeed, he would be bound for ever. He knew that he was bound for ever,—bound for ever to his own Mary; but he desired to have the privilege of thinking over such bondage once more before he proclaimed it even to his dearest friend. He had told her that she tempted him, and she stood before him now as a temptress. But lest it might be possible that she should not tempt in vain,—that letter in his pocket must never be shown to her. In that case Lady Laura must never hear from his lips the name of Mary Flood Jones.

He left her without any assured purpose;—without, that is, the assurance to her of any fixed purpose. There yet wanted a week to the day on which Mr. Monk's bill was to be read,—or not to be read,—the second time; and he had still that interval before he need decide. He went to his club, and before he dined he strove to write a line to Mary;—but when he had the paper before him he found that it was impossible to do so. Though he did not even suspect himself of an intention to be false, the idea that was in his mind made the effort too much for him. He put the paper away from him and went down and eat his dinner.

It was a Saturday, and there was no House in the evening. He had remained in Portman Square with Lady Laura till near seven o'clock, and was engaged to go out in the evening to a gathering at Mrs. Gresham's house. Everybody in London would be there, and Phineas was resolved that as long as he remained in London he would be seen at places where everybody was seen. He would certainly be at Mrs. Gresham's gathering; but there was an hour or two before he need go home to dress, and as he had nothing to do, he went down to the smoking-room of his club. The seats were crowded, but there was one vacant; and before he had looked about him to scrutinise his neighbourhood, he found that he had placed himself with Bonteen on his right hand and Ratler on his left. There were no two men in all London whom he more thoroughly disliked; but it was too late for him to avoid them now.

They instantly attacked him, first on one side and then on the other. "So I am told you are going to leave us," said Bonteen.

"Who can have been ill-natured enough to whisper such a thing?" replied Phineas.

"The whispers are very loud, I can tell you," said Ratler. "I think I know already pretty nearly how every man in the House will vote, and I have not got your name down on the right side."

"Change it for heaven's sake," said Phineas.

"I will, if you'll tell me seriously that I may," said Ratler.

"My opinion is," said Bonteen, "that a man should be known either as a friend or foe. I respect a declared foe."

"Know me as a declared foe then," said Phineas, "and respect me."

"That's all very well," said Ratler, "but it means nothing. I've always had a sort of fear about you, Finn, that you would go over the traces some day. Of course it's a very grand thing to be independent."

"The finest thing in the world," said Bonteen; "only so d——d useless."

"But a man shouldn't be independent and stick to the ship at the same time. You forget the trouble you cause, and how you upset all calculations."

"I hadn't thought of the calculations," said Phineas.

"The fact is, Finn," said Bonteen, "you are made of clay too fine for office. I've always found it has been so with men from your country. You are the grandest horses in the world to look at out on a prairie, but you don't like the slavery of harness."

"And the sound of a whip over our shoulders sets us kicking;—does it not, Ratler?"

"I shall show the list to Gresham to-morrow," said Ratler, "and of course he can do as he pleases; but I don't understand this kind of thing."

"Don't you be in a hurry," said Bonteen. "I'll bet you a sovereign Finn votes with us yet. There's nothing like being a little coy to set off a girl's charms. I'll bet you a sovereign, Ratler, that Finn goes out into the lobby with you and me against Monk's bill."

Phineas, not being able to stand any more of this most unpleasant raillery, got up and went away. The club was distasteful to him, and he walked off and sauntered for a while about the park. He went down by the Duke of York's column as though he were going to his office, which of course was closed at this hour, but turned round when he got beyond the new public buildings,—buildings which he was never destined to use in their completed state,—and entered the gates of the enclosure, and wandered on over the bridge across the water. As he went his mind was full of thought. Could it be good for him to give up everything for a fair face? He swore to himself that of all women whom he had ever seen Mary was the sweetest and the dearest and the best. If it could be well to lose the world for a woman, it would be well to lose it for her. Violet, with all her skill, and all her strength, and all her grace, could never have written such a letter as that which he still held in his pocket. The best charm of a woman is that she should be soft, and trusting, and generous; and who ever had been more soft, more trusting, and more generous than his Mary? Of course he would be true to her, though he did lose the world.

But to yield such a triumph to the Ratlers and Bonteens whom he left behind him,—to let them have their will over him,—to know that they would rejoice scurrilously behind his back over his downfall! The feeling was terrible to him. The last words which Bonteen had spoken made it impossible to him now not to support his old friend Mr. Monk. It was not only what Bonteen had said, but that the words of Mr. Bonteen so plainly indicated what would be the words of all the other Bonteens. He knew that he was weak in this. He knew that had he been strong, he would have allowed himself to be guided,—if not by the firm decision of his own spirit,—by the counsels of such men as Mr. Gresham and Lord Cantrip, and not by the sarcasms of the Bonteens and Ratlers of official life. But men who sojourn amidst savagery fear the mosquito more than they do the lion. He could not bear to think that he should yield his blood to such a one as Bonteen.

And he must yield his blood, unless he could vote for Mr. Monk's motion, and hold his ground afterwards among them all in the House of Commons. He would at any rate see the session out, and try a fall with Mr. Bonteen when they should be sitting on different benches,—if ever fortune should give him an opportunity. And in the meantime, what should he do about Madame Goesler? What a fate was his to have the handsomest woman in London with thousands and thousands a year at his disposal! For,—so he now swore to himself,—Madame Goesler was the handsomest woman in London, as Mary Flood Jones was the sweetest girl in the world.

He had not arrived at any decision so fixed as to make him comfortable when he went home and dressed for Mrs. Gresham's party. And yet he knew,—he thought that he knew that he would be true to Mary Flood Jones.

CHAPTER LXX
The Prime Minister's House

The rooms and passages and staircases at Mrs. Gresham's house were very crowded when Phineas arrived there. Men of all shades of politics were there, and the wives and daughters of such men; and there was a streak of royalty in one of the saloons, and a whole rainbow of foreign ministers with their stars, and two blue ribbons were to be seen together on the first landing-place, with a stout lady between them carrying diamonds enough to load a pannier. Everybody was there. Phineas found that even Lord Chiltern was come, as he stumbled across his friend on the first foot-ground that he gained in his ascent towards the rooms. "Halloa,—you here?" said Phineas. "Yes, by George!" said the other, "but I am going to escape as soon as possible. I've been trying to make my way up for the last hour, but could never get round that huge promontory there. Laura was more persevering." "Is Kennedy here?" Phineas whispered. "I do not know," said Chiltern, "but she was determined to run the chance."

A little higher up,—for Phineas was blessed with more patience than Lord Chiltern possessed,—he came upon Mr. Monk. "So you are still admitted privately," said Phineas.

"Oh dear yes,—and we have just been having a most friendly conversation about you. What a man he is! He knows everything. He is so accurate; so just in the abstract,—and in the abstract so generous!"

"He has been very generous to me in detail as well as in abstract," said Phineas.

"Ah, yes; I am not thinking of individuals exactly. His want of generosity is to large masses,—to a party, to classes, to a people; whereas his generosity is for mankind at large. He assumes the god, affects to nod, and seems to shake the spheres. But I have nothing against him. He has asked me here to-night, and has talked to me most familiarly about Ireland."

"What do you think of your chance of a second reading?" asked Phineas.

"What do you think of it?—you hear more of those things than I do."

"Everybody says it will be a close division."

"I never expected it," said Mr. Monk.

"Nor I, till I heard what Daubeny said at the first reading. They will all vote for the bill en masse,—hating it in their hearts all the time."

"Let us hope they are not so bad as that."

"It is the way with them always. They do all our work for us,—sailing either on one tack or the other. That is their use in creation, that when we split among ourselves, as we always do, they come in and finish our job for us. It must be unpleasant for them to be always doing that which they always say should never be done at all."

"Wherever the gift horse may come from, I shall not look it in the mouth," said Mr. Monk. "There is only one man in the House whom I hope I may not see in the lobby with me, and that is yourself."

"The question is decided now," said Phineas.

"And how is it decided?"

Phineas could not tell his friend that a question of so great magnitude to him had been decided by the last sting which he had received from an insect so contemptible as Mr. Bonteen, but he expressed the feeling as well as he knew how to express it. "Oh, I shall be with you. I know what you are going to say, and I know how good you are. But I could not stand it. Men are beginning already to say things which almost make me get up and kick them. If I can help it, I will give occasion to no man to hint anything to me which can make me be so wretched as I have been to-day. Pray do not say anything more. My idea is that I shall resign to-morrow."

"Then I hope that we may fight the battle side by side," said Mr. Monk, giving him his hand.

"We will fight the battle side by side," replied Phineas.

After that he pushed his way still higher up the stairs, having no special purpose in view, not dreaming of any such success as that of reaching his host or hostess,—merely feeling that it should be a point of honour with him to make a tour through the rooms before he descended the stairs. The thing, he thought, was to be done with courage and patience, and this might, probably, be the last time in his life that he would find himself in the house of a Prime Minister. Just at the turn of the balustrade at the top of the stairs, he found Mr. Gresham in the very spot on which Mr. Monk had been talking with him. "Very glad to see you," said Mr. Gresham. "You, I find, are a persevering man, with a genius for getting upwards."

"Like the sparks," said Phineas.

"Not quite so quickly," said Mr. Gresham.

"But with the same assurance of speedy loss of my little light."

It did not suit Mr. Gresham to understand this, so he changed the subject. "Have you seen the news from America?"

"Yes, I have seen it, but do not believe it," said Phineas.

"Ah, you have such faith in a combination of British colonies, properly backed in Downing Street, as to think them strong against a world in arms. In your place I should hold to the same doctrine,—hold to it stoutly."

"And you do now, I hope, Mr. Gresham?"

"Well,—yes,—I am not down-hearted. But I confess to a feeling that the world would go on even though we had nothing to say to a single province in North America. But that is for your private ear. You are not to whisper that in Downing Street." Then there came up somebody else, and Phineas went on upon his slow course. He had longed for an opportunity to tell Mr. Gresham that he could go to Downing Street no more, but such opportunity had not reached him.

For a long time he found himself stuck close by the side of Miss Fitzgibbon,—Miss Aspasia Fitzgibbon,—who had once relieved him from terrible pecuniary anxiety by paying for him a sum of money which was due by him on her brother's account. "It's a very nice thing to be here, but one does get tired of it," said Miss Fitzgibbon.

"Very tired," said Phineas.

"Of course it is a part of your duty, Mr. Finn. You are on your promotion and are bound to be here. When I asked Laurence to come, he said there was nothing to be got till the cards were shuffled again."

"They'll be shuffled very soon," said Phineas.

"Whatever colour comes up, you'll hold trumps, I know," said the lady. "Some hands always hold trumps." He could not explain to Miss Fitzgibbon that it would never again be his fate to hold a single trump in his hand; so he made another fight, and got on a few steps farther.

He said a word as he went to half a dozen friends,—as friends went with him. He was detained for five minutes by Lady Baldock, who was very gracious and very disagreeable. She told him that Violet was in the room, but where she did not know. "She is somewhere with Lady Laura, I believe; and really, Mr. Finn, I do not like it." Lady Baldock had heard that Phineas had quarrelled with Lord Brentford, but had not heard of the reconciliation. "Really, I do not like it. I am told that Mr. Kennedy is in the house, and nobody knows what may happen."

"Mr. Kennedy is not likely to say anything."

"One cannot tell. And when I hear that a woman is separated from her husband, I always think that she must have been imprudent. It may be uncharitable, but I think it is most safe so to consider."

"As far as I have heard the circumstances, Lady Laura was quite right," said Phineas.

"It may be so. Gentlemen will always take the lady's part,—of course. But I should be very sorry to have a daughter separated from her husband,—very sorry."

Phineas, who had nothing now to gain from Lady Baldock's favour, left her abruptly, and went on again. He had a great desire to see Lady Laura and Violet together, though he could hardly tell himself why. He had not seen Miss Effingham since his return from Ireland, and he thought that if he met her alone he could hardly have talked to her with comfort; but he knew that if he met her with Lady Laura, she would greet him as a friend, and speak to him as though there were no cause for embarrassment between them. But he was so far disappointed, that he suddenly encountered Violet alone. She had been leaning on the arm of Lord Baldock, and Phineas saw her cousin leave her. But he would not be such a coward as to avoid her, especially as he knew that she had seen him. "Oh, Mr. Finn!" she said, "do you see that?"

"See what?"

"Look; There is Mr. Kennedy. We had heard that it was possible, and Laura made me promise that I would not leave her." Phineas turned his head, and saw Mr. Kennedy standing with his back bolt upright against a door-post, with his brow as black as thunder. "She is just opposite to him, where he can see her," said Violet. "Pray take me to her. He will think nothing of you, because I know that you are still friends with both of them. I came away because Lord Baldock wanted to introduce me to Lady Mouser. You know he is going to marry Miss Mouser."

Phineas, not caring much about Lord Baldock and Miss Mouser, took Violet's hand upon his arm, and very slowly made his way across the room to the spot indicated. There they found Lady Laura alone, sitting under the upas-tree influence of her husband's gaze. There was a concourse of people between them, and Mr. Kennedy did not seem inclined to make any attempt to lessen the distance. But Lady Laura had found it impossible to move while she was under her husband's eyes.

"Mr. Finn," she said, "could you find Oswald? I know he is here."

"He has gone," said Phineas. "I was speaking to him downstairs."

"You have not seen my father? He said he would come."

"I have not seen him, but I will search."

"No;—it will do no good. I cannot stay. His carriage is there, I know,—waiting for me." Phineas immediately started off to have the carriage called, and promised to return with as much celerity as he could use. As he went, making his way much quicker through the crowd than he had done when he had no such object for haste, he purposely avoided the door by which Mr. Kennedy had stood. It would have been his nearest way, but his present service, he thought, required that he should keep aloof from the man. But Mr. Kennedy passed through the door and intercepted him in his path.

"Is she going?" he asked.

"Well. Yes. I dare say she may before long. I shall look for Lord Brentford's carriage by-and-by."

"Tell her she need not go because of me. I shall not return. I shall not annoy her here. It would have been much better that a woman in such a plight should not have come to such an assembly."

"You would not wish her to shut herself up."

"I would wish her to come back to the home that she has left, and, if there be any law in the land, she shall be made to do so. You tell her that I say so." Then Mr. Kennedy fought his way down the stairs, and Phineas Finn followed in his wake.

About half an hour afterwards Phineas returned to the two ladies with tidings that the carriage would be at hand as soon as they could be below. "Did he see you?" said Lady Laura.

"Yes, he followed me."

"And did he speak to you?"

"Yes;—he spoke to me."

"And what did he say?" And then, in the presence of Violet, Phineas gave the message. He thought it better that it should be given; and were he to decline to deliver it now, it would never be given. "Whether there be law in the land to protect me or whether there be none, I will never live with him," said Lady Laura. "Is a woman like a head of cattle, that she can be fastened in her crib by force? I will never live with him though all the judges of the land should decide that I must do so."

Phineas thought much of all this as he went to his solitary lodgings. After all, was not the world much better with him than it was with either of those two wretched married beings? And why? He had not, at any rate as yet, sacrificed for money or social gains any of the instincts of his nature. He had been fickle, foolish, vain, uncertain, and perhaps covetous;—but as yet he had not been false. Then he took out Mary's last letter and read it again.

CHAPTER LXXI
Comparing Notes

It would, perhaps, be difficult to decide,—between Lord Chiltern and Miss Effingham,—which had been most wrong, or which had been nearest to the right, in the circumstances which had led to their separation. The old lord, wishing to induce his son to undertake work of some sort, and feeling that his own efforts in this direction were worse than useless, had closeted himself with his intended daughter-in-law, and had obtained from her a promise that she would use her influence with her lover. "Of course I think it right that he should do something," Violet had said. "And he will if you bid him," replied the Earl. Violet expressed a great doubt as to this willingness of obedience; but, nevertheless, she promised to do her best, and she did her best. Lord Chiltern, when she spoke to him, knit his brows with an apparent ferocity of anger which his countenance frequently expressed without any intention of ferocity on his part. He was annoyed, but was not savagely disposed to Violet. As he looked at her, however, he seemed to be very savagely disposed. "What is it you would have me do?" he said.

"I would have you choose some occupation, Oswald."

"What occupation? What is it that you mean? Ought I to be a shoemaker?"

"Not that by preference, I should say; but that if you please." When her lover had frowned at her, Violet had resolved,—had strongly determined, with inward assertions of her own rights,—that she would not be frightened by him.

"You are talking nonsense, Violet. You know that I cannot be a shoemaker."

"You may go into Parliament."

"I neither can, nor would I if I could. I dislike the life."

"You might farm."

"I cannot afford it."

"You might,—might do anything. You ought to do something. You know that you ought. You know that your father is right in what he says."

"That is easily asserted, Violet; but it would, I think, be better that you should take my part than my father's, if it be that you intend to be my wife."

"You know that I intend to be your wife; but would you wish that I should respect my husband?"

"And will you not do so if you marry me?" he asked.

Then Violet looked into his face and saw that the frown was blacker than ever. The great mark down his forehead was deeper and more like an ugly wound than she had ever seen it; and his eyes sparkled with anger; and his face was red as with fiery wrath. If it was so with him when she was no more than engaged to him, how would it be when they should be man and wife? At any rate, she would not fear him,—not now at least. "No, Oswald," she said. "If you resolve upon being an idle man, I shall not respect you. It is better that I should tell you the truth."

"A great deal better," he said.

"How can I respect one whose whole life will be,—will be—?"

"Will be what?" he demanded with a loud shout.

"Oswald, you are very rough with me."

"What do you say that my life will be?"

Then she again resolved that she would not fear him. "It will be discreditable," she said.

"It shall not discredit you," he replied. "I will not bring disgrace on one I have loved so well. Violet, after what you have said, we had better part." She was still proud, still determined, and they did part. Though it nearly broke her heart to see him leave her, she bid him go. She hated herself afterwards for her severity to him; but, nevertheless, she would not submit to recall the words which she had spoken. She had thought him to be wrong, and, so thinking, had conceived it to be her duty and her privilege to tell him what she thought. But she had no wish to lose him;—no wish not to be his wife even, though he should be as idle as the wind. She was so constituted that she had never allowed him or any other man to be master of her heart,—till she had with a full purpose given her heart away. The day before she had resolved to give it to one man, she might, I think, have resolved to give it to another. Love had not conquered her, but had been taken into her service. Nevertheless, she could not now rid herself of her servant, when she found that his services would stand her no longer in good stead. She parted from Lord Chiltern with an assent, with an assured brow, and with much dignity in her gait; but as soon as she was alone she was a prey to remorse. She had declared to the man who was to have been her husband that his life was discreditable,—and, of course, no man would bear such language. Had Lord Chiltern borne it, he would not have been worthy of her love.

She herself told Lady Laura and Lord Brentford what had occurred,—and had told Lady Baldock also. Lady Baldock had, of course, triumphed,—and Violet sought her revenge by swearing that she would regret for ever the loss of so inestimable a gentleman. "Then why have you given him up, my dear?" demanded Lady Baldock. "Because I found that he was too good for me," said Violet. It may be doubtful whether Lady Baldock was not justified, when she declared that her niece was to her a care so harassing that no aunt known in history had ever been so troubled before.

Lord Brentford had fussed and fumed, and had certainly made things worse. He had quarrelled with his son, and then made it up, and then quarrelled again,—swearing that the fault must all be attributed to Chiltern's stubbornness and Chiltern's temper. Latterly, however, by Lady Laura's intervention, Lord Brentford and his son had again been reconciled, and the Earl endeavoured manfully to keep his tongue from disagreeable words, and his face from evil looks, when his son was present. "They will make it up," Lady Laura had said, "if you and I do not attempt to make it up for them. If we do, they will never come together." The Earl was convinced, and did his best. But the task was very difficult to him. How was he to keep his tongue off his son while his son was daily saying things of which any father,—any such father as Lord Brentford,—could not but disapprove? Lord Chiltern professed to disbelieve even in the wisdom of the House of Lords, and on one occasion asserted that it must be a great comfort to any Prime Minister to have three or four old women in the Cabinet. The father, when he heard this, tried to rebuke his son tenderly, strove even to be jocose. It was the one wish of his heart that Violet Effingham should be his daughter-in-law. But even with this wish he found it very hard to keep his tongue off Lord Chiltern.

When Lady Laura discussed the matter with Violet, Violet would always declare that there was no hope. "The truth is," she said on the morning of that day on which they both went to Mrs. Gresham's, "that though we like each other,—love each other, if you choose to say so,—we are not fit to be man and wife."

"And why not fit?"

"We are too much alike. Each is too violent, too headstrong, and too masterful."

"You, as the woman, ought to give way," said Lady Laura.

"But we do not always do just what we ought."

"I know how difficult it is for me to advise, seeing to what a pass I have brought myself."

"Do not say that, dear;—or rather do say it, for we have, both of us, brought ourselves to what you call a pass,—to such a pass that we are like to be able to live together and discuss it for the rest of our lives. The difference is, I take it, that you have not to accuse yourself, and that I have."

"I cannot say that I have not to accuse myself," said Lady Laura. "I do not know that I have done much wrong to Mr. Kennedy since I married him; but in marrying him I did him a grievous wrong."

"And he has avenged himself."

"We will not talk of vengeance. I believe he is wretched, and I know that I am;—and that has come of the wrong that I have done."

"I will make no man wretched," said Violet.

"Do you mean that your mind is made up against Oswald?"

"I mean that, and I mean much more. I say that I will make no man wretched. Your brother is not the only man who is so weak as to be willing to run the hazard."

"There is Lord Fawn."

"Yes, there is Lord Fawn, certainly. Perhaps I should not do him much harm; but then I should do him no good."

"And poor Phineas Finn."

"Yes;—there is Mr. Finn. I will tell you something, Laura. The only man I ever saw in the world whom I have thought for a moment that it was possible that I should like,—like enough to love as my husband,—except your brother, was Mr. Finn."

"And now?"

"Oh;—now; of course that is over," said Violet.

"It is over?"

"Quite over. Is he not going to marry Madame Goesler? I suppose all that is fixed by this time. I hope she will be good to him, and gracious, and let him have his own way, and give him his tea comfortably when he comes up tired from the House; for I confess that my heart is a little tender towards Phineas still. I should not like to think that he had fallen into the hands of a female Philistine."

"I do not think he will marry Madame Goesler."

"Why not?"

"I can hardly tell you;—but I do not think he will. And you loved him once,—eh, Violet?"

"Not quite that, my dear. It has been difficult with me to love. The difficulty with most girls, I fancy, is not to love. Mr. Finn, when I came to measure him in my mind, was not small, but he was never quite tall enough. One feels oneself to be a sort of recruiting sergeant, going about with a standard of inches. Mr. Finn was just half an inch too short. He lacks something in individuality. He is a little too much a friend to everybody."

"Shall I tell you a secret, Violet?"

"If you please, dear; though I fancy it is one I know already."

"He is the only man whom I ever loved," said Lady Laura.

"But it was too late when you learned to love him," said Violet.

"It was too late, when I was so sure of it as to wish that I had never seen Mr. Kennedy. I felt it coming on me, and I argued with myself that such a marriage would be bad for us both. At that moment there was trouble in the family, and I had not a shilling of my own."

"You had paid it for Oswald."

"At any rate, I had nothing;—and he had nothing. How could I have dared to think even of such a marriage?"

"Did he think of it, Laura?"

"I suppose he did."

"You know he did. Did you not tell me before?"

"Well;—yes. He thought of it. I had come to some foolish, half-sentimental resolution as to friendship, believing that he and I could be knit together by some adhesion of fraternal affection that should be void of offence to my husband; and in furtherance of this he was asked to Loughlinter when I went there, just after I had accepted Robert. He came down, and I measured him too, as you have done. I measured him, and I found that he wanted nothing to come up to the height required by my standard. I think I knew him better than you did."

"Very possibly;—but why measure him at all, when such measurement was useless?"

"Can one help such things? He came to me one day as I was sitting up by the Linter. You remember the place, where it makes its first leap."

"I remember it very well."

"So do I. Robert had shown it me as the fairest spot in all Scotland."

"And there this lover of ours sang his song to you?"

"I do not know what he told me then; but I know that I told him that I was engaged; and I felt when I told him so that my engagement was a sorrow to me. And it has been a sorrow from that day to this."

"And the hero, Phineas,—he is still dear to you?"

"Dear to me?"

"Yes. You would have hated me, had he become my husband? And you will hate Madame Goesler when she becomes his wife?"

"Not in the least. I am no dog in the manger. I have even gone so far as almost to wish, at certain moments, that you should accept him."

"And why?"

"Because he has wished it so heartily."

"One can hardly forgive a man for such speedy changes," said Violet.

"Was I not to forgive him;—I, who had turned myself away from him with a fixed purpose the moment that I found that he had made a mark upon my heart? I could not wipe off the mark, and yet I married. Was he not to try to wipe off his mark?"

"It seems that he wiped it off very quickly;—and since that he has wiped off another mark. One doesn't know how many marks he has wiped off. They are like the inn-keeper's score which he makes in chalk. A damp cloth brings them all away, and leaves nothing behind."

"What would you have?"

"There should be a little notch on the stick,—to remember by," said Violet. "Not that I complain, you know. I cannot complain, as I was not notched myself."

"You are silly, Violet."

"In not having allowed myself to be notched by this great champion?"

"A man like Mr. Finn has his life to deal with,—to make the most of it, and to divide it between work, pleasure, duty, ambition, and the rest of it as best he may. If he have any softness of heart, it will be necessary to him that love should bear a part in all these interests. But a man will be a fool who will allow love to be the master of them all. He will be one whose mind is so ill-balanced as to allow him to be the victim of a single wish. Even in a woman passion such as that is evidence of weakness, and not of strength."

"It seems, then, Laura, that you are weak."

"And if I am, does that condemn him? He is a man, if I judge him rightly, who will be constant as the sun, when constancy can be of service."

"You mean that the future Mrs. Finn will be secure?"

"That is what I mean;—and that you or I, had either of us chosen to take his name, might have been quite secure. We have thought it right to refuse to do so."

"And how many more, I wonder?"

"You are unjust, and unkind, Violet. So unjust and unkind that it is clear to me he has just gratified your vanity, and has never touched your heart. What would you have had him do, when I told him that I was engaged?"

"I suppose that Mr. Kennedy would not have gone to Blankenberg with him."

"Violet!"

"That seems to be the proper thing to do. But even that does not adjust things finally;—does it?" Then some one came upon them, and the conversation was brought to an end.

CHAPTER LXXII
Madame Goesler's Generosity

When Phineas Finn left Mr. Gresham's house he had quite resolved what he would do. On the next morning he would tell Lord Cantrip that his resignation was a necessity, and that he would take that nobleman's advice as to resigning at once, or waiting till the day on which Mr. Monk's Irish Bill would be read for the second time.

"My dear Finn, I can only say that I deeply regret it," said Lord Cantrip.

"So do I. I regret to leave office, which I like,—and which indeed I want. I regret specially to leave this office, as it has been a thorough pleasure to me; and I regret, above all, to leave you. But I am convinced that Monk is right, and I find it impossible not to support him."

"I wish that Mr. Monk was at Bath," said Lord Cantrip.

Phineas could only smile, and shrug his shoulders, and say that even though Mr. Monk were at Bath it would not probably make much difference. When he tendered his letter of resignation, Lord Cantrip begged him to withdraw it for a day or two. He would, he said, speak to Mr. Gresham. The debate on the second reading of Mr. Monk's bill would not take place till that day week, and the resignation would be in time if it was tendered before Phineas either spoke or voted against the Government. So Phineas went back to his room, and endeavoured to make himself useful in some work appertaining to his favourite Colonies.

That conversation had taken place on a Friday, and on the following Sunday, early in the day, he left his rooms after a late breakfast,—a prolonged breakfast, during which he had been studying tenant-right statistics, preparing his own speech, and endeavouring to look forward into the future which that speech was to do so much to influence,—and turned his face towards Park Lane. There had been a certain understanding between him and Madame Goesler that he was to call in Park Lane on this Sunday morning, and then declare to her what was his final resolve as to the office which he held. "It is simply to bid her adieu," he said to himself, "for I shall hardly see her again." And yet, as he took off his morning easy coat, and dressed himself for the streets, and stood for a moment before his looking-glass, and saw that his gloves were fresh and that his boots were properly polished, I think there was a care about his person which he would have hardly taken had he been quite assured that he simply intended to say good-bye to the lady whom he was about to visit. But if there were any such conscious feeling, he administered to himself an antidote before he left the house. On returning to the sitting-room he went to a little desk from which he took out the letter from Mary which the reader has seen, and carefully perused every word of it. "She is the best of them all," he said to himself, as he refolded the letter and put it back into his desk. I am not sure that it is well that a man should have any large number from whom to select a best; as, in such circumstances, he is so very apt to change his judgment from hour to hour. The qualities which are the most attractive before dinner sometimes become the least so in the evening.

The morning was warm, and he took a cab. It would not do that he should speak even his last farewell to such a one as Madame Goesler with all the heat and dust of a long walk upon him. Having been so careful about his boots and gloves he might as well use his care to the end. Madame Goesler was a very pretty woman, who spared herself no trouble in making herself as pretty as Nature would allow, on behalf of those whom she favoured with her smiles; and to such a lady some special attention was due by one who had received so many of her smiles as had Phineas. And he felt, too, that there was something special in this very visit. It was to be made by appointment, and there had come to be an understanding between them that Phineas should tell her on this occasion what was his resolution with reference to his future life. I think that he had been very wise in fortifying himself with a further glance at our dear Mary's letter, before he trusted himself within Madame Goesler's door.

Yes;—Madame Goesler was at home. The door was opened by Madame Goesler's own maid, who, smiling, explained that the other servants were all at church. Phineas had become sufficiently intimate at the cottage in Park Lane to be on friendly terms with Madame Goesler's own maid, and now made some little half-familiar remark as to the propriety of his visit during church time. "Madame will not refuse to see you, I am thinking," said the girl, who was a German. "And she is alone?" asked Phineas. "Alone? Yes;—of course she is alone. Who should be with her now?" Then she took him up into the drawing-room; but, when there, he found that Madame Goesler was absent. "She shall be down directly," said the girl. "I shall tell her who is here, and she will come."

It was a very pretty room. It may almost be said that there could be no prettier room in all London. It looked out across certain small private gardens,—which were as bright and gay as money could make them when brought into competition with London smoke,—right on to the park. Outside and inside the window, flowers and green things were so arranged that the room itself almost looked as though it were a bower in a garden. And everything in that bower was rich and rare; and there was nothing there which annoyed by its rarity or was distasteful by its richness. The seats, though they were costly as money could buy, were meant for sitting, and were comfortable as seats. There were books for reading, and the means of reading them. Two or three gems of English art were hung upon the walls, and could be seen backwards and forwards in the mirrors. And there were precious toys lying here and there about the room,—toys very precious, but placed there not because of their price, but because of their beauty. Phineas already knew enough of the art of living to be aware that the woman who had made that room what it was, had charms to add a beauty to everything she touched. What would such a life as his want, if graced by such a companion,—such a life as his might be, if the means which were hers were at his command? It would want one thing, he thought,—the self-respect which he would lose if he were false to the girl who was trusting him with such sweet trust at home in Ireland.

In a very few minutes Madame Goesler was with him, and, though he did not think about it, he perceived that she was bright in her apparel, that her hair was as soft as care could make it, and that every charm belonging to her had been brought into use for his gratification. He almost told himself that he was there in order that he might ask to have all those charms bestowed upon himself. He did not know who had lately come to Park Lane and been a suppliant for the possession of those rich endowments; but I wonder whether they would have been more precious in his eyes had he known that they had so moved the heart of the great Duke as to have induced him to lay his coronet at the lady's feet. I think that had he known that the lady had refused the coronet, that knowledge would have enhanced the value of the prize.

"I am so sorry to have kept you waiting," she said, as she gave him her hand. "I was an owl not to be ready for you when you told me that you would come."

"No;—but a bird of paradise to come to me so sweetly, and at an hour when all the other birds refuse to show the feather of a single wing."

"And you,—you feel like a naughty boy, do you not, in thus coming out on a Sunday morning?"

"Do you feel like a naughty girl?"

"Yes;—just a little so. I do not know that I should care for everybody to hear that I received visitors,—or worse still, a visitor,—at this hour on this day. But then it is so pleasant to feel oneself to be naughty! There is a Bohemian flavour of picnic about it which, though it does not come up to the rich gusto of real wickedness, makes one fancy that one is on the border of that delightful region in which there is none of the constraint of custom,—where men and women say what they like, and do what they like."

"It is pleasant enough to be on the borders," said Phineas.

"That is just it. Of course decency, morality, and propriety, all made to suit the eye of the public, are the things which are really delightful. We all know that, and live accordingly,—as well as we can. I do at least."

"And do not I, Madame Goesler?"

"I know nothing about that, Mr. Finn, and want to ask no questions. But if you do, I am sure you agree with me that you often envy the improper people,—the Bohemians,—the people who don't trouble themselves about keeping any laws except those for breaking which they would be put into nasty, unpleasant prisons. I envy them. Oh, how I envy them!"

"But you are free as air."

"The most cabined, cribbed, and confined creature in the world! I have been fighting my way up for the last four years, and have not allowed myself the liberty of one flirtation;—not often even the recreation of a natural laugh. And now I shouldn't wonder if I don't find myself falling back a year or two, just because I have allowed you to come and see me on a Sunday morning. When I told Lotta that you were coming, she shook her head at me in dismay. But now that you are here, tell me what you have done."

"Nothing as yet, Madame Goesler."

"I thought it was to have been settled on Friday?"

"It was settled,—before Friday. Indeed, as I look back at it all now, I can hardly tell when it was not settled. It is impossible, and has been impossible, that I should do otherwise. I still hold my place, Madame Goesler, but I have declared that I shall give it up before the debate comes on."

"It is quite fixed?"

"Quite fixed, my friend."

"And what next?" Madame Goesler, as she thus interrogated him, was leaning across towards him from the sofa on which she was placed, with both her elbows resting on a small table before her. We all know that look of true interest which the countenance of a real friend will bear when the welfare of his friend is in question. There are doubtless some who can assume it without feeling,—as there are actors who can personate all the passions. But in ordinary life we think that we can trust such a face, and that we know the true look when we see it. Phineas, as he gazed into Madame Goesler's eyes, was sure that the lady opposite him was not acting. She at least was anxious for his welfare, and was making his cares her own. "What next?" said she, repeating her words in a tone that was somewhat hurried.

"I do not know that there will be any next. As far as public life is concerned, there will be no next for me, Madame Goesler."

"That is out of the question," she said. "You are made for public life."

"Then I shall be untrue to my making, I fear. But to speak plainly—"

"Yes; speak plainly. I want to understand the reality."

"The reality is this. I shall keep my seat to the end of the session, as I think I may be of use. After that I shall give it up."

"Resign that too?" she said in a tone of chagrin.

"The chances are, I think, that there will be another dissolution. If they hold their own against Mr. Monk's motion, then they will pass an Irish Reform Bill. After that I think they must dissolve."

"And you will not come forward again?"

"I cannot afford it."

"Psha! Some five hundred pounds or so!"

"And, besides that, I am well aware that my only chance at my old profession is to give up all idea of Parliament. The two things are not compatible for a beginner at the law. I know it now, and have bought my knowledge by a bitter experience."

"And where will you live?"

"In Dublin, probably."

"And you will do,—will do what?"

"Anything honest in a barrister's way that may be brought to me. I hope that I may never descend below that."

"You will stand up for all the blackguards, and try to make out that the thieves did not steal?"

"It may be that that sort of work may come in my way."

"And you will wear a wig and try to look wise?"

"The wig is not universal in Ireland, Madame Goesler."

"And you will wrangle, as though your very soul were in it, for somebody's twenty pounds?"

"Exactly."

"You have already made a name in the greatest senate in the world, and have governed other countries larger than your own—"

"No;—I have not done that. I have governed no country.

"I tell you, my friend, that you cannot do it. It is out of the question. Men may move forward from little work to big work; but they cannot move back and do little work, when they have had tasks which were really great. I tell you, Mr. Finn, that the House of Parliament is the place for you to work in. It is the only place;—that and the abodes of Ministers. Am not I your friend who tell you this?"

"I know that you are my friend."

"And will you not credit me when I tell you this? What do you fear, that you should run away? You have no wife;—no children. What is the coming misfortune that you dread?" She paused a moment as though for an answer, and he felt that now had come the time in which it would be well that he should tell her of his engagement with his own Mary. She had received him very playfully; but now within the last few minutes there had come upon her a seriousness of gesture, and almost a solemnity of tone, which made him conscious that he should in no way trifle with her. She was so earnest in her friendship that he owed it to her to tell her everything. But before he could think of the words in which his tale should be told, she had gone on with her quick questions. "Is it solely about money that you fear?" she said.

"It is simply that I have no income on which to live."

"Have I not offered you money?"

"But, Madame Goesler, you who offer it would yourself despise me if I took it."

"No;—I do deny it." As she said this,—not loudly but with much emphasis,—she came and stood before him where he was sitting. And as he looked at her he could perceive that there was a strength about her of which he had not been aware. She was stronger, larger, more robust physically than he had hitherto conceived. "I do deny it," she said. "Money is neither god nor devil, that it should make one noble and another vile. It is an accident, and, if honestly possessed, may pass from you to me, or from me to you, without a stain. You may take my dinner from me if I give it you, my flowers, my friendship, my,—my,—my everything, but my money! Explain to me the cause of the phenomenon. If I give to you a thousand pounds, now this moment, and you take it, you are base;—but if I leave it you in my will,—and die,—you take it, and are not base. Explain to me the cause of that."

"You have not said it quite all," said Phineas hoarsely.

"What have I left unsaid? If I have left anything unsaid, do you say the rest."

"It is because you are a woman, and young, and beautiful, that no man may take wealth from your hands."

"Oh, it is that!"

"It is that partly,"

"If I were a man you might take it, though I were young and beautiful as the morning?"

"No;—presents of money are always bad. They stain and load the spirit, and break the heart."

"And specially when given by a woman's hand?"

"It seems so to me. But I cannot argue of it. Do not let us talk of it any more."

"Nor can I argue. I cannot argue, but I can be generous,—very generous. I can deny myself for my friend,—can even lower myself in my own esteem for my friend. I can do more than a man can do for a friend. You will not take money from my hand?"

"No, Madame Goesler;—I cannot do that."

"Take the hand then first. When it and all that it holds are your own, you can help yourself as you list." So saying, she stood before him with her right hand stretched out towards him.

What man will say that he would not have been tempted? Or what woman will declare that such temptation should have had no force? The very air of the room in which she dwelt was sweet in his nostrils, and there hovered around her an halo of grace and beauty which greeted all his senses. She invited him to join his lot to hers, in order that she might give to him all that was needed to make his life rich and glorious. How would the Ratlers and the Bonteens envy him when they heard of the prize which had become his! The Cantrips and the Greshams would feel that he was a friend doubly valuable, if he could be won back; and Mr. Monk would greet him as a fitting ally,—an ally strong with the strength which he had before wanted. With whom would he not be equal? Whom need he fear? Who would not praise him? The story of his poor Mary would be known only in a small village, out beyond the Channel. The temptation certainly was very strong.

But he had not a moment in which to doubt. She was standing there with her face turned from him, but with her hand still stretched towards him. Of course he took it. What man so placed could do other than take a woman's hand?

"My friend," he said.

"I will be called friend by you no more," she said. "You must call me Marie, your own Marie, or you must never call me by any name again. Which shall it be, sir?" He paused a moment, holding her hand, and she let it lie there for an instant while she listened. But still she did not look at him. "Speak to me! Tell me! Which shall it be?" Still he paused. "Speak to me. Tell me!" she said again.

"It cannot be as you have hinted to me," he said at last. His words did not come louder than a low whisper; but they were plainly heard, and instantly the hand was withdrawn.

"Cannot be!" she exclaimed. "Then I have betrayed myself."

"No;—Madame Goesler."

"Sir; I say yes! If you will allow me I will leave you. You will, I know, excuse me if I am abrupt to you." Then she strode out of the room, and was no more seen of the eyes of Phineas Finn.

He never afterwards knew how he escaped out of that room and found his way into Park Lane. In after days he had some memory that he remained there, he knew not how long, standing on the very spot on which she had left him; and that at last there grew upon him almost a fear of moving, a dread lest he should be heard, an inordinate desire to escape without the sound of a footfall, without the clicking of a lock. Everything in that house had been offered to him. He had refused it all, and then felt that of all human beings under the sun none had so little right to be standing there as he. His very presence in that drawing-room was an insult to the woman whom he had driven from it.

But at length he was in the street, and had found his way across Piccadilly into the Green Park. Then, as soon as he could find a spot apart from the Sunday world, he threw himself upon the turf; and tried to fix his thoughts upon the thing that he had done. His first feeling, I think, was one of pure and unmixed disappointment;—of disappointment so bitter, that even the vision of his own Mary did not tend to comfort him. How great might have been his success, and how terrible was his failure! Had he taken the woman's hand and her money, had he clenched his grasp on the great prize offered to him, his misery would have been ten times worse the first moment that he would have been away from her. Then, indeed,—it being so that he was a man with a heart within his breast,—there would have been no comfort for him, in his outlooks on any side. But even now, when he had done right,—knowing well that he had done right,—he found that comfort did not come readily within his reach.

CHAPTER LXXIII
Amantium Iræ

Miss Effingham's life at this time was not the happiest in the world. Her lines, as she once said to her friend Lady Laura, were not laid for her in pleasant places. Her residence was still with her aunt, and she had come to find that it was almost impossible any longer to endure Lady Baldock, and quite impossible to escape from Lady Baldock. In former days she had had a dream that she might escape, and live alone if she chose to be alone; that she might be independent in her life, as a man is independent, if she chose to live after that fashion; that she might take her own fortune in her own hand, as the law certainly allowed her to do, and act with it as she might please. But latterly she had learned to understand that all this was not possible for her. Though one law allowed it, another law disallowed it, and the latter law was at least as powerful as the former. And then her present misery was enhanced by the fact that she was now banished from the second home which she had formerly possessed. Hitherto she had always been able to escape from Lady Baldock to the house of her friend, but now such escape was out of the question. Lady Laura and Lord Chiltern lived in the same house, and Violet could not live with them.

Lady Baldock understood all this, and tortured her niece accordingly. It was not premeditated torture. The aunt did not mean to make her niece's life a burden to her, and, so intending, systematically work upon a principle to that effect. Lady Baldock, no doubt, desired to do her duty conscientiously. But the result was torture to poor Violet, and a strong conviction on the mind of each of the two ladies that the other was the most unreasonable being in the world.

The aunt, in these days, had taken it into her head to talk of poor Lord Chiltern. This arose partly from a belief that the quarrel was final, and that, therefore, there would be no danger in aggravating Violet by this expression of pity,—partly from a feeling that it would be better that her niece should marry Lord Chiltern than that she should not marry at all,—and partly, perhaps, from the general principle that, as she thought it right to scold her niece on all occasions, this might be best done by taking an opposite view of all questions to that taken by the niece to be scolded. Violet was supposed to regard Lord Chiltern as having sinned against her, and therefore Lady Baldock talked of "poor Lord Chiltern." As to the other lovers, she had begun to perceive that their conditions were hopeless. Her daughter Augusta had explained to her that there was no chance remaining either for Phineas, or for Lord Fawn, or for Mr. Appledom. "I believe she will be an old maid, on purpose to bring me to my grave," said Lady Baldock. When, therefore, Lady Baldock was told one day that Lord Chiltern was in the house, and was asking to see Miss Effingham, she did not at once faint away, and declare that they would all be murdered,—as she would have done some months since. She was perplexed by a double duty. If it were possible that Violet should relent and be reconciled, then it would be her duty to save Violet from the claws of the wild beast. But if there was no such chance, then it would be her duty to poor Lord Chiltern to see that he was not treated with contumely and ill-humour.

"Does she know that he is here?" Lady Baldock asked her daughter.

"Not yet, mamma."

"Oh dear, oh dear! I suppose she ought to see him. She has given him so much encouragement!"

"I suppose she will do as she pleases, mamma."

"Augusta, how can you talk in that way? Am I to have no control in my own house?" It was, however, soon apparent to her that in this matter she was to have no control.

"Lord Chiltern is down-stairs," said Violet, coming into the room abruptly.

"So Augusta tells me. Sit down, my dear."

"I cannot sit down, aunt,—not just now. I have sent down to say that I would be with him in a minute. He is the most impatient soul alive, and I must not keep him waiting."

"And you mean to see him?"

"Certainly I shall see him," said Violet, as she left the room.

"I wonder that any woman should ever take upon herself the charge of a niece!" said Lady Baldock to her daughter in a despondent tone, as she held up her hands in dismay. In the meantime, Violet had gone down-stairs with a quick step, and had then boldly entered the room in which her lover was waiting to receive her.

"I have to thank you for coming to me, Violet," said Lord Chiltern. There was still in his face something of savagery,—an expression partly of anger and partly of resolution to tame the thing with which he was angry. Violet did not regard the anger half so keenly as she did that resolution of taming. An angry lord, she thought, she could endure, but she could not bear the idea of being tamed by any one.

"Why should I not come?" she said. "Of course I came when I was told that you were here. I do not think that there need be a quarrel between us, because we have changed our minds."

"Such changes make quarrels," said he.

"It shall not do so with me, unless you choose that it shall," said Violet. "Why should we be enemies,—we who have known each other since we were children? My dearest friends are your father and your sister. Why should we be enemies?"

"I have come to ask you whether you think that I have ill-used you?"

"Ill-used me! Certainly not. Has any one told you that I have accused you?"

"No one has told me so."

"Then why do you ask me?"

"Because I would not have you think so,—if I could help it. I did not intend to be rough with you. When you told me that my life was disreputable—"

"Oh, Oswald, do not let us go back to that. What good will it do?"

"But you said so."

"I think not."

"I believe that that was your word,—the harshest word that you could use in all the language."

"I did not mean to be harsh. If I used it, I will beg your pardon. Only let there be an end of it. As we think so differently about life in general, it was better that we should not be married. But that is settled, and why should we go back to words that were spoken in haste, and which are simply disagreeable?"

"I have come to know whether it is settled."

"Certainly. You settled it yourself, Oswald. I told you what I thought myself bound to tell you. Perhaps I used language which I should not have used. Then you told me that I could not be your wife;—and I thought you were right, quite right."

"I was wrong, quite wrong," he said impetuously. "So wrong, that I can never forgive myself, if you do not relent. I was such a fool, that I cannot forgive myself my folly. I had known before that I could not live without you; and when you were mine, I threw you away for an angry word."

"It was not an angry word," she said.

"Say it again, and let me have another chance to answer it."

"I think I said that idleness was not,—respectable, or something like that, taken out of a copy-book probably. But you are a man who do not like rebukes, even out of copy-books. A man so thin-skinned as you are must choose for himself a wife with a softer tongue than mine."

"I will choose none other!" he said. But still he was savage in his tone and in his gestures. "I made my choice long since, as you know well enough. I do not change easily. I cannot change in this. Violet, say that you will be my wife once more, and I will swear to work for you like a coal-heaver."

"My wish is that my husband,—should I ever have one,—should work, not exactly as a coal-heaver."

"Come, Violet," he said,—and now the look of savagery departed from him, and there came a smile over his face, which, however, had in it more of sadness than of hope or joy,—"treat me fairly,—or rather, treat me generously if you can. I do not know whether you ever loved me much."

"Very much,—years ago, when you were a boy."

"But not since? If it be so, I had better go. Love on one side only is a poor affair at best."

"A very poor affair."

"It is better to bear anything than to try and make out life with that. Some of you women never want to love any one."

"That was what I was saying of myself to Laura but the other day. With some women it is so easy. With others it is so difficult, that perhaps it never comes to them."

"And with you?"

"Oh, with me—. But it is better in these matters to confine oneself to generalities. If you please, I will not describe myself personally. Were I to do so, doubtless I should do it falsely."

"You love no one else, Violet?"

"That is my affair, my lord."

"By heavens, and it is mine too. Tell me that you do, and I will go away and leave you at once. I will not ask his name, and I will trouble you no more. If it is not so, and if it is possible that you should forgive me—"

"Forgive you! When have I been angry with you?"

"Answer me my question, Violet."

"I will not answer you your question,—not that one."

"What question will you answer?"

"Any that may concern yourself and myself. None that may concern other people."

"You told me once that you loved me."

"This moment I told you that I did so,—years ago."

"But now?"

"That is another matter."

"Violet, do you love me now?"

"That is a point-blank question at any rate," she said.

"And you will answer it?"

"I must answer it,—I suppose."

"Well, then?"

"Oh, Oswald, what a fool you are! Love you! of course I love you. If you can understand anything, you ought to know that I have never loved any one else;—that after what has passed between us, I never shall love any one else. I do love you. There. Whether you throw me away from you, as you did the other day,—with great scorn, mind you,—or come to me with sweet, beautiful promises, as you do now, I shall love you all the same. I cannot be your wife, if you will not have me; can I? When you run away in your tantrums because I quote something out of the copy-book, I can't run after you. It would not be pretty. But as for loving you, if you doubt that, I tell you, you are a—fool." As she spoke the last words she pouted out her lips at him, and when he looked into her face he saw that her eyes were full of tears. He was standing now with his arm round her waist, so that it was not easy for him to look into her face.

"I am a fool," he said.

"Yes;—you are; but I don't love you the less on that account."

"I will never doubt it again."

"No;—do not; and, for me, I will not say another word, whether you choose to heave coals or not. You shall do as you please. I meant to be very wise;—I did indeed."

"You are the grandest girl that ever was made."

"I do not want to be grand at all, and I never will be wise any more. Only do not frown at me and look savage." Then she put up her hand to smooth his brow. "I am half afraid of you still, you know. There. That will do. Now let me go, that I may tell my aunt. During the last two months she has been full of pity for poor Lord Chiltern."

"It has been poor Lord Chiltern with a vengeance!" said he.

"But now that we have made it up, she will be horrified again at all your wickednesses. You have been a turtle dove lately;—now you will be an ogre again. But, Oswald, you must not be an ogre to me."

As soon as she could get quit of her lover, she did tell her tale to Lady Baldock. "You have accepted him again!" said her aunt, holding up her hands. "Yes,—I have accepted him again," replied Violet. "Then the responsibility must be on your own shoulders," said her aunt; "I wash my hands of it." That evening, when she discussed the matter with her daughter, Lady Baldock spoke of Violet and Lord Chiltern, as though their intended marriage were the one thing in the world which she most deplored.

CHAPTER LXXIV
The Beginning of the End

The day of the debate had come, and Phineas Finn was still sitting in his room at the Colonial Office. But his resignation had been sent in and accepted, and he was simply awaiting the coming of his successor. About noon his successor came, and he had the gratification of resigning his arm-chair to Mr. Bonteen. It is generally understood that gentlemen leaving offices give up either seals or a portfolio. Phineas had been put in possession of no seal and no portfolio; but there was in the room which he had occupied a special arm-chair, and this with much regret he surrendered to the use and comfort of Mr. Bonteen. There was a glance of triumph in his enemy's eyes, and an exultation in the tone of his enemy's voice, which were very bitter to him. "So you are really going?" said Mr. Bonteen. "Well; I dare say it is all very proper. I don't quite understand the thing myself, but I have no doubt you are right." "It isn't easy to understand; is it?" said Phineas, trying to laugh. But Mr. Bonteen did not feel the intended satire, and poor Phineas found it useless to attempt to punish the man he hated. He left him as quickly as he could, and went to say a few words of farewell to his late chief.

"Good-bye, Finn," said Lord Cantrip. "It is a great trouble to me that we should have to part in this way."

"And to me also, my lord. I wish it could have been avoided."

"You should not have gone to Ireland with so dangerous a man as Mr. Monk. But it is too late to think of that now."

"The milk is spilt; is it not?"

"But these terrible rendings asunder never last very long," said Lord Cantrip, "unless a man changes his opinions altogether. How many quarrels and how many reconciliations we have lived to see! I remember when Gresham went out of office, because he could not sit in the same room with Mr. Mildmay, and yet they became the fastest of political friends. There was a time when Plinlimmon and the Duke could not stable their horses together at all; and don't you remember when Palliser was obliged to give up his hopes of office because he had some bee in his bonnet?" I think, however, that the bee in Mr. Palliser's bonnet to which Lord Cantrip was alluding made its buzzing audible on some subject that was not exactly political. "We shall have you back again before long, I don't doubt. Men who can really do their work are too rare to be left long in the comfort of the benches below the gangway." This was very kindly said, and Phineas was flattered and comforted. He could not, however, make Lord Cantrip understand the whole truth. For him the dream of a life of politics was over for ever. He had tried it, and had succeeded beyond his utmost hopes; but, in spite of his success, the ground had crumbled to pieces beneath his feet, and he knew that he could never recover the niche in the world's gallery which he was now leaving.

That same afternoon he met Mr. Gresham in one of the passages leading to the House, and the Prime Minister put his arm through that of our hero as they walked together into the lobby. "I am sorry that we are losing you," said Mr. Gresham.

"You may be sure that I am sorry to be so lost," said Phineas.

"These things will occur in political life," said the leader; "but I think that they seldom leave rancour behind them when the purpose is declared, and when the subject of disagreement is marked and understood. The defalcation which creates angry feeling is that which has to be endured without previous warning,—when a man votes against his party,—or a set of men, from private pique or from some cause which is never clear." Phineas, when he heard this, knew well how terribly this very man had been harassed, and driven nearly wild, by defalcation, exactly of that nature which he was attempting to describe. "No doubt you and Mr. Monk think you are right," continued Mr. Gresham.

"We have given strong evidence that we think so," said Phineas. "We give up our places, and we are, both of us, very poor men."

"I think you are wrong, you know, not so much in your views on the question itself—which, to tell the truth, I hardly understand as yet."

"We will endeavour to explain them."

"And will do so very clearly, no doubt. But I think that Mr. Monk was wrong in desiring, as a member of a Government, to force a measure which, whether good or bad, the Government as a body does not desire to initiate,—at any rate, just now."

"And therefore he resigned," said Phineas.

"Of course. But it seems to me that he failed to comprehend the only way in which a great party can act together, if it is to do any service in this country. Don't for a moment think that I am blaming him or you."

"I am nobody in this matter," said Phineas.

"I can assure you, Mr. Finn, that we have not regarded you in that light, and I hope that the time may come when we may be sitting together again on the same bench."

Neither on the Treasury bench nor on any other in that House was he to sit again after this fashion! That was the trouble which was crushing his spirit at this moment, and not the loss of his office! He knew that he could not venture to think of remaining in London as a member of Parliament with no other income than that which his father could allow him, even if he could again secure a seat in Parliament. When he had first been returned for Loughshane he had assured his friends that his duty as a member of the House of Commons would not be a bar to his practice in the Courts. He had now been five years a member, and had never once made an attempt at doing any part of a barrister's work. He had gone altogether into a different line of life, and had been most successful;—so successful that men told him, and women more frequently than men, that his career had been a miracle of success. But there had been, as he had well known from the first, this drawback in the new profession which he had chosen, that nothing in it could be permanent. They who succeed in it, may probably succeed again; but then the success is intermittent, and there may be years of hard work in opposition, to which, unfortunately, no pay is assigned. It is almost imperative, as he now found, that they who devote themselves to such a profession should be men of fortune. When he had commenced his work,—at the period of his first return for Loughshane,—he had had no thought of mending his deficiency in this respect by a rich marriage. Nor had it ever occurred to him that he would seek a marriage for that purpose. Such an idea would have been thoroughly distasteful to him. There had been no stain of premeditated mercenary arrangement upon him at any time. But circumstances had so fallen out with him, that as he won his spurs in Parliament, as he became known, and was placed first in one office and then in another, prospects of love and money together were opened to him, and he ventured on, leaving Mr. Low and the law behind him,—because these prospects were so alluring. Then had come Mr. Monk and Mary Flood Jones,—and everything around him had collapsed.

Everything around him had collapsed,—with, however, a terrible temptation to him to inflate his sails again, at the cost of his truth and his honour. The temptation would have affected him not at all, had Madame Goesler been ugly, stupid, or personally disagreeable. But she was, he thought, the most beautiful woman he had ever seen, the most witty, and in many respects the most charming. She had offered to give him everything that she had, so to place him in the world that opposition would be more pleasant to him than office, to supply every want, and had done so in a manner that had gratified all his vanity. But he had refused it all, because he was bound to the girl at Floodborough. My readers will probably say that he was not a true man unless he could do this without a regret. When Phineas thought of it all, there were many regrets.

But there was at the same time a resolve on his part, that if any man had ever loved the girl he promised to love, he would love Mary Flood Jones. A thousand times he had told himself that she had not the spirit of Lady Laura, or the bright wit of Violet Effingham, or the beauty of Madame Goesler. But Mary had charms of her own that were more valuable than them all. Was there one among the three who had trusted him as she trusted him,—or loved him with the same satisfied devotion? There were regrets, regrets that were heavy on his heart;—for London, and Parliament, and the clubs, and Downing Street, had become dear to him. He liked to think of himself as he rode in the park, and was greeted by all those whose greeting was the most worth having. There were regrets,—sad regrets. But the girl whom he loved better than the parks and the clubs,—better even than Westminster and Downing Street, should never know that they had existed.

These thoughts were running through his mind even while he was listening to Mr. Monk, as he propounded his theory of doing justice to Ireland. This might probably be the last great debate in which Phineas would be able to take a part, and he was determined that he would do his best in it. He did not intend to speak on this day, if, as was generally supposed, the House would be adjourned before a division could be obtained. But he would remain on the alert and see how the thing went. He had come to understand the forms of the place, and was as well-trained a young member of Parliament as any there. He had been quick at learning a lesson that is not easily learned, and knew how things were going, and what were the proper moments for this question or that form of motion. He could anticipate a count-out, understood the tone of men's minds, and could read the gestures of the House. It was very little likely that the debate should be over to-night. He knew that; and as the present time was the evening of Tuesday, he resolved at once that he would speak as early as he could on the following Thursday. What a pity it was, that with one who had learned so much, all his learning should be in vain!

At about two o'clock, he himself succeeded in moving the adjournment of the debate. This he did from a seat below the gangway, to which he had removed himself from the Treasury bench. Then the House was up, and he walked home with Mr. Monk. Mr. Monk, since he had been told positively by Phineas that he had resolved upon resigning his office, had said nothing more of his sorrow at his friend's resolve, but had used him as one political friend uses another, telling him all his thoughts and all his hopes as to this new measure of his, and taking counsel with him as to the way in which the fight should be fought. Together they had counted over the list of members, marking these men as supporters, those as opponents, and another set, now more important than either, as being doubtful. From day to day those who had been written down as doubtful were struck off that third list, and put in either the one or the other of those who were either supporters or opponents. And their different modes of argument were settled between these two allied orators, how one should take this line and the other that. To Mr. Monk this was very pleasant. He was quite assured now that opposition was more congenial to his spirit, and more fitting for him than office. There was no doubt to him as to his future sitting in Parliament, let the result of this contest be what it might. The work which he was now doing, was the work for which he had been training himself all his life. While he had been forced to attend Cabinet Councils from week to week, he had been depressed. Now he was exultant. Phineas seeing and understanding all this, said but little to his friend of his own prospects. As long as this pleasant battle was raging, he could fight in it shoulder to shoulder with the man he loved. After that there would be a blank.

"I do not see how we are to fail to have a majority after Daubeny's speech to-night," said Mr. Monk, as they walked together down Parliament Street through the bright moonlight.

"He expressly said that he only spoke for himself," said Phineas.

"But we know what that means. He is bidding for office, and of course those who want office with him will vote as he votes. We have already counted those who would go into office, but they will not carry the whole party."

"It will carry enough of them."

"There are forty or fifty men on his side of the House, and as many perhaps on ours," said Mr. Monk, "who have no idea of any kind on any bill, and who simply follow the bell, whether into this lobby or that. Argument never touches them. They do not even look to the result of a division on their own interests, as the making of any calculation would be laborious to them. Their party leader is to them a Pope whom they do not dream of doubting. I never can quite make up my mind whether it is good or bad that there should be such men in Parliament."

"Men who think much want to speak often," said Phineas.

"Exactly so,—and of speaking members, God knows that we have enough. And I suppose that these purblind sheep do have some occult weight that is salutary. They enable a leader to be a leader, and even in that way they are useful. We shall get a division on Thursday."

"I understand that Gresham has consented to that."

"So Ratler told me. Palliser is to speak, and Barrington Erle. And they say that Robson is going to make an onslaught specially on me. We shall get it over by one o'clock."

"And if we beat them?" asked Phineas.

"It will depend on the numbers. Everybody who has spoken to me about it, seems to think that they will dissolve if there be a respectable majority against them."

"Of course he will dissolve," said Phineas, speaking of Mr. Gresham; "what else can he do?"

"He is very anxious to carry his Irish Reform Bill first, if he can do so. Good-night, Phineas. I shall not be down to-morrow as there is nothing to be done. Come to me on Thursday, and we will go to the House together."

On the Wednesday Phineas was engaged to dine with Mr. Low. There was a dinner party in Bedford Square, and Phineas met half-a-dozen barristers and their wives,—men to whom he had looked up as successful pundits in the law some five or six years ago, but who since that time had almost learned to look up to him. And now they treated him with that courteousness of manner which success in life always begets. There was a judge there who was very civil to him; and the judge's wife whom he had taken down to dinner was very gracious to him. The judge had got his prize in life, and was therefore personally indifferent to the fate of ministers; but the judge's wife had a brother who wanted a County Court from Lord De Terrier, and it was known that Phineas was giving valuable assistance towards the attainment of this object. "I do think that you and Mr. Monk are so right," said the judge's wife. Phineas, who understood how it came to pass that the judge's wife should so cordially approve his conduct, could not help thinking how grand a thing it would be for him to have a County Court for himself.

When the guests were gone he was left alone with Mr. and Mrs. Low, and remained awhile with them, there having been an understanding that they should have a last chat together over the affairs of our hero. "Do you really mean that you will not stand again?" asked Mrs. Low.

"I do mean it. I may say that I cannot do so. My father is hardly so well able to help me as he was when I began this game, and I certainly shall not ask him for money to support a canvass."

"It's a thousand pities," said Mrs. Low.

"I really had begun to think that you would make it answer," said Mr. Low.

"In one way I have made it answer. For the last three years I have lived upon what I have earned, and I am not in debt. But now I must begin the world again. I am afraid I shall find the drudgery very hard."

"It is hard no doubt," said the barrister, who had gone through it all, and was now reaping the fruits of it. "But I suppose you have not forgotten what you learned?"

"Who can say? I dare say I have. But I did not mean the drudgery of learning, so much as the drudgery of looking after work;—of expecting briefs which perhaps will never come. I am thirty years old now, you know."

"Are you indeed?" said Mrs. Low,—who knew his age to a day. "How the time passes. I'm sure I hope you'll get on, Mr. Finn. I do indeed."

"I am sure he will, if he puts his shoulder to it," said Mr. Low.

Neither the lawyer nor his wife repeated any of those sententious admonitions, which had almost become rebukes, and which had been so common in their mouths. The fall with which they had threatened Phineas Finn had come upon him, and they were too generous to remind him of their wisdom and sagacity. Indeed, when he got up to take his leave, Mrs. Low, who probably might not see him again for years, was quite affectionate in her manners to him, and looked as if she were almost minded to kiss him as she pressed his hand. "We will come and see you," she said, "when you are Master of the Rolls in Dublin."

"We shall see him before then thundering at us poor Tories in the House," said Mr. Low. "He will be back again sooner or later." And so they parted.

CHAPTER LXXV
P. P. C.

On the Thursday morning before Phineas went to Mr. Monk, a gentleman called upon him at his lodgings. Phineas requested the servant to bring up the gentleman's name, but tempted perhaps by a shilling the girl brought up the gentleman instead. It was Mr. Quintus Slide from the office of the "Banner of the People."

"Mr. Finn," said Quintus, with his hand extended, "I have come to offer you the calumet of peace." Phineas certainly desired no such calumet. But to refuse a man's hand is to declare active war after a fashion which men do not like to adopt except on deliberation. He had never cared a straw for the abuse which Mr. Slide had poured upon him, and now he gave his hand to the man of letters. But he did not sit down, nor did he offer a seat to Mr. Slide. "I know that as a man of sense who knows the world, you will accept the calumet of peace," continued Mr. Slide.

"I don't know why I should be asked particularly to accept war or peace," said Phineas.

"Well, Mr. Finn,—I don't often quote the Bible; but those who are not for us must be against us. You will agree to that. Now that you've freed yourself from the iniquities of that sink of abomination in Downing Street, I look upon you as a man again."

"Upon my word you are very kind."

"As a man and also a brother. I suppose you know that I've got the *Banner* into my own 'ands now." Phineas was obliged to explain that he had not hitherto been made acquainted with this great literary and political secret. "Oh dear, yes, altogether so. We've got rid of old Rusty as I used to call him. He wouldn't go the pace, and so we stripped him. He's doing the *West of England Art Journal* now, and he 'angs out down at Bristol."

"I hope he'll succeed, Mr. Slide."

"He'll earn his wages. He's a man who will always earn his wages, but nothing more. Well, now, Mr. Finn, I will just offer you one word of apology for our little severities."

"Pray do nothing of the kind."

"Indeed I shall. Dooty is dooty. There was some things printed which were a little rough, but if one isn't a little rough there ain't no flavour. Of course I wrote 'em. You know my 'and, I dare say."

"I only remember that there was some throwing of mud."

"Just so. But mud don't break any bones; does it? When you turned against us I had to be down on you, and I was down upon you;—that's just about all of it. Now you're coming among us again, and so I come to you with a calumet of peace."

"But I am not coming among you."

"Yes you are, Finn, and bringing Monk with you." It was now becoming very disagreeable, and Phineas was beginning to perceive that it would soon be his turn to say something rough. "Now I'll tell you what my proposition is. If you'll do us two leaders a week through the session, you shall have a cheque for £16 on the last day of every month. If that's not honester money than what you got in Downing Street, my name is not Quintus Slide."

"Mr. Slide," said Phineas,—and then he paused.

"If we are to come to business, drop the Mister. It makes things go so much easier."

"We are not to come to business, and I do not want things to go easy. I believe you said some things of me in your newspaper that were very scurrilous."

"What of that? If you mind that sort of thing—"

"I did not regard it in the least. You are quite welcome to continue it. I don't doubt but you will continue it. But you are not welcome to come here afterwards."

"Do you mean to turn me out?"

"Just that. You printed a heap of lies—"

"Lies, Mr. Finn! Did you say lies, sir?"

"I said lies;—lies;—lies!" And Phineas walked over at him as though he were going to pitch him instantly out of the window. "You may go and write as many more as you like. It is your trade, and you must do it or starve. But do not come to me again." Then he opened the door and stood with it in his hand.

"Very well, sir. I shall know how to punish this."

"Exactly. But if you please you'll go and do your punishment at the office of the *Banner*,—unless you like to try it here. You want to kick me and spit at me, but you will prefer to do it in print."

"Yes, sir," said Quintus Slide. "I shall prefer to do it in print,—though I must own that the temptation to adopt the manual violence of a ruffian is great, very great, very great indeed." But he resisted the temptation and walked down the stairs, concocting his article as he went.

Mr. Quintus Slide did not so much impede the business of his day but what Phineas was with Mr. Monk by two, and in his place in the House when prayers were read at four. As he sat in his place, conscious of the work that was before him, listening to the presentation of petitions, and to the formal reading of certain notices of motions, which with the asking of sundry questions occupied over half an hour, he looked back and remembered accurately his own feelings on a certain night on which he had intended to get up and address the House. The ordeal before him had then been so terrible, that it had almost obliterated for the moment his senses of hearing and of sight. He had hardly been able to perceive what had been going on around him, and had vainly endeavoured to occupy himself in recalling to his memory the words which he wished to pronounce. When the time for pronouncing them had come, he had found himself unable to stand upon his legs. He smiled as he recalled all this in his memory, waiting impatiently for the moment in which he might rise. His audience was assured to him now, and he did not fear it. His opportunity for utterance was his own, and even the Speaker could not deprive him of it. During these minutes he thought not at all of the words that he was to say. He had prepared his matter but had prepared no words. He knew that words would come readily enough to him, and that he had learned the task of turning his thoughts quickly into language while standing with a crowd of listeners around him,—as a practised writer does when seated in his chair. There was no violent beating at his heart now, no dimness of the eyes, no feeling that the ground was turning round under his feet. If only those weary vain questions would get themselves all asked, so that he might rise and begin the work of the night. Then there came the last thought as the House was hushed for his rising. What was the good of it all, when he would never have an opportunity of speaking there again?

But not on that account would he be slack in his endeavour now. He would be listened to once at least, not as a subaltern of the Government but as the owner of a voice prominent in opposition to the Government. He had been taught by Mr. Monk that that was the one place in the House in which a man with a power of speaking could really enjoy pleasure without alloy. He would make the trial,—once, if never again. Things had so gone with him that the rostrum was his own, and a House crammed to overflowing was there to listen to him. He had given up his place in order that he might be able to speak his mind, and had become aware that many intended to listen to him while he spoke. He had observed that the rows of strangers were thick in the galleries, that peers were standing in the passages, and that over the reporter's head, the ribbons of many ladies were to be seen through the bars of their cage. Yes;—for this once he would have an audience.

He spoke for about an hour, and while he was speaking he knew nothing about himself, whether he was doing it well or ill. Something of himself he did say soon after he had commenced,—not quite beginning with it, as though his mind had been laden with the matter. He had, he said, found himself compelled to renounce his happy allegiance to the First Lord of the Treasury, and to quit the pleasant company in which, humble as had been his place, he had been allowed to sit and act, by his unfortunate conviction in this great subject. He had been told, he said, that it was a misfortune in itself for one so young as he to have convictions. But his Irish birth and Irish connection had brought this misfortune of his country so closely home to him that he had found the task of extricating himself from it to be impossible. Of what further he said, speaking on that terribly unintelligible subject, a tenant-right proposed for Irish farmers, no English reader will desire to know much. Irish subjects in the House of Commons are interesting or are dull, are debated before a crowded audience composed of all who are leaders in the great world of London, or before empty benches, in accordance with the importance of the moment and the character of the debate. For us now it is enough to know that to our hero was accorded that attention which orators love,—which will almost make an orator if it can be assured. A full House with a promise of big type on the next morning would wake to eloquence the propounder of a Canadian grievance, or the mover of an Indian budget.

Phineas did not stir out of the House till the division was over, having agreed with Mr. Monk that they two would remain through it all and hear everything that was to be said. Mr. Gresham had already spoken, and to Mr. Palliser was confided the task of winding up the argument for the Government. Mr. Robson spoke also, greatly enlivening the tedium of the evening, and to Mr. Monk was permitted the privilege of a final reply. At two o'clock the division came, and the Ministry were beaten by a majority of twenty-three. "And now," said Mr. Monk, as he again walked home with Phineas, "the pity is that we are not a bit nearer tenant-right than we were before."

"But we are nearer to it."

"In one sense, yes. Such a debate and such a majority will make men think. But no;—think is too high a word; as a rule men don't think. But it will make them believe that there is something in it. Many who before regarded legislation on the subject as chimerical, will now fancy that it is only dangerous, or perhaps not more than difficult. And so in time it will come to be looked on as among the things possible, then among the things probable;—and so at last it will be ranged in the list of those few measures which the country requires as being absolutely needed. That is the way in which public opinion is made."

"It is no loss of time," said Phineas, "to have taken the first great step in making it."

"The first great step was taken long ago," said Mr. Monk,—"taken by men who were looked upon as revolutionary demagogues, almost as traitors, because they took it. But it is a great thing to take any step that leads us onwards."

Two days after this Mr. Gresham declared his intention of dissolving the House because of the adverse division which had been produced by Mr. Monk's motion, but expressed a wish to be allowed to carry an Irish Reform Bill through Parliament before he did so. He explained how expedient this would be, but declared at the same time that if any strong opposition were made, he would abandon the project. His intention simply was to pass with regard to Ireland a measure which must be passed soon, and which ought to be passed before a new election took place. The bill was ready, and should be read for the first time on the next night, if the House were willing. The House was willing, though there were very many recalcitrant Irish members. The Irish members made loud opposition, and then twitted Mr. Gresham with his promise that he would not go on with his bill, if opposition were made. But, nevertheless, he did go on, and the measure was hurried through the two Houses in a week. Our hero who still sat for Loughshane, but who was never to sit for Loughshane again, gave what assistance he could to the Government, and voted for the measure which deprived Loughshane for ever of its parliamentary honours.

"And very dirty conduct I think it was," said Lord Tulla, when he discussed the subject with his agent. "After being put in for the borough twice, almost free of expense, it was very dirty." It never occurred to Lord Tulla that a member of Parliament might feel himself obliged to vote on such a subject in accordance with his judgment.

This Irish Reform Bill was scrambled through the two Houses, and then the session was over. The session was over, and they who knew anything of the private concerns of Mr. Phineas Finn were aware that he was about to return to Ireland, and did not intend to reappear on the scene which had known him so well for the last five years. "I cannot tell you how sad it makes me," said Mr. Monk.

"And it makes me sad too," said Phineas. "I try to shake off the melancholy, and tell myself from day to day that it is unmanly. But it gets the better of me just at present."

"I feel quite certain that you will come back among us again," said Mr. Monk.

"Everybody tells me so; and yet I feel quite certain that I shall never come back,—never come back with a seat in Parliament. As my old tutor, Low, has told me scores of times, I began at the wrong end. Here I am, thirty years of age, and I have not a shilling in the world, and I do not know how to earn one."

"Only for me you would still be receiving ever so much a year, and all would be pleasant," said Mr. Monk.

"But how long would it have lasted? The first moment that Daubeny got the upper hand I should have fallen lower than I have fallen now. If not this year, it would have been the next. My only comfort is in this,—that I have done the thing myself, and have not been turned out." To the very last, however, Mr. Monk continued to express his opinion that Phineas would come back, declaring that he had known no instance of a young man who had made himself useful in Parliament, and then had been allowed to leave it in early life.

Among those of whom he was bound to take a special leave, the members of the family of Lord Brentford were, of course, the foremost. He had already heard of the reconciliation of Miss Effingham and Lord Chiltern, and was anxious to offer his congratulation to both of them. And it was essential to him that he should see Lady Laura. To her he wrote a line, saying how much he hoped that he should be able to bid her adieu, and a time was fixed for his coming at which she knew that she would meet him alone. But, as chance ruled it, he came upon the two lovers together, and then remembered that he had hardly ever before been in the same room with both of them at the same time.

"Oh, Mr. Finn, what a beautiful speech you made. I read every word of it," said Violet.

"And I didn't even look at it, old fellow," said Chiltern, getting up and putting his arm on the other's shoulder in a way that was common with him when he was quite intimate with the friend near him.

"Laura went down and heard it," said Violet. "I could not do that, because I was tied to my aunt. You can't conceive how dutiful I am during this last month."

"And is it to be in a month, Chiltern?" said Phineas.

"She says so. She arranges everything,—in concert with my father. When I threw up the sponge, I simply asked for a long day. 'A long day, my lord,' I said. But my father and Violet between them refused me any mercy."

"You do not believe him," said Violet.

"Not a word. If I did he would want to see me on the coast of Flanders again, I don't doubt. I have come to congratulate you both."

"Thank you, Mr. Finn," said Violet, taking his hand with hearty kindness. "I should not have been quite happy without one nice word from you."

"I shall try and make the best of it," said Chiltern. "But, I say, you'll come over and ride Bonebreaker again. He's down there at the Bull, and I've taken a little box close by. I can't stand the governor's county for hunting."

"And will your wife go down to Willingford?"

"Of course she will, and ride to hounds a great deal closer than I can ever do. Mind you come, and if there's anything in the stable fit to carry you, you shall have it."

Then Phineas had to explain that he had come to bid them farewell, and that it was not at all probable that he should ever be able to see Willingford again in the hunting season. "I don't suppose that I shall make either of you quite understand it, but I have got to begin again. The chances are that I shall never see another foxhound all my life."

"Not in Ireland!" exclaimed Lord Chiltern.

"Not unless I should have to examine one as a witness. I have nothing before me but downright hard work; and a great deal of that must be done before I can hope to earn a shilling."

"But you are so clever," said Violet. "Of course it will come quickly."

"I do not mean to be impatient about it, nor yet unhappy," said Phineas. "Only hunting won't be much in my line."

"And will you leave London altogether?" Violet asked.

"Altogether. I shall stick to one club,—Brooks's; but I shall take my name off all the others."

"What a deuce of a nuisance!" said Lord Chiltern.

"I have no doubt you will be very happy," said Violet; "and you'll be a Lord Chancellor in no time. But you won't go quite yet."

"Next Sunday."

"You will return. You must be here for our wedding;—indeed you must. I will not be married unless you do."

Even this, however, was impossible. He must go on Sunday, and must return no more. Then he made his little farewell speech, which he could not deliver without some awkward stuttering. He would think of her on the day of her marriage, and pray that she might be happy. And he would send her a little trifle before he went, which he hoped she would wear in remembrance of their old friendship.

"She shall wear it, whatever it is, or I'll know the reason why," said Chiltern.

"Hold your tongue, you rough bear!" said Violet. "Of course I'll wear it. And of course I'll think of the giver. I shall have many presents, but few that I will think of so much." Then Phineas left the room, with his throat so full that he could not speak another word.

"He is still broken-hearted about you," said the favoured lover as soon as his rival had left the room.

"It is not that," said Violet. "He is broken-hearted about everything. The whole world is vanishing away from him. I wish he could have made up his mind to marry that German woman with all the money." It must be understood, however, that Phineas had never spoken a word to any one as to the offer which the German woman had made to him.

It was on the morning of the Sunday on which he was to leave London that he saw Lady Laura. He had asked that it might be so, in order that he might then have nothing more upon his mind. He found her quite alone, and he could see by her eyes that she had been weeping. As he looked at her, remembering that it was not yet six years since he had first been allowed to enter that room, he could not but perceive how very much she was altered in appearance. Then she had been three-and-twenty, and had not looked to be a day older. Now she might have been taken to be nearly forty, so much had her troubles preyed upon her spirit, and eaten into the vitality of her youth. "So you have come to say good-bye," she said, smiling as she rose to meet him.

"Yes, Lady Laura;—to say good-bye. Not for ever, I hope, but probably for long."

"No, not for ever. At any rate, we will not think so." Then she paused; but he was silent, sitting with his hat dangling in his two hands, and his eyes fixed upon the floor. "Do you know, Mr. Finn," she continued, "that sometimes I am very angry with myself about you."

"Then it must be because you have been too kind to me."

"It is because I fear that I have done much to injure you. From the first day that I knew you,—do you remember, when we were talking here, in this very room, about the beginning of the Reform Bill;—from that day I wished that you should come among us and be one of us."

"I have been with you, to my infinite satisfaction,—while it lasted."

"But it has not lasted, and now I fear that it has done you harm."

"Who can say whether it has been for good or evil? But of this I am sure you will be certain,—that I am very grateful to you for all the goodness you have shown me." Then again he was silent.

She did not know what it was that she wanted, but she did desire some expression from his lips that should be warmer than an expression of gratitude. An expression of love,—of existing love,—she would have felt to be an insult, and would have treated it as such. Indeed, she knew that from him no such insult could come. But she was in that morbid, melancholy state of mind which requires the excitement of more than ordinary sympathy, even though that sympathy be all painful; and I think that she would have been pleased had he referred to the passion for herself which he had once expressed. If he would have spoken of his love, and of her mistake, and have made some half-suggestion as to what might have been their lives had things gone differently,—though she would have rebuked him even for that,—still it would have comforted her. But at this moment, though he remembered much that had passed between them, he was not even thinking of the Braes of Linter. All that had taken place four years ago;—and there had been so many other things since which had moved him even more than that! "You have heard what I have arranged for myself?" she said at last.

"Your father has told me that you are going to Dresden."

"Yes;—he will accompany me,—coming home of course for Parliament. It is a sad break-up, is it not? But the lawyer says that if I remain here I may be subject to very disagreeable attempts from Mr. Kennedy to force me to go back again. It is odd, is it not, that he should not understand how impossible it is?"

"He means to do his duty."

"I believe so. But he becomes more stern every day to those who are with him. And then, why should I remain here? What is there to tempt me? As a woman separated from her husband I cannot take an interest in those things which used to charm me. I feel that I am crushed and quelled by my position, even though there is no disgrace in it."

"No disgrace, certainly," said Phineas.

"But I am nobody,—or worse than nobody."

"And I also am going to be a nobody," said Phineas, laughing.

"Ah; you are a man and will get over it, and you have many years before you will begin to be growing old. I am growing old already. Yes, I am. I feel it, and know it, and see it. A woman has a fine game to play; but then she is so easily bowled out, and the term allowed to her is so short."

"A man's allowance of time may be short too," said Phineas.

"But he can try his hand again." Then there was another pause. "I had thought, Mr. Finn, that you would have married," she said in her very lowest voice.

"You knew all my hopes and fears about that."

"I mean that you would have married Madame Goesler."

"What made you think that, Lady Laura?"

"Because I saw that she liked you, and because such a marriage would have been so suitable. She has all that you want. You know what they say of her now?"

"What do they say?"

"That the Duke of Omnium offered to make her his wife, and that she refused him for your sake."

"There is nothing that people won't say;—nothing on earth," said Phineas. Then he got up and took his leave of her. He also wanted to part from her with some special expression of affection, but he did not know how to choose his words. He had wished that some allusion should be made, not to the Braes of Linter, but to the close confidence which had so long existed between them; but he found that the language to do this properly was wanting to him. Had the opportunity arisen he would have told her now the whole story of Mary Flood Jones; but the opportunity did not come, and he left her, never having mentioned the name of his Mary or having hinted at his engagement to any one of his friends in London. "It is better so," he said to himself. "My life in Ireland is to be a new life, and why should I mix two things together that will be so different?"

He was to dine at his lodgings, and then leave them for good at eight o'clock. He had packed up everything before he went to Portman Square, and he returned home only just in time to sit down to his solitary mutton chop. But as he sat down he saw a small note addressed to himself lying on the table among the crowd of books, letters, and papers, of which he had still to make disposal. It was a very small note in an envelope of a peculiar tint of pink, and he knew the handwriting well. The blood mounted all over his face as he took it up, and he hesitated for a moment before he opened it. It could not be that the offer should be repeated to him. Slowly, hardly venturing at first to look at the enclosure, he opened it, and the words which it contained were as follows:—

I learn that you are going to-day, and I write a word which you will receive just as you are departing. It is to say merely this,—that when I left you the other day I was angry, not with you, but with myself. Let me wish you all good wishes and that prosperity which I know you will deserve, and which I think you will win.

Yours very truly,

M. M. G.

Sunday morning.

Should he put off his journey and go to her this very evening and claim her as his friend? The question was asked and answered in a moment. Of course he would not go to her. Were he to do so there would be only one possible word for him to say, and that word should certainly never be spoken. But he wrote to her a reply, shorter even than her own short note.

Thanks, dear friend. I do not doubt but that you and I understand each other thoroughly, and that each trusts the other for good wishes and honest intentions.

Always yours,

P. F.

I write these as I am starting.

When he had written this, he kept it till the last moment in his hand, thinking that he would not send it. But as he slipped into the cab, he gave the note to his late landlady to post.

At the station Bunce came to him to say a word of farewell, and Mrs. Bunce was on his arm.

"Well done, Mr. Finn, well done," said Bunce. "I always knew there was a good drop in you."

"You always told me I should ruin myself in Parliament, and so I have," said Phineas.

"Not at all. It takes a deal to ruin a man if he's got the right sperrit. I've better hopes of you now than ever I had in the old days when you used to be looking out for Government place;—and Mr. Monk has tried that too. I thought he would find the iron too heavy for him." "God bless you, Mr. Finn," said Mrs. Bunce with her handkerchief up to her eyes. "There's not one of 'em I ever had as lodgers I've cared about half as much as I did for you." Then they shook hands with him through the window, and the train was off.

CHAPTER LXXVI
Conclusion

We are told that it is a bitter moment with the Lord Mayor when he leaves the Mansion House and becomes once more Alderman Jones, of No. 75, Bucklersbury. Lord Chancellors going out of office have a great fall though they take pensions with them for their consolation. And the President of the United States when he leaves the glory of the White House and once more becomes a simple citizen must feel the change severely. But our hero, Phineas Finn, as he turned his back upon the scene of his many successes, and prepared himself for permanent residence in his own country, was, I think, in a worse plight than any of the reduced divinities to whom I have alluded. They at any rate had known that their fall would come. He, like Icarus, had flown up towards the sun, hoping that his wings of wax would bear him steadily aloft among the gods. Seeing that his wings were wings of wax, we must acknowledge that they were very good. But the celestial lights had been too strong for them, and now, having lived for five years with lords and countesses, with Ministers and orators, with beautiful women and men of fashion, he must start again in a little lodging in Dublin, and hope that the attorneys of that litigious city might be good to him. On his journey home he made but one resolution. He would make the change, or attempt to make it, with manly strength. During his last month in London he had allowed himself to be sad, depressed, and melancholy. There should be an end of all that now. Nobody at home should see that he was depressed. And Mary, his own Mary, should at any rate have no cause to think that her love and his own engagement had ever been the cause to him of depression. Did he not value her love more than anything in the world? A thousand times he told himself that he did.

She was there in the old house at Killaloe to greet him. Her engagement was an affair known to all the county, and she had no idea that it would become her to be coy in her love. She was in his arms before he had spoken to his father and mother, and had made her little speech to him,—very inaudibly indeed,—while he was covering her sweet face with kisses. "Oh, Phineas, I am so proud of you; and I think you are so right, and I am so glad you have done it." Again he covered her face with kisses. Could he ever have had such satisfaction as this had he allowed Madame Goesler's hand to remain in his?

On the first night of his arrival he sat for an hour downstairs with his father talking over his plans. He felt,—he could not but feel,—that he was not the hero now that he had been when he was last at Killaloe,—when he had come thither with a Cabinet Minister under his wing. And yet his father did his best to prevent the growth of any such feeling. The old doctor was not quite as well off as he had been when Phineas first started with his high hopes for London. Since that day he had abandoned his profession and was now living on the fruits of his life's labour. For the last two years he had been absolved from the necessity of providing an income for his son, and had probably allowed himself to feel that no such demand upon him would again be made. Now, however, it was necessary that he should do so. Could his son manage to live on two hundred a-year? There would then be four hundred a-year left for the wants of the family at home. Phineas swore that he could fight his battle on a hundred and fifty, and they ended the argument by splitting the difference. He had been paying exactly the same sum of money for the rooms he had just left in London; but then, while he held those rooms, his income had been two thousand a-year. Tenant-right was a very fine thing, but could it be worth such a fall as this?

"And about dear Mary?" said the father.

"I hope it may not be very long," said Phineas.

"I have not spoken to her about it, but your mother says that Mrs. Flood Jones is very averse to a long engagement."

"What can I do? She would not wish me to marry her daughter with no other income than an allowance made by you."

"Your mother says that she has some idea that you and she might live together;—that if they let Floodborough you might take a small house in Dublin. Remember, Phineas, I am not proposing it myself."

Then Phineas bethought himself that he was not even yet so low in the world that he need submit himself to terms dictated to him by Mrs. Flood Jones. "I am glad that you do not propose it, sir."

"Why so, Phineas?"

"Because I should have been obliged to oppose the plan even if it had come from you. Mothers-in-law are never a comfort in a house."

"I never tried it myself," said the doctor.

"And I never will try it. I am quite sure that Mary does not expect any such thing, and that she is willing to wait. If I can shorten the term of waiting by hard work, I will do so." The decision to which Phineas had come on this matter was probably made known to Mrs. Flood Jones after some mild fashion by old Mrs. Finn. Nothing more was said to Phineas about a joint household; but he was quite able to perceive from the manner of the lady towards him that his proposed mother-in-law wished him to understand that he was treating her daughter very badly. What did it signify? None of them knew the story of Madame Goesler, and of course none of them would know it. None of them would ever hear how well he had behaved to his little Mary.

But Mary did know it all before he left her to go up to Dublin. The two lovers allowed themselves,—or were allowed by their elders, one week of exquisite bliss together; and during this week, Phineas told her, I think, everything. He told her everything as far as he could do so without seeming to boast of his own successes. How is a man not to tell such tales when he has on his arm, close to him, a girl who tells him her little everything of life, and only asks for his confidence in return? And then his secrets are so precious to her and so sacred, that he feels as sure of her fidelity as though she were a very goddess of faith and trust. And the temptation to tell is so great. For all that he has to tell she loves him the better and still the better. A man desires to win a virgin heart, and is happy to know,—or at least to believe,—that he has won it. With a woman every former rival is an added victim to the wheels of the triumphant chariot in which she is sitting. "All these has he known and loved, culling sweets from each of them. But now he has come to me, and I am the sweetest of them all." And so Mary was taught to believe of Laura and of Violet and of Madame Goesler,—that though they had had charms to please, her lover had never been so charmed as he was now while she was hanging to his breast. And I think that she was right in her belief. During those lovely summer evening walks along the shores of Lough Derg, Phineas was as happy as he had ever been at any moment of his life.

"I shall never be impatient,—never," she said to him on the last evening. "All I want is that you should write to me."

"I shall want more than that, Mary."

"Then you must come down and see me. When you do come they will be happy, happy days for me. But of course we cannot be married for the next twenty years."

"Say forty, Mary."

"I will say anything that you like;—you will know what I mean just as well. And, Phineas, I must tell you one thing,—though it makes me sad to think of it, and will make me sad to speak of it."

"I will not have you sad on our last night, Mary."

"I must say it. I am beginning to understand how much you have given up for me."

"I have given up nothing for you."

"If I had not been at Killaloe when Mr. Monk was here, and if we had not,—had not,—oh dear, if I had not loved you so very much, you might have remained in London, and that lady would have been your wife."

"Never!" said Phineas stoutly.

"Would she not? She must not be your wife now, Phineas. I am not going to pretend that I will give you up."

"That is unkind, Mary."

"Oh, well; you may say what you please. If that is unkind, I am unkind. It would kill me to lose you."

Had he done right? How could there be a doubt about it? How could there be a question about it? Which of them had loved him, or was capable of loving him as Mary loved him? What girl was ever so sweet, so gracious, so angelic, as his own Mary? He swore to her that he was prouder of winning her than of anything he had ever done in all his life, and that of all the treasures that had ever come in his way she was the most precious. She went to bed that night the happiest girl in all Connaught, although when she parted from him she understood that she was not to see him again till Christmas-Eve.

But she did see him again before the summer was over, and the manner of their meeting was in this wise. Immediately after the passing of that scrambled Irish Reform Bill, Parliament, as the reader knows, was dissolved. This was in the early days of June, and before the end of July the new members were again assembled at Westminster. This session, late in summer, was very terrible; but it was not very long, and then it was essentially necessary. There was something of the year's business which must yet be done, and the country would require to know who were to be the Ministers of the Government. It is not needed that the reader should be troubled any further with the strategy of one political leader or of another, or that more should be said of Mr. Monk and his tenant-right. The House of Commons had offended Mr. Gresham by voting in a majority against him, and Mr. Gresham had punished the House of Commons by subjecting it to the expense and nuisance of a new election. All this is constitutional, and rational enough to Englishmen, though it may be unintelligible to strangers. The upshot on the present occasion was that the Ministers remained in their places and that Mr. Monk's bill, though it had received the substantial honour of a second reading, passed away for the present into the limbo of abortive legislation.

All this would not concern us at all, nor our poor hero much, were it not that the great men with whom he had been for two years so pleasant a colleague, remembered him with something of affectionate regret. Whether it began with Mr. Gresham or with Lord Cantrip, I will not say;—or whether Mr. Monk, though now a political enemy, may have said a word that brought about the good deed. Be that as it may, just before the summer session was brought to a close Phineas received the following letter from Lord Cantrip:—

Downing Street, August 4, 186—.

My dear Mr. Finn,—

Mr. Gresham has been talking to me, and we both think that possibly a permanent Government appointment may be acceptable to you. We have no doubt, that should this be the case, your services would be very valuable to the country. There is a vacancy for a poor-law inspector at present in Ireland, whose residence I believe should be in Cork. The salary is a thousand a-year. Should the appointment suit you, Mr. Gresham will be most happy to nominate you to the office. Let me have a line at your early convenience.

Believe me,

Most sincerely yours,

Cantrip.

He received the letter one morning in Dublin, and within three hours he was on his route to Killaloe. Of course he would accept the appointment, but he would not even do that without telling Mary of his new prospect. Of course he would accept the appointment. Though he had been as yet barely two months in Dublin, though he had hardly been long enough settled to his work to have hoped to be able to see in which way there might be a vista open leading to success, still he had fancied that he had seen that success was impossible. He did not know how to begin,—and men were afraid of him, thinking that he was unsteady, arrogant, and prone to failure. He had not seen his way to the possibility of a guinea.

"A thousand a-year!" said Mary Flood Jones, opening her eyes wide with wonder at the golden future before them.

"It is nothing very great for a perpetuity," said Phineas.

"Oh, Phineas; surely a thousand a-year will be very nice."

"It will be certain," said Phineas, "and then we can be married to-morrow."

"But I have been making up my mind to wait ever so long," said Mary.

"Then your mind must be unmade," said Phineas.

What was the nature of the reply to Lord Cantrip the reader may imagine, and thus we will leave our hero an Inspector of Poor Houses in the County of Cork.

Made in the USA
Middletown, DE
23 August 2023

37230633R00124